The Sweet Temptations Collection

MARILYN BRANT

Twelfth Night Publishing

CONTENTS

Acknowledgments i

On Any Given Sundae 1

Double Dipping 183

Holiday Man 429

Excerpts: Perfect
Match & Perfect Bet 595

About the Author 601

ACKNOWLEDGMENTS

My heartfelt thanks to the friends & family members who inspired these stories and encouraged my writing of them.

For *On Any Given Sundae*, my appreciation goes to Simone Elkeles & Sara Daniel for reading it first and for offering such thoughtful writing advice.

For *Double Dipping*, my lifelong gratitude to my brother Joe for being such an inspiration, especially in the areas of health & fitness.

For *Holiday Man*, my love and thanks to my husband Jeff, who's a fan of the film *Holiday Inn* & who can croon "White Christmas" as beautifully as Bing.

And, as always, my deepest gratitude to my readers for being so incredibly supportive and for making this collection a *USA Today* bestseller. Thanks to each & every one of you!

On Any Given Sundae

~CHAPTER ONE~

It was long, Elizabeth Daniels noted. Without a doubt, Jacques's was several inches longer than most.

She leaned in, scanned it and ran her index finger along its prodigious length. She heard Jacques's quick intake of breath.

Silken to the touch, yet deliciously firm. Broad. Sleek. Inviting. She nodded her approval, swallowed and brought her lips to its soft-brown side. A thick, creamy droplet poised on the tip. She moaned, anticipating the coming moments. Her tongue snaked out to lick the end clean.

"Mmmm," she murmured.

"C'mon. Go for it," Jacques urged, tension filling his voice. "Pleeeeease. You're killing me."

"I shouldn't."

"Elizabeth, I'm pleading with you."

"Oh, all right." She licked the tip again, inhaled deeply and took a big bite.

Jacques exploded next to her. "Well?"

"Incredible," she declared. "This is the single best éclair I've had in months." She glanced at Jacques's expression. "Years," she amended.

"And?"

"And you're absolutely right. This new recipe is even better than your last batch. It has to be featured in the book. In fact, I'm giving you the cover spread for the pastries chapter."

"Yes! Yes!" The portly, thirty-six-year-old French chef did a little jig in the front aisle of Tutti-Frutti, the ice cream parlor and confectionery shop where she and Jacques worked part time. Elizabeth's uncle and his business partner owned the place, and they'd turned it into "The Coolest Hotspot" in Wilmington Bay, Wisconsin.

Elizabeth grinned at her good friend's jubilance. Jacques's enthusiasm was one of the many things she adored about him. Another thing was that, despite the remnants of Jacques's French accent, they spoke the same language—a vernacular inhabited by fillo dough, shaved almond bark and imported spices. As one of the few people she could be herself around, the Frenchman was worth his weight in dutched cocoa.

Jacques pranced around a little more, his receding hairline becoming more prominent when he jumped. "I knew you'd love it, *chéri*," he said. "Didn't I tell you you'd love it?"

"You told me."

Elizabeth wiped the chocolate frosting and custard splotches off her chin before scribbling a few cursory comments in her notebook. She hadn't exaggerated in her assessment. Every one of Jacques's creations was bigger and better than the competition. She needed her first solo dessert cookbook— *Perfect Pastries, Pralines and Parfaits*—to do the same.

He gave her a saucy wink. "You know, I think you need to take my marriage proposal more seriously, *ma petite brioche*. Just imagine the two of us together. We could bring tasty comfort to millions of people daily. Sweet-toothed folks the world over," he raised his voice and waved his oven mitt in the air with fervor, "will flock to Wilmington Bay to see where this wonder all began." He beamed at her. "Jacques and Elizabeth— Saviors of the Dessert Deprived."

"Please tell me that's not going to be our slogan."

He shrugged. "I will leave the naming up to you, but I'll be hurt if you don't think it through just a bit. Our possible engagement, I mean." He couldn't disguise the mischievous glint in his eye. "Friendship is the key to long-lasting love. I'd be honored to marry such a good friend as you, Elizabeth." His voice dropped. "If you'll have me."

She walked to where he stood behind the counter and threw her arms around him. "You are an amazing man...and yet, totally, unbelievably insincere on this subject." She punched him on the shoulder. "But thanks for trying to cheer me up. I may have given up looking for love, but one of these days you'll find someone worthy of you."

"Nonsense. You're just saying 'no' now because you want the empire all to yourself, you greedy girl!" He dipped her backward, as if in a finale to a dance routine, and planted a brotherly kiss on her forehead. "In another year or two you'll be ready for me."

She laughed and they stepped apart. Their conversations were peppered with moments like this: Jacques tossing a half-hearted proposal her way and her waving him off until next time. There was truly *no* romantic chemistry between them, but loneliness made people play these kinds of games. They'd spent hours recounting their relationship woes, alongside their other close friends, Nick and Gretchen. All of them had known too many years of heartbreak.

"So, it's a bright and lovely Sunday morning. What else is on your agenda today?" he said as he walked over to the oven and pulled out a steaming batch of fresh cranberry croissants. Elizabeth could feel the butter clogging her arteries from across the room.

"I've got some rewrites to do on the pecan-praline cookies," she told him. "I had Nick try out the lead recipe, and he said the tops burned if we left them in at three hundred seventy-five degrees for the whole twelve minutes. They're only supposed to be 'golden brown.'"

"It's always something."

"Exactly." She sighed.

"I'll bring you one of these to taste when I'm done," Jacques said, taking the croissant tray into the backroom to decorate the pastries with icing.

Just then, her uncle, Siegfried Finklehooper, burst through the front door. From the look on his face, she knew bad news had crossed his path, and now it was going to cross hers.

"Hi, Uncle Siegfried," she said. "What's wrong?" She brushed a strand of frizzy reddish-brown hair away from her eyes and stared at him. His blue eyes flashed with strange brightness.

"I need your help, *Liebling*," her uncle said, using his native German endearment for "darling," which would've made her smile at any other time. He'd called her mother that, too, when she was alive.

"Of course," she said.

"I must go back to Bavaria."

"When? Why?" Elizabeth's worry gene jumped into gear and her pulse picked up speed. She could only think of one reason he'd have to go to Germany. "Is it Aunt Anita?"

He nodded, and Elizabeth knew he'd be flying out

immediately. He'd promised his late wife, Elizabeth's wonderful Auntie Bette, he would never let her sister Anita die alone. But at age seventy-two, that wouldn't be an easy trip for Uncle Siegfried to make.

"I can come with you," she blurted. "Let me go home to pack and—"

"No, no, *Liebling*. You have a deadline on your cookbook, and I must be gone for several weeks, maybe a month. Either until she recovers or until..." He let that distressing thought trail off. "Pauly's going with me."

"I, um...*really?*" she said. Pauly Carrera, her uncle's business partner of forty years, was a full-blooded Italian a few years older than Uncle Siegfried. He was also cantankerous, prickly and on the opposite side of obliging. "But, who's going to run the shop then?"

Pauly chose that moment to make his entrance. "Did you tell her yet?" he said in a gruff voice to her uncle.

Uncle Siegfried shot him an irritated look. "We leave tonight, *Liebling*," he explained to Elizabeth. "And we were hoping we could count on you to be in charge while we're away."

"*Me?*" Her pulse halted mid-beat. As it was, she would barely make her deadline on the cookbook but, looking at her uncle's face, she knew she'd have to burn a lot of midnight oil this summer because she couldn't say no to him. "Oh, sure— if—if that's what you think is b-best." There were also her nerves and her "minor" public-speaking problem, but she'd just have to deal with those issues too.

"Thank you," Uncle Siegfried said. "You're one of the few people we'd trust with Tutti-Frutti, and you know we could never afford to close the shop for that long."

"Don't worry," she said, rubbing gently the paper-thin skin on her uncle's hand, praying she could handle this task. "I'll take care of everything."

Pauly coughed and patted his chest with his fist. "Well, it's not like you'll have to do it all alone."

"Why?" Elizabeth couldn't disguise her surprise at this

news. "Who else will be here?"

Pauly shot her a curious stare. "Didn't your uncle tell you anything? You know my nephew? Roberto Gabinarri?" He rolled his R's in that deeply Italian way. It sounded beautiful, but all she could think was, *Oh, my God. No!*

She took three very deep breaths. "Y-You mean R-Rob?"

"Yeah, yeah, that's what he always goes by, I guess," Pauly said with a shrug. "Well, he's coming up to help, too. Between the two of you, you shouldn't have any problems keeping the place together for a few weeks."

This wasn't happening. She wasn't hearing his name again after all of these years. Ten years, for goodness sake. There was absolutely no way she could—or would—work with him. None. She'd never be able to speak a coherent sentence in his presence.

"You've already t-t-talked to him?" God help her. If Pauly set things up with Rob, there'd be no way for her to get out of this without looking even more foolish than she felt.

Pauly nodded vigorously, and Elizabeth's heart sank to her toes. "In a manner of speaking," Pauly said.

She opened her mouth to question him but her throat clenched up. It was like high school all over again. Before she could force the words out, Uncle Siegfried interrupted.

"We're so grateful to you, *Liebling*." Her uncle waved a sheet of paper at her. "I wrote down Anita's home phone number and address, in case any questions come up."

Pauly shot a rare grin in her direction. "But don't worry. This will be easy for you. And Roberto—he's a wiz at these things."

"Um, w-when will he be here?" she managed to ask.

Pauly pulled out his cell phone. "Let me just check on that now." He rushed out of the room.

Uncle Siegfried gave her a fierce hug and dropped the shop's keys in her lap.

Rob Gabinarri was enjoying the sound of his own voice in his latest battle of wits with Miguel, the style consultant for his Chicago restaurant, when the phone rang.

"Rob Gabinarri, proprietor. The Playbook," he said into the receiver, feeling the usual pride at the words. He never got tired of announcing his ownership of this place.

"Roberto!" his Uncle Pauly said.

Rob checked the date. It wasn't his birthday. It wasn't Christmas. It wasn't the NFL Playoffs or anytime close to the Super Bowl. Something must be wrong with somebody.

"Uncle Pauly, how are you? Is everything all right in Wilmington Bay?"

"Great, great."

"Everyone in the family? Mama and Tony and Maria-Louisa and the kids and—"

"Oh, they're all fine. Just fine. But I need your help."

This stopped Rob cold. The last time his independent uncle had asked for anybody's help, big hair and legwarmers had still been in fashion. No matter what, there was no way Rob could decline. Family always came first.

"Of course. What do you need?"

"You're the boss of that hotshot restaurant, right?"

"Right," Rob said, his pride wavering a bit as apprehension seeped in.

"You make the rules and set the schedules, right?"

"Right."

"So, what you say is what goes, right?"

The last of his pride was now replaced by full-fledged anxiety. "Uh, right."

"So, you could take some time off now, couldn't you, Roberto?"

"I, well...sure. I guess so, but..." *Please, please don't tell me I need to leave the safety of downtown Chicago and return to suffocating small-town Wilmington Bay. Please, no.*

"I need you to come back to Wilmington Bay for a coupla weeks. Help us out here in the shop."

Damn! "I—well, I'm not so good with sweets, Uncle Pauly.

7

Is there anything I can do for you from here? Anything I could send up? Supplies, maybe? I could hire a person who could step in for a while and—"

"*Dire sciocchezze*. You're talking nonsense, boy. You're great with sweets, and we need *you*."

Rob stifled a heavy sigh. "Okay. When do you need me?"

There was a pause on the line. "Is three hours too soon?" his uncle asked, his brusque voice unusually cheerful. "How about four?"

Elizabeth rarely swore aloud but, in her mind, she was cursing not just a blue streak, but also a red, orange, yellow and green streak. She was, in fact, well on her way to a complete blasphemous rainbow, and Rob Gabinarri hadn't even arrived yet.

Of all people. She never thought she'd have to make it through so much as a ten-minute soda pop break with *him* again. The boy who'd broken her heart and didn't even know it.

Or maybe he did know it.

She couldn't decide which was the greater tragedy.

A snazzy red Porsche convertible squealed to a stop behind her sensible blue Toyota Camry, and the town's Golden Boy stepped out of the car and into the empty sweets shop.

"Hey, Lizzy. Long time, no see," he said, glancing around the shop in a frantic kind of way.

"E-Elizabeth," she corrected automatically.

"Oh, all right. Sorry."

She stared at him, which of course he didn't notice because he was too busy looking at everything else in the place besides her.

He walked into the backroom then out of it again.

He peered into the washrooms.

He opened and shut a few closets.

He paced back and forth, sat down in a booth, got back up and paced some more.

8

The guy was as tall and muscular and breathtaking as he'd been a decade before when he used to saunter through the unremarkable halls of Wilmington Bay High School, oblivious to anyone and anything beyond the football field and his bevy of admirers. If it were possible, he seemed even more youthful and in command now than he did at age eighteen.

And she felt about as queasy as she'd felt the last time they'd been face to face.

Finally, his pacing stopped. "Where is my uncle?" he asked in a husky whisper, directing the query at a tray of chocolate-dipped sugar cookies. "Uncle?" he called out. "Uncle Pauly?"

She wanted to tell him, but the words were lodged in her esophagus and, anyway, he wasn't talking to her.

He strode into the backroom again, as if convinced the elderly Italian man could be found hiding behind a jar of candied cherries or a vat of butterscotch syrup. The long black eyelashes blinked in confusion when he emerged into the main shop once again, his gaze and those nutmeg-brown eyes directed at her.

"Don't tell me he left already." This was more a threat than a question. He shook his head at her as though that gesture alone would discourage an affirmative reply.

She held her breath and nodded.

"*Where* is he?"

She pursed her lips, just as she'd learned in her special speech tutorials so long ago, formed the first letter and tried to push it out of her mouth. But she stuttered anyway.

"L-Lufthansa. F-Fl-Flight four-oh-three."

He cocked his gorgeous head to one side and stared at her in the way she'd grown so accustomed to during her miserable school years: *Poor Old Lizzy*, the look said. *What a geeky dweeb.*

"What time is it scheduled to depart?" he asked her with an affected gentleness that made her want to rip out his vocal cords.

She tapped her watch and gathered her courage for whatever might happen next. "T-Twenty m-m-minutes a-ago."

"Oh, bloody hellfire!" Rob shouted, adding several inventive phrases to his curse before pausing to take a breath.

Elizabeth had managed to squeeze out a few additional syllables of explanation, but Rob was quick to catch on to the full meaning, she noticed, even when words were left unspoken.

"Uncle Pauly said he'd be gone only a couple of weeks." He rubbed his palms against his eyes. "Not a freaking *month*. And he never mentioned *Europe*." He pounded his fist on the ice-cream-window part of the counter three times in rapid succession. "He said everything would be explained when I got up here." He turned toward her. "Guess you were elected to supply the details."

If she'd been capable of it, she would've laughed. Oh, yeah. Now that was a first. One for the record books. Elizabeth Daniels: Verbal Disseminator of Information. Hee-hee. Ha-ha.

"S-Sorry," she said.

He paused. "I didn't mean it like that. I'm just..." But words must have defied him, too because he left the sentence uncompleted.

A jangling of bells broke the silence.

"Howdy, folks," the chatty old florist from down the block said. "Hey, Pauly, Siegfried," he called. "Need to get me a double scoop of Cherry-Almond S—" He stopped mid-speech and surveyed Rob from the top of his dark Italian head right down to his pricey black-and-white Nikes. "Holy Hydrangea. Is that really Roberto Gabinarri standing in front of me?"

Rob grinned but a look of something other than gratification (wariness, perhaps?) slid over his face like a well-formed mask. "Good to see you again, sir. You're looking fit as ever."

The gentleman shook his head as if disbelieving the sight. "Been blazing a hot trail through Chicago, I hear. But, we've all missed you in Wilmington Bay, son. Does your uncle know you're back?" He didn't wait for Rob to answer. "Pauly! Siegfried!" He raised his palms. "Where are they?"

She watched Rob inhale several slow breaths. She could almost see him selecting his words with precision, the way a pastry chef might chose just the right filling for a pie.

"They're taking a much-deserved vacation," he said, nodding sagely at the older gentleman and motioning him closer as if letting him in on a deep family secret. "And we couldn't let them close the shop now, could we? During June?"

The florist's eyes grew large. "Oh, no."

"Of course not. Especially since their best customers were counting on them." Rob winked at the man and grabbed an ice cream scoop. "This cone's on the house," he said, digging into the tub of Cherry-Almond Swirl and piling the sweet concoction in massive, if inexpert, blobs atop a sugar cone. "Uncle Pauly's orders."

So Rob was going to start bribing and spin-doctoring, was he? Fine. She'd play along. In fact, she had to hand it to him. Considering the look of bliss on the talkative florist's face, the gossip he'd inevitably spread about them could only be in their favor. She clamped her mouth shut and did her part by passing the man a paper napkin and shooting him a closed-lipped smile.

"Why, thank you, dearie," the florist said to her. "Gotta get back to talking to my geraniums and begonias before they start complaining." He licked his cone and twinkled his delight at her with his eyes.

She waved him off without uttering a sound, a trick she'd perfected through years of social avoidance, then she grabbed her notebook and ripped out the page she'd been working on. She handed it to Rob.

"What's this?" he said, slumping against the counter.

With her pen, she pointed to the heading she'd written in block letters.

"A schedule? For what? The shop?" He stared at her as if this were the most foreign of concepts.

She nodded.

"For us? To divide up the opening and closing times?"

Good. He could read. She nodded again.

"But who's going to work the shifts in between? Last time I talked with Uncle Pauly, he said he and Siegfried were doing most of the serving themselves. Said they didn't trust many people and they'd only hire out part-time helpers during really busy times or when one of them was sick."

She knew this, which was why she'd have to rely more heavily on Jacques, and why she'd called both Gretchen and Nick and told them they absolutely *had* to come over tomorrow to help her with this. She was desperate.

"M-M-My fr-friends will be w-working here," she said.

"Well, great," he said, looking relieved. "Hey, I mean, if you think you can handle all of the organizing, get trustworthy people to take the over shifts and all, you can count on me to chip in with other things. Funding their salaries for the month. Doing all the stock ordering. Sending out publicity notices. Anything you need, just so I can be back in Chicago soon."

She winced. She'd been especially dreading relaying this part of Pauly's parting message. Although she didn't know the precise reason, she sensed Rob wouldn't like the news. "Y-You can't l-leave."

"Why not?" he said, but the uneasiness in his tone convinced her he wasn't surprised there might be a complication.

"P-Pauly called your m-m-mother. T-Told her to expect you for Sunday d-d-dinner tonight. And every n-night."

"Oh, hell."

She pushed her long, unruly hair out of her eyes and blinked at him. Funny, she'd never before seen the Golden Boy's rugged olive complexion look quite so peaked.

"Lizzy," he said, setting her carefully constructed schedule back on the counter. "You're looking at a dead man."

And with that, he collapsed into a six-foot heap of hunky male onto the floor.

~CHAPTER TWO~

Rob lay on the ground after his pratfall, eyes closed and enjoying the coolness of the parlor's tiles against his neck and his arms. Everywhere, actually, that the thick fabric of his shirt couldn't protect.

He might as well stay here.

With his uncle and his mother conspiring together, he'd have a better chance of surviving a month in Wisconsin if he were eyelevel with the native fauna. Badgers might have a vicious streak, but they were good burrowers. They knew how to hide when necessary.

He heard the sound of rapid footsteps crossing the room and a worried "R-Rob?" coming from somewhere above him.

He bit his lower lip. *Frizzy Lizzy. Imagine seeing her again after all this time.* She looked different, not like the quiet teen he remembered, but the aura she projected was the same. Too damn competent. Women like that scared the bejesus out of him. They always did.

Of course, her impressions of him couldn't be much to brag about. He opened his eyes to see her peering down at him with a look of pure horror from above the countertop. She must think he'd turned into a nutcase.

"I'm fine," he told her. "Just resting. Trying to gather my

strength." Which was the truth. He loved his mother, but he knew he'd need more than familial affection to get him through the next four weeks of The Matriarch Dinner Inquisition. He'd need something he didn't have and didn't want: A serious girlfriend.

"Oh, okay," she said, her big green eyes squinty with confusion. This was the first time she hadn't stuttered since he'd gotten there. Must be a sign that she wasn't scared of him anymore...just annoyed.

He pushed himself to his feet and faced her, the barrier of the counter the only object between them. She was fiddling with her schedule. He slid the paper aside and lightly rested his hands atop hers, deciding that making amends was always done best when done right away.

"Hey, I apologize," he said. "I didn't mean to freak you out a minute ago or let my frustrations loose on you when I got here. But this whole thing came as kind of a shock, and I'm still trying to get readjusted. The schedule you did looks real good and—" He stopped. Her green eyes had grown so enormous they became the only feature on her face he could see. "You okay, Lizzy?"

She didn't answer. She just pulled her hands out from under his and buried them in that long, frizzling hair of hers. Lovely reddish-brown strands, come to think of it.

"Um, Lizzy?"

"E-E-Eliz-zab-b-beth."

"Oh, right. Sorry. Elizabeth, are you okay?"

She shook her head. "I n-n—" She squeezed her eyes shut, her face flushing a deep pink. "I n-need to g-g-go." She thrust the schedule and some keys at him. Then, waving a lightning-fast farewell, she sprinted out the door before he could even say, *So long, now.*

Women. Wasn't that just the way they operated?

Well, an enforced vacation in Wilmington Bay hardly lived up to his dream of a relaxing beachside resort—the Virgin Islands was more his speed—but a Gabinarri had to do what a Gabinarri had to do.

14

With a sigh, he grabbed his cell phone and punched in The Playbook's landline.

"Miguel? Yep, I'm here and, nope, I didn't bring up nearly enough clothing. I could use some of my casual wear. Any chance you could go to my condo and FedEx up a few of my favorites tomorrow?"

Miguel, good man that he was, said he could, and that he'd throw in a few cheery surprises as well. "Where do you want it sent, Boss Man?"

Rob pinched his chin and rubbed the pad of his finger over the day-old stubble. He recited his brother Tony's address. He'd square this with Tony and Maria-Louisa soon, but he had to at least have the appearance of a man who knew what he was doing and where he was going before sitting down to dinner with Mama tonight. Twenty-eight years of experience told him no one got away with being wishy-washy around Mama.

"Thanks, Miguel. Keep an eye on my restaurant for me, will you? I'll be back as soon as I can."

"Will do. Oh!" Rob heard the unmistakable sound of diabolical laughter on the line.

"What?"

Miguel kept laughing even as he spoke. "The new menus. Guess you'll have to trust me on the design of those now, huh?"

Rob groaned. It wasn't that he was worried at the final look. Miguel excelled at anything having to do with artistic photography, décor and style. It was just that Rob wasn't fond of losing his place at the center of the action. He'd once been a quarterback, after all. Old habits died hard.

"Have fun in the Land of Cheese, Boss Man," Miguel said before clicking off.

No doubt about it. A month back in Wilmington Bay and his brain would look like hunks of Swiss, his body like clumps of curd and his patience like shreds of mozzarella.

He shook his head and punched in his brother's phone number.

Elizabeth speed-dialed Gretchen on her cell only five seconds after she closed her car door. No chance her hands would stop shaking, though, for five *thousand* seconds, at least.

"M-Meet me at my place in half an hour," Elizabeth told her.

"You sound crazed," Gretchen said. "What's going on?"

She swallowed. "He's back."

"Who?"

"Rob," Elizabeth whispered.

Gretchen gasped. "Roberto Gabinarri? The 'Hot Calzone' of Wilmington Bay High?"

"The very one."

"Hold onto your oregano, honey, I'll be right over."

By the time Elizabeth's heartbeat had slowed to a mere Fred-n-Ginger tap-dance pace, Gretchen arrived, her presence announced by a healthy pounding at the door.

She strode in—tall, strong, big-boned but without flab, shoulder-length blond hair, bright blue eyes, peachy-cream skin with natural rouge spots on her cheeks—bearing a box of her famous truffles and a tin of cocoa. All she'd need to complete the Original Swiss Miss look was a white ruffled apron and a backdrop of the Alps behind her.

Gretchen thrust the chocolate offerings at Elizabeth. "So, tell me about this dude. You two graduated together, right?"

"R-Right."

"What's so bad about him?"

Gretchen was a few years older and had gone to high school in a neighboring town. She'd heard of Rob, of course, like everyone, but she'd never been under his spell.

"Everything. Seeing him again—it's worse than I thought. Even worse than it was in the beginning."

"Let's start there then. The beginning. You met him, when?"

"The s-summer I turned five."

Gretchen's eyebrows popped up to the middle of her forehead. "You've known him that long?"

"Uh-huh." The years spun like a pinwheel through Elizabeth's mind with images of Rob flashing in full color on every panel. "My Uncle Siegfried and his Uncle Pauly were celebrating their seventeenth anniversary of being in business together. Rob and his family lived in Wilmington Bay already but my family had just moved here so I could start school in the fall. We were all invited to a Tutti-Frutti party."

"And it was love at first sight, right?" Gretchen said.

"Not even close. I was terrified of him. He seemed like a creature from the Klingon Empire...and he never stopped talking. And m-me—" She looked into Gretchen's face and saw the caring, loyalty and sympathy an intensely private person like herself came to count on in a friend. The feeling of safety warmed her soul, even while her head still twirled in panic. "You know how hard words can be for me around people I don't trust. People I'm not comfortable with."

"I know, honey. I know." Gretchen put a gentle arm around her shoulders. "So, did he ever stop talking so much?"

She shook her head. "It's remarkable, really. The guy doesn't shut up. He wasn't in a homeroom class with me until third grade but, even before then, I could always recognize his voice in the hall. Hear his laughter."

"Did he bug you in third grade?"

"No. He was nice. Nice to everyone," she said, remembering the smiling dark-haired kid Rob was back then. "There was this one day when he'd lost his pencil. It was a Friday afternoon. He was sitting next to me at the Number Four table and Mrs. Klausen had asked us twice already to get our writing utensils out. Teddy from across the table said, 'Hey, Rob, you can have one of my dinosaur ones,' and he rolled it over to him. But I held my best pencil out to him. It didn't have any fancy designs on it or anything, but it was sharpened just perfectly. And he took mine instead. He said thanks to both of us, though, before rolling Teddy's pencil back. He laughed and talked to me through the whole project, and he told me a story about his little sister and some peas. I forget how that relates. And then, when the bell rang, he returned my pencil to me. He said, 'Thanks for giving me the best one,' and he left."

"So he noticed," Gretchen said.

Elizabeth felt the usual sliver of pride when she thought about that day. "Yeah. He noticed."

"Was he extra nice the next day?"

"The next school day was a Monday and Mrs. Klausen changed the seating chart. She put me at the Number Three table and Rob at the Number One table. Until that day, she'd been my favorite teacher."

Gretchen laughed. "So that was when you fell in love with him, wasn't it?"

She nodded. "That was the first time."

"When was the second time?"

"Senior year of high school. English class."

Gretchen pulled open the truffle box and waved it and its tantalizing aroma under Elizabeth's nose. "Eat one," she commanded. "And talk. What did he borrow this time? A thesaurus?"

Elizabeth shook her head then selected a morsel of gorgeous hand-dipped chocolate. "Mmm," she said as the rich cocoa butter and hazelnut flavors mingled delectably on her tongue. So heavenly. So unbelievably high in fat grams and calories. And so...oh, so what? "I love these." She reached for another one.

Her friend snatched away the box. "Not until you tell me about twelfth-grade English. What'd he do then?"

She groaned. "Don't be cruel, Gretchen."

Gretchen gave Elizabeth her best Elvis sneer.

"Oh, okay," Elizabeth said, laughing. "But only because you're an amazing chocolatier." Gretchen edged the box toward her a few centimeters, but it was still out of reach.

She sighed. "It was in the middle of the year, just before Christmas. Mr. Shane had assigned us these essays to write on holiday traditions, and I wrote mine about a precursor of the winter solstice celebrations—the ancient Roman Saturnalia feast. It was so fun to research with all the incredible foods to describe and the revelry of the people. Anyway, Mr. Shane read three of our essays aloud, and mine was one of them."

"Because those were the best, right?"

She shrugged, but the sliver of pride grew a little larger at that memory, too. "Anyway, I was nauseated through the whole thing. I mean, I'd been in pullout speech therapy since preschool, and I was terrified Mr. Shane was going to make me answer questions about my paper afterward. But he didn't." She paused. "Rob came up to me, though. After class."

Gretchen edged the truffle box forward again. Getting closer. "And?"

"And he said, 'Your paper was really cool. You're a great writer.' I was speechless, which wasn't surprising, but still. And then his girlfriend at the time, Tara Welles, who'd never spoken to me once in high school until then, materialized like a phantom witch next to us. She said, 'I guess *you'd* know a lot about *food*, Lizzy,' and she wrinkled her snobby nose at me, which made it look sharper and more witch-like than usual, and she made a big show of looking me up and down. You know, like she was cataloging the twenty extra pounds I shouldn't have been carrying on my hips and thighs. Then she pulled Rob away, and he pretty much avoided talking to me for the rest of the semester."

"Do you think he was scared of her?" Gretchen said, finally moving the truffles to within easy reach.

Elizabeth popped one in her mouth and melted with it. "Mmm. I don't know, but how could he miss the message she sent? 'Frizzy Lizzy' wasn't the kind of girl a guy like him should ever take seriously."

"*Frizzy Lizzy?*" Gretchen said, incredulous.

"Yep. That's what they called me." She fluffed out her naturally curly, naturally disastrous hair. "Nice nickname, huh?"

"No wonder you insist on being called Elizabeth."

She grinned. "Yeah, well. Anyway, I know that was all a long time ago, but there's just something about Rob that gets to me. In one sense, we practically grew up next door to each other, but the reality is that I've always been worlds away from him. I know Uncle Siegfried must've thought having someone else to help with the shop would be a relief for me, but he should've known better. He knows darn well how self-conscious I am."

"Maybe Pauly insisted and Siegfried couldn't say no. Rob is Pauly's nephew, after all. And," Gretchen added gently, "Rob is reputed to be a pretty successful businessman."

"Oh, I know. But can I help it if I want to avoid him as much as possible? Maybe someday I'll be calm and capable enough not to get so tongue-tied around him. But that day is not today. Or tomorrow, for that matter."

Gretchen rubbed her temples, a sign she was in deep thought. "After your uncle dropped this bomb on you, you called and told me you were going to make up a schedule, right? One that Nick, Jacques and I could help you with. Did you do it?"

"Yes. And I purposely planned my shifts so I'd work with any one of you except for him. I'm not working with him, Gretchen."

"Okay, okay. Not a problem." She laughed. "You say he talks a lot? I hope you stuck him with Nick as often as possible. That boy could talk the ears off of corn. The two of them ought to cancel each other out."

Elizabeth had to agree. "I don't even remember what I wrote anymore, except that Rob and I are at opposite ends of the day. I made sure I worked around all of your busiest times, though. Nick's got his brother's restaurant during the day—"

"Ah, yes. Jason the spanakopita god. Nick's learning from the best. I never thought I'd come to love spinach but...mmm."

"I know. And Jacques has the bakery in the morning."

"That man's talent amazes me. And his accent makes me giddy, although not nearly as giddy as those incredible fig cookies he makes. You know, he told me he puts a teaspoon of—"

"Gretchen! Stay with me here. And *you* have to work at Chocolate Heaven every afternoon, right?"

"That's true."

"So the general plan should work. I scheduled myself to do

the opening shift and the next one. Rob has to do a midday shift and also close the shop."

"So, see, you *can* avoid him."

Elizabeth sighed. "Maybe, but the problem is that twenty-four hours are nowhere near enough time for everything I have to do. Whether I open or close, I've got a ton of writing left to finish for this cookbook. My deadline's August first. And some recipes need to be rewritten. Camden has to fly out here to shoot the pictures. I want to make sure my best friends—" she squeezed Gretchen's arm, "get their creations highlighted in the book in a way that makes sense..."

"Just stop worrying. Nick and Jacques will be there tomorrow morning, too. Between the four of us, we'll put the Hot Italian in his place and figure out a way to get you some quality writing time. Okay, um, Lizzy?" her blond friend said with a saucy grin.

"Oh, don't you start." She gave Gretchen a light smack. But she felt better already. Thank God for true friends. Especially friends who could make such wicked things with chocolate.

She grabbed one last truffle then closed the box.

Ten a.m. Tutti-Frutti time. And they were all assembled at the ice cream parlor. Except for Rob.

"I can't wait to meet the infamous Roberto Gabinarri. The guy was amazing on the football field," Nick declared, fingering his black sideburns and looking especially Greek this morning.

Elizabeth marveled at the twenty-two-year-old's classic features. Turn him into marble and prop him up by the Parthenon. No one would suspect he didn't belong there.

"He was a legend you know," Nick said in Part Two of his Roberto Dissertation. "I read about his senior season in the Wilmington Bay High School record books. Do you know he *averaged* fourteen points per game as a quarterback and that during game three of the regional playoffs he scored a record thirty-two points? And isn't it just amazing when you think—"

"For a gay guy, isn't it just amazing how into sports he is?" Jacques interrupted in a loud whisper to Elizabeth and Gretchen. "Good thing he can at least make a mean baklava or all would be lost."

Nick shot him a pitying look. "Don't go all stereotypical on me, man. The body is a *temple*." He punched Jacques's small paunch. "And from what I've heard about Rob, he's got a body on him that makes everyone drool."

"Is that true, Elizabeth?" Gretchen asked her, one eyebrow cocked.

"I regret to inform you all that, yes, he's the epitome of 'hot.' I refuse to be witness to any drooling, however."

"I won't drool," Jacques promised.

"I make no such vows," Nick said, hip-hopping around the tiles. "So, I hope I'm on lots of shifts with him." He checked his watch. "Damn. Ten after ten. When will he get here?"

"Look, I don't know," Elizabeth said, the nervousness rising like soda fizz inside her. "The only thing I'm certain of is that I will never get done with my draft of *Perfect Pastries, Pralines and Parfaits* if I have to spend an entire five hours per day in this shop. Aside from not getting the features and recipes finished, I'll probably gain back all the weight I lost eight years ago. Some of us—" she tossed Nick her most evil look, "are not natural athletes. Three half-hour sessions of *X-treme Abs and Thighs* is all I can handle each week. No way am I doing more just because I can't resist ice cream and éclairs."

"It's all right, *chéri*," Jacques said, patting her arm. "We all know how you're trying to help us by featuring our specialties in your cookbook. We're here to help you, too."

Gretchen and Nick both nodded, and Elizabeth felt the familiar tightness in her throat, but this time it was because of the affection she felt radiating from her friends. They choked her up and left her buoyant. They made her feel as though she could handle this enormous responsibility. And she wouldn't freeze the next time she had to talk to Rob. No! She'd be cool, like ice cream, and smooth and—

"Hi, everyone," Rob said, surprising them by entering

through the backroom door. "Sorry I'm late, but I picked up bagels and coffee for all of us." He deposited his goody bags on one of the tables and managed to elicit Oohs and Aahs from her cadre of helpers. The traitors.

Her friends introduced themselves to Rob and then quickly turned their attention to the treats. As they spread strawberry cream cheese on their cinnamon-raisin bagels and doctored their coffees to their liking, she watched Rob watching them, and she realized she hadn't heard the backdoor bang before he entered. Had he just gotten here? Or had he been here already, lying in wait, listening to them? Had he overheard their discussion of his 'hot' body?

The possibility of this made her blush, and she suddenly wished she hadn't given him his own set of keys to the shop yesterday in her panic. Then he wouldn't have been able to sneak up on them today.

"Good morning, *Elizabeth*," he said, speaking her name with noticeable deliberateness. "And how are you doing on this bright Friday?"

"F-F-F—" *Oh, hell!* "F-Fine." She gestured an "And you?" with her nearest hand.

"Long night, last night, to tell you the truth," he said. "Kind of stressful, actually. I locked up the shop about a half hour after you left. Spent some time with my family. Dinner. Discussions. More discussions..."

She couldn't help but notice the way he eyed her every move while he spoke. Goodness, what was he looking for? Did he think she had any connection to his family? She barely knew them.

"What did you do last night?" he said.

"I-I—" She made a scribbling motion in the air but Nick took this opportunity to jump right into their conversation. Bless him.

"Oh, man, she's an awesome writer. She's only twenty-seven and she's co-written a couple of books and gotten a three-book contract for her own dessert cookbook series." Nick turned to her. "I know your deadline's during the summer, but when's the publication date for book one? Thanksgiving?"

For a reason she wasn't able to analyze, her voice unfroze. "No, just before Christmas. The s-second book is supposed to be released b-by Thanksgiving next year."

"That's right," Nick said. "And the third one around Halloween of the year after."

"And the first one is going to be *fantastique*," Jacques added, "because my éclairs will grace the cover of the pastries section."

"His are long," Nick said appreciatively.

And Gretchen laughed, which made Elizabeth laugh, which made Rob look at them all like they were more than a little psycho.

"So, we should get organized here," Gretchen said. "Elizabeth needs to get a lot of work done, and all of us have other part-time jobs to return to. Who's got the opening shift today?"

Rob pulled out the schedule Elizabeth had scrawled on the notebook paper yesterday. "Looks like Elizabeth and Gretchen are on the docket for round one. But—" He waved the page in the air before dropping it and letting it float to the tabletop.

"But what?" Jacques asked.

"But it seems to be in all of your best interests to have Elizabeth concentrate her time on finishing this cookbook. Isn't that right?" Rob said, scanning their faces as he spoke.

"Oh, absolutely," Gretchen agreed heartily.

"You bet, man," Nick said.

Jacques squinted at Rob. "But of course. This is why we're here. This is what friends are for."

Rob gulped down some coffee and turned his gaze fully on Elizabeth. "And your having to work these extra shifts is dramatically cutting in to your writing time, right?"

"R-R-Right, but—" she began.

"Well, how about I take over your shifts," Rob said. "I could handle them, too, if..."

"Oh, no. That's not fair to you. I-I'm willing to work—"

"Let the man speak, Elizabeth," Nick said. "My baklava is

being featured on page sixty-five. I'm protective of this book."

She glanced at Gretchen, who winked unhelpfully.

They all turned their eyes to Rob, but Elizabeth sensed his offer of help wasn't quite as altruistic as it seemed.

"Here's the thing," he said. "I can see you're signed up for the first two shifts today, Elizabeth, first with Gretchen from ten to twelve-thirty, and then with Jacques, twelve-thirty to three. If I take over both of those, would you be able to help me for just two and a half hours tonight instead?"

"S-Sure. You mean do the closing shift for you, from eight to ten-thirty?" This she could handle. It would be like her schedule before Uncle Siegfried left, with only half the time away from her computer screen. And Rob would, obviously, be somewhere else. Nighttime party plans, no doubt.

"Not exactly," Rob said. "I can still do the mid-afternoon and late-evening shifts you assigned me as well. What I need from you is the time between five-thirty and eight. I need you to come to dinner with me." He paused. "At my mother's house."

~CHAPTER THREE~

"**W**-What?"

Rob took in Lizzy's—no—*Elizabeth's* stunned expression, but if a little trickery was required to get Mama off his case, he wasn't too proud to stoop to it. Last night had been an evening of enjoyment right up there with a toasty visit to Hades. He had no intention of repeating it. Ever.

"That seems like a more than fair trade," the young guy Nick said to her.

The Frenchman nodded his approval.

Only the blonde looked dubious.

As for Elizabeth, she opened her mouth several times but not a single word emerged after that first "What?" This surprised him. Here was, after all, the woman who apparently could talk up a firestorm without stuttering when among her friends...

He grimaced. So she thought he had a hot body, huh? Wasn't that always the case with the Wilmington Bay crowd? Rob the Hunk. Rob the High-School Football Star. Rob the Popular Guy. Just about anything but Rob the Intelligent. Hell, he'd even settle for Rob the Occasionally Bright. But it was always about his body and his face, never about his mind.

Which hurt sometimes. Especially when he was trying to

talk to a woman as smart as Elizabeth Daniels.

"So, what do you say?" he asked her. "Do we have a deal?"

"I-I—"

"Of course you do," Nick said for her. "Why don't you leave right now, Elizabeth, and get back to typing?"

The blonde started to speak, but Elizabeth stopped her. The ladies did some eye-contact thing and Gretchen said, "Elizabeth?"

Elizabeth said, "B-B-Bye, e-everyone." She waved and headed for the door. Always one for abrupt departures.

"Pick you up here at five-thirty sharp," he called after her. She shot him a worried parting glance, but she nodded.

"L-Later," she said, but he wasn't sure if she was talking to him or addressing Team Tutti-Frutti.

The moment she was out the door, Gretchen started whispering to Jacques rapidly and, it seemed, in code because he couldn't figure out from their words why Gretchen was acting so panicky. He might've gone ahead and asked her if their first customer of the day hadn't shown up.

"Roberto Gabinarri? Is that really you?" his mother's favorite hairstylist said. "Just look at how you've grown up. Such a fine young man." She sparkled at him and, yes, actually pinched his cheek.

He heard Nick stifle a laugh before the Frenchman said to him, "C'mon, Nick. It's Gretchen and Rob's shift now. You promised to help me with the Grand Marnier tortes."

"Okay," he said to Jacques. "Need to be at Jason's Joint in two hours, though." Then, to Rob, "See you later, man. I've got some football questions for you this afternoon."

"All right," he said, turning his attention back to Mama's hairstylist and to Gretchen, who lobbed an ice cream scoop at him, and none too gently either.

Elizabeth stared at her iMac's blue screen, heaved in gulps of air (in an unsuccessful attempt to prevent hyperventilation)

and mentally retraced the past half hour for evidence of personal psychosis. Dinner with his *family?* Good heavens, how could she have let that happen?

Her cell phone rang. Gretchen.

"Oh, God, Elizabeth! I'm so sorry I couldn't stop it. I'm going to wring Nick's neck later. There's no way you have to go through with this. We'll think of something to get you out of—"

"Where are you?" Elizabeth asked her. "I thought you were working this shift?"

"I am," her friend said. "I told the Hot Calzone that I needed a bathroom break. Look," she said, lowering her voice, "I can see why you get tongue-tied around him. He's pin-up-boy gorgeous."

Elizabeth groaned. "He's a scheming deviant."

"That, too," Gretchen said.

"And he wants something—something more than a live body to take along to dinner at his mother's house—b-but I don't know what it is yet."

"We'll find out." She paused. "Elizabeth, I know this all has you rattled, but there's no reason we can't come up with some excuse for you to skip tonight. People get sudden cases of the measles or rheumatic fever or Asiatic flu or…or elephantiasis without warning, all the time probably."

"*Elephantiasis?*"

"Or something," Gretchen insisted. "My point is, you can come down with a contagious disease almost immediately. I can ring up my brother and ask him to give me a list of really vile-sounding symptoms. In fact, he's on call at St. Andrew's right now and I'll bet he knows—"

Elizabeth sighed. "Thanks, Gretchen, but you know I can't."

"Why not? Rob tricked you. That's…that's entrapment. And, anyway, Nick was the one who said yes for you. You didn't say anything. You never actually agreed."

"Quite true, literally, but my silence was my agreement. And I nodded. And I left. Not staying to work my shift confirmed my acceptance of the terms of his deal, however bizarre. So, even if this means long years of psychotherapy are in my future,

I do have to go tonight. But just tonight." Unless...did Rob mean for this to last longer than one night? The very thought made her shudder.

"But Eliz—"

"Look, you know I need the writing time, Gretchen. For all of our sakes."

"Damn. That's the real reason you did this, isn't it? You agreed for *us*. That's why you didn't say anything to him."

"I didn't say anything to him because my throat closes up like the space inside a cream-filled donut whenever I'm around him. And I need the cookbook to succeed as much or more than you or Jacques or Nick do," she said, which was the truth. "I'll be all right for an evening," she added, which was a monstrous lie.

There was a long pause. "Thanks, Elizabeth."

"You're welcome. Now, I have to get back to work, and so do you." For good measure, Elizabeth made a few clicking noises on her computer keyboard.

"Okay, but one more thing—"

"Yeah?"

"If he tries any fresh moves on you, just tell me," Gretchen said. "I'll have him bound and gagged so fast he won't know what hit him."

Elizabeth laughed and hung up. How could she tell Gretchen that doing this very thing to Rob had been the cornerstone of many of her high school fantasies? Rob bound. Rob gagged. Rob all hers.

She rested her head on her arms, thought about the terror-inducing event that stretched out before her tonight and began hyperventilating in earnest again.

Five-thirty wasn't The Witching Hour in anybody's book, but Elizabeth decided it ought to be renamed.

She dressed carefully and conservatively in a pale pink shirt and dress slacks, adding a light summer sweater to camouflage the inevitable sweat rings—from nervousness not high temperatures. Then she packed herself and the pastries she was bringing into her Camry, drove over to Tutti-Frutti with all of forty seconds to spare and eased her way out of the car.

"Perfect timing," Rob said, emerging from the sweets shop before she had a chance to change her mind and speed away. "I'm parked across the street."

"H-How did the shifts g-g-go?"

He took her elbow and led her toward his sporty red car. Her pulse shot up to well over a hundred, and it surely had nothing to do with taking her first ride in a Porsche.

"Awesome," he said. "People were real friendly and had lots of questions about our uncles. They wanted to know where in Europe they were headed, what kinds of sites they'd planned to see, and I told them I'd have to ask you because you're the keeper of all those details." He grinned at her, opened the passenger's door and continued his monologue. "Oh, yeah. And the florist was back for a repeat of yesterday's double scoop. And I had an interesting conversation with your friend Jacques about the making of éclairs. He promised to bring me a sample to taste tomorrow."

"D-Did he?"

Good heavens. Jacques must've really taken a liking to the guy if he offered freebie treats to a non-chef. She glanced at the man sitting next to her as he put the car into gear. So confident. So smooth. So very charming. It was no wonder Rob Gabinarri wormed his way into everyone's good graces. She tried to imagine what it would be like to be that comfortable in her own skin. A virtually impossible daydream.

"Yes, indeedy," he said. "Oh, and I gathered, after talking with Jacques, that Gretchen is some kind of sorceress with truffles." He nodded in her direction but didn't actually require her response, for which she was grateful. "My buddy Miguel in Chicago has a real sweet tooth, so he's always bringing in new desserts for me to try. Plus, he makes a wicked Mexican Hot Cocoa—with cinnamon and chili pepper and a bunch of other things I can never keep straight. Man, I tell you, it is *spicy*, but one of the most magnificent creations imaginable on a freezing January morning when the wind chill is twenty below."

She swallowed, trying to channel "winter" but not succeeding. Even with the cool breeze blowing through the car window, she was broiling. Her body temperature must be hovering somewhere dangerously high. And, jeez, she didn't even want to know her blood pressure.

Rob yakked about the parade of thrilled visitors who'd entered and exited the shop, about the delightful summer weather, about how refreshing it was to be in a small town again (albeit briefly) after the frenzy of a metropolis, and he jabbered on about fifty other things during the winding drive to his mother's house. Stream-of-conscious chatter.

Except...

Well, she almost missed it, but she didn't. She tried to ignore it, but she couldn't. Rob talked twenty miles a minute, fast enough to do a snow job on a polar bear, except there was something in the cast of his expression that seemed to do battle with his words. The set of his jaw, maybe. The cloudiness in his eye. Whatever it was, Elizabeth got the distinct impression that all was not as amusing or as agreeable as it seemed. But, for the life of her, she couldn't figure out why it wouldn't be. Rob lived a charmed existence. Only, by the time they'd parked in front of his mother's two-story Colonial, she was convinced he didn't think so.

"W-Why did y-y-you ask me here?"

A trace of panic flashed across his face then disappeared. He shot her one of his oh-so-divine grins. "Mama said she hadn't seen you since you were a little girl and, when I told her we were working together at the shop, she said it would be so nice to have Siegfried's niece over to dinner." He patted her hand. "And I really appreciate you coming, too."

This time she didn't get blown off course by his touch. Well, she did, but she also kept her focus on his face. Rob Gabinarri was hiding something. If only she could articulate her questions, she could get to the heart of it.

But, before her lips could form the words, Alessandra

Gabinarri came bustling out of the house.

"Roberto!" she cried, arms flung open. "Little Lizzy, all grown up!"

Elizabeth glanced at Rob and he studied her face for a moment. He looked surprisingly serious. Contemplative.

"She likes to be called Elizabeth," he told his mother as they got out of the car and he handed over the bottle of red wine (from him) and the box of pastries (from her). "And I'm Rob, remember?"

The large woman wrapped Elizabeth up in her ample arms and squeezed her before planting a kiss on either cheek. "Welcome, Elizabeth," she said. Then she embraced her son in a similar manner. "Your brother and his family are here." She eyed the two of them. "Show her around the house and the garden, Roberto. Dinner will be on the table in ten minutes."

"Sure, Mama," he said. "And everyone calls me Rob now."

His mother shrugged. "I named you. To me, you're Roberto. Live with it." Then she grinned at them and went inside.

"Impossible woman," he muttered, but Elizabeth heard the affection in his voice.

They ambled around the yard for a few minutes as Rob pointed out the fruit trees and various flowers his mother took pride in. Elizabeth thought of her own mom, who'd loved to plant her annual vegetable garden. And not just tomatoes and cucumbers either. Weird stuff. Eggplant. Summer squash. Rutabaga. The dreaded okra. A pang of longing swept over her again. How she'd love to make just one more phone call to her mom to chat about the merits of harvesting sweet fruits versus bitter veggies.

"Gotta warn you," Rob said as they headed toward the house and passed by a prominent Mother-and-Child stone statuette. "Mama's really big into the whole Madonna thing, so don't be too shocked when we get inside."

Elizabeth understood the allure of religion and knew how prayerfully many Catholics regarded the Virgin Mother. She gave him a solemn nod and walked through the backdoor.

Rob wasn't lying. There were Madonna images everywhere… The *pop singer* Madonna. On refrigerator magnets. Tacked to the pantry door. A huge glossy poster of the singer, circa 1984, dressed in white lace and ruffles in the foyer.

Rob nodded. "See. She's almost a groupie. 'Like a Virgin' is still her favorite song."

Elizabeth stood in place and laughed.

"What?" he said. "Some people are Elvis fanatics and my dad used to think the Beatles were the best band since—"

"No, Rob. I-I just thought you meant your mom was really into the Holy-Mary-Mother-of-God Madonna, not the Kabbalah-practicing-ex-wife-of-Guy-Ritchie Madonna."

Now he laughed. "Well, she thinks highly of them both, but none of us are real clear on the Virgin Mother's singing voice, so…"

Their gazes met and the strangest thing happened. A look passed between them—a knowing, conspiratorial look—one tinged with laughter and camaraderie. Elizabeth's heart leapt.

A lanky guy, who could only be Rob's younger brother Tony, peered around the corner at them. He'd been a sophomore when they were high school seniors and had grown about seven inches since she'd last seen him. He stepped forward. "Roberto!" he said.

"Antonio!" Rob said back with raised eyebrows.

"Okay, let's cut the crap," Tony said. "Promise to call me Tony tonight. No more taking Mama's side like you did yesterday."

"Golden Rule, bro," Rob said to him.

"Yeah, I know." Tony slapped his back and turned to Elizabeth. "Hey, Lizzy. Or—sorry—Mama said it was Elizabeth now. Great to have you here."

"Th-Thanks."

"You've got to meet my wife Maria-Louisa. She's in the basement with the kids but they'll be up any minute." And he launched into a story about something one of his boys did in school last month with a jar of black ants…and how the teacher had been wary of him ever since…and how the woman must surely be counting the hours until school got out for the summer.

Another gabby Gabinarri.

Then, before Elizabeth knew what was happening, she got tossed into a whirling, swirling tornado of gabby Gabinarris. A pack of them—four, no *five* children—emerged from the basement and descended upon Tony and Rob and her, too, followed by a petite woman about Tony's age (Maria-Louisa, no doubt) with a bright smile and, evidently, an unlimited supply of energy.

"Time for dinner," the family's matriarch called from the kitchen. And, at those words, the tornado spun toward the dining room.

Elizabeth looked long and hard at Tony's wife and her pounding heart eased at the sight. That must be heaven, 3-D and in full color. Being the mother to a troupe of exuberant children who loved her unconditionally, and whom she could love in return. When Elizabeth was around kids, all of her self-consciousness drifted away. Children were real and open and honest. They didn't hide their emotions or play games with hers. She bit her lip. If only immaculate conceptions were possible in this modern age.

"Elizabeth," Rob and Tony's mother said. "Please sit here." She pointed to a chair across from Rob and in between two of the Gabinarri youngsters: A dark-haired, giggling Camilla and a sandy-haired, hiccupping Sammie.

"Hi!" Sammie said to her. Hiccup. "I'm five." Hiccup. He covered his mouth, his eyes bugging out with laughter and the astonishment of a bodily process that couldn't be controlled. "How old are you?" Hiccup.

"T-Twenty-seven," she said. "Almost twenty-eight."

"Oooh!" Camilla said. "So, you get to have a birthday soon."

Sammie hiccupped again.

"I just turned seven three weeks ago," Camilla added. "When's yours?"

"In July," Elizabeth admitted. "The fifth. The day after

Independence Day."

Hiccup. "Cool," Sammie said. "My birthday's not—" Hiccup. "Until November. That's too far away."

Elizabeth smiled at him then snatched a glance at Rob. He was staring at her curiously.

"This is my sister-in-law Maria-Louisa," he said as the petite woman sat down.

"Nice to meet you, Elizabeth," Tony's wife said. "I see you're getting to know Camilla and Sammie. These are the triplets." She pointed to the cluster of three identical boys jumping on either side of her. "Matthew, Mark and Michael. They're three and a half."

A chorus of Hi 'Lizbet's greeted her. She looked deep into their brown eyes and fell instantly in love.

"Hello, boys." She gave them her warmest smile. "Are you three ever b-big. Are you going to sit right here with us?"

"Of course," Alessandra Gabinarri broke in. "Everyone should gather 'round the same table. To give thanks. To eat. To talk about the day. I wish the others were here, too." She turned to the triplets. "Boys, sit down."

Her grandsons did as she commanded but, Elizabeth couldn't help but notice, nothing could keep their little bodies from squirming.

"Antonio, time to eat. *Now.*"

"Yes, Mama," Tony said, looking sheepish as he sauntered into the room and took his place at the head of the table, between two of his children and opposite his mother.

For a moment, Elizabeth wondered about this. Tony was only two years younger, it was true, but didn't the head of the table traditionally go to the eldest male present? Maybe being a married father carried extra weight with Alessandra Gabinarri.

She caught Rob staring at her again and being surprisingly silent amidst the family chaos. Elizabeth, meanwhile, answered questions galore from Camilla, Sammie and even an occasional triplet. Dishes clattered as roasted potatoes, manicotti with meat sauce, grilled carrots and tossed salad with crouton cubes were passed back and forth. Hunks of bread slathered in garlic butter were distributed to the crew. Wine or soft drinks were offered. Nobody dared refuse anything.

"None of that stinking low-carb stuff for us Gabinarris," Tony whispered to her with one eyebrow cocked while his mother heaped several spoonfuls of potatoes onto little Sammie's plate.

Alessandra stopped abruptly, ladle in the air. "What happened to my music?" She looked accusingly around the table. "Roberto, was it you?" she said.

Rob shook his head, wide-eyed but with upturned lips, and his mother's gaze fixed on Tony.

"Antonio?"

"Oh, all right. Yes, it was me." Tony rolled his eyes and threw his hands in the air.

His mother continued to glare at him.

"I'll go put it back on," Tony said.

"You do that, Antonio." She set down her bowl and crossed her arms. "Fooling with my CD player," she muttered until the strains of Madonna's classic "Get into the Groove" floated into the dining room. "Hmm. That's better," she said when Tony returned. And the clattering, clanking, chattiness and general chaos resumed again at the table.

Fifteen minutes later, Elizabeth had managed to mostly relax. The children's queries kept her occupied and Marie-Louisa tossed encouraging smiles her way. She released a deep, pent-up breath. She'd almost done it. She'd nearly made it through the meal without saying or doing anything too embarrassing, thank goodness. In another half hour she'd be able to go home.

She glanced around the lively table. The triplets were making a game of poking holes in their bread. Sammie was still hiccupping. Camilla and her mother were giggling about something they'd seen in a Disney video. Rob and Tony were in the midst of a rousing debate over the previous NFC and AFC champs and the players who'd make the best draft picks for the fall season. Everyone grinned, talked, munched. She took a big bite of manicotti.

"So, Elizabeth," the family matriarch said loudly, "don't you think my son should get married soon?"

She gulped her half-chewed pasta too fast, which plunged her into a fit of coughing.

"Oh, let me get you some water," Maria-Louisa said, jumping to her feet and rushing into the kitchen. The kind young woman returned a moment later with a full glass. "Drink this."

"Th-Th-Thank y-you," she managed to say between coughs. She could feel her face flushing and knew it must be a delightful shade of scarlet by now.

"Mama," she heard Rob say. "I don't think—"

"Oh, nonsense, Roberto. She's your girlfriend, after all. Don't you think the lady's got an opinion?"

Elizabeth choked on the water. *His girlfriend!* "H-H-His—" was all she could get out before Rob interrupted.

"It's okay, sweetie," he told her in an unfamiliar, ultra-soothing tone. "I told them about our long-distance relationship, and how glad I was to be able to spend the month up here with you while we were helping out our uncles."

WHAT? "Wh-Wh—" she began, seeing him leap out of his seat and walk around the table toward her.

"You know, maybe you need some hot tea instead," Rob said, the pleading note in his voice starting to break through as he reached her. "I know you're still getting over that awful cold." He put his arm around her shoulder and began steering her out of the room. "Hey, everyone, why don't you guys just continue eating while I make Elizabeth a steaming mug of tea to *quiet* her cough."

"I've got some Earl Grey in the cabinet," his mother said.

"Thanks, Mama." He all but pushed Elizabeth into the kitchen. "Anybody else want some?" he called over his shoulder.

No one did.

"Okay. See you all in a few minutes," Rob said cheerfully.

She swiveled around to face him once they were alone, pointed her index finger at his broad chest and tried to speak. "H-How could y-you t-t-tell them—"

"Shh. Please, Elizabeth, just listen to me," he whispered. "I know I made up a whole bunch of stuff about our relationship, but could you please, please, please find it in your heart to play along?" He didn't wait for her to answer. "I'm in way over my head here, and I didn't know what else to do. A *month*. My God, a month with my mother trying to set me up with every available woman in Wilmington Bay. I just couldn't do it again. Last time I was home only for a weekend, and she called her friends and managed to get me three dates in less than forty-eight hours. No way will I survive a whole month."

He pointed frantically in the direction of the dining room.

"I love my brother with all my heart and soul, but that guy in there is killing me. *Five* kids! Who, by age twenty-six, has five kids? I'm older than Tony and not even married. Not even engaged. Hell, the last time I had a steady girlfriend was when I was still in college. I like the single life. I like being unencumbered. Kids scare the shit out of me, and every woman I've ever dated wants like twelve of them."

He inhaled several gulps of air.

"I come from a family of six siblings, Elizabeth. Only my little sister Ginny is still unmarried, and that's just because she's a college junior. But even *she's* got a serious boyfriend. Andy-something-or-other. And he looks like the type who'll propose the second after he crosses the graduation podium. The others are scattered around the country, but they call Mama. They speculate about me and exert their pressure on me long distance."

He ran his fingers through his thick dark wavy hair and looked at her with the closest thing to "fear" she'd ever seen on his handsome face.

"I know this has to be really awful for you," he said. "But would you please pretend you're my girlfriend, just for a few weeks? We can break up when our uncles come back from Europe. I'll go back to Chicago and won't ever bother you again. And I promise I'll make it seem like I'm the bad guy so you don't have to deal with my family's wrath or resentment if you run into any of them in town." He paused. "I'd be forever indebted

THE SWEET TEMPTATIONS COLLECTION

to you, Elizabeth, and in the meantime I'll work all of your shifts so you can finish your cookbook. I—I own a restaurant. I know how to make really great sandwiches. I can bring lunch over to you on my break. If you've got a dog, I can walk him. I do windows. I'll have Jacques teach me how to make éclairs and—"

"Rob?"

"Yeah?"

"W-Would you please shut up now?"

He clamped his lips together so comically she was seduced into laughing. And then, despite the absolute horrendousness of his idea, she found herself agreeing to "be his girlfriend" (and, yes, coming to family dinners as such) for the month of June.

How did her life get so out-of-control all of a sudden? So bizarre? Oh, that's right. Roberto Gabinarri came back into town.

"How's your throat, dear?" his mother asked upon their return. "Did the tea help?"

"Um, y-yes. I-I'm fine."

"Good. So, where were we when you left?" Alessandra Gabinarri paused and glanced around the table filled with her clan. She smiled with warmth at everyone. "Ah, yes. My son. Don't you think he should get married soon?"

~CHAPTER FOUR~

Rob couldn't believe he'd talked Elizabeth Daniels into this. A smart lady like her posing as his girlfriend. Probably the most intelligent female in his high school graduating class. Jeez, she must think he and his family were criminally insane.

But if she did, she didn't show it.

He watched her from across the table, still holding his breath as she fielded a slew of questions from his mother. Despite her longstanding difficulty speaking, she bravely fought through the stutters and tried to answer diplomatically.

"I-I think m-marriage is only right when two people are r-r-really in l-love." She glanced at Tony and Maria-Louisa as she spoke these words and, for the first time ever, he felt a surge of something like envy at what his brother had going. The guy was still in love with his wife, and it showed in Tony's every glimpse at her and at his passel of children.

"But there comes a time when a man needs to settle down," Mama insisted. "Don't you want a husband? A house? Children?"

Elizabeth nodded. "S-Sure."

"See?" His mother raised an eyebrow at him. "Women are smart. They know what they want. It's men who need to get their act together."

And at this, shy, sweet Frizzy Lizzy actually snickered. Mama beamed at her.

He didn't know which Madonna he should pray to tonight, but he was willing to send invocations to them both to keep his dear mother from planning a fall wedding.

Shortly after they devoured one of Mama's trademark tiramisus, he said it was time to go.

"Elizabeth has a cookbook to write," he told them, knowing how impressed they'd be by this fact. "And I have the closing shift at Tutti-Frutti to get to."

"Thanks for the d-delicious dinner."

Elizabeth's words were met with a gigantic squeeze from Mama who said, as he knew she would, "You must come every time with Roberto. He will be here tomorrow night, too, and I'm making a big lasagna." She gestured to show the enormous size of the tray. No exaggeration, either. Mama cooked large. "Please join us."

His new "girlfriend" stole a look in his direction before saying, "I'd b-be delighted."

"Fantastico!" And with that promise to hold close, Mama let the two of them go for the night.

"See you later, Rob," Tony said to him, and he knew his kid brother would have the sofa sleeper already pulled out and made up for him when he got in tonight after his closing shift. He was one lucky dude, having a brother like that. Even if the guy made him look like a slacker when it came to relationships.

"Thanks, Tony." He gave his mother a kiss and the family a parting wave. Then he lightly took Elizabeth's arm and led her to his Porsche.

"Whew," he said, when they'd driven a mile away from the house. "We did it." He turned to her. "Thank you. You were amazing. Brilliant. No one suspected a thing."

She looked at him for a long moment, her expression unreadable. "Roberto Gabinarri, that was the most deceitful, underhanded, lousy trick I've ever seen anyone play on their mother, and I think you should be ashamed of yourself. Both for trying to fool her and for manipulating her emotions in such a disgraceful way."

He felt a stab of pain in the vicinity of his heart. Damn it if she wasn't right, but this wasn't something he wanted to admit. Or intended to.

"And that was the longest sentence I've ever heard you say to me without stuttering," he said, striking back without thinking, and then wishing he could slap his own mouth for his thoughtlessness.

"I-Is that why you chose m-me?" she asked, pulling her lovely lips into a tight, unforgiving line. "Not because I wouldn't want to say no to you, but because you thought I *couldn't?*"

He pulled the car over to the side of the road and turned off the engine. It killed him that she'd think so poorly of him, that he'd hurt her like this, especially when she was trying to help him. It killed him worse that, in some small way, she was right. Not that he'd admit that either.

"I am so sorry, Elizabeth. No, that wasn't why I chose you. My comment was rude and inexcusable, and I hope you'll forgive me. Sometimes I speak without thinking."

"I never do," she whispered.

He nodded but the lump of self-recrimination in his throat kept him from replying.

"So, w-why did you choose me, th-then?"

Her question was a fair one, but he didn't have an honest answer. He'd already stretched the truth a bit. Yes, her inability to speak quickly and freely *had*, he was ashamed to admit, passed through his mind when he formed the idea of taking her to his mother's. With a family as chatty as his, and Elizabeth being so naturally quiet, he thought he might be able to direct the conversation with no one being the wiser. That had backfired, of course. But he'd also counted on Elizabeth's warm heart to see him through if he got caught. Which he had.

"I knew that, even if you were furious with me, you'd still back me up. That you wouldn't throw wine or ice water or hot tea in my face. That you wouldn't embarrass me in front of my family." All this was true, and he tried to project every ounce of his sincerity in saying it. "Thanks for being someone I could count on. Even though we haven't seen each other in years, you're still just as I remembered you."

At this, something dark passed behind her clear eyes and she looked down. "It's almost eight," she told him, belatedly touching her watch although she was clearly well aware of the time. "You'd better drive us back to Tutti-Frutti."

"Okay," he said, and let it go. He'd make this gaffe up to her. Hell, he'd have a month of dinners to do it. Maybe he'd even confide in Tony at the end of the month, ask him if he knew of any nice guys to set Elizabeth up with after he hightailed it back to Chicago.

Although there was something vaguely unsatisfying about that thought. Probably because she was a truly *nice* girl, and he wouldn't want her to get hurt by some of those creeps out there. God, there were a lot of bad dudes on the prowl.

They got back to the sweets shop and Elizabeth, after waving to Gretchen and Nick, slipped into her car and sped away.

"Hey, my sporting man," Nick said. "Glad you're finally here. Over two hours with the Gretch and I'm sick to death of hearing about reality TV shows and couples falling in love on islands in the Carrib—"

Gretchen gave him a powerful slug in the arm.

"Ow." Nick glared at her. "I totally hate it when you do that."

"And I 'totally hate it' when you shoot your big mouth off without so much as a thought passing through that sports-festering brain," she said, thrusting her ice cream scoop into a water bucket and wiping her fingers with a paper towel. Then she kissed Nick on the cheek. "Good thing I love you anyway," she told the young man as she reached for her handbag. "Where's Elizabeth? Did she leave already?"

"Yeah, I think so," Rob said.

"Were you nice to her?" she asked, giving him a threatening look.

He swallowed. "I tried to be."

Gretchen grinned. "Okay, then." She turned toward Nick.

"In that case, you can talk about sports with Rob."

"Like I need your *permission*," Nick said, but he blew her an air kiss.

She waved goodbye to Nick and surprised Rob by winking in his direction on her way out. This was one weird crowd Elizabeth hung with. But, he had to admit, they were growing on him.

"The guy's demented!" Gretchen shrieked on the phone when Elizabeth explained what had transpired over the past two and a half hours. "And you're going along with this? Someone ought to knock some sense into that—"

"Listen, Gretch, this was, without a doubt, one of Rob's least stellar ideas, but what could I do? His mother is this warm, jovial Italian lady who hums Madonna's 'Lucky Star' while she's buttering her garlic bread. I just couldn't make a scene in her home tonight. Not after she'd been so welcoming to me."

Gretchen harrumphed on the line. "But you can't possibly continue with this charade for four weeks, can you?"

Elizabeth sighed. "I doubt it. Actually, I doubt Rob will want me to. I'm betting he'll find someone to date for real within the week, and then this whole agreement will be history. Plus, I think his brother's on to us. But, for now, I might as well make the most of the extra writing time he's giving me."

"You're really okay?" her friend asked.

"Yeah. I'm okay," she said, collapsing into a chair and marveling at how quickly she'd grown accustomed to lying.

The next day at eleven a.m., after four straight hours of morning typing—preceded by six hours of restless sleep spent dreaming about Rob and typing, and four hours of late-night typing the day before—Elizabeth decided it was high time she took a break and peeked in on the happenings at Tutti-Frutti.

Just long enough to make sure everything was running smoothly, she told herself.

But, of course, with Rob in charge, nothing was running according to *her* version of "smoothly."

Loud music greeted her ears as she pulled into a nearby parking space.

People jammed their bodies against the windows, gawking at something inside the shop and pausing to laugh.

A line snaked its way through the doorway, passed the hedges, across the sidewalk and close to the street.

Elizabeth held her breath and plunged into the mayhem. What she saw stopped her in her sneakers.

For the first time in the shop's forty-year history, there were jugglers—that's right, *more than one*—making spectacles of themselves by spinning, twirling, throwing and catching colorful beanbag ice cream cones, all to the amazement and delight of the gathering Wilmington Bay crowd. It was all she could do to push her way passed the horde and begin hunting for the Gabinarri responsible for this mess.

"Th-This is crazy. What are all these people doing ins-s-side?" she hissed in Rob's ear as he put a swirl of whipped cream on a chocolate malt.

"Having fun is not crazy. It's a good promotional tool. Look." He pointed with his elbow at a mom with two preschool girls. All three were eating double-decker ice cream cones and laughing at the jugglers' antics. Then he nodded in the direction of another grouping, this time six teens, each holding either a strawberry sundae or a Neapolitan ice cream sandwich.

"B-But, Rob, this is a very small shop. I don't know what the exact c-c-code regulations are, but I know we're only allowed an indoor capacity of twenty-five customers." She glanced around and tried to count heads. "There are over f-fifty people in here!"

"They'll be out the door and on their way home soon," he said. "But, the thing is, they'll all come back in search of new surprises and more great-tasting ice cream. And it won't be en masse like this. They'll return in little clusters. They'll talk amongst themselves and tell their friends. Slowly, our daily visitor average will increase. By the end of the month, we might even double profits. And won't that just make your uncle and mine do a happy jig in Europe?"

He didn't give her a chance to answer.

"Sure it will! Before long they'll be making more money than they know what to do with. Maybe they'll open up a branch in another Wisconsin town...or even spread their franchise into Illinois or Minnesota or Iowa. The possibilities, my little naysayer, are limitless."

"Who hired these jugglers?"

"Nobody," Rob said, starting on an order for a triple fudge ice cream sundae.

"They j-just came in here and started juggling by themselves? Without warning?"

He shot her an irritated look. "No, Elizabeth. The two of them dropped by for a cone and we all got to talking—"

"God, I should've known," she muttered.

"—and I found out they were professional jugglers from Milwaukee, so I asked to see some of their best stunts. And they were great." He grinned at the two performers appreciatively. "So, I sent Jacques out to buy the ice cream beanbags from the Hobby Shoppe on Fourth and Main—"

"Where *is* Jacques?" She scanned the room but didn't see him. Rob just kept on chattering.

"—and I told these guys they'd get free ice cream or a complimentary pastry anytime they came into the shop if they did fifteen minutes of juggling for our customers." He checked his watch. "Although, I think they decided to use this as practice time because they've been at it for over a half hour."

A beanbag whizzed by her ear, narrowly missing her head. She frowned at Rob.

"They might be getting ready for their grand finale now," he said.

Amidst a wild flurry of flying beanbags, she gritted her teeth and ducked while searching the room. Her gaze finally came to rest on Jacques who, in time to the hip-hop sounds blaring from the jugglers' portable stereo, was rolling his shoulders and swiveling his hips as he delivered a tray full of orders to a table of kids and their pleased-looking grandma.

Oh, brother.

"Th-This kind of blatant showmanship is going to get us in trouble, Rob, if anyone complains or if the authorities start checking up on us. We could get f-fined for breaking capacity codes."

He leaned toward her, his gorgeous brown eyes widening with good humor and impertinence. He pressed his full lips together and got so close she could see the tiny perpendicular lines on their ruddy red surface. The lips twisted into a devious grin, and one heavily lashed eye winked at her, which sent her heart rate on a skyrocket mission to Venus.

"Lighten up, Lizzy," he whispered in that low, ultra-sexy voice of his.

She tightened her Plain-Jane lips and narrowed her own lackluster eyes at him. "Elizabeth," she insisted.

He grinned bigger. Leaned closer.

"Oh, my gosh! Rob Gabinarri! Is that really you?"

They both turned toward the counter where a familiar woman stood beaming at Rob. Elizabeth hadn't seen Rob's high-school flame in years, but the sight of the bottle blonde put her right back into her chubby senior-year stretch pants and seized her voice.

Rob, of course, didn't miss a beat.

"Tara Welles? Hey, how are you?"

"Absolutely wonderful," his old girlfriend cooed. Her eyes swept over him. "And don't *you* look fabulous."

"Thanks. Want an ice cream? An éclair? Some chocolate-covered macadamia nuts?"

"Ooh, maybe just a *tiny* little something," Tara said, perusing the selections. "A double chocolate-caramel sundae with peanuts and sprinkles on top."

"You got it," he said. "Can you help me with that, Elizabeth?" He motioned for her to grab another ice cream scoop.

She tried to whisper "Sure" but couldn't quite manage it.

Tara's cool blue eyes surveyed her from head to toe and back again, then the blonde let out a muffled laugh. *"Lizzy?* Lizzy Daniels? Oh, heavens. Imagine seeing you again."

Elizabeth succeeded in raising her hand for a brief wave. She refused to be goaded into opening her mouth, however.

"You look—" Tara paused as if searching for just the right scathing adjective, "—the same but...smaller."

Terrific. But what had she expected? A high compliment?

She worked on Tara's sundae, replacing the requested caramel with butterscotch, skimping on the chocolate ice cream and putting only half a teaspoon of nuts and one shake of sprinkles on top. She handed it to Tara with her best imitation smile and the single word she could form. "H-Here." *Take it and don't come back.*

"Mmm." Tara dug her spoon in and lasciviously licked it clean, her gaze fixed on Rob. She did this several times. Now, to be fair, she may have merely been preparing for an Adults Only performance at the Hasty Tasty Bar and Strip Club, but Elizabeth doubted it. It seemed as though Tara had set her sights on Rob again and, from the attentive look on his face, she was well on her way to getting what she wanted.

"Holy Smokes, the rumors are true," a male voice boomed. "Gabinarri's back."

And the morning's only getting better. She sighed and tried to bring her vulnerable heart back into protective custody.

"Burk. It's been a long time," Rob said, his voice tightening.

Elizabeth stole a few glances between the two men. Lance Burk had been about the dumbest-acting of the dumb jocks at Wilmington Bay High and a football rival of Rob's since sixth grade—even when they were playing on the same team. A good-looking guy, empirically speaking (except for that thick neck), he stood about half a foot taller than Tara and placed his hand possessively on her shoulder. She brushed it off, her lust-filled eyes never leaving Rob's face.

"Heard you opened a diner somewhere," Lance said with a bored expression.

"The Playbook is a restaurant on the top story of one of

Chicago's tallest buildings, Burk. It's not a diner."

Lance shrugged. "Whatever." He hooked his thumbs in the loops of his jeans and spread his legs apart in a territorial stance. It reminded Elizabeth of a pit bull readying his attack—only pit bulls could be warm and cuddly on occasion. She'd never known Lance Burk to be either.

"Did you have an order?" Rob asked.

"Nope. Not today. Just wanted to see you in your new digs." Lance scoped the room and caught a beanbag as it rocketed toward the counter. He tossed it in the air a few times and chucked. "You're really moving up in the world, Gabinarri." He flung the silly beanbag at Rob then tapped the blonde on her tanned and toned upper arm. "Let's go, Tara."

Tara batted her eyelashes at Rob one final time. "See you soon. Real soon."

He waved her a quick farewell while Elizabeth busied herself with filling orders. Once the Dynamic Duo walked out the door, though, she had a chance to study Rob's face. His expression was completely unreadable, but she knew what his stony façade must mean: Jealousy. Tara looked as stunning as ever (much as Elizabeth hated to admit it), and she was with Lance, Rob's former opponent, on some kind of casual date. Rob must surely want her back, even if he didn't want to get married or have kids this year. And, if Elizabeth read Tara's signs and signals correctly, Rob wouldn't have much difficulty getting his wish.

But, on a high note, the jugglers finally stopped juggling, the music got turned off and the customers went back to their regularly scheduled lives.

She breathed a sigh of relief.

When the tile floor was clear of townspeople, Jacques bounced in her direction. "Exciting day, no?" he said, still gyrating his hips and snapping his fingers. "Rob's *extraordinairement* ideas make me want to dance."

"Everything makes you want to dance," she said.

He tried to engage her in a hip-hop boogie next to him, but the customers and the noise had drained her of every last ounce of sociability. Plus, she needed to save her strength for another evening with the Gabinarris. She pulled away and Jacques bopped off without her.

Rob was cleaning some of the utensils in the backroom and had become uncharacteristically silent. Brooding, no doubt. Or, maybe, plotting Tara's easy seduction. Elizabeth was preparing herself to return home and settle down to another four or so hours of typing when her cell phone rang.

"Camden, how are you?" she said to her photographer.

"Good, good, darling. Remarkably, unbelievably good. I'm in love."

"Oh, that's...that's terrific. Wow." This was saying something. A statement for the record books, in fact. Camden was not one to easily fall. "I'm so happy for you. Who's the lucky lady?"

"My Annabelle. She's the most gentle, delicate creature I've ever seen, hiding inside the buffest, most sculpted body imaginable."

Elizabeth heard some loud splintering noises on the line. It sounded like a ceiling beam had just crashed into the floor. "Cam, my goodness! Are you okay? Where are you? Please don't tell me you're on assignment in a war zone."

"No, no. I'm at Annabelle's karate studio in Idaho. She's amazing," he said, his tone blanketed with an awe she'd never heard from him before.

"Um, well, I'd love to meet her sometime. Maybe when you come over to do the photos next week she can—"

"Oh, right," he said. "That's why I called. There's no way I can make it out to Wisconsin next week or, really, anytime this month. Annabelle and I are going on a little jaunt out to Yellowstone where I'm going to shoot her doing karate poses in nature. Can you be a darling and let me reschedule for early or mid July?"

"W-Well, sure, I guess. I'd hoped we could have the shots taken and developed well before the publisher's deadline, though, just in case anything needs to be redone."

"Not a problem. Not a problem. We'll have plenty of time

to re-shoot if necessary. But you know I'm a one-shot wonder."

Elizabeth heard another booming crash over the phone line.

"Ohhh," he groaned. "Just watching her kick those muscled legs so high...and break bricks with a slice of her fragile hand...and flip unsuspecting opponents in the air the way I'd toss my Nikon bag over my shoulder... Man, it's like hottest foreplay ever."

"Thanks for sharing, Cam."

"What?"

"Nothing," she said. "Okay, so we'll talk in a few weeks and set the date. Jacques here is especially excited to get his éclairs immortalized on Kodak paper."

Another bash, bang, boom. "Fine. Fine. Tell him we'll get it done. Gotta go now. Thanks for being so flexible, darling." And on that note, Camden hung up.

She stashed her phone in her purse and stepped onto the sidewalk. A young man and woman strolled by holding hands. Teen lovers, oblivious to the world, made out on a bench across the street. An elderly, longtime married couple window-shopped in the stores nearby.

And Camden was in love with Annabelle the Karate Queen.

And Rob was probably daydreaming about Tara.

And she was still alone...and needing to go to yet another heartbreaking dinner at the house of the man who only wanted her to *pretend* to be his girlfriend.

~CHAPTER FIVE~

Could this day get any worse? Rob thought as he cleaned up after his three to five-thirty shift and prepared to hand the reins over to Nick and Gretchen.

Tara Welles and Lance Burk. Now there was a pair who deserved one another.

He shook his head remembering their visit.

Seeing Tara was like running into a pesky little sister, but seeing Burk always inspired him to violence. To want to sack him. It was the very *way* of him. So. Damned. Annoying.

He spotted Elizabeth's car pulling up in front of the shop. Punctual, as usual.

Jacques stood by the counter, chatting it up with Gretchen. Nick played a final round of his favorite electronic game on his smart phone. Some sports thing, of course. A couple of customers lingered over waffle cones and sodas. Rob slipped out unnoticed.

"Hey," he said to Elizabeth. "Recovered from the rappin' jugglers yet?"

One small corner of one side of her mouth lifted into a very literal half-smile. It was a funny thing. For someone who didn't talk much, the lady sure had a way of expressing herself.

"Ah, don't worry," he said. "They've got gigs lined up for

weeks. We probably won't see them again."

She stepped out of the car and he saw she was wearing a long skirt. A nice one in a pretty shade of green. Very delicate ankles.

"Th-That's not what w-worries me, Rob."

"What worries you?"

She raised a brow at him and sighed. "Let's just go."

He put his palm on her shoulder to stop her from turning away. "No, c'mon. Tell me. Please."

Some kind of private battle duked it out on her face, but she seemed to give in to his request. "This m-m-morning, what you did, getting those jugglers. I-I didn't like it. It was risky and it made me nervous, but—"

"But what?"

"But it was also k-kind of ingenious. How you p-pulled it off. It's not something I would think of. Ever."

A pride he didn't want to admit, but couldn't deny, crept into his spine and crawled up it, making him stand taller. "Thanks, I think," he said.

"You're welcome. Sort of," she said back.

"Anything besides that on your mind?" he asked her, hoping it might be something else good but fearing it probably wasn't.

"No," she answered quickly and, before he could fish for more compliments, she slid into his car, sank into the leather seats and angled herself away from him. Great. They'd make a believable couple, all right, just not a couple still in the throes of infatuation.

He cracked his knuckles, revved up the engine and played his part by pretending to ignore her, too. And, so, onward to Mama's for a second dinner they went. Two meals down. Only twenty-eight to go.

As promised, a huge pan of lasagna awaited them. The aroma of oregano, basil and garlic greeted them at the door like a butler, while the "Material Girl" sang cloyingly through the speakers of Mama's stereo. Home again.

Mama was busy in the kitchen and the kids were with

Maria-Louisa in the basement again, but Tony ushered them in, took the plate of cookies they brought, clapped him on the back and smooched Elizabeth lightly on the cheek.

"You look smashing tonight," his brother told Elizabeth, giving her the Male Eye-Scan (face, chest, legs, chest).

She grinned at Tony. Tony winked at her.

"Knock it off," Rob said to him. "You're a married man. You don't get to ogle or wink or flirt." At this, Elizabeth turned her big, surprised eyes on him.

"What?" he said to her. "You're my girlfriend, and my brother ought to be checking out his wife, and his wife *only*. There are rules."

She and Tony made eye contact, and Rob heard her whisper to Tony, "You know the truth, don't you?"

Tony reached over and took her hand, then he kissed it gently. "You're an amazing woman, Elizabeth, and my brother is a world-class idiot."

She didn't say anything to that, she merely sighed.

"What the hell are you talking about?" he said to Tony, lowering his voice in case Mama snuck in on them.

But it wasn't his brother who answered him. It was Elizabeth.

"He knows w-we're not really a couple," she whispered. "He's sharp. He figured it out last night."

Panic gripped his throat. "When last night?"

"During dinner, would be my guess." She motioned to Tony with her palm.

"Before, actually," Tony said. "When we all talked in the hallway."

She nodded. "Maria-Louisa knows, too, d-doesn't she?"

Tony shrugged. "Probably. We didn't discuss it."

"Liar," Rob said. "You two discuss everything." *Dammit.*

"Okay, fine, but you fooled the kids," Tony said, his voice taking on a hard, dangerous edge. "And, of course, you sure bamboozled Mama. That's gotta make you proud, big brother."

"Well, hell, you know how she gets when—"

"That's neither here nor there," Tony said. "But, since

Elizabeth was willing to play your game to help you, I won't snitch on you. Not this time. But you'll owe me."

Rob may have missed Tony's moment of realization last night, but he didn't miss the threatening note in his brother's tone tonight, nor could he avoid seeing the sadness lingering in Elizabeth's eyes as she looked away from him and headed toward the dining room.

He felt like the idiot his brother claimed he was.

The trampling of little feet thundered up the stairs and beelined straight for the table. Jeez, did those kids ever slow down? After a chorus of enthusiastic Hi's and Hello's to and from Maria-Louisa and the kids, Mama marched into the room.

"Oh, *good*. Our Elizabeth is here again!" Mama held her tight, and "Frizzy Lizzy" embraced his mother with a warmth she might have reserved for her own dear mom.

And now he felt like guilt-ridden fool.

"Roberto." Mama kissed him. "How was your day at the shop? You want to follow in your Uncle Pauly's footsteps now? Work at Tutti-Frutti?" Hopeful, futile questions.

"I like what I do in Chicago, Mama. And, besides, Siegfried and Uncle Pauly will be back before we know it." He said this to try to convince himself, but four weeks still seemed like an eternity of two-and-a-half hour shifts.

"Tell her about the j-jugglers," Elizabeth said with a crafty look made all the more wily because she routinely passed herself off as such an innocent.

He narrowed his eyes at her before turning back to his mother.

"We've been having a little fun at the shop and doing some different things," he explained without really explaining. "Some jugglers entertained us today for a while. No big deal. I doubt they'll be back and, besides, I'm sure our uncles will go on doing things their same old way when they come home. That's what works best for them."

His mother raised a dark eyebrow.

"I'm not trying to interfere or change things too much, Mama. There's no room for another person's vision anyway.

Too many chefs and all that."

Mama tweaked his nose. "So sure of yourself, Roberto, aren't you? Now go wash your hands for dinner."

He sighed and did as he was told.

Strange night, though, and he didn't know why exactly. A certain vibe shimmied between him and Elizabeth. Maybe because he sat next to her tonight instead of across the table from her. Maybe because they had this shared secret. Or maybe just because the moon grew fuller as the June nights grew longer, making weird ions hang in the air everywhere. Or something.

Anyway, for whatever reason, all through the meal he felt himself being hyper-attentive to her: The way she talked (so sweetly) to his niece and squirmy nephews. The way she interacted (so politely) with his Mama and Tony and Maria-Louisa. The way she emitted (so surprisingly) a very grown-up sensuality that seemed both innate and unpretentious.

He'd never allowed himself to think of her like *that*. Like a potential conquest. Partly because they'd roamed in such different spheres during high school, but mostly because she'd never been the kind of girl who threw herself at him.

She still wasn't.

But, he remembered overhearing her say he had a "hot body" yesterday. That was something, he supposed, although not nearly as promising as the "kind of ingenious" compliment she gave him about getting the jugglers today. And once, during their junior year, she'd called one of his world-history project ideas "very clever" after class.

He smiled at that.

"Why are you laughing, Uncle Rob?" Camilla the little pixie asked him.

"I wasn't laughing."

"Yes, you were!"

"I was smiling," he said, noticing all the eyes at the table turning toward him and looking more interested than they needed to be. Elizabeth, in particular, seemed pretty damn curious.

"Why were you *smiling*, then?" Camilla said.

"I just had a happy memory."

"Oooh! Was it from your birthday?"

"No," he told the girl. "It was from a long, long time ago." Then, taking a chance, "It was from a conversation Elizabeth and I had when we were in high school."

He put his hand over Elizabeth's jittery one and gazed into her shocked green eyes. Hey, what was the use of pretending to have a girlfriend unless he acted somewhat affectionately toward her, right? He had to make the show believable, if only for his mother's benefit.

"Remember history class with Mr. Monroe?" he said to Elizabeth, rubbing the top of her hand and feeling the soft skin with the firm bones just beneath. "I remember how you used to know the answers to just about everything in there. Really impressive."

She tried to tug her fingers away. No way was he letting her. He held fast with one hand and began stroking gently with the other.

"I-I d-didn't know all th-the answers."

"Sure you did." He traced her tiny blue veins with his fingertip and grinned at her. "You sat two seats away from me, so I always noticed what you were doing. Most of the time you were looking at the clock or staring out the window. You were at least three million light years away. Then Mr. Monroe would ask a question about World War II or the Russian government or something. If you heard it, you'd slink down in your seat behind Kent Grommer. If you didn't, you'd just keep on daydreaming. He'd ask a bunch of people, but they wouldn't know the answer. Then, when he couldn't stand it anymore, he'd call on you or on Matthew Landers. And, no matter what, whether you'd been paying attention or not, you could answer the question. It was freaking amazing."

She shot him a glare, which confused him. He'd kill for a compliment like that, but she was clearly sending an I'm-Pissed-Off vibe in his direction. And also still trying to get him to release her hand.

He tried to put it another way so she'd get his meaning. "Look, everybody wished they could do that, too. Be acknowledged as the smartest one. That's why girls like Tara Welles were so jealous of you."

She stopped both tugging and glaring. "W-What?"

"Well, yeah. I mean, I couldn't do what you did either, and I even liked history. I'd concentrate as hard as I could, but I could barely follow Mr. Monroe's train of thought. For you, it didn't even seem as tough as breathing."

Her hand lay like a limp dinner roll beneath his. Her blank expression gave away nothing. "Y-You're kidding?"

He shook his head. "Nope." Then he turned to Tony. "Tell her. Wasn't she like a legend in high school?"

Tony didn't speak. He merely answered with one of his sage nods and a grin.

Camilla piped up, "Was that your happy memory, Uncle Rob?"

"Kind of," he said, knowing he'd be too embarrassed to explain the real recollection. He turned to look deep into Elizabeth's eyes and saw a flash of something there. Her big brain must be hard at work trying to process his words, evaluate their merit. What her conclusion would be was anyone's guess, though.

"Ah, young love," his Mama mused, standing to clear away the dessert dishes. "Why don't you all go relax on the patio?"

"Th-Thank you, Mrs. Gabinarri," Elizabeth said, almost jumping to her feet, "but I have to g-get back a little earlier tonight."

"You do?" Rob said. She hadn't mentioned this to him before.

Her head bobbed vigorously. "Work."

Like hell.

"Okay, sweetheart." He patted her hand, which was clenched tight again. What had he done to get her so angry and why was she shorting him forty-five minutes? Not that he didn't want to leave, too, but they had a *deal*. "Sorry, Mama. I guess Elizabeth's cookbook project can't be put off any longer."

"Well, that's all right," Mama said. "We'll see you both again tomorrow, yes?"

Elizabeth smiled at his mother. "Of course."

"Absolutely," he said at the same time.

Mama disappeared into the kitchen. Elizabeth snatched her hand away from him once and for all and turned abruptly away.

He glanced at his still-seated family members, and he saw how Camilla tilted her little head in thought. And Maria-Louisa squinted at him. And Tony, never one to hold back, rolled his eyes and pressed his knuckles to his own lips.

"Have a terrific night, you two," Tony called after them as they walked out the door. Although, Rob could tell his little brother expected the remainder of the evening to be just the opposite.

❦ ♥ ❧

Elizabeth massaged her temples and took full, body-cleansing breaths in Rob's car.

"Thanks for springing us early," he said a few blocks down the road, "but what happened back there?"

"N-Nothing." What could she tell him? That having him caress her hand the way he did at the table was torturous and hurtful since he didn't mean it? That his preposterous fib about her being envied by girls like Tara was even more so?

The tips of his ears turned an attractive shade of pink, but Rob's temper seemed to run several degrees hotter. "Nothing? You practically sprinted out of my mother's house. We may be playing a charade in there, but be straight with me here."

"B-Be straight with y-y-you?" She clasped her fingers together and shook them in front of her, imagining she had them around his neck. "Rob, you've d-done nothing but lie to me since you came into town."

"What? I didn't—" He swerved the car over to the side of the road and parked it.

Oh, goody. This was becoming a nifty nightly ritual.

"Okay, now you listen up, Elizabeth Daniels. The only thing

I lied about was telling my family we were a couple. With Tony and Maria-Louisa guessing the truth, the only person I'm lying to—and asking you to lie to—is my Mama. And yes, yes, I know that's still scummy of me, but I have my reasons, and I already told those to you. I haven't lied to you about a thing since then."

"We're also lying to the k-kids."

He shrugged. "But they don't really care."

"They do. Camilla does especially."

He narrowed his eyes at her. "That's why you're mad? Because of them?"

It was partly the truth, but she didn't clarify, which also made it partly a lie as well. Still, she wasn't going to explain that if he touched her again she might have to choke him to make him stop. Every cell inside her body went haywire with desire for him when their fingers joined together. And looking into her eyes, so sincerely it seemed, for those few nanoseconds before she realized he was just acting...that almost did her in at the Gabinarri house.

"Huh. You really like kids, don't you?"

"Yes," she said.

"How much do you like them?" he asked, his voice laced with suspicion. "When you get married, how many children do you want to have?"

Well, there was no denying it. She wanted what she wanted. *"If* I get married, I w-want four."

"Four! For real?"

She nodded, shrugged and turned to look out the window.

"Jeez," he said. "What is it with you women?"

She figured this was a rhetorical question he didn't expect her to answer. She was wrong.

"Elizabeth?"

"What?"

"Explain this to me. Why on earth would you want a brood of little rug rats tearing up your house? They make messes everywhere. They ask a gazillion questions. They fight and bicker with each other until you're crazed with wanting to get away from them. Granted, they're cute and all, especially when they're asleep, but that's hardly a reason to have so many of them living with you."

She thought about her mom—the delightful messes they made together in the kitchen when she was little, the long walks they took while asking questions about each other's day, the warmth and closeness they'd always shared. Motherhood was such a special relationship. A gift to treasure. Then, knowing she'd sound like a Hallmark card but not caring, she said, "Because p-parenting is about real and true love."

This comment seemed to halt his wagging tongue.

"So what's wrong with getting a dog or a cat or a pet alligator?" he said finally. "You could fall in love with a baby black widow. I've seen it happen. This guy in my college dorm treated his spider like royalty. He named her 'Legs' and he kept her in a golden—"

"Rob."

"What?"

"That's not the same thing. At all."

He sighed. "I guess not. I just—well, it's hard for me to imagine I'd ever feel ready. That I'd ever know I could handle the problems that'd come up. My mother—she's amazing. She knew when we were really sick and when we were faking. She helped us with our schoolwork even though English was her second language. When Dad died, she kept the family together, despite her own sorrow. I mean, she must've just wanted to crawl into bed and hide in her room for three months, but she didn't. She worked. She made our meals. She let us be sad or angry or whatever we felt." He gave her a serious look. "I wouldn't be able to pull off something like that."

Elizabeth remembered when Rob's dad had died, just before their senior year in high school. She hadn't imagined he'd been so haunted by it, though. That it would have affected his decision whether or not to be a father. Then again, the deaths of her parents had affected her as profoundly—only in the opposite direction.

"You'd b-be able to do it. No matter what, I think everyone

has fears about being a parent."

"Maybe," he said.

"Tony must've had worries when he became a dad. Did you talk to him about it?"

An odd look came over his face. "Umm, not recently. Look, we've got some time before I have to be back at the shop. If you're able to stay away from your computer for another half hour, I could buy you some coffee or something. What do you say?"

What could she say?

"O-Okay."

"Great. Let's get out of here."

A few minutes later they were seated at Karen's Koffee Shoppe on First and Central. She'd gotten a handful of cappuccinos here over the years, but she'd never ordered and sat in a booth. Least of all with a guy. She always took everything to go. And this...this...*outing*, or whatever it was with Rob, felt suspiciously like a date.

Too bizarre for words. Though most things were.

"So, where do you usually hang out on Saturday nights when you aren't surviving stressful family dinners with old high school friends?" Rob said.

Stressful dinners, she wouldn't argue, but old high school *friends?* Is that what he thought they were?

But she didn't say that. She said, "Gretchen, Nick, Jacques and I get t-together sometimes. We have Treat Swaps."

"Treat Swaps? What's that?"

"We each bring something we m-made to share. Tortes, crepes, chocolate, pastries...anything good...and we taste test."

"Mmm. That sounds fun." He licked his lips and she felt her attraction to him rise from her belly, still churning with suppressed anxiety, to her own lips, which trembled strangely but, she hoped, unnoticeably.

"It is," she said. And, then, to her own astonishment, she added, "M-Maybe you can join us sometime."

His eyes lit up like a little kid being handed his first triple-decker ice cream sundae. "Thanks, Elizabeth. That'd be great.

Just let me know when you're going to do it again. I can't promise to make anything fancy like you guys do, but I'll bring along something for everyone, too."

She nodded and took a long sip of her cappuccino. *He's only here for a few weeks*, she reminded herself. *Don't think you can adopt him into your little group. Don't think he'll become your new best friend. Don't think someone like Rob Gabinarri will stay around for a second longer than he has to.*

But it was hard to deny that niggling little hope, that unruly wish that she'd get the answer wrong for once.

They got on the subject of kids again, a topic Rob couldn't seem to move away from.

"So why, if you like children so much, didn't you become a teacher or something? You seem really at ease when you're around Tony's kids, and they listen to you," he said.

At this she had to laugh. "Don't you realize how much t-talking is involved in teaching? I'd freeze."

He squinted at her as if trying to figure out a Great Mystery of the Universe. "I've heard you with them, though. Your speech is really smooth." Then he paused as if weighing his words. "You don't stutter then, Elizabeth."

Well, at least he was able to openly acknowledge her disability. Two points for him and a big brownie with chocolate chips on top. At least he wasn't one of awful people who pretended to ignore her stuttering while looking like they were going to crawl out of their skin with impatience. Or, even worse, one of those people who spoke *louder* when they talked to her.

"I'm c-comfortable with the kids. I don't feel the kind of pressure from th-them that I do with adults. Unfortunately, teaching is not just doing art projects with seven-year-olds and a bunch of Popsicle sticks. There are the parents and the staff members and the administrators." She took a breath after her long explanation. "Writing lets me p-put everything on paper first. Even most of my communication with m-my editor is done through e-mail. That works best for me."

"Okay, fair enough. But I've also heard you talking to Gretchen, Nick and Jacques. You barely ever stumble with them."

She squeezed her lips shut. How to explain this? If she said that they were her friends and that's why she could speak freely in their presence, would he be offended? He seemed to think of the two of them as friends, too and, yet, she was anything but at ease with him.

"I've known them a long time," she said.

"You've known me a longer time." He raised his eyebrows at her in challenge, but the smile on his lips told her he was still in good humor. "What's the difference?"

She took another sip of cappuccino to buy a few seconds. "Did y-you ever run into someone after a f-few years had gone by and, when the two of you started talking, it was l-like those years disappeared? You felt the same feelings you felt before just by being around that person?"

He grinned. "You mean the way I feel like I'm ten again whenever I'm back at Mama's house?"

"Kind of. Yes."

"Well, sure. Certain people pull you back into the context of whatever time period you shared. When I get together with my college roommates, it's like we're twenty-year-old slackers again, just interested in playing football in the courtyard and watching action flicks on TV and drinking beer at a sports bar."

She nodded and watched his handsome face as realization slowly dawned.

"You mean, being with me puts you back into high school mode? Makes you feel like you're there again?"

"Now you're on it, Detective Holmes," she said.

He crossed his arms, shooting a faux-scowl in her direction. "Did that snide, stutter-free comment really come from *you*, the reputedly oh-so-sweet-and-not-very-communicative Miss Lizzy Daniels?"

A giggle escaped her lips without permission. "Elizabeth," she told him.

He laughed then gulped down some of his own coffee. After a few moments he said, "Was it that bad for you back then? I always kind of thought *not* being in the spotlight would've been a little easier. But what do I know."

It had been bad but, no, she didn't plan on telling him that. He didn't need to know about the nasty "observations" popular girls like Tara made about her or the unkind remarks sports-hero guys like Lance said to other, similar, sports-hero guys. Guys like Rob. If he didn't remember it for himself, she sure as heck wasn't about to remind him.

"Y-You didn't like being adored by the masses?" she asked instead. "You didn't want everyone drooling over your opinion of just about anything or...or driving out in droves to watch your Midas touch on the football field?"

He fingered his stirring stick and flicked a few coffee droplets on the napkin in front of him. "I'd have traded it for something else in a heartbeat."

"What kind of 'something else,' Rob? There weren't that many choices for cliques. And, c'mon. You c-can't expect me to believe you wished you'd been unpopular."

He looked up at her, his dark eyes intense. "Okay, maybe not 'unpopular' but I sure could've lived without that Golden Boy crap. That was a lot of pressure to live with. People projecting their wishes on you all the time. No one taking you seriously in any area but sports. Feeling like every single move you made was being watched and recorded by somebody who wanted something from you, but you were never sure what it was. God, I hated that."

None of his characteristic good humor remained. He was in full glowering form. But, for the first time, it occurred to her that maybe they both craved the same thing: To be seen as they were now, not as they once had been.

"I guess neither of us felt too happy w-with our lot in life back then," she admitted.

"Ain't that the truth." He squinted at her. "So, why did you stay? Why not ditch Wilmington Bay the minute you could blow town?"

"Like you did?"

He nodded.

Why *did* she stay? "I guess there are a few reasons. Living here is 'the devil I know,' so to speak. I don't spend much time out and about the town, but when I do, I know my way around. My only living relative is Uncle Siegfried, and he's here. My three best friends are here, too. I wouldn't want to start all over in a new place. Plus, Wilmington Bay has some g-great memories for me also, especially of times I'd spent with my parents."

"Okay, I get that. But aren't you ever nibbled by the wanderlust bug? Want to go out and see what else the world has to offer?"

"Maybe a little," she admitted. "I went with my parents to California once. To a spot my mom really loved. Mendocino. I wouldn't have minded spending more time there. It was beautiful. But Wilmington Bay is home. I don't plan to ever move away."

"Hmm." He stared at her for a second, brows pushed together, and then pointed with his chin to her cappuccino. "Want a refill to go? I have to get back to Tutti-Frutti before your 'longtime friends' skewer me with a swizzle stick for tardiness. Scary, those people."

"Are not."

"Are, too," he insisted. "But I like them, and I can see why you like them." He gave her a long, scrutinizing look. "I can also see why they like you."

He grabbed a second round of coffee for each of them and tossed away their trash before driving them back to the ice cream parlor.

"Thanks for the evening," he said, opening her car door and helping her out. Not that she needed help. She was just too stunned to refuse.

With her second cappuccino in one hand and his fingers gripping her other one, it was all she could do to step onto the sidewalk and nod her thanks at him.

He smiled and brought his lips to the back of her hand, making every nerve fiber tingle. "See you tomorrow, Elizabeth," he said. "Sweet dreams."

Oh, yeah. That was going to happen all right. Damn.

~CHAPTER SIX~

"**D**id you like your surprise, Boss Man?"

"You're the best," Rob said on the phone to his favorite Chicagoan, admiring the three big boxes of milk-chocolate-covered fruit slices Miguel had stashed between the folds of his requested casual attire. "You know just what I like. Now, tell me about my restaurant. What disasters are happening down there in my absence?"

Miguel huffed on the line. "There are no disasters with me at the helm, oh, ye of zilcho faith. The staff's hopping around like rabbits trying to keep up with demand. We've been booked solid every night since you've been away."

"We were booked solid every night *before* I went away, too," he reminded his buddy, "but thanks for keeping up the good work. Maybe I'll give you a raise."

Miguel snorted. "I already gave myself one."

"Way to stay one step ahead," Rob said. "Hey, you guys need anything down there?"

"Can you spare any of your uncle Pauly's ice cream? It's been Death-Valley hot this weekend and the coolest dessert we have on the menu this month is flan."

Hmm. Rob hadn't considered putting ice cream on the menu before. He figured it wouldn't strike customers as the kind of chic selection that epitomized a hot spot like The Playbook. Too commonplace. But Uncle Pauly and Siegfried had a local supplier, one who made the ice cream thicker and creamier than store-bought brands. Several of the flavors were, in fact, made the Italian way, chockfull of fat and sugar and undeniable goodness.

"Tell you what," he said to Miguel. "Add a section on the new menu. Call it 'Gelato,' the Italian name for ice cream. By tomorrow, I'll get this local guy to ship out three sample flavors for you to test on next week's crowd. If it goes over, I'll send down some more, and maybe I'll throw in a box or two of Greek pastries. There's a kid working here who makes some amazing baklava. Give me a ring later and let me know how it's working out."

"You got it." Then Miguel laughed. "Pretty soon we're going to have an international menu, what with all the foreign words you've got me adding to it."

Rob thought of Jacques (a French import), Nick (a first-generation Greek), Gretchen (whose ancestry was Swiss), Elizabeth (a descendent of Germans and Englishmen) and then of his own Italian background. "That's kind of what my life's about right now," he said. "I'm living in Wisconsin's version of the United Nations."

"Well, be a good boy and try not to aggravate any of the natives or foreigners, okay? It would mess with your America's Least Wanted image."

"What's that supposed to mean?"

"C'mon, Boss Man. I know you're Italian, but you act as White Bread as they come. You never rock the yacht. You charm the cleats off everybody. A straight, good-looking guy like you doesn't need to try so hard to be All-American inconspicuous. Now me, on the other hand, a hot Latino gay brother—I need to be more careful. I need to blend."

Rob imagined Miguel prancing around the restaurant while saying this, striking poses in front of the mirrors and twisting his gold jewelry. It made him grin but, at the same time, there was an uncomfortable truth behind his friend's words that stopped him from brushing off the comments. Maybe he had put too much of his Italian heritage aside since he'd left Wilmington Bay. Maybe he'd gotten a little far from his roots.

Not a bad thing, he argued. A man needed to stretch his skills, test his limits.

But, until he'd been back in Wisconsin, he'd forgotten about some of the things he'd missed: Mama's exceptional lasagnas and tiramisus, the warmth of a close family, the physical demonstrativeness they shared so naturally. Life in Chicago had lots of culture to offer, but it didn't have those things he'd always loved so much from home.

It also didn't have anyone railroading him into marriage.

"Thanks for sharing," he told Miguel dryly. "Now get your butt back to work."

"If you persist in talking to me in such an uncouth manner, I'll—"

"Quit?" Rob finished for him. "Don't you dare, man. I need you."

There was a long pause on the line. "Oh, see? Now there you go saying something sweet. You're a man of many facets, Rob Gabinarri."

"So are you, Miguel."

The self-titled Hot Latino Gay Brother blew him a kiss on the line and hung up.

Somehow, and Elizabeth still didn't know how, she made it through the next two weeks of this crazy schedule:

Write and revise all morning and afternoon.

Nibble only on fruit and veggies during the day in preparation for an evening of feasting.

Flutter around in an hour-long panic over which outfit to wear to the Gabinarris' house at night that they hadn't yet seen.

Meet Rob in front of Tutti-Frutti at five-thirty and spend the most pleasurable and most anxiety-producing two and a half hours of her day with his family and, briefly, alone with him.

Fall into a fitful sleep, dreaming about a man she should know better than to love.

But tonight there was going to be a break in the routine. Rob's mother was going out of town for the evening, staying overnight at Rob's uncle's sister-in-law's house in Milwaukee for some kind of Summerfest concert series. No, Madonna would not be performing, but apparently some band from Michigan would be there doing covers of all her big hits. Alessandra Gabinarri and her distant relative were beside themselves with excitement.

Elizabeth was beside herself with uncertainty. Her first night in half a month without obligatory dinner plans and she didn't know what to do.

Rob, who'd been ever-pleasant but hadn't gotten any closer to her since that hand-kissing incident, breezily announced that she was "off the hook" for this evening. That he had "some stuff to do."

Gretchen had some artsy-craftsy thing planned with her siblings in nearby Kenosha.

Nick had a basketball game up in Port Washington that he'd talked Jacques into going to with him.

They'd even closed Tutti-Frutti early for once. Everyone had plans for the night but none of them included her.

It was simply ridiculous. She used to spend almost all of her nights alone. She'd read. She'd work on new cookbook ideas. She'd watch Jane Austen classics on A&E. She'd tend to her herb garden—plants she kept in small pots on her windowsill. And, occasionally, she'd meet up with her friends at one of their apartments for a Treat Swap night. Regardless, she'd go to sleep at a reasonable hour, and she'd never, ever meander around her place like a chef without her spatula just because she didn't have a pseudo date for the evening.

Okay, so maybe it was difficult getting used to loneliness again after being a part of lively family camaraderie for two weeks. But still. This silliness had to stop.

She tossed on one of her favorite DVDs—*Rachael Ray's Fasta Pasta*—and sank into the sofa. She lasted ten minutes.

She fixed herself a steaming mug of hot cocoa with shaved bits of chocolate on top. She didn't savor it. She gulped it down and found herself scanning the room for her purse and keys. What she needed was a *real* date, but she wasn't going to find it here.

She threw on a semi-fashionable ensemble, strode out the door and slammed it shut behind her.

For the first time ever in Elizabeth Daniels's personal history, she was going out on the town, and maybe, if she played her cards right, she'd pick up a man while she was at it.

Elizabeth sniffed the air of Hauser's Grill and Ale. Wisconsin's Garden Spot, this wasn't. Budweiser's Basement was more like it but, though she'd made no promises to herself to stay late, she did vow she'd give the experience at least thirty minutes. How hard could it be to have a few drinks, meet a few people and, maybe, make out with some guy that she'd probably never see again? Other women did stuff like this all the time.

She bravely marched up to the bar and placed her order. White wine. She just couldn't go for the hard stuff. Imagine *her* drinking scotch or whiskey or bourbon!

No. Now that was the problem right there.

She *should* be able to imagine herself doing anything she darn well pleased. Maybe she'd work her way up to a martini next. Or maybe she'd settle for a rum and Coke. But if she wanted to try a Brandy Alexander, who was going to stop her?

"Lizzy Daniels?"

Elizabeth turned. The not-so-sweet voice belonged to the not-so-sweet mouth of the not-at-all-sweet Tara Welles.

"What are *you* doing here?" Tara inquired, her razor-thin eyebrows raised like mini-boomerangs, waiting for the answer to come back to her.

"W-Wine," she said. "Very thirsty." And, to underscore her point, she took a long sip. "Mmm."

Tara swept her sneering glance from side-to-side, in search of something. "Is Rob here with you? I haven't seen him tonight."

"Nope."

Tara's beady little blue eyes brightened. Well, no. That was a lie. They weren't actually beady. They weren't actually little either. They were big, round, blue...

"Well, where is he?"

...like dinosaur eggs, of the Tyrannosaurus Rex variety.

"C-Couldn't tell you," she said before taking another swig of wine. Yeah, where was he? What "stuff" was he doing tonight? Not that she had any hold on him or any say in where he went or what he did, but she was curious. In an Old High School Friend sort of way.

Ah. That was a lie, too.

Tara, dressed in a skintight jungle-print miniskirt and a sage-green blouse, took a couple of slithery steps forward on her spike-heeled sandals.

"You need to stop monopolizing him," she hissed. "I've seen him at your uncles' shop, you know. And every time I ask him about his plans for the night, he says he *has* to do something with you. I can tell it's some kind of chore you've concocted to get him to go out with you."

Elizabeth drained her wineglass and ordered a martini. "Really?" she said through gritted teeth.

"You've always been so transparent, Lizzy. Having a crush on Roberto Gabinarri. Honey, he wouldn't seriously go for someone like you in this or any other lifetime."

The truth, Elizabeth thought, always hurt just a little more when it was about something you prayed you could keep hidden. She chewed the olive from her martini and regarded the terrible lizard standing before her.

"A-Appreciate your insight, T-Tara."

"Hey, Elizabeth! Over here."

She turned to see, of all people, Maria-Louisa waving at her from a table in the corner. Never had Rob's considerate sister-in-law felt more dear to her than at that moment, even if the woman was sitting with a group of six strangers who were bound to make Elizabeth nervous.

"Hi," she called back in her cheeriest, most confident voice and took a healthy gulp of her second drink. Alcohol. Definitely helpful in situations like these.

"Come join us!" Maria-Louisa shouted over the din of country-western music. To emphasize the invitation further, she motioned with not one, but both hands. "It's Rob's girlfriend," she explained loudly to her group of friends, and soon all of them were calling her over.

Elizabeth looked between Tara, who was staring at her with a kind of mild horror melded with bewilderment, and Maria-Louisa's grinning, girlish face and waving arms.

No contest.

"L-Later," she said to Tara as she walked toward the table of women, half-full martini in hand, ready to do a little partying with an as-of-yet unknown Wilmington Bay crowd.

She took a very, very deep breath.

Hey, she could be spontaneous and *fun* if she wanted to be. She could act like a popular girl. Goodness knows she'd watched women like them long enough to be able to approximate how they behaved. All it would take was another dr—

"We're drinking strawberry margaritas, Elizabeth. Can I pour you one?"

"A-Absolutely," she said, shining her best smile at Maria-Louisa and then greeting the woman's merry band of friends. "I was just thinking of trying something else."

"Ooh, these are the best," one of the other ladies said. "Jimmy, over there at the bar," she pointed, "makes ours extra sweet and—"

"Extra potent," another woman finished.

All the ladies at the table giggled and raised their glasses in agreement.

"Sounds exactly l-like what I'm looking for," Elizabeth declared, polishing off the martini and gratefully reaching for the margarita. She took a good look at Jimmy the bartender. He was pretty cute. And their waiter—his nametag said "Ivan"—was even cuter.

Mmm. This night had a lot of potential. She sipped her new drink, smiled again at everyone and winked at Ivan.

Rob and Tony sat in front of the TV, beers in hand, discussing in intimate detail the parts of the visiting-team pitcher's anatomy that they'd like to eviscerate, since he caused the Brewers to lose again. Rob grinned through the goriness. He missed spending nights like this with his kid brother.

"I keep envisioning a baseball version of *Braveheart*," Tony said, tossing his empty beer can into the trash. "But I guess TV can't show everything."

"Guess not." Rob checked his watch. "Hey, it's after nine. How long is your wife going to be out?"

Tony shrugged. "Late. She gets it into her head that she needs an outing with the girls once a month and, you know, with five kids at home, I don't blame her."

"You don't mind doing everything by yourself for an evening, though? Putting all the kids to bed and all?" he asked.

Tony laughed. "Look, Maria-Louisa does it all by herself during the day. Every day. I'd give her the whole night off three times a week if she asked for it. Once a month is nothing."

Rob thought of the five children sound asleep upstairs. Sammie, when Rob poked his head in on him an hour ago, was actually snoring. And one of the triplets—Michael—was talking to a PBS dragon in his sleep. It was kind of cute, he had to admit. In a Family Channel sort of way.

He got up to stretch his legs. "Hey, you feel like cookies or ice cream or something? I can run out and pick up a half-gallon or two for us."

"I'd love some, but aren't you sick of that sweet stuff after all the hours you spend scooping it up every day?" Tony stared at him with one of his deep, penetrating gazes. This question wasn't intended to be literal.

"Yes and no, Tony," he admitted. "You know how I like to talk to people, so that part of it has been fun. The shop itself is running fine, and Elizabeth is so organized that we have on hand anything we need days before we actually need it."

"Ah, yes. Elizabeth."

He groaned. "Oh, c'mon. Don't start on me. I can't tell Mama the truth yet. That's the part that hasn't been going so well. I mean, Elizabeth's been awfully kind about helping me fake this relationship, but soon Mama's going to have to know that it could never happen for real."

"Because?" Tony prompted.

Man, let me count the ways. "Because we're not of the same type. She's quiet and reserved and straight-laced. A class act. I'm loud and extraverted and a little on the wild side."

Tony indicated his agreement of that last point.

"She's a brain who writes. I'm a jock who does business. She wants to live out the rest of her life in Wilmington Bay. I want to get the hell back to Chicago at the end of the month, preferably sooner. She wants four kids, and I don't want any if I can help it—"

"Whoa, big brother. Slow down." Tony blinked his dark eyes at him. "You two talked about kids?"

"Just theoretically."

"No, no, *no*. There's no such thing with women." His brother crossed his arms. "Who brought it up? You or her?"

Rob thought back over their coffee shop conversation a few weeks ago. "I did, I think."

Tony nodded. "Bad move, bro. You've got her thinking and evaluating now. Plus, with all that playacting and your lovey-dovey hand massaging... Don't fool yourself, Rob. This may be harder to break off than you think."

"Hey, I was totally open with my intentions. I've never led her on with this in any way. She knows it's a game. I don't think she'll be heartbroken when it ends."

His brother laughed. "I don't think she will be either. I wasn't talking about her. I was talking about *you*."

"What? That's—that's—"

"Not nearly as crazy as you may believe," Tony finished for him, although that wouldn't have been how he'd have chosen to end the sentence.

He and Frizzy Lizzy together? For *real?*

He thought about her kindness to his family, her understated prettiness, her sweet nature and the way she was slowly relaxing around him. He remembered her soft, soft hands and the attraction he'd felt for her that night of the coffee outing—an emotion he'd worked hard to suppress because, well, because they just didn't mesh. They were too different. Right?

A jolt of "So what?" smacked him in the gut.

So what if they had polar personalities?

So what if she could spin rings around him intellectually?

So what if he did want to kiss her on the lips, just once?

Not that he'd admit any of these things to Tony.

"I'm going to get that ice cream now," he informed his brother. "Either suggest a flavor or I'll have to pick one for you."

Tony smirked. "Avoidance is the devil's game. Play it at your own risk."

Rob took several pointed strides in the direction of the door. "I'm leaving."

His brother crossed his arms and leaned back against the sofa. "Okay, Peaches and Cream or Butter Pecan, then."

"How very wholesome of you."

"Not especially," Tony said. "I just like what I like. But since you're going out, could you do me a favor?"

"I'm not picking up *Happy Feet* for you or any other heartwarming kiddie DVDs, no."

"Wasn't what I was going to ask. Did you always jump to conclusions like this or is it a recent development?"

He sighed. "What do you want?"

"Maria-Louisa's mom called earlier and their hair appointments got canceled for the morning. She's either got her cell phone clicked off or it's too hard to hear it at Hauser's 'cause I can't reach her. Could you swing by there and give her the message? She'd appreciate being able to stay out later tonight knowing she'll get to sleep in tomorrow."

"Yeah, okay," Rob said, pondering how frightening it was that Tony was so taken in by his petite wife that he'd urge her to stay out later on a Saturday night and sleep in longer on a Sunday morning.

And tomorrow was *Father's* Day.

He squinted at his brother and shook his head. The guy was whipped.

He walked out of their House of Love and into Hauser's a few minutes later still thinking about this. About having a totally loving, accepting relationship like Tony and Maria-Louisa's. About what that would be like on a day-to-day basis.

He inhaled the pungent aroma of extinguished cigarettes by the door mingling with half-empty pints of beer. He felt the vibration of the classic Garth Brooks song, "Friends in Low Places," from the tips of his ears to the tips of his toes. People snickered in one corner, laughed in another, argued in a third. But it was the group in the fourth corner that stopped him like a ten-foot stone wall.

They were chugging strawberry margaritas as though they expected Diane Sawyer to announce a world-shortage on the news tomorrow.

They were flirting with one of the waiters, hooting over his jokes and then dissolving into giggling aftershocks.

They were rising up en masse and dancing in place for fifteen straight seconds before collapsing into their chairs again, arms flung to the sides, glasses dangling precariously in delicate-looking hands. Someone dropped one and they all roared with laughter. The waiter called for another to be sent over.

They were people he knew, or so he'd thought.

Soft-spoken Maria-Louisa. Her cousin Angelica. Her best friend Sandy, who'd been maid of honor at the wedding when he'd been best man. Three of the young neighbor women, all with preschoolers, who'd brought over casseroles and cakes so very primly the week he'd arrived back in town. Nice, sensible people. Usually.

But it was the last lady there whose name caught in his

throat. He struggled to say it aloud. He whispered it at first, but no way could she hear above this racket. He spoke it a second time, louder, but still no luck. Finally, he resorted to shouting.

"Elizabeth!"

Heads from all four corners of Hauser's turned to stare at him. Conversations ground to a halt. Then they all turned back and continued their chattering. Except for the group of women he knew (or thought he knew). They pointed their polished fingernails at him. Shrieked. Hollered cheerful greetings he couldn't quite catch. Motioned him over, waving their margarita pitcher in invitation.

His feet sent him staggering toward The Sirens.

"Rob!" Elizabeth said, beaming a cute but somewhat sloppy grin aimed in the vicinity of his left shoulder. "How are you? I'm really g-good."

"She's wonderful," Angelica gushed, sploshing some of her pink drink on her cream-colored blouse. "And so am I. And we think you're wonderful, too."

"Well, um, thanks," he said.

Maria-Louisa popped in with, "Wanna join us? We've got lots here." She examined the almost-empty pitcher. "Well, more's coming." She grinned at him. "How's my darling hubby? At home asleep yet?"

"No, not yet." He relayed Tony's message about her mom and the canceled appointments while studying with new eyes the absolutely, falling-over-drunk Elizabeth Daniels.

"Goody!" Maria-Louisa shouted. "I just hate getting my hair cut!"

This inspired a chorus of "Me, too"s from the women and an "I *especially* hate it" from Elizabeth.

Which led to a moment of hushed sympathy before a burst of:

"Oh, it must be really, really hard to find someone who can cut long, curly hair."

"But it's so beautiful. What do you do to tame the waves?"

"My sister in Minneapolis uses one of those special conditioners that reduce frizziness while still strengthening the roots and stopping split ends..."

He watched Elizabeth glance around the group and grin.

"Gotta try that stuff then," she said before chugging the rest of her margarita.

"More all around!" Maria-Louisa proclaimed, batting her eyelashes in appreciation at the waiter's arrival, a fresh pitcher on his tray.

"How are you all getting home?" Rob asked.

"Stevie's picking us up in his minivan," one of the neighbor ladies said of her husband. "He wanted that tank. He got it. Now he has to use it for something worthwhile."

They all started laughing again for no good reason.

"Wait," Sandy said. They paused.

"Another Garth Brooks song!" four of the ladies shouted at once. The whole group rose and began wiggling and jiggling. Elizabeth's moves were even wilder and freer than the rest.

His supposedly reserved sister-in-law spun into him. "Dance with us, Roberto. Shake that booty."

Additional hoots and hollers followed. He stood motionless.

Elizabeth grabbed his hand. "Oh, come *on*, Rob. We've all got the beat." And she pulled him toward her, raised his arm above her head and twirled underneath it.

"I think that was the Go-Go's, not Garth," one of them said, swinging her hair in a full 360°.

"Who cares?" said another.

Elizabeth twirled again, lost her balance and lunged right for his chest. He caught her and pulled her close to steady her. She gave him a death squeeze and he automatically hugged her tighter. Then her grip relaxed and her soft body wilted in his arms. She buried her face in the Brewers jersey he'd snitched from Tony's closet, snuggled up to him like a baby bunny and sighed.

"I'm really tired," she whispered.

He smoothed her luscious hair with his fingertips. "I can drive you to your apartment," he said, fighting the image of those beautiful reddish-brown curls fanned out on a white silk pillow.

"Hmm. Okay." She rubbed her eyes and yawned. "It was going to be too late before Ivan got off his shift anyway."

"What?" *Who the hell was Ivan?*

She pointed vaguely in the direction of one of the waiters. "I'll pick him up next time," she said, turning to say her goodbyes to the group as he stared at her dumbfounded. She was going to pick up some other guy? Not a chance! He shot Ivan a death stare and the laughing waiter took a few worried strides back toward the bar. *That's right, bucko. Stay away if you know what's good for you.*

Meanwhile, Elizabeth thanked the women for the fun time and forced his sister-in-law into taking some money for her share of the margaritas. Then she leaned into him again, slipped her little arm around his waist and stumbled a few steps forward.

"Off we go," she said. She ran her free palm against his abs. "Mmmmm."

"Mmm, what?" He took one final glance around the room and caught Tara Welles's stunned gaze and dropped jaw a few feet from them. He looked away.

"You've got one hot body, Rob Gabinarri," Elizabeth said. Loudly. The ladies' group wolf-whistled. "Now, take me home."

Holy Cannoli.

~CHAPTER SEVEN~

Elizabeth felt strange. Lightheaded. Her feet rocked under her as if she were standing in a kayak. The world looked fuzzier around the edges, like an old-fashioned photograph, although the colors weren't variants of gray. They were more a muted pastel, airbrushed with powdered sugar.

And, for the first time ever, it seemed, she couldn't take time to focus on her stuttering, couldn't take mental energy away from more pressing matters, like walking upright and in a straight line. Weird.

Oh, and Rob was with her. Holding her.

What a night. It seemed as if it should be unforgettable and, yet, she was already losing track of some of the details. Like how she'd ended up with Maria-Louisa's group, or talking with that waiter Ivan, or at Hauser's in the first place, and how much alcohol she'd consumed. And why Rob looked so very *tense*.

"Are you okay?" she asked him.

He laughed.

"What?"

"Nothing," he said. "That's just funny."

She didn't see why it should be so hilarious but, then again, who understood the minds of men?

When they got to her apartment complex, Rob walked her up the stairs, shuffled through her purse to locate her keys (because she just couldn't *find* them but she was *sure* they were in there) and swept her into the place and onto the sofa.

His face was really, really, unbelievably close to hers as he pulled off her shoes and laid her down on the cushions. She could see the dark shadow on his chin, the tiny whiskers bursting out of his tanned skin. His pores looked so *huge*—but they were a *sexy* huge. His eyelashes were maybe half a mile long. His hazel eyes had these little black speckles in them if you looked extra close. Kind of like staring at two very small double-chocolate chocolate chip cookies. Mmm.

This whole drinking thing had a definite cool side. She could really *see* things that she would've missed before.

Her gaze traveled to his lips. They were moving, talking, asking her something. She motioned him even closer, so as to get a super-magnified view of that amazing mouth. And, while he was up there, her lips thought they should connect with his. It wasn't her idea. Really. Her lips were working with their own irrepressible logic.

It was a warm, magical, delicious kiss. Like hot bread pudding with a dash of rum. She didn't want to stop her lips from tasting more.

Only, Rob stopped her.

"What're you doing?" he whispered, pulling away and breathing in this odd, almost winded manner.

"I don't know."

This was a pretty truthful answer because she *didn't* know why her lips did the things they did tonight. She raised her head, her lips trying to touch his again. He leaned down and then, at the last second, snapped his head away. Huh.

"I can't kiss you, Elizabeth...or do anything else with you tonight."

His voice came out kind of strangled, she thought, but maybe her hearing had been affected by the margaritas right along with her eyesight.

"Why not?" This was a reasonable question, right?

But he sighed like it wasn't reasonable. "Because you've had a little too much to drink."

She struggled with this logic but, try as she might, she couldn't see the connection. How did drinking a couple of...three or four margaritas have anything to do with kissing? No relation that she could figure.

"So?" she said.

"So, you don't know what you're doing."

He said this in that gentle voice parents used to try to get their boisterous darlings to go to bed when they should've really been in bed an hour before, but they just wouldn't go and ended up being overtired and sort of hysterical. She always hated that voice when she was a kid.

She tried being indignant. It wasn't difficult and she kind of liked it. "I do *too* know what I'm doing."

He kissed her forehead. A feathery brush, but that was it. "Do not," he countered. "Goodnight, Elizabeth. Sleep tight. Don't let the bedbugs bite. And you might want to take a couple of aspirins tonight with water, and drink lots and lots of coffee tomorrow morning. The strong, caffeinated kind. See you at five-thirty for dinner."

Then he stepped back and regarded her with that very, very, exceptionally tense look again. His eyes squinty. His full, kissable lips pulled tight. A moment later, he turned and all but raced out the door.

Huh.

"Oh. My. God."

Elizabeth cradled her head in both hands, but the migraine-like aching was impressive in its intensity. It would stop for no woman. No aspirins. No caffeinated beverages either.

The morning light shined unmercifully through her blinds, even when closed, and the sounds of the Father's Day brunch bustle on the street clanged like enormous gongs, their voices like the rumble of deep bassoons in her ears.

"Oh, my God," she said aloud again.

Her first hangover. So this was what one felt like. Not a repeater experience and, if she had any brain cells left, she'd try to remember that.

She vaguely recalled being bored last night. At loose ends and in need of some adventure. Going out to Hauser's. Seeing Tara, the nasty witch. Seeing Maria-Louisa, the friendly angel. Meeting a bunch of really nice, really funny strangers who were wild about Garth Brooks and who danced whenever one of his songs played in the bar. Having a laugh or two with that cute waiter. And then Rob taking her home...

Did she really kiss Rob?

No, she couldn't have. She must've imagined it.

Hard to keep straight what was merely a remnant of high-school fantasy and what was the current reality. She'd been slipping into daydreams about him again. Never a good sign.

The phone across the room rang like a school bell. She clapped her hands over her ears, but it wouldn't stop.

"I know you're there," Gretchen's obnoxiously cheery voice said on her answering machine. "Pick up, pick up."

Elizabeth struggled to get over to the phone, strained to pick it up. Damn. What a Good Girl she was. Always doing what she was told. Well, she didn't last night.

"Hi, Gretch."

A pause greeted her on the line. Then, "Do you have the flu or something?"

"No." Elizabeth explained her hangover in as few syllables as humanly possible.

"*You* got drunk last night?" Gretchen roared.

She moved the phone away from her ear and curled into a ball on the floor, but Gretchen kept talking and exclaiming.

"You, the woman who considers drinking New Year's Eve punch and eating English trifle with sherry on the same night 'over-imbibing'?"

Elizabeth groaned. "What's your point in calling me on a day when you should be annoying your immediate family members instead? You have a father in good health. Go jabber at him."

"Already did that," Gretchen said. "I'm an early riser. What are you doing tonight?"

"Hmm—"

"Nothing, right? So let's have a Treat Swap. Jacques and I were talking about it yesterday. He said Nick was up for it after his closing shift. We could ask Rob if he wants to join us. I mean, if you want him to join us."

She groaned again and clutched her stomach. Rob... She'd talked with him about this not so long ago. About him tagging along for one. Snippets of that conversation were still in her long-term memory.

"I guess he could come," she said.

"Okay. I switched shifts with Jacques for today, so I'll be at Tutti-Frutti in an hour. I'll tell Rob. Maybe we can put up the 'Closed' sign, shut all the blinds, light some candles and have our little party right there in the shop."

"Fine." Oh, God, she was going to throw up.

"Hey, can't wait." Gretchen's delighted voice was too much for her to take. "I've been dying for an excuse to try these amazing little jam tartlets I saw in *Feasting* magazine—"

Oh, cripes. Don't talk about food. Please.

"—and maybe some chocolate-covered Brazil nut clusters or strawberry-flavored truffles drizzled with a creamy—"

NOT strawberries!

"Bye, Gretchen."

She hung up and raced to the bathroom.

Five-thirty and Rob's nerves jangled like ice cubes in one of The Playbook's crystal goblets. Five-thirty and the rain just transitioned from a light sprinkle to a downpour. Five-thirty and she wasn't here yet.

Damn.

Five-thirty-*five* and Elizabeth's stocky little Toyota pulled up in front of the shop.

"Sorry. R-Running late," she said, sprinting up to the sidewalk, her hair more frizzly than usual, cascading down her shoulders like rainwater off the awnings.

Other than looking a bit paler than normal, though, she acted completely, frighteningly as if nothing had happened last night. As if she hadn't gotten drunk, told him to his face (and without even stuttering) that she'd pick up *Ivan* another time but that he had a hot body. So she lured him into her apartment (well, okay, that part's an exaggeration—he went in willingly) and then kissed the air out of him until he was forced, for honor's sake, to put a halt to it.

"Ready to go t-to your mom's house?" she asked, holding out a fruit salad to take along and smiling at him pleasantly but with her typical aura of competent detachment.

Oh, hell. Now he understood. She didn't remember.

"Sure," he said.

Man, had she been *that* drunk that she couldn't recall the charge zipping through their bodies when their lips met? Or, maybe, hers didn't feel that charge. Maybe this was a one-sided thing. Maybe...

He needed to be more careful. Something was happening here. With him. She was beginning to get to him. And he didn't like it.

Dinner started. Dinner ended. Rob sat through it with the jarring disbelief he'd felt the first time he watched a movie through 3-D glasses. Everything was too overwhelming to see, to concentrate on, so he blanked out into a kind of hazy non-awareness.

Mama talked nonstop about the Summerfest concert. Conversation from him was not required, even though Tony, Maria-Louisa and the kids weren't there. (She was fixing him a special Father's Day dinner at home.) How his five-foot-two, 110-pound sister-in-law could even stand straight today was the big mystery, but she'd been bright-eyed and cheery when he'd last seen her this morning.

Women.

He glanced at Elizabeth, hugging his mother goodbye. Strange, incomprehensible creatures. Who knew how their minds worked?

His kissed Mama his thanks, too, and they hopped into his car.

"Can we drop by m-my apartment for a minute?" she said.

An icy fear ran through his fingers as he remembered the feel of her beneath him on the sofa last night. He gripped the steering wheel tighter. "Why?"

"I n-need to pick up my dessert for the Treat Swap. You can wait in the car. I'll be quick."

"Oh. Okay."

He'd been excited about this thing when Gretchen mentioned it this morning. He had his sweets stashed and ready to share at the shop already. Now his gut was churning a little, though, making him wish he hadn't eaten that second helping of fettuccini primavera at Mama's.

When they walked into Tutti-Frutti, Gretchen and Nick were filling orders for nine teenagers, a family of five and an older couple. They looked swamped, so he grabbed an apron and an ice cream scoop and dug in.

"Thanks, Rob," Gretchen said. "But I've got another five minutes left on the clock."

"That's okay," he said. "I want to help." Well, he wanted to have something productive to do with his hands or he might grab Elizabeth and pin her against the wall.

He stole a long glance at her as she swung open the refrigerator to store whatever dessert she'd brought over. She caught him looking at her legs and sent him a mystified but kind of distracted smile.

He still couldn't believe it. Not a single meaningful reaction in over two freaking hours. She remembered nothing. *Nothing!*

He attacked the Mocha Madness, giving the five-year-old kid a scoop so large the little guy's eyes crossed. A couple of teens saw this, left Nick's line and crossed over into his.

Jacques walked in carrying an aluminum-foil-covered tray.

"Hello, everyone," the Frenchman said. "Looks like the

party's starting early."

And, to Rob's amazement, this appeared to be true. Jacques came early, Gretchen didn't run out when the clock struck eight and Elizabeth didn't hightail it home to write. They all just hung around with him and Nick during their shift, pitching in with orders, chatting in a lighthearted, neutral way when the customers were there and in a baser, more personal manner when they weren't. Nick, especially, had a mouth on him, talking and digging up stuff like a Roto Rooter.

At about ten minutes before closing, when things were winding down, Nick said to the group, "I gotta tell you all, when this guy first came back to town—" He gestured at Rob. "I thought for sure he'd be some arrogant, hotshot ex-Wilmington Bay dude, a quarterback legend and all, but too far into his own super-cool world that he wouldn't stick around to see this gig through for the month. But—"

"What?" Rob said, having already been good-naturedly attacked six times in the past hour about his choice of pricey casual wear, his taste in gourmet coffee and haute cuisine, his quick departure from the rarified environment of southeastern Wisconsin when he was eighteen and whatever else Nick wanted to rib him about.

Nick held up his palm. "Wait, wait. *But*, I was just going to say, that you surprised me, man. I think you surprised all of us. Hanging out here for the past few weeks, working so hard, getting into town life. You done us proud."

"Well, uh, thanks," he said. What else could he say? *Nice of you to mention my sense of duty, but no way am I hanging around here for twenty-four hours longer than I have to.* Yep. That'd go over well.

Nick pointed at Elizabeth and laughed. "And *she* was so *nervous* about you coming here. Now aren't you glad it all worked out this way?" he said to her.

Elizabeth, who until a minute before had been sharing a laugh with Gretchen at the counter, opened her mouth. No sounds immediately came out.

Then, finally, "I-I—well, um..." She paused, stared at him in an intense way that made his toes squirm and then tried again. "Rob's done a g-great job with the s-shop."

"But, I mean, aren't you glad you've gotten to know him again so personally?" Nick said. "Now that you're both all grown up and out of high school? That's gotta be such a trip. I mean, he was this amazing football star and you were this total academic. You guys probably had, like, *nothing* in common, and now you're here together handling your uncles' business and being friends and all." He nodded at them and grinned. "That's so cool, isn't it?"

A look of something—man, it seemed like fright—flashed like a lightning bolt across her face. And it occurred to him that, no matter how many how many family dinners she went to, it was no easy task getting her to feel comfortable with their "relationship." That the supposedly *real* one—their friendship—was probably just as much a sham as the dating game they'd been playing for Mama's benefit.

But, then again, it was a friendship that wasn't quite so pure anymore. There'd been that one kiss, after all. Even if she didn't remember it yet.

A final customer came in, silencing Nick temporarily, but Rob couldn't help but notice the way Elizabeth's gaze kept finding his own at odd moments during clean up. She kept shooting these confused looks in his direction and, when Nick pulled out a bottle of ouzo to accompany the gooey baklava he'd made, she stared at the licorice-flavored alcoholic beverage and then at Rob again.

As if she'd made some connection between the two.

As if memories were floating back to her.

As if chunks of last night's experience, ones that'd broken apart from her now-frozen memory and drifted away for the day, were returning and melting into her consciousness.

Well, she *should* remember, dammit. He was a memorable guy. He wasn't someone who could just be kissed and forgotten.

Jacques pulled back the foil from his tray. Rows and rows of little jam tartlets.

"Gretchen talked me into making these," he explained, popping one into the blonde's mouth.

"Mmm," Gretchen moaned. "These are even better than I imagined when I saw that recipe. Pretty please will you let me make them with you next time?" she asked Jacques.

"My pastry knives are at your disposal, *chéri*. Now, what kind of truffles did you bring us tonight?"

Gretchen opened up a large tin box of perfect dark chocolate confections with green squiggles across the top of each one. "Irish crème. Two dozen." She popped one of her creations into Jacques mouth.

"Mon Dieu. This is heaven."

Rob broke open the milk-chocolate-covered fruit slices Miguel sent up, and the gang's Ooohs and Ahhhs indicated their delight. Relief and a little pride swept over him. This was quite the culinary crowd.

Only Elizabeth's contribution to the Treat Swap remained. She unveiled it: Cherry cheesecake.

"Oh, my! Did you really?" Gretchen said. "It's been so long since you made it. I know it must have brought back memories...were you okay?"

Elizabeth nodded.

"Well, it looks positively sinful," Gretchen said, hunking off slices for everyone and putting one on each plate, right next to the generous slabs of baklava Nick dished out. "When did you have time to make it?"

"A month ago," Elizabeth admitted. "I made three in May and gave one of them to Uncle Siegfried and one to the lady collecting donations for the hospital bake sale. This one I froze for all of you."

Jacques leaned over and kissed her, which left a prickly aftertaste in Rob's mouth, despite the silken truffle he'd just devoured.

"You are a saint among women," Jacques said. "A goddess." Then he paused and his tone turned serious. "This was your mom's recipe, *oui?"*

She nodded again.

"Then it's going to be the best cherry cheesecake we've ever had." And something in Jacques's voice indicated that no one had better to disagree.

Nick splashed ouzo into glasses, Elizabeth made sure all the plates were loaded with treats, Jacques dimmed the lights and Gretchen pulled a few candles and a pack of matches out of her handbag.

This troupe was beyond weird, but Rob had to admit he was getting into it. Elizabeth's face and hands looked softer and smoother than ever in the candlelight. Her eyes glowed a bright green, and the smile that touched her lips appeared more relaxed than he'd ever seen her. This was familiar territory for her. This was home.

He'd tried the Greek ouzo once before—"It's like Good & Plenty for adults," Nick told them—but it'd been years ago and, even then, he hadn't tasted more than a few sips. Elizabeth, he noticed, regarded her glass of ouzo skeptically. He doubted she'd planned on drinking much of anything tonight, but Nick wouldn't shut up until he got them all playing a grownups' version of "Truth or Dare."

"What's the dumbest thing you ever did in a car?" Nick said. "Either tell or drink."

Jacques spoke first. "I tried eating soup while you were driving," he told Nick. "A *très* stupid idea."

Nick laughed. "And you got cream of chicken with broccoli and rice all over my passenger's seat. Yeah, that one ranks high for me, too, but probably the stupidest thing I did was pick up a hitchhiker."

"You did that?" Elizabeth said, her sweet lips parting in surprise.

"Yep. That's how I met Micah."

"His first long-term partner," Jacques explained to Rob.

"I was an idiot," Nick said and, even though he'd "told," he drank a few swigs anyway. "What about you, Elizabeth?"

Her brows creased in concentration. "Mmm. I think it's got to be trying to transport an ice sculpture of this beautiful angel to Milwaukee, in the m-middle of a July heat wave, in my old

Plymouth."

"Oh, my gosh," Gretchen said. "The car that had no air conditioning!"

"She was a fallen—and a melted—angel," Elizabeth said with mock sadness.

"Let us all pray," Nick said, raising his glass solemnly. He drank again. "Rob?"

He'd done many a stupid thing in his day, the worst being the night he and Tara had almost...well...they hadn't but... "I'd better drink," he said, taking a small sip of the clear liquid that tasted like licorice-infused lighter fluid. Elizabeth shot him a wide-eyed glance.

"Gretchen?" Jacques said.

She pressed her lips together, shook her head and brought the rim of the glass up to her mouth. She took a drink and grimaced. "Jeez, Nick! You trying kill us?"

Nick laughed and poured some more alcohol into his glass, the only one that was now empty. "Next question. Who did you have the biggest crush on in high school? For me, it was Andy Northrop, the biggest, meanest and, unfortunately, straightest hockey player at Wilmington Bay High. But, oh, what a sexy slap shot he had." He paused as if in awe, remembering. "How about you, Elizabeth?"

Gretchen looked at Elizabeth, kind of oddly, Rob thought, before interrupting. "Oh, but I wanna go next," Gretchen said. "For me, it was Jeremy Alexander Brennan. He sat right behind me in sophomore geometry and would trace shapes on my back with his fingertip." She shivered. "It was *such* a turn on. What about you, Jacques?"

"I was in love with Mrs. Larousse." He grinned. "She was young—maybe twenty-five—and was the school cook. Her *quiche végétarien* was unbelievable."

They all laughed.

"Rob?" Gretchen said.

"Had a thing for Heidi Klum," he said, which was only a partial truth, but close enough. He had no intention of drinking any more of that stuff if he could avoid it.

"Elizabeth missed her turn," Nick said, his voice getting louder and more insistent. "So, who was your high-school fantasy?"

Elizabeth looked around their small group, caught Gretchen's eye for a split second and then wrinkled her nose. She sniffed the ouzo, turned an interesting shade of pale before taking a sip...and then a few shades paler after it.

"N-Next question," she said, her green eyes watery and her voice a little hoarse.

Three rounds later, they all were laughing, no one more heartily than Nick, who'd downed five or six full shots of ouzo in under an hour.

"Oh—oh, I know the next question," the guy said, flopping to the ground and covering his eyes with his palms for a moment. "Who was the first person you ever slept with?" He raised his head and glanced at everyone with a silly expression. "Oh, wait. You don't have to answer that one, Elizabeth."

"Why not?" Rob said, noting the strange dynamic bouncing between Elizabeth, Jacques and Gretchen at this question.

"I'll go first," Jacques said, trying, from the look of it, to cut Nick off.

"Anybody want more cheesecake or tartlets or anything?" Gretchen asked, waving a few sweets at them. "Oh, and don't forget the baklava, truffles and chocolate-covered fruit. We have lots of—"

"Because she's a virgin," Nick explained loudly, to which Gretchen sighed, Jacques slugged Nick's arm and Elizabeth squeezed her eyes shut.

"Ow," Nick said.

"I'll t-take a truffle to go," Elizabeth said, getting up. "It's pretty late and I didn't sleep v-very well last night." She tossed a few things in the trash and said to him in a strained voice, "Rob, could you please lock up when you're all ready to go home?"

"S-Sure," he said, stuttering for probably the first time since he was a toddler. A virgin! Oh, God. And since this wasn't news to any of them—except *him*—the reason for her embarrassment and quick departure was because of him, too.

He had to let her know somehow that this was all right. That it was admirable even, especially in this day and age when restraint was rare. That—that he was grateful, of all things, that she hadn't given herself to someone who wasn't special to her. But she wouldn't look at him.

"Okay, t-thank you. Gretch and Jacques, could one of you drive Nick home? I don't want him to die a horrible death before I can kill him."

"You got it," Gretchen said.

Elizabeth sprinted out the door. One of the candles extinguished itself when the wind rushed in. The room seemed darker.

Jacques slugged Nick again.

"Ouch. Stop it, would ya?"

Rob got up and handed the keys to Jacques. "Could you lock up for me? There's something I've got to take care of."

The Frenchman gave him a hard look, but he swallowed and nodded slowly.

"Thanks."

Rob said goodbye to all of them, even the nearly passed out Nick on the floor, and told them he'd do all the cleaning up in the morning. Then he ran out after Elizabeth.

He caught up with her by her car. "Can you hold on a minute?" he said.

"Why?"

"Because—because I've got something to—to tell you." And in his mind he spoke very eloquently about how much he admired her and appreciated her moral strength and intelligence and how he thought she was just lovely, both now and even back in high school. But none of those words would come out.

So, after an unbelievably long moment of her staring at him and him saying nothing, he reached out to her and drew her body to his. Her eyes became the largest spheres he'd ever seen on anyone's face, but he figured if she wanted to stop him she would.

He gave her another five seconds to push him away, if that

was her choice. When the time ran out and she hadn't, he brought his mouth down on hers.

Hang on tight, sweetheart. This is one kiss you're damn well going to remember.

~CHAPTER EIGHT~

Elizabeth had racked up plenty of experience with lightheadedness in the past twenty-four hours. A long, thorough kiss with Rob Gabinarri, however, did more than make her feel woozy and unsteady on her feet.

She felt like she could fly clear to Tibet.

This went beyond fantasy. This surpassed any daydreams she'd ever had of Rob during high school, or even this summer. This couldn't possibly be for real.

"W-What are you d-doing?" she managed to ask him when he let them break for air.

"Last night's kiss wasn't a good idea. You were drunk and I wasn't. Tonight, babe, we're both pretty sober, and it's a different story."

He looked at her all serious and sincere. She squinted at him. What the heck was he saying?

"That kiss really happened yesterday?" she said.

Now he was the one who squinted. "You've got me going out of my mind here, Elizabeth. Do you or don't you remember kissing me last night?"

Oh, God. She hadn't dreamed it after all.

"I-I-I thought I'd j-just imagined—"

He shook his head and smiled slightly. "Nope."

Their few moments on her sofa came rushing back to her, as if all she'd needed was the confirmation that she hadn't been hallucinating to solidify the baffling memory into reality. Oh, heavens. In her dream she'd practically attacked him last night. Only, if it wasn't a dream then...

She buried her head in the fabric of his shirt. "S-Sorry."

He pulled her away from her hideout and stared her down. "I'm not. Not about last night and not about now. Not unless—" He paused. "Unless you'd rather be with Ivan."

"Who's Ivan?"

At that, Rob laughed a little and brought his lips to hers again for another long, slow, involving kiss that sent her soaring far away from Wilmington Bay, above the trees, over Lake Michigan, across the country and toward the ocean, while all the time embracing her firmly on their little plot of pavement and keeping her safe on the ground.

"Get a room," some snotty teen boy in a passing car shouted. Rob didn't even look up.

But, eventually, the summer heat grew too warm for them, even at nearly midnight, so he tucked her into his car and sped them over to her apartment.

"Show me to thy sofa, woman," he whispered in her ear.

The heat in his voice made her body ripple with waves of wanting. She did as he asked.

"Where were we yesterday like now?" He tugged off her shoes and laid her down on the cushions. He brought his face up close to hers. He looked at her expectantly. "You're supposed to kiss me. You're missing your cue," he reminded her. "Hurry up."

Although she'd been kissing him virtually nonstop since they'd left Tutti-Frutti, she obliged. But, oh, there was something about this horizontal position that performed devious stunts on her weak flesh.

Her blood pulsed differently, sending shivers of longing spurting through every vein and artery and bodily extremity.

Her lips tingled with desire for more of him. More firm lips. More hungry tongue. More joining of their two beings.

Her vision clouded over, like a kind of fog screen or hazy filter between them and the harsher outside world.

"You n-need to keep doing this all night," she told him. "I won't let you stop."

"Okay by me."

And so the fever continued, with a furor of warring nerve fibers that were unable to decide where to concentrate sensation. There was so much to feel, so many points of contact where her body and Rob's intersected. If only she could get rid of these restrictive clothes, there would be even more locales where their merging would be possible.

She yanked his shirt free from his Levi's…taking Step One in a recipe she'd never made. She lifted it over his head and tossed it on the floor. Step Two. She unfastened his belt buckle—with some difficulty—and snapped open his jeans. Step Three. She wrenched them down over his narrow, sexy hips. Step Four.

He unbuttoned her blouse…unlatched her bra…pulled off her slacks…and had his fingers poised at the waistband of her ivory panties…in a record-breaking Step Five.

When they were underwear-to-underwear, he pressed his erection against her. She gasped, never having felt anything like *this* before, and his gaze flew up to meet hers.

"Oh-oh," he said, his voice thick. "I bet I've crossed some uncrossed boundaries already."

"Ah-huh. About five more than have ever been breached."

He grinned. "Can't say I'm sorry, Lizzy."

"Elizabeth," she told him, then she snapped the waistband of his smiley-face boxers.

"Ow. That was so not nice of you," he murmured in her ear before he nipped at her lobe. Then he traced the outside of her ear with his wicked tongue, shooting sparks of need from that one tiny corner of her body all the way down and around to everywhere else. And, as if that weren't enough sensation, he ground his hips into hers a second time.

"Oohhh, Rob."

Then he did it again and again, and it occurred to her that this extreme level of awareness might overpower her. That her longing for him could get so strong that her flimsy underused circuits would overheat and shut down. That she could *die* from this degree of wanting.

He surged against her another time and she almost broke. "Oh, Rob. I-I can't—"

She tried to say, *I can't take it anymore, I'm about to ignite,* but Rob took her at her literal words, clenched his jaw and pulled himself off her.

"I know. I'm sorry," he said.

She reached up to try to pull him back. To explain how he'd misunderstood.

"You're right to wait for someone special," he said. "Someone who'll love you and stick by you and be here for you next month and next year."

She let her arms flop down on the sofa. She wished she could cover her ears without offending him. She knew for sure she wasn't going to want to hear what was coming next.

"I want you like a crazy man tonight, Elizabeth, but you know Chicago is home to me now. You know after our uncles come back next week I'm going to have to leave."

Her throat was dry and unresponsive, so she just nodded. Yes, yes, she knew he'd leave.

"And you've waited for so long. I don't—I don't want you to waste this gift of yourself, of your first time, on me."

Oh, how she wanted to tell him he was wrong. That with him it would never, could never be a wasted offering. But, as usual, her voice didn't cooperate.

"Or," his expression turned hard, "on some random waiter at a bar, okay? Your moral courage is inspiring. I don't know many women who would wait until they were twenty-seven, almost twenty-eight to—"

"Shhh," she said finally, her voice raspy with the burden of unfulfilled desire.

Oh, God, she wanted him *in* her.

Her shocked body ached for him. Her heart, too. How could she explain aloud that her current state of virginity had much less to do with "moral courage" than with good old "lack of guts"?

Besides, what did it matter? In the end, he didn't want her long term. Maybe it was better this way—stopping now. Maybe. Maybe not. But he'd taken the choice away from her.

She watched as he slipped his shirt over those great shoulders and picked up his jeans. He eyed them apprehensively.

"Um, getting myself back into these is going to be too much of a task in my current...condition." With the merest flush of embarrassment, he glanced down. One of the smiley-faces on his boxers had a nose like Pinocchio's. "I just—well, could I grab a quick shower?"

She got him a towel and, fifteen minutes later, he was out the door, promising to pick her up tomorrow before his opening shift so she could retrieve her car.

His parting kiss was so tender, though, she almost called him back. "Stay with me," she whispered to the empty hallway. "Don't ever go."

But even she knew there was a time when fantasy stopped and reality hit full force. She'd just had a major collision with it.

Elizabeth combated the earthy elements of grogginess and lust the next morning. She told herself she could deal with whatever the day threw at her, but fear crept in and curled into a ball in her stomach. It was The Morning After—or, at least, the biggest Morning After she'd ever had so far. How would Rob greet her? With friendliness? With heightened sexual hunger? With avoidance or shame?

But he surprised her because she hadn't guessed it would be...with warmth and a bouquet of flowers.

"Thank you," she said, accepting the pink roses.

He said his "You're Welcome" to her by collecting her in his arms and kissing her without a breath for ninety seconds at least. He pulled a couple of inches away and pointed at her with a stern index finger.

"You weren't just dreaming last night, got it?" he said, narrowing his eyes in a mock threat. "It was all real. And I don't want to hear any talk from you that you 'aren't sure' of what happened or what didn't happen, understand?"

As if she could forget. "I got it," she told him and gave him her best morning smile. He beamed at her in return.

Oh, she loved this playful side of Rob. Loved it in him. Loved that he brought out something similar in her.

"But I *was* dreaming," she added, amazed at the evenness of her own voice. "After you left, I dreamed this very handsome Italian-American businessman visited me and took me out for an ice cream. A really large sundae with three ice cream flavors, loads of whipped cream, hot fudge sauce and a big red cherry on top."

"Is that so?"

"Oh, yes." She offered him her sweetest smile. "He said he'd personally make it for me. In my dream."

"C'mon." He put his arm around her and nudged her toward the door. "We'd better make this frozen fantasy of yours come true before Gretchen gets there. I've got a feeling both of us are going to be in front of the firing squad today after our quick departure last night." He gave her a pointed look. "Your friends aren't afraid to shoot their toughest questions at a guy, you know."

"I know."

So, to Tutti-Frutti they went.

"Did that 'handsome Italian-American businessman' select the three ice cream flavors for you, or did he ask you what you wanted?" Rob said to her, his lips upturned and looking rather smirky. "In your dream."

"He asked me which ones I wanted, of course."

"Okay. Which ones do you want?"

"I want *your* top three favorite flavors. Please."

His brow wrinkled. "*My* favorites?"

"Yes. And any other toppings you think are good."

He shrugged and loaded the sundae bowl with Pistachio Paradise, Chocolate Brownie Chunk and, finally, the sweet shop's namesake.

"Tutti-Frutti is one of your favorites?" she said. "Why?"

"You disapprove?"

"Not at all. J-Just curious."

He leaned across the counter and kissed her on the nose. "Because I like stuff that's kind of complex. That has little surprises in it."

He ladled spoonfuls of hot fudge sauce over the ice cream, made another layer with caramel, then slathered her entire sundae in whipped cream. He added a couple of fat fresh strawberries to the massive dessert along with the big red cherry she'd requested, plopping it right on top. Then he pushed the concoction across the counter toward her, followed by a napkin and a spoon.

"May I have another spoon please?" she said.

"That one's not dirty, is it?" He reached to grab her spoon back, but she did something she never done before. She put her hand on his and stopped him.

"No. I m-meant, I wanted one for you."

He stared down at her small hand resting on top of his for a moment, then he brought her fingers to his lips. Still holding her hand, he pulled out another spoon and dug into the giant sundae. But, instead of eating it himself, he offered the first scoop to her. Amazing. The man, not the ice cream.

Well, the ice cream, too.

She filled her spoon up and rubbed it against his bottom lip so driblets of hot-fudge sauce clung to that manly mouth. So luscious.

"Mmm," she said, watching him eat it.

He reached toward the sundae, snatching a strawberry and using it as a decorating tool to dot her nose, chin and cheeks with whipped-cream freckles. Then he kissed them off one at a time and fed the strawberry to her. Her heart slammed hard against her chest.

Or, maybe, it was the door that slammed.

"My, isn't this...cozy," Gretchen said, her voice registering an odd combination of amusement, surprise and suspicion.

"Customers will be here in ten minutes, though. Maybe you two should take this...this *activity* into the backroom...provided it's consensual."

Elizabeth turned to look at her good friend, whose blue eyes were wide and questioning and whose body language indicated she could just as easily throw her arms around them in a bear hug of congratulations as she could throw a hard punch that might knock Rob over.

"I-It's okay, Gretch. We're, um, we both—"

Rob cleared his throat. "What she means is that we're giving you the morning off today. Elizabeth's going to work this shift with me." He stared at her until he'd forced a nod out of her. Gretchen raised her eyebrows and shot them both dubious glances, but Rob continued, "You've been working real hard and probably have better things to do than watch the two of us make fools of ourselves for the rest of the morning. We're going to be pretty self-involved here."

A smile played on the far corners of Gretchen's lips. "And who's going to tend to the customers?"

"We sincerely promise not to ignore them," he said. "Not much, anyway."

"Elizabeth?" Gretchen asked.

She nodded at her friend, knowing darn well she hadn't been able to keep the wonder and delight off her own face.

Oh, the victorious thrill of love!

Gretchen's smile broadened. "You sure you don't need a chaperone?"

Elizabeth shook her head at the same time Rob said, "Look, Gretchen, Elizabeth and I have only got a week left to be together before our uncles come back from Europe. We're just enjoying the little time we have before I return to Chicago."

Oh, the defeating agony of reality.

Some of the remarkable animating force that'd kept her running hot these past ten or so hours, drained out of her. A chill took its place.

"Alrighty, then." Gretchen swiveled on her robust heel and marched to the door. She flipped the sign from "Closed" to

"Open" and called over her shoulder, "Play safely, kids. I don't want anyone to get hurt."

Well, neither did Elizabeth, but preventing it was impossible. She waved her friend off and returned her sole attention to Rob, who was holding an ice-cream-covered spoon two inches from her lips again. He'd managed to get some of every layer of the sundae on it, plus, he dangled the maraschino cherry by its stem just above it.

"Open up, Lizzy," he said.

She got as far as "Eliza—" before he dropped the sweet fruit in her open mouth and followed it up with the spoon of ice cream.

"That's a good girl," he said. "Just like that."

She tugged the cherry off its stem and chewed, appreciating the sensation of being fed for the first time since she was three. He made her feel giddy and childlike and not at all like the serious adult that she had the reputation of being. Bless the man.

If she weren't such a good girl, she'd consider making a bargain with the devil to keep Rob here in Wilmington Bay for a little longer. Then again, she probably couldn't hold his attention for more than another week or two, and all she'd get in the end would be the pain of watching this miraculous thing that'd happened between them dissolve and the misery of seeing him fall for someone else—someone prettier and more interesting—before taking off for good.

No. She'd make no bargains. No promises. No vows. She wouldn't let her hopes get all tangled up in this astonishing relationship. She'd just enjoy it for however long it lasted...and then let it go.

Yeah, right.

They worked side-by-side all morning, filling orders and eating up that sundae and two others, before Nick ambled in around noon. He wore dark sunglasses and hadn't yet shaved for the day.

"Hey, guys," he said, his voice raspy. "Gretchen called me and ordered me—I mean, she said I could find you both here. I, um, look—I got really drunk last night, which I think you know, so I'm sorry if I embarrassed you, Elizabeth, or offended you, Rob, or did anything especially stupid because—"

"It's okay," she said, cutting him off.

Rob pretended to punch Nick in the gut. "All's forgiven. This time," he said.

Nick looked more than mildly relieved but also a tad confused. "You sure?"

"Yep," Rob said.

"Oh, yeah," she agreed.

"Okey-dokey—I mean, that's good. Thanks." Nick slouched against the counter, his hands cradling his dark head. "I'm gonna go back to bed then. I'm making my brother Jason give me the day off, but I'll be back at five-thirty for my first shift."

"Terrific." Rob waved him toward the door.

Nick took a few steps backward then scowled at them. "Look, I know I'm majorly hung over right now, but is there something going on here that I don't know about?"

Rob rested his arm on Elizabeth's shoulders then pulled her in tight toward his to-die-for body. "Like what?" he said to Nick.

"Like—I don't know. I'm just getting a weird vibe, but that's probably crazy, right?"

"Right." Rob turned Elizabeth to face him, leaving not a millimeter of space between them. Every single bit of her skin in connection with his tingled. He leaned in and kissed her. A good, long, hard one.

Nick pulled off his dark glasses and squinted at them. "What the hell? When did that happen?"

"Thanks for your help, Nick—I mean, your apology," Rob said with a broad grin. "You can go now."

Her Greek buddy opened his mouth to speak but, for once, closed it again. He smiled, saluted them and was out the door before you could say "Spanakopita."

Rob laughed and kissed her again.

"Promise me you'll work every opening shift with me this week," he said when the coast was clear of both friends and customers. "Please. I know you've still got a lot of writing to do, but I love having you here beside me."

Despite her vow not to make any promises, there was no way she could refuse an appeal like that.

"You're on," she told him. "But I want a promise from you, too." She knew she couldn't ask him to stay beyond the date of their uncles' return, but she felt pretty safe with this one. "I-I want one of your specialty ice cream sundaes every morning. With the works. Do I have your complete consent?"

"You do." Rob looked at her, something intangible in his expression. "And you should know, this handsome Italian-American businessman is a man of his word."

Ah, yes. And a man of her dreams.

One hour and forty-seven minutes into their Thursday morning shift, the phone rang.

Rob ran over to grab it, but he was too late. Whoever called had hung up. He shrugged and returned his gaze to tracing visual patterns on Elizabeth's sexy legs. Oh, the things he wanted to do to those legs...and to about two hundred of her other body parts.

Ever since midnight on Sunday—hell, even before that— he'd been crazed with wanting her, but they'd confined their physical activities to making out, feeding each other ice cream, making out, holding hands at his Mama's house and making out some more. Even Tony admitted to Rob in private that their relationship sure didn't look like a charade now.

Well, it wasn't. The fact that it couldn't last the week didn't make the bizarre sensations he was feeling any less memorable. She was a phenomenal lady. And she was brilliant, so it was better that she didn't have him hanging around for long. Her infatuation with his body would wear off soon enough.

Jacques had all but told him she'd only accept true, long-lasting love before committing herself. "She's got high principles," he said earlier in the week, his voice so icy as to be almost threatening. "She won't put up with shallowness or weak promises."

Rob didn't argue with him, but Jacques made it clear that even if he liked Rob well enough in the sweets shop, he disapproved of Rob's romantic connection to Elizabeth.

Gretchen, although basically supportive, eyed him distrustfully when she thought he wouldn't notice.

And Nick...well, he was still pretty oblivious.

The phone rang again and, this time, Rob got it.

"Hello? Tutti-Frutti," he said.

"Roberto!"

"Uncle Pauly?"

"Buon giorno! How are you?"

"Good. Great. All is well. Tutti-Frutti is doing just fine, although everyone in town misses you both. How has your trip been going? How is Siegfried? What about Anita? And, oh, do you have the details yet on when your flight comes in this weekend?"

"Ah, Roberto, such a responsible boy you are. We knew we made the best choice when we chose you and Elizabeth to run the shop. Isn't that right, Siegfried?"

Rob heard some words to the affirmative and several delighted exclamations in German. An unidentifiable *something* in his uncle's tone niggled at him, though.

"So, uh, your flight?" he asked again.

"Is little Elizabeth around there anywhere?" Uncle Pauly said instead.

"Ah, yeah, sure." She'd just finished with a customer, so he motioned for her to come by him.

"Good, good," Uncle Pauly said, somewhat distractedly, Rob thought.

The two uncles were whispering back and forth on the other end of the line and, when Elizabeth got to the phone, Siegfried took over.

"Liebling?" Siegfried said to her.

She and Rob held the receiver so both could hear. "Hi, Uncle Siegfried. We miss you. How is everything going over there? Is Aunt Anita recovering?"

"Wonderbar! Yes, Anita is doing so well, we are all very pleased. And Europe—being back in Germany again—it's a magnificent thing. There is nothing like home."

This statement was followed by no less than eleven straight long-distance minutes of description, on everything from local landmarks to regional restaurant delicacies to friendly visitors who came by to see Anita, with interjections by Uncle Pauly on all things Italian, as gleaned from the European cable channels and the occasional tourist.

During the uncles' one-sided conversation, Rob caught Elizabeth's eye. Not one, but both of hers were open wide and looking very green and worried.

So, she sensed something was up, too. Terrific.

It finally came out about three minutes after the Bavarian food report.

"So, we decided to stay on a little longer," Siegfried said cheerfully. "Since Anita's health is improving steadily, we thought we might take a little excursion to Italy, for Pauly's sake. So he, too, can enjoy a visit to his homeland. And then we'll return to check on your aunt again. Make sure she's still recovering."

Neither Rob nor Elizabeth opened their mouths.

"Liebling?"

Uncle Pauly's voice boomed over the line, too. "Roberto?"

Elizabeth was the one who'd gained enough composure to actually speak. "Uh-huh?"

Well, so it wasn't exactly eloquent, but she sure had one up on him. He couldn't make a single damn sound.

"You said everything was going well, Roberto," his uncle said. "This is true, isn't it?"

He managed a "Yeah," but that was all.

"Okay, good. So, say hi to your Mama, and we'll see you both in early August then."

"Maybe mid-August," Siegfried corrected.

"W-W-What?" Elizabeth squeezed her eyes tight and clenched the phone until her knuckles shown like hard ridges.

"WHAT!" Rob yelled into the line a heartbeat later.

"Oh, sorry," Siegfried said. "The connection must be getting bad. I said we'd be back in August sometime. Don't know the exact date yet, but Pauly and I will keep you both posted. Thanks for all you're doing. We'll be in touch."

"U-Uncle S-Siegfried!" Elizabeth said in the loudest voice he'd ever heard her use.

"Oh, yes, I almost forgot. I love you, too, *Liebling.*"

"Bye, Roberto!"

And then their crafty old uncles hung up on them.

"Oh, bloody hell," Elizabeth whispered.

His sentiments exactly.

~CHAPTER NINE~

Rob decided, from that moment forward, he wasn't going to let anything throw him.

He spent the next week making vows:

He'd deal with life in Wilmington Bay for as long as he had to, knowing he'd get to leave as soon as the two uncles returned. But, in the meantime, he'd...

Relax.

Be positive.

Enjoy what there was to enjoy.

And try to keep his emotions on an even keel with Elizabeth. Just because they had a little more time together than he'd thought, it didn't mean the expected end wasn't going to happen. And so, he'd just have to find a way to liven up the summer a little more. Distract them both a bit.

"Another customer headed up the walk," Jacques said, still using his frosty voice more often than not.

"I'll get this one," Rob told him. "Why don't you take a break from the counter and finish up the stuff you were doing in the backroom with the lemon bars?"

The Frenchman muttered his agreement in a way that was not exactly rude, but not exactly warm and fuzzy either.

Rob missed the easy camaraderie he and the other man

had shared prior to him and Elizabeth going public with their relationship. Now there was always something in the air between him and Jacques. If Elizabeth hadn't said she considered Jacques simply a good friend, he'd have thought there'd been some kind of romantic history between them.

"Hi, Rob," one of the regulars said. "Can I get a scoop of Vanilla Fudge Almond and one of Raspberry Burst in a waffle cone please?"

"Coming right up," Rob told the guy. "Want a topping today? We've got nuts, sprinkles, chocolate chips, crushed cookies...you name it."

"Got any chocolate-covered raisins?"

He shook his head. "We don't carry that one, but it sounds like it'd be good."

The man nodded vigorously. "Oh, it's the best. How about candy cane slivers? My wife loves that."

He shook his head again. Man, by comparison, their in-house toppings were starting to sound kind of boring. "Sorry, but you're giving me a lot of good ideas."

"What about those candy-coated sugar rocks that jump and pop around like fireworks in your mouth?"

"No, sorry."

"Ah, I'll just take my cone plain today," the guy said. "Maybe you'll have some different selections soon and I'll give those a whirl."

As the customer paid, the spark of an idea began to take form in Rob's mind. A way to add some needed excitement to the coming week.

"Do you think," he asked the man, "that other people in town would be interested in being creative with their toppings, too? That some of them have other unusual favorites?"

"Heck, yeah. You should meet my sister Leah. She puts caramel apple slices on her ice cream. And her husband Cal likes—and I'm serious about this—toasted blueberry waffles, cut up into cubes, sprinkled on top of his ice-cream bowl like croutons."

Rob nodded. "Weird."

"No kidding, but it ain't bad tasting either."

"You think if we asked the good people of Wilmington Bay to bring in a sample of their favorite ice cream toppings, they'd do it?"

"Oh, absolutely." The guy licked his cone and waved farewell. "Sounds like good fun."

"Hmm," he said as he watched the man leave. Fourth of July was coming up in a few days. People were always milling around the shop. This might give them something new to talk about. Kind of like a Treat Swap for the community.

He pulled out a huge piece of tag board from the storage closet and grabbed a few markers. He stared at it and tried to think of the best way to advertise the event. He was still staring when a couple of teen girls came into the shop.

"Either of you any good at drawing?" he asked them.

The tall blue-eyed one pointed at the short brown-eyed one. "She's awesome."

He told them what he wanted to convey and handed the art supplies over to them. "You each get a fudge brownie and a double-dip ice cream cone on the house if you can figure out how to make this sign look good."

The girls hooted their delight and set to work.

Ten minutes later, some high school guys showed up.

"Hey, what're they doing?" one of them asked Rob, pointing to the teen artists, deep in concentration.

He told them.

"Got anything else you need done?" another boy asked. "Fliers, maybe?"

"I've got a killer graphics system on my computer," the third boy said.

Rob grinned at the young entrepreneurs, gave them the event information and a free ice cream sandwich each. "You get another one when you come back with the fliers."

"We could distribute them, too, if you want," the first kid said eagerly.

"I want," Rob told them. "Just name your sweet reward when you're done."

"All right!" the boys said, racing out of the shop. "This is way cool."

"Yes, it is," Rob said. Then, over his shoulder to a slightly scowling Jacques, "Don't you think so?"

Jacques bowed his head. "I do think so," he said, his voice no longer icy, just kind of defeated. "But I'm not sure Elizabeth is going to agree."

Oh, yeah. Elizabeth.

"What were you thinking?" Elizabeth said to Rob "Mr. Big Idea" Gabinarri. "I thought we w-went over this before. There's a limit to the number of people we're legally allowed to have in the shop."

He looked at her with the exuberant, unapologetic gaze of a religious revivalist. "So, we'll have the First Annual Tutti-Frutti Topping Taste Test outside at the park. There's no limit to the number of people who can hang out there."

"Exactly. There are no parameters for control either. Not everyone is g-going to be there for the right reasons, Rob. Some people just crave chaos and will want to create it—at our expense. The Wilmington Bay police force doesn't have the budget, the manpower or the time to have a security team on hand for events like these."

"Relax, Elizabeth. You're overreacting. It'll be pure fun with no worries." He grinned at her and pulled her to him, giving her the kind of kiss that always made her unable to speak for a solid minute afterward. "You sure have a suspicious nature, don't you?"

"Yes. I guess I do. It—it's just—quiet people like me watch other people a lot. We see what they do. And, sure, there are lots of really great, really respectful Wilmington Bay citizens out there, no doubt. But I've also seen what lengths some people will go to in order to get attention." She shuddered. "Plus, I hate crowds."

She knew he didn't believe there would be any problems

with his Topping Taste Test, but jovial guys like Rob rarely took the time to look at the social undercurrents created by the events they hosted. They were too busy flitting around, laughing about things, chatting as though their words might stop flowing if they ceased talking for two whole minutes. They must be attuned to a completely different set of nonverbal messages than the ones she focused on. Which wasn't to say hers were right and his were wrong.

Not exactly.

But they sure were dissimilar, and she wished she could get him to open his eyes to what lay beneath the surface of a supposedly "pure fun" social gathering.

Unfortunately, it was too late now to do anything to stop it. Colorful fliers advertising the event were tacked up all over town, and a big poster hung in the window of the shop. She'd just have to deal with it.

"No one's going to try anything out of hand at this event," he said, running his fingers through her hair and nibbling a little at her neck. She lost her train of thought and didn't bother to try to argue with him further.

The doors jangled as someone entered.

"Gabinarri," Lance Burk's distinctive sneering voice said loudly. "I see you're still in town—" he shot Elizabeth a disgusted look, "and still fooling around. As always. Why haven't you packed up your last-year's-model sports car and headed back to Chicago? Could it be there's not much left to return to?"

"You're full of it, Burk" Rob said. "As always."

But she couldn't help but notice the way Rob pulled away from her then, completely severing their physical connection in Lance's presence. Was Rob ashamed to be seen with her in front of his old high-school rival? In front of the guy who was now dating the ever-popular and pretty Tara Welles? Elizabeth clenched her fists and began cleaning up serving utensils.

"Know what I think?" Lance said.

"Nope, and I don't want to," Rob replied.

Lance ignored him. "I think things at your little food place went to crap and now you're up here mooching off of your family." He held up one of the Topping Taste Test fliers. "I mean, jeez, what the hell is this? If you handled your diner the way you're handling this shop, it's no wonder you went bankrupt."

Rob's jaw grew taut. "First of all, since you seem unable to remember it, I'll have to spell it out. The Playbook is not a D-I-N-E-R. It's a R-E-S-T-A-U-R-A-N-T. Second, I did not go bankrupt. I'm just up here helping out for a while. The Playbook is well cared for and going strong back in Chicago, thank you." He glared at the other guy and said through gritted teeth, "Now, do you have an order or were you just leaving?"

Lance laughed. "You're losing your touch, Gabinarri. Not so hot now, are you? Where did the Wilmington Bay Golden Boy go?" The coward strode out before Rob could answer him.

"I hate that guy," he said.

"He hasn't changed since high school," she said, trying to make him feel better. "He's still the same dumb jock he always was, only now he's also meaner and more desperate. He doesn't think he's going to have many more chances to ride high on the image he worked so hard to project when we were in school. Time's running out for him to hit it big, and you represent everything he's not, so he has it in for you. That's all."

Rob gave her a long, befuddled stare, and she knew she'd said too much. That he'd think she was more of a geek than ever now, spouting off psychobabble that way.

But then he hugged her, and she was no longer so sure what he thought. Although, when he walked out of the room a few minutes later, she could've sworn she heard him mutter, "The same dumb jock..." under his breath. But she could've been wrong about that, too. She just didn't know anything anymore.

The jugglers were back in town.

They came in Monday morning while Rob struggled to get the tubs of ice cream packed into a portable freezer to take to the park. It was a much more complicated task than he'd expected, and he wished to heaven he had some juggling skills of his own right about then.

"Hi, guys," he told them, taking a moment to shake their hands and welcome them warmly. "Good to see you both again. What can I get for you?"

"Saw your signs for the Topping Taste Test," the taller of the two said. "Are you in need of any entertainment?"

"You two have some free time? On the Fourth of July? Man, this must be my lucky day."

"We've got a gig tonight," the other guy said. "But we did all our daytime gigs over the weekend. It's great when the Fourth falls on a Monday."

"Hey, if you're willing to be there, I'm more than willing to accept the offer," he said. "You two were probably the biggest hit Tutti-Frutti has had in forty years. We'd be honored for you to be part of the event."

"Are the terms the same?" the tall juggler asked with a grin.

Rob laughed. "Oh, you'll get all the free pastries, candy or ice cream you can eat, all right, with whatever toppings tickle your fancy. But I'll also throw in a monetary bonus on the side this time, too, for every hour you're out there. You both deserve it."

And damned if those jugglers didn't help him figure out how to pack up that freezer in under five minutes.

When they arrived at Wilmington Bay's Town Park, Jacques and Gretchen had already managed to set up the majority of the decorations. The picnic tables were covered with patriotic-themed tablecloths, there were red, white and blue carnation centerpieces (courtesy of their florist pal, who was a regular customer) and the voting sheets for "Best Topping" were stacked neatly next to a tin of miniature pencils and a giant ballot box.

"Looking good, you guys," he told his coworkers, parking the portable freezer next to the head table. He handed the container filled with ice-cream-shaped beanbags to the jugglers, who immediately flipped on their music and began practicing. "Where are Nick and Elizabeth?"

"Nick's picking up the plastic bowls and spoons," Gretchen explained. "And Elizabeth wanted to bring in some helium balloons for the kids."

He smiled. That sounded like her.

The music and the flying beanies were already drawing a crowd, despite the fact that the Topping Taste Test wasn't set to begin for a half hour. Rob's palms itched with excitement. This was going to be a wild day.

Thirty minutes later, he amended this thought: It was going to be a *very* wild and wacky and probably totally out-of-control day. And Elizabeth wasn't pleased.

"I still don't understand what you're trying to prove by doing this," she hissed at him as citizens of Wilmington Bay reveled in the loud rhythmic music and prepared to show and tell their favorite toppings.

He gently stroked her smooth shoulder, trying for the reassurance pat. "This'll bring in business." He pulled out a cordless microphone to do the announcing and watched as her complexion turned almost as green as her eyes.

"T-Tutti-F-Frutti was already a s-s-successful shop. N-Not that I don't think it's great th-that you're taking such an interest in im-improving it but, c'mon, Rob. C-Couldn't you have aimed f-for something l-lower k-key?"

Her stuttering was back full force with him after weeks of nearly perfect speech. He tried to catch her eye, but she was staring at the mike as if it might jump out of his hand and bite her. He hid it behind his back and made her continue.

"T-This is more like spring b-break in Fort Lauderdale than Fourth of July in W-W-Wisconsin."

He glanced around. Sure enough, there were women in bikini tops wiggling every part of their bodies to the hip-hop beat, men flinging Frisbees back and forth, open coolers, kids and dogs running rampant...and Tara Welles snaking toward them through the crowd, dressed in a skimpy red top and cutoff jeans. Hell, maybe Elizabeth had a point after all. This may not have been the best idea.

"I've g-got to g-go," Elizabeth told him, even though she hadn't seen Tara yet. "I n-need to finish s-setting up." She pointed toward his arms, which camouflaged the mike. "K-Keep that th-thing away from m-me please."

"Anything you say, babe." And, for Tara's viewing benefit, he kissed Elizabeth, intense and slow, before letting her run off. Tara was on him in a heartbeat.

"You know, Rob," she said, flicking her blond hair away from her face and trying to project a coy look, "I've got to give you credit. I didn't think you'd be able to handle being with Lizzy Daniels for this long."

"Why's that? You don't think I'm up to the intellectual challenge?"

Tara looked confused. "Well, Lizzy *is* smart, I suppose. She's always had that, but—"

"But what?" He didn't need to have another vote of no confidence in his ability to handle Elizabeth's brilliant mind. He knew he wasn't at her level. Constant reminders hurt.

"I guess I'm just surprised you'd be so blinded by someone like her. The two of us talked at Hauser's that one night."

"You did?"

Tara gave a bored sigh. "Well, yeah. Lizzy knows she's not really your type. You two just don't seem quite right. Together, I mean. Separately, of course, you're fine. Well, *you* are. She's in a different sphere altogether."

Light years ahead of him, Tara meant. A dumb jock like him couldn't hold the interest of a woman like Elizabeth Daniels. Not for long.

"Look, I've got to do some work right now," he told her.

She took three quick steps forward and put her palm on his forearm. "Do you need any help, Rob?"

"Uh, no, thanks."

He looked up and caught Lance Burk glowering at them from halfway across the park.

"Maybe I'll see you later then?" she said.

Later. Much, much later. "Yep. Enjoy the Topping Taste

Test."

He sprinted away from her and up to his place at the head table. He checked his watch—time to start—and clicked on the microphone.

"Hello, Everyone! Welcome to Wilmington Bay's First Annual Topping Taste Test."

Everyone cheered like maniacs and one guy tossed his Frisbee high into the air as a form of enthusiastic salute. Someone else's golden retriever ran after it, barking happily while everybody stopped to watch.

Rob laughed. Community stuff like this was what made Wisconsin life so endearing. Sometimes the simplest things were what made him smile the most.

Tony was in the crowd, Maria-Louisa and the kids in tow. His brother caught his eye and grinned. It was like him saying, "Welcome Home, big brother."

His Mama was there, too. She looked so proud of him. For all his Windy City accomplishments, this was the one thing— besides his wedding—that he knew she'd dreamed of seeing: Him in the Wilmington Bay spotlight again...which, he had to admit, felt pretty good right now. But he also knew how easily it could become suffocating. How quickly he could be categorized and dismissed. He'd worked for a decade to shed that "dumb jock" label, but look how fast it came back?

He held up the mike and waved at the crowd. Finally, they became silent.

"Okay, folks, this is what's going to happen," he told them. "Pretty soon we're going to call up all the people who brought out their favorite toppings for the Taste Test. Everyone who wants to will taste them on free scoops of Tutti-Frutti ice cream, we'll vote on them and we'll award the winner with a prize. Now, let's hear a shout out from everybody who brought in a topping for your friends and neighbors to try."

A roar went up around him. Whoa. He was going to have to divide this clan into smaller groups. No way could all of them come up at once.

Elizabeth whispered frantically in his ear about separating

the crowd alphabetically, with each of them—Gretchen, Nick, Jacques and herself—taking a table with about a fourth of the alphabet and leaving Rob to be emcee.

"We can have semi-finalist voting at each table, with the four winners competing for the grand prize at the end," she said.

Bright lady.

So that was how they announced it and, soon, the chaos was quartered.

No doubt about it, though—it was still chaos.

Elizabeth served up gobs of ice cream and watched as the citizens with last names beginning with the letters A through F devoured the toppings and debated the taste of each. At her table, it was a race to the death between candied pineapple bits and crushed chocolate-covered cherries. Gretchen waved at her holding up a box of Cracker Jacks, which apparently had taken the lead at her G through M table.

Nick had his hands full with the N through S bunch, a couple of whom were in an all-out war over the merits of cashews versus pecans. And Jacques had the T through Z clan, who were rather subdued by comparison. Then again, maybe that was because there were fewer of them.

She watched as Rob deftly handled most of the social chitchat as well as wielded that dreaded microphone. He was so at ease speaking in public—it was amazing. So unlike her. Not that this was much of a great revelation, considering their longstanding history. She'd known how different the two of them were ever since she was five.

Lance Burk sauntered up to her table and plopped a plastic bag of chocolate-covered somethings on one corner.

"If you guys are wild about those chocolate cherries, you've gotta give these here a try," he told the group. "Hand me a bowl of that ice cream, Lizzy."

No courtesies from Lance. No please or, when she gave

him a bowl, no thank you. But what did she expect? This was the same guy who'd stopped speaking to his own father because he didn't get the specific car he'd wanted for graduation. And he'd never been nice to her in his life.

"Mmm. Crunchy," one avid taster declared before moving on to the sliced star fruit.

"What *are* these?" asked another, gingerly holding up one of the chocolate blobs between her fingers.

"Try 'em, you'll like 'em," Lance said.

Not the kind of forthcoming response Elizabeth wanted to hear. She went over and picked up Lance's bag to get a closer look.

"Oh, here. Let me feed you one." Lance snatched the bag out of her hand and waved a chocolate something in front of her mouth. His spidery fingers rolling the "treat" back and forth.

"N-No th-thanks," she said, taking a step back.

He laughed. "What a timid little wallflower you are, Lizzy Daniels. Gabinarri is even more of a fool than I thought."

Rob Gabinarri, she had learned, was far from being a fool, so Lance was, once again, pointing out how incompatible she and Rob were. Everyone, even a jerk like Lance, knew she wasn't up to Rob's usual girlfriend standard.

But now wasn't the time to get thrown off course by her own insecurities. Everyone at her table wanted to try the topping Lance brought in, but she had a bad feeling about it. When he put the bag on the table again, she snitched a sample.

She turned it over in her palm and broke it in half. As she studied the inside, the pit of her stomach dropped to her toes. Although well concealed in considerable chocolate, Lance's topping bag was entirely filled with insects.

She pulled the bag off the table.

"Hey, Frizzy Lizzy! What d'ya think you're doing?" Lance marched over to her and tried to yank it back, but she resisted.

"Don't eat these," she told her crowd. "They're c-c-crickets."

A few people gasped, a couple of them coughed, one gagged and went behind a tree, but most started yelping and flinging the chocolate-covered crickets off their ice cream and onto the grass. Several just tossed away their entire bowls and began complaining. The other groups stopped eating to watch her table's total upheaval.

Lance laughed.

Rob came striding over. "What's the problem here?"

An enraged lady in fuchsia was quick to fill him in, agitated in equal parts by the fact that she had to throw away perfectly good ice cream and that she was a vegetarian who'd now eaten insect flesh.

"Why did you go and do that, Burk?" Rob asked him. "This is a family-friendly event."

Lance waved a rainbow-colored flier at him. "It says right here—" He pointed. "'Bring your favorite topping to share.' That's just what I did."

"Get out of here," Rob said in a low, dangerous voice.

Lance raised his light eyebrows. "You can't kick me out of a public park. Besides, I didn't do anything wrong. I didn't force anyone to try my favorite topping. It's not my fault if they didn't like it." He laughed again, daring Rob with his insolence to make the next move.

"Leave now, or I'll call the authorities," Rob said.

Lance shook his head and crossed his arms as if rooting himself to the spot. "You're a freakin' idiot, Gabinarri. This whole event is just a stupid stunt you're using to try to distract people from noticing what a failure you are. You always played that same game on the field, too, so the fans wouldn't notice your poor form when you threw a long pass or how you rarely scored any points in the final quarter." His eyes narrowed. "You haven't changed a bit. Still more show than substance. Still dumb as a rock."

To Elizabeth's horror, Rob didn't answer him back right away or put that Lance bastard in his place. He just stared at him with the oddest expression. A yard away, Nick's fists were clenched, however, and despite not being much of a fighter, she knew her Greek buddy wouldn't hesitate to throw a left hook or two if it came to blows.

It looked like Rob was thinking. Planning. But something had to be done. And fast.

Before she could talk herself out of it, she stepped up beside Rob and pried the microphone from his fingers. Most of the Wilmington Bay residents were eavesdropping with unabashed interest, so she had a ready audience. She flicked on the mike, gulped some air and said a prayer to both Madonnas for wisdom in using this thing.

"H-Hi everyone," she said, the loudness of her amplified voice making her want to cower under the red-white-and-blue-covered table, but she pressed on. "I-If you haven't cast your vote y-yet for the semi-finalist round, pl-please do so now. But, before we m-move onto the f-finals, I just wanted to say, on behalf of all of us at Tutti-Frutti, how much w-we appreciate such a fine group of people coming out for our special event t-today."

She paused to take a few long breaths and was surprised when people started clapping. She glanced around at the cheering crowd before noticing Lance's fallen expression. She'd deprived him of his spotlight. Well, good.

She felt a small smile rise on her lips. She could do this. Yes, she really could. If she just pretended she was talking to Rob alone, maybe she could trick herself out of this fear for a minute. She fixed her eyes on him.

"I also w-want to add that, in Tutti-Frutti's long history, we've never had the p-privilege of having someone like Rob Gabinarri on staff. He's so clever. He's always thinking of ways to bring fun and entertainment to our little sweets shop. F-For one thing, he brought us these amazing jugglers." She pointed toward the two men, who were quick to do a couple of terrific, showy stunts involving back flips and flying beanbags. The crowd went wild. Rob turned his attention away from Lance and stared at her.

"And, of course, y-you all know that today's Topping Taste Test was Rob's idea, too." She paused for more enthusiastic cheering. "So, thanks, Rob," she said to him, her voice echoing across the park.

"THANKS, ROB!" the crowd parroted back.

Rob waved his arm in response, but he didn't say a single word. He just kept looking between the gathered taste-testers and her, seemingly surprised and very, very uncharacteristically silent.

She couldn't help it. She laughed. She suddenly thought of about five thousand things she wanted to say to the good people of Wilmington Bay, starting with how remarkable it was to finally see Rob Gabinarri speechless.

But she didn't. He shot her a questioning look, and she responded by sending him a love letter with her eyes. After a very long moment, he rewarded her with a blazing smile.

Maybe it was crazy but, at least for today, she didn't care that their relationship wouldn't last the summer. For the first time in over twenty years, she understood something about the guy she'd once idolized: Rob also needed someone to believe in him. And he needed it just as desperately as she did.

Lance Burk stalked off, dragging a whining Tara away, while the rest of them returned to their tasting and voting.

"I—um—" Rob tried to say.

"We'll talk later," she promised him. He nodded slowly and returned to tallying the ballots, the serious expression never quite leaving his face, though.

Jacques slipped over to her. "Nice speech, *chéri*."

"Thanks."

"Tell me," he said in her ear, "is he worth it?"

"What do you mean?"

"Is he worth your heart of love, *ma petite brioche?* Because that's what's happening to you, isn't it? You're beginning to fall in love with that boy all over again?"

She looked into her dear friend's kind eyes and bit her lower lip. "Oh, Jacques. That's the worst part. I never stopped."

~CHAPTER TEN~

Rob knew Elizabeth was falling in love with him. She'd braved the microphone and public speaking for him, and if that wasn't a grand gesture of love for someone like her… Well, this had to stop.

Although he'd only been biding his time before punching out that idiot Burk, he owed her for standing up for him. For putting herself out there in his defense. And the best way he knew to reward her was to steer her clear of him.

The fireworks would be starting soon.

Team Tutti-Frutti closed up shop at dusk that night to gather on a blanket under the canopy of stars, which would soon be replaced by the rockets' red glare, the bombs bursting in air and the mosquitoes buzzing everywhere else.

She sat no more than a foot in front of him, the glow from the distant streetlights caressing her hair. He felt his arm rise, lifting his hand toward the shimmering waves, but he forced it back down. He had to pull away from her.

"Birthday torte?" Jacques said, passing around a cookie tin stocked with his delectable apricot concoctions. He blew Elizabeth a kiss and handed her a special one with the number "28" on it.

"Thanks, Jacques," she said. "Please tell me I don't have to wait until my birthday officially starts at midnight to eat this gorgeous thing."

The Frenchman grinned. "Enjoy, *mon amie.*"

When the tin reached him, Rob grabbed a torte for each hand to keep himself from seizing Elizabeth instead.

Nick popped a big one in his mouth. "Mmm, man, these are awesome."

"Gretchen helped me with them," Jacques said. "You should see that woman brandish a pastry crimper. She's frightening. Comes snapping at you like a one-pincered lobster."

Gretchen retaliated by giving him a hard shove. "Don't forget, I'm going to do the tartlets with you, too. You promised, and you'd better be nice about it or I'll cut off your supply of amaretto truffles."

Jacques shuddered. "Cruel woman. Okay, you win. We'll do the tartlets in the next week or two and let you all try them. They're fairly safe. Only slight crimping is involved."

Gretchen made a comic face and the group laughed. Rob smiled before remembering that pretty soon their future plans wouldn't include him. Sure, he wanted to return to Chicago but, at the same time, there was a growing list of things he'd miss about Wilmington Bay.

"Oh, you guys," Elizabeth said. "Don't forget, Camden rescheduled. He's now coming out on the fourteenth to do the photographs, so leave that following weekend open. He'll probably be here Thursday through at least Saturday finishing the shots. We're going to need lots of good ones from all of you." She paused and grinned at him. "We'll except for you, Rob. We won't make you bake us any desserts, but we'll probably need you to tackle most of the shop's shifts alone during those days."

"I can handle it," he told her. "No problem." But, yeah, how could he not feel a little left out?

"Oooh! Sparklers," Gretchen said to Elizabeth. "Wanna get some?"

"Sure," Elizabeth said. "How about you guys?"

Nick shook his head. "Sissy stuff. You two enjoy."

So they went off together leaving Rob alone with the other men for a few minutes. There was a long silence.

"So, about Elizabeth's cookbook," he began. "Why is this project so important to her? You two know her writing history better than I do."

Well, that wasn't entirely true. He was trying to butter them up a bit. He'd always paid extra attention when one of Elizabeth's essays was read in class and, on the infrequent occasion when she wrote a story for the school paper, he always read it two or three times because the way she explained things on the page was in the same voice she used when she spoke, which was a rare occurrence back then. He liked "hearing her," if only on paper.

Jacques, of course, got right to the heart of it. "She's dedicating it to the memory of her mom. It's Elizabeth's farewell offering and, in her mind, it has to be perfect. An absolutely flawless project."

"Yeah," Nick said. "She was close to her dad, too, but her mom was the one who taught her how to bake. I guess Mrs. Daniels was a great lady, although I never met her."

"I met her," Rob said. "A few times, but it was years ago, when we were still kids. She was always very nice to me."

"I met, too," Jacques said quietly. "More recently. She and Elizabeth acted like sisters. Elizabeth didn't make her mother's cheesecake recipe for two years after she lost her." He paused, as if trying to decide how much Rob could be trusted to know. "Elizabeth is also completely self-supporting now. Only a tiny amount from the will remained after expenses were paid and, since she normally only works a few hours per week at the shop to relieve her uncle, her Tutti-Frutti salary is also very small. So, the advance and the royalties on her cookbooks are her major source of income. She can't afford to be irresponsible."

The way he said it, it was like an accusation. As if Rob were one of Elizabeth's few bad choices. It was an insinuation he sure could have lived without.

The ladies returned, sparklers in hand.

"We brought some to share with you boys, even though

you said they were for sissies." Elizabeth gave Nick an especially saucy grin. "I'm willing to bet you won't be able to resist once we light them."

Nick laughed and snatched one of the packs away from her.

"See," she said, pointing at him.

Rob watched as they lit a few, the sparklers brightening up their little corner of the park and casting a warm glow wherever the light shined. He noticed Elizabeth's facial expression. How different it was tonight. Not because of the bright sparklers' light but because of her growing confidence. That look of self-assurance flattered her, enhanced her natural quality of competence by adding a dash of poise.

She may fancy herself in love with him, but it was clear she'd do just fine without any dumb jock hanging on her sleeve. He was seeing her transformation from the fearful, stuttering duckling to the secure, dignified swan right before his eyes. She didn't need him to rescue her. If truth be told, she'd been the one rescuing *him* today. She didn't need his help.

Hell, *nobody* needed his help.

Miguel assured him (at least twice a day when Rob checked in via cell phone) that The Playbook was doing just fine, despite him being over a hundred miles away and in another state. He'd worked long hours for years—hiring the right people, organizing every aspect of the restaurant, automating as many procedures as possible—so he wouldn't be indispensable forever. Now, he wasn't.

Mama, Tony, Maria-Louisa and the gang were great, as always.

His other siblings, in a variety of conversations and e-mails, declared they, too, were in terrific shape. No problems on their end, thanks.

Tutti-Frutti required only a warm body to open and close the place, so even there he was nobody special.

Maybe when the uncles returned he should close his eyes, throw a dart on a map and go somewhere new. Nothing pressing was holding him to either Wilmington Bay or to

Chicago...other than a sense of duty and a bunch of old habits.

The fire chief made the announcement that the first set of fireworks would be going up in a few moments. Elizabeth scooted next to him—so damned close his pulse started racing—and she nudged his side to get her expected hug. He knew he should pull away. He wasn't going to stay in Wisconsin. He'd break her heart...but he just couldn't do that to her tonight. Not now. Not when she was so confident for once, so sure of his eagerness to hold her.

And the worst part was that he *did* want to hold her on this, the eve of her twenty-eighth birthday. Tightly, passionately, desperately.

He wanted more than that, too.

Boom!

The opening display shot ribbons of colored light through the blackened sky, like streamers chasing each other then disappearing in a game of tag.

Another boom. And another.

Fireworks poured out of the heavens and rained down on them in a flamboyant thunderstorm. They looked up at it, awestruck.

Elizabeth pressed harder into him and ran the tip of her nose along his cheek. He caught his breath and tried to resist, but he was as powerless against her as he was against the falling beams of light from the sky.

He turned his head and their lips met for a deep, thorough, tantalizing kiss that made his mouth burn from the heat and his erection pulse against his zipper. He imagined laying her down on the velvety blanket beneath them, wishing away her friends and the entire Wilmington Bay Fourth-of-July crowd, unfastening all of these binding garments, sliding his fingers against her smooth skin and into damp and very intimate places before taking her...gently and undeniably...into full womanhood.

"Rob."

He wanted to hear her scream his name in passion and feel her pulling him onto her, into her. Beautiful Elizabeth.

He wanted to smell the musky scent of their lovemaking on

his skin and taste the tears of her pleasure when she cried out in climax. He wanted to run his tongue along her neck and—

"*Rob.*" Elizabeth cupped his cheek and tickled his chin until he stopped kissing her neck.

"Um, yeah?"

She raised her eyebrows in the direction of the rest of Team Tutti-Frutti. The three of them were smirkily avoiding establishing eye contact and focusing way too hard on the fireworks finale.

"Oh," he said.

"Let's get out of here," she said. Or, at least that was what he thought she said.

"What?"

"Let's. Go," she told him, enunciating both syllables. "To my place. Now."

And, see, this was the problem: He knew damn well that she didn't *really* know what she was propositioning. That she ought to wait for a better first-time candidate. That he'd, nevertheless, find it impossible to resist her under the unrestrictive conditions of an empty apartment.

And, yet, he couldn't make himself stay in the nice, safe, noisy park with all those prying eyes. He couldn't turn her down to save his life.

Elizabeth knew exactly what she was doing.

Well, okay, there were a few technicalities that she was certain Rob's expertise would make easier, but she knew she wasn't making a mistake in her choice of a first-time lover. Even if it were doubtful he'd hang around long enough to be her last one.

They collapsed onto her sofa. One of these times they ought to try her bed, she supposed, but the sofa was pretty comfortable and it had the added advantage of being several yards closer to the door.

"Take off everything," he whispered. "It'll distract me

enough so I won't talk you out of this."

"Okay."

She stripped down to her underwear, and Rob assisted with unbuttoning, unlatching and other undoing activities. She always did appreciate a man who knew how to be helpful.

"Your turn," she told him, loosening his belt and flicking open the snap on his jeans. She saw the waistband of a different pair of boxers. Mmm. A true patriot. "Love those stars and stripes."

"Repeat after me, Lizzy. 'I pledge allegiance to the flag...'" He paused to kiss behind her ear. "I don't hear you repeating."

"I used to stutter through saying the Pledge in elementary school until I began mouthing the words." She yanked the boxers off him. He gasped. "I'll let my allegiances be known later."

"Alrighty then."

He took a shuttering breath and Elizabeth's heart almost stopped. *Please don't back out on me now*, she pleaded silently.

"Okay, look, I only have the strength to ask you this once." He pulled back and gazed deep into her eyes. "Are you absolutely sure you want to do this...with *me?*"

She still had her own cream-colored panties on. The new Victoria's Secret extra-lacy ones she'd gotten with Rob in mind. Or, rather, with Rob *discarding them* in mind.

She took his long, strong hand and placed it on her hip, his fingers brushing against the lacy leg opening at her right thigh. Oh, she wanted him so much, yet *still* he waited and made her wait. If her nonverbal green lights weren't enough of a clue, she'd just have to add on the words as bluntly as possible.

"Rob, if you don't make love to me *right now*, I may have to poison your next ice cream sundae," she said. How was that for a threat?

"I'll take that as a yes." And her panties were gone before he reached the end of his sentence.

While it was true she'd kissed a handful of boys before this particular night, and she'd even begun moving around those proverbial bases with them, Rob had long ago dragged her far into new territory. He was now taking her into an outfield she'd never explored except within the pages of an occasional romance novel. She couldn't help but feel hyperaware of each and every movement, of the way his body's contours connected with her own.

His slightly roughened hand slipped between her thighs, abrading the sensitive, previously untouched skin and making her nerves jitterbug.

"Relax," he told her.

Yeah, that was going to happen.

His warm lips overtook hers, his tongue darting in and out of her mouth like a kind of kinky foreshadowing. She wished she didn't like it quite so much. It made the strange tugging reaction of her lower regions feel more urgent. Her hips lifted to meet his fingers.

He encircled the delicate folds with a fingertip, and she could feel her pulse in every part of her body. She heard herself moan.

"Say my name." He rubbed more insistently and moved his kisses to her breasts.

But these first impressions of genuine physical foreplay took too much of her energy. Speaking was a difficult thing for her under the best of circumstances, but this—

He pushed one of his fingers slowly inside her and her breath caught. Oh, Lord, this was going to be something...something unforgettable. What was she supposed to do next?

"Say my name." His finger began to thrust in and out. Just when she'd begun to get used to the rhythm, a second finger entered and joined the first in its dance.

"R-R—" she said, not saying at all what she'd intended. Her earlier bravado began slipping away. Fast. What had she been *thinking* trying to take on a man like Rob? This kind of intensity couldn't be safe. At least she hadn't expected to feel—

"Elizabeth. Say. My. Name."

She had to pull herself together. Refocus. "R-Rob," she whispered.

His fingers thrust hard into her and she gasped for air.

"Rob, y-you have to s-stop." She put her hand on his. He stopped moving so abruptly the world felt as though it'd crashed to a halt.

He slid his fingers out of her, pulled back and looked down at her with a combination of stunned disbelief, hurt and, she had to admit, incredible self-control. "E-Eliz—"

She touched her fingers to his lips. "C-Condoms," she managed to say. "Do you have any?"

"Well, yes, but—"

"Good," she told him. "I-I need you in me now. No more of these preliminaries."

The pallor that had come over him a minute ago disappeared and he nodded, snatching at the wallet in the back pocket of his Levi's. A moment later, she got her wish.

The thing was, she'd imagined the reality of this experience, what it would be like, for years and years. At least ten years of wondering seriously: Would it hurt? Would she be driven mad with desire? Would her partner? So, to be honest, what she got wasn't exactly what she'd expected.

First of all, yes, there was a bit of an achy tenderness when he first entered fully, but not like the painful tearing she'd spent a decade worrying about. She doubted there'd be much—if any—blood. And that was kind of a relief. There was definitely something to be said for being *really* turned on. It seemed to ease everything.

Secondly, she could say without reservation that, yes, she was being driven mad with desire, but she'd expected that desire to be all consuming somehow, and it wasn't. Not all consuming enough, anyway, to keep her from contemplating everything. She used to think, when this time came, she wouldn't be aware of anything aside from the feelings The Man (whoever he was) brought out in her.

Rob (a.k.a. The Man, in this particular and rather singular instance) brought out an overwhelming range of emotion in her, but she could still hear the clock ticking, the cars swishing outside on the street, the rumble of her food-deprived stomach because she hadn't eaten since lunch. Well, no. She'd had one of Jacques's tortes, but she was still starving.

And she was having stray thoughts like these. Thoughts about *pastries*. What the hell was that all about?

Finally, she didn't know, and couldn't comment on, whether Rob was being driven mad by desire. And this really wasn't something she could ask him either.

He *did* seem to be getting into the experience, what with all the moaning and grunting and other noises indicating his interest in continuing, but there was no way for her to know if his enthusiasm was because of *her* specifically or just because sex was an all-around, feel-good, never-turn-it-down-if-remotely-possible activity for a hot-blooded, twenty-eight-year-old, all-American, extremely-patriotic male.

She did know that the thrusting, tugging, tightening and tension-filled physicality of the whole lovemaking thing shattered her ability to focus on any one feeling. It was too much conflicting sensation, and still too new to her.

Not that she was finding it unpleasant or anything. Oh, no. Just really, really...well, overwhelming.

As for Rob, his body's urges seemed to have taken over every other part of him. He mumbled her name a few times. He kissed her mouth, her earlobes, her neck, her breasts—all the while still moving his hips in a slow grind that made her so dizzy that she was relieved to be lying down. He cupped her bottom and pulled her up into him, in time to a deliberate rhythm her heartbeat was beginning to copy. He covered her—inside and out—with himself.

And she knew if she could just *concentrate*, she could reach the same, nearly mindless state he was in. But she couldn't bring herself into that kind of focus.

Then the rhythm changed.

It became faster. More insistent. Urgent.

"Elizabeth!" he cried out, seeking her mouth, devouring her, trying to pull her into his passion. She wanted to do it for him, to jump in and join him, but she was still outside herself, still taking it all in. Her very first time...

"Please. Try." His voice was pleading.

So she tried, but it was too late for this go around.

With a curse he shuddered in a moment of wildness, and then his body went very, very still. Once again, he pulled back and looked down at her, his eyes serious and full of concern.

"I'm sorry," he said. "I waited as long as—"

"I know." She hugged him tight. "I'm—I'm still learning about—about this."

He kissed her. "I know." Then, after a beat, "I guess we're gonna have to rest up and try it again." He glanced down at his watch, which showed it was after midnight, and sent her a naughty grin. "Ready for your present, Birthday Girl?"

~CHAPTER ELEVEN~

Rob gulped his air, as he'd been doing for the past half hour, and very gently pulled out of her. He'd tried to be as careful as he could tonight. He'd tried to keep things slow, sensual. He'd done his damnedest not to crush her under his weight. But he'd actually never slept with a virgin before, even when he'd been one himself, so if anyone had some learning to do...

Although, technically, she was no longer virginal now, was she?

He felt a bizarre combination of pride and all-out guilt at this fact. At the very least, he had to make this first time end right for her.

He slid to the side and ran his fingertips along her smooth hip, trailing them across her belly and further down to her beautiful, caress-able thighs.

"Ohhh," she said. "Y-You don't have to, um—"

"Shh," he told her.

This time, with his own hunger somewhat sated, he had patience completely on his side.

His fingers tingled as he first found, and then traced, a series of ever-shrinking circles over her most sensitive flesh. Not altering the pattern. Letting her become accustomed to it until she began to predict it, began to need it.

Her hips started to move with the pattern. She became one with it. He smiled. It was only a matter of time.

He knew, when he heard the catch in her breathing, the time had almost arrived. Now his fingers moved in circles so small they barely pulsed. He let her find them, let her cling to them. He wanted to kiss her so badly, but he was afraid to interrupt her. He didn't want to spoil the spell they'd both worked so hard to achieve.

And then she broke.

"Rob," she cried out.

The surprise on her face both delighted and confused him. What had she expected? That it would be awful? That he wouldn't work until dawn, if need be, to satisfy her?

Then he remembered, once again, that this was her first time. She had no experience, only expectations, and those were probably based on extremes. Novels or films or fairy tales—all either glorifying the perfect lover or admonishing the insensitive rogue for his disregard of the lady's needs.

Rob was no hero or villain.

He gave in now to his acute desire to kiss her. A long Happy-Birthday-To-You soul kiss. Afterward, she turned toward him and snuggled in his arms, yawning. His heart jumped around like a jackrabbit as he tried to identify the weird sensations he couldn't name—at least not all at once and in a jumble like this.

Yeah, there was passion.

Yeah, he could pick out pure lust and admiration and affection, too. But there was more.

Friendship, for sure.

A sense of protectiveness toward her. That one he wasn't certain he should be feeling, but there it was.

Sentimentality at all the years they'd known each other. That quiet little kindergartener with the wispy, wavy hair from way back, even before they started school. That third-grade girl with the expressive and oh-so-observant eyes. That young lady she became, still so much of her own spirit—not part of the high-school collective mind.

And these thoughts were followed by a solitary one he couldn't believe actually passed through his sex-fogged brain: *To have a child with a woman you deeply love must be amazing. To see your features and hers combine—awe-inspiring. To create a joint heritage, in the form of a baby, by this act of lovemaking, would be a kind of miracle.*

Maybe Tony wasn't so out of his mind with the five kids after all.

Rob watched Elizabeth slip into the tranquil slumber of the innocent, and he shook his head. He was going to need a twelve-step program or a year of sessions with a damned shrink to straighten himself out when he got back to Chicago, just so he could be a normal happy bachelor again.

He put his head down next to hers and closed his eyes. He didn't, of course, manage to fall asleep, though.

The Morning After. A real one, this time.

Elizabeth tried to wrap her mind around this fact because, in all truth, she felt *way* more woozy today than she'd felt after their first totally conscious kiss or even after that margarita hangover.

And her back was sore. And her joints were stiff. And though this sofa was comfortable as sofas go, it was not the kind of furniture choice two people should sleep on long term. She rubbed her neck and tried not to wake up Rob.

One dark eye fluttered open despite her efforts.

"Morning, Birthday Girl," he said, a slow grin rising on his tantalizing lips. Oh, how she remembered those lips.

"Morning," she said back. "Is it a good one?" She literally held her breath waiting for his reply.

He didn't answer in words. He leaned over her, brushed away the quilt he must have flung over them some time in the night, and then the handsome rascal licked and nipped and kissed her worries away for what felt like an hour, although it was probably only five minutes.

"Mmm, good answer," she said.

He winced. "You know, my right hip and elbow are killing me."

She pointed in the direction of the hallway, hoping he'd understand.

"Ah," he said. "You have a bedroom? How convenient." He pulled her upright and rubbed some of the worst kinks out of her neck and shoulders. "Please say you're going to lead me there, Lizzy."

She laughed. "Call me Elizabeth."

"Why?"

"Why not? You prefer to be called Rob."

He nodded. "True. But Roberto marks me as someone ethnic when I'm really pretty American. There's not that kind of distinction between your two names."

She tugged him toward her bedroom, praying she'd remembered to clean it up yesterday. "But the names have different vibrations. Th-They send off different signals. You know how Madonna sort of changed her name to Esther for a while? At the time, she said she wanted to attach herself to the energy of a different name. That's kind of how I feel. Lizzy is that frizzy-haired chubby girl from high school. Elizabeth is still frizzy-haired, but a grown up. Marginally less awkward."

He lifted her onto her neatly made (Thank God!) double bed and leisurely ran his hands over her waist and hips. No way could he, in the bright light of morning, think those hips of hers were attractive.

"I never thought you were chubby," he said, looking sincere, but she couldn't entirely believe him. "In fact—" He lightly pinched the skin around her belly and frowned. "I think you're probably too thin now. I think you're going to need some chocolate today. Several servings. Just to break even."

"To break even?"

"Because of all the calories you're going to burn this morning." He grinned big. "As I recall, we have a Take Two to do."

"Oh, yeah. That's right." She raised her eyebrows at him

and waited to see what he'd do next.

"You bet that's right. Oh." He got up and wandered out of the room—totally, gloriously naked!—returning a moment later with his wallet. He flicked one condom on her nightstand and scowled. "We may actually have to leave your bedroom today, much as I don't want to. I only had two of these in my wallet and we used the first one last night."

She decided to let him sweat it out. He could find out about her unopened box of Trojans later, when it suited her to be forthcoming with information. "Guess we'll just have to make this one last a while," she said, giving him her most demure smile, batting her eyelashes for extra effect.

His jaw dropped a little and his eyes narrowed. "You're kind of a devilish one, aren't you? This 'Elizabeth' that you are now. You like to play at being so sweet, but really I'm starting to see a trend. When you get comfortable with someone, that whole Miss Innocent act starts to melt away, doesn't it? You're able to speak your mind way too clearly. In fact, I'm starting to think that you—"

"Rob?"

He smirked. "If you're trying to shut me up, sweetheart, let me tell you someth—"

"I-I have this fantasy."

He stopped smirking and shut up.

She hadn't intended to do this. Not this soon. Heck, probably not ever, but she'd leaped into it without thinking. (See what kind of trouble a big mouth got you into?) And now it was either follow through or have him call her bluff.

She sighed, got out of bed and pulled open her bottom dresser drawer. There she drew out three long silk scarves. Roberto Gabinarri...to be all hers. Bound and gagged, finally. Now *that* was a birthday present.

"I've had this, um, fantasy about you for a long, long time." There, she'd finally admitted it and, yet, Rob didn't look repulsed. He looked downright intrigued.

"R-Really?"

She grinned. It was so great to hear him stumble on a word

for a change. When a gabby Gabinarri was reduced to stuttering, emotion must be dancing around in there somewhere. Now, if she could just get him to stop chattering altogether for a while, maybe he'd finally be able to hear her heart speaking to him over the incessant talking.

"What, um, do you want to do?" He blinked at her and got into bed again, his expression utterly eager.

She slid in next to him and held out the first scarf, touching it to his mouth. "I want you to listen—not talk." She dangled the other two. "And I want you to stay in one place when you're doing it."

For a long moment he paused, his eyes scanning her face with the most incredulous look. Then, at last, he laughed out loud. "Why, you little minx," he said, reaching for the scarves and twining one thoughtfully around his wrist.

But, for the next hour, those were the last words he said.

Over the following week, Elizabeth tried hard not to think about *only* Rob.

Instead, her mind chose to contemplate the highly exciting things Rob could do, with or without scarves. The way Rob's obscenely sexy body felt against hers, whether they were on her bed or on her sofa. The various adventures they had with sundae toppings in the privacy of her apartment. (She'd come to have a special fondness for whipped cream.) The witty conversations with Rob that made her head spin, either at the shop or at his mother's house or just at some random location in town. And how being in Rob's very presence could make her forget to breathe.

Stuff like that.

At Gabinarri family dinners, she had to remind herself to clean her plate and talk about only topics of conversation suitable for young ears. Although, admittedly, Rob's mother looked at her as if she were the new family savior, and the woman would've probably forgiven her just about any infraction. Alessandra Gabinarri had bridal bouquets in her bright brown eyes whenever she glanced in Elizabeth's direction.

With Nick, Jacques and even Gretchen, she was cryptic in her explanations of her whereabouts, and she knew she was being discussed behind her back. Gretchen and Jacques, especially, would stop talking abruptly almost whenever Elizabeth walked into a room.

They were her best friends so, naturally, they wouldn't be blinded to the obvious. They plied her with sweets whenever she saw them, but she knew what they were doing. She could almost hear them saying:

"*Mon Dieu*. Rob's going to break her heart."

"I know, but will that girl listen?"

"She's the dearest *chéri* but, face it, she's not in his league. Nowhere close."

"Few are. Maybe I'll make her some crème-orange truffle parfaits and she'll forget about him."

"Good plan. I'll whip up a few pastries, too. What do you think? Blackberry tarts or caramel-apple turnovers?"

Elizabeth would've gained ten pounds from all their love and concern if she weren't burning off hundreds of calories every night. And, no, she couldn't credit her *X-treme Abs and Thighs* DVD. It was collecting dust by the TV.

On the morning of the fourteenth, she and Jacques were at the bakery he worked at when he wasn't moonlighting at Tutti-Frutti. Both nervously awaited Camden's arrival. Time at last for the photos, and Jacques, a man who typically possessed a storehouse of excess energy, paced and fidgeted in uncharacteristic agitation.

"Ready?" she asked him, her own anxiety taking a different form than her friend's. What was Rob doing right now? When could she see him alone?

"But of course," Jacques said, his eyes darting restlessly between his pastries and the door. "I've got it all laid out. Just look at these plump, delectable—"

Her cell phone rang.

She and Jacques glanced at each other before she answered it. Camden.

"W-What's going on?" she said. "Where are you?"

There was a torrent of "Sorry, sorry darlings" and an almost convincing "I'll really, really make it up to you." Elizabeth felt her temper rise.

"Camden, *where* are you?"

He moaned on the other end of the line. "Annabelle and I missed our flight out of Banff. We—we were kind of—um—busy in the private lounge and didn't hear the last boarding call. There's not another Midwestern-bound flight until late tomorrow, and by the time I get out there it'll be too late to do everything we need to get done. Please, please forgive me. I've got another break later in the month, can I still come out then?"

She sighed. Ten days ago she wouldn't have understood this type of mindless passion. The kind of desire that obliterated all other responsibilities and left her feeling vulnerable to its tempest. Ten days was a lifetime ago.

"Okay, we'll reschedule," she heard her voice say with surprising calm. "But remember the deadline is August first." Camden blessed her and hung up.

"Merde." Jacques sliced a picture-perfect éclair in half and stuffed one part in his mouth. He waved the other at her dispiritedly. She took it.

Yet, despite her disappointment, she could think of only one thing, and it ran like tickertape through her brain: *I get to spend more time with Rob this weekend! More, more, more!*

Yep. She'd made up for twenty-eight years of sexual restraint by turning into a nymphomaniac over the course of ten days. Nice.

"Let's go to Tutti-Frutti and console ourselves with ice cream and a couple of caramel-pecan rolls," she suggested.

Jacques complied immediately.

On the street outside the sweets shop, Jacques ran into an acquaintance and chatted with him for a minute. Elizabeth knew she could go inside if she wanted to but, instead, she decided to mill around, enjoy the summer sunshine, smell the roses. She peeked in the shop's window, though, which was empty except for two elderly couples and a middle-aged lady, all of whom had already been served. Then she noticed Rob and Gretchen.

They were standing behind the counter, close to each other. Leaning in. *Very* close to each other, she clarified. A lump, belonging to an emotion she didn't like, lodged itself in her throat.

Gretchen—tall, blond, beautiful Gretchen—put her hand on his shoulder and whispered something in his ear. He laughed and looked at her as though her blue eyes made starlight dim by comparison.

Then Rob motioned her close again with a come-hither gesture that Elizabeth thought he used only with *her*. He whispered a response back in Gretchen's ear. She, in turn, clasped her hand over her mouth, as if to hold in the hilarity, and her cheeks flushed. Even across the shop and through the fingerprint-smudged window Elizabeth could tell flirting when she saw it.

She heard a gasp behind her.

She looked over her shoulder to see Jacques, the color draining from his face, staring at the giddy couple inside Tutti-Frutti. He gave her a horrified look.

Oh, what a perfect little fool she'd been. She'd been trying so hard to ignore the obvious—that a man like Rob Gabinarri wasn't for her—but she went ahead and fell in love with him anyway. Idiot.

Consciously, unconsciously, the guy attracted attention from other women. He couldn't help it. No matter what he whispered to her in the middle of the night, when he thought she wasn't watching him during the day, he could freely give in to those natural flirtatious impulses of his. And, eventually, when the novelty of being with her wore off, wouldn't he choose someone beautiful and confident like Gretchen over someone plain and fretful like her?

Elizabeth closed her eyes. Of course he would.

There was no way she could face them now. Not any of

them.

Not Rob, whose opportunity to cheat would always be plentiful, whether or not he ever planned to act on it.

Not Gretchen, whose betrayal was surely unintentional. Elizabeth doubted her friend even realized she was next in line for Rob's attention. But Elizabeth knew no one escaped his magnetism unscathed, so it still hurt to see her with him.

Not even Jacques, whose empathy had him turning several shades of sickly pale.

She race-walked down the block and back to her car. She got in, drove as far as the park, found a shady spot and killed the ignition. Then she sobbed nonstop for forty minutes.

Elizabeth was acting weird as hell tonight. Rob figured she must still be pissed at Camden for canceling the photo shoot at the last minute. But Jacques, who Rob had thought was warming up to him again after the Fourth of July, was back to being very, very chilly, which made no sense at all. Those moody Frenchmen.

Nick was off in his own world most of the time, no doubt dreaming of some gay hockey-playing fantasy lover who could down a shot of ouzo without clutching his stomach and grimacing at the potency.

Only Gretchen was being her normal self. When he'd asked her for details about Elizabeth's experience as a cookbook writer this morning, she'd told him sidesplitting stories of some of Elizabeth's earliest recipe attempts. Customers with delicate sensibilities were in the shop, so they had to keep their voices down...her tales involved proclaiming several very descriptive swear words, which Gretchen claimed Elizabeth hadn't used since. But Rob laughed and laughed just imagining his sweet woman letting loose with a range of profanities a Green Beret might find offensive.

He just loved those contradictions in her. She usually surprised him and challenged him as a result. But here they were at dinner and, try as he might, he still couldn't figure why she could act with perfect pleasantness toward every member of his family and, yet, give him the cold shoulder. Even Tony noticed the change.

"You two get into a fight?" Tony whispered to him.

"Not that I'm aware of."

His brother winced. "Oooh. Those are the worst kind. Hey, man, take my advice and just apologize now."

"For what?" he said. "I didn't do anything."

"Yeah, you did. You just don't know it yet. Nip it in the bud and say you're sorry. It's easier that way. Really. Trust me on this."

But games like that made Rob mad, so he ignored his brother's wise counsel, only to regret it on the car ride home.

"You need to keep your eyes on the road," she informed him when he leaned over to kiss her at a stoplight.

"O-*kay*." He snapped back to the driver's seat and stared straight ahead until the light changed and he could floor the accelerator. A Porsche can go damn fast.

"S-Slow down," she hissed, crossing her arms and looking all irritated.

What was this? Driving 101?

He didn't slow down.

"Rob, what do you think you're doing?"

He slammed on the brakes and pulled over to the side of the road. He shoved the car into park with a force that probably wouldn't be looked upon too favorably by the manufacturers.

"What the hell do you think *you're* doing?" he said, none too quietly. "What is up with you tonight? I did not do anything wrong, and I'm not going to apologize. So *there*." Okay, well that last part came across as kind of childish, but he really wasn't in the mood to care much.

Her green eyes narrowed. Her lovely lips tightened. Her soft hands clenched together so hard he worried a few of her fingers might get dislocated.

"I saw you flirting with Gretchen this morning." Her words were pointed, precise, as accusatory as they came and without a stutter anywhere. "She is my friend, you know, and if you're leading her on or—"

"You think there's something going on between me and *Gretchen?*" WHAT? "Hell, Elizabeth, she's the only one of you guys who isn't acting like a nutcase today."

Oooh, she didn't like that comment. Whoops.

She snatched at the handle of the passenger door and began to pull it open.

"Would you just wait a minute?" He tugged at the hem of her blouse to keep her in the car.

Oooh, she didn't like that move either, and he was rewarded with a glare that could freeze water in Aruba.

"Why should I wait?" she said.

"Because this is ridiculous! There is nothing—I repeat, *nothing*—going on between me and your best friend. Gretchen's fun to talk to, that's all. She tells goofy stories and they make me laugh."

Oooh, man, was he ever striking out tonight. Now she looked hurt and he remembered—too late, of course—that she was sensitive to the whole speaking thing. Not that he ever thought of her as having a speech impediment anymore. And the two of them talked constantly. How could she forget that? How could she act like an insecure seventh grader?

Women were these crazy-making beings, which reminded him of why he'd stayed clear of them in the first place.

"Please drive me home," she commanded.

"Fine." He put the car back into gear and got them the hell out of there. Not that it helped any. A change in location didn't change her attitude toward him.

"I'm still very angry with you," she said primly when they reached her apartment complex. "I'd rather you didn't come up tonight."

As if! "You don't have to worry, sweetheart. I could use a good night's sleep for a change." He heard—and cringed at—the bitterness in his own voice.

Clearly, she heard it, too. Something in her expression telegraphed both fresh pain and confusion.

"I'm s-sure you'll have plenty of restful n-nights soon...back in Chicago." Her tone was sad, regretful even.

If he'd have stopped right there and apologized for losing his temper—and let her apologize, as he sensed she probably wanted to—he could've gone up to her place with her and they could've made love and their kisses would've removed the stingers they'd thoughtlessly inflicted on each other.

But, dumb-ass that he was, he didn't stop there and apologize for his part in letting this silly battle escalate—even though she was wrong about the flirting. Oh, no.

Instead he said the genius line, "My nights in Chicago aren't restful at all. I've been taking it easy up here."

The fury in her eyes told him he'd better get used to Tony's sofa sleeper again. The hurt on her face told him that they were now paying the price for a relationship that should've never happened in the first place. He could see her practically computing the hours until she could watch him leave the city limits of Wilmington Bay—and leave her alone.

Tony cocked an eyebrow at him when he returned to his brother's house that night after a ten-day absence.

"I told you, you should've apologized. No questions asked," Tony said.

"I don't want to talk about it."

"Ah-huh." Tony flung some sheets and blankets at him. "I believe you. Really."

Something in his head exploded. "Women are *crazy*."

Tony nodded like a freaking TV shrink. "Yep."

"They get these damn fool ideas into their heads about something and they won't listen to logic or to reason or to anything that remotely makes sense."

"Sounds familiar."

"And I was *not* flirting with Gretchen."

Tony laughed. "Oh, boy."

"I am really pissed off." He massaged his temples with his

fingers and collapsed onto the sofa sleeper.

His brother slapped his shoulder on his way out of the room. "Love does that to you," Mr. Family Man said.

"Dammit," Rob said back.

And, just for the record, he did not have a restful night.

Elizabeth knew Jacques didn't own much black—it didn't suit his coloring—but, whatever he'd collected in mourning colors, he was wearing all of it the next day.

"I haven't been much of a friend lately, have I?" she said to him in the early-morning, pre-opening-shift hours at Tutti-Frutti. She enjoyed coming up here before the crowds. It was peaceful, and she needed that these days. She'd be long gone before Rob and Gretchen waltzed in at ten.

She leaned against the counter and finished filling out the order forms she had to complete. Then she handed Jacques one of the blueberry muffins she baked oh-so-late last night when she was *not* with Rob.

"I've been pretty self-absorbed with my own bizarre life, and I'm sorry," she told him. "I know something's bothering you. Do you want to talk about it?"

He took a deep breath then a big bite of muffin. "Mmm," he said without enthusiasm.

She smiled slightly. "Are they that bad?"

His brow wrinkled. "Well, *chéri*, let's just say they aren't your best effort."

"I was mad when I made them. And sad. And...well, I don't know."

"Just as it was in that film *Like Water for Chocolate*. How the family's reactions to the foods the heroine served depended on her emotions when she cooked them." He sighed. Jacques was a longtime fan of foreign flicks that played at independent artsy theaters.

Of course, in this case, he was probably drawing an accurate comparison.

She snatched the muffin plate away. "Better not eat these then. I don't want you suffering through my reactions from last night."

"Rob—he's a short-term thing, yes?" He looked up at her with big worried eyes.

She hated to admit it, but she couldn't lie to her good friend. "I suppose so."

He reached past the plates and papers and gave her a long hug and then a soft kiss on her cheek. "You know, my marriage proposal—it still stands. We could be very, very happy together. Good friends, comfortable. Not this constant and unpleasant churning of emotion." He smiled at her. "Why don't you marry me, Elizabeth?"

She glanced at him sharply before being distracted by a noise. "Did you hear something?" she said.

He shook his head then grinned a little wickedly. "Just my beating heart."

"Nice try." She thought about his words. What he'd described as a "constant and unpleasant churning of emotion." He wasn't just talking about her feelings for Rob. Something was definitely up with him. Then it suddenly hit her. "Jacques, are you in love with someone?"

He gave her a stricken look. "It doesn't matter. I don't like this. I don't want this."

"You *are* in love with someone." And she knew, with certainty, that this someone wasn't her. For a moment she felt a sting of hurt, but she and Jacques had always worked best together as friends. She knew that even before Rob Gabinarri returned to put a big crimp in her life.

Jacques still wasn't talking.

"Why won't you tell me?" she asked him. "You know you can trust me."

"Oh, I know. It's just—I'm just—" He paused and she saw actual tears in his eyes. Tears she knew he wouldn't let fall. "She's a good friend, too, but there was always something...more to it. A spark of something beyond friendship, which made everything more frightening."

Elizabeth covered her mouth as the connections in her brain began to zig and zag and reach an amazing—but not really so unbelievable—conclusion. "Gretchen?" she whispered.

Jacques nodded. "For maybe two years now," he admitted. "She's like the smell of bread dough rising. Like thick chocolate icing on a fresh pastry. Like powdered sugar on Mexican wedding cakes." He gave her a small smile. "Like all the things I love best."

"Does she know how you feel?"

A single tear escaped his eye, but he brushed it away before it rolled down his cheek. "I was going to try to tell her yesterday. Then I saw her with Rob. And I realized that, even if there's nothing between them, she has higher standards than just me." He looked utterly, inconsolably miserable.

"Jacques, don't say things like. It's so, so not true. You're a wonderful man who's incredibly caring. Gretchen, or any woman, would be delighted to know you were interested in her. Even when I knew you were just playing around with the marriage proposals, I was still flattered that you'd thought enough of me to pretend." She took his hands in her. "Please, d-don't sell yourself short."

"Guys like Rob are tall. They have a head full of hair, muscles and no flab. They don't have a silly accent and they know how to play all sports. There's no comparison between him and me."

"But Jacques, you and Gretchen can literally see eye-to-eye. She laughs when she's with you and has told me a trillion times that she loves your French accent and wishes it were even thicker."

This made him grin. "Really?"

"Oh, yes. And you know darned well that appearances aren't everything. Hair and flab don't matter where there's true affection."

He tilted his head to one side and regarded her strangely. "You believe this?"

She paused for a moment of personal honesty. "Well—" she began.

"You're saying *you* believe, although your hair was so frizzy and you were a little chubby in high school, that these things didn't matter? That a boy who cared about you wouldn't have cared about those features? What you always considered to be your flaws?" He shook his head. *"Mais non, il n'est-ce pas vrai.* It's not true that you believe this."

"But that was *high school*, Jacques, not *now*. That same kind of shallowness doesn't hold up anymore. We're all smarter and wiser. At least most of us are." She grinned at him and tried to make herself project total belief in this position despite all of her evidence opposing it.

If only Rob would have ever said that he thought she was beautiful to *him*. He must've said a thousand times he thought she was brilliant. But, to her, that was decades-old praise. And, perhaps her grand wish was just an expression of human nature. Everybody craved the one compliment they never got.

Jacques still looked sad as he stood up and tossed the rest of his blueberry muffin in the trash. "Ah, *mon amie*, thank you for the advice. I will consider every thought. Although—" He grinned. "I'll wait for the next batch of muffins you bake, if you don't mind. Those were dreadful, you know."

"I know," she said, pitching the remaining ones into the trash bin one at a time as Jacques left. Without Rob, most everything was dreadful.

~CHAPTER TWELVE~

Rob found himself on US-41 driving a good twenty miles per hour above the speed limit. He didn't care. He was headed southbound to Chicago and, by God, he couldn't get there soon enough.

There were times in a man's life when standing and fighting were the best options. There were also times to head for the hills. Or, in his case, a high-rise condo overlooking the Windy City's Lake Shore Drive. Go Bears.

Even now, an hour later, he still couldn't believe what he'd overheard. Monsieur Jacques saying so breezily to his secret love interest, "Rob—he's a short-term thing, yes?"

And Elizabeth—damn her!—saying, "I suppose so."

And then the two of them mumbled some stuff he couldn't hear because he was too busy picking his heart up off the floor. Oh, except for the last, extra-special bit: "Why don't you marry me, Elizabeth?"

Why? He could sure give good ole Jacques a few hundred reasons why *not*...in English or in *français*, for that matter. He'd taken two whole years of French in high school. He could put a few fairly graphic sentences together if he ever found his battered old dictionary.

He stepped a little harder on the gas pedal.

Huh. So that's how it was, then. Elizabeth...and *Jacques*. He knew there'd been something simmering between them, even if she hadn't fully opened her eyes to it. Why had he ever overlooked, overruled, overridden his first impression? The casual friendship those two shared. All that time spent baking and talking about recipes together. They had mutual interests. And what could he add to the conversation? "I used to play football a lot. Cool, eh?"

Rob saw the police siren before he heard it but, no doubt about it, the black-and-white car was headed toward him.

"Oh, hell."

He pulled over and the officer got out and sidled up to his Porsche.

"Nice car," she said.

And he thought, Nice body, nice lips, nice skin... But he said, "Thanks."

She asked for his driver's license. "You realize you were going close to thirty miles above the speed limit, Mr. Gabinarri, don't you?"

He nodded then managed to shoot a warm smile at her.

She grinned back. Attractive lady, no doubt. But, dammit, not his *particular* type of attractive these days.

"No way are you getting out of this speeding ticket," she told him. "And it's going to be an expensive one."

He sighed and squeezed his eyes shut while she did all of her police officer stuff back in the squad car. A few minutes later she came back, notepad in hand.

"Here you go," she said, scribbling down the rest of his ticket information. One that probably would have his insurance company tossing him in driving school.

"Um, thanks," he said, when she handed the paper to him. He noticed an address scrawled on the top and glanced up at her in question.

She winked. "If you're free after five, I'll be a little place called the Silver Stallion, a bar about a mile and a half east of here." She pointed to the street address she'd written on the page. "It's easy to find. Any chance you might be able to swing by?"

He struggled with his answer. Not because he didn't want to tell the truth, but because he desperately wanted his lie to *be* the truth. "I don't think so, ma'am. There's a woman at home who's waiting for me."

She shrugged and gave a good-natured laugh. "Oh, well. Lucky lady." She waved him off but, before she walked back to her squad car, she added, "Drive back to her safely."

Rob thought about that comment (as he headed south and still further away from Elizabeth) for another ten miles before pulling off into a gas station along the side of the highway.

"Hi, Miguel. How's it going down there?" he said into his cell phone, but he was thinking: *I'm only about seventy minutes away. Tell me you need me back right now. I need a good excuse to leave Wilmington Bay for twenty-four hours and you're my only chance, buddy.*

"Awesome, Boss Man."

So much for that idea.

"Hey, have you got any more of that Fourth-of-July topping?" Miguel asked. "That Hawaiian Mix? The Playbook's dinner crowd is going crazy for it."

"Sure, I could get some to you, though it's pretty easy to make," Rob said.

He explained to Miguel that the winner of the Topping Taste Test had brought a combo of macadamia nuts, dark chocolate chips and coconut shavings. The runner-up was the person with the candied pineapple bits. Put them all together and you get what they'd been calling the Hawaiian Mix for the past two weeks. It'd been Tutti-Frutti's biggest hit since the contest, and he'd shipped some down for Miguel to experiment with at the restaurant.

"Why don't I bring you down a tub of it?" Rob suggested hopefully.

"Nah, no need. I'll get the dessert guys on the case now that I'm sure of the ingredients. You just deal with whatever you need to deal with up there. All's well here." His friend paused. "Unless you want to come back, Rob. I mean, I'm not trying to keep you away. It's your place, after all."

He thought about it, going purely on gut instinct. Did he want to go back to Chicago, or was he just trying to escape Wilmington Bay? Two different things, weren't they? And, oh, the answer was obvious.

"Guess I'll stay here a little longer then," he told Miguel. "I promised Uncle Pauly, after all. But call me if anything comes up."

"Likewise. And we'll see you for sure in a few weeks."

"Right," Rob said. But, for the first time, there was no thrill, no satisfaction associated with this thought. For the first time in a long time he was rearranging his definition of the word "home."

He got back on the Interstate, taking the northbound ramp, and began driving back to his hometown...at a very responsible speed.

Elizabeth called Gretchen.

"Hey, Gretch, any chance we could talk?"

"Sure, what's up? Everyone's been acting so moody lately. Must be something they slipped into that Lake Michigan water." She laughed at her own joke then sobered up. "Is there something serious happening, Elizabeth? Something I don't know about?"

Gretchen's voice was so concerned, so very caring, that Elizabeth almost burst out with an apology for entertaining, even for a second, the idiotic notion that her best friend might try to sneak around with her boyfriend behind her back. If Rob even was her boyfriend anymore.

One thing was certain, though. She owed Rob an apology for what she'd said to him.

"No," Elizabeth told her. "I—I just wanted to thank you for being such a true and loyal friend. And—and if you ever need someone to listen to you about relationship things, then I hope you'll come to me."

Elizabeth thought she heard Gretchen sniff on the other end of the line.

"Thanks," Gretchen said. "But I think it'll be a good long time before anyone's interested in me. I'm glad Rob's smart enough to see in you all the wonderful qualities that we've always known about. He's a great guy. Gorgeous, too." She paused. "But I don't know if anyone is out there who'll look at me that way. The men I'm attracted to...well, they have a tendency to think of me as their buddy. I'm too tall, too strong, too big-boned. Not one of those cute feminine women like you."

"*What?* Gretch, you're totally beautiful! And not all men want a woman whom they can easily overpower. Trust me on this. You should hear Camden talk about Annabelle, Karate Queen Extraordinaire. He loves how strong she is."

"Camden isn't the man I'm attracted to, though. I'm telling you, this guy thinks of me as a friend and that's all. I mean it. Every time I start to wonder if there might be something more there, he backs away. He's trying to protect me from myself, I just know it. He doesn't want to break my heart."

Elizabeth's eyes pricked with tears—tears of joy for two of her best friends who were about to realized they were meant for each other.

"Uh, Gretch? Is there any chance that I know this guy-friend of yours?"

There was a long pause.

"Gretchen?"

Then came a very small voice from the other side of the line. *"Mais oui."*

Elizabeth grinned and let the tears stream down her face.

Inspired by the new love blooming between Jacques and Gretchen, and by their heartfelt declarations (albeit not yet to each other), Elizabeth decided she should try to make amends with Rob. So she called his mother.

Alessandra Gabinarri greeted her suggestion with a whoop of delight and told her to come over immediately.

She also called Tutti-Frutti and spoke with Nick, who'd switched with Jacques and was working an earlier shift today.

"Nick, could you please tell Rob not to pick me up for dinner tonight? I'll meet him at his mom's."

"Sure," he said. "I'll tell the man just about anything you want once he comes in."

She looked at her watch. It was one o'clock. "What do you mean? He was supposed to be there three hours ago."

"Yep. But Gretch said he never showed for the first shift, and he's still not here. He left a way weird message on my voicemail, though. Said he'd be 'back when he was back.'"

Her throat tightened. "Did he sound hurt or in trouble or anything?"

"Nope. Just kind of pissed." Nick paused. "But, hey, if you wanna contact him so bad, why don't you call his cell? Speak to him in person or leave a message?"

"Um, that's okay."

"Why?"

How about: Because she was scared. Because she didn't know if Rob would ever want to talk with her again after her little tantrum. Because sometimes love just wasn't enough to overcome every obstacle.

"B-Because I'm running late," she said instead. "So, uh, thanks for your help. Please just tell him what I said if he comes in." *And if he doesn't come in, then what? Will it be because he's taken off for good?*

"Okey-dokey."

Then, thinking worst-case scenario thoughts, Elizabeth drove to the Gabinarri house.

Rob meandered back toward Wilmington Bay, stopping at just about every roadside antique shop or cheese-n-sausage store in southeastern Wisconsin, and reacquainting himself with the native experience. Decided it was high time he bought himself a new "Badger" t-shirt and he'd been fresh out of salami cheese for probably eight years. He'd forgotten until today how much he'd liked them both.

As he tossed his J.Crew shirt in the back seat and pulled on his new Badger one, he wondered about that. Wondered why people let certain things go, even when they loved them. Sometimes, maybe most times, it was because they wanted to move on to other things. Finer, maybe more preferable things.

But sometimes that wasn't the case at all. Every once in a while it was just because they'd gotten caught up in something that was different, but not necessarily better. Sometimes the original stuff was still the best.

Feeling unbearably philosophical for someone who was neither drunk nor wearing a white clerical collar, he sat on the curb in the gift store's parking lot, bit off a hunk of salami cheese and tried to figure out what to do with the rest of his life.

His cell phone rang.

"Hi, Mama," he said, swallowing.

"Don't spoil your appetite, Roberto. We're having a nice dinner tonight."

He looked around his Porsche for a hidden camera. How did she always know when he was doing something wrong? Not that eating between meals was a crime but—

"Roberto?"

"Yeah?"

"I don't know where you are right now, but I want you come home early tonight."

"Um, well..."

"And you need to pick up some wine, too, *capiche?*"

He groaned. "Yes, Mama, I understand."

"Good," she said, sounding fairly satisfied. "Red wine, please. And don't worry about getting Elizabeth."

Of course not. He could just imagine how Elizabeth had decided not to come and very politely extricated herself from anything to do with his family now and forevermore. He was probably in for the lecture from hell tonight on the subject of How Men Are Stupid Beings And Don't Know How To Keep Their Women Happy. But, he wanted to know what Mama knew—all the better to be prepared—so he said, "Why?"

Mama gave him a you-must-be-joking huff and lowered her voice. "Well, because she's already here."

Rob jumped up, threw the Porsche into gear and hightailed it back to Wilmington Bay.

He smelled garlic, oregano, basil and simmering tomato sauce when he walked through the door, but Mama didn't rush over to greet him as usual.

He set the wine down on the table and was about to head into the kitchen when Tony appeared out of nowhere and snagged his shirt from behind.

"Don't go in there," his brother warned. "We're not allowed."

"Why not?"

"Just listen."

Over the din of Madonna's early hit "Borderline," he heard the distinctive bubble of feminine laughter. Four voices. Four very different timbres. Mama. Maria-Louisa. Camilla. And—his heart hurt to hear it—Elizabeth.

He shot Tony a sideways glance. "What's going on?"

"Female bonding." Tony paused. "They're cooking...I think. At least that's what they told me they were doing when I arrived with the boys, though it's just as likely that it's some kind of spell-conjuring witchcraft. And they've been at it for hours. But—"

"Hours?"

His brother shrugged. "Oh, yeah. There's something weird in the air tonight, bro. My wife's been edgy with me since we got here. The few times I was allowed to talk with her, that is. It's kind of a goddess thing, I think."

Rob stared at him for a long minute. "What the hell does

that mean?"

"Well, you know. Women getting in touch with their inner power and all that New Age stuff. I figure they gain energy in groups or something. Most of the time, when Maria-Louisa does it, I don't have to see it. She's at Hauser's or out shopping with her cousins. So by the time we talk the next day, she's pretty much back to normal." He gave a long-suffering sigh. "Tonight's gonna be a different story."

"Terrific."

Tony squeezed his eyes shut and nodded. A high-frequency wave of women's laughter vibrated through the swinging kitchen door.

Oh, man.

About a half hour later, young Camilla emerged as the emissary of the female delegation and announced that dinner was about to be served. So, everybody had better wash their hands and sit down quick because the ladies weren't going to stand for any "dallying." Her words.

The kid was serious, self-possessed and every inch a Mystifying-Woman-In-Training. Rob got a no-nonsense glimpse of what Camilla would be like as a teenager and it didn't make him envy Tony. Not one little bit.

Except...she was absolutely beautiful, even when spouting off orders. She radiated capability and intelligence and personal strength. And—despite differences in age, height and family background—she reminded him very much of Elizabeth. *His* Elizabeth.

Then the woman he was thinking of came out. She held a platter of hand-rolled ravioli and was followed by Maria-Louisa bearing an enormous tray of chicken Parmesan. Camilla disappeared and then returned with a basket of hot garlic rolls and a large mixed green salad tossed in a spicy vinaigrette dressing. Mama brought up the rear with a casserole of grilled vegetables and sirloin cubes covered in a zesty Sicilian sauce.

All the Gabinarri males, young and not-so-young, stared at this display, and Rob knew they all must be thinking the same thing: How did we get so lucky?

The ladies served everyone, moving from place to place as if of one mind. When Elizabeth got to him, she looked deep into his eyes and his pulse almost stopped.

"H-Hi," she whispered. "Ravioli?"

"Yes, please."

She spooned several plump pasta squares on his plate and ladled the hardy meat sauce over it.

"Thanks," he said.

"You're welcome." She glanced around the table, as if to ensure no one was listening, then said, "I'm sorry about yesterday."

He forgave her in an instant and wished he could kiss the worry and sadness off her lovely face, but he also wondered still about what he'd heard that morning. With Jacques. He was proud of the fact that he knew enough not to say anything about it, though. At least not here.

Instead, he just smiled at her and whispered, "Can we talk after dinner?"

She nodded, although reluctantly, he thought, before moving on to Sammie's plate. Tony sure was right. There was a charge in the air. Something different. And he found himself watching the interplay between the women very closely. They seemed to be in agreement on every point, so much so that when the subject of marriage came up Rob couldn't have been more surprised by the commentary.

"I'm not sure marriage is for every man," Mama said with an earnestness that made him want to reach out and feel her forehead for fever.

"Oh, I agree," the ever-so-calm (except when drunk) Maria-Louisa added. "Some men are far too self-centered to handle the obligations that are a part of such a commitment. Not just the household duties inherent in sharing a life, but also the emotional responsibilities." She paused. "Tony, of course, has done okay with it."

Rob eyed Tony who, apparently, knew it was his job to take the half-compliment in silence because his teeth were firmly clamped onto his bottom lip.

Camilla added solemnly, "Yeah. Daddy's a pretty good guy."

Tony stuffed a forkful of chicken Parmesan into his mouth and chewed hard.

Mama nibbled on a bread roll. "I think Elizabeth has got the right idea, waiting before settling down. A woman can't be too careful these days."

Rob almost choked on his ravioli.

"Oh, are you okay?" Elizabeth asked sweetly. "Do you need some water? Hot tea, perhaps?"

He shook his head, coughed a bit more and downed half his glass of red wine.

"Yes," Mama said. "It's not worth it to be stuck with a man who can't handle commitment. Your father—" she looked pointedly at him and Tony, "was a remarkable man, bless his soul. But, he had his faults, too. It probably would've been better for him if he'd been given another few years to grow up before we got married."

"R-Really?" Rob managed to say. Tony kicked him under the table but he didn't retract the question. This was the first time he'd ever heard his mother suggest that getting married wasn't the end-all, be-all relationship experience. And that his own father had lost points in Mama's eyes for not doing it exactly right. What the hell was the world coming to?

"Oh, yes," Mama stated, as though she weren't completely contradicting everything she'd ever said to him in the past ten years. "I loved your father, but every day I wished I didn't have to be the one to teach him all the basics. When to give me some space. How to express his own feelings. When to do a household chore. How to really listen." She shrugged. "That was kind of exhausting."

To his surprise, he saw both Elizabeth and his sister-in-law nodding as if these complaints about men were common knowledge. Tony kicked him again and, this time, he held his tongue.

Just before Mama brought out the biggest and most delectable tiramisu ever, Elizabeth said to Maria-Louisa, "So, are we still on for tomorrow night?"

"Yep. Hauser's Grill and Ale. Seven o'clock sharp. Be there or be a tee-totaler."

The ladies laughed. Rob, remembering Elizabeth's last margarita night, felt uncharacteristically queasy. He shot a panicked look at Tony.

His brother mimed pressing his lips together and shook his head in warning. Though Rob hated to admit it, he suspected his kid brother was pretty wise. He wondered if his other married siblings had amassed this level of perception. Maybe he ought to give the rest of them a call. Collect some serious advice.

As Mama dished up the dessert, she said, "I'm so pleased Elizabeth came up with this idea of us women cooking together. So much better than just bringing different dishes to pass." She nodded at the ladies. "Although, next time, it'll be the men's turn of course."

At this, even Tony had to really fight to keep from commenting aloud. "Think pizza," he whispered in Rob's ear when he passed him a bowl of tiramisu.

Rob nodded. Yeah, everything good required some kind of work in return, didn't it?

When dinner finally ended, he walked Elizabeth to her car.

"I'll be done with my shift at ten-thirty as usual," he told her. "Can I come and see you afterward?"

She gazed at his mother's house for a moment before turning those green eyes back on him. "I have some work I should finish," she said. "I spent a lot of time here today, and it was great, but I didn't get any writing done and my deadline's in two weeks."

"Oh, okay," he said, feeling a pang of disappointment in his gut, but what could he say? "Got any time tomorrow?"

She shook her head. "I'm so sorry, Rob, but I really don't. Your mom already knows I can't come to dinner tomorrow night, since I'm meeting Maria-Louisa and the gang at seven, and before that I'm revising and then helping Gretchen make one of her trickier truffle parfaits."

Dammit. She was avoiding him. It must be because of

someone else, namely the wily, torte-making Frenchman. Man, he was going to pulverize that guy tomorrow.

"Are you and Jacques...involved?" he asked her directly, applauding himself on his immeasurably cool demeanor.

But she looked at him as if he were demented. *"What?* No! What kind of a—I mean, where on earth would you—" Then she was utterly speechless for a minute. "Jacques and Gretchen are in love, Rob. They're sorting that out tonight and I—well, I'm really sorry I jumped to c-conclusions about you and Gretchen yesterday. I misinterpreted what I saw, and I guess I g-got jealous, and it was all very foolish of me." She stopped and regarded him with another of her regretful looks.

He had to repeat one sentence, though, just to clarify. "Jacques and Gretchen are *in love?*"

She nodded and the relief he felt was palpable. Thank God for small miracles, like other people's irrational emotions.

She glanced at her watch. "I know you've got to go, so I won't keep you. Maybe we can meet up again in a few days, grab a cup of coffee or something."

A few *days?*

He pulled her into his arms. She let him, but he could feel her holding herself back, not allowing herself to sink into his embrace. That restraint just about killed him. "What's really going on here, Elizabeth? What have I done wrong?"

She looked everywhere but at his face. "You haven't done anything wrong. It's just...I-I've been thinking and..." She sighed in a way that indicated whatever she'd been thinking wasn't good news for him. "You were upfront with m-me from the beginning, Rob. You told me, and you were really clear on this, that you w-wanted to go back to Chicago. That you didn't want to stay in Wilmington Bay after our uncles got back from Europe. That's still true, right?"

He wasn't exactly sure if it was still true but, since he had no idea what other options there were yet, he sort of nodded.

She blinked a few times then gazed directly into his eyes. "See, here's the problem. I'm in love with you, Rob." She paused and let her words sink in. His heart soared for a split second. "But—" Never a good word to hear after an I Love You.

"But what?" he managed to say over his hammering pulse.

"B-But you and I want different things. We're very different people, w-which I know isn't a newsflash. And I've been getting really attached to having you around, even though I know in a few weeks you'll be g-gone." She put one soft hand on his cheek. "I don't regret a single thing that's happened between us. Not one thing that we've shared. But I think you were right from Day One. We're friends. And, as much as I'd like it to be otherwise, that's probably all we should be."

He opened his mouth to speak. He didn't know what he could say in response, but that was a moot point because not a single damned syllable came out.

"Remember how you said last month that before you left Wilmington Bay you'd tell your mother you broke up with me, you know, s-so I wouldn't be the 'bad guy'?" She gave him a weak smile. "I don't think you should do that. I th-think you should tell her the truth. Tell her it's my fault. Explain that I can't handle a long-distance relationship, but that I want to stay good friends. And please tell her that I've loved being with her and your family nearly as much as I've loved being with you."

He swallowed hard but he still couldn't talk. He bobbed his head a little, though, which she took as his answer.

She kissed him lightly. "Thanks," she said. Then she got in her car and drove away.

~CHAPTER THIRTEEN~

Rob spent the next week feeling as though he'd lost a lot of yardage in the relationship game and had been benched indefinitely. He could see a bunch of action happening on the field with his teammates, but he wasn't allowed to play. Elizabeth—head coach of their organization—had given him one helluva time out.

Jacques and Gretchen, by contrast, were starters in every play. With their newfound relationship out in the open, they laughed like psychotic hyenas. They tangoed in Tutti-Frutti's backroom. They sipped from each other's milkshakes. They made a general nuisance of themselves with all their damn humming and smiling. Rob considered locking them up in the dry-storage pantry. On several occasions.

They had it too easy, what with living in the same town and everything. There was no real challenge involved because— come on—if they had to deal with what he and Elizabeth had to deal with, they'd suffer under the intense pressure of indecision, too. Wouldn't they?

Sure they would.

Still, for the first time in a long, long time, he didn't feel like distracting his insecure self with social interactions and chatter. Not even in debates with himself. It hurt too much to watch

Elizabeth breaking away from him, setting her sights on another man who could deliver what she needed.

The fact that this new man hadn't yet materialized was little consolation to him. A perfectly respectable, unattached Wilmington Bay male would appear in record time to snatch her away for good. And, because Rob had nothing permanent to offer her here, he couldn't do a thing about it.

But then the phone rang. Elizabeth.

And, after days of moping, something finally happened that gave him a shred of hope.

The phone rang.

Elizabeth picked it up only to hear Camden's distraught voice on the other end of the line.

"Darling, darling, please—before you kill me—let me explain," he said.

She was going to kill him. He was due in town two hours from now. Everyone had worked like maniacs to get the food ready for the shoot. "C-Camden—"

"Oh, I know. You hate me. You never want to speak with me again let alone work with me on any big project. I'm a scourge amongst men. My presence is a blight upon your otherwise flawless writerly existence. I—"

"Cut the dramatics, Cam. What happened this time, and *where the hell* are you?"

He breathed heavy on the line. "Oh, my dear, I've made you swear. I am so screwed."

"You bet you are. My deadline is in eight—count them— *eight* days. You *promised* me you'd be here. Why aren't you?" Worried she'd snap the receiver in half, she loosened her grip on the phone just a notch, but she didn't even try to unclench her jaw. She was going to KILL him.

"I'm in the hospital. I'm very, very sick."

Oh, God, please forgive me. She said a short prayer that his condition wasn't terminal.

"I have the measles," he said. "My parents, darlings that they were, were hippies in the seventies who didn't think you should ever trust the government or the establishment or any other '-ment.' Not a bad philosophy. But they also didn't believe in vaccinations. I just found out this morning what an unfortunate thing that was for me. I'm in San Diego. I'm highly contagious. I'm under quarantine and not allowed to go anywhere."

She squeezed her eyes shut. "Oh, Cam…"

His voice softened. "I am so sorry, honey. I know you were counting on me. I can try to get released in a few days, but there's no guarantee they'll let me fly anywhere or that, even if I could, I'd be able to do everything we need to do in time. I can call your editor and explain and maybe—"

"No. Look, you just concentrate on getting well. I—I'll see what I can figure out here. Maybe I can find a local food photographer on short notice." Well, this was doubtful, but she didn't want Camden sitting and worrying in his hospital bed. "Otherwise, we can get the deadline extended a week or two. It's just, I've never worked with anyone besides you, so…"

"Whatever you decide to do, it's fine with me. If you can get someone else to take the shots, he or she should get the credit in the book. If the editor will let you wait for me, I'll make sure—no matter what—that I'm there. You just do what you need to do, okay?"

"Okay," she said, pretty sure the world was on its way to disintegrating before her eyes. She hadn't told Camden this of course, but her editor had been very firm on this deadline. With the cookbook's release date being in mid-December, they were cutting it close as it was. If they were late getting the photos in, the book wouldn't make it to production on time and its release would have to be delayed until another spot opened up.

Jacques, Gretchen and Nick stared at her in fury, shock and horror respectively. She herself could barely see in color. One of them, she couldn't tell who, whispered, "What are we going to do? I don't know any professional photographers?"

Another one said, "Who does?"

To which the obvious person popped into her brain. The man who knew everyone and whom everyone knew in turn. The man she'd been avoiding for his own good...and for hers.

"I'll call Rob," Elizabeth said.

Ten minutes later, after explaining to him the dire predicament Cam and his measles had put them in, Rob was on the job.

"I have just the photographer you need," he said. "I'd trust this guy with my life, and I've already got him on payroll. Just give me a half hour to make some calls. We'll get him up here in a few hours so don't panic. Okay, Lizzy?"

The way he said her old nickname, all warm and worried for her, made her broken heart pound for wanting him. He'd done almost the impossible and made her *love* that stupid name when it came flowing off his lips. He'd given her a wealth of new memories to associate with it. For once, she didn't bother to correct him.

"Thanks, Rob," she said quietly.

"Anything for you, babe," he whispered before hanging up. "Anything for you."

Ah, if only that were true.

By two p.m., a sprightly and very sharp-dressed young man came gliding into Jacques's bakery where they were all gathered. His dark features were Hispanic in origin, but his clothes were pure Armani. Elizabeth heard Nick's jagged intake of breath next to her.

Gretchen detached from holding Jacques's hand long enough to rap Elizabeth's arm and whisper, "Get a load of that hottie."

Jacques scowled and pulled her back.

Rob came rushing in a few paces behind the dapper dude, and said, "Everyone, this is my good friend Miguel. He's been managing The Playbook for me while I've been up here, but he's a wiz kid." He grinned. "His current resume says he's one of

Illinois's top style consultants, which is true, but I won't let him work for anybody else. He's studied business, fashion and, most importantly for us today, photography."

Elizabeth felt tears prick her eyes. If this Miguel guy had earned Rob's loyalty and respect, they might just have a chance...not only of getting the photos taken, but also of getting them taken well.

Miguel smiled at the group. "Happy to be here." He waved and smiled politely through the introductions. Then he glanced around the bakery and specifically at Jacques's perfectly formed éclairs. Immediately Miguel's demeanor changed.

"Boss Man," he commanded of Rob, "we need to get the equipment from the car. Now. There's lots of work to do." And he began rustling around the room, giving orders, inspecting pastries, flicking on the special spotlights he brought, setting up his camera on the tripod.

"I need a helper. Fast," Miguel demanded and, before anyone else could so much as unbend a finger, Nick had pounced into position by his side.

Miguel's eyebrows raised a fraction of an inch as he got his first really good look at Nick. Elizabeth could feel the pheromones flying.

Pretty soon photographs of the various desserts were being snapped faster than any of them could say "Tutti-Frutti," which—incidentally—was closed midday, in honor of these special circumstances.

Elizabeth saw Rob tap his buddy on the shoulder during a short break in the shooting. "Nice work, Miguel," he said, edging out Nick for a moment, who was hanging on every word they said two yards away.

Miguel huffed. "I don't do *nice* work. I'm a perfectionist. I do *exceptional* work."

Rob laughed and caught Elizabeth's eye for a moment before responding to him. "Okay, then. Exceptional work, Miguel."

"Oh, I know. I just gave myself another raise and trust me, Boss Man, I'm still a bargain."

The two men looked at each other affectionately for a second then Rob slapped him on the back and strode away. Nick pranced over to Miguel again where they resumed a discussion of either clothing or sports—Elizabeth kept losing track. But one thing she knew for certain: Nick wouldn't be lamenting the loss of ex-lovers a moment longer.

She wished she could say her love life looked remotely as promising.

This past week had been the kind of torture she wouldn't have cursed an enemy with (well, maybe Tara Welles), but she knew she couldn't take back her words to Rob. Watching him stomp around the room now, so strong, so masculine, so confident...she realized he'd given her an extraordinary gift. Some of his freedom of speech had rubbed off on her, even if it had been only a tiny bit. She found she was finally able to say what she meant. That she could, at last, speak up for herself.

And she desperately hoped something good of hers had rubbed off on him, if only so he wouldn't forget her too quickly.

The next few days passed in a blur of activity. Rob returned to handling the ice cream parlor. Nick, Gretchen and Jacques took turns having their specialties featured. Other local cooks that Elizabeth had contacted, gladly provided delectable-looking samples of their creations to accompany the recipes selected to be in the book. She herself made several batches of sweets, including her mother's cherry cheesecake from scratch, and had them photographed by Miguel.

By the fifth and final day of the project, Nick and Miguel were an inseparable pair with plans to take their relationship to the next level.

"Wisconsin has the Brewers, the Badgers, the Bucks, the Green Bay Packers—" Nick began in his plea to get Miguel to consider a relocation to the Dairy State.

"But Illinois has the Bears, the Sox, the Cubs, the Blackhawks and the Bulls," Miguel said over him.

"We used to have Brett Favre," Nick said.

"And we used to have Michael Jordan," Miguel shot back, his tone taunting and more than a hint sarcastic.

Nick squinted at him. "Chicago is a serious two-and-a-half hour drive away, Miguel. For me, it's doable but, man, my family would kill me for ditching them."

"I've got Blackhawks season tickets," Miguel said simply, no doubt having already heard Nick's fantasies about hockey players. "Section 113. On the glass."

Nick's eyes grew wide. The clock ticked for three seconds. "I'm so there."

And with that Elizabeth realized how quickly and easily other people could solve their long-distance relationship problems if they were motivated to do so. Maybe songwriters through the ages had gotten it right:

Love is all you need.

Love will keep us together.

Love will find away.

Love is the answer.

And, so, since nothing remotely that simple applied to her relationship with Rob, perhaps she'd overestimated the strength of not just his emotions, but also her own.

Well, no. She was pretty darn sure she loved him. But sometimes, well, sometimes...*Love just ain't enough.*

While Nick was packing the following day and Miguel was gathering up the last of his equipment, Elizabeth snuck into the backdoor of Tutti-Frutti to grab some more order forms. They'd been so busy with the photo shoot that she hadn't restocked in a week, and they should never be allowed to run low on Mocha Madness.

Plus, she needed an ice cream treat herself. Today was August first and she'd just e-mailed her editor the text of her cookbook with the jpegs of the photos. And, for good measure, a hardcopy of everything was set to arrive in New York City via express mail the next morning, too.

She snitched an ice cream sandwich and was just about to be her stealthiest and leave unnoticed when she heard a familiar female voice.

"Hi, Rob. How are you, handsome?"

"Tara. Hi. Nice to see you as always."

Blah!

"I heard through the grapevine that you finally ditched Frizzy Lizzy and you're a free man again. That's true, right?"

Elizabeth couldn't see her, but she could almost hear Tara's incredibly high-wattage smile beaming rays of intense desire at him. She felt nauseated.

Rob, however, was probably staring lustfully back at Tara, so he didn't answer her question.

"Rob, honey, why don't you come with me to the Beer-N-Brat Fest in Milwaukee this weekend? We'd have so much fun together. It'd be just like old times when we—"

"Why don't you take Lance to it, Tara?" Rob said.

"Lance? What does Lance have to do with any—"

"The guy's crazy about you," he replied. "He goes insane with jealousy whenever any other man so much as looks your way. I know you've been more casual about dating him than the other way around, but think about it. Think about the attention he pays to you. You're his kind of woman. You always were. Even in high school. And, unless you don't feel anything toward him at all, he's the man who should get the honor of spending time with you now."

Elizabeth listened to this statement without taking a breath. Wow. He pushed Tara away, too. He must really be set on heading back to Chicago soon. Tara must also have realized this because she didn't speak for a full fifteen seconds. Then she said, "But what about you and me?"

"There's no you and me," Rob said simply. "Here, have an ice cream cone on the house. And have fun in Milwaukee at the Beer-N-Brat Fest. With Lance."

Elizabeth heard a pause and some rustling of paper napkins or other such things.

"Well, um. Bye, Rob. Good luck with everything," Tara murmured. Footsteps clicked toward the door and the bells jangled as she left the shop.

After a lengthy moment of silence, Elizabeth heard Rob mutter, "So long, Tara-rantula."

In spite of herself, she almost laughed. *Tara-rantula?* And all this time she'd thought Frizzy Lizzy was a bad nickname. Nothing like perspective.

Elizabeth knew she needed to get out of the shop before Rob discovered her back there, eavesdropping and guiltily holding a frozen novelty. Still, it was hard for her to creep out the backdoor—which she did very, very quietly—and head toward her car after overhearing what she did. Rob didn't sound like himself. He was breaking away from everyone. Not only her, but the Wilmington Bay townspeople, too. He wasn't the gabby Gabinarri who'd strode so confidently into the shop in June. She felt sad for him. And for herself.

Outside, she took a big bite of her ice cream sandwich. Creamy. Sweet. But not nearly as good as one of Rob's kisses. Sometimes in life you had to settle, huh? At least he was still here with her for a little while longer. At least she got to look at him and admire him and remember everything they shared together, which was helpful when her days seemed bleak.

But the thought of their lost relationship gave her knots in her stomach again and, suddenly, the dessert didn't taste so good after all. She was about to toss it in the trash when she heard a chuckle followed by a distinctive *"Liebling!"*

Startled, she accidentally dropped the ice cream sandwich on the ground and a curious squirrel nabbed it. "Uncle Siegfried. You—you're back."

"Roberto! There you are."

Rob almost stopped breathing. "Uncle Pauly? When did you get home?"

"Just a coupla hours ago." He marched up to where Rob was standing at the counter and threw his hefty arms around him. "The place looks great."

The last time Uncle Pauly had hugged him that

enthusiastically, Rob had been under five feet tall. He shot his mother's big brother a suspicious glance. "Uh, thanks. How was the trip?"

"Oh, great, great. Anita's feeling real healthy now. She invited us back sometime soon. Maybe we'll take your Mama along with us next time. She'd love it."

"I'm sure she would," Rob said, feeling the oddest combination of emotions. If Uncle Pauly went back to Europe—and Siegfried and Mama went with him—he and Elizabeth would have to run the shop again. He'd be stuck returning to Wilmington Bay, which hadn't turned out to be so bad after all, and he'd get to be with Elizabeth for another few months, which had turned out to be damn terrific. Until very recently.

So maybe all they needed was a little more forced time together and then...and then what? He wasn't sure how much she really wanted a guy like him in her life, but more time to figure out the truth couldn't hurt, right?

"When are you thinking of doing that, Uncle Pauly? The fall, maybe?"

His uncle shrugged. "Eh, I dunno. Maybe next summer. Maybe not."

"Oh." And Rob had to face the fact that there was only one feeling he was experiencing now: Disappointment. He didn't want to wait until next summer—or whenever it was convenient for everyone else—to be with Elizabeth again. He didn't *want* to leave her. Period.

"So, Siegfried and I are going to sleep off our jetlag and then we'll take over tomorrow. You can go home to Chicago and not worry about us old men up here. You left everything in great shape, Roberto. *Grazie.*"

"You're welcome," he said automatically, but he felt dismissed. He wasn't needed anymore. He could go. And no one would miss him.

The bells jingled.

"Hi, Rob," Elizabeth said, looking strangely pale and walking in the shadow cast by her own smiling uncle. She greeted Uncle Pauly, and Rob said hi to Siegfried. "It's great to have them both back, isn't it?" she asked him.

"Oh, yeah. Definitely." *Hell, no.*

"Uncle Siegfried just told me that we should close the shop early today." She glanced at her uncle and he nodded earnestly.

"You two have done so much work for us," Siegfried declared. "Why don't Pauly and I help you wrap things up for the day, then we can all relax. I know Pauly and I need some sleep. *Liebling,* you must have some writing business to finish up and, Rob, you'll probably want to start packing."

Rob clenched his jaw. Everyone was trying to get rid of him. "That's...thoughtful," he managed.

"Great." Siegfried turned the sign on the door to "Closed" and began washing the metal cookie sheets and ice cream scoops. Pauly grabbed a broom and did a quick sweep of the floor.

Rob and Elizabeth looked at each other. Their Tutti-Frutti rein was officially over but, somehow, despite weeks of anticipation and waiting for this moment to arrive, he got the distinct sense that she was feeling the same reluctance to end it as he was.

The tiny bit of hope that lived inside him, the part that remembered the ecstasy of their lovemaking and the thrill of her saying she loved him, began to grow bigger. Maybe it all just came down to believing it could be done. Maybe when a choice was made in favor of intimacy, most barriers bowed down to a superior power. Maybe he just had to really *look*...and to really *listen* to what she was saying.

He decided to take a chance and see if his theory proved true. "I'll head back to Chicago in the morning," he told Elizabeth and watched for clues.

She shuttered her eyes and tightened her lips before nodding slowly. "I-I understand," she said.

But she didn't.

There was a tremor in her voice that had nothing to do with stuttering, and a tiny, almost imperceptible catch in her breath. There was a rigidity in her posture that suggested she was working extra-hard to keep her shoulders from drooping.

Rob felt a couple of obstacles shattering in front of his eyes. She knew him well enough by now to know what she was getting into with him. He was loud. He was talkative. He was into sports. He wasn't as smart as she was by a long shot.

Yet, every nerve fiber told him she didn't want him to leave. And, hey, he was catching up in the brilliance department. When given a chance and a little time to think, he could make good choices. He was going to try his damnedest to make an excellent one now.

He pulled her into the backroom, away from the prying eyes of their uncles. "Are you doing anything this Friday night?" he asked and, again, scanned her face and her body for any signs that might give away what was really going on in that whirling mind of hers.

Her forehead wrinkled. "I...can't think of anything. Why?"

Total confusion on her part. Cool, ultra-reserved voice. Not exactly good, but not bad either. He'd have to make his intentions clearer.

"I'm going to go to Chicago tomorrow, but I'm going to come back up on Friday night." He held her soft hands in his and looked deep into her gorgeous green eyes. "I'd like to take you out on a date."

The eyes got significantly wider, and her luscious lips parted in surprise. But those same lips turned up at the corners, just the slightest bit, in an indication of pleasure at the news. And her fingers tightened in his palms. And when she said, "Oh, okay," her tone warmed up about forty degrees.

He grinned and kissed her hands first and then her forehead. "I'll see you then, sweetheart."

Elizabeth reviewed Rob's parting line about, oh, seventeen thousand five hundred and eighty-three times between that moment and Friday.

Why did he want to leave immediately to Chicago? Why did he want to come back after only a few days? How long did he intend to stay here? What was he hoping to *do* on Friday night—and did his plans also include Saturday morning? Was this a guilt visit or more of an attempt to prove to her that he valued her friendship? And, most perplexing of all, what did he *mean* when he called her "sweetheart"? A term of genuine affection...or a sweet nothing?

Try as she might, she didn't know any of the answers for sure. But she intended to find out within the first fifteen minutes of his arrival.

He only made her wait five.

They were at her apartment, sitting a respectable distance apart on the sofa, when he turned to her.

"Elizabeth, I have a few questions for you."

She didn't trust herself to speak so she just nodded.

"Okay," he said. "Here goes." He fiddled with his wristwatch and gulped some air. He looked even more nervous than she felt, which made her anxiety rise to match it.

"J-Just say it, Rob. Please." If it was going to be something unpleasant—like that this was his last visit to Wilmington Bay for a while—she just wanted to get it over with.

"Remember that day when we were in third grade together and you loaned me your very best pencil and we talked and talked all through the art project?" He looked up at her with bright, expectant eyes.

She smiled slightly. "You talked and talked. I listened. But, yeah, I remember."

"Good, because I thought you were the most wonderful creature to walk the planet that day." He took her hands in his and they were shaking. Not her hands, but *his*. "I still think that."

Okay, this was going differently than she'd expected. Better, but way, way differently.

"Um, thanks," she said.

"You're welcome." He paused. "All right. Let me try this again. Remember how I said that I couldn't imagine having a whole houseful of kids? That I thought this was a really strange female thing and that Tony's ability to procreate little Gabinarris was way beyond me?"

She remembered.

"Well, I've kind of changed my mind."

Her heart did a weird little tap dance. She squinted at him. "Seriously?"

"Yeah. Not a *lot* of them, mind you, but I could handle one or maybe even two...I think. Especially if they're half as sweet as their mother."

He didn't give her even five seconds to process this before he said, "And you know how I was really glad to leave Wilmington Bay and live in the big city far away from my dear mama who was trying so desperately to marry me off?"

She remembered that, too.

"Well, to be honest, that part is still kind of up for grabs. So, I wanted to know..." He reached into his coat pocket and pulled out a sheet of paper he quickly unfolded. "Are you afraid of flying?" he read from the list.

She shook her head. She'd done it a few times and, while not exactly her favorite pastime, she wasn't too scared.

"Good. Are you in any way opposed to leaving Wilmington Bay for a week or two every few months? Perhaps an occasional spontaneous weekend away every now and again?"

"No, but why—"

"Super. Moving on then. Could you be happy being the mother of, say, only two children instead of four?"

A happy premonition she couldn't name began to spread inside her like chocolate frosting on a hot peanut-butter bar, but she kept a straight face. "Well, that all depends on who the father is, Rob. Now why are you—"

"I'm getting there. Are you uncomfortable having these children with a man who's not as smart as you are?"

"Rob!"

"Well?"

Now her hands were trembling, too. "I would only share my body with a man I considered both very clever and extremely kindhearted. Period."

He looked pleased with her answer. "Okay, then. Last

question. Will you marry me, Elizabeth?"

"No," she said without hesitation and watched his expression fall. "Not Elizabeth. It's Lizzy to you." She smiled her sweetest smile at him. "Try it again."

He recovered after a few deep breaths and shot her a dangerous look. "So, *Lizzy*, will you marry me?"

"Oh, yes, Roberto," she said, again without hesitation. "I'm yours forever."

"Damn right," he muttered, pulling her into his arms and pressing his mouth hard against hers. "And don't you forget it."

"With you," she whispered, "I never forget anything."

He hugged her tight. "Elizabeth, I love you, and only you. You're the most beautiful woman I've ever known, and you've had a piece of my heart ever since you were a shy five-year-old. I don't ever want to be without you."

She looked into those warm eyes of his and saw sincerity there—an incredible, almost inconceivable truth. And she knew if a thousand women as pretty and tenacious as Tara Welles threw themselves at him it wouldn't matter. As long as he loved *her*, she didn't have a thing to fear. Rob's loyalty to those he loved beat like a drum in his chest.

She kissed him back even harder. When they came up for air, she finally got to ask, "Now, what's all this about flying?"

"Oh, I'm planning to turn over management of the Chicago branch of The Playbook to the capable hands of Miguel who, along with his new assistant—this Greek-American guy named Nick—" he paused to raise a cocky brow, "are taking the patrons by storm with a bunch of sticky new desserts and some spinach appetizer thing."

She grinned. Nick's brother Jason would be so proud.

"And I decided to start a second restaurant out in northern California, in a hot spot I'd heard from a reliable source was just incredible."

"Mendocino?" she said, almost gasping out the four syllables.

"Yep. That's the place," he said, making a show of feigning indifference. She wanted to kiss and strangle him at the same time. "It'll need to be checked up on, though," he added. "We may need to fly out there a few weekends a month to make sure it's running smoothly—especially in the beginning." Then he gave her a serious look. "So, do you think you're up for it?"

"I do," she told him. And she was.

Across town, Siegfried Finklehooper and Pauly Carrera were reviewing their books at the shop.

"They did a great job," Pauly said, noting the increase in profits over the past two months.

Siegfried read over his shoulder. "Well, we knew they would."

The two men looked at each other and laughed. "Those two kids have been meant for each other for twenty years," Pauly said, patting his belly and grinning at his longtime friend and business partner. "That European idea was inspired, Siegfried. I thought so. Anita thought so. Even Alessandra thought so. She couldn't believe we'd found a way to hook Roberto."

"Ah, well, your sister has a bright son. I know my *Liebling* will be very happy with him. He's already brought about wonderful changes in her."

"Think they'll be pleased with their engagement gift?" Pauly said, still grinning.

"How could they not adore it?" Siegfried said, handing the other man a card that read:

Congratulations, Rob and Elizabeth! Tutti-Frutti is yours with love... Your Uncles.

Double Dipping

~CHAPTER ONE~

STEP 1:
To make a delightful, delicious, delectable batch
of my regionally famous ice cream,

"Chunky Cherry-Chocolate Jubilee,"
you must first gather the following ingredients:
eggs, sugar, milk, heavy cream, real vanilla extract,
cherry-flavored syrup, sliced candied cherries,
milk chocolate chips, shaved dark chocolate...
and some air-blown kisses for good luck.
~From *Mr. Koolemar's Top Secret,*
Kool Kreme Ice Kreamations Recipe Book, pg. 97

Caitlin Walsh knew good men were hard to find, so she rarely had high expectations. After all, what average American male could possess Cary Grant's debonair charm, Gregory Peck's effortless intelligence or Jimmy Stewart's boyish enthusiasm?

That's right, none. So why bother with them?

But that afternoon, as she sweltered in her second-grade classroom and scanned the new financial director's end-of-August memo, she realized the average American male had just sunk to a new low.

Cait rubbed her eyes. "Jenna, please tell me I didn't read what I think I did. That this is some rotten joke."

Her best friend and fellow Ridgewood Grove Elementary teacher, Jenna Murray, crossed the tiles of Cait's classroom, handed her a pint of premium ice cream and a spoon and said, "I couldn't believe it either...so I got us these."

Cait stared at the ice cream, then back at the memo—unable to speak, unsure of what to do next. With the new school year starting tomorrow, she'd been prepared for the typical changes. But, Good Godiva, she'd never imagined anything this disastrous.

She tossed the awful memo onto her desk and, despite the excess calories her "full-figured" (in Jenna's diplomatic words) body didn't need, she yanked open the pint of Raspberry Truffle Swirl and plunged her spoon into it. Ah, creamy heaven.

In this tiny southeastern corner of Wisconsin, where the town's motto was "Sundaes Save Souls" and the local doctors prescribed "two scoops" instead of aspirin, comfort was as close as a grocer's freezer.

After a few medicinal spoonfuls, she recovered her voice. "How could this Ellis guy cancel the Harvest Hoopla? He hasn't even been the financial director for a week and already he's cutting our favorite school festival?" This was *her* festival, dammit. The one she hosted. The one her students loved best.

Her friend dug into her own sweet pint. "He's despicable."

Cait tightened her grip on the spoon. "The children are going to be crushed. The staff up in arms. I've already made arrangements with half the vendors and...oh, God, my *mother!*"

"It's real crummy, no doubt about it." Jenna's voice dropped to a whisper. "But maybe if we talk to him, tell him how important this event is...the community spirit it builds...maybe he'll reconsider. Sonja said the superintendent hired him after only one meeting, so he's got to have a brain."

"But does he have a heart?"

Jenna shrugged. "Who knows? But if he *did* this, he can *undo* this. And, if all else fails, we could make an appeal to Ronald."

Cait thought of the school's aged principal Ronald Jaspers. Not a bad man, but not an effective administrator either. "Doesn't the financial director's authority in these matters go over Ronald's head?"

"Probably."

Cait sighed and ran her fingers through her hair, certain the blond must be turning to gray after her horrid afternoon. "Well, Budget Man Ellis has to show up by tomorrow. You'd think the guy was a fugitive. Has *anyone* seen him recently?"

"Nope."

Other than tidbits their secretary Sonja divulged last week, Cait didn't know much about Garrett Ellis, but she was willing to bet the elusive financial director was hiding out in a cave somewhere with his calculator, crunching numbers and dreaming up new methods to wreak havoc on their fall plans.

Another teacher rushed through the classroom door. "Did you hear? Can you believe it?" the usually calm Marlene said indignantly. "What kind of an idiot would—"

"We know," Jenna said around a mouthful of Butternut Pecan.

"Well, someone's gotta put a stop to this." Marlene shook a wiry fist. "And where *is* that guy anyway?"

Loni, one of the older teachers, marched in from her classroom across the hall. "You ladies talking about the Harvest Hoopla?" She waved her copy of the memo in the air. "I almost had a coronary when I read this thing."

Cait reread the memo. "He's canceling the Hoopla but keeping the Open House Parents' Coffee. Why?"

"Who's running the Coffee this year?" Loni asked.

"Mrs. McAllister," Jenna said, rolling her eyes.

Loni winced.

Marlene pretended to gag.

Cait groaned. She couldn't bear the sight of that school-board-member-slash-socialite Shelley McAllister. Her obnoxious perkiness. Her smoldering red hair. Her evil attempts at sweet talking the administrators during meetings. That had to stop.

"Mrs. McAllister certainly has a way of getting what she wants. We should insist on getting *our* way, too," Cait said.

"How?" Marlene asked. "Have you got a plan?"

"Yeah?" Jenna's grin turned devious. "Forget using the proper channels, is there a way to get rid of a financial director without leaving any evidence?"

"Sure," Cait said, enjoying the momentary slide into silliness. "Consider a non-detectable poison. Villains have tried that in countless films. Only, with our nasty Mr. Ellis, some clever heroine won't be there to figure it out and save him."

Jenna chuckled. "Super. Glad to see you're putting your realistic Movie Channel knowledge to good use."

"Reality is for people who lack imagination," Cait shot back. She licked her last spoonful of ice cream with a ripple of regret. "But it's hard to do away with someone you can't identify. We have no idea what Garrett Ellis even looks like."

"Too true." Jenna flicked a mass of dark hair away from her face and grimaced. "Guess it won't work then."

Cait tried to fight the familiar feeling of powerlessness, but it was no use. She had to do something useful. Grabbing the stapler, she pounded the edges of her calendar into the bulletin board. "My mom's been talking about doing the children's face painting again at the Hoopla ever since we wrapped up last year's festival," she told her friends. "It's one of her clearest memories from the past school year, and I can't come up with many activities like that anymore."

The other teachers nodded, sympathy etched on their faces.

"Is her memory loss getting worse?" Marlene asked.

Cait inhaled and bobbed her head. Damn that Budget Man. On top of the kids' disappointment and the staff's frustration, how would she explain the Hoopla's cancellation to her mother?

She stabbed straight pins into a "Second Grade Welcomes You" poster and tacked it to the wall with a sense of permanency. "School administrators are as bad as deceitful politicians," she muttered, a memory bubbling to the surface of her politically ambitious ex-fiancé Fredric. The callous jerk.

She snatched the financial director's vile memo, crinkled it into a ball and lobbed it toward the trash...missing by half a foot. Well, sports never were her strong suit.

Loni looked defiant. "We'll get Ellis to change his mind."

"Or maybe we'll just *get* him," Marlene said.

Cait cringed and tried to tear her thoughts away from fruitless revenge fantasies. She could count on nothing but hard work, which was her life's salvation alongside ice cream and MGM. But every time she'd played by the rules someone underhanded and conniving muscled his—or her—way into the center ring. She hated to make trouble, but if she didn't stand firm for once she'd get shoved aside and forgotten.

Again.

"You think this Ellis guy's got any secrets?" she asked.

"Besides that he's bound to be an ogre?" Jenna asked. "No."

Marlene and Loni shook their heads.

"Well, I'm going to find out." Cait pressed her fists to her sides and stood firm, her extra-decisive pose. "When The Ogre shows up, I'll pick his brain, cunning and ugly as it may be."

"You go!" said Loni. "Snoop in his office. Peek in his car."

"Exactly," Jenna said. "Ask some pointed questions and, Cait, don't be so nice and polite like you always are."

"Yeah!" Marlene threw herself into the cause. "Give the creep a hard time. The opportunity's bound to present itself. Pester Ellis until he's forced to consider our point of view."

Her friends were right. She'd do it! She'd make that man listen. The easy way or the hard way. His choice.

"I'll try," she murmured.

"Do more than try," Jenna said. "Remember, he's not our boss or anything, just a math geek they've got squirreled away somewhere. We'll probably never see him except at monthly staff meetings."

A twist of self-doubt turned circles in her gut. "What if I can't get him to change his mind?"

"I'm betting you can." Jenna looked at the other teachers. "Give it a shot and we'll have a quart of Fudge Triple-Ripple Decadence waiting for you in the teacher's lounge freezer—"

"A gallon," Loni corrected.

"A gallon," Jenna agreed. "Maybe two." She crossed her arms and gave Cait an expectant look.

Cait walked over to where the crumpled memo lay on the floor and stomped on it good and hard. "Okay, ladies. You've got yourselves a deal."

Outside the building, Garrett Ellis swiped a few beads of sweat off his brow and tried to provide the school district's anxious superintendent with the calm reassurance he needed.

The hefty administrator ran his thumb between his belly and his belt buckle before leaning in and whispering, "I think you've got a good handle on the situation, Garrett. The stolen money is being siphoned off through extracurricular school events, not big-budget programs. Whoever's doing it would have to either look for another channel or stop stealing altogether if that avenue is blocked."

"Which is a big reason why this year's Harvest Hoopla has to be the first thing to go," Garrett said. "All records point to that event as having the highest potential for thievery."

The superintendent nodded sadly. "There's gonna be a lot of disappointed people, but you're right. We have little choice."

"Well, if they're disappointed, maybe a few of them have motives that aren't as pure as they should be."

The superintendent rubbed a bloodshot eye then dropped his gaze. "I wish I didn't have to suspect the people I suspect."

"I know," Garrett told him, feeling a stab of empathy for the man and his difficult situation. "Don't worry. I'll investigate everyone's expenditures. Even those marginally involved. If someone's gotten a kickback from previous festivals, human nature says they'll find a way to keep the cash flowing. They'll get careless. And when they do, I'll be there to catch them."

The older man looked miserable. "Thank you. I know this is a challenging job, but I'm sure I chose the right person for it. Your reputation precedes you, Garrett."

Really? Says who? Garrett swallowed the unasked questions and said instead, "Thanks, sir."

"I appreciate both your skill and your discretion in handling this matter." The superintendent extended his palm.

Garrett shook it. "I'll do my best to find the culprit."

And he would. He was a big believer in hard work on the job. At least when it came to jobs he had some skill at and marginally enjoyed. But he couldn't stop wondering just who had recommended him for this position. It must've been one of the East Coast CEOs he'd worked for earlier this year, though none of them had mentioned anything. He sure hadn't gotten an endorsement from his father.

The older administrator shuffled away before Garrett could work up the nerve to ask and, besides, he wasn't about to look a gift horse in the mouth.

He knew the superintendent had given him an opportunity to right a district wrong and, equally pressing, he'd given him a chance to prove himself to his dad. A chance Garrett desperately needed. Because one thing was for damned certain, with his father's angry statements still ringing in his ears, he couldn't go back to Connecticut if he failed here in Wisconsin.

With added resolve, he took a deep breath and marched toward the school.

Cait whipped the lid off an activity box and dropped it to the floor with a clunk. She tossed some folders onto a kid's desk and glanced up again at the clock. Another twenty minutes gone and still no Ogre-ish Budget Man. Huh.

She'd tried to find the guy, but his office was locked. Figured. So she'd scribbled a message for *him* to find *her*, tacked it to his door and took out her fury on the remaining boxes.

In an unpacking frenzy, she displayed the puzzles, put away the new stash of construction paper and arranged the language arts worksheets. Where the heck would she get the money to purchase the rest of the supplies she needed, though? The ones the school was too thrifty to buy this year?

Pain-in-the-neck Budget Man at it again, no doubt.

Still, she surveyed her mostly completed room with pride. Here were concrete lessons. Well-organized activities. The one place in the world where she felt in control.

At the double knock, she turned toward the door. A man stood in the doorway—a lean, tall figure, claiming the space.

She froze. A visceral reaction rooted her sneakers to the ground. Dark, wavy hair. Chipped-chocolate eyes. Enticing lips. A distinguished jaw line. And somehow she knew instinctively it was The Ogre. Only he wasn't, was he? The man before her might be pure evil, but Holy Hollywood, he was Cary Grant reincarnate.

She drew upon her most assertive teacher voice. "Hello. I'm Caitlin Walsh."

He quirked a brow in apparent surprise. "If this is Room Number Eight, I guess you would be." His rich baritone swirled around her. He offered his hand along with a shrewd, resolute look. "Garrett Ellis," he said, his gaze sweeping the room collecting details. "Looks like you're ready for the first day tomorrow."

"Not quite," she murmured. Whoa. *This* was Budget Man?! That cologne...it had to be something expensive, European. Goodness. She'd gotten a whiff of Italy when their hands touched, and her fingers practically tingled from the contact. "You got my message, finally."

He narrowed his eyes at her, very slightly, but she noticed.

"Yes. I understand you're disappointed by the cancellation of the Harvest Hoopla."

Now there was a genius remark. Making it out to be *her* problem. His insinuation made her curse power-hungry males everywhere for their absurd games.

"I'm disappointed, of course, but also concerned." She kept her tone neutral. "The funding we need to get the festival up and running is nominal. We've always held it on school grounds, so there's no additional charge for location and—"

"Not quite. There are set-up and clean-up costs." He appraised her with an adversarial confidence.

"But not *many*," she shot back. "The vendors use cafeteria tables and share a percentage of their profits to offset expenses. We photocopy the fliers at school—"

"Which means you'd need reams of paper, the use of the district's copy machines and—"

Her temper flared. "I'd appreciate your attention without interruption." She waited until he closed that mocking mouth of his. "As I was *trying* to say, Mr. Ellis, only a small portion of the school's extracurricular budget is used for decorations, advertising and incidentals." She raised her palms in question.

He raised his eyebrows in response.

Okay, so he was a tad slow. She'd try again. "For an educational event that brings pleasure to the children, business to the community and overall goodwill, the benefits of the Hoopla are clear. I can't understand why you'd choose to let it go."

Cait didn't think men in their early thirties still snorted, but Garrett Ellis was an exception.

"We're talking about the *same* event, right? The one where kids wear 'goblin ears' and run around painting pumpkins and eating caramel apples until their teeth rot?" He snorted again. "I read about it in the old newsletter files. Very educational."

His sarcasm made her skin itch. "Well, we also have a storyteller," she said.

"For fairy tales?"

She paused, imagining an evil sorceress turning him into a *real* ogre—one with warts and two heads—but she only said, "No, Mr. Ellis. Ghost stories."

"I see."

"And Ridgewood Grove's balloon artist comes, too. There's face painting..." She thought of her mom and sucked in a few gulps of air. "And caricature drawing. And the Jenkins family runs the Harvest Vegetable Taste Test, which is amazing."

"Baked squash is amazing?"

She couldn't help but laugh, remembering. "It was brown-sugar 'n' cinnamon-spiced squash. Last year they also made sweet potato dumplings, zucchini pie and Mr. Jenkins's specialty—rutabaga al formaggio."

He creased his brow, clearly unimpressed.

She sighed, grabbed a pen, then squeezed and twisted it. "Look, if it's a matter of money, I'm sure the vendors would be willing to contribute a little more to offset the startup costs. They rely on events like this to attract new customers. Or, though we've never had to do it before, we could have a small admission fee for adults and students. I'd be willing to donate something, too, in addition to doing all of the organizing."

An odd expression crossed his face. "Sorry, Miss Walsh, but there's more to it than that." Of course he didn't deign to elaborate. He took a couple of steps forward and picked up the crumpled, trodden memo. "Mine, I presume?" He actually had the nerve to wink at her before tossing it in the trash.

She felt her face flush. She should've pitched the darn thing earlier. She took a few breaths until she could speak calmly.

"Mr. Ellis, I'm sure you have your own, um, *logic*, but you've yet to tell me one good reason why you—"

"What's this?" He pointed to her list with the words STILL NEED written in red marker along the top.

She'd have thought it was self-explanatory but, perhaps, he needed that spelled out for him, too. "It's for supplies I don't have yet. Things the school district won't pay for but that the children still need. Now, about the—"

"The school district won't pay for them?" He seemed taken aback. "But the parents will buy these items instead then, right?"

"The parents have already been sent a list of over twenty school supplies they need to provide. I didn't put these things on their list because, in past years, the school has purchased them. Not this year, though." She crossed her arms. What would Budget Man say to that?

He scrutinized the list with a mystified expression. "Ridgewood Grove Elementary can certainly afford to buy felt, yarn and glitter bottles." He mumbled the names of the other things then looked her in the eye. "Let's go get these for you."

She almost dropped her pen. "What? Now?"

"Sure. Why not? You got other plans?"

"Well, um, no," she admitted. "But—but wouldn't that contradict the 'streamlined' office-supplies budget you set up?"

He shook his head. "I may have canceled your little festival, but I didn't set up the supplies budget. Some blunders actually preceded me, though you may find that hard to believe."

He seemed strangely sincere about it and, to top it off, he'd just given her the perfect opportunity to snoop a little into his life. She should grab it. But she still had questions. "What about the other teachers? They need these supplies, too."

"One problem at a time, Miss Walsh. And you're first on my list."

Now what did he mean by *that*? That her problem had come up first, or that *she* was a problem? She couldn't help but wonder if Garrett Ellis was really trying to help her, or if he was merely acting supportive because he wanted something in return. Maybe he was trying to buy her silence...

She studied him. He had the classic glint in his eye of a player. The kind of man who'd switch allegiances—or women—like airport rent-a-cars if someone got in his way or if his ego got neglected for five minutes. She knew men like this. Guys just like her ex-fiancé Fredric. They didn't spill secrets easily, and they always, *always* had ulterior motives.

She needed to clarify terms. "So, you're saying the school is going to buy these things for me after all?"

"If the school doesn't cover it, Miss Walsh, don't worry. I will."

Garrett watched the curvaceous blonde throw a few last things together, and he shook his head behind her back. This was exactly the kind of individual who could get away with skimming budget funds if she wanted to. No one would suspect someone as lovely and as, well, *wholesome-looking* as Cait Walsh. Not of fiscal misdeeds.

Still, it would be bad form to deny a teacher her glitter. The school board had approved the office supplies change, but he wondered who'd orchestrated it and why. Something seriously strange was afoot in this district.

He studied Cait. She was young, dynamic and closer to his sister's age than his. Twenty-five, maybe. But unlike Sis, this shapely woman was a neat freak who used round vowel tones as weapons. She challenged him with that reserved posture, that combination of clarity and caution. With those huge gray-green eyes, freckle-splattered nose and forehead creased in concentration over God knew what, she was cute as hell.

Which annoyed him. He had too much to do. A leak to pinpoint. He had no intention of finding *anyone* "cute as hell." Least of all a potential embezzler from Wisconsin.

He saw her lift a bulky beige tote with the letters "CLW" stitched in green. It looked as heavy as a golf bag, but shorter and twice as dense. She had it crammed with papers, scratch 'n' sniff stickers, lots of stuff he couldn't see. He'd have offered to carry it for her, but she grabbed it tight. Didn't look like she'd trust the FBI with that thing. Huh. Suspect behavior.

"What's the 'L' stand for?" He pointed to her monogram. "It wouldn't be Lynn, would it?" He squinted. "Leigh? Or Loretta?"

"None of the above." Cait locked her classroom door.

Then again, maybe secrecy was just part and parcel of being a woman. They always thought they had to be so mysterious.

"So, what? You're not going to tell me? Think I'll laugh?"

She nodded, standing still and staring at him in the hallway.

He puffed out some hot air. He'd have to brush up on his chitchatting. Not a good idea to alienate the staff so soon, even if he had suspicions about somebody. He'd known her for...what? A whole fifteen minutes? And already she pretty clearly despised him. Well, never let it be said he couldn't make a strong first impression.

"I won't laugh." He tried to radiate sincerity.

She gave him a thorough once-over. "Livie," she mumbled. "After my grandmother Olivia."

"Oh." He shrugged. "That's not so bad. Olivia's nice, too. Why'd your parents shorten it?"

At this she chuckled. "Think about it, Mr. Ellis. You couldn't have grown up around here. Even in Wisconsin—the 'Dairy State'—having the initials C.O.W. is hardly a woman's deepest desire."

A laugh erupted from deep within him. So there was a sense of humor behind the snow queen façade. Good. Maybe she'd thaw a bit, they could talk, he'd figure out her angle and, hopefully, discount her from his investigation. He needed to concentrate on forwarding his career...and on keeping his father from disowning him. Ogling attractive women was his brother's department, not his.

"You have bright parents," he said finally. "Bet you appreciated their foresight."

"I did." She surprised him with a grin that lit up her whole face. For a moment he was rendered speechless.

They strolled outside toward the parking lot.

"Okay," she said. "Now that you know my secret, what's *your* middle name?"

Sheesh. He hadn't been thinking. Sharing his middle name could only land him in boiling water. "Mine's not real interesting."

The light in her face vanished. She turned huge, distrustful eyes on him. "So?"

He grimaced. "My middle initial's 'M,' how 'bout you guess?"

"What? I practically told you mine outright. There's no reason to hedge with me. It couldn't be *that* terrible."

"Oh, don't be so sure. Your parents altered yours from your namesake's to be less embarrassing, my parents did nothing of the kind." He hesitated, praying she'd back off. The name recognition, he knew from years of painful experience, could be instantaneous.

But no such luck. This Miss Walsh was a persistent one.

Her forehead crinkled. "Hmm. Well, it couldn't be Michael or Matthew, could it? Those aren't unusual enough to upset anyone. Max, maybe? What about Mitch? Or, Marvin?"

"I wish," he muttered. And he did. For maybe the ninety-thousandth time he wished he came from a family that wasn't internationally famous.

They reached their vehicles, and he changed the subject. "Look," he told her, "why don't you jump in with me? It'll be easier than taking two cars. I can drive you back here later."

"Oh, um...sure."

He opened the passenger door of his red BMW and held it for her. She slid into the black leather seat, her eyes bulging at the rows of gadgets on the dash. He knew how impressive it looked. He liked his cars complicated, his women simple. Yet another reason the chilly and changeable Miss Walsh posed a problem: She did *not* seem simple. But someone was meddling with funds and, although instinct and experience told him Cait didn't have the bearing of a ringleader, she might know who was at the center of these thefts.

He slipped into the driver's seat and retrieved a second list from the glove compartment. Time for a test.

He pasted on a grin, wondering how invested she was in this silly fall festival. If he could draw her off track, it might not be much. "Now that we're out of school, I hope you don't mind one addition to our plans. I need to grab a few things from the bookstore before they close. Is it okay if we head there first?"

She gave a curt nod and laced her fingers together, looking about as enthusiastic as a shop mannequin.

Within ten minutes, he had them parked in front of Bookends. First they'd book shop, then they'd drive to the supplies store. His two-part strategy to relax, converse, slide into informality. He'd try to find out what she knew, if anything. If he could rule her out, he could get back to investigating the problem. Alone.

Garrett leaped out of the car. "You coming in?" he asked as she sat, pensive, in the passenger's seat.

"No, I'll just wait here for you."

Damn. "Are you sure? If you don't want to browse, there's a nice coffee bar and snack area inside. You could relax a little."

She glared at him like he'd suggested a round of strip poker. "I'm fine here. *Really*. Get what you need. Take your time."

"Okay." What could he do? Garrett tossed her his car keys. "If you want music, feel free to pop something in. CDs are in a case under your seat." At that she looked almost intrigued.

"Thank you." Cait doled out one of her angelic smiles. It made him tense, uncomfortable and kind of...warm. Aw, hell.

He took a few brisk strides across the street toward the shop. He had a job to do, he reminded himself again. He didn't need complications like, oh, lady swindlers.

But he hoped to heaven she was innocent and he could maintain a friendly distance from her. Something about this woman just got to him. A point underscored by the fact that, as he entered the bookstore, he found himself wondering what he might buy her to make her smile again.

At him.
Like that.

~CHAPTER TWO~

STEP 2:
Crack a couple of eggs into a stainless-steel bowl
and whisk them until they're good and fluffy.
~From *Mr. Koolemar's Top Secret,*
Kool Kreme Ice Kreamations Recipe Book, pg. 97

Cait watched Garrett disappear into the store, his body gliding athletically with every step. His lean thigh muscles teased the thin fabric of his slacks. His broad shoulders defined the white dress shirt. His tasteful silk tie embraced his neck. For a moment she almost envied the inanimate object. Then his long fingers brushed through the dark hair casually, leaving a feathered streak of hair-upon-hair in the back.

He was masculine beyond belief. How provoking. There shouldn't be any impulse of attraction at all. She should despise him. She shouldn't want to squeeze him like a double-roll of Charmin.

Darn it. It'd been so much easier to hate him before they'd met.

Yet every minute she spent with the guy raised her curiosity, and not always in a good way. He had to be hiding something. What influenced his decision to cancel the festival?

How could she find out?

She pursed her lips and turned her attention to the dashboard. More gadgets than a flight simulator. An excessive, irritating display. But one thing seemed certain: From the look of his car and his clothes, the guy had money coming in from somewhere. School gossips told her he'd worked with companies out East in the past year, but she sensed there was more to the story.

She stared out the front windshield. A moth and a fly played tag on the other side of the glass. Hard to say who was winning. But after twenty seconds and sixteen glances at the door to Bookends, she no longer watched their chase. The coast was clear.

She set to work inspecting the back of the car. Twisted gum wrappers clung to the seats, an empty pizza box jutted out of one foot well and several unopened candy bars were lodged in the door pockets.

Conclusion? Garrett Ellis was a junk food addict.

She gingerly used his keys to unlock the glove compartment. She'd never done anything like this in her life and her heart pounded as she shuffled through the papers. The other teachers talked big, but were they here to help now? No.

She reminded herself of the festival and her mom, took a deep breath and then scanned the sheets before her. Nothing unusual. An insurance card made out to Garrett M. Ellis of New Haven, Connecticut. The address didn't ring a bell. No elaboration on that middle name. Why didn't he want to tell her what it was?

She relocked the box and reached below her seat, sliding the black fabric case out to a spot between her ankles. What kind of music did Budget Man listen to? She lifted out a couple of CDs.

Aretha Franklin. The *Les Misérables* soundtrack. She replaced those, grabbed another handful. Big Band Hits of the 1940s. Elvis. The Beatles. Huh.

Garrett's collection ranged from '60s classic rock to weird stuff by foreign groups with names she couldn't pronounce.

There were no patterns. Her head spun trying to assimilate the variety.

Devo alongside Def Leppard.

Michael W. Smith next to Moby.

Sinatra and Sting.

What did such diverse, almost frenetic musical preferences say about a man? Could his opinions be swayed easily?

"'Every Breath You Take' is a great tune, huh?"

She jumped. Garrett peered at her through the open window as she looked between him and the Sting CD in her hand.

"It's a little stalkerish, but I like the beat, and it'll always be a favorite of mine, even though he was with The Police then," he said, scrutinizing her every movement.

"Eclectic musical collection," she admitted, wondering what to do with this new information about her adversary. She didn't like how this knowledge personalized him. How she'd forever associate Sting with him. She *liked* Sting.

"I've got varied and unusual tastes. In all things." He grinned at her.

Not just talking about pop culture now, was he? She felt the unfamiliar sizzle of sexual chemistry between them. The hairs on the back of her neck sprang to attention. The oxygen in the car ceased to be abundant enough to support human life forms.

Oh, God. No. Anything but an ambitious, power-hungry man. Anyone but someone who'll lie to me again and break my heart. She forced her eyes shut and tried to block out the uninvited emotion. She'd fight it! But the knowledge was already inside her, changing her perception of everything.

Garrett hopped in the car, a bag of books in his hand. "Toss these in the back for me, will you?" he said, dropping it onto her lap. "But before you do, look inside. I got you a gift."

Weighted down by the mass of plastic, she blindly slid the CDs back into their case and eyed him from head to toe, not bothering to conceal her wariness. "What is it?"

He didn't answer.

She riffled through the bag. There were two books on watercolor painting, something on art history, a map of the Midwest, a canister of hazelnut coffee and way too much other junk for a ten-minute store visit. She glanced at him. Uh-huh. He had the look of an impulse buyer.

He laughed. "Still haven't found it?" His eyes scanned her. "Trust me, you'll know it when you see it."

Trust him, he said. Yeah, right. She'd heard that one before and what did it get her? Fredric and his assembly line of ready-made fabrications. She fingered through a handful of bookmarks, a copy of *Rolling Stone*, a clip-on book light, a purple notebook with mini-cows emblazoned on the cover and—*cows!*

"Very, very funny, Mr. Ellis." She pulled out the notebook and waved it in the air as he laughed.

"It reminded me of you," he said, his voice way too sweet. He reached for the keys on her lap, sending a gush of shivers through her legs. Then he put the car into gear.

Whamp! She slugged him upside the head with the notebook, horrified and delighted by the sound it made. "And now I'll know what to use it for." She dared him with a glance to retaliate.

"Ah, I'd like to get even, Miss Walsh, but I'm a man who bides his time." He rubbed the top of his head. "So, I take it you weren't thrilled with your present?"

She lifted the notebook again, threatening him. Before she knew it, he reached up and grabbed her wrist. His touch was gentle, but the masculine firmness combined with the warm, slightly callused fingers against her softer flesh made her arm weak. The notebook fell, landing between them.

He let go of her and raised a cocky eyebrow. "Point taken," he said. "I'll use better judgment in my future gift-giving."

"That would be wise." But, in spite of herself, she smiled and discretely massaged her flesh where his fingers had touched her.

That was the problem with trying to snoop. It put her in situations like this, and the novelty of it caused bizarre internal reactions. She felt faint, probably from lack of food. Hunger combined with unnatural sneakiness would reasonably explain the odd tremors beneath her skin and strange racing pulse. The uncharacteristic wooziness and peculiar inability to concentrate. Right?

"So..." She fought to keep the trembling from her voice. "Are you ready to go to the supplies store?"

He nodded, a mischievous twinkle in his eye.

Thirty-five minutes later, Garrett's back seat overflowed with tag board, drawing paper, brass fasteners, dry-erase markers, glitter, Scotch tape rolls, felt squares and skeins of yarn.

"I think we aced this list," he said, and Cait had to admit they'd not only gotten everything she needed, but the time they'd spent together had gone well. Almost too well. If he were purposely trying to beguile her, it'd nearly worked.

Still, she had plenty of unanswered questions. Despite his generosity, the guy was as slippery as she'd feared. Every time she mentioned the budget or festival he managed to deflect her.

She looked out the windshield, planning her next strategy and taking in the surroundings. He wasn't driving the usual way back to school, but she knew they'd get there sooner rather than later. Ridgewood Grove was a town the size of a TV sitcom's soundstage.

The sun inched toward the horizon. She could smell the distinctive scent of charcoal and late-summer barbeques in progress through the open car window. Her stomach rumbled softly.

"We're heading back to school now, aren't we?" she asked.

"Not quite." He motioned with his chin to the Giuseppe's Pizza Parlor at their right, then pulled into the parking lot and looked at her expectantly. "What do you like on your pizza? Meat lover's, vegetarian, double cheese, Hawaiian—you name it. You waited to get your supplies until after I'd picked up the other stuff I needed. I owe you some dinner, or at least a snack."

"That's not necessary," she said, panic rising at the prospect of dining with someone who looked like a film icon. "I'm not at all hungry. You don't owe me anything."

"Sure, I do. I learned a valuable lesson in budgeting for school-district supplies. The same mistakes won't be made again next year." His lips twitched. The devil with the squeezable shoulders and the even more squeezable derriere was trying to derail her. This was bad. She couldn't let him win. If only she weren't starving...

"Well, I really can't. I've got more work to finish before the kids come tomorrow and—" But her stomach rumbled again, louder this time, quashing the debate.

He smiled in victory, the way Cary Grant sometimes looked at Katharine Hepburn. Cait often wished she were as spunky as *that* Kate. Wished she could come up with just the right one-liner on command. There was no script of perfect lines to say around men like Garrett Ellis.

She conceded her loss of this round. "Okay, thanks. Just one of their vegetarian slices."

"That's it?"

She nodded.

"Hmm. Well, in that case I'll run in and grab them to go." He jumped out of the car. "Don't leave."

She didn't. Where would she leave *to?* There was nowhere besides school, her closet-sized apartment and her mother's house. And, if truth be told, all three could wait another ten minutes.

In record time, he was back. Warm brown paper Giuseppe's carryout bag in one hand, white untitled plastic bag in the other.

"Decided we needed dessert, too, where we're headed," he said, driving into the street with a surprising sense of purpose.

Alarm and curiosity battled it out inside her. "We're going

somewhere *else?*" She stared at her watch and felt her blood pressure spike to unhealthy levels even as she admitted her growing excitement to herself. "But it's nearly six."

"Yep," he said smoothly. "Warned you, didn't I? I'm a man who bides his time. You have to pay for your misbehavior now." He grinned big, looking pleased with his skewed sense of justice. "Caitlin Livie Walsh, consider yourself mine for the evening."

Garrett took stock of Cait's stunned expression and prepared to give her the fuller explanation he knew she deserved after such a line, but he wanted to watch her every reaction while he did it.

"Don't worry," he said, trying to project reassurance from the driver's seat. "It's just to the beach for an hour or so. To talk. To relax." *And to gather information, sweetheart.*

He knew she hadn't anticipated this much of a time commitment—that much was clear from her rabbit-quick glances at her wristwatch. But, hell, who was he to let an opportunity like this slide by? The superintendent declared he should go to *any legal length* necessary to investigate potential thieves and, by God, he was going to take his duty seriously. What was Little Miss Walsh like on a personal level?

Oddly, any lingering distress drained from her eyes. "Sure, Mr. Ellis." She twisted her lips. Looked at him in a curious, calculating way. Made him wonder just who was setting up whom.

"I think we passed the formal stage a while ago. Please, call me Garrett."

"Okay, Garrett." She arched one delicately curved eyebrow. Too damn pretty. He fixed his gaze back on the pavement.

He turned down the gravel road heading to the beach. Other than a few stragglers in the distance, they had a good chunk of sand and surf to themselves. He eyed a picnic table on the higher ground and pointed to it as they hopped out of the car.

"Dignified picnic table or casual coastal rocks? Your choice. Comfort versus excitement." He nodded toward the flat, increasingly wet rocks along the shoreline.

She glanced at him then at the beach. From the firm set of her jaw, he figured she knew a dare when she heard one. "Rocks," she said.

He watched her well-rounded calves and ankles fight the resistance of the sand while he followed her tracks to the shore. He forced his pulse to slow down. Damn. He must be getting out of shape. There was no other explanation for his jumpy heart rate.

He gave her a hand up onto a massive shale block and climbed after her, clutching the food bags.

"A veggie lover's for you, pepperoni for me." He pulled the still-hot slice boxes out of the brown paper bag and handed over napkins. "But put those aside for now—they'll stay warm— and try these first." He fished two cold tubs out of the plastic bag, pausing a moment to build suspense. Then he turned the containers around so she could read the labels.

"Kool Kreme Ice Kreamations! But how did you get—"

"A Mr. Alan KOOLemar, according to his nametag, must've talked the Giuseppe's staff into letting him sell samples at a side table. Seems he's got a homegrown business and was hoping to expand. Everybody in the place was eating it up. Literally."

"Oh, Mr. Koolemar's a darling. Everyone in town likes him. He's a regular Harvest Hoopla vendor," she added with a pointed look. "He was once a chemist by trade, but now he has his own ice cream workshop." She touched one of the pints reverently. "He's much appreciated in this corner of the state. We consider our town 'The Creamery' of America's Dairyland, you know."

He laughed at her saucy expression. "I didn't know, but I guess I do now."

"Yes, indeed. And Mr. Koolemar makes the most original flavors I've had anywhere, and I've sampled a lot of cones."

The lady took her ice cream seriously.

"Ah," he said. "Well, you're right about Koolemar's original flavors. I've never heard of Tangy Citrus-Pumpkin Mélange before." He squinted to read the fine print on the white-and-pink tub. "'A blend of cool pineapple, orange, grapefruit and lemon flavors with the warmth of sweet roasted pumpkin.'"

"I haven't tried it yet. Sounds unique. What's the other?"

"So-ho-ho Supreme. 'New York cherry melded with wintergreen and peppermint.'" He brandished his plastic spoon. "I'm starting with this one."

He plunged his spoon into the creamy concoction and brought it to his mouth. Chewy and crunchy textures teased his tongue while the flavor of mint-infused-cherry overwhelmed his senses. His sinuses tingled, clearing more than they had in months. Better even than a York Peppermint Patty, it was like breathing December air in August. He stared at the container then looked up at Cait. "This is amazing."

"I know. His Bananarama Cream Pie is incredible, too, and don't get me started on his classic Orange-Cranberry-Walnut Fiesta. It's impossible to forget one of Mr. Koolemar's Kreamations."

He shoved the pint over and motioned for her to dig in. "Give this one a try." He watched as she dipped her spoon into the container and tasted it. Still watched as the irresistible sensation overtook her. Her eyes fluttered closed, her full lips curved with pleasure. He noted with acute discomfort his powerful desire to kiss the smudges of white, red and green ice cream off those delectable lips. She opened her eyes, catching him staring.

"What?" she said.

Garrett shook his head and breathed in. He had to get a grip. "It got to you, too, didn't it? You looked ecstatic for a second there, like—" *like a climax*, "—uh, like skiing down a black diamond slope in the Rockies." *Let me take you there*.

She nodded. "Well, I've never skied anything more challenging than the bunny hill at Devil's Head, but I think you've got a point. The flavor makes me want to dig out my parka from the back of the closet. Mr. Koolemar knows ice cream." She hijacked his breath with a radiant smile, and he knew this was at least one gift for her he'd gotten right.

They finished the So-ho-ho Supreme and tried the very odd Tangy Citrus-Pumpkin Mélange. Despite the combination of flavors, it tasted fabulous. He reread the label and shook his head. Remarkable.

By the time the pints and pizza boxes were empty, the sun had dropped to a comfortable spot on the horizon behind them. It brought shimmers of glitter to Cait's hair and a golden luster to her skin. The tide forced an occasional water spray as it inched higher on the rocks and closer to their dangling feet, but Garrett wasn't ready to let her go for the evening. It was all in pursuit of a larger goal, solving the financial problem for the school district, he told himself. But a part of him knew he was being a damned liar.

"So, did you always want to be a teacher?" he asked, trying to get the insight he needed into her motives, but also imagining what it might be like to dribble some So-ho-ho Supreme on her bare legs and lick it off.

"Yes. I wanted to make a difference in children's lives. To be like Meryl Streep in *Music of the Heart*."

Ugh. Sappy old chick-flick. "Moving film."

She nodded. "How about you? Were your parents educators?"

He saw a gorgeous, dreamy smile cross her lips, and she appeared to finally be relaxing in his presence. How could he have thought her cold? Maybe she'd just been hungry.

With the ice princess act melting away, she seemed genuinely curious about him. What surprised him, though, was how much he wanted to impress her, to gain her approval. Not enough to tell her a whole lot about his family, of course, but enough to take a step in that direction.

"No, they're in business," he said glancing at the lake. *A Fortune 500 nightmare.* He took a stab at a partial truth. "We're all into math but I didn't want to use it to buy and sell things."

She ran her fingers through the flaxen strands that swept against her pretty face and shoulders. Oh, hell. She was killing him.

"And I really like being around kids. I get a kick out of them," he admitted, realizing he'd probably never told anyone that. Not even his brother Jacob, whom he'd trust with his life.

"Did you ever consider teaching?" she asked.

He shook his head. "That takes a special kind of person. One with patience. But I always wanted to help kids. Support them in the things they needed."

"Adults need support, too, though. Why choose to work with a school district and not some big-name corporation?" She watched him so intently he had to force himself not to squirm.

"I tried it and it wasn't for me," he said simply. He cleared his throat. "So, are you still happy with your choice of profession, Cait? Teaching, while emotionally rewarding, is hard work and it isn't always financially lucrative."

"But it's where I feel I belong. I know I'll never make millions, but if making money had been my goal I'd have chosen another field. Business of some kind, maybe. But like you said, it wasn't for me. I still believe that."

There. Nothing she said indicated she wanted to divest the school district of its cash. Moreover, it showed a genuine dedication to her field. He'd go over her classroom receipts and past year's expenditures tomorrow, page by page, but he sensed she'd come up clean. Her attachment to the Hoopla must be for some other reason. What else could be important to her?

He made a goofy face, trying to short-circuit that serious look of hers. "Schools have great built-in vacation times. Another advantage. What do you like to do with yours?"

"Oh, I read, watch movies with friends, work ahead on my lesson plans, spend time with my family." She smiled again. "And you? What do you do on your holidays?"

"Travel, listen to music, learn new things. And I love sports. I ski in winter. Play golf in summer."

She raised an eyebrow at this. "You bought watercolor books earlier. Are you an artist as well?"

He chuckled. "Hell, no. My sister is. She does graphic

design in Philadelphia. She's coming in on a late flight tonight to check out my new place." *And to hound me about going home.* "I wanted to get her something I knew she'd like." *A bribe gift.*

Cait looked surprised. Almost touched. As if it hadn't occurred to her that he'd go out of his way for his own sister. This galled him. He was a good guy, dammit. He was nice to his sister. Even when she didn't deserve it.

"So tell me about her," she said. "What's she like?"

"Marianne?" There was no easy way to describe her. A bohemian mother hen? A bighearted nut? "She's very...unique. She lives on yogurt and kiwi fruit, has more energy than a preschooler and just moved out to Pennsylvania to live with *Dr. Daniel Bentley IV,*" he purposely exaggerated the name, "of the Philadelphia Bentleys. He's a museum-loving, up-and-coming cardiologist. They make a bizarre couple."

"So," she gave him another of her pointed looks, "would you say you and your sister are close?"

Jeez. Who was doing the investigating here? "Of course," he shot back. "But enough about my family. What about yours?"

Cait studied Garrett in bewilderment. Conversation with him was a minefield. True, he'd answered many of her questions, and the facts she'd begun collecting about his life were piling up, but some topics were clearly off limits. The festival. His family. Specifics about what he did prior to this year.

What was his agenda? What was he hiding? The odd thing was he mostly had the appearance of honesty, which, if it were real, would be unusual in a school administrator. Or, heck, in any man.

"I have an older brother, Seth," she said at last, feeling a splash of water on her calves and brushing it away. "He's an electrical engineer. His wife's a statistician who works from home. Math people. You'd like them," she added, then instantly regretted it. She didn't want to come across as too casual.

He cast her an unnerving grin. "They have any kids?"

She nodded. "A darling three-year-old. Very active girl."

He laughed. "Sweet-looking, not always so sweet-tempered?"

"Exactly." She allowed a quick chuckle before clamping her mouth shut. He was making her laugh more often than she wanted to. Making her speak too freely. Aggravating ability.

She inhaled and decided to probe a bit further into *his* life. "Where exactly do you live, Garrett?"

"I just got a place in New Brighton. It's only ten miles away, so the commute isn't bad. You go there much?"

"Often, actually. It's my hometown. My mom and Seth still live there."

This piece of knowledge inspired him to chat in a charming way about his impressions of the Midwest. She listened to the cadences of his speech, picking up on a hint of sophistication a person inherited rather than developed through study. It perplexed her. Maybe it was an East Coast thing.

"What about your father?" he asked later. "You didn't mention him. Does he live somewhere else?"

"Dad died of a stroke four years ago. He was a construction worker and not big into doctors." She paused, not sure she should tell him more but impulsively deciding to trust him with this. "My mom's just beginning to show signs of decline now, too. High blood pressure. Arthritis. Memory loss."

"That's hard," he said and gave her a look too masked to interpret. "Losing a parent you're close to must be difficult."

She nodded as the familiar pain coiled inside her. "Do you have any other siblings besides Marianne?"

"Yep," he said, his eyes troubled, distant. "I've got a big brother. Jacob."

"Where does he live?"

"Connecticut."

"Is that where you're from originally?"

"That's where I grew up, but originally? No." He glanced over at her with a thin smile. "I was born in faraway Melbourne."

"*Australia?*" Her throat constricted as she recalled her first and last trip to that country. Fredric was Australian, the fiend.

"Florida."

She allowed her breath to escape, surprised by her relief. "Well, Florida's not *that* far away."

He scoffed. "Far enough."

As they talked, Garrett let his eyes sweep the edges where the sand and water merged. He inhaled, feeling the pungent aroma of the lake enter his system and mix with his blood. Thinning it. Making it flow more rapidly. Being here with *her* was doing something to him, creating a moment of odd fusion. An intangible desire came over him. A longing. He wanted something he'd never had, but he didn't know why. His family's expectations, the superintendent's wishes...they all faded into unimportance. But Cait—she didn't. Somehow she was connected to all of this. To this feeling of wanting. They were in some weird dance together.

He looked at her anew, wondering who she was and what *she* really wanted. He speculated about what had brought them both here to this moment. Together. Aside from his maneuverings, of course, and her persistence with the festival. He had questions. But what he wanted to know was becoming too personal to ask.

Instead he made a few jokes, tried to lighten things up. She laughed like the tinkling chimes of the xylophone Marianne had played for two weeks when they were kids. Like the chortling of angels.

He laughed with her. Their hands rested dangerously close to each other on the dark gray rock. He snatched his away and began computing factorials in his head to distract himself.

"Ever travel across the country? Or overseas?" he asked her.

She stiffened and turned silent. He waited. Felt the spray of a small wave. Wiped away the droplets.

After a few seconds she said, "I was in the Sydney, Australia for a few weeks last summer with the guy I was engaged to. Fredric. It didn't work out."

Excellent. "That's too bad." The dude must've been an idiot. Garrett considered gliding his palm over the back of her hand. As a gesture of comfort. He talked himself out of it.

She shrugged, seeming to warn him off such clichéd conduct. "*Some* people," she said with an unmistakable edge to her voice, "are unable to distinguish between truth and lies. They'll do anything, no matter how deceitful, to get what they want."

"I take it there's a reason for that strong opinion?"

She gave a humorless laugh. "Oh, yeah. Fredric didn't have a real firm grasp on honesty. He even lied about his last name. Neglected to mention it had been legally changed when he was ten. Which, you know, makes a difference on a marriage license. There are things about him I never would've found out if—"

"If what?"

"If I hadn't been forced to look closer," she murmured. "If I hadn't insisted on answers." Her gaze traveled from the blue of Lake Michigan to his face. She tilted her head to the side and her eyes twinkled at him. He felt an unwelcome jolt of arousal.

"What?" he said.

"You know, Garrett, if you thought I'd forgotten about your middle name and the fact that you didn't tell it to me yet, you'd be almost right." She half smiled. "You've gotten me completely off track with your errands, questions and unexpected excursions. But now I've got to know. What does the 'M' stands for?"

Her gaze never wavered, her expression triumphant. How could she shift moods so quickly? He could usually peg a woman's type in under an hour, but she wasn't at all typical. The women he'd dated in the past were easy to categorize: Like Clarissa Hughes, the urban intellectual sophisticate. Or Shell Oliver, the gold-digging, too-skinny Southern belle. Or Amelia Trilling, the stereotypic ditzy blonde. And there were others. Many others.

Cait might be a blonde, but she wasn't a flake like Amelia. Maybe her Midwestern upbringing played a part, or not, but she wasn't like any of them. She was sharp-witted yet sweet. Alluringly voluptuous rather than sticklike thin. Professional yet with a touch of playfulness. Still, if she knew his background she'd change her behavior around him in a heartbeat. Women always did.

"My middle name is…Marvin," he said, ruining the lie by hesitating.

She pierced him with a withering glare. "It is *not*. I guessed Marvin earlier and you said that wasn't it." Her lips formed a comical pout, but there was a hint of dead seriousness underneath. "Tell me the truth."

The hell with it, and damn the consequences. "Okay, Caitlin Livie Walsh. If you must know, it's Macauley. Happy now?"

"Garrett Macauley Ellis," she said, testing it out. "That's not bad at all. In fact, there's kind of a familiar ring to it. Like a movie star's name, maybe." She beamed a delighted grin at him.

Believe that if you want, sweetheart. "Or the name of a hapless character some movie star played," he suggested, deciding to throw her a nice, fat, red herring.

"Yes, that's it! Like Jimmy Stewart's character, Macauley Connor, in *The Philadelphia Story.*" She gave him a knowing look. "Of course, he was pretending to be a friend of the bride's brother just to get a top-secret story. He wasn't all that honorable at first, but then…then he turned things around and started to fall for Katharine Hepburn. And he kissed her by the pool."

She sighed and looked impassioned about it, like she'd given the love lives of a troupe of fictional 1940s film characters actual thought. He rolled his eyes, recalling the classic movie. So she was a romantic at heart. Why did women always go for those creepy romantic types? If a real-life guy swept a woman off her feet—particularly a woman he barely knew—and kissed her, the guy would get slapped or screamed at, not idolized. No doubt about it.

"You watch too many movies," he said.

She shrugged and stared into the darkening sky.

He took a devil-may-care breath and let his fingers, which were in close proximity to hers again, *accidentally* brush against her. She trembled and looked up at him in surprise. He leaned

in to kiss her cheek, his lips inches from her creamy skin.
Then the wave hit, drenching them both.

~CHAPTER THREE~

STEP 3:
Measure out 3/4 cup of sugar.
If you go a teeny bit over—that's okay.
A little extra sweetness makes people happy.
~From Mr. Koolemar's Top Secret,
Kool Kreme Ice Kreamations Recipe Book, pg. 97

"**S**weetie, where did you put my coffee mug?" Cait's mother asked in New Brighton later that night, her knobby fingers shaking slightly as she waved them through the thick gray hair.

Cait admired the beauty of her mother's soft features with the usual pang of envy. They were freckle-free, unlike her own. She noted also the natural gracefulness of Georgina Walsh's demeanor, something to which she'd always aspired.

She regarded her mother with compassion before scanning the kitchen. The hot mug was only the third item her mom had misplaced this evening. Inevitably, as sleepiness swept over the elderly woman, there would be more lost objects.

"It's not in here," Cait said with a sigh. "Perhaps you left it on the hall table when you got the mail?"

"No, no. Oh, I don't know." Mom shook her head, puckered her lips and strode out the opposite door to the living room.

Cait sighed again and followed her. "Your bedroom, maybe?"

The clouds of frustration in her mother's eyes cleared as she spotted a blue-and-white porcelain mug perched carelessly on the edge of an end table. "Here it is!" Her expression of triumph turned to puzzlement. "But it's empty."

It was the wrong mug of course, but Cait wasn't about to tell her that. "Why don't I refill it for you, Mom."

"Thank you, honey. Oh, did I tell you? Eleanor showed me a new book of designs she bought. It has dolphins, penguins and other cute things the kids'll love when we do the face painting at the Hoopla."

"That's great," Cait said faintly, rushing out of the room before her mother could sense anything amiss. "Be right back."

On her roundabout route to the kitchen, Cait strode through a few rooms and hallways before spotting the evasive object in the bathroom. She picked the bright, floral-patterned mug full of lukewarm coffee off the counter, dumped it in the sink and brought both empty cups to their final resting spot in the dishwasher. If only her mother would remember to turn it on this time, she thought, closing her eyes and squeezing back a few tears.

It wasn't supposed to be like this. She should've had emotional support from a lover, a soul mate, at moments like these when her mom's needs were overwhelming her. When things in her life didn't go as planned. She should've been happily married right now and been "Mrs. Lloyd," celebrating her first wedding anniversary tonight with Fredric in a cozy place of their own.

"I love you utterly, eternally," he'd said with his adorable Aussie accent, dropping his R's at every turn, no word was safe. "You're so exquisite. My number one gal."

Three days later he was gone.

In light of everything he did:

Lying to her about himself and his affections so he'd have companionship while in America.

Cheating on her with his ex-girlfriend Paige (a well-connected, impossibly tiny-waisted, size-two redhead).

Laughing about her lack of sophistication.

Caring more about money, career and social position than being her true love.

Not appreciating her...

It was impossible to mourn the real man. Just her illusion of him. Just the memory of what should have been a happily-ever-after tale, but wasn't.

Cait thought of other men she'd known. A stray image of Garrett Ellis materialized in her mind. The way he'd tried to dry her off with a paper napkin after the wave soaked them. The way he'd befriended her in one minute then abruptly pulled away in the next. The way natural electricity jumped from his skin's surface to hers like static shock, first when they shook hands and later when their fingers touched at the beach. The way he leaned in as though he were about to kiss her—but then didn't.

Maybe there was a scene in some romantic comedy that was like this, but to her it was such a foreign sensation it should've had subtitles.

"Did you move my yellow sweater from the recliner? I can't find it."

Cait brushed the tears off her cheek. "Let me help you look for it, Mom."

Back in her Ridgewood Grove studio apartment, Cait couldn't sleep. It was more than night-before-school jitters. Something tugged at her mind.

She threw off her quilt and moaned, thinking of her canceled festival and the wondrous sense of belonging and connection she'd experienced last year. How her mom and Eleanor giggled with the children, dabbing paint on them. How the excited "goblins" told her of their adventures. How the community joined in a spirit of togetherness and fun. Everyone appreciated the Hoopla and, in doing so, they appreciated her.

Cait sat up and played with the fringe of her quilt. If only she could get to know Garrett better, his motivations would be revealed. She knew she could change his mind if she had enough time, but there was a new problem. He didn't seem real impressed with the festival's offerings. His facial expression when she'd described the brown-sugar squash had rivaled even board member Shelley McAllister's last year, who'd looked horrified when Mr. Jenkins explained his recipe for rutabaga al formaggio.

What a piece of work *that* woman was. The way she dressed like she was one of the Pussycat Dolls—her focus on hair and makeup, too—convinced Cait that Shelley cared more about appearances than education. Why would she even *want* to serve on the school board?

Cait sighed, thinking about all the vendors and all the terrific treats they'd miss out on now. No grilled bratwurst or strawberry-rhubarb pie. No caramel apples, spiced cider or Mr. Koolemar's Kreamations.

The Tangy Citrus-Pumpkin Mélange she and Garrett tasted that afternoon haunted her. Reminded her that she'd hoped to feature baby pumpkins and oranges at this year's Hoopla, placed in cornucopias, along with apples and pears, maybe walnuts and cranberries, too, to highlight the harvest theme and the vivid fall colors.

Too bad she couldn't do that now.

She poked at her pillow and closed her eyes, still sitting upright. She should go back to sleep, but she couldn't stop thinking of Garrett. Over and over. He'd sidetracked her. He'd told her nothing about the real reason behind the canceled festival. True, he bought the classroom supplies for her, but then he absconded with her to the beach. She barely had time to tie up the loose ends for tomorrow, which should've made her furious.

Instead...it didn't.

He'd been charming, mystifying, oddly humorous and, well, almost likable. She hated to admit it. And he might've kissed her. And she might've let him.

For heaven's sake, what was she thinking?

It couldn't be a good idea to get personally involved with an administrator, even if he wasn't her boss.

But his joking nature put her at ease. His thoughtfulness surprised her, as did his interest in her background. Even that silly cow notebook was kind of funny.

She smiled, remembering.

Still, there was something so disturbing about him. Maybe the way he smelled, all sumptuous and sensual, as if they were in an Italian villa on the Adriatic and not merely at the edge of a Great Lake. But that wasn't what triggered the recognition. It was something about his face, about his name. She couldn't quite put a finger on it.

Impulsively, she got out of bed and hopped on the Internet, scrolling through the online white pages in sleepy absentmindedness.

Ellis.

Her fingers, squeezing the mouse, paused in mid-click—her memory finally catching up with her intuition.

Cornucopias...or maybe baskets? Fruit and nut gift baskets?

Holy Mackerel! He can't be related to THAT Macauley Ellis, can he?

The advertisement was located at the top of their company's webpage. "From Our Family To Yours," or so said their slogan. "We ship our Nutty Fruit gift baskets anywhere in the world. Order online or call our toll-free number 24 hours a day, 7 days a week. The Ellis Corporation delivers to your door."

They certainly did, she thought dryly. Right to her classroom door. Garrett Macauley Ellis—no doubt one of the heirs to the Ellis Fruit and Nut Gift Basket Empire. Base of operations? Why, New Haven, Connecticut, of course.

She whipped the phone over and punched in the numbers. Ellis wasn't exactly an uncommon name. Maybe Garrett was a second cousin or something to the big wig. God, her mother loved those ridiculous baskets. She held her breath as the phone rang.

"Ellis Corporation. The Nutty Fruit," the cheery young thing answered. "How may I assist you?"

"I—um—hi."

"Hi, ma'am."

"I was just wondering about...about your gift baskets. Are, um, pumpkins or...kiwi fruit ever included in one of your fruit and nut combinations?" Cait was rarely this impulsive and felt woefully unprepared for conversation with a real, live human at this time of night. She covered her eyes with her palm, glad the girl couldn't see her.

"I don't believe we have either in any of the standard baskets, but we can surely create one to suit your preferences if you wish to make a special request. Do you have a particular occasion in mind, ma'am, or a list of produce you wanted to order?"

"Ah, well, I'm...not sure. What's available?"

"Oh, our selection is huge. You might enjoy checking out our Ellis website at www.TheNuttyFruit.com, or I'd be happy to send you a copy of our international catalogue."

There was a long pause as the girl waited for a response.

"Ma'am?"

"Yes. Yes, the catalogue would be great," Cait said finally, reciting her address. Then, screwing up her courage, she added, "The, um, *family* mentioned in the ads—you know, 'From our family to yours.' I wondered, how many people are in that family?"

"It's a family of five, ma'am. Mr. and Mrs. Ellis, of course, and their adult children Jacob, Marianne and that rascal Garrett." The cheery girl's voice rose an octave as she giggled his name.

"Uh, thanks," Cait murmured. She let the phone sink into its cradle.

Damn him for lying to her. After everything she told him...

In business, he'd said of his parents. In business, indeed. A multimillion-dollar corporation kind of business. And he'd been questioning *her* about not choosing a lucrative profession.

How did he manage to keep that juicy piece of background information from the small-town rumor mill? She knew he'd been hiding something, but even she hadn't expected it to be something like this. It was more than an understatement. It was a huge lie of omission.

Everyone knew of the successful Ellis Corporation. Macauley Ellis, Garrett's father, had been featured often enough in *Opulence* magazine to have his own display rack. She should know. It was Fredric's favorite publication. He read it with the fervor a devout minister reserved for reading scripture.

As for Garrett, she couldn't care less if he was as wealthy as a Rockefeller. More troubling was that he was some East Coast corporate heir masquerading as a small-town financial director. He could leave at any time with little or no consequence to himself. For the district's sake, she hoped he wouldn't act irresponsibly.

But how could she forgive and forget how he'd lied to her today? How he'd probed into her family life, asking all kinds of questions, yet hadn't been willing to share an enormous part of his personal history with her. He had to know she wasn't some fortune hunter after him. God, *he* was the one who'd made the first move. He nearly kissed *her!*

And, even after he knew how she despised being misled, even after he knew she recognized his name from somewhere, he pretended he was just some average person. Someone like her. But all the while he must've been laughing at her ignorance of his background, hiding behind his ultra-suave veneer.

Damn him, he was *just* like Fredric.

Another tall, dark, handsome liar who'd snicker about her behind her back and make her miserable until he moved on to "better things." Never again.

She wove her fingers through her hair and pulled, cringing. Garrett might be more subtle, might even be more personable than Fredric, but he had the deceitful part nailed down. And, for reasons she couldn't quite put her thumb on, he made her ten times as angry.

Her first impressions of the man had been correct after all. She could never let her guard down with him. But, oh, if he thought he was going to try another slick evasion move on her, he didn't know a single thing about the woman he was dealing with.

Her friends weren't going to have to bribe her with ice cream to dig into his life any more. She'd get him back for this. No additional incentives needed.

Garrett stood outside Milwaukee's Mitchell International Airport and speed-dialed his brother's number on his cell phone.

"Yo?" Jacob said, clear as a bell one thousand miles away.

"Yo, yourself. Listen, I just heard about the leg. How are you?"

"Ah, I'll heal. Damned Jet Ski. But this is nothing. You, little brother, are in real trouble. Mom and Dad want you home."

"Really? Did Dad tell you to call me on his behalf?" Garrett couldn't quash the smidgen of hope that rose at the thought.

Instead of answering, Jacob asked, "How the hell could you leave the East Coast to go live in Wyoming?"

"Wisconsin."

"Wherever," Jacob said. "Point is, we've barely seen you since last New Year's Eve and Mom and Dad want you back in Connecticut."

"They've got *you*." Which was so true even Jacob couldn't shoot off a quick comeback. After all, who needed a second son to run the family company when the first son did such a spectacular job? Even in a hip-to-toe cast.

Jacob moaned loudly on the line.

Concern pulsed through Garrett's body. "You okay?"

"Oh-ohhhh," Jacob groaned. "Mindy was expecting a romantic evening for our three-week anniversary tomorrow. A. Very. Romantic. Evening."

Garrett rolled his eyes. "She'll live. If she loves you, she can wait until you're not quite so bruised."

His brother scoffed at this. "Love has nothing to do with it. You know women are only after our stock portfolios. I'm talking short-term erotica, Bro. High performance. And I'm at my peak."

"You're well over a decade beyond your peak, Jacob."

"That age seventeen thing is an old wives' tale. Now listen, have fun on your Midwestern adventure for a few days then get your butt back to New Haven before Mom has another conniption."

No mention of Dad, huh? Something bitter clenched at Garrett's throat. The hurt of his father's disapproval seeped back in, hard as he tried to shut it out. He couldn't go back. Still, he hated to let his brother down.

"I can't," he managed to say.

"Why? And this better be good."

"You know why. But besides that, it's because I've got a job to do. Because I made a promise. Because I'm under contract. Take your pick."

Jacob huffed on the line. "Nothing against the school, but so what? Our company's an international phenomenon. We need you more than some minuscule elementary district in Wichita."

"Wisconsin."

"Right, right."

"And it's not *that* tiny, Jacob. We're close to Milwaukee—"

"Brewers, Bucks, beer and *Happy Days*," Jacob chanted.

"—and if I solve the financial problems here, I can work with larger school districts next year or maybe a few universities."

"How exciting," his brother said in his driest voice.

"To me, yes, it is."

Jacob sighed. "Well, okay then, but I won't give up on you."

"Oh, I know you won't. Just take care of yourself so you can get back to being the Ellis Corporation's latest, greatest CEO."

There was a pause. "Truly, Bro, we could share this," Jacob murmured. "No matter what *anyone* says."

Garrett cringed at the idea of turning down the brother he'd looked up to for thirty years, but it had to be done. "Thanks, but no thanks. You're the man who gets to wear the company crown. And it looks good on you."

"But—"

"Look." Garrett cut him off, unwilling to have this same argument again. "Stop worrying about me. I've got my own empire."

His brother sighed again. "Yeah, I know. Out in Winnipeg. All right, catch you later. And tell Marianne I said hi." Jacob hung up.

"Bye, big brother," Garrett said to the dial tone. "I will. And it's Wisconsin."

Fifteen minutes later, Garrett was thrown to the floor of Terminal Three by a force he'd long ago ceased trying to tame.

"Hiya, Sis," he said, the words muffled by the fuchsia sweatshirt she carried, a sleeve of which happened to be caught in the corner of his mouth. His head connected with the turf-like carpeting, making a dreary thud.

"How's my favorite big brother?" Marianne asked, grinning as she brushed the carpet dust from her jeans and began to stand up.

"Forget the flattery. I've heard you say that to Jacob, too. And I was fine until about ten seconds ago. Now I think I've got a concussion." He rubbed the back of his head.

"Oh, you. Don't pretend you didn't know I'd be excited to see you. Finally. It's been ages." She punched his arm in the familiar playful manner she'd perfected when they were kids, but something in her eyes looked serious. He felt a very adult foreboding.

"Marianne—"

"Don't feed me any of your excuses, G. I'm not Mom, and I'm not going to be waylaid by your pretty speeches about dedication to this latest venture of yours. I know the financial director thing is a big deal, and I'm happy for you. I really am."

"But?"

"But Mom and Dad miss you. *Both* of them."

"Is that a direct quote from Dad, Marianne, or are you just interpreting?" He damn well already knew the answer, though.

She looked down in classic gaze evasion.

"Listen, kiddo. Just because I don't want to help run the family company, it doesn't mean I don't want to be a *part* of the family. Isn't there a way to have the latter without the former?"

Her shoulders slumped. "I don't know. But I do know Mom and Dad need you, and they want to see you sometime soon. Hiding out in Wisconsin isn't going to make up for what happened last year."

"Really beating around the bush tonight, aren't you, Sis? What else is on your agenda? Gonna tell me I'm getting too fat? My hairline's receding? Maybe I no longer have that winning personality you adored so much during our ill-fated youth?"

"Stop being so dramatic, although—" she tilted her head and scanned his torso, "maybe you did put on a pound or two."

"Thanks."

"Anytime, G. So, it's late. You taking me back to this quaint village of yours? Ridgeburg Grove?"

"Ridge*wood* Grove and, no, I'm not. My condo's in New Brighton, remember? And don't get any funny ideas about inspecting the school. Or surprising me with a mural for my office wall. Or telling nasty stories about me to my new colleagues. You're not allowed within ten miles of the town."

"We'll see about that," she said, slipping her arm around his waist and squeezing—hard. "I've missed you, Garrett."

He kissed the top of her head, picked up her carry-on luggage and nodded toward the baggage claim area. "Missed you, too, Sis."

"They're coming. They're coming. The children are coming!" Jenna announced the next morning, breathless from her sprint down the hall.

"We've got a few more minutes, don't we?" Cait scanned the classroom, frantically thrusting a handful of newly sharpened pencils into a mug on her desk. A loud bell rang. Eight o'clock.

"Aaaahh!" the two teachers shrieked.

They race-walked out of the room toward the gym just as the mad charge of scurrying feet reverberated through the foyer.

Cait took her place in the second grade section next to Loni and readied herself to meet her new group of second graders.

She eyed each one of the twenty-five children as they scampered, skipped, darted or meandered toward her line.

A blond boy and his grinning buddy were already getting into mischief, snickering over a toy one had stashed in his backpack.

A little girl with the hugest blue eyes wrinkled the shirtsleeves of her mother while squeezing a last farewell.

A couple of girls with sparkly sunglasses and Barbie T-shirts discussed a new Disney flick.

A heavy-set boy near the back of the line clutched his Batman lunchbox. He sat on the floor, brown eyes cast down. Cait felt a surge of compassion and wished she could give him a hug.

A second bell rang. The children squealed and stood to attention.

Ronald Jaspers tore himself away from his greeting station at the gym's entrance. "Welcome everyone," he intoned, patting the sweat off his pallid brow, glancing around the room and projecting his authority to anyone in doubt. "We have a thrilling new year in store for us."

He paused and motioned for everybody to clap. "For those who may not know me, I'm Mr. Jaspers, Ridgewood Grove's principal, and all of us here—" he waved his hands in the direction of the teachers, "join together in making *every* day of this school year an *exciting* day."

She watched the way Ronald scanned the room while the parents applauded politely. Did he even notice the four frightened kindergarteners sobbing in their mothers' arms? One distraught youngster had to be escorted out to the hall, but nothing seemed to stop the droning of his inspirational, first-day discourse.

After saying the Pledge together, Ronald dismissed the

crowd.

In the section to Cait's right, Loni set to work perfecting the straight lines for which her classes were notorious. At Cait's left, Marlene flocked her first graders together with a waving motion. And straight ahead, Cait saw Jenna's third grade class bouncing out of the gym in merry imitation of their enthusiastic new teacher.

She chuckled, gathering her own class into a respectable line. "I'm Miss Walsh," she told them. "I'm delighted to be your second grade teacher. Let's go back to the classroom and get to know each other better." Then she gave them an obvious wink. "I've got lots to tell you, and I brought treats."

The children's cheer went up behind her as she made her way out of the gym and down the hall. She saw Garrett, ever attentive, as they passed by the office. Her chin rose a notch. He waved in greeting.

She was calm.

She was in control.

She was onto him.

Mr. Fruit and Nut must have sensed it, too, because, when their eyes met, he wore an odd expression—a combination of confusion, surprise and something else. Something she hoped was one man's unparalleled fear at having angered a woman.

"Hi, I'm Marianne," a bubbly, russet-haired lady said to Cait at lunchtime when the kids were still at recess. She thrust out an enthusiastic hand and her light-brown eyes did a sweep of the classroom. Cait could tell she wasn't one to overlook a detail.

The resemblance was striking. Even without the benefit of hearing a last name, Cait knew an Ellis when she saw one. She took in the vision of the willowy stranger, grasped the outstretched palm and introduced herself.

"Great classroom," Marianne gushed. "G said your room was like a piece of artwork and, for once, he was right on target."

He talked about her classroom to his sister?

"Thank you. Are you looking for Garrett, umm, *G?*"

"Heck, no. I'm hiding out from him, but Sonja let me slip in. He's forbidden me to come to the school. As if I need to listen to a word that slacker says!" She laughed so zealously it seemed she might topple over. "Big Brother's always watching me back home. Now it's payback time. Got any dirt on him?"

Cait busied herself with a few pages on her desk, warming to the lively visitor but also struggling to look more indifferent than she felt. What could she say? Everything about Marianne's brother touched a nerve, but the things most surprising to her wouldn't be news to his sister. Mutely, she shook her head.

"Too bad," Marianne said. "Maybe you'll think of something later." She shot Cait a devilish grin. "I'll be sure to give you my card, just in case."

They heard footsteps echoing down the hallway and turned expectant glances toward the door as the man in question strode into the room.

"Cait—" Garrett said, then stopped and glowered at his sister. "How the hell did you get here? I thought I locked you in the condo. You had watercolor books, enough food for a month, seven new DVDs—"

"Next time use stronger locks. Ever hear of something called a *bus*, G? The experience was so interesting. This nice old lady in the building next to yours explained to me all about how the red line works. First it goes to the businesses in downtown New Brighton, then it stops at Clairmont—"

"Oh, shut up, Marianne." He scored his fingers through his hair and exhaled very, very slowly before raising a thoughtful gaze in Cait's direction. "This is my sister."

"We've met," Cait replied. Seeing Garrett's discomfort made her spirits soar. Not so suave now, was he? She awarded Marianne her most brilliant smile. Marianne sparkled in return. Two against one.

He looked from one to the other, shifting his weight as he leaned against the doorjamb. "Time for you to go now, Sis.

Don't you have to poison red apples or cook up an eye-of-newt brew somewhere?"

"Nope. My afternoon's pretty open." Marianne stood a little straighter, crossed her arms and shot him a glare.

Cait's decision to jump in was instantaneous. She took a step forward, pointing toward Marianne but looking at Garrett.

"Your sister and I were just discussing...art," she said. "I hoped to enlist her help in the development of some ideas I had." She glanced at Marianne, raising an eyebrow in question.

Garrett's sister gave Cait a cheerful thumbs-up, then scoffed at the displeased figure blocking the doorway.

"I see," Garrett said, scowling.

"You're welcome to join us," Cait said. "I was thinking of making an autumnal centerpiece for the back table. One overflowing with fresh fruit. A handful of nuts here or there would be a nice touch, too. What do you think...*G?*" She gave him her most mocking smile. He looked like he was going to strangle her. Then again, maybe she was second in line.

"You *told* her?" he roared, his accusing glare focused on Marianne.

"He told you?" said his sister at the same time, staring at Cait with a look of growing admiration. "Wow, you must be special. He never tells anyone."

Garrett's expression fell just short of murderous. Marianne looked gleeful. Cait figured she better step back into the fray before someone got hurt.

"No one told me anything," she said. "I just put a few pieces together last night, that's all." She stole another look at Garrett, whose face became a study in un-readability, then added gently, "Everyone I know thinks they're great baskets."

"Oh, they *are* great," Marianne said. She swung a perceptive glance between her brother and Cait, struggling, it seemed, to suppress her natural mirth. "Don't be too hard on him for withholding information, Cait. Big Brother here was never much into the family business." She threw a casual arm over Cait's shoulders and winked at her brother.

Garrett rewarded her with a very thin smile. "It's probably

wise for you to line up allies while you can, Sis, considering you're still in big, big trouble. Your junk's lying all over my place and, unless you meet me in my office in ten minutes, you'd better have an arrangement with that Nice Old Lady In The Next Building 'cause that's where I'll be dropping off your stuff."

He leaned in toward Marianne. "Catch your act later." He was halfway out the door when he swiveled back, tempering his expression only slightly. "Good talking to you yesterday, Cait."

The two women waited until the sound of his footsteps had diminished to a distant set of thumps before laughing openly.

"Poor, poor G," Marianne said, her body wracked with giggles. "I've always been such a trial for him."

Cait downshifted to a simple smile, relieved by this latest turn of events for some reason she wasn't prepared to analyze. "If he carries through on his threat, you can stay with me."

"Thanks, but G's not as bad as he likes to appear. He's just a little extra sensitive about our family's company. I think he was worried I might spill the beans."

"Why is that?" Cait asked. "Why doesn't he tell anyone about it? I'll admit, I was pretty surprised by the omission."

"Long story." Marianne shrugged. "I found my niche in the Ellis Corporation by doing graphics for the Nutty Fruit. I love what I do and could take on even more responsibility." Her eyes looked wistful. "But it was never a clear path for G. Growing up as a younger brother to Jacob was difficult. Jacob's gotten most of our dad's attention, and he's more involved in running the company. Jacob's a lawyer, you know." She paused to flick her eyes upward. "He thinks he's pretty hot stuff. Despite this, G always adored him, trailed after him for three decades. But during the holidays this past year there was a big argument. G got more distant from our folks and he left New Haven..."

Marianne's gaze was lost in the colorful pattern of a spelling-vocabulary bulletin board for several long seconds. She bowed her head. "Anyway, Mom and Dad want him back home, or at least in the general vicinity. But he's still too angry or too stubborn or something, and I'm stuck trying to be peacemaker again."

For a split second Cait thought she detected a trace of bitterness in her voice. But just as quickly it was gone.

"I love both my brothers, you know, but even when we were kids I was always a little more worried about G," Marianne said.

"It must be hard to be caught in the middle. To try to deal with situations where family members are talking to you but not to each other," Cait said.

"Exactly. In some ways it's like losing someone." She paused then looked up at Cait with startled eyes. "Oh, I'm sorry. G told me you'd lost your father. I didn't mean to put this Ellis feud in the same category as that."

"It's okay," Cait said, surprised again that Garrett had spoken about her so freely to his sister.

Marianne seemed to sense this. She grinned. "G talked about all the new staff he'd met, but your name came up a few too many times for it to have been a coincidence. Look," she said, laughing, "as you might've guessed, I'm not shy. My flight back to Philly leaves at six a.m. tomorrow, so this was my only chance to get out here and see the school. And also to meet you, Cait." Her eyes crinkled in merriment. "Now, were you at all serious about wanting a fall centerpiece?"

Five minutes later Marianne was out the door, pressing her business card in Cait's hand, promising to keep in touch and to send her a special fruit and nut basket for the classroom.

"Ciao. Call me if you need anything else," she said, waving, "or if you ever wanna hear about the stupid things G did when he was a teen. I've got stories!"

Cait grinned, pocketing the card. For a couple of lovely seconds, the imposing new financial director didn't seem half as powerful as his little sister.

And this knowledge gave her a few admittedly devious ideas.

~CHAPTER FOUR~

STEP 4:
When the eggs are nice and light,
start adding a little pinch of sugar at a time into the bowl
while continuing to whisk.
~From *Mr. Koolemar's Top Secret,*
Kool Kreme Ice Kreamations Recipe Book, pg. 97

The afternoon smelled of heat, cookies and urgency.

Cait's students, dismissed an hour early for this first day, were already on their school buses or bikes headed home. They'd been pretty good, all things considered. No major accidents. No stomachaches, not even after they'd polished off the two packages of chocolate-covered Oreos she brought in as a treat.

Spread in front of her on the table, the manila file folders stuffed with students' learning assessments, contact information and photos called out to her like giant cards in the game of Memory. She needed to match the names and educational needs.

She opened Jimmy's folder, the one for the boy who held himself back from the others. His parents had gotten divorced a year ago, and he needed some serious self-esteem building.

She'd just begun jotting down notes on ways to help him gain confidence when His Royal Nuttiness swept into the classroom.

"Hi, Cait."

"Hello, Garrett. Or should I address you more formally now? Mr. G. Ellis? Sir? Honorable CEO?"

He groaned. "Oh, please. Somehow I knew you'd figure it out, but I'd appreciate your not making it public. Even Ronald Jaspers doesn't know the whole story. If he did, he might hold it against me. The usual 'I must've had it easy because my family's famous' deal." He gave her an exasperated look. "You don't know what it's like having your life tied to those damned baskets."

"That's true. I don't."

A look passed between them that was almost friendly. Conspiratorial. Cait studied him, realizing her anger had diffused a bit after having met his sister. Okay, so the guy couldn't help his upbringing. Maybe he wasn't trying to be the lying, game-playing bully she'd feared. She could, perhaps, give him the benefit of the doubt. Let him off the hook again. But three strikes and he'd be out. No more chances.

He seemed to be studying her, too. Cautiously. He said, "So, you were a big hit with my sister. She talked about you all through lunch." He fingered his hair, brushing it away from his forehead. "Thanks for tolerating the intrusion."

"It was no intrusion at all. I liked Marianne."

"Hmm." He expelled the air as if it were something mildly distasteful.

"I *did*," she insisted. "I hope you weren't too nasty to her. Older brothers can be a real pain."

"I'd like to hear you say that to your brother's face. I bet Seth puts up with quite a lot from you, and I just wonder what he'd say if I asked him about it."

"Well, that's an unlikely meeting, don't you think?"

Garrett only lifted an eyebrow at her, and Cait remembered too late that both he and Seth lived in New Brighton—a town with a population smaller than some extended Italian families.

"Anyway," he said finally, "I'm glad we could get your supplies yesterday. Anything else you need?"

"Yes." She looked him in the eye. "I need you to change your mind about the Harvest Hoopla. It still doesn't make sense to me why that event was targeted. You said it was about more than just the money needed to operate it. So what is it? What's going on behind the scenes?"

"Look, I'm still new here. There's a lot I don't know."

"And you don't want to rock the boat finding out."

"That's not fair, Cait. The force of your conviction—and you sure are persistent on this issue—might give me reason to reconsider if the situation were different, but it's not."

"Why is the situation 'different', as you say, this year?" She crossed her arms and glared at him.

He exhaled deeply and shook his head. "I'm not at liberty to explain. I'm sorry. Maybe you need to just let this one go."

It was hard to let it go. Besides her mother's constant and enthusiastic anticipation, the children had asked her about it already that day. They'd seen the students in her previous two classes get to be the Harvest Hoopla's official "goblins"—the lucky kids who passed out fliers to visitors, delivered messages to vendors, dashed around the site flinging goblin dust (a glitter and confetti mix) on the participants. To a seven- or eight-year-old this was unspeakably exciting. The kind of school memory that long outlasted the spelling tests and the math homework.

"Just give me one explanation, Garrett. Even a partial one. Just one good reason."

He wrinkled his nose and pulled up a kiddie chair next to her. It looked funny—his long legs nearly reaching his chest while he tried to sit in the tiny chair. She suppressed a giggle.

"There's something I'm working to figure out and, to do it, I needed to give your goofy autumn festival the ax. In the end, it may make no difference at all but, to the best of my knowledge, this method has the greatest potential to lead me to what I'm looking for. So, please, accept my apology and try to move on."

She swallowed hard. Too many pieces were still missing, but he'd done as she'd asked. He'd given her a partial explanation, even if it didn't make any sense whatsoever.

"Just tell me this one last thing," she said. "You don't have any underhanded reasons for doing this, do you? Some secretive connection to the school board? Or a conflict of interest somewhere?"

He shook his head.

She paused and thought of Mrs. McAllister getting to keep her Open House Parents' Coffee. "And this isn't some game of privilege, is it? A situation where the big people in positions of power get what they want and the ordinary little teachers don't?"

He shook his head again.

"And you're not just agreeing with me now to get me to fall into line and be a team player, are you?"

"How much longer is this 'one last thing' line of questioning gonna last?"

She stared at him, unsmiling.

He sighed. "Cait, I know this must be frustrating for you. I'm not trying to make it more difficult, and that's the truth."

Cait sighed, too. She didn't want to do this. She didn't want to relent. But it didn't seem as though any argument would change his mind. She shut her eyes and swallowed again.

"Well, I suppose—" she began.

Loud voices in the hall interrupted her. A woman's champagne-bubbly laugh. A raucous male reply. She and Garrett turned their heads in the direction of the doorway as Ronald Jaspers shuffled through it.

"Ellis, there you are. Got someone here who's anxious to talk to you." The principal beamed at him. "Oh, and, uh, hi, Cait," he said, friendly, but clearly as an afterthought.

Cait squinted up at Garrett as he began to stand, the long legs unfurling from the chair.

"So, Ellis, the school board members came here special to greet you." Ronald gazed out into the hallway and put on another fat smile. "Just one more minute," he called to some impatient person out in the hall. "I'm getting him."

While Ronald's attention was still directed outside the

room, Garrett cocked his head to one side and listened to the voices. Cait watched him. After only a moment, he blanched at the sound, looking as guilty as a Vegas card shark in Omaha.

What now? He shot her an imploring—almost disbelieving—look, which she didn't understand.

Meanwhile, the champagne-voiced lady had moved closer. Cait rose from her chair. The vocal tone was distinct, identifiable in seconds. Cait grimaced. Clicking heels tortured the tiles. A familiar menace breezed into the room.

"Ah, Mrs. McAllister—" Ronald began, no doubt preparing to pull out some ever-ready flattery suitable to the occasion. But the woman waltzed past him with her long legs, stilettos and a daring cerulean mini. She glided into the center of Cait's classroom and struck a pose.

"Garrett, darling, you look so good," she drawled, flicking her flaming red curls off her navy blouse, achieving the effect of a comet streaking the night sky. "How charming to see you again after all this time." She blew him a hot kiss.

No connection to the school board, eh? She watched Garrett's eyes widen. Cait narrowed hers. She didn't buy his innocent act this time, though. He might feign surprise, but he had to have known that woman was a board member. He was a liar, liar, liar. Just like Fredric.

Three strikes, Mister. You're out.

She heard him draw in a raspy breath before whispering, "Shelley? Shell Oliver?"

Damned if this wasn't the worst possible moment Shelley could appear, Garrett thought. Just when he was close to getting Cait on his side. He'd checked her classroom expenditures. Clean as a whistle. If she'd proven her trustworthiness, too, he might've even confided in her before long and enlisted her help.

Wasn't going to happen now, he realized, as Cait continued to glare daggers at him.

Garrett turned his attention to his slinky ex-girlfriend and pondered life's inscrutability. Of all the school districts in the country, Shell Oliver had to show up at this one.

The redhead, however, did not seem the least surprised by his presence or by the disruption she'd caused.

"Why, yes, darling," she said. "Only, my name's been Mrs. McAllister for three whole years now. The charms of the Midwest are pervasive, aren't they?" Her blue eyes flirted unabashedly with him. She even grinned at the principal. Garrett noticed she ignored Cait entirely. Shelley took a couple steps closer to him.

"Three years?" he said, clearing his throat. "I had no idea you've been out here that long, Shell."

"I suppose I should be offended," she drawled. "How could your parents have overlooked telling mine how close we are—in proximity?" Shelley reached out and brushed exquisitely manicured scarlet nails down the forearm of his suit. She wrapped her fingers around his bare wrist and squeezed. It felt like the death-grip of a cobra.

He caught Cait's eye but he couldn't explain this to her. He wasn't even sure he could explain it to himself. Not that he'd be able to talk any sense into Cait now. She looked like she wanted to throw the nearest heavy object at him. He scanned the room. Yep. He could see her reaching for her stapler.

Ronald Jaspers coughed twice, breaking the silence. "Well, now. I didn't realize you two were so *well* acquainted. Maybe we should relocate this reunion to the conference room where the other board members are waiting." He coughed again extra hard, as if to underscore the point. "Ellis. Mrs. McAllister."

Garrett nodded. Shelley McAllister grasped his elbow with her other hand and steered him toward the door. He threw a last-minute backward glance at Cait before he left, trying to apologize nonverbally, but he couldn't tell from her expression if he'd succeeded in making his regrets known.

"Have a good evening, Cait. I'll talk with you later," he said before Shelley all but shoved him out of the room.

Cait didn't respond. Damn.

Cait pursed her lips, unclenched then re-clenched her fists. Garrett Ellis could just keep his lies and his career games to himself. If he could be taken in by a devil in a blue dress like Shelley McAllister, then he was no better than Ronald, an unthinking, wishy-washy puppet of the board, who could get sweet talked into anything in under three minutes.

Darn it. Did Garrett ever *date* that snippity, uppity, superficial woman? God, it seemed that way. If so, Mr. Fruit and Nut deserved what he got...and he wasn't nearly as intelligent as she'd given him credit for.

Not that it mattered.

Not that she cared.

It just took away any concern she might've felt for his position, especially now that she was going to defy every single word the hotshot financial director said.

"The Packers are gonna go all the way this year, I just know it," school board president Mike Firenzi announced to Garrett and the other males in an impromptu huddle in the conference room. "And I'll be watching it live and in person. Got the season tickets my grandpa used to have on Lambeau's 30-yard-line."

Board members Jason Lenox and Doug Chippenak looked appropriately appreciative. Garrett nodded, trying his best.

Mike grinned. "See how they decimated the Lions on Sunday's preseason game? It's almost like when Favre was playing."

"They'll be engraving those Super Bowl rings before long," Jason chimed in.

"I heard the coach interviewed on ESPN yesterday...no, a couple nights ago, I believe," Doug said, rubbing a graying sideburn and nodding leisurely. "And while they were talking, he said to the sportscaster..."

Garrett ceased listening. Doug's monotone had a tendency to inspire drowsiness. He glanced over at Shell Oliver or, rather, Shelley Oliver McAllister with growing surprise. Wasn't she still supposed to be out East terrorizing rich graduates of the Ivy Leagues? She might have great legs—all three of the Oliver sisters did—but she used them to walk all over people.

His mother had prattled on about her not that long ago. But most of his family couldn't get the Midwestern cities straight. He only knew Shelley had left Atlanta, but he never much listened to gossip about which state she'd relocated to.

He cringed.

Man, oh man, he could only imagine what she'd been up to in this sweet, unassuming town for three years. The woman was a barracuda when she went after something.

"Coffee, boys?" Shelley said, handing Garrett and the others steaming mugs of black brew. "Skim milk and sugar substitute are over there." She pointed to the table behind her with a hot red fingernail, managing to make even that motion a seductive one.

The men's huddle disbanded so they could fix their coffees, but one distasteful form of small talk replaced another as Shelley attached herself to his arm again.

"How's your lovely sister Marianne doing?" she asked, tilting her fiery head to the left and smiling like Wile E. Coyote with Bugs Bunny in sight.

"She's happy. She lives in Pennsylvania now."

"Oh, yes. That's right. Mama mentioned she'd moved in with that dashing doctor, Daniel Bentley—the *Fourth*."

He eyed her, irritated with the conversation already. His memories of Shell Oliver, the cute Georgia State coed he met at Hilton Head the summer before his senior year at Princeton, were coming back to him. Hard to believe their relationship lasted a whole four weeks. Marianne practically beat him up when she learned he and Shelley were dating. Those two were about as close as a snake and a mongoose.

Garrett took a deep breath. "So, how did you meet *Mr.* McAllister?"

"You mean Chucky-darling," she all but squeaked. "Oh, my. Well, he was out visiting Atlanta on bank business. He's the VP here in Milwaukee…"

Appropriate. Shelley would, of course, snag a banker.

"…It wasn't more than four months after his divorce, and I was working at the downtown branch of First Liberty National. So, we just got talking, and he showed me photos of his two adorable girls. He has full custody," she said with a knowing nod. "We hit it off real well, ate out at vegetarian restaurants, went jogging together…"

Aha. He remembered her fixation on athletes. He wasn't surprised "Chucky" was a runner type.

"…Later he invited me up north to visit. Then he gave me this." She waved around a diamond the size of an Olympic hockey rink and looked at him victoriously. "We celebrated our third anniversary in June."

"Congratulations, Shell. Your folks must've been pleased." He thought of her stiff, stock-portfolio-assessing parents whom he'd met at the beach so long ago.

"Yeah, they were." She glowed.

"How was it that you got so involved with the school board?"

Shelley took a dainty sip of her coffee. "I have ideas, you know. Plus, Chucky thought it would be good for me to occupy myself with community issues, so I decided to run." She sighed. "Everyone's been so nice to me, real friendly and all, but it's a little—" she leaned toward him to whisper, *"provincial."* She batted her eyelashes, curved her full lips into a pretty smile. "Of course it's much less so now that you're here."

Garrett was rescued from having to respond by Ronald's return. The older man balanced a plate of cookies in one hand and a box of pastries in the other. A few chocolate crumbs clung to the corners of his lips.

The guy had the look of someone who could potentially pad his pocketbook with district funds, Garrett decided. This, in fact, was the superintendent's biggest concern. The two went way back. But, despite that longstanding friendship, the head honcho suspected the principal above all others and told Garrett so.

Not that he should be too quick to discount Shelley.

He watched as she sauntered toward Ronald and hastily took the tray off his hands. The two shared a laugh over something Garrett couldn't hear.

"Now that all the refreshments are in the room," Ronald said, "maybe we can relax and swap some ideas." He held out the pastry box. "Cinnamon roll, anyone?"

On Thursday morning Cait hung up her classroom telephone, fuming. Just why securing a location permit should be this difficult was beyond her. Every open venue in the town of Ridgewood Grove either had size restrictions that would keep out the kind of crowd the Hoopla would draw, or it didn't allow food to be served, which was a given at the festival, or it was already booked for the first Saturday in October, the date she needed.

The only privately owned facility both large enough and available on that day was the Four Gates Country Club, which belonged to school board president Mike Firenzi and his family. And that venue had to be crossed off the list simply because it was too expensive.

The children would be returning from gym class in ten minutes, and Cait still had no idea how to turn the situation around. She slumped in her desk chair, flopped her head onto her folded arms and closed her eyes.

"Stay up too late watching *Casablanca* last night, Cait?" Jenna asked, popping into the room. "Hey, what's wrong? Is everything okay with your mom?"

Cait managed a short nod. "Mom's doing the same, but now I've got other problems." She filled Jenna in on yesterday's conversation with Garrett, her permit predicament and the lovey-dovey connection between the financial director and the redheaded school board member.

"But we can't give up on the Harvest Hoopla!" Jenna said.

"We won't, but I need some help brainstorming."

"Have you tried talking with Ronald?"

"Yes, this morning. He doesn't understand the festival's cancellation either and he seems really disappointed, but he won't go against what Garrett says. So we can't host the Hoopla on school grounds. And now, it seems, we can't host it anywhere in the town. Indoors or out."

"How about out of town?" Jenna's lips twitched, her forehead wrinkled—sure signs that she was thinking hard. "What about a familiar town but one without so many restrictions?"

"You mean, New Brighton?"

"Well, why not? You know it like the inside of your shoe closet. You're there all the time because of your mother anyway. It's not too far away so children and families who want to go from Ridgewood Grove can still attend, but it's far enough not to be under the jurisdiction of the formidable Mr. Ellis…"

For the first time in twenty-two hours, Cait grinned. "So, my dear Mrs. Murray, you wanna be an honorary goblin?"

Jenna wiggled a hand behind each ear and laughed aloud.

"Cait!" Garrett called out to her in the parking lot.

She cringed, but turned away from her car long enough to nod at him. Argh. She'd hoped to escape the building without a confrontation today. Ridgewood Grove Elementary School had been blissfully free of Garrett Macauley Ellis for the whole day. But of course he had to show up now and ruin it.

"How are you, Garrett?" she said in her coolest voice as he jogged up beside her. He stood way too close for comfort. His body heat made her skin prickle.

"Fine, thanks. Look, I'm really sorry we were interrupted yesterday, and I was at a meeting with the superintendent all day today, so I didn't have a chance to talk with you." He tried to give her one of those charming grins, but she wasn't fooled.

"Anyway, I hope you're not still disappointed about the festival. Maybe it'll turn out for the best this way and—"

"So, you don't have *any connection* to the school board, do you Garrett? Fascinating. Really."

He swallowed, gave her an odd look and took a small step backward. "Look, Cait, about that. I was—"

"You were lying, weren't you?"

The surprise in his dark eyes and his heightened color let her know she'd touched a nerve. "Hey, what is this? Do you really think I had any idea Shelley was going to show up and—"

"You're answering a question with a question, Mr. Ellis." She forced herself to keep her tone even. "But while we're at it, let's get back to what you just said. Why, exactly, would it be 'for the best' not to host the festival?"

"Well, you—" He stared at her. "I can't tell you but—"

"But nothing. You've got your agenda, some big political plan, no doubt, complete with whatever career-ladder-climbing rationale you need to pull it off. Good Ole Boys scratching each other's backs and all. And the only one it would be 'for the best' for is *you*." She leveled her angriest look at him. "I take my work seriously," she added. "More seriously than most people, maybe. I won't let down those children, or the people I care about, because of some hypocritical administrator."

"Cait, I never intended to deceive you, I just meant—"

"You just meant you expected me to fall into line based upon what you, our superintendent or certain members of our school board want. That I wasn't supposed to fight any of you or even question your actions. That I have no resources available other than what you oh-so-powerful, righteous individuals have to offer. Isn't that it, Garrett?" She opened her car door and shoved her tote bag inside. "Well, think again, because I *am* running the Harvest Hoopla. I figured out a way. And you can tell that to your *darling* friend Shelley McAllister!"

He grabbed her by the arm, not roughly but firmly enough to keep her from jumping in the car. His expression was gray and grim. "Listen, you can't do that. You'll ruin everything I'm trying to do."

"Which you, of course, refuse to tell me. I'm supposed to trust you and your judgment, but you won't trust me in return."

Cait shook herself loose from his grip and glared at him, a barrier of raw emotion inside of her bursting. Just who did he think he was? One thing was certain, she'd be damned if she'd repeat past mistakes and get forced into doing some man's bidding based merely on faith in him.

"Don't you ever—EVER—tell me what I can or cannot do." She pressed her pointed index finger against his chest, the lean and hard muscles creating a formidable, infuriating wall against her attack. "Your work extends to the boundaries of the school district only, not beyond it. Certainly not into my private life or thoughts. So don't think for a second you can push me around."

She slipped into the car and slammed the door, pleased to see his too-handsome face turning an unnatural pink. She drove off without so much as a backward glance.

~CHAPTER FIVE~

STEP 5:
Add 1 cup of milk.
Make sure it's fresh, wholesome and from
America's Dairyland (that's Wisconsin, of course).
~From *Mr. Koolemar's Top Secret,*
Kool Kreme Ice Kreamations Recipe Book, pg. 97

"I don't know what to do with her anymore," Cait's brother said over the phone, his voice a combination of worry and annoyance. "I was over there this morning, and Mom had left the front door wide open. God knows who could've walked in. And now half the food in the basement freezer is spoiled because she forgot to close it completely." Seth exhaled heavily. "We need to talk with her."

"I know," Cait whispered. She was on the phone in her mother's living room while the lady in question was freshening herself up in her bedroom upstairs. "I'm really frustrated, too. She's losing everything, and I'm afraid to let her go out of the house by herself for fear she'll forget the way home...not to mention the dangers involved with her driving."

"No kidding. An accident at her age would be a nightmare."

Cait shuddered to think of their mother trapped in her Ford

Escort. Maybe they'd just been putting off the inevitable. She needed time to collect herself. Seth must have felt this too because there was a long pause on the other end of the line.

"What are you thinking, Seth?"

"I was wondering if you're free tomorrow night," he said. "Maybe we can both meet there, have dinner together. Talk, just the three of us."

"Okay. I'll tell Mom we're going to have a little family meal. She and I can get some groceries later this evening."

"Sounds like a plan. Well, a *start*, anyway."

"Yeah," Cait said. "Give kisses to Dianne and Mia for me."

"Will do. See you tomorrow."

Cait put down the phone moments before her mother came in wearing a somewhat odd mix of garments.

"Did you borrow my green and gold scarf, dear? I can't seem to find it."

The red scarf her mom was wearing provided a discordant contrast to her pink blouse, but Cait doubted the green and gold one would have been much of an improvement.

"No, Mom. I can help you look later, but first we need to head to the market." She pointed to the telephone. "Seth just called. He was hoping to pop by for dinner tomorrow night so the three of us could chat."

Her mother clasped her hands together in her typical gesture of excitement. "Oh, wonderful. Let's make stuffed peppers. You know how my little boy loves them."

"Great idea." Cait chose not to remind her mom that her "little boy" was a married father and dangerously close to thirty.

After a twenty-minute search for house keys, they strolled the few blocks to Pummelhof's Market, grabbed a blue basket and began sniffing and squeezing peppers. They selected six near-perfect specimens—firm to the touch, green like a palm leaf and possessing the distinctly scented aroma of roasted cactus. At least, that's what Cait always thought roast cactus should smell like.

They'd just moved on to the tomatoes when a familiar tuft of dark hair nabbed her attention. Her surprised gaze collided with Garrett's. He, however, recovered an instant sooner and set his lips in a rigid line of incivility.

"Good evening, *Miss Walsh*," he said, sounding maliciously formal.

Clearly she wasn't forgiven for the day's earlier comments. Not that she needed his forgiveness. So, okay, maybe she'd been a little rude. Normally she'd feel awful. Heck, normally she'd never resort to shouting or insult slinging. But none of her reactions to Garrett Ellis were remotely normal and, anyway, it was too late to take back her words.

"And how are you, Mr. Ellis?" she said, proud of her reserved voice. Then, stating the obvious, "Out grocery shopping?"

He looked fleetingly amused. "Why, yes, Miss Walsh. Even we hypocritical administrators eat broccoli on occasion." He held up a baggie of Mr. Pummelhof's best organic broccoli and swung it between them for a moment of show-and-tell. "And you?"

"Peppers."

"Ah."

Cait noticed her mom watching their exchange from a few feet away with some confusion. Finally, the older woman stepped up to them and put a finger to her lips, her gray-eyed stare riveted on Garrett. "Why, I know your face, young man. Were you one of Cait's high school boyfriends?"

"Mom!"

Her mother ignored Cait's vigorous head shaking. "I've seen your picture, that's what. Were you a college buddy of Seth's? Maybe in our photo album at home—"

"No, Mom. I don't think so. This is Garrett Ellis, our new financial director. You've never met him before." She turned to Garrett. "This is my mom, Georgina Walsh."

Garrett circumnavigated a mound of tomatoes and extended his hand to Cait's mother. "Nice to meet you, Mrs. Walsh." Then tossing a significant glance at Cait, he added, "Working with your daughter has been an enlightening experience." While he wasn't exactly smiling, his voice didn't have the same edge as before.

"How wonderful," her mother gushed. "It's so nice when you can work with people you enjoy. Cait's fortunate to have you in her school district."

Cait stifled a snicker.

"But you look so very familiar, I can't get over it. Do you do house painting?"

"Mom, no. Mr. Ellis did not paint our house. Ever. I'm sure of it."

"Hmm," her mother said, then abruptly walked away, picking up a large grapefruit in a bin and regarding it thoughtfully.

Garrett squinted at the older woman as if trying to solve a jigsaw puzzle without the reference picture. He then glanced at Cait. "Got enough angst out of your system today, Miss Walsh? Think you'll be ready to play nice with all the big kiddies tomorrow?"

"I don't know," Cait shot back. "But, honestly, I wouldn't count on it. Maybe you'd better just keep your distance if you don't want to get caught in the crossfire." She closed her eyes briefly, but when she opened them it was to the vision of her mother hopping up and down near a selection of fruit baskets. Oh, no.

"You're one of fruit and nut kids!" her mom said, pointing excitedly at him. "I *knew* I knew you from somewhere!"

Cait saw him clamp his lips together and bow his head. "Yes, ma'am. That's me. One of the fruit and nut kids." She had to concede he used considerable restraint. Under his breath, however, he added, "I'll force my father to cut me out of that damn basket photo tag if I have to turn his own lawyers against him."

Cait gave a short laugh. "A gift, from *your* house to *his?*"

"You're hilarious," he murmured. In a regular voice he said, "Pleasure to meet you, Mrs. Walsh. Hope you have a good evening."

"You, too, Mr. Ellis." Her mom waved from the pineapples.

Garrett looked once again at Cait. "See you tomorrow," he

said stiffly, heading to the checkout before she could reply.

"What a nice young man the fruit and nut kid is," Georgina said ten minutes later on their walk home. "And so attractive, too. Did you say he was your boyfriend, dear?"

"Financial director."

"That's right." Her mother inhaled. "What a delicious night. Something in that brown paper bag smells wonderful."

"The green peppers, perhaps?" Cait suggested.

"Yes, that's it. I like peppers, but Seth loves them."

"He sure does. Since Dianne isn't much for cooking them, I think he'll really enjoy his dinner with us tomorrow night."

Her mother tilted her head in bewilderment. "Seth's coming for dinner tomorrow?"

Cait's brother Seth burst through the back door, spotted her and grabbed her for a quick squeeze, lifting her feet off the kitchen floor in the process.

"Put me down!" she shrieked, kicking him once or twice on the shin until he finally relented. All in all, not much had changed since they were kids.

"Hey, Cait. Where's Mom?"

"Upstairs changing her outfit again. Every time she tries anything on, she's reminded of another garment she's misplaced. We search the closets and drawers until we find it, she puts it on and then remembers something she wore in nineteen seventy-two." Cait felt ready to collapse and it was only five-thirty. "I'm a little worn out," she admitted.

"I can see that. Dealing with this is exhausting as hell." Seth sniffed the warm kitchen aromas. "Stuffed peppers," he said, grinning at her. "My favorite."

"Yeah, yeah. I know."

He reached over and sandwiched her right hand between both of his. "So, you for sure think it's dementia setting in, huh?"

She fought the tears that had been threatening to come

out all day and nodded at her brother. "She has all the classic symptoms although, fortunately, she's neither depressed nor argumentative. At least not yet. But it seems like she's moving through the stages quickly. It's more than typical age-related memory loss, Seth. We've got to get her in to see Dr. Zimmerman next week."

"I live closer. I'll take her on Monday." He stopped. "No, wait. Monday's Labor Day. I'll make sure she gets in Tuesday."

"Seth, I'm scared. If the decline in her memory continues at this rate, soon she won't be able to take care of herself at all. What are we going to do then?"

"Let's wait and see what the doc says but, if need be, we can hire a nurse to come here to be with her. For peace of mind. Ours, of course." He shrugged. "Mom probably wouldn't be wild about giving up her independence. She's like someone else I know." He winked at her. "But maybe Dianne and I can convince her to move in with us eventually. We've got plenty of room, and Mia would be in toddler heaven with Grammy there."

Seth pulled her into a long hug and tried to lure her into a conversation about teaching. She resisted at first, but he finally managed to drag the problem out of her.

"So, you need to find a large, open space to host this event, the Harvest Hoopla? And you need to find it in New Brighton?"

"Exactly. I'll probably spend the weekend making inquiries."

"Consider them made."

What was he up to now? She leveled her most suspicious look at him.

"Would two acres of apple orchard be large enough?" he asked.

Then she remembered. "You didn't! You finally bought the property next door? When?"

"Once they started seriously hinting about selling, we put in an offer. They accepted our bid a month ago, but we weren't going to say anything until closing."

"Which is?"

"Next Wednesday," Seth admitted with a devilish grin.

"Things have been so crazy around here..." He shrugged and kissed the top of her head. "So, you didn't answer me. Will the orchard work?"

"Are you sure you—"

"Yes. And I can check downtown about permits, if one is even required for private property. You like?"

She hugged him. "It would be perfect."

Later, back at her apartment, Cait placed the keys to her mother's Escort in her jewelry box. After a long discussion, she and Seth had convinced their mom to forgo driving, and they gently wrestled away both sets of car keys on the condition that they'd ask Dr. Zimmerman's opinion next week. Cait already knew what he'd say, though. Her mom's memory was regressing in every way. Soon stop signs would be a mystery. She took a few yoga-like cleansing breaths, but they didn't help.

On the brighter side, this was one step in the right direction, and they'd all be together again on Monday for a little family Labor Day picnic. With Dianne and Mia there, too, her mother would be in high spirits.

Although Mom had managed to retain her positive attitude so far, this had to be hardest of all on her. Cait sighed. Her mother needed moments like Monday's event to cherish and look forward to, and Cait planned to provide them whenever possible. No matter what.

Fortunately, the arrangements surrounding the Harvest Hoopla were looking up. Despite Sour Grapes Ellis. She'd seen Garrett a time or two in passing, but mostly he'd avoided her during school that day. No big surprise there. But with Seth offering the use of the orchard, she and the other teachers finally had a starting point in their attack.

Now all she had to do was contact the vendors. Find out if they were willing to relocate to New Brighton. Ask if they could bring their own tables. Get in touch with members of the community who might donate supplies, services and decorations. Communicate the changes to the children and their parents while maintaining her professionalism. (Or, at least, not openly railing against the shortsightedness of the school's financial director in public.) Oh, and she had to figure out how to publicize the event without cost or the usual channels of support.

Not much work, eh?

Cait collapsed into her cozy armchair, an ugly burnt orange dinosaur that had once graced her father's den. If she put her nose up against the worn fabric, she sometimes thought she could still smell him there. Campfire smoke, hot coffee and paint chips.

Maybe she could call a Racine or Kenosha radio station for advertising, since neither New Brighton nor Ridgewood Grove had one of its own. This would cost money though. She and the children in her class could make signs and post them. It would be cute, but a lot of information needed to be conveyed on a single poster. She wondered if there was anyone in the community who might volunteer to make eye-catching...

Cait shot a look at the clock. 8:16PM Central Standard Time. That would be 9:16 Eastern. Not too terribly late. She fished in her tote bag, pulled out a tiny lavender business card, then she punched in the area code and telephone number. It rang twice before a chipper young woman answered.

"Hello? Hello?" the upbeat voice asked.

Cait inhaled and gathered her courage. She wasn't really being bad, she told herself. This was divine justice. "Hi, Marianne. This is Cait Walsh from Ridgewood Grove. I'm calling to ask you for a little help."

"Well, heck, yeah! It's about time. Ask away, girlfriend."

Garrett had a headache the size of the New England Patriots' home field. He was about ready to strangle his sister, who'd just lectured him long distance for damn near an hour. He wished Unlimited Minutes and Family Discounts had never been invented by enterprising phone company employees.

He opened the fridge. *Oh, hell.* No milk. No bread. No meat of any kind. Just some mustard packets, week-old leftover tuna salad and a half-empty jar of green olives with lost pimentos floating on the bottom. He checked the freezer. Ice cubes.

He grabbed his wallet and his keys. He should've known to buy more than a bag of broccoli and a bunch of grapes when he was out at Pummelhof's Market Thursday night, but seeing Cait there threw him. Now she and Marianne were in cahoots over this ridiculous Harvest Hoopla festival, the superintendent would be pissed when word of its covert reinstatement got out, he'd be back to square one in the search for the person siphoning money and, to top it all off, he couldn't so much as make a sandwich for the noontime Denver-Dallas game.

It was a quiet Sunday morning when Garrett entered the bakery. He'd picked up a few choice items from the deli next door and shifted the bag containing them from one hand to the other. Would Asiago cheese loaf or sourdough baguettes go better with smoked turkey and pepperjack? He was leaning toward the sourdough when the bell rattled, and he found himself face-to-face with Cait's mom. He could tell she recognized him.

"Good morning, Mrs. Walsh. How are you?" he said, feeling the edges of discomfort returning as he remembered his last conversation with her feisty, pain-in-the-ass daughter.

"Why, good morning, Mr. El—um, El—" She broke off looking perplexed.

"Ellis," Garrett supplied.

"Yes, Mr. Ellis. The fruit and nut kid!"

"That's right." He glanced around, glad the place was almost empty. "Please, call me Garrett."

"I came in here to buy some nice rolls for our Labor Day picnic tomorrow. They have wonderful honey wheat rolls. Have you ever tried them?"

"No," he said, "but I'm sure they're very good." He snatched three sourdough baguettes and lunged toward the counter. He needed to get out of here, and fast. Where the mom was, the daughter might follow.

"Oh, regular grocery stores don't carry freshly baked breads like these. Hank and I used to enjoy coming here after church, especially when the children were little. Cait loved smelling the sweet rolls, fresh out of the oven. Hank would lift her up so she could see them all." Mrs. Walsh sighed, a wistful look smoothing away some of the worry lines across her forehead. "She was Daddy's Little Girl for so many, many years."

Garrett stepped a little closer to her. The expression on Georgina's face revealed something he'd felt himself, more than once, whenever he'd remember what he and his grandmother did together. Grandma Maria didn't treat him like a second-rate kid. She didn't ignore him or threaten to never speak to him. The only bad thing she ever did was up and die when Garrett was twenty-one and leave him without a family advocate.

Garrett whispered, "I'm very sorry for your loss." Mrs. Walsh looked up at him. He was pained by the tears he saw glistening in her eyes.

She sniffled. "Well, never mind." She dug into her purse. "There was another important thing I wanted besides rolls, and now I can't find my list. You're such a nice young man, Mr. Ellis—Garrett—could you please look for me?"

She surprised him by thrusting her unzipped handbag at him. Garrett laid his bread down on the counter and sifted through lipstick and a bunch of female gunk before discovering a folded half-slip of paper.

He handed it to her along with the heavy brown purse. "Here you go, Mrs. Walsh. The paper says, 'Honey wheat rolls and cinnamon-raisin bread.'"

"Thank you." She was really staring at him now, no longer lost in memory. In fact, she looked alert and altogether too attentive. "You know," she said, "our lunch picnic is tomorrow from eleven to three. We're at Two-Thirty-Six West Lawn Avenue. I'd be delighted if you could join us."

Garrett inhaled. "Well, that's very kind of you, but—"

"Oh, I know you young people are always so busy, with so many plans, even on a national holiday. But Cait will be there, and I'm sure she'd be thrilled to see you. You haven't met my son Seth yet, have you?"

He shook his head.

"My, would he ever enjoy getting to talk with one of Cait's new colleagues! And you could meet his wife, Dianne, and my precious little granddaughter, Mia." Mrs. Walsh plunged into her purse and retrieved a photo. She flicked the image of a pigtailed cherub in sturdy toddler overalls at him and beamed. "Please join us."

While he could imagine just how thrilled Cait would be to see him at a private family function, he had to admit the idea appealed to his more devious side. Turnabout was fair play. Plus, she'd have to talk with him in her mother's home. He grinned at Georgina Walsh.

"I'll be there," he said. "Thanks for the kind invitation."

Cait parked in her mom's driveway behind Seth and Dianne's Land Rover and rushed to the door for the picnic. She loathed being late, but she'd been stuck in a discussion with the storyteller, who was excited to tell ghost tales at the Hoopla's new location. An hour of conversation couldn't sufficiently express his delight.

She clutched a tub of homemade potato salad and a bottle of sweet apple cider in one hand, unlocked the front door with the other and entered a house under siege. Mia's puppy Gibberish, a chunky golden lab, sprang high off the stairs with his three-year-old owner in hot pursuit, both missing Cait by inches as they rounded the corner toward the family room. Cait heard laughing voices in the kitchen. She smiled.

"Hello, everyone," she called out, flushing a bit from her hurried arrival and striding toward the kitchen with the expectation of seeing Seth in his usual spot snitching chips, Dianne leaning against the doorframe chatting while folding paper napkins and Mom giving the chili a final stir. Cait burst into the room and her smile froze.

Seth tossed a chip in the air, catching it in his open mouth. Dianne leaned over and smacked him in the nose with a stack of unfolded napkins. Her mother giggled before turning back to the pot on the stove. And Garrett Ellis, a paring knife in one hand and a cantaloupe wedge in the other, let his baritone laugh ring out across the kitchen as Seth said to him, "Your turn, buddy."

The potato salad tub slipped from Cait's fingers and landed unopened on the wood floor. She managed to re-grasp the apple cider bottle just in time. The delicate art of speech, however, was beyond her.

"Uh…" she said.

"Hi, Cait. Little klutzy today, aren't you?" Seth grinned at her, swooping up the potato salad and giving her shoulders a squeeze before lifting and swinging her as usual. Cait was too shocked to protest.

"Hi, Cait," Dianne said, her blond curls springing around her face like golden ribbons on a Christmas present. "I'd better make sure Mia and Gibberish haven't broken anything out there." She pointed toward the family room and left with a twinkling laugh.

"Hello, honey," Mom said, radiating the happy look of the innocent—even when she couldn't possibly be. Cait squinted at her mother then further narrowed her eyes at Garrett. He couldn't mask his triumphant gleam nor, she noticed with irritation, did he try.

"So good to see you, Cait," he said, putting the knife and fruit down with a fluid yet exacting motion. "Your brother has been challenging me to a little contest of skill." He pointed at the bowl of chips. "While I'm usually a popcorn man myself, I agree with Seth that these work pretty well, too."

He grabbed a chip, held it up for Seth's inspection, then tossed it high into the air, catching it neatly between his teeth. He grinned at her brother before crunching it with the smile of a satisfied tiger.

Seth laughed. "This guy's great. He hasn't missed yet and we've been at it for ten minutes." He slapped Garrett's shoulder. "I'm getting the grill started. See y'all in the backyard soon."

Ten minutes! How long had he been here?

Cait recovered her voice. "I'm sorry I was late. It seems I've been missing all the fun." Her tone was chilly, she knew, but she couldn't help it. She eyed her mother who searched in agitation for something near the stove. "What is it, Mom?"

"Where's the pepper grinder?" Her eyes brightened. "Oh, maybe on the dining room table." Mom skipped out of the room.

Left alone in the kitchen, Cait turned on Garrett. "And you're here...why?"

"Now, now, that's not very hospitable of you." He gave her a prickly look. "Keep up that attitude and you might just give me the impression that I'm unwelcome. I'm here only because I was personally invited. By your very own mother, I might add." He twisted his lips and began slicing cantaloupe again.

"Cripes, I knew it," she said under her breath, but not quite softly enough.

Garrett's eyes widened. "Am I that much of a disturbance in your life? No one else seems to be upset by my coming today. Your mom put me to work chopping fruit right away, figuring a 'fruit and nut kid' like myself would be an expert. Mia's sweet, Dianne's been friendly and your brother Seth's a riot."

He smiled—almost sincerely.

"It's so *nice* getting to know a colleague's siblings, isn't it?" he said. "I may just have to call up my new buddy sometime and chat with him about you." His grin turned into a glare. "Thought *you*, of all people, would approve of that tactic."

Cait put the apple cider on the counter with a bang and took four long strides closer. The man looked substantially more dangerous than usual, and she couldn't attribute it entirely to the paring knife he clutched in his fist.

"So that's what this is all about," she said. "You left me with very little choice, Garrett. I suddenly have no administrative support and not a penny that can be allocated by the school budget to run the festival. Mysterious resistance is plentiful, however." She put her hands on her hips. "I needed to use the few resources available to me. Marianne offered her help when she was here and—"

"Oh, don't talk to me about Marianne!" He slammed the knife down. "I mean it, Cait. You dragged my *sister* into this. I'm sorely tempted to get even with you. If your family weren't so damned nice, well..." He inhaled, picked up the knife again and made several very controlled incisions in the unlucky cantaloupe.

"Well...what?" she asked, biting her lower lip.

He shook his head, removed some rind and skewered a stray melon cube.

"Garrett—"

"Look, I'm trying to understand your point of view even though you're undermining everything I'm working toward. Marianne ranted for an hour yesterday about how you had to move the festival here to New Brighton and how I should've been more helpful. But neither of you understand the circumstances."

"Then enlighten me."

He leveled a stare at her. "You accused me of asking for your trust but yet not trusting you in return. If I tell you about the problem, Cait, I'm going to need both your absolute trustworthiness and your total discretion."

This took her aback, but she nodded solemnly.

And then he told her about money being skimmed out of district accounts. Fifty dollars here, a couple hundred there. How incidental items and extracurricular activities were the thief's main targets—the places where the discrepancies were most clear. Situations where a series of individuals were involved. Events like, oh, the Harvest Hoopla.

She stared at him, stunned.

"So, by canceling the festival, you'd hoped to draw out the person or people involved?" she said. "Hoped they'd try to get the money from another source?"

"Yes. I'd planned to limit the areas where more than two or three people require payment. Overcharging vendors, for instance, would be easier to check, and those people with access to the accounts would, likewise, be limited." He paused. "At last year's Harvest Hoopla alone, several hundred dollars were unaccounted for when the proceeds of the event were compared with its expenditures. The vendors, in particular, were shortchanged. I just discovered that by going over all the records this week, although I'd had my suspicions before."

"Wait. You can't be thinking that I—"

"No, not anymore," he told her. "Every penny you spent you documented. But at least seven other people had access to school district money for that event, and none of the others were as meticulous in their record keeping as you, Cait."

"Oh, boy." She thought of all the people who, in one way or another, were involved in the organization of last year's Hoopla. There were administrators, board members, other teachers. Jenna, Marlene and Loni, just to name a few. And Ronald, of course. She caught Garrett's eye. "Is this why the superintendent keeps meeting with you? Does he have a list of people he wanted you to check out?"

"You could say that." Garrett glanced away from her and, finally, she understood.

She felt her cheeks heat up. "So all of your questions and interest in talking to me—that was only because you wanted to find out if I was a thief?"

He looked her in the eye. "I apologize. Clearly that's not the case. I know I misjudged you initially, but I had to do my job, and I tried to correct my error quickly."

His *error*. As if his assessment of her character was as inconsequential in his eyes as an adding miscalculation on a piece of scratch paper.

It hardly mattered now, though. The hurt was already there. The thin veil of trust she'd allowed to creep in had, once more, been torn to shreds. Then again, she couldn't throw stones with a clear conscience. She'd snooped in his car after all.

"Cait—"

"I tried to investigate you, too," she blurted out. "I

searched all over your car. I'm sorry."

"My car?" He looked confused, then light dawned in his eyes. "Oh, you mean when I was in the bookstore?"

She nodded.

He flashed a grin. "That'll teach me to leave you alone with my possessions. Learn anything good?"

"You like Sting."

"Good detective work, Nancy Drew," he told her and went back to slicing melon. He acted nonchalant about it, but she sensed he, too, was hurt by her insincerity that day.

One thing she had to admit, though: Seeing him interact so genuinely with her family in those few moments when she first came in...that had shaken her up. It was as though he fit with her clan. As though he were one of them. That perhaps, in some areas, they weren't so far apart.

"Um, about Marianne," she said. "I wasn't trying to put a wedge between you two."

He cocked an eyebrow.

"Okay, but just a *little* wedge," she conceded. "She seemed so receptive when we met, and I needed an artist sympathetic to the project."

He looked at her, laughed and popped a skewered chunk of melon into his mouth. "I'd say you two were flawless in your choice of allies. I give up. I can't keep fighting you both." He shook his head again, sliced another piece of melon and offered it up to her on the end of the paring knife like a pink flag of surrender. The fruit floated on stainless steel a millimeter away from her lips. His eyes challenged her to accept it.

Her stomach flipped and an unknown magnetism made her lean in, pull the melon off with her teeth as daintily as she could and chew. Very sweet.

"Thanks," she whispered. She wiped away the little stream of juice escaping from the corner of her mouth and glanced up at him. He watched her every move, his expression serious.

Then one of those moments happened. One of those "she knew that he knew that she knew..." moments. Neither said a word, but their eyes confessed things and, against every act of reason, she knew their attraction to each other was real, mutual and not part of some charade.

Garrett finally broke the spell.

"Mind you," he said, those beautiful lips of his curving into an expression of open mocking, "you'd better watch that sassy behavior. I'm betting I could meet Seth for a round of golf and, after two beers or less, get the inside scoop on your childhood. In fact, if I were you, I wouldn't get too comfortable tonight, sweetheart, what with that big, long shelf you've got in the family room filled edge-to-edge with photo albums. Why, I think your mother would be more than happy to—"

Her mother breezed into the room carrying a new bright blue dishtowel, but no pepper grinder. Garrett closed his mouth but didn't stop smirking.

Tearing her gaze away from him, Cait turned her attention to Mom. "Did you find it?"

"Find what, dear?"

"The pepper grinder. Was it on the dining room table?"

"Oh, darn it. I didn't look." Her mother swiveled around and marched out the doorway again.

Dianne popped her head in ten seconds later. "I'm letting Mia and Gibberish loose outside. You two want to join us?"

~CHAPTER SIX~

STEP 6:
Add about 2 cups heavy cream.
(None of that whimpy low-calorie stuff, please.)
Whisk some more.
~From *Mr. Koolemar's Top Secret,*
Kool Kreme Ice Kreamations Recipe Book, pg. 97

Seth grilled the bratwurst to tawny perfection, Cait thought. Mom's chili, even without that extra hint of pepper, was satisfyingly spicy. The spread included corn on the cob, green beans and bakery rolls, as well as the apple cider, potato salad and cantaloupe.

After the main meal, Dianne went inside to mop up Mia, whose grass- and food-stained outfit looked like a Van Gogh painting. She also brought out dessert. Dianne had made brownies and Garrett, Cait gathered, had brought some kind of cake.

Mom spirited Seth away to get the Vanilla-Mocha Swirl from the basement freezer while she busied herself loading up the dishwasher and brewing coffee. She assigned Cait and Garrett the task of outdoor cleanup.

Cait collected the burnt tinfoil from the grill and a handful of dirty paper napkins from the picnic table then tossed them into a trash bag. But something significant nagged at her, and she decided it was high time she figured out the truth.

"What's your history with Shelley McAllister?" she asked him, knowing full well it wasn't any of her business, but she couldn't discount the relationship.

His dark eyes focused on her. He put down the grill scraper, grimaced and exhaled slowly, like he had to compose a legally binding document and needed the concentration.

"Our families have known each other a long time," he said, "and she and I dated, briefly, years ago. But I like to think I'm a better judge of character now than I was as an adolescent."

"So, you're not still...in touch?"

He laughed openly. "You're adorable when you're jealous."

"I'm not jealous." She was *not* jealous, damn him. Not exactly.

"Okay. Whatever you say. And, no, we're not remotely in touch. Truth is, I forgot she was living around here now, and I didn't recognize her new name when the superintendent showed me the list of board members." He shrugged. "She, of course, wouldn't have had any trouble recognizing mine once I was hired."

Cait tied the top of the Hefty bag and set it down. "Garrett, you realize she and several other board members had access to the Harvest Hoopla money last year. Are you prepared to investigate her as thoroughly as you were me?"

He didn't hesitate. "Absolutely."

"Then why can't we meet both our goals in this? I'm already set to host the festival, but the change in location ought to be enough to establish different precedents as far as organization and funding. Why not trap the offender in a controlled environment? One he—or she—knows well? One that worked for the thief before...instead of trying to create a new opportunity?"

He gave her a curious look. "Why is this event so important to you?"

"Because...I love it. My students love it. It's all about

celebrating autumn's abundance." She tried to put into words the meaning of the festival from her viewpoint, but she knew it was something he had to experience to understand.

"It's really fun, Garrett. But it's also more than that. It brings the community together. People look forward to it all year and, for some, it's their favorite seasonal event. It's certainly mine. And my mom's. She loves to participate in it, and I need to do things with her while I still can."

"You two are that close?"

"Well, yes. She's my *mother*. I'm afraid before long she won't remember all the things we used to share."

Something in his expression softened, but he turned his head before she could read the emotions she saw there.

"All right, all right," he said after a moment, sighing and motioning her nearer. His fingers brushed the tops of her shoulders making her pulse race. He leaned in, even closer than he'd been at the beach, and whispered, "I'm a ten-minute walk from here or, if you wanna give me a ride, a two-minute drive. We can go to my place and talk strategy."

Cait nodded, her heart hammering in her chest. "After dessert?"

"Okay," Garrett murmured, just as Mia came sprinting out of the patio doors.

Dianne emerged behind her daughter with a plate of brownies and Garrett's Black Forest cake. Seth trailed them carrying a half-gallon of ice cream, bowls and spoons. Their mom followed closely behind.

"So, when you come out to this Harvest shindig my sister's organizing, you'll have to stop by our place," Seth said, plunking down the ice cream tub. "We're in the green, mauve and white painted lady in the lot next to the orchard."

Garrett shot Cait a mischievous and rather exultant grin. "Love to see it, Seth," he said. "Hell, maybe you and I should get together even before the Harvest Hoopla and go golfing or something."

Cait scowled at her brother but he didn't take the hint.

"Sure," Seth said. "Sounds like fun."

Once in his condo, Garrett led her up to the fourth and highest floor, welcoming her into his home.

She was beyond nervous. She pinched at the cuff of her blouse and twisted the fabric to try to take the edge off her anxiety. It didn't work.

"See my iPod station over there?" Garrett pointed to a shelf that held his iPod and speaker system plus a few books and magazines. "I just got a new dock for it and plugged it in, but the rest of the shelf isn't organized yet. In fact," he looked around ruefully, "I wasn't expecting company today, so nothing in here is organized to impress guests. You'll have to ignore the mess."

Cait swiveled from side-to-side, trying to give the impression of observing the room but not really seeing the details. "I think it looks nice. Very spacious," she said, forcing a tiny smile.

"Well, thanks. I appreciate elbowroom." Garrett indicated the iPod again with a flick of his wrist. "Best thing about this place are my new speakers, though. I'm going to grab a few sheets of paper from the other room. Pick something good to listen to." He strode out the door thus granting her a few moments to collect herself.

She eyed the furnishings more attentively now as she meandered over to the music and books. Garrett lied. Other than a pyramid of candy wrappers on the far side of the counter and a few scattered magazines, no real mess existed anywhere.

Actually, if the few items he had in the room weren't of such fine quality, it would've appeared spartan. One long black leather sofa. A few essentials like lamps and a trash bin. A Persian throw rug over the parquet floor. Only one piece of artwork—a framed watercolor of three children playing by the beach.

She stepped closer to the picture. Two boys, roughly eight and twelve years old, and a girl who looked about four. Cait read the title at the bottom and the artist's initials. "Nantucket—M.E."

Marianne. It must have been painted from a photograph taken some long-ago summer. She looked closer. Garrett as a boy—dark hair, devilish grin, long tanned limbs, sand in his toes and on his shirt. Happy. The older boy, which must be Jacob—with hair a little lighter, limbs a little longer—running up ahead, gesturing for Garrett to follow. And the young girl, the chubby preschooler Marianne, sitting quietly with her pail and shovel, playing at the water's edge.

Tears pooled in Cait's eyes for no good reason. She tried to blink them away, tried then to rationalize why the image would make her cry. She was tired, maybe. Frustrated, certainly. Angry about what had happened to the school funds. Worried about her mother. Lonely...and alone. All these things might be the cause.

Only she knew they weren't.

It had more to do with something else. With life's preciousness and its temporal nature. How beautiful moments can exist in time and in memory, but can't necessarily last outside of them. About the innocence of three small children, blissfully unaware of future pain.

She swiped at her eyes and scrolled through his iPod's song list. Incubus. Shinedown. Amy Grant. Bob Dylan. The Fray. She did a double-take when she saw a handful of old classic tunes from *Singin' in the Rain* on his list, though, and clicked on the title track.

Garrett returned a minute later, smiling. "Interesting choice. It's sunny out."

She handed him the iPod, their fingers rubbing in the exchange. Cait's spine turned to Jell-O. "I like Gene Kelly, Debbie Reynolds and Ronald O'Connor," she said, moving a few steps away from him. Such close proximity had a strange effect on her lumbar system. "Besides, old movies always make me feel better," she muttered, sinking into his sofa.

He fiddled with the volume then asked, "Why? Are you feeling ill?" He held eye contact with her the way he might grasp a rope in a game of tug-o-war. She could tell he wasn't going to be the first to let go, so she shook her head and immediately pointed to the watercolor.

"That's beautiful," she said. "When did Marianne paint it?"

"Last year. I liked it, so she sent it to me as a late Christmas gift." Garrett skimmed his fingers along his jaw, his eyes on the painting, but he seemed focused on something farther away.

"You didn't see her last Christmas?"

"She spent it with her boyfriend's family. I'd intended to see her for New Year's but...there was a change of plans. I left a few hours before she arrived."

They didn't speak for a few moments.

"So," he said, "are you doing okay now that you've had a chance to relax?"

Cait nodded though this was, of course, a blatant lie. The cheery voice of Debbie Reynolds sang about dreaming of someone "the whole night through" in the background.

She held her breath. This man she'd been resisting in person, and even more vehemently in her mind, had wedged his way into every form of her consciousness. Her blood cells pranced inside of her, pulsing against the walls of her arteries as if to announce their heightened interest.

Garrett sat in the space next to her and slid over a few inches until their arms brushed lightly.

All he did was look at her, touch her. Bone, sinew, marrow, flesh, the tiny hairs blanketing her skin—every part of her began to join in the dance. She'd fought valiantly, but it was clear this was a battle she'd been destined to lose from the beginning.

"I need to find out who's behind the leak," he said.

She sighed. Ambition first, again. Another Fredric Lloyd situation—take two. If she could control it, she'd banish for good every emotional and physical reaction she had toward Garrett. He might enjoy many things, but the dream man she'd always wished for, the one who placed her ahead of all worldly goals, the soul mate who made her feel second to no one...this was not him.

Garrett had too many plans that didn't include her. And a

life out East to eventually return to.

Cait forced herself to concentrate on strategizing. "Okay, let's work through this. We need to keep track of everyone who makes any claim on the money earmarked for the festival. I've already set certain things up differently, though, because it's not going to be held on school grounds."

"Somehow, we need to alert the vendors to be careful without explaining all the details," he said. "To make sure they're getting the funds allocated to them but not accidentally tipping off the thief." He grabbed a pen from the end table and began scribbling some names down on his paper.

"What are you doing?" she asked when she saw her name written in red.

"These are people I've confirmed who requested money or wrote checks for the past three big festivals—last year's Harvest Hoopla, the Valentine Carnival of Love and the May Day Festival."

Cait read the names besides her own. Jenna, Marlene, Loni and Ronald were on it, just as she remembered. Shelley McAllister, of course, and two other board members, Doug Chippenak and Mike Firenzi. Oh, and Sonja their secretary. "So nine, including me."

"Right. You're in a position to know the teachers much better than I ever could. Do any of them have any financial woes at the moment? Any cash-flow problems?"

Jenna had four kids so, of course, money was always tight. But Cait knew her like a sister and couldn't imagine she'd steal from the district. She didn't know Marlene or Loni quite as well, but her intuition didn't lead her in their direction either.

She shook her head. "Not anything serious, Garrett. Nothing I know of anyway. Do you have any suspicions about the board or the administration?"

He wrinkled his nose. "Shelley's been after money as long as I can remember, but she married rich. Her husband's some kind of high-level banker, so she should be firmly in the black now, unless greed is an issue. As for Mike and Doug—both are successful businessmen. Mike has the Four Gates Country Club, which charges an arm and a leg for entry. Doug is vice president of Chippenak Chemical, a company owned by his uncle, so he's not hurting for cash either."

"And Sonja's simply too good natured to be involved in something like this," she said.

"Well, though this may be true, I needed harder evidence than that. With the superintendent's blessing, I read through all of her receipts and records from the past six months. They all checked out clean."

"Which leaves Ronald," she said.

"Yes." He sighed. "He makes an administrator's wages, but he's maxed out his credit cards and doesn't have any rich relatives to bail him out."

"That's true of a lot of people, though. Few people come from families remotely like yours."

He shot her an irritated look. "You've got that right."

Cait was reminded, once again, how little she really knew about Garrett's family life. True, his father was a pillar in the financial world, but those kind of men rarely blabbed about their home lives. And, sure, Garrett had a chatty sister, but even Marianne hadn't divulged in any detail the nature of the problems he faced. She wished she could ask him what went wrong and why he fled his home state.

"What did the superintendent say?" she asked instead.

"Ronald is his leading suspect, but the principal also spends a lot of time around the board members—especially Shelley, Doug and Mike. Of course, that could all just be for school politics."

An awful thought came to her. "Garrett, you don't think Shelley and Ronald are getting together in any other, um, manner...than in a political sense, do you?" She held her breath, stunned by the mental picture of the pale Principal Jaspers passionately linked with the scarlet Mrs. McAllister. Would their spouses believe it? Would anybody?

He looked at her, amused, then shook his head. "Not that I wouldn't put it past either of them, but I doubt it. Shell's got a tendency, as you well noticed, to hang on people she's interested in and ignore those she's not. I watched her with Ronald for two hours, and there was a friendly camaraderie but little else. At least not on her side. She and Doug Chippenak seemed to catch each other's eye fairly often. But I don't know if there's any kind of romantic history between them."

Cait swallowed, still trying to shake off the prior image. "Doug and Shelley?" she repeated. "It's not impossible, but I doubt it. Doug is such a low-key guy. Not too flashy. Kind of, well, boring."

"Exactly. Not Shelley's usual type. Without fail, she goes for high fliers and athletic men, which puts Mike Firenzi into the watch zone. With her, we shouldn't rule out anything."

Cait sank further into the sofa. The firm leather was soothing beneath her skin. She ran her hands along the cool black surface, closed her eyes and enjoyed the ending strains of the latest song. When she opened them again Garrett was watching her.

A few seconds later, he stretched his lean legs out in front of him and closed his eyes. She couldn't pull her gaze away from the way his Levi's clung to his muscles, making contact with all the important bends and straight-aways, defining them like a dictionary.

Garrett slid another two inches toward her and glanced down at the page with heavy concentration before setting it aside on the end table.

Gene Kelly crooned in the background as Garrett's attention turned on her. Her stomach spun around a few times before it flipped.

"Are you tired?" he asked.

She glanced at her watch. It wasn't even a quarter past four, but her body felt wrung with exhaustion. *Admit to nothing*, her rational brain screamed. "Not at all," she said.

Garrett slid toward her another couple of inches, and she realized her mistake. He shifted to face her. He reached over and gently tugged on her shoulder, maneuvering her into eye-to-eye contact. She held her breath, sure that even the dust particles had stopped falling.

"Cait," he whispered, "we're on the same side."

"I know," she said. And she knew that their strategizing and tenuous alliance underscored this truth. He'd chosen to let her fight on his team.

"Cait, I'm going to kiss you."

She nodded, feeling every internal vow shatter. This, too, she couldn't deny. "I know."

He trailed his thumb down the side of her face with a stroke as tender as if he were frosting a sugar cookie. His fingers came to rest just under her chin. He used them to tilt her jaw higher until her lips were just beneath his.

She felt the pressure of that extraordinary mouth against her own, the well-formed ridges indenting her lips as they merged. His mouth looked softer than it did from a distance. Ruddy. Red. Just a hint of roughness. It astonished her that within seconds she'd lost the ability to tell which part of the kiss belonged to her and which to him.

He drew the tip of his tongue along the fullness of her lips, and slipped between them to a warm welcome. He pressed against her with tantalizing gentleness—memory lost, future strategies forgotten, only this moment seemed real. "Oh, yes," she said.

"Cait", he said, the fingers of one hand effortlessly parting her legs and coming to rest like a hot iron on her upper thigh. Everything in the vicinity began to burn.

"I don't know if we should do this yet," she whispered, or tried to. But that was her logical mind talking. Her body made her add, "But I really want to."

To Garrett's ear, Cait mumbled something, but he didn't care if they never spoke in words again. His mouth delighted at being occupied this way, and his fingers itched to talk in the most primitive form of sign language.

He'd lost a bunch of memories in a second—all that indecision, resentment, discontent. Every unpleasant feeling was swiped clean, and he was left with a mystifying awareness of bliss. It'd been ages since he'd let someone, anyone, get this close. Admire a beautiful woman? Sure thing. Invite her to rummage through his soul? He almost laughed. Not hardly.

Once or twice, with a few fingers laced in Cait's spun-gold hair and others happily squeezing the softness of those supple leg muscles, Garrett tried to pull back his mind, his emotions. He knew his body was a lost cause. But there was something about being with *her* that made a deeper connection possible. That made him briefly consider a romantic life beyond the short term.

Her lithe body slid underneath him, and he grew vaguely aware of his role in assisting. He rocked on top of her carefully. Every delicate bone became a newly discovered treasure. They were fully clothed, and he wanted nothing more than to undress her. He flicked open a couple of buttons near the top of her white blouse, released the front clasp on her bra, traced the upper crest of her nipple with his fingertip. His tongue followed.

"Yum," he said.

Cait gasped. She couldn't believe what she was feeling. Fredric had never inspired sensations this intense. Nothing close. And, besides, any other kiss but Garrett's felt like a trillion light-years ago.

But the simple, invading memory of Fredric was like the jolt of real-life bad news upon awakening from a joyous dream. How could she forget the hurt she'd felt when a relationship that appeared good turned out to be a lie?

And as for Garrett...oh, boy. She'd already fought for control and lost. With him at the helm, she'd be left to count the minutes, hours, days until this new dream turned nightmarish. She had to put a stop to it now.

"Hey—" she began. Then he did something especially creative with his tongue and all she could say was "Ohhh."

Garrett delved deep into fantasy, reenacting the kitchen love scene from a movie he once saw. He became aware of a few more murmurings coming from Cait and kissed her harder. He slipped a hand between them, brushing the snap on her jeans and the top of the zipper. The film's characters had tried erotic experiments with black olives, syrupy cherries, rotini pasta, and...yes, oh yes...honey. But, first, restrictive garments had to go.

The snap flipped open with an insistent push of his thumb. "That's right," he told her jeans. He reached for the zipper, but five firm fingers clamped his wrist.

He pulled back and slid to the open side of the sofa, a dangerously narrow place, and tried to keep his heart from racing like an Indy 500 frontrunner. "Is everything okay?"

The beautiful woman in front of him exhaled heavily and reclaimed her own lips with a quick darting of her tongue. "This is all a little fast for me," she told him.

He swallowed. "I like you, Cait."

"Well, I like you, too."

Cait realized she was speaking the truth aloud and it threw her. Fear seeped into her arteries and began a frenetic race through her bloodstream. She grasped at her open shirt, eyeing Garrett with growing anxiety, and he studied her expression in return. Something unspoken passed between them and she knew that he knew…

"It's just—" she began. "I told you I was hurt before. Seriously hurt, Garrett. I thought I'd worked through that but—but, I guess, I'm afraid if—"

"I get it." He leaned in and gave her forehead a smooch. "You're not sure you wanna eat breakfast here yet. Is that it?"

She gave his shoulder a tiny squeeze. "Yeah, that's it."

"Okay."

Garrett forced in a few lungfuls of air, laboring to get his fantasies of her naked out of his mind for thirty seconds. "We'll cool it. For now. But I've got a question."

"Yes?"

He looked at her and grinned. She was so lovely…and so tense. Her face was splotched with patches of heat, and her brow was all scrunched up. "Have you got any allergies I should know about?" he asked her, using his innocent voice.

"None I'm aware of."

"Good," he said. "Because I've got this really tremendous fantasy for us someday involving vanilla ice cream and fresh strawberries where…"

Cait gave his chest a hard shove.

"...where...aaah!" He fell on the floor with a thump.

She wasn't exactly smiling, but there was a light in her eyes that gave him hope.

"That's okay," he said. "Blueberries'll work, too."

~CHAPTER SEVEN~

STEP 7:
Add about 1/4 cup of cherry-flavored syrup.
Mmm, mmm, tasty!
~From *Mr. Koolemar's Top Secret,*
Kool Kreme Ice Kreamations Recipe Book, pg. 97

Cait had no idea how she'd managed to drive home. Ten long miles in a blizzard of emotions counted as unsafe conditions. There should've been signs: "Hazards Ahead—Beware." "Slow Down." Or, like the old Bon Jovi album, "Slippery When Wet."

What was she going to do?

She hadn't felt this vulnerable since, well, since that chilly morning at Sydney's Kingsford-Smith Airport when Fredric said, "So sorry, Cait, but Paige and I were meant for each other. I didn't realize it until I was back home again." Back home.

Garrett lived out of his element now, too. What would happen when the other girlfriends of his past resurfaced? The other tenacious Shelleys, who held their collective breaths, waiting for him to get bored with the Midwest? Cait knew she was just a stand-in until the real thing came along for him. Someone to amuse him until he returned home. To the East. To his family's multimillion-dollar corporation. To where he belonged in society.

Oh, she knew how it'd start. He'd say he was going back "just for a visit," but ambitious men behaved in predictable patterns. What would happen next was a given: He'd leave her.

She felt a cramp in her gut that traveled upward, painting her body from chest to head in rising achy strokes. The grief was already there, priming her.

She groaned. Heartbreak aside, other problems existed in the world. Nearly forgotten in the midst of their lip-lunging was the odd connection between Shelley and Ronald. Or maybe Shelley and Doug. Or Shelley and Mike. Yikes. What was going on there?

Then there was her mother. It seemed Mom had been forgetting to take her high blood pressure medication. Seth found a full bottle in the bathroom cabinet, almost untouched from her last prescription refill in June. His first call tomorrow morning would be to Dr. Zimmerman.

She stumbled into her apartment, collapsed on the bed and curled into a fetal ball. She tried to breathe deeply. To let the anxieties go. But her fears pelted her until she fell into a fitful sleep, haunted by unsettling dreams.

Marlene, perched on one of Cait's classroom desks before school the next morning, raised her fist in a victory cry as she spoke. "Hurray for the Hoopla! Long live its fearless leader!"

"To Cait Walsh," Loni said. "Hip, hip..."

"Hurray!" Jenna and Marlene cried.

Cait grinned, glad she was able to make them all so happy, but unable to tell them the real reason she'd pulled it off. Garrett had sworn her to secrecy.

"Thanks, ladies," she said. "It seems the financial director was not as unreasonable as we'd all thought."

"Good thing," Marlene deadpanned, "or we'd have had to kill him."

Loni slapped her knee and laughed, but Jenna didn't take

her eyes off Cait. She seemed to be waiting for something. A sign of some kind, maybe. Cait smiled at her and turned her attention back to the chapter books she was sorting.

"You know, Cait," Jenna said, speaking up at last. "Maybe the guy likes you. Maybe that's why he changed his mind. Why he was so reasonable."

"Oh, I don't think—" she began.

"Oh, but I do." Jenna grinned. "He's hot."

"Shush, *Mrs*. Murray," Marlene said. "You're married."

"And so are you," Jenna told Marlene. "Doesn't mean we aren't allowed to notice these things." She focused her gaze on Cait. "I think you should ask him out."

Loni, the oldest teacher in their group, gasped and looked at Jenna as if she'd suggested hosting a rattlesnake exhibition. "That's insane. Sure, the man's handsome, but teachers shouldn't date their administrators."

"Teachers shouldn't date their *bosses*," Jenna corrected. "But Garrett isn't her boss. It's not against the law, or even school policy, for them to go out. What do you think, Cait?"

Cait glanced at her friend. The woman probably wore that saucy expression in her sleep. It was just Jenna's nature. "Save your matchmaking skills for someone worth using them on," she told the dark-haired teacher. "I'm not the best candidate."

"It's been a year now, Cait. You're young. And the Fredric thing is long past. It's time to try again."

"I don't think so."

Jenna grinned at her but wisely let the subject drop...until Marlene and Loni left the room ten minutes later.

"Okay, girlfriend," Jenna said, firmly shutting the classroom door. "No more censored small talk from you. Gimme the real story about you and the financial director, and gimme it now."

"There's no story to—"

"Cut the bull." Her eyes bored right through Cait's attempt at a stony façade. "He kissed you, didn't he?"

"How did you—"

"When will you learn? I'm all knowing," her friend said with a laugh. "I'm the mother of *four*. I know how to read faces."

Cait knew it was futile to withhold information now. She threw her hands up and filled Jenna in on the Labor Day luncheon and the romantic highlights, careful to leave out Garrett's reason for being hired and downplaying his family's background.

"We kept running into each other and butting heads," she explained. "Then my mom and brother got involved and I met his sister... It's one of those cases of people being thrown together too much, or something, but it's not like there's anything between us. We're not a *couple*. We're just two people trying to figure out how to make the festival work. On a limited budget," she added, since restricted funding was the reason she gave for Garrett having canceled the Hoopla originally.

"Yeah, and I'm a royal princess from the House of Windsor," Jenna said. "But hey, if you say that's your intention, I'll take your word for it." She winked. "But I wonder, is that really *his*?"

Cait shrugged and tried to be honest where she could. Jenna had a way of hitting too close to home.

"I don't know," Cait admitted. "Garrett's different than I first thought. He's smarter. Funnier. Kinder. But I don't know what he's looking for. And if it's only going to be another short-term thing, something to keep him busy until his need for social parity kicks in, I'd rather skip it."

"Cait, Fredric didn't leave you because you weren't up to his social level, and you know it."

"But Paige was from—"

"Paige was the high school girl that got away. Yes, she was from an upper-crusty family, but the real reason Fredric went back to her was because he was a social-climbing scumbag who wanted quick money and an easy life. You were too good for him, and as for Garrett, you're better than anyone he could dredge up from Connecticut...or from any other state for that matter."

"That's nice of you to say."

"It's not nice, it's true. God, I wish you'd have punched out that Aussie bastard when you had the chance. If I'd have been standing next to you—"

"I know, I know, Jenna. You'd have left-hooked Fredric right there at the Qantas gate."

"Exactly. And a broken nose might've jostled that idiotic brain of his into a few moments of reflective thinking."

Cait picked at her thumbnail and paused before speaking. "I wouldn't want him back, you know."

"I know."

"But I miss some of the memories."

"I know that, too," Jenna said, reaching out and giving Cait's arm a gentle squeeze. "Which ones most?"

She swallowed. "Ah, a few romantic things here and there. Having someone to cuddle with and talk to. The poetry maybe. He could quote Wordsworth." She grinned at her sympathetic friend. "Mostly the ice cream we ate on our walks."

Jenna giggled. "Well, from what you've told me, Garrett's also an ice cream lover."

"That he is. I'm already getting sentimental about the Ice Kreamations we've shared."

"They're the best, aren't they?" Jenna sighed, her lashes fluttering dreamily. "The Volcanic Mocha Explosion is orgasmic."

Cait laughed out loud. "I guess I'll have to add that one to my list of new flavors to try."

"Don't miss it. Mr. Koolemar's originality is unsurpassed."

Cait couldn't help but wonder, were she to be alone again with Garrett, if *his* originality would be equally inspiring.

"Can I have a bunch of fliers to take home, Miss Walsh?" Miranda asked later in the day. "I'll put 'em up in good spots."

Cait smiled at the tall girl with adorably frizzy long brown hair. "Of course. My friend sent plenty."

Massive understatement. Marianne's FedEx package arrived at the school that morning and must've contained five hundred brightly colored posters announcing the Harvest

Hoopla and all the pertinent details of the event. She also sent a beautiful autumnal centerpiece for the classroom. Cait opened the package in class and hung one of the posters on the bulletin board for her students. They screeched with delight.

"Can I take some, too?" Jeremy shouted out, then belatedly raised his hand, his freckled face looking hopeful.

This spurred a chorus of "Me, too"s and "I want some"s.

"Class. *Class.* Everybody please take your seats," Cait said, raising her voice only slightly. "As I just told Miranda, we have more than enough fliers. Everyone may take home a stack. Just be patient, please, while I pass them out."

After a mad dash to equitably distribute the fliers before the children left to music, Cait collapsed at her desk. But she only allowed herself a few seconds. There was no such thing as "rest" in a busy teacher's day. She grabbed the blueberry muffin she didn't have time to eat at lunch and bundled up the pages she had to Xerox during this prep period. She raced to the copy room.

Alone for a few brief moments, she alternated nibbling on her muffin with pressing buttons. Her breath caught as she remembered Garrett's reference to blueberries, and she felt her face turn hot. She was glad the copy machine was the only witness.

She finished eating, reached for the math sheet she planned to assign for homework that night and gave her watch a quick check. Nine minutes until she needed to pick up her class from music. She fiddled with the colored paper drawer and set her teaching master on top of the glass plate.

A sniff tickled the back of her neck. She swiveled around, eyes wide, her hands flying automatically upward.

"Kinda jumpy today, aren't you, Cait?" Garrett said, paying no attention to personal-space conventions as he leaned in and gently shoved her out of the line of sight from the hallway. He closed the copy room door.

With the Xerox machine taking up half the space and boxes of unopened paper stacked on the floor, there was no room to stand. She couldn't maneuver. Her gaze darted to the door then to Garrett's grinning face.

"What are you doing?" she said. "Someone could come in."

He wet his lips, bent down and, with the gentlest flick of his tongue, he licked her bottom lip, igniting flames in her mouth as he traveled from one corner to the other. She couldn't breathe. She couldn't speak. But she felt herself drawn back into him. It was as if the intervening twenty-four hours hadn't happened, and they were at his condo once again...on that black leather sofa, arms around each other, bodies entwined.

She'd been avoiding him today, but those lonely hours were irrelevant and forgotten when he brought his whole mouth onto hers. She was certain the second hand of her wristwatch stopped ticking until Garrett finished kissing her.

He pulled away and she immediately missed him.

"I got a lead," he whispered. "Sonja mentioned in passing that Shelley and Ronald are meeting tonight. I thought maybe we could observe them. See where they go and what they do."

"You mean *spy?*"

"Well, I like to think of it more as 'information gathering.' It's part of my job." He wrinkled his nose. "Yep, spy, I guess."

She laughed. "What upstanding, moral citizens we are."

"Want to come with me at five o'clock?"

She bit her lip, considering. What if they got caught? "O-okay," she found herself saying anyway.

Garrett squinted at her. "You sure? It's all right if you don't want to. I can tail 'em myself," he said, in a voice reminiscent of a character on *NCIS: Los Angeles*. She couldn't help but laugh again.

"No, I'll go. I want to." Which was foolishly true.

He ran his finger down her forearm. Her mirth turned to shivering and then to a delicious burning as the sensation set in.

"Good. Catch ya later, doll." In an instant he was gone.

She didn't move for a precious minute. She closed her eyes, breathed. These fantasies must stop, she told herself severely.

Cait opened her eyes and pushed the green copy button, trying to push away her desires for Garrett Ellis at the same time.

A red Beemer wasn't the best choice for traveling incognito, Garrett decided as they pulled out of the school parking lot a few minutes before five. He eyed Ronald's ugly beige Seville and thanked heaven that the principal didn't seem too observant.

"Who the hell drives Cadillacs anymore anyway?" he said to Cait, wincing at the way Ronald handled his vehicle. "Did you see that wide turn? You'd think the guy was steering a semi."

She laughed. "Not everyone can afford a fancy sports car. And not everyone who buys one knows how to drive theirs like you do." She gave him a gliding, head-to-toe once-over. "You're just too cool for words, aren't you? Spiffy car. Tailored clothes. Hotshot attitude." She sniffed the air. "Delectable cologne."

He shot her his most irresistible grin and leaned in her direction, hoping to tempt her into a kiss. "Like it, do you?"

"Mmm-hmm." She blushed and looked out the window, ignoring his silent offer. He snaked his hand onto her lap to squeeze her fingers. She squeezed back then said, "Keep your concentration on road, Cary Grant."

Now he laughed. Yeah, if only he were so smooth. Maybe then he wouldn't be spending the night alone.

But, okay, he'd admit it. He liked to think of himself as moderately debonair. Her words, however, held a hint of censure in them despite the cologne compliment. She might admire his looks, but she wasn't a woman impressed by extravagant purchases, designer labels or swanky digs. It would take qualities of more substance to win her over, and he didn't have a lot of experience with that kind of lady.

He focused on the road, keeping a respectable distance from Ronald's tank of a car. So far, tailing him proved easy.

"Where do you think he's meeting Shelley?" Cait asked. "Any educated guesses?"

"You looking for fill-in-the-blank, true-or-false or a five-hundred-word essay?"

"None of the above. Think multiple choice."

"Okey-dokey." He ran through a mental list of options. "(A) Secret School Board Meeting at Posh Restaurant, (B) Steamy Lovers' Rendezvous at Sleazy Motel, (C) Pastry-Eating Contest at French Bakery or (D) Wild-n-Wacky Martini Happy Hour at Hot Local Bar."

Just then the Seville turned into the entrance of the Four Gates Country Club. He heard Cait gasp next to him.

"Oooh," she said, eyeing the Members Only sign and the subsequent list of entry restrictions. "How about (E) Lack of Connections and/or Insufficient Funds to Determine Answer?"

He nodded. This might be tougher than he'd anticipated.

"Gotta admit," he said, "I hadn't expected them to be going to an aerobics class. But the explanation is probably simpler than we think. Ronald and Shelley must be meeting Mike Firenzi here for dinner. I gather they've got some kind of healthy-gourmet café inside."

"For people who like their tofu with a side of caviar?"

"Exactly." He surveyed the lot. True to its name, the Four Gates Country Club had four separate entrances, each manned by a guard in a box next to an electrically controlled steel gate.

Ronald's car pulled through one entrance and, after waiting for another vehicle to pass through, Garrett drove up.

"Good evening, sir. What's the purpose of your visit tonight?" said a pompous-looking college kid in a tux.

Putting on his best prep-school voice, Garrett tossed him a smooth lie, "We're considering membership at the Club and wished to see the facility." He gave Cait a quick look and she added a convincing nod.

"Very good, sir, ma'am. Do you have a tour invitation from Mr. Firenzi or, perhaps, a visitor's pass for the evening?"

"I work closely with Mike Firenzi," Garrett said, purposely cryptic. "The Club came highly recommended."

The boy gave him a tight smile. "Mike Firenzi doesn't usually forget his father's request to hand out advanced passes, but fortunately the elder gentleman is in tonight. I'll alert him to your arrival, Mr.—?"

"Ellis. Garrett Ellis."

"One moment please." The kid looked like he was auditioning for a part in a spy flick, whispering into the phone with covert precision, protecting the free world from danger.

Cait nudged him and he saw the principal descend from the Seville and vanish into the entrance. *Dammit, kid. Hurry up.*

"You may park in the lot to your right, Mr. Ellis. The Club's owner, Anthony Firenzi, will meet you both in the lobby. Please wait for him there."

He gave the kid a curt nod, tapping a finger on the steering wheel while the Boy In Black took a lifetime lifting the gate.

Finally parked, Garrett turned toward Cait. "Look, we've got to move fast on this. I think we should split up and try to get information where we can." He paused. "Plus, it probably wouldn't be good for us to be seen together snooping."

She nodded and slid out of the car. "Okay. If I'm detained somehow, you'll be on your own. And vice versa."

He leaped out of his side at the same time. "But wait—how will you get home if we're separated?"

She pointed an index finger at the cabs lined up near the side entrance. "I'll be fine."

He winked at her, and they began racing toward the glass front doors, only to see Shelley McAllister inside the lobby, her arm around Ronald. She was leading him toward the private members entrance that signaled "Spa and Fitness" to the left and "Dining Room" to the right.

"I'll go in first," he told her.

"Fine. I'll head through the service entrance on the side and see if I can spot them in a bit." She granted him a dazzling smile that sent his pulse skyrocketing. "Good luck, Garrett."

"You, too."

Garrett tailed the board member and principal through the center of the lobby and into the hallway where a member's pass was required for admittance at a door about ten yards away. Shelley sashayed down the hall, Ronald waddling by her side. She held up a plastic card for the computer eye to scan. It beeped, the heavy door swung open and they both walked through.

Garrett took two steps in their direction, hoping to grab the door before it locked shut, when he felt a tap on his shoulder.

"Mr. Ellis?"

Garrett turned to the voice. "Um...yes?"

A white-haired, stern-looking gentleman held out his hand, flanked by a bald younger guy with a glossy green folder, a clipboard and a Membership Staff nametag.

"I'm Anthony Firenzi," the elderly man said as Garrett clasped the roughened skin. "I hear you know my son."

Damn. Thwarted in under a minute. "Yes, indeed, sir," he said with a final regretful glance at the swinging door.

"Where's your wife?"

"My what?"

"The woman accompanying you in the car? My young man at the gate said to expect two visitors."

"Oh...my *friend*. She dropped me off and...left." *Wife?* Sure, he liked Cait but... He let that thought go for now. He prayed she'd stay out of sight or, better yet, take a cab home.

Anthony Firenzi grinned. "So you have some time to devote to this tour then?"

Garrett acknowledged his defeat silently before pasting on an enthusiastic smile. "That's right, sir. I do, and thank you for meeting with me on such short notice. I've been looking forward to seeing the Four Gates Country Club for some time."

Cait managed to gain admittance through the service entrance by holding the door for a couple of young workers struggling with garbage sacks. Being that they seemed unconcerned with protocol, unlike the snooty guy at the gate, she slipped inside without a second glance and probably without a second thought.

She took in her surroundings. She stood in the midst of a

small room with clean walls and a tiled floor. There were four doors: one leading outside and three others with brass placards above them reading *Kitchen*, *Equipment* and *Laundry*, respectively.

She peered through the kitchen one and saw that it led to a hallway. The same was true for the equipment door. This place was big on hallways. She'd just reached the laundry door when she heard the kids with the garbage bags coming back. She slid into that hallway and began striding with faux purpose toward its end, which led to...another room.

This one also had clean walls and a tiled floor, plus fifty shelves stacked with "FGCC"-monogrammed fluffy white bath towels. They reminded her of stuff she'd seen in glossy interior designer magazines. She touched one gingerly. It engulfed her finger in warm fibers and sprang back into shape when she pulled away.

Cait could hear the sounds of washers, dryers and chattering females one room over. She searched for an escape from the Downy-fresh chamber but jumped when a voice materialized beside her. The voice said, "Oh, good. You're early. Kendra, right?"

"Umm..." Cait said swiveling to look at an older woman dressed in gray, one with lynx-soft footsteps.

The lady didn't give Cait a chance to answer. "I'm Doris, the head of laundry services. Mr. Firenzi told me to expect you." The woman gave her a warm smile. "Once you've changed into your uniform, you can begin by taking a cart of clean towels down to the women's locker room." She pointed to a metal cart near the far wall. "You might need to make a couple trips. These woman go through 'em real fast."

"I, um..." Cait wanted to explain, but what would she say? *I'm not the new maid, ma'am. I'm just breaking and entering.* She opted for a deceptive but at least fairly innocuous question. "What's the quickest route to the women's locker room?"

"Ah, a speedy worker then, are you?" The woman laughed. She explained the directions, pulled out a folded Four Gates uniform and handed it to Cait with a pat on the shoulder. "Just ask me if you have any other questions, dear."

"Uh, thanks, Doris."

The lady walked briskly and soundlessly into the other room leaving Cait to stare at the light gray uniform in her arms. Great. What would a Bond Girl do in a situation like this?

She gulped some air and followed Doris's instructions to the women's locker room, debating whether she should take the ruse a dangerous step forward by actually changing into the uniform. Would she really sneak around under the pretense of being a maid?

Good God, no!

She slipped into the room and shoved the uniform into an empty locker before glancing around. It was a fancier changing area than what might be found in a five-star hotel. Really over the top. Golden baskets of toiletries hung conveniently on the modern-art-inspired walls. Little bottles of salon-quality shampoos and conditioners. Disposable razors. Packets of Q-tips.

Cait rolled her eyes. She'd take her showers at home, thank you. But those fluffy towels mesmerized her. She stood near a rack of them and poked at another one. It sprang back. *Boing!*

The door flew open.

Cait turned her back to the door, grabbed a towel and threw it over her head, rubbing as if drying her hair. Oh, yeah. She was a master of disguises all right. How could she get out of here fast?

She crab-walked in the direction of the exit. The woman who'd entered was humming to herself in a voice Cait would recognize on a mountain in Tibet. Shelley! Oh, damn.

One thing she knew for certain, Shelley would not be divulging school district secrets to herself alone in the women's locker room. Cait held her breath until she heard one of the toilet stalls lock shut. Now was her chance to escape.

She flung the towel into the laundry hamper, raced out of the door and down the hall. She didn't spot Ronald anywhere, thank goodness, but Garrett was nowhere to be seen either. This was one massively failed operation, and she felt both guilty and cowardly. She hated to imagine Garrett's disappointment in her, but she couldn't pull this off any longer.

She skittered to the "service" area, evading Doris, and burst out the door and into the night. She hailed a cab for home.

When she got there, she grabbed her mail and trudged up to her apartment, her heart still pounding. Thoughts of Garrett rolled through her mind. What had happened to him? Where was he now?

Swallowing, she glanced at her mail. The heaviest item was, ironically, the Ellis Corporation Catalogue she'd requested for The Nutty Fruit Gift Baskets. She flipped through a few pages, looking for photographs of the Ellis family, but there weren't any. Just lots of picturesque displays of fruit.

Towers.

Pyramids.

Cornucopias.

One display featured a heaping arrangement of nuts and dried fruit in a turkey-shaped basket tub. She smiled, set the thick catalogue down and checked her answering machine. No messages.

So Garrett must still be out in the field.

She sighed and decided she needed a hot shower after her day. A long one. With her own shampoo and her non-monogrammed towels. So what if they didn't "spring" back? They were warm, familiar.

An hour later, when she finally emerged from the bathroom, her message light was blinking. She pressed the PLAY button.

"Hi, Cait." Garrett's voice filled the studio apartment and, though she knew he couldn't see her, that he wasn't even on the line any longer, she glanced nervously around room as if he could. She straightened her papers and brushed dust off the counter.

"So, I guess I'm not much of a secret agent, because I not only lost sight of our suspects the minute I ran into the Club, but I got finagled into purchasing a two-month trial membership. I sure hope you fared better." His laughter surprised her. He sounded so natural, so at ease with his own blunders. By contrast, she never forgave herself for the slightest miscalculation. She always felt, maybe arrogantly, that she should know better.

"Firenzi Senior gave me a never-ending tour, but I didn't catch sight of our people again. When last I saw them, they were headed for either the fitness center and spa or the dining area. Knowing Ronald's sweet tooth, I doubt he was getting a facial. Wish I had more news. Give me a call later, and we can compare notes. Oh, and Cait—let me know if you're up for a game of golf sometime. Their course is damned impressive."

"So, how's it going in Washington?" Jacob asked Garrett over the phone.

"Wisconsin."

"Oh, yeah. I heard Marianne couldn't even convince you to come home for a visit," his brother said, sounding incredulous, though that news shouldn't have surprised him.

"Nope," Garrett said.

"Didn't I already give you the We-Really-Need-You-Here speech? Or how about the It's-So-Boring-Without-You plea?"

"Glad I add entertainment value. It's always a laugh to watch me and Dad battle it out, isn't it? Microwave some popcorn, grab a soda and kick back."

"That's not what I meant," his brother said quietly.

"I know." Garrett cradled his head in his palm and squeezed his eyes shut to block out that familiar ache.

"You'll come back for my birthday, won't you? No one will have to even know it's you. Or me, for that matter. I've got a Spiderman mask."

Garrett laughed. Jacob always had the best birth date, although it was hard to believe the guy was turning thirty-four. He acted like he was fourteen.

"Halloween or not," Garrett said, "who'd ever believe

Spiderman could break his leg? Isn't that against Superhero rules or something?"

"Maybe, but I'm an original."

No kidding, Garrett agreed silently. *He* was the one who was the imitator. And apparently a screw-up at that, as their father had so succinctly put it last New Year's Eve. Maybe he deserved to be cut loose from the family. He couldn't do the things Jacob did, or do them as effortlessly. And his own talents had been regarded as irrelevant for so long he'd almost forgotten he had them.

Resentment rose inside him, and he had to remember not to take it out on his brother. His father's favoritism was never Jacob's fault. Garrett wouldn't let it poison a good sibling relationship.

"Look, I won't promise about Halloween, but I'll think about it. If I can wrap up a few things here, maybe I'll be able to get away for the weekend. I'll buy you a birthday beer—or whatever Spiderman's having that night."

"I'll keep my tentacles crossed that you'll show up." Jacob drew in a long, noisy breath. "Hey, I know this is kind of a crazy thing, but Marianne was prattling on about some Cait person you'd met. You aren't—" He hesitated. "I mean, the reason you're staying away isn't because of a woman, is it?"

"No," Garrett answered honestly. Well, at least that'd been true up until now, but Jacob didn't have to know the details.

"Thank God. 'Cause you know women. They'll screw you up good if you give them a chance."

"I've heard this lecture before."

"But were you paying attention?" Jacob said. "Learn from my experience. Keep it hot. Keep it fresh. Keep it short-term."

Garrett had played this very game under Jacob's tutelage for years. He understood it and could see the sense in it from his brother's point of view. But there was something vaguely unsatisfying about that lifestyle. He could, if he worked at it, think of Cait in those terms, but he doubted she'd think of him in that way. He couldn't imagine her consenting to a mere fling.

No, she had Long-Term Commitment written all over her

luscious body.

He shook his head to himself. He and Cait didn't have anything permanent going. It probably wouldn't work if they did, despite her sweetness, brightness and cuteness. He was just in the mood to be contrary to everything typically "Ellis" tonight.

But the devil in him had to ask his brother one more thing. "So, how are you and Mindy doing these days?"

"Mindy? Oh, her. We broke up *days* ago. Been seeing this nurse. Patricia. She does fantastic things with latex gloves..."

~CHAPTER EIGHT~

STEP 8:
Add 1/2 teaspoon of real vanilla extract.
Absolutely no skimping on tasteless imitation stuff,
you hear?
~From *Mr. Koolemar's Top Secret,*
Kool Kreme Ice Kreamations Recipe Book, pg. 97

"**O**kay, let's talk motives," Cait whispered over her platter of cheese fries and a thick hamburger. "It's time we put our intuition and imagination to work, instead of relying on pure logic."

Garrett glanced around the New Brighton diner, appreciating their corner booth. The red vinyl was as cheesy as the greasy, cheddar-covered fries, but it was a nice secluded spot. For a public locale, anyway. He'd have preferred his place, her place or a locked broom closet, but Cait was playing it cool tonight, and he'd have to take what he could get.

He reached for a fried mozzarella stick and dipped it in the vat of marinara sauce. Delicious.

"Mmm," he told her. "You picked the perfect restaurant for a Friday night dinner."

She plucked the pickle off her burger and glared at him. "I

know. Now, c'mon. You insisted on getting together to discuss the investigation. Let's discuss."

"Okay, okay." He took a bite of his own juicy burger and a slurp of his banana-chocolate milkshake. Incredibly rich. At this rate, he'd gain ten pounds before the end of September. "Well, common sense says that money is the draw. We need to find the person who has the most to gain from an increase in fortunes."

She shook her head. "That may be true, but step away from reason, logic and common sense for five minutes. What if it's not about the money? What if it's about something else—like revenge? Does someone have a chip on his or her shoulder? Something that might motivate an attack on the school district?"

Sheesh. She had a good point. "All right, let's say this whole mess is not *solely* about getting cash. How then, do we determine where the hidden source of resentment lies? Some kind of 'job satisfaction' test?"

She raised her eyebrows, a motion that made his pulse race and his blood heat up every damn time. It drew attention to her clear, intelligent eyes. But, from the look in them, was she thinking about hot passionate nights in his arms? No. She was thinking about Motives For Revenge. He snapped off the end of a fried mozzarella stick with his teeth and watched those eyes widen.

"What if we *did* give a test? What if we asked some specific questions geared at determining why, for instance, Shelley McAllister wanted to be a board member? That would have to give us some clues, wouldn't you say?"

"I already asked her that."

Cait felt her blood pressure rise when Garrett said those words. Of course he'd already asked Shelley. They must've had ten thousand conversations since he came to Wisconsin. She forced her voice into neutral. "What did she say?"

"That she had 'ideas' and wanted to occupy herself with community issues." He shrugged. "She didn't elaborate, and I wasn't in the mood to get into a long discussion with her."

Yeah, right. "Oh."

"But she's got stepdaughters in the district, so that's a reason right there. Mike's got three kids in school, too, and Four Gates is a major business in the community. Doug's not a parent, but his uncle's company is a heavy contributor to the school. They paid a large chunk of the building costs for that new gym a few years ago."

He paused and speared a cheese fry with his fork. "Sonja's been cleared. Ronald needs to be seriously investigated regardless. So, that just leaves the teachers. Are they happy with their jobs?"

Good question. "Jenna's absolutely never in a bad mood at school. She's always bouncy and optimistic. I've never seen anyone more enthusiastic when it comes to being with her students. Loni and Marlene—" She paused.

"Yeah?"

"Well, I don't know. They don't seem any less happy than I am, but we only know each other during the school day, not beyond it. Marlene is laid back. Things rarely agitate her, although she was mad when she thought the Hoopla had been canceled."

She gave Garrett a significant look and he rolled his eyes.

"Loni is more structured, a bit higher strung," she said. "Both are very well respected teachers, though."

"We need more evidence to exonerate them than that."

"Well, did you check out their expenditures, like you did mine?" She knew her voice had an edge to it, but it still hurt when she thought about their first meeting. About his motives for wanting to spend time with her.

He was busy drinking his milkshake, oblivious to her feelings, of course. "Sure," he said. "But you were more conscientious than anyone else. I already told you that. Although Sonja did a nice job with her records, too. Nothing's clear—one way or another—on the others."

"How do we make it clear?"

"I think a job satisfaction test might be just the right idea. Let's brainstorm on that next. But—" he squinted at her, "I've also been doing a little research into the vendors, and I came across one glaring problem that needs to be examined further. What are you doing tomorrow morning?"

The trees in Ridgewood Grove's town park provided ample Saturday morning shade as they walked with purpose toward the residence of Alan Koolemar. Garrett found himself enjoying the bright day and the company he was keeping even more, mysterious lady though she was.

He'd been behaving. Keeping his distance. And his restraint seemed to be paying off. Cait wasn't exactly warming up, but she wasn't bolting away from him either.

He straightened his collar and said, "I don't want to frighten Mr. Koolemar, but I think we'll have to talk with him candidly. My analysis showed that, based on the number of customers he reported, his business was continually shortchanged at these festivals. Maybe because he drew in the most people and likewise had the most to lose."

She nodded. "I always thought buying tokens at one booth location for the festival made purchases easier to monitor and everything simpler for vendors and festival-goers. The vendors could charge what they thought was fair—three tokens for an ice cream cone, for instance, or two for face painting—and not have to worry about making change. The festival-goers could buy in advance however many tokens they thought they'd need and could use them more easily than cash."

Although he'd already researched this, he listened as she explained the system employed during prior events, paying special attention to the distribution of the final profits.

After festival expenses were deducted, the total profit was determined. This he knew. The tokens' worth, however, was based upon the final profit, and this fluctuated from year to year. This part was news to him. Proceeds were split evenly between each vendor and the school district, and vendors could begin redeeming tokens for cash once general expenses had been subtracted. The plan, of course, was for everyone to make a fair profit in the end.

"Doesn't it all seem straightforward to you?" she said.

"It does," he agreed. "Unless the total number of tokens is being tampered with or the amount of cash in the booth is reduced. Then the vendors and school district get less and someone else—a person posing as a vendor, perhaps—gets something for nothing."

"I want to get to the bottom of this."

"Me, too." Then he grinned at her. "But I also want a pint of Mr. Koolemar's Chocolate Chip Peanut Brittle Bonanza while we're there. The Four Gates golf caddies highly recommended it."

She laughed briefly. God, he loved that sound. He tried to keep his eyes focused on the sidewalk, but they kept defying his higher brain's orders and sneaking glances at the two open buttons on Cait's blouse instead.

That lower brain of his couldn't get enough of the way the light breeze pushed against the thin, white material, allowing him to see translucent wisps of lacy lingerie underneath. It was too tantalizing a promise to ignore for long.

But this morning he was going to have to ignore it. They'd reached Mr. Koolemar's house, and he had to concentrate on strictly professional matters. At least until he could get Cait alone in his condo again.

Cait took a deep breath and rang the bell. A middle-aged lady answered the door. She had hair spun like cotton candy, piled in a hive of frosted gold on her head and lips painted the shade of a painful sunburn.

"How can I help you kids?" she said in breathy syncopation.

Garrett introduced them both and asked for Mr. Koolemar.

"My Alan's down in his workshop," the woman replied. She radiated a hot pink smile at them. "Wanna come in and see?"

"Yes, thank you, Mrs. Koolemar," Garrett said.

So the older lady pushed the screen door wider to let them in. "Just call me Audrey, dear."

They trailed behind her into a ranch house right out of the

1950s and followed her down the stairs until she came to a stop in front of a door with the words "Kool Kreme Ice Kreamations" written in dripping white letters on a pink plaque.

"This is my Alan's ice cream workshop," she said proudly. "He's licensed." She swung open the door.

Inside, a large wooden tub sat between a long tan counter and six tiers of wall shelving. The shelves were crammed with glass jars of every sweet imaginable, from chocolate chips to crushed cookies to colorful sprinkles. There were also decanters of multicolored syrups, bottles of natural extracts and a myriad of measuring tools stuffed in a small cardboard box on the lowest shelf. Cait's mouth dropped open at the sheer variety.

"Hi, folks," Alan Koolemar said.

To Cait's eye, Mr. Koolemar appeared to be his usual cheerful self as he ushered them further into his workshop. Open boxes littered the floor. Spilled candy and chocolate bits gave the linoleum tiles a sprinkled effect. Dribbles of syrup decorated the counter like a Jackson Pollock original. Tasty artistry at work.

Audrey gave her husband a kiss.

"Thanks, sugarplum," the man said, his eyes twinkling.

"If anyone needs anything else, y'all just holler," Audrey said, breezing out the workshop door with a sway of her abundant hips and a toss of her cotton-candy hair.

Mr. Koolemar wiped away a butterscotch squiggle from the counter and grinned at them. "You two here to learn about ice cream making or did you just want to buy a few pints?"

"Both," Garrett said quickly.

Cait added, "You know I love your unique flavors, Mr. Koolemar, and I always stop at your booth first when you're at the school carnivals. All of my students rave about your cones, too."

"And I've been a fan since we met at Giuseppe's last month," Garrett interjected.

Cait noted Mr. Koolemar's look of pride. "I also appreciate your willingness to go to New Brighton for the Hoopla in a few weeks," she said, "but there's something we're worried about."

She took a deep breath. This was so much harder to say than she'd imagined last night when she rehearsed this question in her head. She'd feel terrible if she frightened the kind gentleman, but forewarned was forearmed.

"Are you aware of anyone who might've tried to cheat you of profits in the past?" she asked him. "Is there anybody, perhaps even someone from the school during the festivals, who might've stolen some tokens from your booth?"

Mr. Koolemar's bushy salt-and-pepper eyebrows merged for a moment of deep contemplation. He pressed his lips close together. "I've had a lot of offers for scooping helpers since I started churning up the ice cream maker a few years ago. But that's because I'm pretty liberal about giving away free samples to anyone who works for me. I always collect the tokens, though—"

"Any suspicious, unusual or uncharacteristic behavior among those workers?" Garrett asked.

"If my memory serves me, a few of the sixth grade boys fought over who'd get to work in the booth last year."

"Any adults react that way?"

"No." He gave them a serious look. "Say, kids, why don't you tell me what this is all about?"

Garrett gave him a succinct version of the leaking district funds and the superintendent's suspicion that someone working in or around the festival last year might be responsible.

Garrett crossed his arms. "How well do you know Ronald Jaspers?"

Mr. Koolemar squinted, his puzzlement apparent. "I've talked with the man a few times. Seen him at all the festivals and around town. I remember he asked for a double scoop of Igloo Almond-Cherry Crème at the Carnival of Love. But he hasn't bought anything from me for a few months."

"How about any of the school board members? Do you know Shelley McAllister, Mike Firenzi or Doug Chippenak, for instance?" Cait asked, holding her breath.

"Shelley got the Coconut Carob Ripple once. Said it was good but still too rich." He whistled. "I say, that woman's a foxy one, isn't she?"

Garrett laughed, much to Cait annoyance. She glared at him, but he was too busy agreeing with Mr. Koolemar to notice.

Mr. Koolemar continued, "Anthony Firenzi, Mike's dad, said something to me about stocking a few flavors at Four Gates. He's a big fan of Pistachio-Raisin-Chip Gazpacho, but we haven't worked out the details yet. Mike's a regular Hazelnut Highway customer. Gets my triple-scoop parfait every time. As for Doug—" he smiled, "we go way back."

This hooked her attention. "You and Doug Chippenak go way back?" Cait asked. "How far back?"

"Oh, very far. Thirty years or more. His uncle and I are pals. We went to the same university. We're all three chemists, you know."

"That's right." Garrett gave him a sharp look. "Tell me more."

"Why, sure," he said, a warm grin making the corners of his eyes crinkle. "We all get together now and then, swap ideas."

"What kinds of ideas?" Garrett asked.

"Oh, the usual. New techniques for plant growth. Splicing, grafting and so on. Topical treatments for skin injuries or mosquito bites. Mmm...the latest research on DNA engineering. And, of course, cooking, wine and ice cream making."

"Is their business thriving?" she said.

Mr. Koolemar nodded. "Normal ups and downs and all, but Doug and I talk frequently. He's a great one when it comes to investing. They're doing all right for themselves."

Garrett shot her a look that telegraphed uneasiness, but Mr. Koolemar had turned his attention back to his frosty creations and began chattering about toppings. He seemed to have lost interest in their investigation, so they let the subject drop for the time being.

"One thing I've always wanted to know," Garrett said to the man, "is what's the secret to making really fine, premium ice cream. Is it an ingredient or a process? One thing or a combination?"

Mr. Koolemar laughed. "The basics are simple, young man.

You need fresh milk, eggs, sugar, heavy cream, spices, vanilla extract, syrup flavors you love and toppings that excite you. You need a rock-salt freezer—if you like the old ways—a hardening freezer, too, and some clean utensils. And you need patience. But, there's more to creating exquisite ice cream than chemistry, extracts and candy. Takes heart and soul, too." He blew a kiss in the direction of his mixing bowls. "A little love needs to go into every batch."

Garrett caught Cait's eye and winked at her. Her heart started fluttering. Then he turned to Mr. Koolemar. "That's what must make your brand extraordinary. I can taste the love."

The older gentleman's grin broadened. "Taste the love. Spread it around. That's what I always say." And he blew them a kiss also. "Wanna try some flavors I've been experimenting on?"

"Yes!" she and Garrett said together. Then, when Mr. Koolemar turned his back to open the silverware drawer, Garrett pulled her close and kissed her hard.

"Taste the love. Spread it around," he whispered.

The fluttering in her heart became pounding.

Mr. Koolemar grabbed three ice cream dishes from the cabinet and some spoons. "I've been working on an action flavor line." He lifted the hardening freezer's lid. "We got pints of Orange Mango Jitterbug left. I see some Double Dark Chocolate Sleepwalk and Runaway Mint Paradiso. Umm, Lemon Burst Sundae Stroll and Strawberry Whiplash, too. Which do you want to try?"

"No more Chocolate Chip Peanut Brittle Bonanza?" Garrett asked, his voice registering only slight disappointment as he leaned against the counter and eyed the flavors inside the freezer.

"Sorry," the older man said. "But I'll add it to my special request list." He scribbled a few words on a clipboard.

"Well, I don't think I can leave in good conscience without trying Double Dark Chocolate Sleepwalk," Garrett said. "Cait?"

"Strawberry Whiplash please," she said.

Mr. Koolemar smiled merrily at them. "Good choice, kids."

An hour later, after they thanked the Koolemars for their

hospitality and all the delicious ice cream, Cait trailed Garrett through the park again and toward his fancy car.

She exhaled. "I know we must be getting warmer, but I feel as though there's a major piece missing somewhere. For instance, could there be a connection, besides an old friendship, between Chippenak Chemical and Mr. Koolemar's Ice Kreamations?"

"I don't know," Garrett said. "But I think we're going to have to keep a particularly close eye on those board members just in case. And—" he eyed her, "we're going to need to look deeper into the teachers' backgrounds and motives, too."

"I know."

He rubbed his washboard-flat stomach. "But if I keep eating like this, I'm going to have to spend more time working out at Firenzi's country club."

Cait had devoured three bowls of ice cream herself, so she knew what he meant. Still, it wasn't all the sweets that were making her nauseated.

She couldn't help but worry that someone she knew was involved in something underhanded. All the roads leading to the school board members hadn't turned up anything definite so far, although Shelley was certainly devious enough.

Yet, if Cait were completely honest, she had to admit she considered Jenna to be the brightest of the people potentially involved. More so than even Loni and Marlene. If anyone could mastermind such a plan, her best friend had the brains to pull it off. But hopefully not the motivation.

Sonja, their sweet secretary, had the most opportunity, however. She was the one who'd purchased all the tokens. But Garrett said he'd checked her out and all was well.

Ronald...well, Cait still couldn't figure him out. He did seem to be worthy of suspicion, though.

She sighed. Where, like in movie mysteries, were all the clues?

There were sweet rolls, fruit and vegetable trays and ice cream sundaes the following Thursday night at the Open House Parents' Coffee, but whoever brought the ice cream wasn't thinking. It was conventional and store-bought. Cait didn't bother with it.

She stood near a wall. Rubbed her temples with the pads of her fingers. Tried to remember to breathe deeply. All the way to the bottom of her lungs. In on a count of five. Out on ten.

"Well, you sure look stressed," Jenna whispered in her ear. "You doing okay?"

"I'm hanging in there. But look—" Cait pointed to Doug Chippenak and Shelley McAllister huddled together in a corner of the auditorium. People milled around them, laughing over coffee and snacks, but those two were engrossed in a very private tête-à-tête. "What do you think they're talking about?"

"My guess? Malicious intent to take over the Universe."

Cait nodded. "Good answer." Even though Cait couldn't confide any of her suspicions of board-member thievery to Jenna, it was no secret that Mrs. McAllister was universally despised amongst the teaching staff. Mr. Chippenak was merely considered bland as sawdust.

They watched silently until Shelley and Doug parted ways a few minutes later.

Cait eyed her friend, and her concerns about Jenna's involvement in the money leak rocketed back to her.

"How are you, Paul and the kids doing?" She watched Jenna's reaction, hunting for the slightest indication of discontent.

Her friend laughed. "Good. Great, actually. Paul got a promotion back in the spring. He's been putting money aside. Says he wants to take me on a real vacation this Christmas. Just the two of us." She grinned. "Somewhere warm."

Cait grinned back.

"I've been looking into good deals online. What do you think of Aruba? Or maybe Turks and Caicos?"

"Wish I knew more about the Caribbean, Jenna. I'm sure they're all good.

"You know, that's what I think. Besides, the most important part is just to be together. I'd be happy to be alone with Paul at a Holiday Inn in Madison, eating cheese curds and drinking cheap wine from a bottle."

"That sounds great, too." And it did. Cait smiled at her friend, and she knew—just *knew*—there was no way Jenna would get herself involved in something unpardonable. She refused to entertain the notion again. Ever.

The other teacher leaned in and said, "So, what's up on the Garrett Ellis front? You two going out regularly now or what?"

"Our relationship clearly falls into the 'or what' category."

"Go on," Jenna said.

"He's respecting my wishes to take things slowly. In fact, even though we spent time together this weekend, he's barely touched me since the copy room."

"The copy room!"

"Oops. Didn't I tell you about that?" Cait quickly filled her in on what had happened by the Xerox machine. She could tell Jenna was disappointed that what had transpired wasn't bawdier.

"So you think he'll try to get you alone in the janitor's closet next—"

Cait nudged her friend. A few yards away, Garrett walked down the aisle and handed a cup of coffee to Shelley. He appeared not to notice anyone else in the room.

"He says he doesn't like her. Doesn't trust her. Yet, look at how natural they are together." She sighed, the old insecurities flooding back in. But, no denying it, Garrett was a *guy*. Even though Shelley was married and Garrett knew her history, how could he fail to recognize all the things other men found attractive about her? The red hair. The fabulous body. The full chest shown to advantage in that spicy V-neck.

Cait looked down at her own more modest chest, which was concealed in a prim button-up summer sweater. So teacher-y. Okay, maybe the baby blue was a striking color on her, but she knew it couldn't compete with Shelley's black, plunging-collar blouse.

A tall, trim guy in his mid-forties with a dark ring of hair across the back of his bald head, strode up to Shelley and Garrett. Cait looked on, mesmerized. The guy couldn't be called attractive, not by Cait's definition, but he had an air about him. She saw him pull the cup from Shelley's hand and speak with a hint of displeasure to Garrett, but they were too far away to hear specifics.

"Who is that guy?" Jenna asked.

"I'm going out on a limb here, but I'm guessing that's her 'Darling' Chucky," she said.

"No one outside of a bad horror movie calls *anyone* Chucky."

"Apparently Shelley does. I'm pretty sure that's her husband."

"*That's* Charles McAllister? The big banking dude?" Jenna regarded the man in the distance with a rueful shake of her head. "Hey, Cait, take a peek to your left."

Cait turned just fast enough to see Doug shooting Shelley an intense, lingering look before slipping out a side door. So maybe Garrett had it right. Maybe those two were having an affair. Hey, stranger things happened every day.

Yet almost any debauchery was better than the thought of Shelley together with Garrett...or even with Ronald Jaspers, who, at that very moment, was shaking the hand of a Ridgewood Grove parent with his right and holding a giant chocolate-almond Danish with his left.

Chuck McAllister, who'd been eyeing the room with irritation, shot Ronald a look of disgust. He put a proprietary arm around Shelley and led her out of the room. Garrett caught Cait and Jenna staring at him and gave them a long, mysterious look before turning to talk to the parents of a high-needs third grader.

"Maybe we'd better separate now," Cait whispered.

Jenna took a step toward the center of the auditorium. "Mix-n-mingle, girlfriend," she mouthed over her shoulder.

Garrett couldn't get Shelley's comments out of his head. As the parent in front of him droned on about the need for a restructuring of the IEP/special-ed budget, he reviewed what Shelley told him before her jerk of a husband showed up.

"Nice job running the Open House, Shell," Garrett had said, handing her a coffee with milk but no sugar, just like she'd had it at their last administrative-board meeting. He figured he'd butter her up before he grilled her. "Want me to get you an ice cream sundae?"

"Heavens, no, darling. I can't believe Ronald let the PTA bring in all those hideous desserts."

"I saw fruit and vegetables up there," he said, pointing to the treat table.

"Well, of course. I brought those. But no one's eating them." She scanned the room with a glare. "Ice cream, of all things," she muttered. "That's the worst. The butterfat in the cream, the egg yolks, all that sugar." She shivered. "The chemical additives used to stabilize the ice cream and improve its texture in commercial products can be extremely unhealthy, not to mention the coconut oils and unnatural flavorings."

Garrett narrowed his eyes. Technical words sounded so strange coming out of her mouth. He remembered the young Shell Oliver. That girl was exacting when it came to fingernail polish and designer clothing, but she wouldn't have been able to pass a basic chemistry exam if her Prada handbag depended on it.

"You seem to know a great deal about ice cream production for someone who doesn't like the stuff," he said, careful to present it as curiosity not accusation.

"Oh, I know all about it," she said cryptically.

Before Garrett could question her further, Charles McAllister showed up.

"What are you drinking, honey?" Good Ole Chuck said.

Shelley offered her cup to him. He took a sip and grimaced. He looked around with a sour expression. "When does this end?"

"Only another half hour," Garrett offered before introducing himself.

The jerk tried to out-muscle him on the handshake.

"So, do you lift, Ellis?"

"Lift?"

"Weights. Free standing? Nautilus?"

As if he'd actually compare workout notes with that dickhead. "Both, on occasion," Garrett said.

Chucky sniffed, turned his attention to his wife. "I just saw Doug. Need to talk to you. Alone."

The two of them stalked off and Garrett was left with the uneasy feeling he'd just missed the punch line on a joke. He spotted Cait spying on him across the auditorium. He was tempted to walk over there, politely dismiss Jenna and then squeeze all the worry out of his blond angel, but he had to control the urge.

As it was, she was pulling away from him instead of being charmed and moving nearer. In past relationships, he'd lost his temper fast with the hot-and-cold routine and brushed off the offending lady as gently as possible. But Cait wasn't as easy for him to shake. She looked like a sea nymph in that soft blue sweater. It enhanced her thoughtful, questioning eyes and reminded him of her sharp mind and warm heart. A heart that was beautifully cushioned by the lovely swell of her breasts. And the sweater displayed them to perfection, too.

She was gorgeous inside and out. The way she cared about her family, the children, the community—everything she did showed her kind spirit. He knew she liked him, at least a little. He'd let her know in a hundred ways how much he liked her. Okay, not in a let's-get-married-and-stay-together-until-the-end-of-time sense, but he didn't feel that way about anybody.

Still, even after all the time they'd spent together, he couldn't get a clear read on whether she wanted him. Why not?

The parent called his attention back with a question about budget allocations for academically challenged learners. But, though Garrett was talking like a financial director, he was thinking like a teenage boy. His eyes followed Cait out the room.

~CHAPTER NINE~

STEP 9:
And, finally, everyone involved in the preparation
of this lip-smackingly good recipe
needs to blow a kiss into the mixure.
Whisk well.
~From *Mr. Koolemar's Top Secret,*
Kool Kreme Ice Kreamations Recipe Book, pg. 97

Johnny Appleseed Day was on her heels. Although no special all-school event was scheduled to commemorate the notable September twenty-sixth birth date of John Chapman, eighteenth century apple-tree planter extraordinaire, Cait still needed to get things ready for her class. She jotted down a list of possible apple activities for tomorrow:

*counting the number of seeds and graphing the results

*tasting the differences between apple types and rating them

*measuring their heights and circumferences in centimeters

*slicing apples widthwise so the "star" is visible and dipping them in tempera paint to create apple-star patterns on paper *sticking toothpicks with raisins and marshmallows on them into the apples to make Scary Fruit Monsters

*coring them, adding a cinnamon-sugar filling, then baking...

Since making Scary Fruit Monsters topped her personal favorite list, Cait circled the asterisk by it but soon found herself doodling on the edge of her paper. She deserved a moment of laziness this week. She needed it. It was imperative for her mental health to take time away from serious school tasks and worrying about Mom to...draw the perfect depiction of an enormous marshmallow-mouthed Macintosh with beady raisin eyes who, if given the opportunity, would plan a hostile takeover of Milwaukee.

She tilted her head to consider its proportions on the page. Goodness, the thing kind of looked like Ronald Jaspers.

"Nice piece of artwork you got there," Garrett said, balancing a heavy-looking box on his shoulder. He'd entered the room so stealthily she didn't see him until he spoke.

She covered up her drawing with the first folder she could grab and leaped from her desk. "Umm, hi. What's in the box?"

"C'mon and see," he said, setting the mass of cardboard down on Daisy's desk and motioning her over. She opened the box and peered inside. "Oh, wow! Garrett, your sister's amazing."

"Psychotic is the word I usually use," he said, pulling out an individually wrapped gift basket, "but she does know her art."

"These are beautiful." Cait ran her fingers along the carefully crafted leaf-shaped basket. It was constructed like a large, curved maple leaf that formed a bowl for the fruit. Inside, the apples, tangerines, peaches and baby pumpkins were arranged to highlight the brighter fall colors, while walnuts and chestnuts accented the composition with browns. The entire piece was wrapped in transparent gold plastic wrap and tied with long red and yellow ribbons. "Did Marianne design this?"

"Yep."

She pulled out eight baskets. Little Styrofoam balls went flying. "Gracious, she already sent me a display basket for the classroom. Are all of these centerpieces for the Hoopla?"

"Nope."

"Oh...well, that's okay." Cait tried to hide her disappointment. "Even one or two would be lovely, so—"

"No, sweetheart. What I meant was, you can use them for centerpieces, sell them for profit, make Carmen Miranda hats out of them—I don't care. I doubt Marianne cares. They're her gift to you. But there are five more boxes in my car."

He glared at her with a look of good-natured irritation. "And if either of you think, for even ten seconds, that I'm storing damn near fifty of these eyesores in my condo for over a week, you've got me confused with some other Ellis."

"She sent us *six* boxes?"

"Yes, ma'am. The UPS guy looked insanely cheerful to get rid of them. Good thing I could work from home this morning and be there to help unload." He pointed to a corner of the room. "You can have them here, or I'll transfer them to your place. Your choice, but I want my Beemer smelling like empty pizza cartons and Tootsie Rolls again real soon—not fruit salad."

Cait giggled imagining Garrett's fancy car filled from leather seat to sunroof with the pretty baskets. A memory tugged at her. She glanced at the place where the ribbons were fastened around the plastic wrap. "Hey, no photo tags on these."

"Damn right. If there's only one thing Marianne and I agree on, it's that our last family portrait sucked." He laughed. "That was taken three years ago and it was the last time we all agreed to pose for Dad's photographer. Marianne hated it even more than I did. Pretty sure she snipped the tags off herself," he said, eyeing the ribbons with suspicion. "She's taken to going into supermarkets with a pair of scissors stashed in her purse, just in case."

She shook her head. "Oh, I don't know. I thought you all looked really nice in it."

He opened his mouth to speak but was interrupted.

"Hi, Miss Walsh!" Robbie Cranz waved from the door with a couple of his fourth grade friends in tow. "Hi, Mr. Ellis. We got a pass from library 'cuz we wanted to see if you needed any extra help with the Harvest Hoopla."

"Yeah," another kid said. "Anything at all."

She grinned at them. Robbie, now nine, had been a student in her very first class two years ago. Seeing his confidence and abilities grow had been a private joy.

"Well, I'm going to need lots of assistance on the day of the festival, and you boys—because you're mature fourth graders—will be able to do things my students might not be able to do. Can you get to New Brighton a little early to join the set-up team?"

"Oh, yeah!" Robbie rubbed his palms together, and the other two boys echoed his enthusiasm.

"Wonderful. I'll be counting on your help." She glanced at the clock. "I need to pick up my class from art in about twenty minutes, and there's not much more we'll be able to do this afternoon—"

"Unless," Garrett interjected, "you've decided to house your sweet treasures here..." He gave her a hopeful look. "I could use some real manpower lifting those boxes." Cait saw Robbie swallow twice in anticipation of her answer.

"Why, Mr. Ellis, what an excellent idea," she said. "I'll just clear away a corner spot and leave the hard work to you four gentlemen."

A few squeals escaped the boys mouths, but they stuck out their chests and strode up to Garrett.

Garrett appraised them like a general overseeing his troops. "Let's go, men," he said to them, jingling his car keys.

Tears stung her eyes as she watched them exit. Garrett casually placed a hand on one boy's shoulder, gave another a grateful nod and ruffled Robbie's light-blond hair. Three pairs of eyes gazed up at him as if they'd just met Superman.

He was a natural with them, she realized. As the big boxes made their way into the classroom, the image of Garrett with kids of his own materialized before her like a daydream. She blinked and looked away.

When the boys had safely returned to the library, Garrett said, "I know we only have a few minutes before you have to get your class, but I wanted to ask—did you dig a little more into Jenna's motives?"

She sighed. "I did. I didn't find anything. And, Garrett, I'm not *going* to find anything. If there's only one thing I'm certain of in this whole crazy money-leak mess, it's that Jenna's not involved."

He leaned closer. "How could you possibly know that? You sure you're not being blinded by your friendship?"

"I'm not blinded. I just *know*."

He rolled his eyes.

"I *do*," she told him. "It doesn't happen to me very often, I'll admit, but there are people I can trust with my whole heart. Jenna's one of them."

She saw a hard-to-decipher light in his eyes. "And how did she manage to achieve that remarkable feat?"

"With time. And loyalty. And genuine friendship," she whispered. And with honesty, commitment and appreciation, she added silently.

He nodded. "Okay, then. Jenna's off the hook. But perhaps later you can clue me in as to what logical processes back up your intuition. And Marlene and Loni are going to need a closer, more in-depth examination. We'll have to put into play that plan we talked about at the diner. Deal?"

"Fine." She glanced at the clock. "I've got to get going."

"All right. Last thing. There's a new development from the school board sector you should know about."

"What is it?"

He dipped his head and lowered his voice. "I spotted Chuck and Shelley out on the golf course together over the weekend. There were lots of people at Four Gates, but those two were playing with none other than Doug Chippenak and Ronald Jaspers. It looked like an intense foursome, and Mike Firenzi showed up for a while to chat, too."

"Did you hear anything?"

"Unfortunately, no. I was busy batting off one of the Club's too-enthusiastic personal trainers." He shook his head. "Scary, those dudes. So I couldn't watch for long, and I was too far away to catch any direct quotes. I just thought you should know they've all been very, very cozy lately."

"And maybe not just *lately*..."

The next afternoon, Cait drove to New Brighton, her car so familiar with the road it steered, shifted and braked by itself. She entered her mother's house only to catch the tail end of a jovial conversation.

"So, what did he say then?" Garrett's smooth voice prompted.

"Oh, then my dear Hank told the gentleman that, no, we weren't looking for olive groves but *orange* groves. And the man said, 'Well, you could've told me that in the first place!' So we finally got the directions to Tampa, after every possible delay, and made the tour bus just in time."

Mom and Dad's famous Florida trip the year before Seth was born. Cait sighed. She loved that silly story and was jealous, suddenly, of Garrett getting to hear it without her. What the heck was he doing here, anyway?

She walked into the family room and gave him a questioning look.

"Oh, Cait, dear. You're back from the market already?" her mother asked.

"No, Mom, that was yesterday. I went to the market yesterday afternoon. Today I just came straight from the school." Garrett's eyes found hers, and he shared an understanding smile with her.

"Fine, dear. That's fine. Mr. Ellis was so nice to stop by. He brought us a delicious treat from the bakery."

Garrett lifted his shoulders in a modest shrug. "It's nothing big. Just an apple pie to celebrate a holiday only elementary kids know about. Goes great with cinnamon ice cream."

"Mr. Koolemar's Cinnamon Sticks 'N Scones, no doubt?"

"Yep. It's in the freezer downstairs. We didn't want to start without you."

Ice cream and pie seemed as necessary to her as oxygen and fresh water right then. She backed out of the room. "I'll go get everything set up."

"Oh, all right, Cait," her mother said, waving her away.

She tried not to feel offended by the easy dismissal, but the pang of hurt lodged in her chest and blended with the sadness already lurking there. Why did children always have to feel so powerless in situations like these? She knew her mother couldn't help losing the present, but did she have to exclude her daughter from recollections of the past as well?

"Mrs. Walsh," Garrett stage-whispered, almost as if he'd heard Cait's thoughts, "you promised to tell me about Cait's adventures with the housepainters when she was a toddler."

"Oh, no you don't, Mom!" Cait shouted from the hallway, but her mother's delighted laugh rang out, and Cait could hear Garrett encouraging her.

"If you wanna do damage control, Cait," Garrett called, "you'd better step to it."

In spite of the sadness, she couldn't help but smile at Garrett's efforts. She hurried down the stairs. On her way back up, ice cream in hand, she heard her mom begin, "My, my, was that ever an aggravating day. Cait was wearing these adorable panda overalls, and I'd just put her hair up in pigtails when the doorbell rang..."

Seth popped the cap on a lite beer and held it out for Garrett before pulling another bottle out of the fridge for himself.

Garrett took a swig, letting the liquid coat his tongue until he couldn't stand to keep it hostage in his mouth any longer. The taste was so familiar it was strange. It belonged to another time. To late nights shared with Jacob during their wild youth.

He heard rustling noises upstairs and an occasional shriek as Cait and her mom hunted through a box of her childhood memorabilia. Seth had come over during the pie eating and stayed to keep Garrett company while the two women slipped into an earlier decade.

"Oh, my God, my N'Sync poster!" Cait exclaimed.

Seth raised his eyebrows at Garrett in an expression of long-suffering sibling exasperation.

"So, pardon my ignorance of this," her brother said to him, "but you're a financial director for a school district after having worked in a big corporation. Big change, or no? Is what you're doing now what you'd expected?"

"The math challenge is still there," Garrett said. "But it's a different atmosphere being around kids and teachers during the day and living on my own out in the Midwest. Those were changes I'd anticipated, and I like them." He paused, figuring he'd let Seth infer what he wanted about his romantic relationship with Cait. He didn't have anything to hide. Well, not much.

But honesty made him add, "In another sense, though, there are things I didn't expect. I sure didn't think it'd take this long to discover the source of the financial problem." He knew Seth well enough now to trust his discretion, so he explained briefly about the money leak. "I'd hoped to have it wrapped up by now."

Seth took a few swigs of his own beer and nodded. "What about your family's company? Will you be part of that operation again?"

He and Jacob had had this talk as well...too many times to count. It had never been a serious consideration from Garrett's viewpoint, but after New Year's it was nonexistent. Jacob never gave up trying, though. The guy was brilliant, generous and funny. Garrett's personal hero. Who the hell could compete with his awesome brother?

"I doubt it," Garrett said to Seth. "But I've learned never to say never." Hopefully he could snag the culprit before the holidays. Before the next time his parents would want to "talk." Prove himself to be a success in something, and maybe then the pressure would stop.

Cait's brother plunked a basket of chips in the middle of

the table, straddled a chair across from Garrett and pointed to the snacks. "Wanna play a round or two while we wait?"

"My *Saved By The Bell* DVD!" Cait's elated voice floated down the stairs.

Garrett chuckled. "Yeah."

"Good." Seth lifted his chin toward the ceiling. "We'll give 'em fifteen more minutes before we make those two reenter the twenty-first century. Then I'm kicking you and Cait out." He gave Garrett a friendly nod and nabbed a chip. "Not to be rude, but I need to speak with my mom privately, and I sure as hell don't need my sister bringing out her old American Girl dolls in the middle of the conversation. Take her out to dinner or something. Anything. Just get her out of my hair for tonight."

Garrett tossed a chip in the air, caught it expertly between his teeth. "You got it, Seth."

For some reason, Garrett insisted on stopping at Pummelhof's Market on their way into Milwaukee. Cait checked her watch—quarter-to-six—and wondered when they'd actually end up at the "incredible bistro" Garrett had raved about at her mother's house.

"What's the name of the place we're going to?" she asked, getting suspicious, and watching as he selected an eggplant, a handful of yellow onions, three large potatoes and garlic cloves.

"The Grecian Taverna." Garrett studied several ripe tomatoes before selecting two. "Could you grab a cucumber please?" He pointed to the other side of the store. "And a head of lettuce?"

When she rejoined him, a tub of ripe Kalamata olives and a container of ruby-red strawberries had found their way into his basket. Garrett strode toward the register.

"We're not going to Milwaukee, are we?" She gazed up at him.

"Nope. Never said The Grecian Taverna was in Milwaukee. You just inferred that part back at your mom's house."

"Where would this exciting dining establishment be located?"

"New Brighton."

"I know every place in New Brighton and there are only a handful of ethnic spots. None are Greek."

His lips twitched. "It just opened up."

"Where?"

"My condo."

"That's what I was afraid of."

He tried to give her a wounded look. "Listen here, Miss Walsh. I picked up a pound of ground lamb yesterday, and I've been itching to make good use of it. You can come to my place and have *moussaka* with me, or you can go home and eat some frozen-solid mystery meal. Your choice, sweetheart."

She knew she could never turn down an offer like that.

Back at his condo, Garrett unloaded the food and told her to make the musical selections. She consulted the iPod and decided on some Elton John. She also washed, sliced, diced and followed his orders willingly, for once.

"I didn't realize you were such an expert chef," she said, slivering the eggplant into thin circles.

"I'm not."

She laughed openly. "Since when does any cooking-challenged man know how to whip up a *moussaka?* You're hiding something."

He stirred the cream sauce at low-heat over the burner and shook his head. "I can make two complicated things. This and Sicilian-style lasagna. Grandma Maria taught me. Meat-based layer dishes. But that's the extent of my gourmet training."

"So, most of the time then you eat...what?"

"Sandwiches. Ice cream. Uncomplicated fruits like bananas or grapes." He began frying the eggplant in olive oil. "You?"

"I can make tacos." She chopped up a tomato and watched as he flipped an eggplant slice then gave the ground lamb a quick stir in its pan. "Mom taught me chili, spaghetti, stuffed peppers, things like that, but mostly I'm a Lean Cuisine girl. I'm too lazy."

"You, Caitlin Livie Walsh, are *not* lazy." He gave her a thoughtful, intense look before turning his attention back to the stovetop. "Chop the lettuce for the salad," he commanded.

An hour later they were seated at the small dining table and eating. The scent of allspice roused her, infiltrated her pores, reminded her there was a world beyond this little corner of Wisconsin. If Odysseus could take a voyage of discovery, maybe she, too, should set sail sometime. Toward adventure, for once, not running from it.

Moussaka, complemented by a salad tossed with oil and vinegar, made for a wonderful meal. It tasted warm and spicy and like a summer night on Mykonos. Not that she'd ever been there, but she could imagine.

Garrett eyed her quizzically and poured glasses of red wine for them as "Goodbye Yellow Brick Road" played.

When they were done eating, he took their plates to the kitchen and told her to put on something upbeat. "We've listened to enough laments about relationships gone bad, Cait." Then he demanded that she stay the hell out of the kitchen until he brought out dessert. "Just sit on the sofa and relax, would you?"

She did as he asked. Well, she *sat*. Relaxing was impossible.

Ten minutes later, he entered the room and turned down the lights. He carried a plate of washed strawberries and a glass bowl of something white and creamy.

"Mr. Koolemar's Polar Bear Freeze ice cream," he explained.

He pulled her onto the Persian rug with him, setting the food on the parquet floor. He picked up one large berry by its stem and swirled it in the ice cream. Then he lifted the whitened tip and ran it along her lower lip until she licked it.

"Open up for me, Cait."

The chill and sweetness burst into her mouth when she bit down on the strawberry. The flavor was so strong, her eyes watered. Every sensation was super-sized. Garrett nibbled on the second half of the berry then fed her another one. When she'd swallowed, he dipped a third berry in the cold treat and decorated the corners of her mouth with it. He leaned in and kissed the white cream away, lingering as if time were never a consideration.

The heat of his mouth deliciously contrasted the frostiness of the cream, melting the sweet dots and dashes into a cool lotion on her skin.

S.O.S., her logical brain cried out. But her emotions ignored the plea. Every normal feeling had gotten jumbled.

He grew more ambitious and trailed a line of white from her lips over her chin to the hollow of her throat, sending tender kisses to erase the pathway he'd created.

Every one of her cells shimmied. Her hands had a private agenda and began tracking the movements of his body with hers. Her fingertips pressed into his chest and traveled on an exciting voyage.

"Lie down," he whispered, helping to ease her to the floor. Her head, her body, cushioned by the thick rug, sank into the colored threads and melded with them.

His nimble fingers unbuttoned her shirt and drew it off. The ivory lace bra was unlatched and likewise discarded. He traced each nipple with his pinky, leaning back for a clear perspective.

"You're beautiful, Cait." Then he kissed her on the mouth immediately, as if to keep her from blurting out a denial. It was a hot, deep kiss that shorted out her fears and her memories of loss for longer than she felt was prudent.

Distrust, betrayal, pain—they still lingered deep inside her, but they were all finally put back in proportion to life's easier emotions. Even conjuring up Fredric's image wasn't enough to distort them again.

Garrett picked up another strawberry. Maintaining his role as scribe, he dipped it into the Polar Bear Freeze, penning words of love over her heart.

"Lovely Lady," he whispered as he wrote. "Sexy Mystery. My Dreamsicle."

She stiffened at the chill of the ice cream, the tips of her breasts hardening, but he licked and sucked and tasted and, soon, all of her turned to flame.

He journeyed down her chest and belly with the white topping, unfastening her navy slacks and sliding them over her hips. She heard him draw in a quick breath.

"You stun me," he murmured.

Garrett's heart was beating at a machine-gun pace. The way Cait's skin flushed under his lips made him gulp in air, but he was sure only a few parts of him had gotten enough oxygen. His arousal was painful. He'd wanted her for too, too long.

He tore his shirt off and tried to ignore the increasing pressure against his zipper. He tucked his fingers into the sides of her ivory panties and removed them. Her gasp almost undid him.

"There's so much I want to do to pleasure you," he whispered in her ear.

He reached for the berry again, swirled it in cream and parted her legs. He painted the soft inside of her thighs, going higher with every stroke. She moaned when he brushed his lips against her, lapping up first the sweetness of the cream and then the sweetness of only her.

"Oh, God, Garrett, I don't think I can...you just can't keep...oh, but please don't stop."

He didn't stop.

Cait murmured under her breath at the torture he inflicted. The cold dessert, the warm air, his hot tongue... The three strands of temperature swirled together outside of her, then inside. And when all three joined forces, the power of that bond ripped her apart. Only the aftershocks of an improbable connection remained.

She pulled him up, clung to him, buried her face in his chest. The heat of her breath nearly made condensation form on his taut skin. His open mouth found hers, and she felt the length and weight of his body meld to her conforming one.

She fingered his belt, unhooked it with one hand, and in the next motion managed to undo the clasp on his pants. She reached for his zipper.

The telephone rang.

"We're ignoring that." His voice was raspy against her ear.

It rang again.

"Your machine can get it, right?"

"Right."

She unzipped his black pants.

Another ring, and another.

The answering machine flipped on.

After Garrett's simple greeting, a familiar voice began to speak: "Hey, G, it's me. I thought you might want to know. Jacob's had a complication with his leg. They just rushed him back to the hospital."

~CHAPTER TEN~

STEP 10:
Transfer the mixture into the stainless-steel cylinder
of a rock-salt and ice freezer.
No matter what newfangled contraptions you can buy
on the Internet these days,
I still say the old ways are the best.
~From *Mr. Koolemar's Top Secret,*
Kool Kreme Ice Kreamations Recipe Book, pg. 97

"**B**-l-o-o-d-y *hell*," Garrett said, springing to his feet and racing toward the phone. He snatched up the receiver. "Hi, Marianne, I'm here," he said on a ragged exhale. "What happened?"

"Well, Jacob's toes were aching more than usual. When he went in to have it checked out, they did an x-ray and discovered a blood clot that broke away and was blocking one of the vessels in his foot. Daniel tried to explain it to me. He said it was called thrombo-something. Thromboembolism, I think. The doctors in New Haven were worried about it traveling to his heart."

"Jesus. Were they able to dissolve it or remove it?" What the hell did they do when something like this happened?

"They're working on that now. I'm still in Philly tonight, but

Daniel and I are driving up to Connecticut tomorrow to see him. We think he's going to be okay. Don't panic. But I didn't want you to find out from anyone else. Figured I'd better call."

"Thanks, Sis." He grabbed for the pen and paper on the counter. "Do you have the phone number to Jacob's room?"

While Marianne hunted for it, he gave Cait's gorgeous naked body a regretful glance. He watched as she reached for her clothes and began pulling them back on. Her eyes looked haunted when she glanced up at him, concern etched on her face. He blew her an air kiss and hoped she'd smile. She did.

Marianne recited the number and he jotted it down. "Okay, I got it. I'll give him a call there."

"He'll be glad to hear from you, G."

Garrett hung up the phone and stared at the receiver. Cait came to stand near him. She smelled like strawberry shortcake. In spite of the news he'd just received, his mouth began to water. He slipped an arm around her waist then told her about the conversation with his sister.

"Do you need to fly back there?" she asked.

He shook his head. "Not just yet. Besides, there's nothing I can do. I'm not a doctor, and he's got a great team working on him." He sighed. "Plus, Marianne's boyfriend Daniel is headed there tomorrow with her. If there are any problems, he'll help the family get it straightened out. He's Mr. Medicine."

He couldn't believe how bitterly those words came out of his mouth.

She shot him a sharp glance. "You don't like Marianne's boyfriend?"

He hugged her tighter and silently kissed the top of her head. "He's okay. Actually, he's a real good guy. Daniel's not the source of the problem. I'm just frustrated with everyone tonight."

He released her and paced around the room, an angry energy seeping into his veins. He was so damned tired of being made to feel guilty. Being told, directly or not, to go back home when he knew it wasn't where he belonged. If he didn't know better, he'd have thought Jacob orchestrated this complication in order to push him on a plane sooner. He scowled at the Persian rug.

"Maybe this isn't a good time for me to be here," Cait said in a small voice. "I'm sensing you'd rather be alone."

He heard the unspoken question she was asking. The question most women ask at some point: "Do you want me here even when you don't need me to be?"

He couldn't answer that tonight, although his body still throbbed from wanting her and the built-up frustration was going to make it a hell of a long evening.

"Look, I'll drive you back to you mom's so you can pick up your car," he said. "I'm sorry."

"It's okay." But she didn't look like it was okay. She still gave him a compassionate glance or two, but she seemed distracted. She waltzed right by the strawberries and didn't even shoot them a second look. It felt as though she'd turned her back on him. As though she'd already forgotten what they shared.

His rational, intellectual side knew the change in the evening's tone wasn't her fault or, really, even his. It wasn't reasonable to blame her for reacting as she did to the interruption or to his consequent irritation with his family, but her easy departure pissed him off anyway.

This just proved the truth again. He needed to concentrate on his job and on things he could control and understand. Letting a woman get too close, letting himself get too attached, that would only make him crazy.

And here was the depressing bottom line: When it came to women, Jacob may have had it right all along.

Cait was tempted to stop at the DVD store on her way back to Ridgewood Grove, but it was late and she had too much on her mind. Alone in her car, she blushed recalling the intimacies she'd shared with Garrett. His touch was gentle but deeply inquisitive. She felt she'd been asked a thousand unspoken questions with his fingertips, and her body had responded by screaming, "Yes! Yes!" in reply to every single one.

She'd wanted him so much tonight. She squirmed in the driver's seat just remembering how close they'd come to making love. But the transparency she experienced in his presence was embarrassing, too. It was more than nakedness or being probed by his eyes, his hands, his tongue. His power to hurt her had increased exponentially by that one little act on the Persian rug.

And then, after everything, his goodnight kiss had seemed downright dismissive, as though he were angry with her but didn't want to admit it. His inability to let her in on his emotions trivialized the romantic moments that came before. He might share his body, but she knew he had no intention of sharing his life.

Marianne's call might've separated them that night, but how long until Garrett would be out the door anyway and back where he belonged? How long before he got bored or the winds of ambition blew him in another direction—far and away from her?

Cait forced her mind back to the Harvest Hoopla and the person responsible for stealing funds. It was a topic that was worrisome on one level but safer on another. Pieces didn't connect, but too many people were involved for the problem to be insignificant.

Less than a week until the event. This was what she needed to focus her attention on. Not on Garrett. Not anymore.

"Tell me they're sending you home soon," Garrett said to his brother. "Tell me they've found the problem, fixed it and are releasing you to your own shoddy care, far away from the hospital staff."

"Why the hell would I want to leave?" Jacob said, laughing on the line. "Amelia's amazing."

"Another nurse?"

"Oh, no."

"A doctor?"

"Guess again, little brother."

"A tax attorney for the hospital?"

"Well, now you're getting closer." Jacob sounded disappointed he couldn't prolong the game. "She's an insurance agent."

"What happened to Patricia and her latex gloves, or was she so last Wednesday?"

"Did anyone ever tell you you're a very *literal* person?"

Garrett sighed. "So you broke up with her, too, huh?"

"Hey, you worry about your own love life and leave me to arrange mine."

"As you wish," he said, although his brother had no idea how much help he needed in that arena. "You sure you're doing okay, Jacob? You sure I can't do anything for you?"

"Other than come home for my birthday, no. I'm fine. Sorry Sis got you all riled up. She worries about us, you know."

"I know," Garrett said. "But she doesn't have to worry. Not really. Not about you and me." He weighted his words with meaning, hoping he didn't need to spell them out. Hoping Jacob would just understand. They were brothers and best friends, after all. Their love for each other couldn't be measured, and it didn't have to be spoken aloud all the time.

"No, she doesn't have to worry," Jacob agreed. "And I'll tell her that when I see her tomorrow."

Garrett's frustrated swing made the ball slice dangerously to the right, veering way off track from the seventh hole of the lush Four Gates golf course.

His golfing partner that afternoon was none other than Cait's brother Seth, a fact that delighted him to no end when he saw Cait's stunned expression at his arrival.

At first she didn't know why he was at her mom's house, appearing suddenly in the middle of a Walsh family gathering.

She asked politely how he was doing. Inquired about Jacob.

But Seth had jumped to his feet and grabbed his clubs when Garrett walked through the front door.

"Wait—you're taking out my *brother?*" she asked, her voice disbelieving then, slowly, quite believing.

"Yep," he told her, enjoying the moment.

Seth, who'd been initiator of the outing, had helped by looking smug and claiming it was all Garrett's idea. But somehow, an hour later, that victory felt hollow.

At his bad swing, Seth cocked an eyebrow in his direction. Garrett reached for his five iron.

"First time out in a while, Ellis?"

"No. Third."

"Hmm."

Garrett felt Seth's sharp eyes assessing him. He'd been playing like an idiot, slicing and dicing so much he should've been in a kitchen. He just couldn't get the touch, the taste, the scent of Cait off his mind... Parts of his body reacted with rigid indiscretion at the memory of those milky thighs.

They walked in silence toward her brother's golf ball. Seth shifted his tall body with surprising grace and gave his ball a PGA-perfect swing. It arched, landing like a gently tossed egg on the green, not more than a yard from the flag.

Seth turned to him. "Woman trouble?"

"No."

"Oh, okay." He glanced over at Garrett, green eyes glowing like a freaking Looney Tunes character. "Well, Dianne's kid brother just got his first serious girlfriend."

"Good for him. Who's the lucky lady?"

"A cute freshman at New Brighton High, like him. Had an officer buddy at the station do a background check on the family." Seth grinned. "They seem like good people."

Garrett laughed. "They'd have to be now, wouldn't they?"

A toothy smile split Seth's face as he shrugged, an unconvincing attempt to appear innocent.

They reached the spot where Garrett's ball rested, mud-splattered and trying to hide from his club. He grimaced as he lined himself up.

"You always check up on the people involved with your family members?" He swung before Seth answered and watched his ball sail impressively into the sand trap. Releasing a deep sigh, he turned to Cait's brother, daring him to comment on the swing.

The corners of Seth's lips quirked, but he didn't take the bait. "Yep," Seth said. "I'm a little protective of the people I love. Especially my kid sister. She's been through a lot. If that Fredric bastard hadn't hightailed it back to Australia, he'd be in permanent traction." He squeezed the iron in his hands and flipped it over his right shoulder as they walked on. The movement was casual, but Seth's knuckles were unmistakably white.

Garrett nodded and took it as the warning it was.

Garrett strode into Cait's classroom at precisely 3:25PM Monday afternoon, just as the two of them had planned. And, just as they'd planned, she was in the midst of discussing Harvest Hoopla decorating ideas with Loni and Marlene.

"Oh! Hi, Garrett," Cait said, in a believably surprised voice. He clenched his jaw then forced himself to relax it. Her ability to playact gnawed at him, despite the fact that this setup was his own damn idea.

Loni said, "Hello."

Marlene gave him a friendly wave.

"Sorry to interrupt your meeting, ladies," he said, holding up his manila folder, "but I got this administrative survey thing in the mail, and I've been scouring the halls for anybody willing to help me with it." He gave them his best self-depreciating laugh. "I really suck at this stuff."

Marlene chuckled and Loni grinned. Cait raised her eyebrows and nodded approvingly, and he wondered if this was yet another act. Was she really approving of *him* or merely the pretense he'd performed so seamlessly? What he wouldn't give to know.

"How can we help?" Loni said.

He feigned a deep sigh. "Okay, it's like this. I need to answer a bunch of questions about 'School Operations' for the central office. Everything from what I think of the efficiency of the hot lunch line to what my opinion is of the condition of our playground equipment." He shrugged and did his best to look mystified. "I've seen the school in action this past month, and I have a few thoughts, but as for the real ins and outs...well, you teachers know the true story better than I do."

"Slow lunch line," Marlene said. "Top-notch jungle gyms."

Cait appeared to give the question some thought. "I agree on both counts. We probably need a new swing set soon, though. What do you think, Loni?"

The older teacher nodded. "The chains are rusting on them."

Garrett opened the file and began scribbling down their comments. "This is great, thanks."

"Any other questions?" Cait asked innocently.

Yeah, sweetheart. When can I make love to you? "Um—yeah," he said aloud, pretending to scan his sheet for a good one. "How about teacher satisfaction? Any general impressions?"

"We've got a fabulous school!" Marlene said with passion and the appearance of total sincerity. "Involved parents, sweet students, honest and dedicated staff. What's not to love?"

Did he spy a look of guilt crossing Cait's face at Marlene's words? True, it had to be hard on her to hoodwink her friends, but he was irrationally pleased to see a crack in her acting veneer.

"That's so true," Loni chimed in. "There are some annoyances here and there but, for the most part, our school is a wonderful place to work. I was in another district for seven years before we moved to Ridgewood Grove, and I can say the atmosphere's not always this cordial elsewhere."

He saw Cait swallow. "Yes...but what about the reduction in office supplies this year? Or the cancellation of the Hoopla?"

She tossed a small, well-rehearsed grin his way before glancing at her colleagues. "Originally, I mean. Before Garrett saw the light. We were all pretty upset about that, remember?"

"Well, sure," Loni said. "But the Hoopla got ironed out—"

"And we've been filing our complaints about the supplies with Sonja, who's really efficient at getting the right words to the right ears," Marlene said, and he knew that was true. Sonja could run the school singlehandedly. "Our concerns won't go unnoticed."

Loni nodded. "Exactly. That's the kind of school we have."

"Good to know." He scribbled some more and gave Cait the high sign that it was okay to move on. He asked them another bogus question or two for good measure and, five minutes later, they disbanded.

Then, just as they'd planned, Cait and Garrett drove separately to New Brighton and met in the Pummelhof's Market parking lot to confer.

"Well, your friends hardly seemed like disgruntled school employees," he admitted to her. "If either has a motive to steal district money, it sure wasn't easy to pinpoint."

"I hated doing that." She picked at her fingernails and looked lost, confused, in need of comfort. From him.

He put his arm around her, and his body heat rose from the contact. "I know, but we needed to do some checking. We can't completely rule them out, but every nonverbal cue they gave off seemed genuine. Any guesses on the others?"

She shook her head and tantalizing golden hair brushed his skin. He bit back a groan.

"I won't even try," she said. "I must not be good at this sleuth thing. I mean, I loved watching Agatha Christie movies when I was a girl, but real life isn't that simple. Figuring out motive and opportunity isn't the straightforward task I'd thought." She sighed. A soft, inviting sound. "I'd have completely failed as a detective."

He couldn't take it anymore. No more talk. No more waiting. No more charades.

"You sure got that last part right, darlin'. If you were any good at gathering clues you'd have deduced by now that I've been waiting to make love to you for way too long."

He heard her breath catch, and he leaned in until he could see the dark gray rims around her irises. He wanted to make sure he had her full attention. That she understood his meaning. "No more detective games, Cait," he said, enunciating every syllable. "You're coming home with me. I want you bad, and I want you now."

Cait's stomach quavered with excitement, anticipation and unappeased desire. "Strawberries and Polar Bear Freeze again?" she whispered once they were inside Garrett's condo.

"No."

Time played relativity games with her mind. Garrett moved at both a rapid speed—locking the door, flipping on lights—while also gliding through the rooms in a bizarre kind of slow motion. Cait wasn't sure which was the reality and which was her skewed, passion-fogged perception. But this she knew: He was focused.

In the end she decided it had been only a matter of seconds since they'd entered the place. He stood in front of her, grasping her fingers, letting his warm brown eyes beam down at her with the intensity of an uncovered fluorescent lamp.

"I made my intentions clear," he said. "If you have any objection, speak now."

"Or forever hold my peace?" Nervousness made her twist a strand of hair.

"Don't mock me, Cait."

"I'm not."

"So, then?"

She approximated a deep, cleansing breath. "Yes."

"Yes?"

"Yes. Absolutely yes."

He relaxed his shoulders and grinned. "Good answer."

And that, she realized, was the end of the discussion. No

preambles about birth control, a detail she doubted a man like Garrett would neglect. No lingering glass of wine to either numb or heighten sensation, not that she could stomach it anyway. No awkward conversations about where to lie down...or was it *lay* down? Oh, God. She couldn't remember even simple grammar rules. He'd shorted every circuit in her brain and body.

"You're thinking too hard," he whispered into her mouth, his lips closing in on her, warming her, throbbing to the beat of his roadrunner pulse as he captured her lips with his. "Stop worrying, Cait. I'm not Fredric. I won't hurt you like he did."

No. But he might hurt her in new, far more painful ways. That didn't surprise her. Her willingness to take a chance on him anyway—well, that was a fresh shock.

The clothes disappeared off her back...and off her chest and her legs, too. She had almost no recollection of him removing them until she felt his skin on hers. The tiny hairs on her arms danced and mingled with his in their embrace.

"We've waited too long," he murmured.

Garrett buried his face in her flaxen hair and felt he was, like the words of some old song he'd once heard, walking on sunshine. Yeah, he thought. It was time to feel good.

There'd be no phone interruptions that afternoon. He'd clicked off the damn ringer. Purposely left his cell in the car. God help anyone, anywhere, who tried to come between them.

For ten seconds or less he debated doing something extra creative. There was a bear-shaped bottle of honey in the kitchen. Something involving a lathery shower maybe. The hallway was a mere two feet from the door and had very thick carpeting.

But he opted for comfort and tradition over originality as he half-led, half-lifted her into his bedroom. She moaned when he ran his tongue over her nipples, first one breast then the other, in leisurely spirals. Her heart pounded underneath. He sensed she was facing down some demon. He refused to disappoint.

Within a few short minutes, Cait had never been further from disappointment.

"This is w-wonderful, Garrett. But what—what can I do for you?" Saying those words cost her several breaths. He'd taken her oxygen away.

He growled at her. "You can let me have my way with you."

The wild thrashings of his tongue, as it neared her belly and then headed further below it, made her claw at the silky bed sheets. They scrunched beneath her fingers.

She heard her own voice cry out to him, her words a jumble. Could he understand her calls of desire? Her admiration of his skill? Her amazement at his gentleness despite his strength?

Her bones, her skin, weakened, loosened. They turned to water just as her internal organs turned to flame. An impossible combination, they shouldn't have been able to coexist this way. But they did. Her body craved release, either in the form of wave or combustion, so long as immediate satisfaction came.

And, oh, it came.

He cradled her once the aftershocks subsided, allowing her to feel the magnitude of him beside her—his hard muscles, long limbs, masculine scents of sweat and musk, lingering aromas of the late autumn afternoon—and she relaxed into his embrace, imbibing him. When he slid away from her, an odd bereavement set in. Their psychic connection had become even stronger than their physical one, and letting him go caused a stab of loss.

The sound of crinkling foil lifted her spirits, though. She'd never before felt this union of emptiness and fullness, anguish and bliss. Not that her sexual past was much to speak of, but to never even guess it could be like this...? God knew, this was more like the first time than the actual first time had been.

He returned to her arms, his arousal obvious. She drew him to her, opening herself up to all of him, being and soul. And he accepted the invitation, entering her slowly, fully.

Garrett's thoughts came in brief, random pulsations. He tried to express them aloud, but his mind was too fuzzy to say anything right.

"To finally be with you, Cait," he whispered. "Heaven."

The best he could do was to let go of reason and then drench himself in only her. Words didn't mean a thing in moments like these anyway. What he had to say to her, he had to say with kisses and caresses.

A groan escaped his lips as their bodies climbed together and journeyed higher and higher. Eyes clenched shut, he felt blindfolded but not sightless. Though he couldn't see through to its end, the path itself grew clearer. And it narrowed, and narrowed further, until he could feel the tautness and the tension in what little space remained.

They sprinted to the top of the peak, whirling over the edge as if the path continued in air, then clung to one another for the slow, delicious descent. Falling brought not fear, but the rarest sense of freedom.

A few hours later, bodies still entwined and sheets twisted, words came back to him.

"How are you?" he said, trying to untangle himself from his now-blueberry-stained linens without losing skin contact with Cait. He licked a dab of fruit off her shoulder, the remains of a tasty experiment during their second (or was it their third?) round of lovemaking that had served as their dinner.

"Mmm?"

"Are you feeling all right, sweetheart?"

She rolled over and looked him in the eye. "Oh, fair."

"Wh-wha—*fair?*" he sputtered, trying to keep the horror from his voice, but knowing he sure as hell wasn't succeeding. *Man! If all she could say about it was—*

Then she openly laughed. "Oh, stop looking at me like I just put peanut butter in your CD player. I don't know about you, but I'm feeling pretty marvelous right now."

So, okay, she was teasing him. He could forgive her.

He kissed her good and hard, and extra long, too. Damned if he'd let her forget *he* was the man who'd made her feel marvelous. He'd only just begun their evening together as far as he was concerned, and he planned to add the adjectives spectacular, splendid, awe-inspiring and magnificent to it before dawn hit. Though, she did give him an idea.

He'd never considered peanut butter before.

"Give me a pair of those," Jenna demanded early the next day, reaching into the box of goblin ears. "Hmm," she said, trying them on and looking more like a dark-haired elf than usual.

"Just got them online," Cait said, passing her a hand mirror.

Jenna admired her reflection and grinned. "There are wacky websites for everything now, aren't there?"

Cait sighed. All the fears she'd put on hold yesterday when she and Garrett made love were now coming back full force. "No, not everything. You can't buy love electronically."

Jenna shot her an inquisitive glance. "You refuse to talk about Garrett, girlfriend, but you plague me with lead-ins like that." She shook her head and dark curls flew. "Besides, you're wrong about e-love. Computer dating is real big, and you never know who you might find."

"E-love, huh?" Cait wrinkled her nose. "Ha. Well, anything seems better right now than *G*-love, but the traditional method is still the way for me, however imperfect."

"Oh, whoa, Cait," Jenna whispered, her eyes big and bright. "You slept with him."

It wasn't a question. Jenna just knew these things. Cait nodded in acknowledgment anyway.

"Oh, boy." Her friend sighed. "Are you falling for him? Falling in love with Garrett Ellis?"

She mentally rehearsed her lie then said, "No."

"Are you sure?"

She hesitated. Breathed. Thought of the countless reasons she had to never fall in love again. Like pain. Suffering. Cheating slime-ball boyfriends. And she realized that logic didn't change a darn thing when it came to emotion. "No."

335

"*Cait!* So you're saying you *did* fall—"

Marlene breezed in, rubbing the drowsiness out of her eyes. Jenna threw Cait a We're-Not-Finished-With-This-Conversation-By-A-Long-Shot look before turning toward the other teacher.

"Morning," Marlene said. "Hey, Cait, remember how you told us to let you know if we spotted any school board members roaming around?"

"Yeah?"

"Well, right now a whole clan of 'em are invading the office."

Garrett gulped down a mouthful of lukewarm coffee to buy time. He gave his watch a deliberate, lengthy stare. "It's only seven-forty," he told a toe-tapping Mike Firenzi. "Can't predict when Ronald will get here. His arrival times vary."

Mike motioned for board member Jason Lenox to join them and shut the door. "Listen, Garrett. Doug and Shelley are doing a quick search of the building, hoping to find him, but we've got to talk to Ronald as soon as possible."

"And it better be today," Jason said firmly. "We've just discovered a big problem."

Garrett cleared his throat. "What exactly did you find?"

"We'd voted over the summer to streamline the office supplies budget," Jason said. "The purpose of which was to save money in that area, put it into an interest-bearing account and start using it to purchase fitness equipment for the staff, one or two pieces at a time. It was a special project we planned to keep as a surprise until the holidays."

"Four Gates is willing to donate a few treadmills and stationary bikes, too," Mike said, "as well as offer trial memberships for teachers at the Club. You know, for New Year's resolutions, that kind of thing. We figured improving district-wide fitness was a more important objective than having an excess of glue sticks or tag board for kiddie projects."

Garrett muttered a "you're kidding" under his breath, but aloud he said, "Really?"

Jason nodded. "But Sonja set us straight this week. Said teachers have been complaining nonstop about the limited supplies. That they all really use that stuff, and regularly. You know, yarn and masking tape and—"

"Glitter?" Garrett added.

"Exactly," Mike said. "But when we went to withdraw some of the deposited money this morning, we discovered the account had been drained."

Garrett narrowed his eyes. "Who was the person responsible for making the deposit? Someone else on the board?"

"No," Jason said. "Since it was for his school, we put it in Ronald's hands. We told him to deposit it, but asked him to keep it a secret."

The words were still hanging in the air when the door banged open. Shelley. She looked like a flaming magnolia, her temper matching her attire. *"Well?"* she demanded.

"Ellis doesn't know where he is." Mike glanced at her and clawed at his necktie. "You and Doug didn't have any luck, huh?"

She shook her head.

"Look," Mike said, "I'm going to give the superintendent a call then, see if he knows anything. I'll be back in a few minutes." Jason marched out of the room, too, but Shelley stayed. She sashayed to Garrett's desk then leaned over it, taking great big, blood-pressure-reducing breaths.

"Garrett, darling, we need to chat sometime soon. Privately." The hot-pink blouse plunged between two very pale mounds of flesh. He couldn't fault the outfit, but he wished Cait were wearing it instead.

"Is this about the missing money from the account?"

"In part," she said, turning coy. A thin smile fought its way to her lips. "What are your plans for this weekend?"

"I'll be in New Brighton." He paused to gauge her reaction. "The Harvest Hoopla is this Saturday."

It looked as though someone cranked Shelley's fake expression a couple notches tighter. "Oh, of course. The festival."

"Planning to attend, Shell?"

"Why, yes, darling," she said, though the words lacked her usual sultry conviction. "I'll be there, I suppose." She swiveled around and sauntered back to the door just at Cait came into view in the office lobby. He didn't know how much of their exchange Cait had overheard but, from the look on her face, he doubted she'd missed anything at all. To add fuel to the fire, Shelley blew him an enormous kiss. Cait's beautiful eyes grew wide.

"See you Saturday then, and plan to spend a few minutes alone with me. I have a favor to ask." Shelley turned, sweeping by Cait as if no one else were there.

He watched the redhead retreat and the blonde take a few hesitant steps in his direction. "Hey," he said softly.

"Hey," she whispered back, her expression impassive now, as if frozen. "What's going on?"

He gave her a quick run-down of his discussion with Mike and Jason.

"This doesn't look good for Ronald," she said, nibbling on her lower lip, her brows creased.

"I know. But a few things still don't add up. I've had my eye on him since August and, other than this situation, I have no hard evidence of wrongdoing on his part." He paused. "The board, however, seems ready to lynch him."

"Shelley certainly seems to have different plans for *you*." Her eyes flared and he was momentarily pleased by her jealousy. He considered reassuring her that she had nothing to worry about, especially after last night, but Cait didn't give him a chance. "Is she really coming to the Harvest Hoopla?" she asked coldly.

"Unless we can bar her from the grounds, yeah, she is."

A humorless laugh escaped her mouth. It stopped as abruptly as it started, though, and she studied him from across the room. "I hope your time alone together will be...pleasurable."

"Oh, well, it might've been the highlight of my fall season except—" he lowered his voice, "I've been having these 'berry incidents' recently that have kinda taken the lead."

He had the satisfaction of seeing her blush before she turned away.

"Berry-picking season is quickly coming to an end," she said, tossing a backward glance at him and speaking far too sweetly, he thought, for anyone with such a sharp glint in her eye. "After the first frost, it's all over."

Somehow he figured this little statement didn't bode well for their love life. He opened his mouth to speak but, in a swivel and a flash, she was gone.

What the hell was wrong with her? Why the sudden cold-shoulder? She couldn't seriously think he and Shelley were still...? No.

He didn't have much time to ponder anything, though, because two minutes later Mike Firenzi strode back into his office.

"Ronald called the superintendent late last night. Said his wife had a death in the family." Mike narrowed his eyes. "He's out of town and unable to be reached until the weekend."

Garrett squinted, too. "Very odd."

"It is. I just wonder what Ronald did with that money."

"Hmm," Garrett said. "And I wonder what we'll have to do this weekend to find out."

~CHAPTER ELEVEN~

STEP 11:
Turn on the rock-salt and ice freezer.
Let the dasher (blade) scrape away the thin layers
of frozen ice cream while pumping air into the mix
as it's whipped up.
~From *Mr. Koolemar's Top Secret,*
Kool Kreme Ice Kreamations Recipe Book, pg. 97

A few days later the sun rose into a flawless October sky, full of autumnal promise. Cait sprang out of bed at five-thirty to begin preparations for the big day.

She'd spent a week of afternoons unloading bags of streamers, leaf-patterned tablecloths, boxes containing the fruit and nut gift baskets Marianne had sent, miscellaneous decorations and various Harvest Hoopla signs into Seth and Dianne's spare bedroom for easier access on this day. Now, it was time to use them all.

With a fuzzy sweater over her shoulders to stave off the morning chill, her hair pulled away from her face into a twist and a clipboard full of notes and lists in hand, Cait stepped onto Seth's backyard patio and surveyed the orchard.

The apple trees, heavy with ripe fruit, glistened in the

slanted morning light. Dappled patterns of sun and shade danced with each other on the grassy carpet. The hums and chortles of wildlife conversation played softly around them. Cait inhaled. If peace had a scent, this was it.

"This is going to be amazing," she whispered to her brother as he set out a picnic-table spread of pastries and hot coffee for the just-arriving volunteers.

"May the day bring you only good things." He pecked the top of her head and gave her a squeeze. "Let's set up the tables."

Garrett parallel parked into one of the spaces along the side of the country highway and began the short stroll toward Seth and Dianne's massive Victorian home. The festival wasn't scheduled to start until nine, but cars were already lining the road.

He meandered to the backyard, setting down the bakery box of fresh chocolate chip cookies he'd brought over. He saw Jimmy, one of Cait's second graders, running his chubby little legs off to deliver a tablecloth to a booth. He hadn't seen the kid smile like that even once when they'd passed each other in the school hallways. In fact, Garrett couldn't remember ever seeing him smile. Must be Cait's magic.

He glanced around. Where was she? She'd avoided him for days, claiming "work" for the festival, but enough was enough.

He eyed Cait's mom wandering around the edges of the property, greeting Seth's neighbors and the Ridgewood Grove volunteers with smiles and donut holes. The orchard was crawling with artists and food vendors unloading their wares and getting their tables organized. Where there weren't caramel-apple-toting adults, watercolorists or craftspeople, there were children. Everywhere. Running around with fake ears the size of Frisbees.

"Hi, Garrett," a lady said.

Seth's wife Dianne stood waving a couple yards away,

strands of hay poking out of her blond ringlets. Mia alternated between twirling in place and running in circles. Gibberish woofed at him then showed off by leaping atop his squealing three-foot mistress. "What are you doing?" he called to Dianne. "Need help?"

"Pumpkin patch set-up," she yelled back, "and yes!" She pointed to several crates of small pumpkins near the patio. "Just grab a bunch and help me hide them over there."

"You got it." In the corner of the lot he could see where a few piles of hay had been dumped for the little kiddie pumpkin patch. Garrett hauled over an entire crate on his first trip across the yard and set to work.

Cait studied her list as she all but sprinted down the orchard's central path, making checkmarks on her sheet every time she passed a completed booth or designated game area.

"What've we got left?" Seth asked, a little out of breath.

"Not much," she admitted, relief just beginning to settle into her tensed shoulder blades. "Mom and Eleanor seem comfortably set up. They've got enough paints and designs between them to decorate about a thousand kids."

"I know. Mom's been so excited. So focused. She's almost like her old self today."

Cait nodded, feeling hope rise inside, inflating her heart.

"How about the others?" he asked.

"We've got a few parents and their kids manning the easier games. Bean Bag Toss. Apple-Bobbing. The Musical Shoe Game."

A group of shrieking goblins ran passed them, and Seth snickered. "I guess the storyteller's already at it."

"He's unbelievable." She smiled. "He started telling spooky tales for the volunteers at seven-fifteen and hasn't stopped to take a breath yet. He'll keep going until we close down at five."

Miranda's frizzy brown hair flew from behind her as she delivered stacks of plastic cups to a booth. Cait waved to the girl then pointed to Seth where Robbie and his buddies stood. "Mr. Jenkins set up the table for his ever-popular Harvest Food Taste Test. Half the kids are hovering around him right now."

He laughed. "What are the featured delicacies this year?"

"I don't know them all, but I could've sworn I heard his son say they made something called Brussels Sprout Quiche."

Seth blanched. "God help us."

"Well, if you try it but don't like the aftertaste, all you need to do is find the Pastry Queen. I ate three pieces of her strawberry-rhubarb pie before I could stop myself last year."

"Now you're talking. I also thought I saw the chef from the BBQ Roadhouse setting up a booth. I take it he'll have grilled bratwurst slathered with Bavarian mustard at lunchtime?"

She nodded. "And at the booth over there—" she pointed, "you can get caramel apples, cookies, jams and spiced cider. Oh, and Alan Koolemar, of course, has his own Ice Kreamations booth."

Her brother opened his mouth to speak but another of Cait's students came rushing up to them. "Is it really true, Miss Walsh? Is Jeremy's dad gonna draw pictures of us?"

"It's true. His table is over there." She pointed deep into the orchard. "I think Daisy put up the sign down this path."

"Thanks!" He raced away, barely swerving to avoid skidding into a mother with handmade quilts and comforters. A few minutes later, she and Seth reached the Pumpkin Patch.

Mia, hanging upside-down with Garrett gripping her ankles, was being swung in a slow arc over the tops of the pumpkins. The little girl giggled and squeaked, her chunky fingertips literally grasping at straws as she passed above the hay pile.

"Whooo-hooo," Seth called out to his daughter. "That looks like a perfect position...for tickling!"

Mia shrieked as Seth wiggled his fingers over her rounded tummy and Garrett continued to hold her, swaying her tiny body slightly from side to side.

Cait was reminded again of how good Garrett was with kids. His behavior with girlfriends, of course, was another matter...but maybe he didn't really understand what she needed from him right now. Maybe he couldn't see the effect his flirtations with Mrs. McAllister had on her. It was bad enough that the school board member was always on the verge of propositioning him, but did he ever consider that his own behavior encouraged it? Did he have to keep *smiling* at the woman? Showering her with eye contact, the kind that said she had his full attention? Her friends might claim she was being paranoid, and a couple of years ago she would have agreed. But now she knew better. She'd been down this road before, and it was better to be paranoid than to be blindsided.

Dianne appeared. "I'll rescue you, darling," she cried, pulling Mia into her arms. "Poor baby. Were they torturing you?"

"Oh, yes, Mommy." Mia's pink lips puckered up as she gave her mother a wet kiss.

Dianne kissed her right back then winked at her daughter. "Ha, ha! Well, I've got you now, and it's my turn." A fresh round of giggling began as Dianne started tickling Mia and then spirited the child off to the house.

"Thanks for keeping an eye on her, Garrett," Seth said. "She loves roughhousing like that."

Garrett brushed the hay off his jeans. "Nah, she was keeping an eye on me. Told me where to hide every single pumpkin." He half smiled at Seth then looked at Cait for a long moment.

"Well, I'd better go inside, too, take care of stuff before things get hopping out here," Seth said. "Catch you both later."

Cait watched her big brother walk away. Seth didn't fool her. He hadn't changed one iota since the day she was fifteen and he discovered her enormous crush on his best friend. He found all kinds of reasons to leave them alone. Until his buddy groped her a bit too freely for his tastes. Then Seth punched him out.

"So, how are you doing, Cait? I can't say I've seen much of you this week," Garrett said, his voice noticeably cool.

"I—I'm doing all right. It's been busy, you know...lately. Planning for the festival and getting everything organized."

He glanced around. "Well, you've done a remarkable job. Every booth, every activity looks perfect." His lips quirked. "Not that I'm surprised. After all *you* were the one in charge."

She could feel her skin heating up. "Thanks."

"Noticed the baskets made their way here safely. Marianne would be pleased to see one monopolizing each table."

"Oh, come on, they're great. Did any of the children tell you what we're doing with them?"

"I can't imagine."

"They're going to make the most wonderful door prizes. The booth owners will draw names from the big cauldron we have set up over there." She pointed. "Each lucky winner will take home a gift basket personally presented to them by one of the goblins."

"Yep. Saw your students. They look like very cute rats."

"Garrett!"

"Okay, mice."

"Hey, that's a mean thing to—"

"Oh, stop trying to be so contrary, Cait." He laughed and hugged her in a way that sent her pulse skyrocketing. Memories of their passionate night together flashed through her mind. The reminder made her joints grow weak. When in his arms, she could almost trust him completely. Almost trust herself, even...

"This is your big day," he said, "and, as you can see, I'm here to help."

"Thanks," she said again, looking at her toes once he released her. She scanned her clipboard out of habit, took three deep breaths then asked the question that had been on her mind for several very long days. "Have you talked to Shelley already?"

"Nope. Haven't seen her."

"Oh." She swallowed. "Any word yet from Ronald?"

"Nope on that, too. The superintendent said he left a bunch of messages at the principal's house. Said he'd call once Ronald responded." Garrett shrugged. "I'll let you know what happens."

"Okay." She looked at her clipboard again. "Well, I guess I

should get back to work. It's really nice of you to be here, even though it seems the offender you were searching for has been found."

"It does seem that way," he told her. "But you never know. Like the saying goes, 'It ain't over 'til it's over.'"

Garrett spotted Shelley and Chuck McAllister arriving together a couple of hours later, but the two separated almost immediately, and their daughters shot off in their own directions once their feet touched the grass and gravel.

As always, Garrett marveled at the mysterious connection that bound Shelley to her Chucky. He suspected it had something to do with a combustible merger between cleavage and stock portfolios.

Well, at least she hadn't spotted him yet. He wasn't in the habit of playing one-on-one with someone else's wife. Hell, even if he were, he still wouldn't be caught alone in a dark pumpkin patch with Shelley Oliver McAllister.

Jacob once said of Shelley's older sister, "Sabrina Oliver's a viper. She poisons her male prey, but—" he expelled a harsh laugh, "she'll lick every inch of his body before she does...and pocket every dollar in his wallet."

"Gold-digging snakes," Garrett hissed to a guiltless pumpkin. It was women like that who turned Jacob into the incorrigible womanizer he became.

"Garrett, darling," Shelley drawled, approaching him.

Oh, sheesh. "How are ya, Shell?"

"Wonderful. What a gorgeous day we have here. And—" she glanced around Seth's lot and the orchard, "isn't this just the quaintest place? Wisconsin is so full of cuteness."

Garrett spied Cait ushering a few children down the path toward the apple-bobbing station. "Yes, it is." He turned to face Shelley. "So, perhaps here, amidst all of nature's wonders, you've got some answers for me. Let's start with whatever it is you needed to see me so privately about."

Her complexion began to pink up. She pursed her lipstick-slathered mouth and lifted the corners for a quick smile. "There's no need to get all agitated, honey. I did want to talk to you, but it can wait if you're not in the right mood. Maybe you need to run around and get some fresh air first."

God, did she think he was seven or something? Well, he could act childish, if that's what she required.

"Get to the point, Shell, before I walk away and tell my mother to tell your mother how you're still playing little games."

Her pouty rosebud mouth dropped open. "Don't get all testy with me and make me sorry I recommended you for this position."

What the hell was she talking about?

"You recommended me for financial director?" he asked slowly.

"Why, sure. The superintendent and I were talking one day last spring. He said the other guy was retiring, and I told him that he should get someone like *you*. I didn't think he was listening, so I was surprised. Not that he hired you, of course, but that he took my suggestion." She flashed a bright smile at him at him. "He usually doesn't. But, naturally, I was right. I knew you were exactly the kind of person we needed here."

He narrowed his eyes at her. "Why?"

She looked at him as though he were as dense as a bowling ball. "Garrett, darling, putting our, um, personal history aside...for the kinds of projects the school board holds close to its heart, we need the *right* kind of administrators in the office. Ones who'd be supportive. Set a good example."

"What *kind* of example?"

"Well, that's what I wanted to talk to you about." She eyed his body up and down. "You know, you're very trim. More people should be that fit."

This left him nearly speechless. "I—uh, thanks."

She nodded. "You always were athletic."

"Yeah, so?"

"So that's what my projects are about, silly." She slapped

him lightly on the arm.

He pulled away and motioned for her to continue.

"I hadn't been living in Wisconsin for two weeks before I realized this was a state with a real consciousness problem."

"The citizens seemed sleepy to you?"

She giggled. "No, Garrett. *Health* consciousness. It's terribly lacking, but how could they help it? What with all these dairy products." She began ticking them off on her fingers. "Cheese, whole milk, butter, milkshakes, ice cream, frozen custard, even many brands of yogurt. They're products so high in fat! Plus—" She covered her heart in a show of shock. "Some people actually *deep fry* their cheese."

"You don't say..."

"It's true! I saw it on the menu the first time Chucky and I went out to dinner here, and I thought, 'Now this is a state that needs a Fitness Fairy.'"

He covered his mouth to keep from blurting out something extraordinarily inappropriate. "A Fitness *Fairy?*" he managed.

"Yes. You know, like a fairy godmother. Helping the unfit residents of Ridgewood Grove get healthy again. Lowering their cholesterol and blood pressure. Getting those glucose readings down. Teaching them how to do high-cardio, low-impact aerobic workouts. It's a tough job," she said solemnly. "And some people—you wouldn't believe how many!—are really resistant to changing their eating and exercise habits."

Garrett thought of the junk food wrappers in his car. "Hmm."

"And events like this are the worst." She motioned toward the Hoopla booths. "They put butter on everything. Caramel on perfectly tasty apples. Cheddar-cheese sauce on vegetables. Brown sugar on *zucchini*, for goodness sake." She shuddered. "And I don't even want to know how much saturated fat and sugar are in those Kool Kreme Ice Kreamations."

"I'm sure it's hideously high," he said, masking his smile the best he could.

"I knew you'd understand. That's why I'd hoped you'd help by being a fitness role model. Maybe taking a few staff members under your wing and teaching them how to lift weights or even golf. Anything to get those heart chambers pumping."

"Well, I—er..."

"It would mean a lot to me." She gave a deep sigh. "I can't tell you how disappointed I am in Ronald. I'd been working *so* hard with him. Getting him to lay off those frosted donuts. Encouraging him to go for walks after lunch. He seemed to really be in favor of the fitness equipment idea. I can't believe he'd take the money out of the fund, but I suppose he didn't expect anyone would be withdrawing from it yet."

"How much was in the account, Shell?"

"Just a few thousand dollars. We'd hoped to grow it faster, though. Ronald was talking to Doug and Chucky about that when we went golfing together."

"At Four Gates?"

"Yes, of course," she said. "Mike has been very, very supportive of everything sports related, but he doesn't know the business side like Doug. Or my hubby, for that matter."

This caught Garrett's attention. "So did, er, *Chucky* have an investment plan for the fund? Something at the bank with a higher-than-average interest rate?"

"Oh, yes, of course. He had great ideas. But Doug said Chippenak Chemical had a terrific savings plan already in place. He was going to discuss some options with his uncle and get back to us. Before he had a chance to, though, this all happened."

"Is Doug anywhere around here now?"

"He said he was planning on coming." She gazed at a few clusters of people in the orchard, squinting at the figure of someone who had Chippenak's average build. "I think that's him over there."

"Good," he said. "I'd be interested in talking with him about his strategy. It may have given Ronald a few ideas."

"Okay," she said. "But, honey, if you could—" She looked pained. "Would you please try to steer people away from Mr. Koolemar's booth? I get cellulite just from looking at it."

❧ ♥ ❧

At the Kool Kreme Ice Kreamations booth, Mr. Koolemar was doing steady business. Cait handed a double-decker cone to a first grader. She smiled at the older gentleman once the child, eyes aglow, had walked away.

"Thanks for letting me be one of the scoopers for a little while," she said. "It's fun to step away from the hosting role and watch all the happy faces leaving here with their cones. You make the best ice cream anywhere."

"Thank you, dearie. It's my pleasure."

Doug Chippenak stepped to the booth, eyes crinkling. "How're you doing, old man?" He gave Mr. Koolemar's arm a friendly pat.

"Doing fine, son. How's your uncle been lately?"

A look like a dark cloud passed in front of Doug's eyes. He brushed his fingers through his hair, a nondescript shade of brown but for a few streaks of gray near his temples. Cait thought she heard him sigh.

"Hanging in there," Doug said. "Had a knee surgery, which was a little rough, but he pulled through. He should be back at the office soon."

"Glad to hear that," Mr. Koolemar said. "You give him my best now."

"Oh, I will. And how about a triple scoop of Honey Crunch Delight?"

"Coming right up." Mr. Koolemar turned to Cait. "This one's on the house. You want to do the honors or should I?"

"I will," Cait said with a smile at the two men.

While she was busy putting the final touches on Doug's enormous cone, she caught a movement out of the corner of her eye. Mr. Koolemar was passing a bag of something to Doug, literally under the counter. Doug took it and slipped it into his shoulder duffle.

She turned to look at them directly, but Mr. Koolemar sent her a guileless grin, and Doug gently withdrew his cone from her hand.

"Thanks," the board member told her. "I'll take it to go." He patted Mr. Koolemar again, winked and said to him, "See you in a few hours." Then, with a parting wave, Doug walked away.

She eyed the older man. "I'm sorry if this sounds nosy," she said, "but what was in that bag you gave Mr. Chippenak?"

"Just some tokens, dear."

Tokens!

"But, when Garrett and I talked to you a few weeks ago about our suspicions of theft from the festival booths, you said you collected your own tokens."

"I do collect them. I just let Doug exchange them for me."

Cait's heart started pounding. "But do you have any idea how many tokens were in that bag?"

He shook his head.

"Did you keep track of your customers? How many stopped by?"

He shrugged. "Oh, probably somewhere between eighty-five and one-hundred-twenty. I get to talking to people and I lose count."

"Mr. Koolemar," she said extra slowly in an attempt to keep from raising her voice, "do you realize what a difference in total profit there would be if someone snatched just a few handfuls of tokens from your bag every time you turned one in?"

An odd look crossed his face. "But I trust Doug. Known the lad since he was six. Why on earth would he wanna steal from me?"

"I don't know, but tell me—did he do the token exchanges for you at the other festivals, too?"

"The past couple of years, yeah. And not just for me," Mr. Koolemar said. "He's got a circuit. Helps out the other seniors, too. We all appreciate not having to run around so much." He tapped his hip. "Creaky bones."

Cait thrust the scooper into a tub of Mocha Madness, gave the old man a tender hug and rushed out of the booth to find

Garrett.

Garrett and Cait tailed Chippenak around the festival, watching from a safe distance as he went booth to booth.

That sneaky ferret. Garrett thought of him at school board meetings. Always so reserved but pleasant. So boringly ordinary. Mundane and seemingly harmless. The guy blended in. Acted appropriately. People tended not to suspect people like that, but they should have. Garrett bereted himself. *He* should have.

Well, he'd make up for his negligence now.

Chippenak stopped at a total of eight booths, seven in addition to Mr. Koolemar's. All booths run by elderly men. He'd chat with the vendors, slap their backs, lean in and whisper a joke of some kind and then take a bag of their tokens. He'd slip the bag with the vendor's name printed on it into a black duffle he'd slung over his shoulder and move on to his next prey.

Working to stay well hidden, Garrett and Cait followed Chippenak for half an hour before they got the proof they needed.

It happened right after the board member bought a spiced cider. He sat under an apple tree in a far corner of the orchard, sipping then gulping the drink until it was empty. Still holding his cup, he set down his duffle and slipped a free hand inside.

What was he doing? It was too far away for Garrett to see exactly, but Chippenak seemed to be tugging on something inside the duffle. Loosening the tops of the eight little bags, maybe? After a few moments, Chippenak pulled a ninth small bag out of his duffle—this one completely empty. He set it near his thigh.

He then leaned back against the tree and closed his eyes. He rubbed his graying sideburns then took a slow sip of his beverage.

From his *empty* cup, Garrett remembered. He nudged Cait to see if she'd noticed. She did.

One "sip" at a time, Chippenak pretended to drink cider but instead dipped his cup into his duffle bag, filling it with tokens. He brought the cup to his mouth as if to drink from it then, lowering the cup carefully, he let the tokens slide into the single small bag he kept near him. From a distance, unobserved, no one would guess the lackluster board member was doing anything but enjoying an autumn drink under a shady tree.

But Garrett and Cait knew differently as they watched Chippenak repeat this procedure a dozen times, transferring hundreds of dollars in tokens from the other bags into his.

On a few occasions the sneaky ferret glanced around, probably scanning for prying eyes, but apparently he didn't see anything that alarmed him.

"For someone who seemed so unobtrusive at school, so normal," Cait said, "he sure is despicable."

"That he is."

"But I wonder, why does he think it's worth it? Stealing thirty dollars from one vendor, fifty from another?" she asked. "So he'll get a few hundred in the end, maybe, but that's still petty cash compared to what big corporations have on hand."

"No kidding," he said. "I checked into Chippenak's employment history. The guy's been making a six-figure salary for a decade. He's not strapped for cash in any obvious way."

"But even if he were, why steal from these old men? Why not do his thievery at Chippenak Chemical where he could embezzle half a million and maybe get away with it because he's the VP?"

"How do we know he's not doing that, too?" Garrett said.

"I guess we don't, it's just—"

"Shh. He's leaving."

They followed him as he wound his way through the orchard and toward the booth where tokens were exchanged for cash.

Cait looked at her watch. "Darn. It's after two o'clock."

"What's the problem?"

"That means the expenses for hosting the festival have already been withdrawn from the purchasing booth. Profits can now be distributed to any vendor who wants to turn in tokens."

"And just look where Chippenak's headed..."

Cait sighed. "This year," she said, "I chose a foolproof person to handle the cash. Someone I trusted implicitly with both her honor and her math competency."

"Your friend Jenna?"

"I'd trust Jenna with my life, Garrett," she said, giving him a serious look. "But for this I wanted someone who wouldn't make even a single mathematical miscalculation, which is why I enlisted a professional statistician. Dianne."

He looked toward the booth and, sure enough, Chippenak was leaning casually against the table, having a friendly conversation with Cait's golden-haired sister-in-law.

"Did you tell her to be on the lookout for any suspicious behavior?" he asked.

"Absolutely, but this wouldn't raise a red flag. The elderly vendors, I'm sure, told Dianne a 'nice young man' would be exchanging their tokens for them around this time. And here he is pulling out not eight but nine token bags."

"And there he is getting the cash back," Garrett said. "What is their value this year, Cait? About a dollar per token?"

"A dollar and fifteen cents."

"Ah," he said. "So calculation work is required on the part of the booth attendants."

"And, thus, we have Hard Workers A, B and C." Cait pointed. "Dianne, Worker A, is faithfully using her calculator, with Marlene next to her, B, trying to quickly count tokens so they can return the correct amount of money. And Loni, C, is scribbling fast, trying to record the names of the vendors to whom the cash belongs. Dianne won't allow anyone to make an error. Period."

"But Doug's brought so much to the booth, and they're all so busy being fast and accurate, none of them have noticed the way he repositioned the bags. The way he pocketed the unlabeled, cash-filled sack after the tokens were counted, so he got the money but didn't have to explain who that ninth token bag belonged to."

"Sneakier than a skunk," Cait said.

"A ferret."

"A weasel."

"A bored board member."

She looked up at him in surprise. "Do you really think that's what it is? That that's what this is all about for him? Boredom?"

"I don't know, Cait. Maybe. But I do believe it's high time we found out for sure." He pulled out his cell phone and got the New Brighton police on the line.

"We have a situation here you need to take a look at," he told them. "Right now."

But, before the local officers could arrive, Doug glanced right at them. He must've sensed they'd been watching because an astonished looked crossed his face. Within seconds, he'd eluded their attempts at long-range surveillance, slipped through the happy festival crowd...and disappeared.

~CHAPTER TWELVE~

STEP 12:
After about a half hour,
add in the sliced candied cherries,
the milk chocolate chips
and the shaved dark chocolate.
What could be a better combination?
~From *Mr. Koolemar's Top Secret,*
Kool Kreme Ice Kreamations Recipe Book, pg. 97

"I feel like an idiot!" Dianne pounded her fist on her living room sofa two hours later. "How could I let him put something like that passed me? I *never* make computation errors."

"It's not your fault," Garrett said, trying to reassure her. "The way Doug played a shell game with those bags, he could've been a professional grifter."

A handful of police officers were now out scouring the town for the missing board member. The one officer who remained scanned the festival grounds through the window, a serious look on his face. "I believe you're right, Garrett. Doug Chippenak clearly had a lot of practice ripping people off, and it's likely his little scam would've gone unnoticed again if not for you and Cait."

The officer turned to address the superintendent, who'd been called in immediately. "Unfortunately, sir, we need to locate the man in order to corroborate what Garrett and Cait witnessed and, of course, to gather the remaining evidence."

Seth stepped forward. "Isn't it enough that you have the token bags belonging to the vendors?"

"Not quite," the officer said. "We don't have Mr. Chippenak's bag. The one Cait and Garrett saw him pocket during the exchange. Nor do we have the cash he took for himself, which was inside it."

"What did he do with the vendors' money?" the superintendent asked, a worry line creasing his brow.

"He left all eight of the cash-filled bags, labeled with the vendors' names, at Mr. Koolemar's booth," the officer said. "He told the gentleman to keep an eye on them and that he'd be back to distribute them to their owners later. Said he couldn't pass up the opportunity to grab a piece of strawberry-rhubarb pie before the lady running that booth ran out."

"The Pastry Queen," Cait whispered.

The officer squinted at her. "What?"

"It's made by the Pastry Queen, and it's really, really great pie," Cait said. "Mr. Koolemar would've believed Doug if he said that. He would've thought Doug was sincere, not a lying thief."

Garrett tried to read her expression. It was a combination of perplexed, determined and outraged. Despite the strain of the afternoon, he couldn't help but smile a little. That was the same expression she'd worn when he'd tried to cancel her festival. That No-One-Better-Mess-With-Me look and, in the end, she'd sure gotten her way. Whether or not Doug realized it, he was toast.

"Well, at least Chippenak didn't run off with the old men's money sacks," Seth said.

Dianne crossed her arms. "In a way, he did. *All* of the cash in the one bag he kept belonged to those elderly gentlemen."

"That's true," the officer said. "When we looked in the bags and cross-checked the amounts allocated to the vendors with the amount of cash given out, we found that he'd stolen close to four hundred dollars. Almost fifty from each."

"I'm beyond saddened," the superintendent whispered. "I never would've imagined Doug capable of something like this."

"But why'd he do it?" Seth asked. "The guy was wealthy. He had no motivation to steal, not unless he had personal cash-flow problems or unless the company was in financial trouble."

The officer shook his head. "We still need to do a full investigation, but no. Neither of those things seems to be the case. Mr. Chippenak's logic is mystifying to us as well." He patted his weapon absentmindedly. "We'll contact you when we know more. 'Til then, if you see or hear anything, give us a call."

"Of course," Dianne said. The rest of them nodded.

Garrett walked the officer out to his squad car, while Seth, Dianne and Cait conversed quietly inside. The superintendent stood by a window, staring at the Harvest Hoopla booths, their vendors and the many locals still enjoying the day of revelry.

Fortunately, few participants even realized there'd been a disturbance that afternoon. New Brighton police officers were swift and discrete. Garrett felt a rush of pride in them.

After the policeman left, the older administrator pulled Garrett aside. "I finally got a call back from Ronald while I was on my way out here. He had no idea what happened to the money in the fitness account, but he admitted he'd put his trust in Doug."

"Why? What did they do together?" Garrett said.

"Ronald was getting ready to deposit the funds in the account when Doug convinced him to go with a 'better investment strategy.' Doug said he'd 'take care of everything' and get the money to gain interest faster. He promised to give Ronald the credit for making the investment, and Ronald had no reason not to believe him."

"So, where did Doug put the money for the fitness equipment?"

"I don't know, Garrett. But I told another officer about it, and he took notes, so the police have it on record."

He thought back to the day the board members raided the

office. Doug's behavior made no sense whatsoever. "But why the pretense of looking for Ronald this week? He and Shelley searched the school for him together. Doug would've known the principal didn't have anything to do with the disappearing funds."

The older man rubbed his temples and sighed. "Don't know the reason for that, either, but the whole day's given me a migraine."

Garrett could understand that. His head ached, too. Once the superintendent went home, Garrett rejoined the three Walshs.

"Are Marlene and Loni still manning the token-exchange booth?" he asked them.

"Yes," Cait said. "And I asked Jenna to fill in for Dianne while we talked with the police."

"I'll go back and help again in few minutes," Dianne said. "But I'm still fuming at the man's behavior. What a slime!"

Seth grinned. "I've heard board members can be slippery." He began rubbing his wife's shoulders to relieve her of the built-up tension. It made Garrett want to do the same thing for Cait.

"Speaking of which," Cait asked Garrett, an undeniable gleam of curiosity in her eye, "I meant to ask earlier—what happened to your conversation with Shelley McAllister? Did she ever find you?"

"Oh, yeah." And, just to tease her a bit, he added, "She had an irresistible proposition for me."

"What was that?" She stared at him, brows pushed together.

"Why, she wanted me to help convert the fitness offenders of Ridgewood Grove to a life of health consciousness."

He got his reward when Cait suddenly laughed. "What?"

"Yep. It's fitness evangelism, let me tell you. I may even get a muscle T-shirt out of it if I'm real good."

Seth and Dianne chuckled at this.

"What do you have to do? Make the staff do wind sprints during their prep time?" Dianne said.

"That's a start. But I'm supposed to choose a few teachers

to 'take under my wing.' Teach them to swing golf clubs or throw balls or do...something aerobic."

"Oh, boy. I'm not touching that comment," Seth said, his body shaking with laughter. "You be careful with my kid sister."

Before Garrett could reply, Cait broke in. "You're saying, all this time, *that's* what she wanted from you? Nothing illegal, immoral—"

"Or even fattening," Dianne completed, and the two ladies dissolved into a fit of giggles.

He shook his head, his spirits rising at the sight of Cait laughing like that again. He'd missed her smiles. Then, deciding to be bold, he turned to face her. "Forget Shelley. What do *you* want from me?" He puffed out his chest and added a winning grin.

"Ooooh, now that sounds like an irresistible proposition," Dianne said, nudging Cait and winking. She eyed the staircase suggestively. "Lots of room to explore your options upstairs."

"Dianne!" Cait cried.

But Seth gave him and Cait a long, thoughtful look. "You know, despite Chippenak slipping away, the Harvest Hoopla turned out to be quite a success." He gestured toward the window. "Look at all those happy people out there. And the goblins—my God, Cait. They were a riot. I've never seen kids have so much fun."

"Seth's right," Dianne said. "Not only did everyone who showed up have a great time, but I haven't seen your mother so delighted with anything in months. When she wasn't painting dolphins on children's cheeks, she was flitting about like her old social-butterfly self. You brought so much pleasure to so many people by organizing the festival."

"And so did you," Cait said, "by letting us host it here." She gave her sister-in-law and her brother a warm look. "Thanks for everything you did. It was just—well, kind of an odd day."

"Which is why you should take a half hour to relax," Seth said. "You need a break."

"But the vendors—" Cait began.

"Shh." Seth patted his sister's head as he might a child's. "I didn't say run off to Tahiti. But go upstairs, sit down, take a few deep breaths before you return. Nothing's going to happen in the next thirty minutes that we can't handle. The police are searching for Doug, so there isn't anything you can do but wait."

"They'll probably get him tonight," Dianne said.

Seth nodded. "And the vendors are only just beginning to pack up, but lots of people are still nibbling on treats outside. It's okay to give yourselves a little time to...regroup...or whatever." His grin broadened. He turned to Garrett and jabbed his thumb in the direction of the stairs. "Get her out of here. Please. I want to spend a few minutes alone with my wife."

Cait blushed but Garrett didn't need to be asked twice. He wanted Doug Chippenak caught but—as Seth said—the police were on it and, anyway, he wanted Cait more. He didn't give her a chance to suggest a counterproposal.

He held out his hand to her, watched as she put her small fingers in his palm, then he tugged her away from the others.

"C'mon," he whispered as he led her upstairs. "I haven't seen any of the rooms up here yet. I think I've been missing out..."

As much as she loved the Harvest Hoopla, Cait had to admit it didn't hold a candle to giving Garrett a "tour" of the bedrooms.

"This is Seth and Dianne's room," she told him, as they peeked through the door.

He scanned the master bedroom approvingly and skimmed his fingers over her shoulder blades until she shivered. "Very nice. Let's move on."

Walking across the hall, she popped open another door. "And this is Mia's room."

He laughed. "Does it double as Santa's workshop? Dolls, stuffed animals, fake food... This kid has everything."

She shrugged. "Only child. Only niece. Only granddaughter."

He kissed the top of her head. "One very loved little girl. Just like her auntie."

Cait's heart skipped a few beats...and then a few more. What did he mean? That she was loved by her family, like Mia? Or that *he* loved her?

He didn't give her a chance to ask. "Next room, please."

"Um," she said, "this is the guest bedroom." The white frilly lace curtains ruffled as the wind blew another gust inside. She watched Garrett appraise the open windows and, then, the firm mattress of the double bed. The structure sat prominently in the center of the room, covered with a matching white frilly lace bedspread. His eyes narrowed and his lips pursed.

He marched over to the windows and shut them with one swift stroke. Then he turned to stand beside the bed, shaking his head and motioning for her to join him. "Close the door."

She did.

"We're not sleeping on this," he informed her.

"We're in my brother's house, Garrett. We're not sleeping on anything."

He glanced around the room, amused. "You're absolutely right." He grabbed her hand and tugged her to his side. "What's in that closet?"

"Nothing. They keep it empty for guests to—"

"Perfect."

And before she knew it, that's where they were. Closet door shut tight, the two of them—not *on* anything—but *up against* the smooth wall, with his mouth on hers, her legs wrapped around his waist and his hands...touching everywhere. Ohhh, good heavens.

She'd never think of storage space the same way again.

At about five o'clock, they heard some loud pounding on the guest room door. Seth called out, "I've gotta talk to you two."

"Okay, um, just a second." Cait's pulse raced, not only from her passionate interlude with Garrett, but from the worried tone of Seth's voice. They managed to slip their clothes back on and emerge from the closet. She swung open the bedroom door. Her brother's face looked ghostly white. "What's wrong?" she said.

"Hey, Cait, Garrett, sorry to interrupt you like this, but we have a big problem. Mom's missing."

"What?" she cried.

Garrett was already racing down the hall and to the staircase, she and Seth at his heels. Jenna, breathless from running in from outside, met them at the bottom.

"We'll find her, Cait," Jenna said, but she looked panicked.

Dianne had a cell phone to her ear and, for the second time in three hours, the New Brighton police were on their way over. Her sister-in-law was ashen. "I feel horrible when I think—" She paused. "The last time I saw your mom, she was talking to Doug Chippenak, of all people."

Seth's eyes bulged out. "Oh, God, honey. When was this?"

Dianne brushed away a few tears. "Around lunchtime. Maybe twelve-thirty, one o'clock."

"That was before Cait and I started tailing him," Garrett said. "When was the last time you saw her, Jenna?"

Her friend blinked. "It was after that. During the time the police were searching the grounds. Two-thirty, I think."

"Thank God," Seth said.

Garrett exhaled deeply. "Doug was long gone by then. But all this means is that their disappearances are unrelated."

Cait held her breath and fought off the guilt she didn't want to acknowledge. "Did any of us see her after two-thirty?"

No one had.

"How about mom's friend Eleanor?" Cait asked.

Jenna shook her head. "She saw her just before I did, and that was her last time, too."

Cait swallowed. "Then we shouldn't waste another minute."

"You need to stop blaming yourself," Garrett said in his gentlest voice, one hand on the steering wheel, the other on Cait's knee. Gone was the passion from the late afternoon. Now, after an hour of unfocused driving, he thought she looked ready to crumple from stress. He reached out and squeezed her fingers. She squeezed back, but he could tell it was a halfhearted gesture.

"Seth and Dianne got on top of things immediately," he said. "They notified the police. Men were put on the job within minutes. You couldn't have done it any faster."

"If only I'd gone out to check on her instead of going upstairs. If only I hadn't been so preoccupied with Doug Chippenak before that. I should've been more responsible. God, I haven't done a single responsible thing in hours."

The sting of her words hurt worse than a smack across his face. His body recoiled from the blow. He jerked his hand away.

Then she noticed him, for the first time, he figured, since Seth's words jolted them out of the closet. Distress, terror and remorse filled her eyes.

"Garrett, I'm sorry. I—I didn't mean—"

"Forget it," he said quickly, hoping he could do the same, but he had to admit to there being an angry, selfish side in him. A side that felt his joy in their coupling had already been tainted.

They rode in silence.

"Look," he said after another fifteen minutes of pointless meandering. "Do you have a list of places you want to check out that the police might not think of? Are there spots she enjoys wandering around in sometimes? Parks, maybe? Friends she might visit? Restaurants or coffee places or that bakery?"

Tears slipped down Cait's cheeks. She shook her head. "Mom's memory...it's vanishing. She no longer follows any of the routines we'd gotten used to for the past four or five years, and I've got no idea." She brushed at the tears, missing a few. They slid onto her blouse and left wet splotches on the front.

"What about before then? About her more distant past?

What would she do on a Saturday evening when you and Seth were kids?"

"Go strolling in town. Stop for a piece of pie or an ice cream sundae. Play bridge or bingo with the church group. She and Dad would go together almost weekly when he was still alive. They went to St. Christopher's on County Highway K-Z. But it's way on the other side of town, much too far for her to walk. Even before we took the car keys away from her, Seth and Dianne would usually pick her up and take her to St. Luke's for senior activities or church services. It's where Mia was christened, where Dad was buried and much nearer to her house."

"How many miles would you say it is from Seth's house to St. Christopher's?"

She looked at him like he was as nutty as a pecan. "Seven, maybe eight. Garrett, there's no way she could've walked—"

"Your mother is really healthy, physically at least. I know she's got the blood pressure thing, but she's also got stronger legs than a lot of women her age." He swung the car around for a not-exactly-legal U-turn. "Plus, she's got determination in her favor, a four-hour head start on us and a very clear memory of her favorite times in her life." He looked at Cait, fear and hopefulness battling it out on her face. "It's not impossible."

They found her wandering in the back corner of St. Christopher's cemetery, the day's last sunlight bathing her hair, her sweater wrapped tight and a wistful smile playing on her lips.

"MOM!" Cait cried, rushing up to her and throwing her arms around her mother's shivering body. "We were so worried about you. How did you get here? Did you get lost? Are you hurt?"

To the flurry of questions, her mom squinted, appearing surprised. "It's a lovely evening, isn't it? A bit chilly, but I think Hank will remember to bring my thicker cardigan when he comes. We like to meet back here before the bingo game, you know. I wanted to show him these pretty pink roses." She pointed to a tangled mass of baby roses in a colorful vase, brought by someone paying tribute to a loved one long departed.

Cait's heart jumped to her throat. *Daddy. Didn't Mom remember he was gone? And buried at St. Luke's, not here...* Four years and Cait still missed him. Would Dad have been disappointed in her? In the choices she made in his absence? In the things she did and failed to do?

"Did you see him?" her mother asked, feverishly bright. "He didn't go into the church already, did he, darling?"

"Oh, Mom." It came out like a sob. "Garrett?"

"Yes," he answered.

"Please...get Seth on the cell phone. *Now.*"

Cait, Seth and Dianne spent the next week taking turns with Mom, staying with her, arranging days off from work and beginning to pack up her most necessary belongings from the house.

Though Cait knew they'd never know the whole story of what happened the evening of the Harvest Hoopla, an extensive medical exam proved there'd been no physical harm done, and her mother had remembered enough to assure them she'd enjoyed her walk to church. She even remembered conversing with Doug Chippenak. "Oh, yes, the nice man with the gray sideburns, just like Hank's," she'd said when questioned. And Cait couldn't deny that, though she would hardly call Doug "nice," he did have graying hair that looked similar to her father's. Which was what Mom would notice.

Still, she and Seth weren't about to take any more chances. Their mother may have been unfazed by the whole experience, but Cait had been shaken to the core.

She stared out her mother's kitchen window, floundering in silence. The shrill ring of the phone broke the deadened air.

"Hiya, Cait. How's she doing?" Seth said.

"Okay. I made tomato soup and grilled cheese sandwiches for lunch and got her to go up for a nap about ten minutes ago. Some moments she seems totally lucid, others are like a return to life in the early nineties. I'm reliving my childhood, not just in packing up the boxes, but in the way she treats me. It's like I'm six again."

"Just hang tight, okay? The movers will be there this weekend, and we've nearly got her room here ready. The most important thing is to keep an eye on her. We'll deal with all the other garbage later. We can talk about selling the house and all that after she's safely transitioned in here." He sighed.

"What else, Seth?"

"Ah, I'm bummed, too. I thought, you know, it'd take longer before we reached this stage. I guess we were in denial about her symptoms for a while." There was a long pause. She sensed her brother was struggling with his own emotional juggernaut.

"Dianne's gonna sort through Mom's clothes tomorrow, to keep out the winter stuff and label everything she won't be able to wear 'til spring," he said. "So, you won't need to bother with the closet or dresser today."

"All right. I'll stick to all the knickknacks, photo albums and things in the living room. Most of it can probably be boxed."

"Sounds good. Any chance Garrett might be able to swing by to help us out on Saturday? There are a few things, like that glass breakfront and the inlaid mahogany coffee table, I'd rather not trust to the movers, even if those pieces are only going to be stored in our basement."

A cold hand gripped her heart, squeezing it tight for a second. *Garrett.* She'd barely spoken to him since the weekend, though it wasn't for lack of effort on his part. Throughout the ordeal of her mom's search, he'd pulled her aside repeatedly and whispered how everything would be okay. He'd called eight times at least in the past three days. And he'd stopped by her classroom for as long as she'd let him stay yesterday as she muddled through school, praised the kids on their work at the festival and tried to keep from having a nervous breakdown.

To call him would only remind her of her own irresponsibility toward her mother. To not call him would mean to hurt the man she'd fallen in love with. Even if his feelings were in no way similar to her own.

Bolstering her courage, she said, "I'll ask him," knowing, since she'd promised Seth, she'd have to do it.

"All right. Try not to get too stressed." He gave a light, forced laugh. "And I'll try to follow my own advice."

Garrett had a mental list of all the things that were pissing him off at work, and it was growing:

1) For the first time since he met Sonja weeks ago, her on-top-of-things manner got on his nerves instead of impressed him.

2) Despite everyone's optimism that Doug would be immediately apprehended, the guy was still at large. He'd left a voicemail claiming to be visiting his sister in Memphis. But one call to Doug's uncle confirmed that Doug's only sister had moved to Aspen three years ago. Lying, stealing bastard.

3) If Ronald handed him one more school improvement folder, his fury might make it spontaneously combust.

4) Mike Firenzi left him three messages—and Shelley had come in personally—to offer him a place on the new "Fit-4-Ever" committee. As if he didn't have enough responsibilities.

5) The superintendent wanted to get together at lunch tomorrow to discuss the Chippenak scandal, so he needed to rearrange his schedule for that.

6) His mother called at noon with her same story, followed by another one of Marianne's Friends and Family lectures. Jacob, not to be outdone, was still harping about Halloween in Connecticut.

7) And then there was Cait, of course.

Cripes! Colleagues. Family. Women. All of them. They were so damned self-centered. They wanted this, they wanted that, they wanted him to do whatever they wanted...whenever they wanted it...and to hell with what *he* might've wanted.

He tried to help. Tried to be a good guy. No matter what, there were complications. With Cait, when he was standing next to her, he was too close. When he gave her space, he was ignoring her. Women were demanding and crazy-making and illogical and—

He heard a knock at the door.

"Hi, Garrett. Am I disturbing you?"

Cait's eyes were red-rimmed from lack of sleep. While she looked presentable enough, the tension radiated from her skin's surface like a low-voltage bulb. Another woman wouldn't be able to pull it off. But, even with all the worry churning around inside her, Cait managed to glow. Man, if Jacob could read his thoughts, he'd say his kid brother was out of his freakin' mind.

"No," he said, setting down a folder with one hand and clenching his other fist under the desk, out of her sight. "What's up, Cait?"

"I-I'm sorry for not being in touch with you much this week."

Not *much?* Not at all. But he said, "Yeah, okay."

Every physical overture rejected. Every phone call scaled down to one-syllable responses. Every visit shrugged off with a chill that'd freeze fire. Why was she stepping in now? What'd she want? "Is there something you need?" he said.

"Um, well, Seth asked me if you might be willing to help us move our mom into his place on Saturday. Of course, I know you must be very busy with everything here, especially after last weekend... I know you spent a lot of time with all of us then, so maybe you've got other plans and other things you need to take care of. I'd understand if you didn't want to commit to—"

"That's fine. I'll be there. What time?"

"Are—are you sure? I mean, you don't have to—"

"Didn't I just say I'd be there, Cait?" He was mad. He knew he looked mad. He saw her take a few steps backward, her forehead creased in concern or anxiety, but he was tired of pussyfooting around each and every emotion.

She shook her head a little, those gorgeous golden strands swinging around her petite face. He remembered running his fingers through them when they'd made love. He remembered holding her, being above her, next to her, inside her. He remembered how their passion spiraled together, bonding them. But it must not have been strong enough to hold them for longer than a moment. It shouldn't hurt. Easy come, easy go. But it did.

She took a labored breath. "Seth said nine or ten would be good. The movers are planning to show up around noon, and Seth hoped we could get a head start with the more delicate items."

"No problem." He clenched his fist again.

"Thanks, Garrett. Look, I'm really sorry about everything. It just hasn't been the best time and—"

"Yeah, whatever. I'll see you Saturday morning, but I should probably finish this stuff now." He pointed to a pile of papers on his desk that contained work he'd already completed, but she didn't know that, and he needed her the hell out of his office.

"Of course," she said, backing out of the room, looking all hurt. Looking like he felt. "I won't keep you."

No. And that was the problem, wasn't it? She wouldn't keep him.

There were so many holidays on the fall calendar. On Saturday at her mother's house, Cait couldn't believe it was already Columbus Day weekend, although it wouldn't be officially observed until Monday when they'd get the day off. Suddenly, days off seemed very important to her.

She idly flipped though one of her mother's photo albums, not really looking at the images, just needing to do something with her hands. She'd spend the week dreaming up exercises to keep her fingers busy. Yesterday, she and her class made cute Nina, Pinta and Santa Maria sailing-boat replicas to commemorate the holiday.

Still, she'd felt a traitorous sense of relief when the final Friday bell rang, releasing her students into the charge of their parents...and letting her concentrate on her own family matters.

It had never been like this before. Though she'd always appreciated the little holidays sprinkled throughout the school year, she'd never *counted* on them to sustain her until now.

She glanced out the window. Maybe she wasn't as dedicated a teacher as she'd thought. Maybe she shouldn't be around impressionable children at all. Or people of any age. She was clearly more irresponsible than a grown woman should be.

Last weekend had proven that.

Maybe living in an underground cavern, somewhere unpopulated, wouldn't be a bad idea. No one would have to know how miserable she felt. And she wouldn't have to pretend not to feel miserable. Because love was kind of torturous. Being in love turned her into a passion-crazed, irresponsible person that she hardly recognized.

Something in the basement shattered.

"Dammit!" Seth bellowed.

"Need some help?" Cait called down to him.

"No!" There was another crash. "God—"

"Are you sure?"

"Yes! Hey, where the hell is your boyfriend? It's ten minutes after nine."

She inhaled sharply. Her boyfriend? Was he really? Or was he just someone she'd had secret sex with in various places? With occasional toppings? Did it indicate any real commitment to—

"Well?"

"Look, Seth, I don't know." She peered out the window for the three-hundredth time that morning. "When are Mom and Dianne returning?"

"I told Dianne to keep Mom out of our hair until after two. Brunch, shopping, some stylist appointment crap, I think. Mia's staying with Dianne's sister for the day."

A flash of red caught her eye as Garrett pulled into the

driveway. She set down the photo album near a packing box and raced into the foyer. She swung open the front door. His finger was poised to ring the bell.

"That was fast," he said. The words were light, but his expression wasn't remotely amused.

"I—um, hi, Garrett. Good morning."

"Morning." He strode into the living room and glanced around. "Where's Seth?"

Before she could answer, she heard a clank. Then a bang.

"Christ almighty!" shouted a voice from the basement.

The corners of Garrett's lips lifted slightly. "Need some help?" he called to her brother.

"Hell, yes. How're you doing, buddy?"

Garrett let out a warm laugh. "Okay, I guess," he said. "I'm coming down."

He walked passed her to the stairs, granting only the briefest nod in her direction and taking his warmth with him. It wasn't for her anyway. It was for Seth. The envy she felt in that instant stunned her.

She heard the deep timbre of their laughter, so male, as they carted up her mother's wedding china—minus a piece or two that didn't survive Seth's butterfingers. She felt superfluous.

And it only got worse.

Every twenty minutes another man arrived. A neighbor friend showed up. His son came a little later. Three of Seth's colleagues. All this help and the movers hadn't even gotten there yet. It was like being the only girl in the guy's locker room.

Shortly after the moving van pulled up, Cait fixed sloppy joes for lunch, setting out chips, salad, sodas and thick chocolate chip cookies on the kitchen counter for the men to help themselves. She melted into the other room, accustomed by this time to being ignored.

One of Seth's closest work buddies, Todd Brayden, sought her out, his easy manner a welcome change from Garrett's coldness.

"Hey there, Cait, thanks for the lunch," he said, using a

potato chip to scoop up some of the hot barbeque on his plate that had managed to escape the bun. He slipped it into his mouth and grinned. "I love this stuff."

"I'm glad," she said. She slid over on the sofa to make room for him. He plopped down next to her, stretching out his long legs in front of him and balancing his plate on his lap. Cait couldn't help but feel her spirits lighten. Ever since she first met Todd at one of Seth's company picnics a few years back, he'd treated her like Seth did. Like she was his "favorite and only" kid sister, too.

His deep blue eyes darted around the living room. "You've done a lot of work here already, haven't you? With it packed up, it doesn't look like the same room we played Scrabble in this spring."

She shook her head, remembering those nights fondly. "Not only that, I feel as though I have to let go of so many childhood memories. I lived most of my life here. Now the things that made this room—this house—our *home* will be stashed in Seth's basement." She shrugged. "But the worst part is knowing that even if the room remained the same, Mom isn't the same anymore."

"Letting go is hard." Todd put a brotherly arm around her shoulders and squeezed. "It sucks, I know. But you'll be okay, kid." With the light streaming into the room, his blond hair took on a sun-god kind of glow, his handsome face compassionate.

Garrett entered the room just then...and froze.

"Thanks for lunch, Cait," the financial director—heck, the man she'd fallen in love with—said stiffly. His eyes turned to coal as he gazed at the union of Todd's arm and her shoulder.

"You're welcome," she said automatically. The muscles in her back and neck tightened, and she expected some further comment from the glowering man blocking the doorway.

Nothing came.

Garrett remained rooted to his spot, his half-empty plate nearly levitating on his fingertips in front of him. Todd glanced between the two of them and, a few seconds later, removed his arm without a word.

Todd cleared his throat and a goofy smile graced his lips. "So, what do you think, Garrett? Can the Pack take it all the way this year or are you hoping the Patriots'll come from behind and surprise us all?"

A strange expression crossed Garrett's face as he eyed the guy sitting next to her. "New England might not have gotten off to a great start, but they've got determination. Green Bay, well—" He twisted his lips into something that couldn't quite be called a smile. "They're often a lot of show, not a lot of substance."

Todd's laugh sounded forced. "Now, I'm guessing that's not a belief you share too often around these parts."

"No," Garrett said coolly, narrowing his eyes at Todd. "But that doesn't make it any less true."

"Huh. But the New England defense...not real sharp this year." Todd popped another chip into his mouth and stretched out his legs even further, taking up as much territory as his six-foot-one, twenty-eight-year-old body could manage.

"But the Packer offense...inexperienced," Garrett countered. He stepped forward three paces and struck an imposing stance.

Cait, not sure the conversation was *at all* about football any longer, stood up. "Well, guys, as stimulating as your sports talk has been, I'll have to leave you to it." She smiled at them as graciously as she could fake. "I've got some things to finish up. Glad you both liked the sandwiches."

She walked toward the kitchen, feeling two sets of eyes boring into her spine. Todd looked at her with concern, but Garrett's gaze was like a switchblade. She glanced back at him and his expression changed from cold fury to shuttered indifference in an instant.

Well, he could be that way if he wanted, but it was unjustified. Unlike Shelley McAllister's overtly flirtatious manner toward Garrett, Todd treated Cait like a sibling, which Garrett should be able to see if he paid any real attention. It hadn't occurred to her that he might be upset by her friendship with Todd, but if he could get jealous that quickly, maybe he wasn't as unaffected as he'd been trying to appear. Maybe, she had to admit to herself, she and Garrett both just had a tendency to overreact and feel threatened too easily. And, maybe, that meant there might be hope for them yet...if they could just get over that knee-jerk defensiveness.

She was about to leave the room to think about this further when Seth walked in and blocked her path.

"Uh, guys," he said to them, holding up his cell phone. "It's Dianne. She says she and Mom just spotted Doug Chippenak."

~CHAPTER THIRTEEN~

STEP 13:
Let the batch mix for another fifteen or twenty
minutes more in the rock-salt and ice freezer.
~From Mr. Koolemar's Top Secret,
Kool Kreme Ice Kreamations Recipe Book, pg. 97

Garrett grabbed his car keys and was halfway out the door when he realized Cait was following him. "What? You wanna come with me?"

She gave him an incredulous, Man-You-Are-Such-An-Idiot stare before saying, "Of course" in her sharpest, most clipped tone.

Great.

"Well, c'mon then."

He let her scurry after him, not slowing down, basically making an ass out of himself, but he wasn't sure how to stop. He was just so damned angry. First Todd (the blond bastard) and now Doug.

Dianne told them Georgina had pointed to Doug Chippenak sneaking out of the bakery and said, "There's the man with the gray sideburns, like Hank. Hank liked pie, too."

Dianne took a closer look and, sure enough, her mother-in-law was right. Although Doug didn't have many distinguishing features, and he tended to blend well in a crowd (unlike *Todd*, whom Cait had no problem picking out right away, damn him), Georgina sure had nailed it. Dianne called the New Brighton police and then home. But Garrett had every intention of being first on the scene.

He began backing out of the driveway before Cait even closed her car door. He'd driven to the corner before she'd fastened her safety belt. He didn't bother with his own. He was already living dangerously.

"Do you think he'll still be there?" she asked.

He shrugged. How the hell should he know? They sped to the bakery.

Cait scanned the streets, checking all four cardinal directions. "Do you see him?"

"No." He didn't see Doug anywhere. Instead, in his mind's eye, he saw *Todd*, draping his arm around Cait, like she was a football trophy or something. That little scene back at the house nearly put him over the edge. He gripped the steering wheel tighter and gritted his teeth. He did not like that guy at all. And he *really* didn't like how he was feeling at the moment. So very out of control.

He drove up and down the block several times, trying hard not to superimpose Todd's cocky face on every man who walked by. But none of that mattered as far the hunt for Chippenak was concerned. The board member was nowhere to be found.

"At least we know for sure he isn't in Memphis," Cait said.

"We always knew he wasn't in Memphis. Or Aspen, for that matter. The uncle contacted the sister, and Doug was never at her house. It seems the weasel is trying to hide in plain sight."

"Dianne said she didn't think he noticed them but that she also lost track of him right away."

"Hopefully, he'll think it's safe now and will be less likely to run again. He'll keep getting more and more careless, and we'll get him."

Careless like *Todd*. Very careless behavior on his part. Any more of that touching-Cait crap and Garrett wouldn't be responsible for his actions.

After forty-five minutes of combing the surrounding neighborhoods and coming up empty, they stopped to talk to an officer in an unmarked squad posted near the bakery.

"Where do you think he's staying?" Cait asked the policeman.

The officer raised his palms. "Could be anywhere, but it's probably within a thirty-mile radius. People do strange things when they feel their backs are against the wall. The fact that he's even returned to New Brighton leads us to believe that Doug is either confident he won't get caught or he's trying to create a more challenging chase. Today, he's succeeded in doing both."

This, of course, bugged the hell out of Garrett. He knew the officers were doing their jobs, following correct police procedure and, eventually, they'd draw Doug out and trap him with the law's long, strong arm. But it ticked him off that the scoundrel had evaded them all yet again. And Garrett didn't need any new reasons to be angry.

He drove Cait back to her mother's house without a word spoken between them. In their absence, Dianne and Georgina had returned from their outing, but all was not well there either.

"What do you need, Mom?" Seth asked.

The older woman's hands shook, her gaze shooting all over the room and, occasionally, alighting on her son's face. "Hank wouldn't have liked this," she whispered. "We only moved twice before, and it was always in the summer. It's too cold now."

Seth motioned for Cait to come over. He leaned in and murmured something in her ear. Garrett saw her nod, glance at her mother and nod again. Then Seth said something else, and Garrett noticed both of them turning their attention to him. What now?

Cait gave a little shrug, like she didn't care, which really pissed him off. A minute later, Seth tromped over.

"Hey, Garrett," Seth said. "The movers are ready to go, and

Todd and the guys are helping me take a batch of breakables over to the house in my car."

He nodded at Seth. Smart move. Get rid of Toddy-boy.

"Would you mind hanging out here for a while with Mom and Cait and our neighbor? Mom's not handling the moving-day experience real well. We kind of figured she might get a little agitated by the chaos at our place, at least until we've had a chance to set things up properly."

Garrett allowed a shallow grin. Seth was a good guy. Not his fault he had an obnoxious friend and a freaky sister. "Sure."

Seth glanced around at the bare living room. "Not much left by way of furniture. I'll grab some lawn chairs from the garage."

"I'll get them." Garrett intersected the room, feeling an uncontrollable heat in his lower body when he passed by Cait. She looked at him in that inscrutable way but didn't smile.

Damn, damn, damn, damn. Women. He wanted her up against that closet wall again, his mouth devouring hers again, their bodies touching and rubbing and joining. He shook his head to try to clear the thought, like a mental Etch-A-Sketch image he desperately needed to erase.

By the time he stomped back into the room with four folding chairs, the other men were already out the door. Good riddance.

Cait and Georgina stood mutely by the window watching them go. The neighbor guy shifted his weight uneasily near a couple of unsealed boxes in the corner of the living room. The rest of the house looked empty as death.

"Have a seat," Garrett said to the man, unfolding a chair for him.

"Thanks, but I've gotta be getting back soon. My wife wants me to take her out to dinner tonight and this time I can't escape it. Her birthday's tomorrow." He raised his eyebrows at Garrett as if to say, "You know how women are, right?"

Garrett nodded sympathetically.

The neighbor said his goodbyes...and then there were three.

In the role-reversal of the century, Cait gave him her best impression of a woman who'd lost her memory, treating him like a stranger who'd walked in off the street. Her mother, suddenly more articulate than her daughter, began grilling him on life as a "fruit and nut kid."

"Did you help your parents quite a bit with the company when you were young?" she asked, settling into an orange-and-yellow-striped lawn chair. Her daughter, meanwhile, stood motionless by the door, as though she might have to flee if the scary stranger got too personal. A fresh blade of anger twisted inside him.

"I tried," he said. "But my big brother was able to do a lot more, and he did it more quickly. By the time I was twelve, I spent most of my time at the company hanging around the staff's break room. Sneaking cookies. Talking to the workers. They'd tell me stories about their lives outside of the Ellis Corporation. I was fascinated by that."

"Don't you have to go back there sometime, to work there, too?"

Now wasn't that just the Million-Dollar Question, hmm? "If my parents have anything to say about it, yes." An awful sense of inevitability settled like a boulder on his chest.

He resisted looking at Cait, keeping his attention focused on her mom. "The corporation is run by a team of people heading each department. Working with the financial sector, as I did, was fairly straightforward. It's just that it wasn't that much fun for me being in a company setting. I like it when the people around me are enthusiastic, energized. The Ellis financial advisers and accountants are very competent, but not real lighthearted."

Georgina smiled at him. "Hank liked doing that, too. Talking to people, hearing stories about their families, helping them. The management side of construction was all right for him, but only because of the people involved." She gave the room a heartbreaking glance, then turned to her daughter. "Cait, sweetie, where are my photos? I—I don't want those stored away."

Cait walked over to her mother, put a gentle hand on her shoulder. "I know, Mom. I just set the albums in these boxes here. Seth said we could put them on a bookshelf in your new bedroom once we get everything else unpacked."

Georgina's eyes misted a bit, clouding over in a way that frightened Garrett. She seemed to be changing mind zones right in front of him.

She jumped up from her chair and clasped her hands together. "Oh, my! What about the loose pictures? The doubles of my favorites. Where are they?"

Her daughter walked her back over to the chair and made her sit back down. "They're also right here. I'll get them for you now if you'd like."

"Yes, dear. Yes."

Cait rummaged through one of the boxes, pulling out a large white envelope stuffed with photographs. "See, Mom? Nothing to worry about."

"I want to look again," Georgina said, stretching her arm out toward Cait and wiggling her fingers like a child asking for a lollipop. Cait placed it in her hands. "Thank you, honey."

The older lady grabbed a fistful of pictures, flipping through them, comparing one to another, holding a few up to display to him and Cait. "The garden in our starter house on Lemming Street, and Seth riding his tricycle in the front yard."

She flipped some more. "Aunt Meg's first wedding—to that horrible Bill from Ohio—but Seth was so adorable as the ring bearer." More shuffling. More show and tell.

After ten minutes of Seth's early years, Georgina said, "Here's my little Cait when she was four." That one prompted Garrett to spring up and take a closer look.

"Hey, cute." He looked over at his blond angel, the one who was barely speaking to him now, and he pointed to the picture. "Love that tutu."

Cait turned almost as pink as the barrettes once clipped to her wispy, preschool hair. She opened her mouth, but no words came out. Finally, she said, "I—oh, give me that!"

She lunged for the photo, but he was faster.

"Got it," he said, snatching it out of the older lady's grasp. "Sorry, Mrs. Walsh, but I may need to confiscate this one from your envelope. I've got the perfect spot for it on my refrigerator."

Georgina laughed, shrugging at her wide-eyed daughter. "Well, Cait, he was too strong and speedy for me, what could I do?"

"You could put the rest away before he gets any other ideas." Cait brushed a few strands of hair away from her face and reached for the envelope.

Seth walked in, interrupting.

"Hi, loves," he said, kissing his mother and sister. Demonstrative family, Garrett thought. "Garrett, hey there." Seth lifted a hand in greeting. "Dianne's running our place like a naval captain, so I just wanted to check in on things here. You all doing, okay?"

"Fine," Cait said too quickly.

Garrett nodded, as noncommittal as politeness would allow.

"We were looking at pictures," Georgina exclaimed. "And, well—" she gave a sly smile, "I was just about to give this envelope to Garrett, so he could see our family over time."

"What?" Cait almost doubled over.

"Thank *you*, Mrs. Walsh." Garrett grinned at Seth and Georgina before granting a deliberate look to the one objector of the family. Her gaze was like granite. "I know I'm going to enjoy borrowing these. Tremendously."

Seth studied him with a half-amused, half-contemplative look. "Anyone here want some pizza? It's been hours since lunch, and I've really got the urge for Giuseppe's peppers-n-shrooms." He pulled out his cell phone. "Garrett, what do you take on yours?"

The idea of having to watch Cait nibble on a slice, the way she did that first night on the beach, was almost too much for his mind and body to take. He'd only want to lick the sauce off her lips, lay her down in the middle of one of the empty rooms and...

"No, thanks," he heard himself say. "Nothing for me. If you don't need any more help, I should probably be heading back." He glanced at his watch to emphasize his point, but couldn't keep the sigh from slipping out.

Seth held out his palm for a firm handshake. "You were a great help today, buddy. Thanks for coming out. Really appreciate the time and all the effort."

"No problem." Garrett touched Georgina's shoulder in gratitude when she handed over the white envelope, then he smiled briefly at Cait.

"See you guys," he said to everyone in general, but he hoped she was paying attention. He'd be damned if he'd chase after her just so she could screw with his head some more. "Let me know if I can do anything else sometime." He waved and slipped outside.

Cait watched her brother curiously. Seth exhaled on a count of ten, waited until Garrett's car was halfway down the street then dragged her by the sleeve into the kitchen.

"Are you out of your mind?" he said.

She blinked at him. What was he talking about? "What are you talking about?" she asked.

"Excuse me, Cait, but unless the circumstantial evidence was extraordinarily misleading, you guys had sex in our *closet* last weekend."

She stiffened. "Your point being?"

"What the hell are you doing to that poor guy?"

"I'm not doing anything to him. Come on, Seth. His mind is on the Chippenak thing. And there's so much for me to deal with here, to take care of, especially with Mom in this condition—"

"Oh, is that ever a buncha crap."

She drew in a long, self-righteous breath. "It is not. I—"

"Yes, it is, and you can shut up and listen to me." He glared at her. "Take a good look around this house. It's empty. Dianne and I are in charge. Your reign is over. Before today's done, Mom'll be tucked into bed in the room next to Mia's. She'll be fine. Or, at least as fine as she'd be anywhere."

He swung an arm around her neck, getting her in a strangle hold. "You, on the other hand, need to move the hell on. Start dealing with your own life. Your past and your future. And I mean *now*."

"Seth—I—look, it's hard. I feel so out of control. Every time I think Garrett and I are headed in the right direction something shifts, and I'm lost all over again."

"I know it's not easy for you to let go, to allow someone else into your inner world after losing Dad and Fredric and now, in a way, Mom, too. But if Garrett's half the man I think he is, he might be worth the effort."

"And if he isn't?"

"I'll beat the living daylights out of him," Seth said.

Cait laughed then bowed her head, thinking. It was comforting to know he'd make good on that threat if she asked him to. It's what big brothers were for. She tried to project all the love she felt for him. "What should I do?"

"Leave. I mean it, Cait. Get out of here and go over to Garrett's and talk about whatever the damn problems are."

He had to be out of his mind. "Not tonight?"

"Hell, yes, *tonight*. Garrett's under a lot of stress, I can tell. He needs you to be there for him."

"But the move—"

"It's done, Cait. A couple more boxes, a few chairs, odds and ends in the kitchen." He shrugged. "You did a whole lot of work around this place, but—" he lowered his voice, "you didn't do the work in here." He tapped his index finger to the left side of her chest. "The time's come. Mom and I are gonna eat some pizza. You aren't."

"Seth, I can't—"

He steered her to the front door and pushed her outside. "Talk to you tomorrow."

Cait circled the parking lot five times before deciding to pull into a space. The sun slid beneath the horizon, and she could see a light flick on inside Garrett's condo. She waited in her car, seatbelt still strapped tight, working up the nerve to approach the building. What on earth could she say to him?

At the entrance buzzer, she punched in his number and stood still, not realizing she was holding her breath until his voice echoed over the system.

"Yeah?" he said, sounding wearier than he'd let on before.

"Garrett, it's me."

There was a click. Silence.

He didn't even respond. He just hung up on her. *Oh, God.* She closed her eyes, the intercom's phone-like receiver still in her hand. Cait rubbed the smooth white plastic, as if it were a genii's bottle, making the same wish three times. *Please, in spite of everything, love me back, Garrett.* She replaced the receiver and stepped away from the door.

Of course that was it. He must not really love her. They might make love, but if his ego didn't get stroked, if he wasn't getting his way, if his needs weren't being met for one measly week, then of course things would come to a halt. If she pulled away, he wasn't going to be the one to humble himself. He wouldn't be the one to follow. Or maybe he just wouldn't follow *her*.

She sprinted across the parking lot. With trembling fingers she unlocked her car door and tossed in her purse.

"Cait!"

She raised her head to the voice. Garrett, clad only in gray sweatpants and some untied leather sneakers, stood breathless by the door, holding it open so he wouldn't lock himself out.

"Get over here now."

She couldn't keep her eyes from him, but the sight of him standing there in that rumpled state had a surreal quality. Could she trust the vision before her? Was there an intercom genii after all? Garrett still looked really mad, so probably not. She continued to stare at him.

He groaned. *"Please."*

Cait relocked the car, walked over and stepped inside. Closer now, she could see beads of perspiration in a neat row along his hairline. Four flights of stairs, she remembered.

She searched his face for clues, explanations. "Why did you hang up on me? And, then, why did you run down here?"

"Cait, you're a stubborn, frustrating-as-hell woman. I didn't want to give you a chance to say anything both of us would later regret." He glared at her.

This was hardly an I-Love-You-And-I-Can't-Live-Without-You-Despite-Your-Faults declaration. She clamped her mouth shut, bowed her head and backed away.

"No." He snatched at the lapels of her windbreaker. "That was the answer to the first question," he said, his breath windy against her cheek. "This is the answer to the second one." His mouth covered hers and they merged, lip-to-lip, tongue-to-tongue, until the only tangible thing between them was heat.

He broke away from her, his skin glistening with a new sheen which she was fairly certain had little to do with his dash down the stairs. He tugged on the waistband of his sweatpants, his body betraying his arousal, and then yanked her into the elevator.

"We've gotta talk," he said. "But there's something else we need to do first."

Cait had a strong working notion of what that "something" might be, but she was thrown off course when, instead of leading her into the bedroom, Garrett marched her into his kitchen. He lifted her on the countertop and handed her a common grocery item.

"Creamy peanut butter?" she said, reading the label.

"Yes, Cait." A slow grin pushed up the corners of his mouth. "Choosy lovers choose Jif."

Garrett stretched his legs out under the sheets, snagging one of Cait's ankles with a sweep of his foot. He caressed her with his toes then pulled her closer. Her hair was still damp from their recent shower, a necessity Garrett didn't mind partaking in after the tasty stickiness of the peanut butter. And the jelly.

"Mmmm," she said, if moans could be counted as words. She tugged him toward her, her arms encircling his waist, and she ran her thumb slowly from the backs of his legs to his shoulder blades. He felt himself getting hard again just from her touch.

They rested their heads on the same pillow, and she nestled into him like a baby bird. Then, as women do, she began chirping.

"Were you ever engaged before?"

"Uh, no," he said.

"Did you have lots of lovers then? More than one girlfriend at a time, that kind of thing?"

He stared at her silky blond head. She wasn't looking at his face but was focused on playing with his chest hairs...and driving him wild with it.

"Hmm, well, I had girlfriends before." He figured that was ambiguous enough but still honest.

"But did you ever cheat?"

He groaned. This wasn't really about him. Women always wanted to make sure they weren't walking into the same trap twice, but he wasn't up for a game of compare/contrast with bloody Fredric. "So, your ex cheated on you, and it still really bothers you, right?"

She sighed and burrowed into him even more. "Right."

"I've never cheated, Cait. I'm not Fredric."

She looked up at him and grimaced. "I know."

"Then why the scary face?"

This made her laugh. "I'm sorry. I just can't let something like that happen again. Do you know what I mean?"

He kissed her forehead. "I know what you mean. But are you over him, sweetheart?" Oh, man, he hoped she was.

"Him, definitely yes. But it hurt. I questioned the ideals of marriage and trust and commitment for a long time."

Garrett still questioned the ideals of marriage and trust and commitment, but he wasn't about to say that aloud. Instead he rubbed her back and let his fingertips wander lower still.

She reached out again, too, tracing patterns on all the areas she could reach. His thighs. His hips. "What happened on New Year's Eve?" she asked him.

Damn. He didn't see that one coming.

He felt the familiar pounding of his heart against his chest, reminding him that the fight-or-flight adrenaline still pumped strong in his arteries. Thinking of that night at his parents' home in Connecticut always inspired a desire to bash in something with his fist then run like hell.

"My father and I 'had words,' as they say, but I don't really want to talk about it." There. He'd explained—kind of—and made his feelings clear. Now she'd drop the subject and they could get back to what they were doing—

"What kind of words?"

"Nasty words, Cait." She might be Miss Persistence, but he had ideas that could distract her. He trailed his fingers from the soft skin of her belly up to the rounded buds of her breasts. She gasped. Instinctively, he licked his lips.

But she put her hand against his cheek to stop him from pursuing his ideas, and she looked him in the eye compassionately, patiently, lovingly. It was the loving part that did him in...and he knew he wasn't going to get out of this discussion.

He sighed. "Look, my father was mad at me. I'd been kind of wild in my twenties, but I was slowly getting my life together. That night, though, I guess I seemed particularly juvenile. Jacob had just handled a big crisis at the company and was looking really mature. He was ahead of me in everything—more skilled, more experienced. It felt like it'd be impossible to catch up."

"Your father expected you to?" she asked.

"He said that Jacob had inherited all of his traits and that Marianne was a lot like our mother. But me, well, he just couldn't figure me out." He swallowed, trying to drown the words and the pain in a gulp. It didn't work.

"And?"

"And that, if I couldn't be a corporate director, if I couldn't lead like a man, then I couldn't be in the family either."

"He threatened to disown you?" Cait stared at him as if in shock.

He gave a short nod, unable to believe he was actually repeating those sentences aloud. "My father said, based on my behavior, that he didn't think I was really his son anyway. He said that—" He had to stop. Clench his fists. "He said he wished I weren't."

Cait's entire body radiated distress over his revelation, and he regretted not keeping his mouth shut. Garrett bent down and kissed her arm from knuckles to shoulder. He tried to refocus on the physical hunger, the sex, the lust. His speeding pulse raced for another reason, though. He'd never told anyone this much before. He'd sure as hell never planned to.

How had he been seduced into letting his guard down? In a flash of memory he recalled how quickly Cait could turn away, change directions, run from him. Jacob had been right on target with things like that. Maybe his brother really *was* that much smarter than him, and he'd been slow to catch on in every aspect of life.

"Oh, Garrett, I'm so sorry," she whispered. "I'm sure he didn't mean it. Not really."

"No," he said, feeling an odd constriction in his throat. "Perhaps not literally. But his expectations were clear. I knew I'd have to prove to be responsible, prove my leadership skills in order to be welcomed back home. I haven't exactly succeeded here yet—"

"That's not true! You've been wonder—"

"Has Doug Chippenak been caught?"

She squinted at him, and he hated the doubt he'd created in her eyes. "Well, no, but he *will* be and—"

"And nothing. Until I've done what I'm supposed to do, until my father finds me worthy of the Ellis name, I've tried to give him his wish. I've removed myself from the family."

Cait felt Garrett withdraw from her, like a spirit leaving its corporeal confinement. They were good at playing lovers' games together. That was easy. But when it got down to unearthing what lurked beneath their own manic drives, neither of them could seem to stay in one place and battle out the emotions to the bitter end. He was still attentive to her, but wary. He still wanted her, but she knew it had to be on his terms.

She felt her heart closing up at this. But she remembered Seth's earlier admonition and restrained herself from flinging on her clothes and bolting out the door.

"Did you discuss what happened with you mother?" she asked him. "How did she react?"

"I'm done talking about this now." His fingers slid off her breasts and slipped between her thighs, rubbing her, pushing inside her, until her mind stopped asking the questions she knew they needed to address—especially the biggest one: When he'd finally proven himself, would he stay here or go back?

But the heat of his mouth burned her nipples and, before long, passion's fire consumed them both.

Yet, despite the steam they'd created, something numb and frozen still lay between them. And Cait already dreaded the day when it would have to thaw.

The thing Garrett hated about his cell phone was that it didn't have a spiraling cord of a landline for him to wrap around his finger. At moments like these, when he was supposed to be listening to his mom, he would've enjoyed the distraction of watching the tip of his pinky turn purple.

No such luck.

"...and, Garrett, I know you're very busy out West, but—"

"It's the *Mid*west, not the West, Mom. There are no

cowboys that I know of in Wisconsin."

"You're really not taking this seriously." She gave one of her hurt sighs followed by a threatening pause. "We've been over this before. Your father and I would appreciate it if you'd come back to New Haven for a little visit. There are so many things both of us would like to discuss with you, and it simply cannot be done over the telephone or the Internet. Can you, in the foreseeable future, allot us a weekend of your time?"

Damn. When she put it like that he could hardly say no. "I'll take another look at my schedule, okay, Mom? I'll figure out something and fly back home soon. Before the holidays, for sure." Or, maybe, he could stretch it to early January. But anything further away than the long Martin Luther King, Jr. weekend was probably pushing it.

When his mother finally released him, Garrett sank back into his office chair and squeezed his eyes shut. He didn't want to go home. That, of course, wasn't new, but his reason had changed recently. He thought of Cait waking up in his bed this morning, as she had almost every morning for the past two weeks: warm, snuggly, beautiful, sweet, intelligent, funny...tasty, no matter what the topping. She was only three hallways away this very instant, but he missed her.

His condo was roomier than her studio apartment, but the main inducement for spending their time in New Brighton was because they could be together there less conspicuously. Few Ridgewood Grove students haunted their takeout places, and it was rare to run into a parent or a staff member ten miles from school. Also, Cait needed to check in on her mom and on her mom's house. She and Seth were preparing to put the place on the market after Thanksgiving.

Garrett was involved in their lives. He wanted to spend every free moment with her that he could. And with her family, too. He didn't want to miss out on a single weekend.

But, hell, who was he kidding? Marianne nailed it right on the head during her visit when she said staying away from Connecticut wouldn't change the past. It was just that, for once, his resistance to going back home had less to do with the problems there and more to do with a real reason to stay here.

And that reason had a name: Caitlin Livie Walsh.

That, in itself, brought its own form of terror, forcing him to weigh which would be the lesser of two evils. Dealing with his father, despite not yet having accomplished his mission here? Or allowing himself to get too attached to Cait?

He looked down at the calendar on his desk and halfheartedly began blocking out potential weekends around Halloween to fly out of Milwaukee's Mitchell International Airport.

~CHAPTER FOURTEEN~

STEP 14:
The batch could be eaten now as soft-serve,
but it's better to pour the mix into a container
and put it in a hardening freezer at -20ºF
for two to three hours.
~From *Mr. Koolemar's Top Secret,*
Kool Kreme Ice Kreamations Recipe Book, pg. 97

Cait flicked her dangly pumpkin earrings back and forth while reminding the Ninja Warrior to stay seated, telling the Pop-Rock Diva and Cinderella to stop whispering and asking the Hawaiian Surfer to please keep his hands to himself.

"Josh," she told Brave Lancelot, "your sword needs to stay in your belt loop or we'll have to put it in your locker."

"Okay, Miss Walsh." He reluctantly withdrew the plastic toy from Erin's Fairy Princess tiara while his buddies, the Werewolf and Peter Pan, looked on and snickered.

Cait knew she'd need a handful of Tylenol after the Halloween Magic Assembly was over. Unfortunately, for it to end, it had to begin. And that hadn't happened yet.

Garrett, on the other side of the auditorium, greeted a few parents who'd stopped by to see the show. He carried himself like a calm commander in an army of costumed chaos. Dealing kindly with children, considerately with parents, respectfully with staff. All this and a wiz with numbers, too. He was well suited to being a positive, influential administrator. She wondered if his own parents knew this side of their son. If they wanted to know it.

Ronald Jaspers tapped on the microphone and the squeal of feedback filled the air. His pallor was striking under the white stage lights. "My apologies for the delay," he said. "It's with great pleasure that I introduce the extraordinary troupe of magicians here to help us celebrate an early Halloween..."

As he spoke, Cait caught Garrett's gaze and smiled. His eyes sent back a look that should only be allowed in a bedroom. Something ethereal in the vicinity of her heart began to tango.

They'd been more or less living together since Columbus Day. It just happened. She still kept most of her clothing at her own apartment and stopped by to water her plants, check mail and listen to messages. But he'd presented her with a toothbrush that first weekend, and she'd purchased extra bottles of her favorite shampoo and conditioner, since she found herself at his place so many mornings. And, oh, he also bought her some special bath towels. Springy white ones, just like those at Four Gates.

They took lots of showers.

It wasn't an entirely secret relationship. Jenna wheedled details out of her daily, and Garrett went with Cait to Seth and Dianne's house frequently enough to be considered a family member. Last week he and Seth went golfing again at the Club. Their third time out. Cait knew she'd never hear the whole story on that afternoon.

They walked in slapping each other's backs and laughing like adolescents. Longing lingered in Garrett's expression for the rest of the night. Was falling in love with her family a prerequisite for him to fall in love with her?

She'd noticed he still held a part of himself back from her. Not physically, of course. There he couldn't be more open. She worried about the emotional side, though. But, oh, their first kiss and all the firsts that followed... If it weren't for Little Red Riding Hood, Cait might've lost herself in daydreams.

"No pinching, Daisy," she whispered.

The girl sighed and flipped up her hood. "Okay, Miss Walsh."

Cait watched an escalating battle between a few boys in Loni's class and was about to nudge their teacher when Ronald's droning voice abruptly stopped.

Everyone directed their attention to the principal—the children expectant, the adults first surprised then concerned. He crushed the index card against his chest. There was an interminable pause.

"And here they are," he whispered at last into the microphone before stumbling offstage.

Cait saw Garrett slip out the side door, following Ronald.

"What the heck was that all about?" Marlene murmured.

"I don't know," she said. "But if you can keep an eye on my class, I'll go find out."

Marlene nodded and Cait hurried into the hall.

"Cait, we need your help," Sonja called, motioning her to the office.

Garrett hovered above the principal, who was sweating profusely in one of the office chairs and clutching Sonja's water bottle in a shaky hand. "We've just called nine-one-one," Garrett said. "Stand here by him, will you, while I get some aspirin."

"Can you tell me what you're feeling?" Cait whispered.

He put his hand on his chest then squeezed his fist. "It's like that," he said. "Like something's wringing my heart."

Garrett was back in an instant. "Take these," he ordered, holding out two tablets. "And don't worry. The paramedics will be here any minute."

"I should've started walking sooner," the older man mumbled. "I promised Shelley I'd walk during lunch three days a week, but I wasn't strict with myself. And I should've followed the doctor's dietary recommendations," he lamented, swallowing the aspirin and some water. "If I recover from this, I swear I'll—"

"Just relax, Ronald," Garrett said. "Just stay calm."

They heard the sound of sirens in the distance. Ridgewood Grove's medics might be small in number, but they were fast.

Mike Firenzi appeared in the doorway, a stunned look on his face. "I—I was just in the auditorium—"

"Thanks for coming in, Mike," Garrett said. "We've got a situation here, but it's under control."

"What can I do for you, Ronald?" Mike asked.

The sirens were closer. Ronald Jaspers reached out and gripped the board president's wrist. "Come with me," he whispered. "I don't want to go to the hospital alone."

Mike looked to Garrett for direction. Garrett nodded.

"That's a great idea, Ronald," Garrett said as two paramedics rushed through the school's front doors.

"Take care of things for me, will you?" the principal said to Garrett. "Please."

"I will," he answered. "Just get yourself better."

Garrett's thoughts weighed him down and drained him to exhaustion by the time he got home. Between his unsuccessful hunt for Doug (three damn weeks of tracking, and still nothing), Ronald in the hospital and the decision to finally have a face-to-face talk with his folks, his stress level hit at an all-time high.

Cait waited for him that night at the condo.

"So, tell me, what's the verdict?" she said. "Did you swing by the hospital after school?"

"Yeah. Ronald's doing okay, but it was definitely a heart attack. He's going to need to stay off his feet for a while. I handled things at school today but, until he returns or the board finds a replacement, the superintendent's going to cover for him."

She sighed, looking relieved. "Well, good. I'm glad both Ronald and the school are in safe hands. What a scare today."

"I know."

"Let's have a wonderful weekend, though." She grinned at him. "We can see a few movies if you want. Go out to dinner, maybe. Or just stay home..." Her eyes twinkled.

He took a breath. Somehow he was going to have to get these next words out. "Listen, Cait. This Sunday is Halloween."

"Yes?"

"I need to go somewhere."

"Okay," she said, that old wariness creeping back into her voice. "Where?"

"New Haven."

"Oh."

"It's Jacob's birthday and back in September I sort of said I...well, I didn't exactly promise him but I kind of implied I'd probably visit him..."

"Yes, of course," she said, standing up, taking a few steps backward. "Naturally, you should go. He'll be glad to see you."

"It's all kind of complicated there now, actually, but—"

"You don't have to explain. It's your family, after all. Your home." She waited a few moments, her face unreadable to him, before asking, "You wouldn't happen to want someone to come along with you, would you? I mean, if you did, I could—"

"No, no, that's okay. Thanks," he said, unable to hide his surprise at her offer, but wanting to spare her the drama of such a visit.

He realized his mistake almost immediately. Her disappointment at his offhanded manner of turning her down couldn't be camouflaged.

"You know, on second thought," he said, "it'd be really great to have company. To hold your hand during takeoffs and landings." He forced a smile. "We could sightsee or bum around Yale or something. Why don't you come with me?"

She gazed into his eyes for a long moment then turned away. "It's okay, Garrett," she whispered. "You don't have to pretend to want me along. I know you have major stuff to iron out in Connecticut. Go and do what you need to do. That's what's important. If you come back, then maybe we'll pick things back up where we left off."

"*If* I come back? What are you talking about? Of course I'm coming back."

She didn't immediately answer.

He glanced at his watch and mentally calculated the hours before his departure. If he didn't procrastinate too much, he shouldn't have any problem getting packed in time. When he looked at her face again, though, he knew he'd just made another mistake. The expression in her eyes was one of dawning realization.

She backed even further away from him, picking up her keys and purse in the process. "So, um, when's your flight, Garrett? Tonight or tomorrow?"

He stared at her. She was fading away from him before his eyes. "I—well there are lots of different flights out there. I can check the schedule to see when—"

"Not what I asked. I want to know when *your* flight is. The one you already booked. Because you *did* book one, didn't you?" The reproach in her voice was as piercing as a foghorn, and he realized that, from her perspective, his behavior must have come across as secretive and excluding. That she thought he'd been hiding the trip from her, which, in a way, he sort of had been.

He didn't know how to respond. He opened his mouth but closed it again.

"Tonight or tomorrow?" she said steadily.

He sighed. "My flight is scheduled to leave at eleven p.m. tonight, but I don't have to take that one. I can change—"

"Don't change anything, Garrett. Good luck out there. Good night. And goodbye—for now," she said, walking out the door. "Have a safe trip, okay?"

Though she added in that "for now," to Garrett's ear it still sounded like an awfully final parting line. "Cait?" he called after her. "You're not breaking up with me or anything, are you? Just because I'm flying home?"

He heard a muffled sound coming from the corridor, but it wasn't clear enough to distinguish whatever word she'd said.

"*Cait!*" he called again, a little too stunned by the rapid turn of events to move. By the time he could force his feet into the hallway, she was already gone.

Something fragile inside her was shattering.

The problem wasn't that Garrett wanted to go back to Connecticut. Cait couldn't begrudge him time with his brother or his family, even if the "going home" thing did tap into her old fears.

No. It was that, despite all the time they'd spent together in the past few weeks, he'd booked his flight, plotted out a trip and all but called a cab to take him to the airport before telling her his plans. And it hadn't even occurred to him to ask her along. Not "I've thought about it and it wouldn't be a good idea for you to come, and here's why," but, rather, "It never crossed my mind to include you."

This hurt, badly. She would be willing to compromise in most areas, but she couldn't be with a man who'd always put her second in his life. Who'd think of her as incidental to whatever his *real* plans were.

She called Jenna.

"I can be over to your place in a half hour," her teaching friend said. "What kind of ice cream should I bring?"

"You don't have to come. I just wanted to talk to someone for a few minutes. A friend who would understand—"

"Cait, you know my hubby put me through hell before we were married. Men just do that kind of thing. They're clueless when it comes to knowing what women want." Jenna paused and let her words sink in. "Triple Ripple or Nutty Almond Fudge?"

Cait sniffled. "Both, please."

"You got it, girlfriend. I'll toss in a classic movie, too."

Women are irrational, crazy making and altogether not

worth the trouble, Garrett thought for the six-hundredth time since yesterday.

He was at Jacob's place in New Haven eating chocolate-bar miniatures and drinking a bottle of birthday champagne in honor of his brother's big day. But his spirit wasn't in the mood for celebration no matter how hard he tried.

"Tell me again, what is it that's so appealing about life in West Virginia?"

"Wisconsin, Jacob. Dammit, it's Wisconsin."

"Okay, *Wisconsin*. Anyway, it's not here."

"That's true, and that's something largely in its favor."

"So that's it? Your reason for choosing to live there is that arbitrary?"

Garrett considered lying. Yes, Wisconsin had seemed pretty far away from Connecticut when the district's superintendent had approached him with the job offer in August. But Garrett knew weeks ago this wouldn't be reason enough to stay beyond his contract. And lately he'd been thinking very long term.

"No," he said finally. And then he spilled his guts to his brother. He told him all about the school district and the goofy Harvest Hoopla and the small-town, tightly knit community he'd become so fond of. Mostly he talked about Cait and her family. How they'd welcomed him. How he'd fallen in love with her despite their misunderstandings and insecurities.

"So, what are you doing hanging out at my place eating Halloween candy?" Jacob asked, giving him a good-natured shove. "You'd better get back there, especially if you think this relationship of yours has a chance of lasting longer than three weeks. I got no advice for you beyond that." He glanced at his Rolex. "There's usually a westbound flight around seven."

"Tomorrow," he said. "After I see Mom and Dad. But tonight's reserved for my only brother. Happy birthday, man. A day early." Garrett raised his glass. "To your next thirty-four years."

Jacob laughed and clinked glasses with him. "And to your next thirty-four hours."

The next day, though, Garrett stood on the steps of his

parents' house, wishing he had a little more time and another glass of champagne to work up the nerve to ring the bell. He'd reserved a ticket on the red-eye back to Milwaukee, figuring he'd need the whole afternoon and evening to square a few things with his folks. He'd come unannounced, to surprise his mom. Hoping to please her.

He was the one who got the surprise.

They were gone. Out of town. No answer on their cell phones.

Not even Jacob knew where they were. But he said they'd sent him a big cake. It arrived after Garrett left that morning with a note saying they'd take him to dinner when they got back.

Garrett returned to Jacob's house, ate cake with him, handed out candy to the neighborhood trick-or-treaters and whiled away the whole of that Sunday until his flight.

Monday morning came and Cait's hands were still trembling. Whether it was from frustration, hurt or too much sugar (both half-gallons of Jenna's ice cream were long gone), she couldn't say. What she did know was that she hadn't seen Garrett last night or this morning. Didn't even know if he'd flown back. He wasn't at school that day, and he hadn't called her or left any kind of message.

Cait twisted a paperclip from her desk and toyed with the idea of her own escape. Now that her mom was safely settled at Seth and Dianne's, she wouldn't be needed nearly as much. Plus, Mia-World had already taken over. No one could compete with a toddler for entertainment, so Grandma Georgina was set.

As for Garrett, he was probably furious with her, and maybe he had a right to be mad because she'd walked away from him on Friday, but he still didn't understand her or know how to let her into his life. You couldn't really need someone you didn't understand. You couldn't really love that person.

Plus, Garrett had the kind of charisma that could draw in

tons of women. Since he was only interested in something short term, sooner or later he'd be glad things between them ended. He'd gotten his Midwestern diversion, and now he could concentrate on his true priorities...of which she clearly wasn't one. Maybe she could disappear for a while. Take a vacation herself. Make it an even cleaner break.

But, of course, leaving was out of the question. She'd never abandon a classroom of students midyear. It went against every notion of responsibility she had. And, besides, this was home. This was where she belonged. This was where she chose to stay.

Garrett would have to make his own choices, and she knew she couldn't control that. It was like that sappy cliché: If you love someone, set him free. If he comes back to you, he's yours...

And if he doesn't—like Fredric—he never was.

She rubbed her temples. Well, at least some wisdom came out of that disastrous relationship after all. She could see that finally and no longer feel the same sting of regret at having had her engagement end the way it did. Maybe one day she'd be able to look at her relationship with Garrett much more philosophically, too.

But for now...oh, it was a difficult morning to be at school. At least it couldn't get much worse than this...this waiting and wondering.

"Excuse me," said a voice behind her. "Are you Cait Walsh?"

Cait swiveled around to greet the visitor. An elderly woman, tall, familiar-looking, but a little too old perhaps to be the mother of an elementary schooler. Had she seen her in the building before? Maybe a grandma? A devoted aunt?

"Yes. How may I help you?"

"My daughter told me about you, and I wanted to meet you myself," she said.

The lady had a decidedly distinguished air, although her lips were pulled tight in a line of worry. It was probably Jimmy's grandmother, Cait thought with a jolt. Jimmy's mom said she and his father were back in court over custody issues again, poor kid.

"My name is Janine," the woman said, stepping forward and extending her hand. "Janine Ellis."

Cait's heart stopped mid-beat. She stared at Garrett's mom, forgetting for a few long seconds that a reply would be required.

"I—I'm pleased to meet you, Mrs. Ellis," Cait said, recovering enough to shake her hand. "You—you're here visiting?"

Her hazel eyes, disguised somewhat by spectacles not worn in the famous gift basket photo tag, were gentle as they assessed Cait. "No, dear. I'm here to bring Garrett home."

This was enough to render Cait speechless again.

"Marianne mentioned you and my son were seeing each other. I hope this isn't too presumptuous of me, but could you tell me, is it a serious thing?"

Cait's lips attempted to form words. "W—well, we, um—" She paused.

"Tough question?" Janine Ellis smiled kindly. "That's okay, dear. Sometimes it's hard to know with Garrett."

Cait located her voice. "That's true, Mrs. Ellis," she said simply. "No formal commitment of any kind has been made, though, if that's what you're wondering."

A sad expression crept into Janine's face. "I don't mean to put you on the spot, Cait. I was just trying to determine the strength of my son's ties to this area. He—he isn't always as forthcoming with information as I'd like. At least not with me."

"I understand," Cait whispered.

"Do you? If so, I apologize on Garrett's behalf. The past ten months have been—" her eyes clouded with sadness. "They've been nothing short of hellacious. None of us have been at our best." She dabbed at her lashes.

"I'm so sorry."

Janine waved her hand as if to brush the grief aside for another day. "I'm afraid if we don't get Garrett back home soon, we'll lose him forever. We weren't as careful with him as we should've been, and I don't know if he understands how important he is to us. He's been in Jacob's shadow for so long…" She seemed to pull herself in tight, not allowing errant emotions to escape.

"Is there something I can do for you? Some way I can help?" Cait wanted to reach out to the woman, but mourning descended upon her own soul. She'd been right from the first. One way or another Garrett would leave her. The fact that she wouldn't get to see him at all soon—not even in a cold, platonic manner—hurt more than she could've imagined.

"No, thank you, dear. My husband's roaming the halls and doesn't know where I've slipped off to," Janine said. "Told him I had to find the ladies' room." The women shared a fleeting smile.

"I don't know if this helps, Mrs. Ellis, but I believe Garrett was just in New Haven. He may still be there. He told me he was flying home late on Friday night, and I was under the impression he wanted to see you, your husband and Jacob over the weekend."

"I didn't realize…" A light of hope sprang into her eyes. "Thank you, dear, for telling me. I can see why Marianne spoke so highly of you, and I'm especially glad I had the chance to meet you in person. Thanks for spending a few minutes with me." She paused. "I'm sorry things didn't work out better for you and my son, though." The older lady gave Cait a hug. "Good luck to you."

"And to you," Cait said, releasing her.

A minute later Garrett's mother was down the hall, and Cait was as alone as ever.

Garrett sat on a sofa still scented by Cait's perfume, groggy from lack of sleep, when he heard the knock at the door.

He'd called in for a personal day off at the last minute because he needed to think things through. When to meet up with his parents, for one thing. And, for another, how to discuss with Cait his growing feelings for her, despite their relationship missteps. He was willing to concede he'd been in the wrong more than once...but she had been, too.

Opening the door and seeing his mother standing there took care of question number one.

"Mom?"

"Hi, honey. May we come in?"

It wasn't until he'd said, "Of course," that he saw his father, leaning against the hallway wall, looking as if he'd aged a decade in less than a year.

"Hello," he whispered to his dad.

"Garrett, how are you?"

"Okay." He paused. "You know, I was just in New Haven this weekend. I stopped by yesterday but—"

"But we'd flown here," his mom finished. "I know. Cait told me, and I just spoke with Jacob, too. We'd foolishly left our cell phones at home."

Cait told her? Garrett felt a rush of conflicting emotions, which jumbled up his thoughts and made every action feel out of order. He offered them sodas, which they politely accepted but didn't drink. He made small talk about Jacob's birthday and Marianne's latest fruit-basket designs.

But, in facing his parents that morning, Garrett couldn't help but feel sympathetic to criminals pushed before a firing squad. They, at least, had the benefit of a blindfold. He, on the other hand, had to suffer through watching his mom's eyes fill with tears every few seconds, which she valiantly fought back, and he had to deal with the grim set of his dad's jaw every time the man tried to speak.

Possible breakups, surprise parental visits, painful memories...all in three days...made for a ceaseless burning sensation in his chest.

"Son," his father said finally, pacing over the Persian rug, "your mother was right. She said, and I admit it's true, I've always focused more on Jacob. His interest in the company was so apparent. For a long time I'd hoped it would be that way for you, too. That your interest would grow."

His father's voice wasn't accusatory exactly—at least

nothing like the way it'd been for the past several years—but his message was clear: Garrett hadn't lived up to his expectations and now, at best, his father was resigned to that.

"I'm sorry if my lack of passion for the business disappointed you," Garrett said gently.

"So you'll try again then," his father said. A statement, not a question. "We'll put the past behind us and work on the company together. I can see you've matured, and you're building a good, strong reputation for yourself. I think we can get beyond our differences now."

"Look, Dad, I don't want you and Mom to think I'm trying to get even with you for whatever you believe you did to me. I'm not pulling away from the company because of some childish vengeance game. But what you said about me maturing—that's exactly the point. In many ways you were right about Jacob being the son best suited to leading the Ellis Corporation through these next decades. And maybe, for a while, I resented the attention he got as a result. But eventually I understood. I grew up, particularly this past year. And I got over it."

He stood, put his arm around his mother's shoulders. "So, I'm not saying no to going back because I'm bitter about my childhood. I'm saying no because I finally found the right niche for me. And it's here."

Another thought of Cait skittered through his mind. The way she was like human sunshine in his life. How her affectionate and warm spirit battled the world for those she loved. The fears that were a part of her, too, which made her vulnerable...and also that much more precious. But, much as he wanted to, he couldn't dwell on her right now. His mom's tears were splashing on him.

"Honey, you've been away for months and months," she said. "First, all over the Eastern seaboard and, now, way out here. You've proven you could do well. Your superintendent's been raving about you to whoever will listen." She smiled through the tears. "But we need you near us. If not in Connecticut, at least closer to home. Why not get involved with the company again? Work with Jacob?"

"I'd be an imposter, Mom. Don't you understand that?" Garrett said, realizing he was speaking the whole truth to his parents at last. "It'd be like when Jacob and I were kids, and how I always had to dress like him, follow him around the house, eat baloney and cheese sandwiches for lunch just because that was his favorite—even though I really loved peanut butter and jelly."

He sighed and held his mom tighter. "I trailed after him all through high school, went to the same college, stopped just short of mimicking his career choice and studying law. But it was obvious that wasn't the profession for me. And that was the first time I knew I couldn't imitate Jacob any longer. It's just taken me years to admit it and act on it."

"But maybe you could find your own manner of being in the business," she said. "Marianne paints fruit, after all. You wouldn't have to lead in the same way Jacob does."

"I couldn't if I wanted to, Mom. My focus was different from the start. You know it was. Dad, as I recall, quickly picked up on that. Even my years working for the company full time didn't change me into the kind of corporate director type you wanted."

Garrett saw the raw pain in his father's eyes. "I don't know what more to offer besides my apology, Garrett. About that night in December—I was angry. I spoke carelessly. You're my son. I would never exclude you from the family." He paused, swallowed. "I hadn't thought what I'd said then would lead to this."

"I know. And I know now you didn't mean those words as literally as I'd taken them, but they got me thinking. They set me on a different course. And, I realized this fall, I'm not entirely disappointed with that. I've found my place. Finally."

The venerable Macauley Ellis sighed. "We'll respect your decision, son. We're proud of you." He paused, and Garrett held his breath. "*I'm* proud of you," his father concluded.

Garrett hadn't dreamed he'd ever hear those words from his father's mouth, at least not directed at him. The tightness gripping his heart eased a little as the sense of peace flooded in. After their awful argument on New Year's Eve, he'd thought their relationship would never recover. But he was wrong. It might take time and effort, but it was possible. Words could hurt, but they could also heal.

"Thanks...Dad."

His father caught his eye at that and held his gaze for a long moment. Then he nodded to him once more before walking out.

Garrett pulled his mom even closer to him. "I love you two very much," he whispered in her ear. "But I've put some thought into this. Wisconsin is where I'm staying."

"If we ever need your help—really and truly—with the company, will you be there?"

"Absolutely. If the Ellis Corporation—or, more importantly, you—*really and truly* need me for anything, you can count on me to be there. I promise." He looked her in the eye. "Although Marianne is a much better choice for second in command. Don't underestimate her."

This made his mother smile. "I won't. I was just thinking about promoting her myself." She squeezed him tight. "You'll come home to visit sometimes? Often?"

"Yes."

"You'll bring your wife back with you, too?"

"I don't have a wife."

"No," his mother said, her eyes bright. "Not yet, you don't. But maybe if you stopped trying to battle the past you would." She squeezed him again. "Don't listen to Jacob when it comes to women. Listen to Marianne, and listen to me. You can trust us."

Somehow he knew what was coming, but he let her say it anyway.

"Cait's wonderful. If she needs you half as much as you need her, the two of you might finally have a chance to grow together." She hesitated. "If you love her, that is."

He nodded. "I love her, Mom."

For Cait, the afternoon was sinking to an unprecedented low. While shopping at the Grocery Mart, she ran into the Koolemars.

"How are you, dear?" Audrey called out. "Hoped you and Garrett might drop by to visit us before now. Hectic schedule?"

Cait almost cried. For a brief time she'd been so happy, so in love, that work had achieved a proper balance with the rest of her life. Things had been easier, though, back when she just threw all her energy into her career. If she returned to that way of living, she'd never again get derailed by a man. She'd never again have to spend another day wallowing in self-pity.

"Until we see you next," Mr. Koolemar said, rummaging through his jacket pocket, "take this coupon. Just had 'em printed up."

Cait read the writing in the light blue square. "Good for One free pint of Kool Kreme Ice Kreamations. Eat and Enjoy!" She looked at the older couple. "For me?" she asked, her spirits lifting a bit.

"Of course. Grocery Mart's stocking six different flavors in frozen foods, aisle five. And here—" he reached in his pocket again to retrieve another slip. "Give this one to Garrett. Or, better yet, tell that boy to get himself over to the workshop. I've got a peach-mint combo he's gonna love."

"Thanks," she said, her spirits plummeting again. "I'll make sure he gets it."

"That goes for you, too, honey-bunch," Audrey said with a wave. "Don't you be a stranger, now."

Cait swallowed back the pain. She picked up a complementary pint of Brazen Raisin-Maple Swirl, enough groceries and tissues to keep her supplied for the next eighteen hours and a stack of Cary Grant, Jimmy Stewart and Gregory Peck films from MovieWorld, the DVD place next door. She was prepared to weep all the way through *Roman Holiday* if she had to. Knowing the end, who wouldn't?

She could feel the tears starting to fall already.

After his parents left, Garrett flipped through the photographs Georgina Walsh had lent him that moving-day weekend. He'd put up a few around the condo to tease Cait when she was here but most were still in the envelope. They weren't his to keep, he knew. They were an offering from a caring mother to her daughter's then-boyfriend. A way to bond them. To connect them through time. But they were meant to be returned.

Garrett picked up the phone and hit the speed dial.

"Hello? Hello?" the familiar voice said.

"Hiya, Sis. What's up?"

She laughed. "Boy, oh boy, are you ever lucky I'm in Philly right now instead of somewhere nearby. Mom called me from the *plane*. Couldn't even wait to land, she had so many questions to ask. You might've given me a little warning you were abdicating the throne completely, big brother."

Garrett grinned. He could hear the pride in her voice, though. "You're the right lady for the job," he said. "Jacob doesn't know what's gonna hit him."

"Oh, don't try to flatter me, G, but...thanks." Her voice was so soft. Sometimes he forgot how vulnerable she could be underneath her tough edges. She'd been overshadowed for too long also. Not by one big brother, but by two.

"You're welcome," he said. "And you can repay me by offering your artistic consulting services on a project I'm doing."

"Is it for Cait?"

"Not directly," he admitted. He wasn't prepared to fill Marianne in on their relationship angst just yet. He wanted a happier ending first. "But I think she'll appreciate the idea."

"Good enough for me. What can I do?"

~CHAPTER FIFTEEN~

STEP 15:
Scoop the ice cream into bowls.
(Use a big spoon.)
Garnish with a cherry on top.
~From *Mr. Koolemar's Top Secret,*
Kool Kreme Ice Kreamations Recipe Book, pg. 97

"Thanks, Dianne, but I'm really not in the mood to drive out there for dinner," Cait told her sister-in-law over the telephone that night, trying to camouflage a teary sniffle with a phony cough.

"Did you come down with a cold?"

"Not exactly. I'm not feeling great, though."

"Well, your mom's been asking about you. She hasn't seen you in four whole days. Your niece wants a playmate, and you know there's no reasoning with a toddler. But, most importantly, Seth and I need a good excuse to order Chinese takeout. C'mon. You'd be doing us all a favor here."

Cait smiled through her tears. The old-movie marathon didn't provide nurturing like the comfort of a family member's voice. "You're trying to be nice, Dianne. I appreciate the call but—"

"I'm not being nice, and saying no isn't an option. Get your body in your car now."

Cait knew from experience the battle was over, so she gave in, switched off *Mr. Smith Goes to Washington* and washed her face until no more tears were visible.

When she arrived at the house, an exuberant Mia greeted her.

"Auntie Cait!" the little girl cried, throwing her body against her and kissing her face three times in a row.

"Hi, sweetie. How are you?"

"Good. I got a fwoggie." Mia waved her new toy puppet at Cait and made the frog's mouth move. "Wibbit. Wibbit."

Mia and her frog raced out of the room chasing Gibberish just as Cait's mother appeared at the bottom of the stairs.

"I heard voices," she said with a drowsy smile aimed in Cait's direction. "How are you, sweetie—"

The doorbell rang.

Cait saw a glance pass between her brother and his wife. She stiffened. "Were you expecting someone else for dinner?"

"Oh, yeah," Dianne said, in a faux-offhanded way. "Garrett called earlier and asked to stop by."

Before Cait could scream, "What?" Seth swung open the door.

"Gawett!" Mia exclaimed, running back into the room and throwing herself at him, the little turncoat.

"Hey, buddy, nice to see you," Seth said, opening the door wider to accommodate the man and the large gift-wrapped package he was holding.

"Hi...everyone," Garrett said. To his credit he seemed genuinely surprised to see her there. Either he didn't plan this meeting or he had an acting background she wasn't aware of.

Since Cait hadn't told Seth and Dianne about her last conversation with Garrett, she tried to gauge the look on Garrett's face to see if he'd said something to them. No expression.

"So, what have you got there?" Seth asked, pointing to the thin, silver-foil-wrapped rectangle.

"It's for your mom," he said. Garrett grinned at her mother. "I hope you like it, Mrs. Walsh."

Mom clasped her hands together. "A present for me?"

"Yep, in a way."

"Is it my birthday?" It was a serious question. Her mom squinted at Cait and Seth.

"No, not yet," Seth said.

"But we can celebrate anyway," Dianne declared.

Garrett presented the package to her mother, who sat regally in Seth's brown-leather armchair.

"Next week it'll be Veteran's Day here in the States," Garrett said. "In Canada and the U.K. the holiday is called Remembrance Day. Everywhere, though, the focus is on the importance of memories—and especially those of people who are no longer with us." He indicated with a gentle gesture that Mom should rip open the paper.

"Oh, my favorite photographs!" her mother cried. "Seth on his tricycle, Cait's first ballet recital, my darling Hank..." She turned the glass-covered and framed picture montage around for everyone to see. The effect was breathtaking.

"Marianne's an infinite source of artistic wisdom," Garrett said. "I asked her a hundred questions about arranging them, so if you're not happy with it...blame her." He smirked. "Then again, she was consulting long distance, so if you don't like it, it's my fault."

"It's beautiful, Garrett," Dianne gushed. "All of these treasured family moments in one place."

"Cool idea," Seth said, scanning the photos and nodding.

Mom's eyes were damp. "Thank you," she whispered to him.

Garrett smiled at her. "You're very welcome. I thought, maybe, you might like it for your new room."

Her mother kissed his cheek, and Cait felt tears spring into her own eyes when she witnessed it. No one could give Mom a firm grasp of the present time, but Garrett had given her a precious depiction honoring her past. His thoughtfulness stunned Cait even more than the hours of work he must have spent on the project.

"What a lovely gesture, Garrett," Cait said.

He moved near her, the tips of their shoes in intimate contact. An anguished expression crossed his face.

"So, you're back," she said.

He nodded. "Since late last night."

Then Seth asked him a question and he turned away. Mia twirled in circles. Dianne made a few light jokes to delight Mom. All this love in the room and, yet, Cait felt disconnected from it while things were so off track with Garrett. He had come back, yes, but the determination she'd seen in Janine Ellis's eyes convinced Cait it probably wouldn't be a permanent return. The sense of loss wrung her soul, and she knew there was just no way she could keep up the pretense of everything being all right for an entire evening.

Slipping on her jacket, she reached in her pocket for car keys and felt a piece of paper crunch. The ice cream coupon.

"I, actually...need to go," she told Dianne.

"But you just got here," her sister-in-law said, looking stunned. "I have dinner waiting in the—"

"Thanks, anyway. I'm sorry to have to rush out. Another time, maybe." She raised her voice. "See you all later." She handed the coupon to Garrett. "This is from the Koolemars. They asked me to give it to you."

She saw Seth and Dianne exchange another look at her reserved manner with Garrett and her sudden departure, but she ignored them and braced herself for the nippy night. She entered it without a backward glance.

Garrett watched her leave, his fingers still clutching the paper she'd handed him. Didn't she know what a hollow pleasure eating a pint of ice cream was now? He resented her escape all the more when Seth and Dianne transferred their stares from Cait to him. He might've been an idiot to call and set himself up for something like this, but he didn't know she'd be there, and he sure hadn't expected the woman to run away from him on sight.

Thanks to that, he was probably in for some kind of lecture on how not to upset Princess Caitlin. Maybe if he could make it through ten more minutes, he could go home, too. He wished he'd have thought to exit first.

Seth's eyes narrowed to a calculating squint. "So, Garrett, want a beer?"

"Why not?" he said automatically. "Thanks." He drank two beers before he remembered why not. Now he couldn't leave in ten minutes. Couldn't drive for at least an hour. And his mind metamorphosed into something all bleary and philosophical.

Dianne handed him a plate of Chinese food he wasn't hungry for and left the room with Mia and Georgina. Seth flipped on ESPN. He knew Seth had to be counting down the minutes until he was weak enough. Then the guy would read him the riot act for sure.

After half of a depressing college basketball game, Garrett couldn't take it any longer. "Just say what you need to say, Seth, will you?"

Seth looked at him blankly then pointed at the screen. "These kids suck." He shook his head. "Both teams. Can't imagine how either of those pudgy bastards can get away with calling themselves a 'coach.' I say bring back the guillotine."

Garrett quirked a brow. "Seriously, man."

"I am serious," Seth insisted. "Those two dudes shouldn't live to see Thanksgiving. They deserve to get the turkey treatment."

"I mean about Cait."

"Yeah? What about her?"

"What did she tell you? She must've told you something. You know, something along the lines of what a bad boyfriend I was, how I abandoned her or kept secrets from her. Stuff like that."

A slow grin slid over Seth's face. He put his feet up on the coffee table in front of them, took a swallow of beer, stared at the screen, kept silent.

"You're not gonna make this easy, are you?" Garrett drained his third beer and rubbed the inside corners of his eyes.

"I'm not gonna punch you in the jaw," Seth said, still grinning, "if that's what's worrying you. I think I finally outgrew that stage."

"Good to know."

Seth aimed the remote at the TV, switching it off. "Too painful to watch." He pointed to Garrett's empty beer bottle. "Want another?"

"I want a case," he admitted, "but I don't need any more."

"That bad, huh?"

He nodded.

Seth changed the subject. "You know, that photo display you made for my mom was great. The past is all she's got right now. It was good, and she's hanging onto it real tight." He paused, a hint of forthcoming revelation in the stiffening of his shoulders.

"But?" Garrett prompted.

"But Cait's different. Her old memories are so mixed— some happy, a lot of them really sad—that now she's only comforted by security. She knows life doesn't come with guarantees or anything, but she still needs to know that wherever she is, she'll have a place in it. A place where she'll be appreciated and not be so vulnerable."

"A commitment, you mean?"

Seth shrugged. "Call it whatever you want."

Garrett thought about Jacob, about commitment, and he cringed. But, then again, while Georgina Walsh was caught in her past, Garrett, by contrast, had been actively avoiding his. And the part Jacob played in it.

He tried to let himself feel his real emotions. Look at his gains and losses straight on through his own lens. Not Jacob's.

He loved his brother and emulated him, true. But he also missed the happier, less suspicious boy he himself had once been. Running away and escaping into work had never been a part of him when he was a kid. Avoiding emotional commitment had been a learned behavior also.

"So, what now, Seth? You gonna give me any brotherly advice?" He'd meant "brotherly" as in Seth's relationship to Cait, but it was like a wallop to the head when he realized he thought of Seth as *his* brother, too. That he considered the two of them to be family already.

Seth closed his eyes, and Garrett wondered if the guy would even answer. Probably thought he was a real loser. Someone he should keep far away from his kid sister.

Finally, Seth said, "Brotherly or no, I don't think anyone can give anyone else advice on love. That would be real dangerous. And to take it, if it's not right for you, would be even worse."

Garrett thought of the people who'd given him advice on relationships recently and how their thoughts often contrasted sharply with each other. He covered his eyes with his palm. He knew what he wanted...what his heart told him. What he didn't know was whether wanting it was enough to make it so.

Seth slugged him not-so-gently in the bicep. "You've gotta look at who you are and who she is. Feel what you feel. Talk to *her*, not to me or to anyone else. Then decide." He slanted Garrett a sideways look and reached for another beer. "But I think you're okay, buddy. Whatever happens."

Cait didn't think it was possible for an early November night to drag on like winter in the Yukon. By the time morning came, she was convinced it should've already been Valentine's or something.

She arrived at school only to have a message in her box saying the superintendent wanted to see her immediately. She stopped in the office and there were two police officers, the superintendent of course and...Garrett...already waiting there.

Cripes. What was going on?

"Thanks for coming in, Cait," the district's top administrator said. "We've just gotten some good news."

She glanced quickly at Garrett, who was studying the faces of everyone else in the room but hers. Then she said to the older gentleman, "I-I'm glad to hear it. What's happened?"

"These officers apprehended Doug Chippenak early this morning."

"Oh, well, that's..." What could she say, 'that's great'? The whole thing was just sad. "I'm, um, relieved."

"We knew you'd want to know," the superintendent told her.

"Despite the unfortunate circumstances, Miss Walsh," the taller officer said, "we wanted to make sure your mother and sister-in-law knew how much we appreciated their tip about seeing Chippenak near the bakery. Knowing they'd spotted him there is the clue we needed to eventually find him."

"I'll be sure to tell them," she said.

The officer grinned at her. "Of course, you and Mr. Ellis are to be commended for your detective work as well. Especially during the festival."

She glanced over at Garrett again. This time he was looking straight at her. She swallowed.

"Um, thanks. But I still don't understand why Doug did what he did. Did he give a statement explaining his actions?"

The other officer nodded. "Best we can figure is that the man is going through a self-image crisis. He apologized for his actions. Said he didn't mean to hurt anyone. Told the Chief he just hated being boring and predictable. Hated that he had this unexciting job with steady benefits. A job he'd gotten just for being the nephew of the company president. He said there were no challenges in his life."

This theory rang a bell. "Garrett suggested that to me," she told the group. "He sensed something like this while we were watching Doug at the token-exchange booth. He said the man just seemed to be bored."

The tall officer's eyes fixed on Garrett with admiration. "Good insight then, Mr. Ellis." He and his buddy turned to go. "Oh, one other thing the Chief mentioned. Said Chippenak confessed to a bunch of other petty thefts. Money he'd wheedled out of the district over the past couple years—"

The superintendent closed his eyes and sighed.

"And," the officer continued, "he was babbling about withdrawing cash from—and I may have this wrong—a *fitness* account. Could that be?" He shrugged and shot the superintendent a perplexed look but didn't wait for an answer. "We can get you his full statement on that later."

"Uh, thanks," the superintendent murmured as the officers left. "What an odd little mess we have here," he told her and Garrett, "but at least it's coming to a close." He smiled slightly at both of them. "I appreciate everything you two did to help resolve this problem."

Garrett cleared his throat before speaking for the first time since she'd arrived. "I was only doing my job, sir, but Cait deserves a lot of credit for going above and beyond the call."

She tried to shake away the praise, but Garrett cut off her nonverbal denial.

"You know your help was essential," he told her. Then he immediately turned to the superintendent. "Did you get an answer from the police on the whereabouts of fitness equipment money?"

"Yes, the Chief called me earlier," the older man said. "Doug actually *did* invest it in a separate account. I guess he's really good with that kind of thing. After hearing what the officers said about him, my guess is that Doug might've just wanted another challenge—but one that wasn't illegal. He'd probably planned to let Ronald in on the location of the fitness fund as soon as he saw him, since he'd promised to give the principal credit."

"But Ronald was gone before the Hoopla and Doug feared getting caught if he'd stayed around to explain," Garrett concluded.

"That's right," the superintendent said. "He wouldn't have actually stolen that account money. He knew we would've been able to trace it back to him after one conversation with Ronald."

Garrett nodded. "This sheds some light on why the other leaks were so hard to pinpoint. Doug Chippenak didn't need money. He just needed a thrill. So he could wait for an opportunity to present itself."

Cait listened with interest to this exchange, glad Garrett was finally getting the closure he'd so desperately wanted on this case. "Speaking of Ronald, how is he doing?" she asked.

The superintendent hesitated as he took a moment to glance at the principal's dusty desk. "He's recovering, day by day," he said. "But I, for one, have learned a valuable lesson." He patted his expansive belly. "The time to get fit is *now*, and I won't be putting it off any longer." He flashed a plastic card at them. "I just joined the Four Gates Country Club."

Although nothing could rival her endless night, the school day wasn't exactly speeding along either.

Of course, it didn't help that the school board members had been meeting in the building the entire day. She saw Shelley McAllister fawning all over Garrett. Hanging on his words the way Ginger from *Gilligan's Island* might cling to a life preserver and her favorite bottle of nail polish.

Cait was making photocopies after lunch when she overheard them in the hall.

"Tell me, Garrett, are you planning to join Four Gates as a full member next month?" Shelley drawled. "Chucky and I would love to meet you there for lunch."

"Don't know, Shell," Garrett said. "I didn't see ice cream on the dessert menu. I doubt I can stomach the alternatives."

Shelley laughed. "You goose!"

Cait heard her smack Garrett playfully. How dare that woman touch his body...

"I simply do not know how you routinely eat that stuff and still stay trim, darling. I'm so much happier now that I'm living a life with minimal toxins." Shelley sighed blissfully.

"You do seem cheerier," Garrett said.

"Oh, yes. Living in Wisconsin's a challenge, though. You know what I recommend to combat it? Yoga," Shelley declared. "It's a terrific relaxant. You should come to my class sometime."

"That's a generous invitation, Shell," Garrett said with such sincerity Cait almost teared up.

He probably wouldn't so much as drink a cup of coffee with her in the staff lounge, but he'd consider going to *yoga* with Shelley McAllister. Cait finished her copying and burst out of the room. She couldn't bear to listen to another word of this.

The redhead's back was to her as she emerged into the hall, but Garrett saw her and must have known she'd overheard them. He gave her a long, indecipherable look before returning his attentive gaze to Shelley—Self-Crowned Fitness Queen of the Midwest.

"When are the classes?" she heard him ask the board member as she sprinted to her classroom.

Cait clutched her papers tighter, whispered calming words under her breath and tried to block Garrett Ellis out of her mind.

By 5:00PM the school building was nearly deserted, but Cait refused to leave. She grabbed her staple remover and began taking down last month's bulletin-board display to ready the area for the children's upcoming Thanksgiving projects. She put away the classroom basket Marianne had sent her, sealing it—with the sound of finality—in a big box of Harvest Hoopla decorations.

Opening up the November/Thanksgiving box, she reached in to get a handful of laminated paper leaves...and one of her favorite decorations, a chunky turkey. She peeled off a long strand of masking tape and glanced around the room for the perfect spot. Where would Gobbler want to go?

"Moving on?"

She swiveled to face the door. "I—um—what?" she asked Garrett, who was leaning against the doorframe in such a familiar way her throat began to constrict.

"It's beginning to look a lot like Thanksgiving around here," he said with a half-grin. "Johnny Appleseed Day, the Harvest Hoopla, Halloween...they're all just memories now, right?"

She tried to force herself to relax. "Well, you know how it is with the children. Once a holiday's been celebrated, we need to move right along to the next one." God, what an inane comment. She exhaled. Hard to believe their relationship had been reduced to such superficialities.

Garrett nodded absentmindedly. He carried a large plastic bag, the kind with a handle, and he reached into it.

"Then maybe it's not too early for me to give you this," he said, handing her a circular piece of brown construction paper with multicolored strips sprouting from it. "Unless…unless it's too late."

She took Garrett's "turkey" card and held it gingerly in both hands. "Y-you made this for me? Today?"

"I did," he said. "I saw the kindergarten classes making them this morning after our meeting with the superintendent. Big brown round bodies…long pointy tail feathers…" He sent her a tiny smile. "It looked like an art project I could handle without Marianne's help."

Cait swallowed, hard. She began reading the words on first of seven colored feathers glued to the paper card. *"I appreciate your kindness."* She looked up at him, not quite believing he was standing there talking to her let alone giving her presents.

"There's more," he whispered.

She blinked and turned to the next one. *"I'm grateful for the way you greeted my sister and my mother—you've made friends for life."* She shot him a curious look. "You knew your mom stopped in here?"

He bobbed his head. "Yep, she told me right away. She's not as naturally sneaky as Marianne is."

She couldn't help but smile at that. She returned to her turkey. *"Your professionalism and creativity are assets to the school."* She took a deep breath and read the next two. *"Your trustworthiness is a gift I treasure."* Then, *"You make days (and nights) fun."*

"Keep reading, Cait."

Feather number six. *"Your family is as important to me as they are to you—I'm glad you've shared them."* The words began swimming in a haze of tears.

"Just one more, sweetheart," he said.

"I'm thankful for you," she read, *"and I love you."* Tears, impossible to hide, slid down her cheeks. She pressed the paper turkey to her heart. "I don't understand. I thought you were leaving. I thought—"

"It'll be Thanksgiving soon, Cait. When I think of all my blessings, all that I have to appreciate in my life, you're at the very top of the list. I wanted you to see my gratitude." He took a deep breath. "See, I made a choice, and I'm not going anywhere. I want to stay in this little corner of Wisconsin with you."

She couldn't restrain herself any longer. He came back to her. He loved her. He was hers. She threw her arms around him. "I'm sorry for jumping to conclusions," she murmured. "I missed you."

"I know," he said. "Me, too...on both counts. Think we can work it out? Talk more. Run away from each other less?"

She nodded into the crook of his neck. "I know we can."

"Good, because I'm not quite finished yet." Garrett took a half step back, rummaged in the plastic bag and pulled out a blue cooler about the size of a large lunchbox. "Open it," he urged.

She flipped the lid on the mini-cooler. The familiar pink-and-white label winked at her from atop a thick ice pack. "Kool Kreme Ice Kreamations," she said. "You saw the Koolemars?"

"Yes. I called in for a special request, and he made this new flavor for us to my exact specifications."

She lifted the ice cream out of the cooler, studying the label. "'Luscious Lovers' Tryst—rich vanilla ice cream swirled with sliced strawberries and warm kisses.'" She blushed deeply. "Garrett, you didn't tell him about that night when we..."

He shook his head. "Just open it up."

She pulled off the lid and saw the smooth, tempting ice cream. Yum.

"I brought two spoons," he said, reaching into the plastic bag again, grinning at her. "I have one more thing, too..." He fed her a truly luscious spoonful of ice cream, then he dug into the bag one final time, retrieving the last item.

"A turkey-shaped fruit and nut basket!" she exclaimed. "I saw one of these in The Nutty Fruit catalogue."

"The basket's from my family," he said, watching as she untied the ribbon and removed the plastic wrap. "They want you to fly out for A Very Connecticut Thanksgiving, by the way. I'm just warning you." He winked at her. "But the velvet box in the center of the basket, should you choose to accept it, is from me."

Garrett handed the dark blue box to her and kissed her lips gently. "Cait, I've never been happier than when I'm around you. Please say you'll consider marrying me."

For several moments, Cait was unable to utter a sound, but she did manage to nod.

"So, you think that's a good idea, then?" He kissed her one more time.

"I do," she said, kissing him back. "I love you, you know that, right?"

"I do now," he said, pulling her close to him.

She let him open the box and slip the ring on her finger. After several moments of losing herself in the warmth and comfort of his embrace, though, she laughed. "Our ice cream is going to melt—I think we should go home. And besides, Mr. Ellis, as I recall, you're a creative, adventurous guy with unusual tastes. Shouldn't we see what other ideas you can come up with?"

"Why, that's excellent thinking, Miss Walsh," he said, smiling. "Are you a fan of s'mores? Because I just so happen to have a brand new bottle of chocolate syrup in my kitchen. And we could pick up a box of graham crackers and a bag of marshmallows on the way back there and..."

~EPILOGUE~

LAST STEP:
This scrumptious recipe for
"Chunky Cherry-Chocolate Jubilee"
makes a generous one-quart serving.
Eat and enjoy with those you love!
~From *Mr. Koolemar's Top Secret,
Kool Kreme Ice Kreamations Recipe Book*, pg. 97

Christmas Day, Two Years Later

The Ellis's house in Ridgewood Grove was filled with people decked in red and green. The bright lights on the Christmas tree illuminated stacks of presents and speckled a cheery banner with flecks of festive color. And little Olivia Gina Ellis sat wide-eyed under her birthday banner, gaping at the display.

Her big cousin Mia, behaving like a proper kindergartener to her left, handed the one-year-old a well-loved frog puppet.

"He doesn't look like it," Mia said, "but I'm sure he's a prince in disguise."

The birthday girl, with owlish, cocoa-colored eyes and wisps of blond hair, shrieked with delight.

"Happy birthday, Livie." Mia gave her rounded cheek a kiss.

One by one the other guests brought gifts to Livie. Her Aunt and Uncle, Dianne and Seth, presented her with a talking alphabet/number machine. Dianne pressed a button to demonstrate.

"One," said the disembodied electronic voice.

"Exactly," said Auntie Dianne. "You're *one* today."

Livie's Auntie Marianne and Uncle Daniel, still acting like the newlyweds they were, kissed each other before offering Livie a huge box of children's art supplies.

Uncle Jacob brought her toddler-sized skis and poles...and an "On, Wisconsin!" jersey.

Proud Grandma Georgina was having one of her rare lucid days. She'd painted an animal/insect menagerie on canvas for her young granddaughter.

First-time grandparents Janine and Macauley lavished Livie with an enormous basket heaped with handmade wooden toys, while honorary Auntie Jenna ruffled the girl's baby blond curls before giving her four gorgeous, color-coordinated outfits.

Cait whispered to her husband, "She's going to be spoiled rotten, and we haven't even opened her Christmas gifts yet."

"I know," Garrett murmured, taking in all the discarded wrapping paper and ribbons, but still pulling out of his desk a package of Disney CDs he was sure his daughter would love.

Cait grinned when Livie opened up the gift from her "Da-da-da," then she handed her baby several carefully selected Winnie the Pooh DVDs.

A knock on the door interrupted the group's merry laughter.

"Oh, good. The Koolemars are here," Cait said as Garrett let them in.

"Hope we haven't missed the cake yet," Alan Koolemar declared, setting down a gift bag on the nearest table. He shrugged off his coat and helped his wife remove hers.

"We were just about to get to that," Garrett said.

"Oh, aren't you just the sweetest little pumpkin," his wife Audrey cooed. Livie gave her a bright, dimply grin and a few photo flashes went off.

A few minutes later the crowd joined together to sing a rousing rendition of "Happy Birthday," while Livie's single candle flickered on her chocolate cake.

"This'll be her first taste of cake and ice cream, won't it?" Grandma Janine asked, pulling out her digital video camera.

"Sure is, Mom." Garrett handed the cake knife to Cait, watching his wife slice the first piece.

"Oh, yes," Mr. Koolemar said, reaching over to pull a pint of ice cream labeled Baby's Birthday Bash out of the bag he brought. "This is for the little lady."

Livie let out an indignant squeal when her mother strapped her wiggling body into the highchair and tied a bib firmly around her small pink neck.

"This is going to be messy, sweet pea," Cait said by way of apology for the confinement.

Livie gurgled, "Ma-ma-ma-ma-ma!"

Garrett let Mr. Koolemar do the honors of putting the scoop of ice cream atop his daughter's piece of cake. Then Garrett set it on the highchair tray with a spoon while everyone crowded around to watch.

The one-year-old jabbed the mysterious food with her plastic spoon then poked at it with her index finger, looking up at her parents questioningly.

"It's okay, sweetheart," her daddy reassured her. "It's good."

"Try it, you'll like it," her mommy encouraged.

So, with an audience of doting family encircling her, Livie took the plunge and filled her baby spoon up with the cold creamy thing on top of that dark spongy stuff. She lifted the spoon in the vicinity of her mouth—missing the first time and decorating her chin instead, but getting it in the right place a moment later.

A few more cameras clicked and film footage rolled, marking the momentous occasion. But Livie Ellis, unaware of the dates and details, knew two things for sure: She was surrounded by big people who loved her, and this slippery stuff on her tray was really sweet and yummy. She wanted more.

Livie grinned her most winning six-toothed smile and dug in again.

❧END☙

Holiday Man

~CHAPTER ONE~

Valentine's Day

Shannon Quinn made a final adjustment to the heart-shaped

banner above the inn's reception desk and sighed.

Valentine's Day.

Yet another holiday weekend spent alone. Well, at work, which amounted to the same thing. If this romantic dry spell didn't let up soon, she'd have to consider investing in an inflatable man.

She slid her clipboard across the counter to her assistant Jake. "You get to register the next set of guests," she told him. "I'm all out of ink."

Jake studied her fuzzy pink Cupid pen with one of his I'm-too-sexy-for-my-ballpoint looks. "And I'm all out of love, babe," he crooned, bringing his palm to his chest as if struck by the romance god's arrow. "I'm *so* lost without you. But, maybe, if you give me a kiss to recharge my batteries, I could—"

"Knock it off," she said, laughing. "A guest might overhear you." The guy brought sexual suggestiveness to every conversation and wasn't above singing sappy love ballads for effect, but she knew better than to take him seriously. Her smooth-talking assistant was a Grade-A flirt.

Which was part of his charm.

But it was the kind of charm best kept out of an employer-employee relationship and better used to keep the young female guests at her Door County, Wisconsin inn amused and intrigued on "holiday" weekends. Jake Marcolis never had trouble scoring girlfriends, and Shannon knew her brush-off wouldn't deter him from finding companionship that weekend. Or any weekend.

The front door swung open and a gust of February chill swirled inside, along with three snow-covered adults. Two men. One woman. An easy registration. Jake could handle this.

Shannon took a few steps toward the backroom to restock the printer paper and grab a couple of new Valentine pens.

"Hi, I'm Trevor Wainwright, and this is my wife Gina," the shorter of the two men said, finger-combing his blond hair with one hand and rubbing the young woman's snowy shoulder with the other. "We have a reservation for this weekend." He winked at his lady, a petite brunette who looked to be about four or five years older than Shannon's twenty-six. "For a room with a king-sized bed."

"Of course," Jake said, typing the name into the computer. "The Wainwrights from St. Paul, Minnesota?"

The blond man nodded.

Jake hit a key to print out the Wainwrights' record. "Here it is," he said, putting the sheet on his clipboard along with a pen covered with red, white and pink hearts. "Please read this over and sign it, sir." To Shannon, Jake said, "That was the last of the printer paper."

"I'll be right back with more," she told him, feeling two sets of eyes on her—the woman's and the other man's. That taller, darker one who wasn't her husband. He was an intense-looking guy with jet-black hair, and he had an unsettling but somehow provocative gaze. It was a Come-here-baby/Don't-touch-me look, the kind Bad Boys who'd grown into Dangerous Men possessed.

"Thanks," Jake said. "And, hey, if you find a plain old Bic back there, that'd be fine by me..."

Shannon just laughed, but she heard Jake mutter something to the male guests about his "masculinity taking a hit with all these froufy pink things lying around." The woman, Gina Wainwright, chuckled slightly.

Shannon raced through her chores in the backroom so she could get back out to the reception desk again, unable to account for her curiosity about the new guests. True, the three of them made an attractive trio, but she wasn't quite sure where the powerful-looking dark-haired man fit into the lovey-dovey couple's weekend's revelries. A threesome? It didn't seem that way, exactly, but she was willing to shamelessly eavesdrop as Jake processed the guy's registration in order to find out.

Hey, it was within her rights. She owned the place, after all. Had to know what kind of guests she was dealing with, didn't she?

She emerged with an armload of paper, refilled the empty printer tray then laid out a few new cutesy pens on the countertop. Gina grinned at her, so she returned the friendly gesture. Then the woman's attention shifted to the unadorned fingers of Shannon's left hand, which still rested on the countertop near the pens.

"Trevor, honey," Gina said sweetly to her husband, her grin broadening. "I want a little tour of this quaint inn. Right now." She raised her eyebrows in his direction.

Her husband raised his eyebrows back. "A fab idea, darling."

Gina glanced pointedly at Jake. "Excuse me, sir. Would you be so kind as to show us around for a few minutes? Perhaps your colleague," she gave a cheery nod to Shannon, "would be able to register our friend? He wishes to settle in for the night in his own room, but we're *so* anxious to explore our surroundings."

Shannon wasn't certain, but she could've sworn the dark-haired man rolled his eyes at this pronouncement. Gina's husband, Trevor, let out a short laugh that he tried without success to cover up with a cough.

Jake peeked over at Shannon, not in on the trio's joke but not opposed to stepping away from his desk duties either. With a smirk that seemed to say *What can I do? A guest's wishes always come first*, Jake stood up and turned to Gina. "At your service, ma'am."

This left Shannon and the tall, unsmiling man just watching as Jake led the happy couple sashaying down the hall. Terrific. Now she was alone with Mr. Intensity.

She cleared her throat. "Welcome to Holiday Quinn, sir. May I have your name, please?"

The man's glance appraised her—there was no other way to describe it—from her chest upward. Granted, her chest, shoulders and head were all that were visible behind the registration desk's counter, but *still*. She mentally fumed over this distinct act of rudeness until she saw his stony face break into a full smile.

"I apologize," he said in a voice that was far deeper and much more resonant than she'd expected. "I could see

432

immediately why Gina selected you as my personal desk attendant for tonight, but you must excuse her matchmaking tendencies. She's incorrigible."

Shannon looked into his sharp hazel eyes, stunned by his candor and even more shocked at being "selected" as any kind of a match for him. Alpha males weren't the type to appear often on her dating radar. And this one was too, too...just too much.

Of something. Of everything.

"Why, th-thank you," she stammered. "I think." Then added, "Your name, please?"

He laughed briefly. "Yes, of course. The reservation is under Hartwick. Bram Hartwick." He paused. "Unless it's under Graybell." His forehead creased and he frowned. "Perhaps try searching under that name first."

Shannon stubbornly typed in "Hartwick" and found his computer file, but it was cross-referenced with, yes, an Angie Graybell—the woman who'd originally made the weekend reservation. Shannon didn't know why, but her stomach roller-coastered downward at this news. From the "matchmaking" comment, she'd foolishly assumed this towering, commanding man was single. Silly her.

"I've found your reservation, Mr. Hartwick. You're from Minneapolis, Minnesota, correct?" she asked him in her most professional voice. He seemed the type to demand a professional demeanor in all things.

He nodded once.

"We're all set, then." She printed out his form and handed him a pen. "Will Ms. Graybell be arriving later tonight, or shall we expect her in the morning?"

The handsome Mr. Hartwick didn't immediately respond, but his face turned to rock-like seriousness again in an instant. He pressed his lips together in a line of clear displeasure, and Shannon was certain of only one thing: This was *not* the kind of man she'd ever want to upset. He looked capable of biting off the heart-shaped heads of all her Valentine's Day pens, starting with the red-sequined one he was holding in a death grip. Not an image she wanted to cling to, thanks.

"Ms. Graybell will not be coming tonight. Or tomorrow. Or Sunday. You may safely remove her name from the reservation," he said stiffly.

Okey-dokey.

"Very well, Mr. Hartwick." And Shannon had to admit to feeling a perverse pleasure in deleting the heretofore-unseen Angie Graybell.

"And what would be *your* name, if you don't mind my asking?" he said to her, still intense-looking but his lips turned up a tiny notch at the corners.

"My name is Shannon Quinn, sir." And why, exactly, did so much as telling him her name make her heart rate speed up and her fingers twitchy? It must be that Bad-Boy/Dangerous-Man Factor again. Truth be told, this trait was starting to bug her.

Bram Hartwick, of course, did not look nervous. He did, however, appear downright surprised, and he couldn't seem keep the shock off his face.

"Is your last name a lucky coincidence, Ms. Quinn, or are you related to the original owners of this charming establishment?"

"The luck of the Irish is always with me," she shot back, determined not to let him intimidate her. "But, yes, I'm a direct descendent. The original owners were my grandparents. They opened the inn back in the mid-1940s."

He quirked a brow. "Fans of the classic film, then?"

She knew what he was asking. Everyone wanted to know if Holiday Quinn was named after the famous Bing Crosby-Fred Astaire movie musical *Holiday Inn*.

"Yes," she informed him. "The picture came out in 1942 and it was one of my Grandma Quinn's all-time favorites. When she and my grandfather opened up their inn a couple of years later, the play on the name was intentional. However, until a few years ago, we were open all year round, not just on holidays. My parents made that change themselves."

"Hmm." He tilted his head, leaned in toward the counter and said, "Why?"

Why? Because, as much as she tried to help them, they could no longer take care of the inn day after day by themselves. Because they loved her and wanted to leave her family's legacy in good condition. Because they deserved to finally retire and enjoy the relaxation their elderly years afforded them.

Only, once they did, they died.

But Shannon wasn't about to confide her personal life story to a man whose face, as far as she could tell, resembled a block of granite.

"Because they had a great sense of humor," she said instead.

"Ah." He glanced around the lobby, a glint of interest in those intelligent eyes. He focused them again on her. "And what about you, Ms. Quinn? Do you have a great sense of humor, too?"

"I'd like to think so, but everyone believes that about themselves. I could be sadly deluded."

Mr. Stonyface actually laughed. "Delightful," he murmured, just loud enough for her to hear. He signed the forms, pushed her copies back across the counter toward her and pulled out his iPhone. After a moment of squinting at it and fiddling with the screen, he said, "So, Gina tells me there are also singles' events at the inn this weekend. What've you got scheduled?"

"We have a High Tea Mix-n-Mingle tomorrow at four, the Queen of Hearts Singles' Dance tomorrow night from eight until midnight and the Valentine's Morning-After Breakfast on Sunday at nine."

"The Queen of Hearts Singles' Dance…" he repeated, staring down at his cell phone again. "That sounds almost promising."

"Almost?"

He gave her one of his cool, assessing stares. "Well, I'd only be sure if I knew who was planning to attend the function." He paused. "Any chance you'll be there?"

A strange but thankfully temporary panic gripped her throat. "Of course, Mr. Hartwick," she managed to reply. "I run the inn. I oversee everything."

He broke into a near-grin, one clearly calculated to subdue women into compliance. "In that case, count on me to show up." Then he leaned forward, as if about to ask a personal question, when the electronic version of an old dance tune, "La Vida Loca," blared from somewhere inside his clothing. Curious choice of ringtone.

He grimaced and reached into his coat pocket. "Excuse me," he told her before clicking on his cell phone. "Hartwick," he said into it. Then, *"Ciao*, Senior Niccolo." He listened, winced and took the room key she extended toward him. He waved his thanks, grabbed his bag and strode in the direction of the stairs. The last words she heard him say were *"Il problema con la sapone in Milano?"*

Italian. The man spoke rapid-fire Italian. How weird was that? And, okay, how very cool. For someone with such a stately façade, she never would've guessed he'd be fluent in a Language of Love. What other surprises hid behind that composed demeanor? She stared after him.

"Yo, Shannon?"

She spun around and to find Jake eyeing her with a curious expression. "Huh?"

"He's not your type."

She blinked. "What?"

"The tight ass who just went up the stairs. Not for you. And besides—" He tapped her nose with the tip of a fuzzy-heart pen. "The guy looks like trouble. He's got Control Freak written all over him. Stick with someone who might actually be fun."

She raised an eyebrow. "Like who?"

"Well, like...*me*," Jake said. "I'm real fun, great at karaoke, a sharp dresser and, I'm told, unbelievably cute," he added with his usual modesty and a fluff of his light-brown hair. "And I promise to fight off any tall, grim-looking guys who glare at the world as if it didn't agree with them."

She laughed. "He wasn't *that* bad."

"Matter of opinion, babe."

Jake was joking around, of course. He didn't care about

Bram Hartwick one way or another, he just wasn't too fond of some other man forcing him to relinquish center stage. Jake delighted in being the main attraction.

Before she could comment again, though, one of the female guests who'd checked in that afternoon sidled up to the counter. The young woman in her early twenties shot Shannon a quick smile before turning toward her oh-so-fun assistant.

"Hi, Jakey." The woman giggled. Svelte, soft-spoken and seductive, this lady had Jake leaning toward her, his expression indicating he was "ready to help" with whatever might be needed.

"Yes, Ms. Malone?" he asked with his ultra-solicitous tone. "Is there a problem with your accommodations tonight?"

The woman bit her lip, brushed a dark curl behind her ear and murmured something only Jake could hear. He cleared his throat as if to suppress a laugh then whispered something back that included the words "late-night" and "fantasy."

Enough already. Shannon walked into the backroom to give them some privacy. Besides, she had late-night fantasies of her own she'd love to indulge in. Finding the right heroic lead for those sexy daydreams, however, proved to be an ever-changing mental pursuit. Sometimes Ryan Reynolds headlined. Sometimes Henry Cavill or Colin Firth. Sometimes a classic actor like James Dean.

Tonight she knew Bram Hartwick would be featured in the starring role. Something about him had her certain that, though he might be too much to handle in real life, he'd be just perfect for a hot night of erotic fantasy. And she intended to enjoy it.

Bram clicked off his cell phone after a full twenty-seven minutes of talking long distance with his European distributor. Seemed there'd been some delay in getting the latest batch of Lathericious Bath Products to Milan, and now they were running low on the scented body oils. The Italians really loved those body oils. Especially "Citrus Cravings."

Bram smiled. As the Minneapolis-based company's founder and CEO, he had a say in the names of all their products, but he usually let the creative team do their thing. His personal favorite, which he'd been known to give as a gift to very special women in his life, was the fiery fragrance "Sin-amon Spice." Nothing like it.

He'd given Angie a bottle, of course. Not that it'd helped heat things up much. At least not in the last few months of this cold freeze they'd mistakenly called a relationship. Damned good thing she finally put an end to their misery. She was already dating again—some accountant in St. Paul.

Bram tossed his phone on the bed, kicked off his dress shoes and twisted open the complimentary split of champagne chilling in the white plastic tub on the table. He took a few swigs and shrugged off his coat, letting the residual snowflakes fall where they may. Then off with his jacket. Next he loosened his tie, imagining Scarlett Johansson—wait, no, that auburn-haired woman downstairs with the huge blue eyes and the soft voice— what was her name?

Shannon.

Imagining Shannon pulling the tie off from around his neck and letting it float to the floor. Then, with those delicate, creamy fingers, unbuttoning his shirt.

When his shirt billowed open, he rubbed his chest with his palm. Would Shannon do that? Would her touch be light and teasing or firm and decisive?

He didn't know, but he'd gotten a good look at *her* chest and, if she were here with him right now, that cutesy hearts sweater she was wearing would be on the carpet mingling with his tie. So would her bra.

Visions of her covered with Sin-amon Spice and Valentine's Day red-hot candies danced through his mind. Mmm.

He loosened his belt, unzipped his pants and let them drop to the floor, too. His fingertips skimmed the waistband of his boxers as his mind drifted back to Shannon. She was the inn's owner, not—as he'd first thought—a subordinate of that glib jerk standing next to her downstairs. A woman full of surprises.

Maybe his scheming friends weren't so wrong to insist he come away on this weekend after all. Maybe he'd just need to make a little time to get to know the inn's attractive owner a bit better. He'd look for her tomorrow. Ask her some questions.

Then Bram's hands dipped lower but, as he closed his eyes, it was Shannon who touched him.

Shannon perused the guests at the High Tea Mix-n-Mingle the next afternoon. Everyone had been served in the Crosby Room and, adding a splash of milk to her Earl Grey, she stirred her drink and kept a watchful eye on the crowd.

"These lemon teacakes are scrumptious," Darlene Baker purred, springing across the parquet floor to Shannon and planting a wet kiss on her cheek. "Keith has eaten four of them already. Somebody make him stop." She paused, raised a thin, white eyebrow. "I want there to be some left for me."

Shannon grinned and leaned in to whisper in the older woman's ear. "Don't tell anyone, but I've got two more trays in the kitchen."

Darlene Baker gasped then giggled.

"No whispering allowed here," her husband's voice boomed with good-natured irritation. "I know you're telling tales about me to our favorite hostess. Said I'd start that damned diet on Monday, didn't I?"

"Yes, honey," his wife replied with a smile in Shannon's direction.

"I'm so glad you're enjoying the Tea, Mr. Baker. How are your accommodations this weekend?"

"Wonderful, as always, Shannon dear," the man replied. "And, for the three-hundredth time, enough with the 'Mr. and Mrs. Baker' nonsense! Call us Keith and Darlene."

"Yes." His wife turned on her, too. "We know no one can top your professionalism, but we insist. We practically live here these days. Heck, we're almost like your relatives."

Shannon felt a pang of longing in her chest—loss entwined

with an unexpected strand of hopefulness. The Bakers spoke the truth. They visited the inn often enough to be both well known and well loved by the Holiday Quinn staff, and they reminded her enough of her parents to almost always break her heart when she saw them. The two couples shared the same warmth of spirit.

"I'd be honored," she admitted to them. "And thank you."

She was about to ask the Bakers their plans for the rest of the afternoon when, out of the corner of her eye, a tuft of jet-black hair snagged her attention.

Mr. Bram Hartwick. Seemingly unchanged since last night. Still tall, dark and intense.

Also unchanged since last night were her growing fantasies of the man. How, in her midnight dream—manufactured for personal arousal—she imagined those strong arms encircling her. The stubble on his chin burning a trail along her cheek. The press of his lean hips against hers as the two of them tumbled between the silky sheets of the Astaire Suite...

She felt a bolt of white heat rush through her just from the memory of that dream.

Darlene Baker tapped her shoulder. "Are you okay, dear? You seem to be blushing."

Shannon brought a hand to her face. Damn her fair skin. "Oh, I'm fine. Fine. Thanks. I'm just, um, a little warm. From the tea."

Keith Baker scanned the room and his gaze came to rest on Bram, who was standing near the door. Keith turned back to Shannon. "Well, that's as good an excuse as any, but to me it looks like the stirrings of young love."

Shannon shook her head to deny such an embarrassing notion.

His wife rolled her eyes. "You're such a romantic, Keith. Don't you know that not every woman spends her days lusting after men?" She shot a glance at Bram. "Even really, really handsome ones?"

"Maybe, maybe not. But men sure lust after lovely women." He paused. "Shannon here doesn't know about our

Tommy yet, now does she?"

"Who's Tommy?" Shannon asked, mostly to be polite. She couldn't seem to keep her gaze from straying to Bram, who held his high-tech cell phone up to his ear with one hand and rolled a chocolate dipped pastry between the fingers of the other. He caught her glance and, for a split second, the air between them sizzled.

"Our youngest son," Keith explained. He then began telling her the story of how their "little" boy's commitment-phobic heart finally got captured for good by a pretty lady in Arizona. "Just when he thought he was safe from the wiles of women, he goes on this wilderness hike, and who should be the trail guide? Why, none other than Mary Ellen. The girl he'd had the hugest crush on back in seventh grade!"

"See, she'd moved away from Wisconsin when they were in junior high, but Tommy had never forgotten her," Darlene said. "They recognized each other right away—I don't know how, but they just *knew*. He asked her out, and they've been together ever since."

Keith leaned toward her. "And every time she looks at him, she blushes. Still."

Shannon laughed faintly. "That *is* romantic. But I'm, um, not in the same situation. At all."

The Bakers grinned as though they didn't believe her, and why should they? No matter what Bram Hartwick's feelings were toward her, her feelings were about as romantic, or at least erotic, as they came.

Why the hell was he still staring at her?

He finally had the cell phone away from his ear. He popped the pastry in his mouth and reached for a cup of tea from the table nearby. Before he lifted the cup to his lips, though, he raised it slightly in her direction. A salute of sorts. Then he grinned.

She felt her cheeks flush warm again.

"If you'll excuse us, dear," Darlene said with a saucy smile. "I do believe I need another teacake."

"Oh, me, too," Keith insisted.

They stepped away before Shannon could utter a sound, and they deliberately steered a path that left plenty of room for the dashing Mr. Hartwick to get through. Darlene winked at Shannon over her shoulder.

Bram took three strides in her direction before stopping in his tracks and grimacing. He put down his teacup on a nearby tray and raised a silent hand at her. What was this? Charades? She hadn't planned any games for the High Tea, but she didn't feel the lack of activities had left the guests wanting.

Then she saw him reach for that blasted cell phone in his pocket.

"Hartwick," she heard him say into the receiver as his long legs carried him out the door.

Well, so much for romance—erotic or otherwise. Bram Hartwick had attractiveness going for him, sure, but he was clearly a workaholic, and nothing seemed capable of pulling him away from that damn phone. The only interaction the two of them would probably have this weekend would be the imaginary face-to-face contact in her mind, featuring him as the lead in her nighttime fantasies.

Not that this was all bad. But the tiny, adventure-seeking side of her had begun, irrationally, to hope for the real thing.

Shannon ladled a few more glasses of pink, champagne-spiked punch into crystal goblets and placed them on the refreshments table for the dancers. The song "Playing with the Queen of Hearts" resonated clearly from the speakers, while newfound couples laughed and made small talk throughout the room. The evening's singles' dance looked to be a success. Too bad she wished herself to be elsewhere.

She couldn't help it. She wanted to be dancing, too, but somewhere more exotic, like on a romantic cruise down the Seine with Paris as a backdrop. Or, on a sandy Caribbean beach, the sun sinking into the water in thunderbolts of gold. Or, maybe—

Jake bustled up to her, interrupting her latest daydream, and reached for a goblet. "The DJ said he was thirsty."

She shook her head and stilled Jake's hand. "I'd be happy to get him any kind of soft drink he'd like but, please, no alcohol for him tonight. He's got to drive back in an hour and the roads are treacherous."

"Fair enough." Jake set off toward the kitchen, grinning at all the single ladies littering the dance floor. Waving. Winking seductively. The usual.

Jake's ease with women was infamous in these parts. He even went as far as to proposition *her* again this weekend. Jake was cute. He was "a catch," of sorts. And some nights the loneliness of not having a real lover left her tempted. Just not tempted enough.

"Why are you always standing on the sidelines, Ms. Quinn?" a deep voice near her said.

She swiveled toward it, her heart rate picking up speed. "Mr. Hartwick. H-How are you? How are you enjoying your stay?"

"Hmm. Answering a question with more questions. That's not the answer I was looking for." He appraised her appearance again, as was his habit, his hazel eyes twinkling as he took in her cream-colored, floor-length evening gown with the gold spaghetti straps. One of the few outfits she felt actually flattered her. "You, of all people, should be out on the dance floor."

"Why?"

"Because you're the loveliest woman in the room."

Her breath caught at these words, but she forced herself to show no overt reaction. God, she hoped she succeeded. Instead, she replied coolly, "You presume too much. This is a singles' dance, Mr. Hartwick. It's for those men and women who are looking for love."

He took a purposeful step closer. "And you're not?" Those serious eyes bored into her, ready to disagree. "Tell me, are you the queen of your own heart or has some lucky man already claimed it?"

A smooth line but, she had to hand it to him, though it might have sounded silly coming out of anyone else's mouth, Bram Hartwick somehow managed to sell it with style.

"Mine isn't a quick or easy heart to claim," she replied. "But there are plenty of other ladies out there who may feel differently." She pointed toward a couple of especially pretty guests, both of whom had stolen not-so-subtle glances at him during this little chat.

He grinned. "I never said I needed either 'quick' or 'easy,' Ms. Quinn, and you deflected my question yet again." He scanned the room then focused those sharp eyes on her. "I'll be more blunt this time. I'd like to dance with you, but I don't want to step on another man's toes or offend your sense of propriety. If you're not free, just say so. But if you are, I hope you'll honor me with the next slow dance."

Direct, wasn't he? Shannon cleared her throat and battled a cocktail of emotions. Sure, she desired him, but he was a weekend guest from another state. How likely would it be that she'd see him again? Not very. And his whole ultra-polished, International-Man-of-Mystery air was slightly on the intimidating side...and, also, a little intriguing.

Okay, a *lot* intriguing.

Still, he wasn't proposing marriage. Just a dance. Only a three- or four-minute dance.

She cleared her throat again. "I'd be delighted to dance with you, Mr. Hartwick."

He smiled. "Bram," he said, reaching for her hand.

"Bram," she repeated. "And, please, call me Shannon."

His smile broadened. "I will."

He led her onto the dance floor as the next slow song began to play. And while Barbra Streisand belted out "My Heart Belongs to Me," Bram caressed her shoulder with his palm and drew her a few inches closer to him. Shannon knew her heart may well belong to her alone but, goodness, her body cast its vote for the dashing Bram Hartwick.

As her skin tingled from his firm but soothing touch, conversation between them ground to a stop. She mentally sifted through their two prior meetings for some clue as to what to ask him. At first, all she could come up with was *When did you learn to speak Italian?* And *How many hours do you spend on the phone every day?* But then she remembered.

"Your friends, the Wainwrights," she began. "Are they enjoying their weekend getaway? I'll confess, I haven't seen them once since they registered."

He laughed. "Well, no, you wouldn't, would you? Not unless you tried to spy on them from their balcony window. They warned me about their plans before we left Minnesota." He leaned in close and whispered in her ear. "They're doing a Lennon-and-Yoko-like 'Love In' this weekend."

Now it was Shannon's turn to laugh. "I believe I like your friends, Bram."

"Yeah, me, too. They can sure be—"

"Excuse me, Shannon, I need your help." Jake stood just to their left, his jaw tight and his eyes narrow. Something must really be wrong.

She broke away from Bram's grasp. "What is it?" she asked Jake. "Is there a problem with a guest?"

He pursed his lips. "I should speak with you privately. If you'll excuse us, Mr., um…"

"Hartwick," Bram supplied. "And, of course. Perhaps I'll have the pleasure of another dance with you later in the evening, Shannon?"

"I'd like that," she told Bram before Jake dragged her away. She'd *really* like that.

"What's going on?" she asked him when they were in the backroom.

"The chocolate hearts aren't here," he informed her. "I checked the kitchen twice, and the candy platters are nowhere to be found."

She squinted at him. "Is that all this is about?"

He gave her a grim look tinged with anger.

Oops. Now she'd offended him. "I mean, there's nothing to worry about, Jake. I thought I told you this, but maybe it slipped my mind. We're doing the candy distribution differently this year and giving out the chocolate hearts at the Valentine's Morning-After Breakfast instead of at the dance. Margaret hired a special chocolatier at The Ashland, and she's bringing over a batch for us at seven a.m. tomorrow. Everything's under control."

Jake shrugged. "Oh. Okay then." He gave her another odd look. "Are you all right, Shannon?"

She laughed. "Yeah, I'm doing great. No problem. How about *you*?"

"Fine, of course," he said stiffly.

"Well, that's...good to hear. So, I'm going to head back into the dance now. If anything important comes up, please let me know."

"Oh, I will," he said, his voice weirdly serious. Jake was in a mighty strange mood tonight.

"Super." And, with that, she dashed back out to the dance to see if Bram was still there.

He wasn't.

And the disappointment she felt surprised her with its potency. She'd wanted that second dance, and not just because it was Valentine's Day. Not just because she was lonely. But because, in spite of herself, she kind of liked him.

Her imagination had always been stronger than her nerve. Time for that to change.

Bram watched Shannon scurry after that assistant of hers—that man with the shrewd eyes and the pesky manners—and he wanted to throttle the guy.

Jake Whatever-The-Hell-His-Last-Name-Was lusted after Shannon—that much was clear. Shannon's feelings toward the assistant were more difficult to ascertain, but Bram would figure it out. He always did.

Why? Because she'd caught his interest. Even if anything beyond tonight was an exercise in futility.

He marched around the perimeter of the dance floor,

trying to imagine his ex-girlfriend at a weekend affair like this. Angie would've wanted to hit every activity. Not miss a single second of excitement, whatever the latest thrill might be. She absolutely exhausted him when they were together, but not because he couldn't handle the events she threw his way.

No. He could handle anything.

But her insatiable need for diversion drained him. It felt like a reflection on him. Made him fear his inability to keep her entertained. And he'd hated that.

Pretty-faced women dotted the dance floor. Several looked at him with those eyes filled with feverish anticipation, an expectation that a love match might be imminent. Well, Bram knew better. Relationships were fine as long as they were kept in their proper place. Something hot. Something short-term. Something with boundaries. Try to make them your top priority and everything else in your life would get shot to hell.

He shuddered, flooded by a need to get away from the hopeful expressions etched on the faces of those single women.

So he strode out into the hallway and lingered by a display cabinet featuring, among other things, a curvy stained-glass vase. It was European. Mid-Twentieth Century. Delicate yet intricate. Colorful but in a tasteful, not discordant style.

Funny. In an odd way it reminded him of Shannon.

Now there was a woman whose company he'd admit to enjoying. But, let's face it, she wasn't exactly available to him. If he were being honest with himself—and he'd made a habit out of doing just that—perhaps this was part of his fascination.

She was lovely, but she wouldn't be capable of making demands on him during his hectic workweek. She represented everything that spelled relaxation in his book: Home and hearth, an out-of-the-way locale, feminine cozy comfort nestled in a charming, rustic environment. She was smart, responsible and in full charge of her own career path.

He could almost convince himself his attraction to her was "wholesome." Almost...because he still loved the allure of her most curvaceous assets. And, after a mere twenty seconds of remembering her in his arms as they danced, he knew their potential physical chemistry played no small part in her appeal.

He stared at the vase again, mesmerized by the swirl of colors whenever a stained-glass chip reflected the light. He squinted at it, and the magnificent rainbow was no longer distinct. The hues bled together like silken watercolors, as if, by a mere change in perspective, all the disparate elements of life could join together as one.

"Well, hello again, Bram."

Shannon. Her voice made him open his eyes fully and drink in the vision of her standing before him.

"Crisis averted?" he asked her.

She smiled. "For the time being." She pointed to the display cabinet. "See anything that intrigues you."

He looked right at her. "Yes." He stared into her blue eyes until she blushed. After another moment he added, "And the vase is nice, too."

"Um, well, that's one of my favorites also. My parents took a trip to New York about ten years ago, and they found it in an Old World antique shop there."

"It's pretty," he said, reaching for her hand and entwining her fingers with his. "But I think it belongs elsewhere. In a private home. Atop a fireplace, maybe. It seems too personal for a hallway, even in an inn this cozy."

She let him continue to hold her hand and even took a step closer to him, but her gaze was focused on the vase. Or maybe on something—a memory—further away. "I guess I'd never thought of that way, particularly since I grew up living here at Holiday Quinn. The entire inn was our house, but, I'll admit, it was never especially private."

Bram brought her soft hand toward his face, looked at her for a long moment and then pressed his lips against that smooth skin.

"So, what does a man have to do to get some privacy in this place?"

A flash of passion ignited within her at these words. He could sense it, feel it burning just beneath the surface. What did he want to have happen here?

A night with her? Yes.

A part of tomorrow? Maybe, maybe not. Goodbyes were difficult...and indefinite. But he'd take his chances on their flame blazing steadily until the morning.

"Bram." His name rolled off her lips in a whisper. He could feel her interest. Her questions. Her deliberation. But he sensed, despite whatever internal battles she waged, she was as curiously enchanted as he.

"Shannon!" Jake called.

And the spell was broken.

Jake jogged up to them. "Excuse me, Shannon, I *hate* to interrupt," he said with frozen, insincere syllables, "but we have another problem."

Shannon sighed and pulled her hand away. Bram's fingers felt the chill of her departure.

"I'm so sorry, Mr. Hartwick," she said with a formality that would have offended him if he hadn't noticed the flicker of disappointment in her eyes. "I'm afraid I have additional business to attend to tonight."

"Perhaps we'll be able to continue our conversation another time," he found himself saying, though he had no immediate plans to return to the inn.

"Perhaps," she replied. Then added, "I hope so."

They smiled at each other before she turned away and trailed her assistant down the hallway.

Damn.

Bad timing. Lost opportunities. Whatever you wanted to call it, it sucked.

Bram returned to his room for a fitful night followed by an early departure with his friends just after breakfast the next morning. He didn't see Shannon or her pain-in-the-ass assistant. But he had to put the weekend behind him.

Time to get back to work.

~CHAPTER TWO~

St. Patrick's Day

"**S**lainte!" the formidable Margaret Ashland said to Shannon, lifting her glass of red wine and looking more like a giddy schoolgirl than a fifty-two-year-old Midwestern hotel-chain mogul. Although there wasn't one drop of Irish blood in Margaret's family tree, Shannon's mentor celebrated the March holiday with enthusiasm. And at least half a bottle of Bordeaux's finest.

"*Slainte,*" Shannon replied, clinking beverages. "And thank you for inviting me over for such a delicious dinner. There's nothing that says 'home cooking' quite like your world famous Roasted Red Potato and Leek Soup."

Margaret laughed. "It's Ricardo's potato soup, and you know it." She waved her palm in the direction of The Ashland Hotel's impeccably clean kitchen, where the talented Chef Ricardo worked his nightly magic. "He's been delighting our guests with it all week."

Ricardo's ritzy, copper-pot-crammed workshop was an extension of the hotel's aromatic-candlelit-glowing dining room, its spacious and sensuous guestrooms and its exotic flowering-plant reception area. The Ashland Hotel, just a few miles down the road from Holiday Quinn, was an example of supreme luxury and flair. In fact, everything about Shannon's home away from the inn bespoke of high class and expensive tastes.

And why shouldn't it?

Margaret Ashland demanded nothing but the best.

"Well, it was as fabulous as always," Shannon said. "It rivals Grandma Quinn's, and that's saying something."

The older woman looked pleased. "Glad to hear it, missy, but you know I always have ulterior motives for plying my top employees with ultra-rich food." She paused and looked Shannon in the eye. "I've got a proposition for you. You ready?"

Shannon had a sneaking suspicion that the forthcoming proposition might involve longer hours along with a sizably increased paycheck, but she didn't mind. She'd worked for Margaret since college, whenever her parents could spare her from Holiday Quinn and, once they were gone, during the weeks when the inn was closed. As a longtime family friend, Margaret had affectionately taken on the role of Shannon's second mother and had made no secret that she was grooming Shannon for bigger and better things.

Shannon nodded. "Fire away."

Her boss laughed. "Oh, there's no firing involved, my dear. Just the opposite. I want you to be a manager."

She squinted at the older woman. Maybe Margaret had imbibed a few too many glasses of that pricey wine. "Um, I already *am* a manager. You promoted me three years ago, remember?"

Margaret laughed again. "Sorry, sweetie. I know that! What I meant was, I want you to be *the* manager. The head manager. Of any one of the country's twenty-three Ashland Hotels. You choose which."

Shannon felt a foreign sensation of excitement bubbling up inside her, along with another emotion—one she couldn't quite identify and didn't have time to analyze. Okay. So this *was* a surprise after all. And a part of her wanted to jump at it. But...but...

"But..." she said aloud, her thoughts racing through all the hows and whys and wherefores.

"No buts necessary. We can take care of anything that needs taking care of—including Holiday Quinn." Margaret looked at her kindly. "You don't have to stay in this little corner of the state simply because the inn is here, Shannon. It'll fetch a sizable price if you sell." She grinned. "And I'm tempted to make the first offer myself. I love that place."

All true words, Shannon had to admit. Margaret had visited the inn countless times when her parents were alive and had always admired it with a professional eye. And the land Holiday Quinn sat on was prime resort-quality real estate. She knew she could make a bundle in profits. But, even though she didn't see herself retaining ownership of the place forever, she couldn't bear to watch some overzealous housing developer tear it down in favor of a bunch of modern-looking bungalows for wealthy yuppies.

Not that wealthy yuppies didn't frequent the inn now. Take Exhibit A: The too-hot-for-his-own-good Bram Hartwick. She sighed remembering the powerful man who still graced her nighttime fantasies and who she'd put on her inn's mailing list in hopes that he'd return. Not that he'd taken the hint yet.

But regular folks like Darlene and Keith Baker could stay at Holiday Quinn, too, as they had just last weekend when Shannon hosted the St. Patrick's Day celebrations at the inn—a few days in advance of the official holiday. There had also been families there and older couples who'd been guests for years. She couldn't disappoint everyone by selling. Even if...even if...

She shut down that burgeoning thought before it could fully form in her mind. There were too many memories still housed at Holiday Quinn—of her parents and grandparents, and of years of celebrating special occasions like this particularly Irish holiday with them. Even when it fell on a Wednesday, as it had this year.

No.

She couldn't just give it up yet. No matter what Margaret said. No matter how much Shannon's spirit soared at the idea of having a grand adventure far away from home.

"Think about it, honey," the wonderful woman sitting

beside her said gently. "Keep the idea open." Margaret shot her a speculative glance. "I know it's hard to give up the past, but you've got a promising future ahead of you. Don't sell yourself short, okay?"

"Okay," Shannon whispered. "And thank you. I'll mull this over for awhile." And she'd try, if only out of respect for Margaret's wishes.

"You do that." Margaret refilled both of their wineglasses and pointed to the dessert menu. "How about some Shamrock Cake? It boasts five layers in different shades of green, and it's topped with a candy four-leaf clover." She leaned closer. "Ricardo has secretly dubbed it 'The Shannon' in your honor."

Shannon laughed, loving that she had a family friend— heck, practically a family *member*—looking out for her when the twinges of loneliness crept into her soul and made it ache with longing. "How could I possibly resist?" she said.

Margaret Ashland's philosophic words flowed out in a gush of whimsical wisdom, enhanced, no doubt, by the warm glow of candlelight and strong vino. "It's my belief, my little Irish rose, that some temptations should never be resisted. This is merely *one* of them."

Across the Wisconsin-Minnesota state line, Bram checked the voicemail on his cell phone for the sixty-seventh-quadrillionth time that day and stared at his frosted mug of unnaturally green beer, which O'Flannery's Pub served only on this annual occasion.

He deleted a few stupid messages, amused himself by shredding an unwanted business card and regarded his two big brothers with detached curiosity.

His brother Alex, the middle child, was muttering to himself while composing what must have been a twenty-page manifesto on athletic shoes into his travel laptop. Alex, founder and CEO of his own company, HighTop Treads, had been at this task for a half hour already. He paused occasionally, but only to stroke the black plastic above the computer screen. Bram was pretty sure Alex slept with that thing.

Meanwhile, their eldest brother Grant had no fewer than two BlackBerrys on the table in front of them and another that he had clutched to his ear, in addition to a paper-filled briefcase, which he'd opened. Bram watched Grant page through a stack of nasty-looking invoices from *his* multimillion-dollar company—Eastern Treasures, Inc., of which he was president, of course—taking an occasional photo of a document and e-mailing it instantly to the unfortunate employee he had on the line in St. Petersburg. His brother took turns swearing (in Russian) at the man, at the papers and at the BlackBerrys, between slurps of his disgusting green beer.

And this was what they called A Night of Family Bonding.

Bram rolled his eyes. He and his brothers were exactly one-sixteenth Irish, but they used to milk that drop for all it was worth on St. Patrick's Days of "olde." They used to talk a "wee bit," too. To each other, in fact, not just to their electronic equipment. When the hell had that changed?

He sighed and glanced a few more times between his two closest relatives. Deciding Grant was a lost cause, he focused his attention on Alex.

"Gonna be done with that script anytime soon, Shakespeare?" he said, aiming for eye contact and a jovial tone of voice.

Alex grunted something at him.

Bram took this as encouragement enough and tried again. "Hey, how's it going with Carrie Ann? You two gonna do the Bahamas again this spring?"

Alex lifted his fingers off the keyboard and stared at him. "What?"

Bram laughed. "Your girlfriend? Vacation? Anything romantic happening there? Hey, I know a great little getaway in Door County, Wisconsin, if you two are interested."

He thought of his visit to Holiday Quinn the previous month and the beautiful woman he'd met that weekend. Shannon. Mmm. He still had regrets about not following her down the hall that night or trying to win a private invitation up to her room.

He'd gotten a postcard from the inn a couple of weeks ago, though, listing the upcoming "holiday" dates. He'd already missed this past weekend's St. Patrick's Day celebration, but maybe Easter...

His brother grimaced and downed about a third of his green beer. "Carrie Ann moved out after Christmas, Bro. Thought I told you."

Bram's eyes widened. Alex damn well *hadn't* told him. He had a million questions: *What had gone wrong? Whose decision had it been to break things off after two years? And what kind of a family was this—keeping secrets for months on end?*

He opened his mouth to ask his cagey brother a few things, but Alex had already resumed his typing.

Okay. End of conversation.

He stared again at Grant, who was currently spouting off to the man on the phone about shipping and how the poor guy would need to—translated loosely from the Russian—"settle things with the company's Moscow distributor if it took him all freakin' day and night."

Grant never thought twice about making those kinds of demands on his employees. He'd do all that work himself, and more, if necessary. He *had* done it. For years, in fact, which was why his first, second and third wives all divorced him, claiming Grant's workaholism had progressed to an incurable illness.

Angie had dared to say the same about him, Bram remembered, which was a bunch of bull.

His cell phone vibrated in his palm.

He clenched his jaw and tried to ignore it. Well, maybe there was a sliver of truth to her words. He worked hard, sure, but he was nothing like his brothers.

Nothing.

He could sit here in this bar and relax, see? Being the CEO of a successful business didn't mean he didn't know how to turn off the daily onslaught of company chaos when he wanted to. It didn't mean he didn't have what it took to make a long-term relationship work. It just meant he and Angie weren't well suited to being together, that was all.

Right?

The phone continued its relentless vibrating.

Damn. Maybe it really *was* something important this time.

He glared first at his brothers, who persisted in their benign neglect, and then at the stupid phone. Finally, he sighed and punched the green button.

"Hartwick," he said into the receiver.

An hour and three phone calls later, Bram stalked out of O'Flannery's with the start of a migraine and a vow to never waste another night this way again.

He wasn't going to be like his brothers, no matter what lifestyle patterns had been set. No matter what performance expectations had been demanded by their competitive parents, whom they almost never saw because their mom and dad were even busier than they were. Bram was his own man, dammit, and he'd make his own choices.

Yeah, right.

His cell phone vibrated against his hip. He muttered a curse and checked the number. Work again. His secretary Miranda this time.

He clicked the button to answer, half listening as she recited the latest snafu at their Italian production center. The lightest snow had begun falling, and couples clad in green skipped past him on the sidewalk. Talking. Laughing. Connecting. In the soft glow of the streetlights, they made a picturesque scene. Like something from a romantic-comedy film set. Both worlds were equally foreign to him.

He sighed. "I'll handle it, Miranda. Thanks for letting me know."

"All right, Mr. Hartwick. There's also a memo that was just faxed in from—"

"I'll read it tomorrow," he told her. "It's almost eight o'clock. Go home."

"Why, thank you, Mr. Hartwick," she said, her voice indicating both surprise and delight. "Are you sure you don't want to hear about—"

"I'm sure." He needed to start doing more delegating in the office. But he thought of something he did want to hear about. "One last thing. Any major trips already set during Easter?"

He could hear the flipping of calendars and the click of computer keys as she checked all possible sources of meetings, appointments, etc. He didn't see anything listed on his iPhone for Easter weekend, but his schedule changed daily.

"I see a trip to London blocked in for the week prior, sir, but Easter weekend looks open at present. Do you want me to book something for you?"

"No, no. Thanks, Miranda. I'll take care of it. Just keep it clear for me."

If a journey of a thousand miles began with a single step, this one was his. He'd visit Holiday Quinn in April, see Little Miss Shannon again and make damn sure something happen between them this time.

And why the hell not? It was just one weekend. And, after all his hopping from one continent to the next, he figured the Easter Bunny had to be on his side.

Shannon slipped out of The Ashland Hotel and meandered down the quiet street. A few fat snowflakes fell and she caught them in her mittens.

So calm tonight. So peaceful. And so lonely.

St. Patrick's Day used to be such a noisy family holiday, what with all the relatives, neighbors and friends showing up to share in it. She'd been too young then to realize how much she'd miss that later in life. How alone she'd be someday.

For maybe the three-millionth time she wished she'd had a sibling. Of any variety. A big brother. A kid sister. Even a step-sibling. Anyone she could count on to stay in her life. This only-child thing stank.

Her car sat conveniently parked across the street, but she couldn't bring herself to return to the depressing, post-holiday silence of the inn just yet, not after such a spirited evening with

Margaret. She needed to connect. With somebody. Then she remembered.

She dashed a block and a half down the snowy sidewalk and tapped on the window of Arpeggios, the secondhand music store Jake managed in between the big holiday weekends.

"Hey, Jake!"

The sign on the door read "Closed," but she could see him through the glass pane, laughing with another guy.

He spotted her and motioned her in. "It's not locked," he called out.

"How are you?" Shannon said, brushing off a few remaining snowflakes and letting the friendly warmth of shop cover her like a winter's coat. Bing was crooning "Danny Boy" from the in-store speakers, and Jake pointed to the younger man who stood across from him.

"My cousin," he said. "Evan, meet Shannon. Shannon, Evan."

As they said their hellos, Jake's college-aged cousin eyed her curiously. "Shannon Quinn?" he asked. "THE Shannon?"

"Umm..." She glanced at Jake, who was smirking from behind a Sinaid O'Connor CD. What the heck was she supposed to say to that? "I imagine so. Why?"

Evan, whose fair complexion seemed capable of showing every change of emotion, turned pinkish. "I've heard about you," he informed her. "Jake calls you The Babe behind your back."

"Shut up, Evan!" Jake said, swatting him with the CD. "That's not true." Then he speared her with one of his most flirtatious grins. "I call her that to her face sometimes, too. Right, Shannon?"

She laughed. "That's right, but your aptitude for flattery is legendary at the inn. No one believes anything you say."

He waggled his brows. "Well, they ought to, babe."

She rolled her eyes. The guy never knew when to stop. "Oh, cut it out. So, what are you two up to tonight?"

Jake shrugged. "Just closing up here then heading down to Green Bay for a little Irish revelry. Wanna join us?"

Shannon looked between the two men and shook her head. "Tempting, but no thanks. I've got to work at The Ashland in the morning. But," she turned to Evan, "have boatloads of fun. And try to keep that wild older cousin of yours in line."

Evan's complexion turned a darker pink this time. "Oh, I don't think that's on the agenda, Shannon. But it was nice to finally meet you."

She smiled at him. "Likewise."

Jake chuckled and walked her to the door. "Drive home safe, babe." Then, lowering his voice so his cousin wouldn't overhear, he whispered, "Just say the word, Shannon, and I'll go to Holiday Quinn with you instead."

For a split second he looked every one of his twenty-six years and fully serious. And for a split second she actually considered his offer. But Jake was a friend and an occasional employee. And, though he was attractive, he wasn't the man who'd been gracing her dreams at night.

So, instead, she shook her index finger at him and said in her most scolding tone, "Try not to break too many hearts tonight, Jake Marcolis. I need you to help me prepare for Easter at the inn in a few weeks, and I don't want to have to identify your body after some angry Irish babe in Green Bay gets through with you."

This made him laugh, as she'd hoped, and she escaped the shop without any further suggestiveness on his part. Jake was easy to brush off that way, which only proved there was little real feeling behind his proclamations of attraction.

Too bad, really. That he couldn't act more sincerely toward her. That she couldn't feel more affectionately toward him. Why wasn't romance more convenient?

Shannon hopped into her car and drove the few miles back to the stretch of land nearby that she'd always called home.

But, even once she'd turned up the heat in her private room at the inn and made herself a hot cup of tea to combat the cold, she couldn't quite shake the chill of loneliness, and she found herself on the verge of regretting her inability to take Jake up on his offer of nighttime companionship.

Yes, she wanted something more for her life, but she was starting to suspect she wouldn't find it here. Not in Holiday Quinn. Not in Door County. Maybe not even in Wisconsin. She'd been living her life in this place, to a large degree, in honor of a family that had either died or moved away. If the situation were right, she'd be open to taking some kind of a risk now. Finally.

Perhaps Margaret's offer of letting her manage another hotel in another state would be the answer after all.

Only, there were impulses inside of her—communiqués from deep within her subconscious—that were trying to bubble up. She could feel them dancing just below the surface. Daring her to acknowledge them. She didn't quite have the energy to excavate just yet, but she knew the day would come when they'd burst out of her. It was a toss up as to whether this prospect made her more excited or more anxious.

She flicked on her computer to scan messages of a different sort, and one in particular caught her eye.

Sender: Bram Hartwick.

He'd formally requested a room reservation for Easter weekend! King-sized bed. No smoking. Fully stocked fridge, please. Yada, yada, yada.

Her gaze followed his typed words down the screen, looking for the one extra detail she needed to know—not only for professional accommodation purposes, but for personal peace of mind.

Number of guests staying in the room: One.

She'd promised herself she'd take just one step. One small step toward adventure. And she'd vowed if ever Bram returned...

Shannon grinned and, for the first time in an hour, felt the tingling of heat all the way to her toenails. Seemed that Holiday Quinn, Door County and the fine state of Wisconsin had joined together to provide all of their risks in one single, dark-haired, six-foot-two package.

And, whether it turned out to be "oh, hell" or "hallelujah" for the holiday weekend ahead, that risky package was headed her way.

~CHAPTER THREE~

Easter

He was late, dammit.

Bram checked his watch. 10:35, Saturday morning. Twelve freaking hours late.

He slammed the door of his silver Lexus, strode into Holiday Quinn and marched up to the reception desk. But was Shannon there? No. Instead he came nose-to-nose with that pain-in-the-ass assistant, a clipboard in his hand, a sour expression on his face. Jake the Prick narrowed his eyes when he saw Bram coming. Bram narrowed his eyes right back.

"Bram Hartwick," he informed the guy, taking particular pleasure in looking down at him. "I reserved a room for the weekend."

Jake slowly perused the sheets on his clipboard. "Ah, yes, Mr. Hartwick." He paused. "However, you were originally scheduled to arrive last night. I'm afraid we've given your room to another guest."

Bram raised his eyebrows at the guy and leaned a couple of inches closer. "Then I'll take a different room."

Jake pursed his lips and let out an arrogant sigh. "This is quite a *popular* weekend, Mr. Hartwick. Our waiting list is several pages long. Guests usually make their reservations

461

months in advance and, if there's a delay in their arrival, they usually have the *courtesy* to let us know when we might expect them." Jake tossed the clipboard on the counter and pushed it away with a bored flick of his fingers. "You can try The Ashland Hotel in town, but I don't believe *we* have any other rooms available for this holiday. Perhaps next time."

Jake turned away like a member of European royalty who'd just dismissed the peons. Bram had dealt with quite enough of this bullshit.

"Listen, Jake," he began, using the tone of voice he reserved only for lousy accountants and lazy office managers, "I haven't slept since yesterday morning, and I've been on the road since one a.m. I would have flown into Green Bay last night if it had been possible to charter a plane at midnight and rent a car from there, but it wasn't. I tried." He shot him a very steely glare. "As I'm sure you know, I sent my credit card information along with my room reservation last month, so I'd be happy to pay for the night I missed. But right now I want a room. And I want a schedule of this weekend's Easter events." *And, if I don't get it, I want your fucking head on a platter.*

Jake turned back and gave an apathetic shrug. "I'm sorry to disappoint you, Mr. Hartwick, but—"

He'd pull him apart. Piece by snotty piece. "Now," Bram interrupted, lowering his voice to a dangerous whisper. "Right. Now. Jake."

A shadow of fear darkened the assistant's green eyes, but he didn't back away. The brave idiot. He didn't know who he was dealing with, did he?

"We're booked, Mr. Hartwick. There are no single or double rooms available. Period."

"Really? Why is it that I don't believe you?" Bram crossed his arms and glared at the lying bastard sitting smugly behind the counter.

"What you believe or don't believe isn't any of my concern," Jake replied, fiddling with the puffy white tail of a stuffed-animal rabbit, which decorated the corner of the reception desk. "I suggest you leave, Mr. Hartwick."

And I suggest you go to hell. Bram took a deep breath and opened his mouth to say something that would probably border on extremely insulting...when he heard a voice behind him.

"I'm so glad you could make it, Bram."

He swiveled in place and saw Shannon Quinn's beaming smile. Man, she was lovely. He'd forgotten just how much.

"Thanks, Shannon. I'm glad I could make it, too. It's nice to see you again." He shot a look at her assistant who, for the first time since Bram's arrival, didn't look disdainful, just defeated. He almost felt sorry for the jerk. Almost.

"Shannon," Jake began, resuming his supercilious tone, "I gave this gentleman's room to Mr. Prescott this morning. We're filled and cannot accommodate him now."

Shannon laughed. "Of course we can. The Astaire Suite is unoccupied. Mr. Hartwick may have that instead."

Bram saw Jake's jaw drop.

"The Astaire Suite?" the assistant said. "But it's *huge*. It's for honeymooners. Anniversary couples. Are you sure you want to—"

"Of course," she said. She turned to Bram. "Unless you have a strange fear of open spaces or something, or if you believe a room of that size will make you nervous."

"I suffer from no such phobias," Bram said. Then, just to make his position on the matter perfectly clear, he added, "I'm greatly in favor of elbowroom at night."

Her grin broadened. "Then it's settled." Shannon reached for Jake's discarded clipboard and a pastel-colored pencil with a yellow baby chick where the eraser should be. She scribbled a few notes on the top sheet then pointed the baby chick's head at her assistant. "Please charge Mr. Hartwick only the rate for the original room he reserved, Jake."

"Why, thank you," Bram said, impressed by her moxie and her seemingly effortless ability to put Jake the Prick in his place. The discount, though nice, was unnecessary. "I appreciate the V.I.P. treatment."

She responded by winking at him. *Winking*, the little vixen. She took a few steps away from the desk, her auburn hair swinging in tempting waves behind her. Bram was aware of Jake watching her every move, just as he did. Neither of them seemed capable of pulling their gaze away.

Shannon turned for a final glance over her shoulder. "You've missed a few activities already, Bram," she informed him. "But the Bakers are leading an Easter Egg Hunt at noon. Feel free to join in, if you'd like."

And he knew right then and there that he'd search every inch of Holiday Quinn, from noon until midnight, for silly chocolate-marshmallow eggs if Shannon would be standing nearby.

"I'll be there," he told her. Exhausted or not.

After she walked out the door, he and Jake shared one meaningful glance that charged the air with testosterone and certainty. They both wanted to have this woman. And they both wanted to have her now.

The race was on, and it didn't have a damn thing to do with Easter eggs.

Shannon's knees shook, but she hoped she'd managed to disguise it well enough.

He was here. He'd made it after all.

Yes!

She'd forgotten the controlled intensity that was Bram Hartwick. When she'd walked in on him and Jake, she could almost feel the room imploding. How did one man manage to upset the ions in the atmosphere simply by standing there? She didn't know, but she couldn't deny its truth. His intense manner was as distinctive as his signature.

She inhaled the mid-April air and drank in the Saturday sunshine. As she scanned the expansive front yard of her inn, she saw the sturdy oaks her grandfather once planted, now with colorful, wind-ruffled ribbons encircling them. The pastel bows, placed by the Bakers for the weekend festivities, added a sense of celebration to the just-awakening landscape. Even in these cold northern reaches, spring had finally come.

She clomped along the newly emerging shoots of grass on the walkway to the backyard and spotted two tall figures bounding toward her.

Darlene Baker arrived first, breathless. "We're all set!"

Her husband Keith jogged up next to them. "We've got it done, Shannon dear, not a thing for you to worry about."

"We're so excited!" Darlene hugged herself through her thick pink windbreaker. "Thanks for letting us lead this activity. We've wanted—"

"To do something like this for years," Keith concluded for her. "And we had such a blast—"

"Coloring the eggs!" his enthusiastic wife said. "Five hundred and seventy-eight of them and—"

"Then hiding them along with all of those chocolate ones," Keith added. "Not to mention the more grown-up treats. Haven't had this much fun since the kids were toddlers."

Darlene grabbed Shannon's hands in her own. "You made our weekend!"

Shannon laughed. "I wish all of my guests would insist on helping out, cheerfully doing hours of work and managing to create a finished product that looked so professional." She paused to grin at them. "Come to think of it, I wish all of my *staff* would do the same. I'm comping your room for this holiday just because you're so darned inspirational!"

"It's our pleasure, Shannon," Keith said, the sincerity of his words evident in his voice and his warm gray eyes.

Darlene released Shannon's fingers and turned to her husband. "Oh, Keith! The baskets."

Keith's glance darted around the backyard. "We've still got to set up the table with the baskets," he explained to Shannon, already striding toward the spot he and his wife had selected earlier. "See ya in an hour, hon!"

So, Shannon left them to their tasks and completed several small chores of her own. The next time she glanced down at her watch, it was five minutes to noon.

When she reached the Bakers, the yard was already

swarming with animated guests of all ages, every one of them as energized as that famous TV bunny, ready to fill their baskets with colored eggs and sweet treats.

At the stroke of twelve, Darlene rang a bell to quiet the crowd. Her husband cleared his throat.

"Welcome to Holiday Quinn's Annual Easter Egg Hunt!" Keith said.

The crowd cheered. Shannon glanced at their faces, hoping to see Bram, but he wasn't outside. A shot of disappointment surged through her. She hadn't wanted to admit how much she'd been looking forward to seeing him having a little child-like fun, especially since there wasn't a thing that seemed remotely child-like about him. She'd hoped to catch a glimpse of a different side of this commanding, authoritative man.

And, well, she also just liked looking at his body.

Keith continued. "Miss Quinn has graciously allowed us to run the event a little differently this year, so we've decided to add a new twist to it."

Shannon grinned. When the Bakers had suggested this change to her, she thought it might be a funny one. She was curious to see if the predominantly adult crowd thought the same.

"Any child under ten gets a basket and free rein to run and collect whatever he or she can," Keith said. Shannon noted the giddy handful of guests that fit into this age bracket. "Everyone over ten must hunt with a partner. And only one member of the team is allowed to touch the eggs, though the other can lead and direct. One more thing—" Keith paused for dramatic effect. "The partner that picks up the eggs and puts them in the basket has to be blindfolded."

A gasp rose from the crowd followed by a bubbling of laughter, which grew louder once Darlene demonstrated the blindfolding process by tying a long scrap of black fabric around her husband's eyes.

"So, you adults out there, choose wisely," Keith informed them, lifting the fabric on one side so he looked like a benevolent pirate. "You'll want to be with partners you trust."

Darlene passed out the baskets to the little ones and then, with her husband's help, made sure all of the adults in attendance had been paired up, with one member of the team securely blindfolded.

Stopwatch in hand, Keith said, "You and your partner get to keep the booty and, adults, some plastic eggs are hidden in higher locations, filled with treats just for you, so enjoy whatever you find!"

Darlene pointed to the stopwatch. "Five, four, three, two, one...GO!"

And off they went. The little ones scurried around, eager and unfettered. The wisest of the adults held hands, the sighted ones leading the way. The Bakers, too, held hands and snuck in a few kisses when they thought she wasn't looking. Shannon sighed. It must be amazing to still be in love like that after so many years together.

"Have I missed it?" a deep, instantly recognizable voice whispered from behind her.

"Hi, Bram," she said, trying to keep her excitement at his appearance in check. "I'm afraid the hunt has already begun, yes. Did something detain you?"

He tapped the cell phone in his hand and shot it a disgusted glance. "Phone call."

Of course. She was talking to Mr. Workaholic, after all. "Well, you can watch the festivities with me, if you want. Here, from a safe distance."

He smiled. "I'd like that."

"Oh, no you don't," Darlene declared.

Shannon, Bram and Keith all stared at her.

Darlene wagged her finger at Bram. "No guest can stand on the sidelines like a wallflower at *our* event. Get a blindfold on and get yourself out there!"

"Like a *wallflower?*" Bram muttered, clearly mystified by having such a term applied to him.

Shannon couldn't help herself. She had to laugh at this. "It's okay, Darlene," she began. "Perhaps if another guest joins in late, Bram can—"

"Who needs other guests?" Darlene said, a devious grin pulling up the corners of her lips. *"You're* not running this event, Miss Shannon Quinn. *We* are." She thrust a blindfold at Shannon and an Easter basket at Bram. "Hurry! Clock's ticking. You don't want everyone else to get all the good stuff, now do you?"

"W-Well, I hadn't planned on—" Shannon said.

Keith, getting into the act, grabbed the fabric out of Shannon's hand and tied it tight around a surprised Bram until his eyes were completely covered. "Go!" the older man commanded.

They didn't dare refuse.

As she tugged on Bram's hand, his large palm engulfing hers, she felt his body heat seep into her skin. Her pores tingled everywhere.

"Uh, what just happened back there?" Bram said, gamely allowing her to lead him toward one of the oak trees at the edge of the property. "One minute we're talking like civilized adults..."

"...and the next, we're being pushed off on this merry chase," she concluded for him.

His grip on her hand tightened. "Well, I'm not complaining. But I hope you're leading me toward something good."

"Guess you'll just have to trust me, won't you?"

He chuckled but didn't reply. More intensity emanated from him, radiating unspoken questions in her direction along with a rising warmth.

What the heck she was doing?

Playing flirtation games with *this* man was like blithely cutting wires on a ticking bomb. And though she wasn't inexperienced in the romantic arts, she was hardly an explosions expert.

She briefly explained the rules of the game and directed him to an area near their feet where a few colored eggs were stashed. "Okay, Bram. There are three eggs along the base of this tree. Two are real. One is milk chocolate filled with caramel. They're all about a six or seven inches from the tips of your shoes." His very nice leather shoes.

He squatted next to her, still holding her hand with one of his. With the other hand, he put the Easter basket on the ground near his foot and blindly reached a few inches in front of him, tapping the grass with the pads of his fingers until he finally touched one of the colored eggs.

"Hey, I got one." He lifted it and placed it into the basket, somehow managing to make every motion provocative.

"Very nice, Mr. Hartwick. You're a quick learner."

He rubbed her palm with his thumb, a wicked grin emerging from the mouth below the blindfold. "You have no idea, Ms. Quinn." He nabbed the other eggs in a flash and stood up. "Where to next?"

Even without eye contact he was still a formidable presence. Shannon felt her pulse speed up and she took a few cleansing breaths. "Um, well, I spotted a couple of plastic eggs between two branches just above us. I can hold the basket for you, but you'll have to be the one to reach for them."

"Sure. Which direction?"

She studied the tree limbs and the juncture between them where a pink and a purple plastic egg sat. If she asked him to swivel around and he turned too far, he could easily hit his handsome head on one of the branches. Didn't want that to happen.

"Okay," she said. "Here's our strategy. The angle is a little tricky. I'm going to have to move your body so you're facing the eggs." She stood behind him, wrapped her arms around his strong torso and slowly pivoted him about 45 degrees to the left. He didn't resist being handled, but he was solid man. Hardly what she'd call "pliable."

"How am I doing?" he said in a low voice. "Am I in the right position?"

She cleared her throat and tried to get her mind out of the gutter. "Yes. You're perfectly positioned."

She caught that wicked grin of his again. "That's what I like to hear."

Inwardly, she groaned. He wasn't making this easy on her.

MARILYN BRANT

Another ten minutes of his innuendos and she was going to rip those designer clothes off his back and start reenacting one of her favorite nighttime fantasies, right here in front of everybody.

"Carefully lift your right arm," she instructed him, "until it's parallel with your shoulder." He did this and waited for her to continue. "Now bend your right elbow and move your hand toward your chin until I say to stop."

"Okay." He followed this direction, too.

"Stop," she said when his hand had cleared the branch. "Now reach up like a crane. A few inches at a time." She watched as he did this. "Higher," she said. "Still higher." His fingers hovered just above the plastic treasure.

"Am I getting closer?" he asked, with no attempt to disguise his amusement by this continued game of intimate insinuation.

"Very close," she said, determined to keep them on task. At least in public. "All you have to do now is pick them up. They're right next to each other, about two inches below your fingertips and a little to the left."

He reached for them and, with his large palm, scooped them both up at the same time. "Got 'em!" But as he leaned over to drop them in the basket Shannon held for him, the purple egg slipped out of his grasp, landed in the grass below and broke open revealing—to Shannon at least—its contents.

Ooops.

"Damn, I dropped one," he said. "Here, direct me. I'll pick it up."

"No, no, don't worry about it." She tugged at his hand. "Why don't we go to the next tree?"

He stopped like dead weight in place and pulled her toward him. "What's in the egg, Shannon?"

"Just, um, just a few condoms."

He let out a short laugh. "How many? Two? Three?"

Shannon blushed, glad he couldn't see her face. She glanced at the broken egg and its spilled booty. "More like seven."

"Seven?" He laughed again, longer this time. "Wow. Optimistic Easter Bunny. Are they colored?"

"Yes."

"Flavored?"

"Um, yes."

"Well, in that case, we're not leaving them here." Bram knelt down and began patting the ground. "A little help, Shannon. Am I getting warmer?"

His fingers were nowhere near the egg, but every part of her turned warm just from standing next to him. "Yes," she whispered, unable to keep the desire from her voice. She knew it the moment he lifted the blindfold from his eyes. He dragged her toward him and toward the side of the tree furthest from the Holiday Quinn crowd.

"So much for playing by the rules," Bram murmured, tossing the scrap of black fabric on the ground and bringing her body flush with his. He leaned against the tree's solid trunk and let his fingers dance along her vertebrae. "Tell me how you want me to move next, Shannon."

Taking chances was a good thing, a tiny voice inside of her whispered. She needed to learn to take more risks, within reason, she reminded her internal critic. This was the only explanation she could give herself for what she said next. "I think you'd better kiss me, Bram. Now. And you can do whatever you want with those fingers of yours."

She didn't need to say more than this. He grunted and simply took over. His mouth was on hers the moment her words had left it. His hands roamed the curves and crevices of her dress slacks, pausing to give special attention to the gap at the back of her waistband. He slid a few fingers in there and massaged her lower spine while pressing the front of her body up against all his hard ridges and planes.

No sensation could rival this. Bram orchestrated his maneuvers with a finesse most men could only dream of mastering. When his lips explored hers and his tongue probed deeper, she felt the rare sense of flight had been gifted to her. She would've sworn in a heartbeat that her shoes had left the ground.

Someone coughed nearby. "Shannon...uh, there you are."

She and Bram broke apart, and she felt her feet crash back to earth.

Jake stood a yard or two away, a shuttered expression on his face and his voice ice cold. "The new caterer has been looking for you, and Margaret stopped by your office about half an hour ago. She left you a message."

She nodded. "I—er—thank you, Jake. I'll check it in a few minutes." She took another step back from Bram and heard his audible sigh. That was when she remembered the chill between the two men earlier in the day. Well, they might not get along, but she still needed to deal with them both. "Perhaps we can run through a few things when I get back to my office," she told her assistant. "I'd like to do something special for the Bakers, since they've helped so much this weekend."

"Okay," Jake said, making no motion to leave.

"So, I'll see you. In my office. Soon," she said, enunciating every syllable, all but forcing him to take the hint, which he finally did.

Once Jake stalked away, Bram returned his mouth to hers, more possessively this time. She almost let herself get pulled under his spell again, but she knew she needed to act like the owner of the inn now, not like a sex-starved teenager on her first date in months.

She put her hand to his chest and leaned away. "Business before pleasure, Mr. Hartwick. I must get back."

His hazel eyes pierced her with fire, golden and untamed. "Understood," he whispered. "But you know where I'm staying. Any chance you could slip away to the Astaire Suite later?"

"I have a major meal preparation to oversee, Bram, and then there's an early evening performance I'm responsible for hosting. It doesn't finish until nine."

He grinned at her. "Yeah, I heard about it on my way outside. 'Green Eggs and Hamlet.' Very clever."

"Entertainment for all audiences," she said.

"That's not the kind of entertainment I crave," he retorted.

He picked up the Easter basket and filled it with the purple egg and its spilled contents. Then, very deliberately, he dropped the black blindfold into the basket, too, and regarded her with a heated glance. "You've been in my fantasies, Shannon. I'd like to turn a few of them into reality tonight. If you're interested."

Oh, boy, was she ever interested.

But she wasn't crazy. This man might spark a blue flame just by entering a room, but they didn't run in the same circles or even live in the same state. There was no future in something like this, no matter how many fantasies—hers *or* his—they enacted in the Astaire Suite. She'd just have to enjoy it as the one-night-stand it would likely be.

Could she live with that?

A part of her wasn't sure, but that wasn't the part of her that was speaking. "I'll see you around nine-thirty," she said before walking away. "And Bram? Hang onto that basket."

No doubt about it, Bram was head over heels in lust. He didn't delude himself with illusions that his feelings were anything more than the obvious: He wanted Shannon in his bed. Tonight. And tomorrow morning. Despite not being an especially religious man, he intended to have a positively divine Easter Sunday.

He took a power nap then fielded a half-dozen or more calls. Some production problems in Zurich had been the cause of his late arrival at the inn, but things seemed to be under control now.

He shot off a few business e-mails, grabbed a plate full of delicious roasted lamb and potatoes at the buffet dinner and caught a glimpse of Shannon inspecting the stage before the acting troupe went on for their performance.

Bram couldn't stomach sitting through a whole G-rated show, not with his mind decidedly elsewhere, but he stared at Shannon until he had the satisfaction of seeing her cheeks blush. Then he went up to his suite to wait for her.

And quite a suite it was. The Astaire featured a four-poster, king-sized bed with silk sheets and a satin-and-down comforter. It was as spacious as three regular guestrooms combined and it boasted an entertainment center, wireless Internet access, a balcony, a Jacuzzi and a fully stocked kitchenette.

Yes, he'd stayed in higher-class, more luxurious accommodations when he'd traveled to Rome or Vienna, but for a small Wisconsin harbor town, this was tops.

He decided he'd book this room every time he visited the inn. What the hell, he could afford it.

At precisely 9:29 p.m. he heard a light knock on his door.

Shannon.

He swung it open and his auburn-haired angel breezed in. "Hi," she said, looking gorgeous but, from the slight fidgeting of her fingers, a little apprehensive.

He closed the door. Locked it.

"Hi," he said back. "I've been waiting for you."

"I know." She bit her lip. "Listen, Bram, I need to tell you something."

Oh, God. She's married or engaged or…who the hell knows what? He held his breath and nodded.

"It's no secret that I'm attracted to you. Very attracted. And I want to be here with you. Tonight."

Well, this wasn't bad news. He released a little of the air in his lungs and said, "But?"

"But I don't know how far we should take things. We barely know each other, and I'm a little new to taking chances on the unknown, so…"

He reached for her hands and exhaled the breath that remained. "Don't worry. Nothing's going to happen in here that you don't agree to, Shannon. I don't want the ghost of Fred Astaire haunting me for the rest of my life. Who knows what noisy havoc he could wreak?" Bram smiled at her and waited for her to smile back. When she did, he brought his lips down on hers.

She wasn't wearing anything silky. Not a sleek evening gown or lingerie. Just your basic business-casual attire. Stuff he'd seen countless times on other women.

Yet, to his touch, it might have been the sheerest, laciest garment on the market because he could feel her luscious curves and softness just beneath the fabric. As he allowed their bodies to melt together, he knew with a flash of pure insight that there was nothing casual about this encounter.

And that made him pull back.

He looked down at her until her blue eyes fluttered open and he could feel the steady blaze of passion behind them. He would have to tread very carefully here. Shannon was not Angie. Shannon was the kind of woman who loved hearth and home, and his lifestyle didn't lend itself well to that. At least, not until now. Maybe...maybe that could change.

"Let's try this sitting down," he suggested, leading her toward the bed. She complied then wrapped her arms around him and pressed her lips against his. He kissed her back—long, hard and thoroughly—bringing her head to rest on the mattress and trapping her legs beneath one of his.

Control.

He had to remember that. Especially now when every cell in his body wanted to release her from those unfussy clothes and ravish her until morning. He knew from her responsiveness that it would take little effort to get what he wanted. He could be inside of her in ten minutes, maybe five.

But then what? Would she have second thoughts later? Would she avoid him when he came back to the inn? And he had every intention of coming back. Soon.

So, he needed to play strategy. Spotting the Easter basket on the bedside table, he reached for his ace—the blindfold.

"It's your turn to wear this," he told her.

She shivered but whispered, "Okay."

He wrapped the black fabric around her eyes, careful not to pull it too tight. Then he kissed her again until she sighed, contented.

"You said you had fantasies about me," she murmured between kisses. "Tell me one."

Bram grinned to himself. She was playing right into his

hand.

"Yes. It starts with this zipper." He dragged down the zipper of her slacks and unsnapped the clasp at the top. Light-blue panties winked at him from between the folds of clothing. Very nice. He'd deal with those soon enough.

"And then what?" she said, her breath quickening.

"Then the slacks come off." He slid them off her until her exquisite skin and all of the light-blue panties were revealed.

"Yes?" she rasped out.

"Then, in my fantasy, I get to place my tongue here." He moved his mouth to her belly button, ringed it with his lips and then licked. "And my hand here." He slipped his fingers underneath the band of her soft undergarments to reach the wetness between her legs. He pressed against her soft skin until she moaned.

"Bram?"

"Mmm-hmm?" He licked and pressed and, finding the warm space just below the pads of his fingers, pushed slightly inward.

"You...you can..." She wriggled beneath his grasp.

"Am I getting closer, Shannon?"

She laughed then sucked in some air. "Yes, dammit."

"Well, good. You're perfectly positioned for what I want to do next." And with that, he thrust two of his fingers in all the way. She gasped. Then, still using his tongue on her naval and adding his thumb to the sensitive area just above his fingers, he grabbed both of her wrists with his free hand and held them firmly. The other hand tangoed with her until he got his fantasy: She screamed his name.

Once she'd had a chance to catch her breath, he loosened his grip on her wrists and helped her tug off the blindfold. She stared at him for a long time before reaching into the Easter basket and pulling out one of the flavored condoms.

"My turn now," she said, stepping onto the carpet and waving the foil packet in the air. "I love strawberry."

He was already as hard as concrete, so whatever flavor she chose would've been just dandy. "Me, too."

She nodded. "Stand up, take your pants off and turn around."

He squinted at her.

"My fantasy," she informed him. "Just do it."

He shrugged and did as the lady asked.

"The boxers, too, Bram."

When he was standing there, his naked ass to her, he felt the familiar scrap of black fabric encircle one wrist and then the other. She tied his hands firmly behind his back then turned him face forward again at the edge of the bed.

"I think you'd better sit down," she said, ripping open the packet and grinning at him.

"A damn good idea," he agreed as she slid the flavored condom over his erection and brought her mouth down on it. And, a few minutes later, he was glad for the soft comfort of the bed as the force of his desire propelled him backward and Shannon's sweet mouth caused his release.

When was the next holiday at this place? Wasn't Earth Day coming up soon? May Day? Cinco de Mayo?

Hell, he'd take any one of them, and he'd tell Miranda to clear his calendar for a month, if that was what it took, to get him back to Shannon.

Shannon crept out of the Astaire Suite at around three-thirty a.m., through the hallway, down the stairs and back to her room.

Her body still trembled in a hundred places from Bram's touch. One glance in her mirror and she saw she looked as tousled and flushed as she felt. And it felt *marvelous*.

She'd never celebrated Easter Sunday quite like this.

Bram had fallen into a deep slumber sometime after midnight and, though they didn't completely join their bodies during the evening, Shannon wouldn't claim to be anything but absolutely satisfied by the experience.

At least from a physical standpoint. That man worked

amazing deeds with his fingers.

He didn't push her farther than she'd wanted to go. He didn't become some guy she didn't recognize once the door was shut. He didn't make her feel anything but cherished for several wonderful hours. A part of her wanted to run back upstairs, wake him up and insist that they fully consummate their union right then and there. Wouldn't that make him want to stay?

She shook her head to clear it. This was exactly the problem. He wasn't going to stay, whether he wanted to or not. And begging him to make love to her until they'd used up all the condoms in their Easter basket wouldn't make the gnawing insecurity of that fact go away.

This defined "risk" for her. She had to learn to embrace the inevitable, short-term nature of things—not cling to known entities just because they were safe.

But, ohhh, she *liked* Bram. She couldn't help herself.

Trying to get to sleep now was futile. She showered, puttered around in her room until a reasonable hour and, finally, went down to her office to get some paperwork done.

A few minutes after seven, she heard knocking. Figuring it must be Jake, she called out, "You know it's open."

The door swung open. It wasn't Jake.

"Why'd you leave so early?" Bram asked her, leaning against the doorjamb, wearing travel clothes and a lazy smile. "I missed you in my bed."

She felt her face and most of her body heat up at his words. "I thought you might need the rest."

He nodded. "What I *need* is to get back to Minneapolis." He held up his cell phone and frowned at it. "What I *want* is to drag you back upstairs with me. Any chance we'll have a next time?"

"I hope so," she said but tried to let go of all expectation.

"Me, too." He took a few steps closer to her. "The Easter Bunny left you a present in my room. You might wanna grab it before someone else gets to it first."

She stood up from her desk and walked over to him. "A hint?"

"Nope. You'll just have to see for yourself. And promise

that you'll think of me when you use them."

Then he kissed her before she could say, "I promise."

She broke away and nodded.

"Good. I've got to go, Shannon, but I'll see you soon, and I'll talk to you sooner than that, I hope." He brought his lips to the back of her hand, which, while a gentlemanly gesture, still felt intensely intimate coming from him. "Happy Easter."

"Happy Easter," she said as he rushed out the door. She trailed his shadow into the hallway wishing she, too, could set off on a journey. Maybe Bram's adventurousness would rub off on her.

"Good morning, Shannon," Jake's cool voice whispered behind her. "Have a restful night?"

"Hmm? Oh, yeah." Liar, liar. Would Bram really come back?

"Seems that way."

She turned to look at Jake, his gaze piercing daggers at Bram's distant form. She grinned at her friend. "Be happy for me, Jake. It's nothing serious, really, but I like him. Okay?"

Jake shrugged. "If you say so, babe." Then, after a few beats, "Okay, okay." He half smirked at her. "But he'd better treat you well, Shannon, or he'll be rooming in the utility closet next time."

She laughed. "Thanks, *Jakey.*"

He rolled his eyes at the nickname she rarely used when addressing him and mumbled a grudging "you're welcome" back to her.

She flashed him a grin, gave his arm a quick squeeze and then raced up to the Astaire Suite.

Bram had hastily made the bed but much remained the same as when she'd left in the wee hours of the morning. In the middle of the table, however, sat the Easter basket, the black blindfold tied in a bow around the handle.

She moved closer to get a better look and discovered the basket was now filled with sumptuous soaps, lotions and body oils, all from Lathericious. Bram's company.

She smiled as she smelled a few of the fragrances, her smile broadening when she spotted the note he'd left her. It read:

Shannon,

Slow, sensual seduction is not only my pleasure...it's also my business. I brought these to Holiday Quinn for you. Please enjoy them at your leisure and imagine my hands rubbing them on you. That's what I'll be imagining.

Don't hesitate to call me at the cell number below, or e-mail me, if you'd prefer. I'd be happy to hear from you anytime. I repeat—ANYTIME.

Bram

Hmm, would right now be soon enough? Shannon sat on the bed next to the phone and punched in Bram's cell number before she could talk herself out of it.

"Hartwick," he answered on the second ring.

"Hi," she said, feeling dangerously daring as she stretched out on the warm bed that still held his scent. "Guess where I am?"

~CHAPTER FOUR~

Memorial Day

*W*hat color, you ask... You mean you can't guess < g >?

I'll leave the visuals to your imagination, Bram, but I WILL tell you their texture. Think soft and satiny from top to bottom, with a hint of roughness around the frilly edges.

Perfect for a summer's evening and, when uncovered, will prove more unusual than what is expected...

Bram couldn't resist reading Shannon's latest message one more time. He laughed and logged off his e-mail for the night before getting ready for bed.

Hmm, bed. Alone.

But he was in Brussels on business and she was in Wisconsin preparing for the upcoming Memorial Day weekend at the inn. And writing, by his account, the sexiest descriptions of cupcakes ever composed online.

Yes, professionally made and creatively frosted, using the smoothest fondant and the most artful designs for her guests. Delicate red-white-and-blue cupcakes...

Not satin panties.

Not sheer lingerie.

Not silky bed sheets.

Oh, how that woman delighted in tormenting him.

They'd played this game for weeks now, starting after Easter with her first phone call from the Astaire Suite. A game of suggestive one-upmanship, which turned out to be more like "one-up*woman*ship" because she so often had him bested. He never would've guessed someone with such a poised demeanor would become this evocative, this bold. This quickly.

Not that he was complaining.

He just wanted to see where her imaginative mind would take them these days, if ever they were face-to-face again.

He threw his tired body down on the mattress and sank into the pillow. He clicked off the bedside light, flipped the blanket over his legs and squeezed his eyes shut.

Nothing.

Well, nothing but Shannon dancing behind his eyelids in a lacy, flowing teddy—probably forest green—while luring him down the darkened hallways of Holiday Quinn for a flaming quickie against one of the banisters.

He swallowed and felt himself harden. No way would he be able to fall asleep without some help.

He dialed room service and had them send up a cup of decaf with cream and a chocolate croissant. Carbs usually knocked him out fast. But the sweet pastry, like virtually everything else he laid his eyes on, made him think of Shannon.

So he tried some strong bourbon from the mini bar. No such luck.

The late-night TV show in Flemish didn't help either. Nor did the French one.

He checked the clock and, counting backward seven hours, he decided there remained only one viable option. He punched in a phone number he'd long since memorized.

"Hello, you've reached the voicemail of Shannon Quinn. I'm unable to take your call right now, but please leave your name and message, and I'll get back to you as soon as possible. Have a wonderful day."

"How the hell can I have a wonderful day?" Bram grumbled after waiting for the familiar beep. "I'm bored, horny and on my way to becoming an insomniac. Call me the second you get this and put me out of my misery. Please." He recited the phone number of his hotel suite and his room number. Then he slammed down the receiver.

Dammit.

This international travel gig had long ago curtailed his social life, but he hadn't resented it quite so much until recently. Trying to stay in contact with someone when you were seven or eight time zones away...who could do that and not go out of their freakin' minds?

Twelve long minutes later the phone rang.

"Hi, birthday boy. How are you?" Shannon's soft voice was like a salve on a wound.

Bram exhaled a breath he hadn't realized he'd been holding. "Not great. And my birthday isn't until tomorrow."

"Isn't it already tomorrow in Belgium?"

He glanced at the clock. She was right. Three minutes past midnight and, having been born a late-night baby, he was less than a half hour away from officially turning thirty-one. He was educated, responsible, highly successful, and yet... God, when had he become so boringly adult?

"Yeah, okay, it's tomorrow here," he said. "But I'm getting impatient in my old age. I wanna kiss you and do other things to you. Tonight. And, sorry, I'm not being subtle but, frankly, I don't care."

She laughed, sort of. "You'll have to come back to the inn then. That's where I am and where I need to be. At least for now."

He heard a touch of something in her voice. Couldn't quite put his thumb on it, but it sounded like yearning, maybe. Which gave him a great idea. "Why don't you fly here instead and meet me? I could e-mail you a ticket and—"

"I'd love to, Bram, really. But you know I can't just pick up and leave. I've got the party coming up this weekend with over a hundred registered guests, and there's just too much to do beforehand." The tone of her voice continued to mystify him. Longing? Resignation? Did she burn to see him or did she merely want to get away?

Bram let his mind drift back to the cozy comfort that was Holiday Quinn. The warm, homey feel of the place, the tasteful décor, the relaxing environment where the hotel was situated. No way would she wish to leave such a sweet spot so, perhaps, it was really him she missed.

Something unfamiliar in the vicinity of his chest soared at the thought. He'd fly back to her in a heartbeat if he could, but business requirements claimed his time and sapped his energy. He was as bound to his world at present as she was to hers. But, hey, maybe there was a middle ground.

"What about the weekend after Memorial Day?" He'd still be in Europe, but he could maybe swing a day or two off and, of course, they'd have the nights.

"I'm working at The Ashland next weekend. I'm off the following one, though. What are you doing then?"

For a split second he was hopeful. Then he checked his electronic calendar. "Dammit. I'll be in Tokyo." And the following week would be spent in Beijing. Lathericious was expanding to the Asian market and he had serious work to do in both cities.

She sighed when he explained this. "Well, it's looking like we'll have to wait until the 4th of July." She paused. "You *are* still planning to visit then, aren't you?"

"Hell, yeah." He'd made Miranda block off Independence Day weekend right after he came back from his Easter visit, since he already knew Memorial Day would be a lost cause. But he hadn't counted on missing Shannon so much in the interim. He looked forward to her phone calls and e-mails like a seventeen-year-old looked forward to driving his dad's convertible on a Friday night in summer.

"Good." He heard her exhale before adding, "So, what does the birthday boy want to do to celebrate his big day?"

Bram almost laughed. The last time he'd done anything worthy of note on his birthday had been a decade before when he'd celebrate legal adulthood by earning his first six-figure salary and, consequently, his financial freedom from his parents. Four years later, he became the owner of his own company, had worked until at least ten p.m. on every birthday since and never once considered it unusual.

Not until tonight.

"I want you to touch me," he admitted before censoring himself.

There was a long pause on the other end of the line. "I'm putting you on hold and going up to the Astaire Suite," she said, her voice low and undeniably seductive.

He waited for what seemed like an eternity, though the digital clock by his bed flipped only one number in her absence. Then her voice returned to the line.

"Hi," she said, a little breathless. "I locked the door and am lying down on our bed."

Our bed.

He swallowed hard at those words, but he, too, had begun to think of the silk sheets of the Astaire Suite's king-sized bed as "theirs." He slid onto his hotel mattress, got as comfortable as he could under the circumstances and whispered, "Yeah? We'll I'm lying down, too. What'cha gonna do with me, sweetheart?"

"Turn off the light."

He flicked off the bedside lamp. "Done."

"Close your eyes."

He did. "They're closed."

"What are you imagining?" she asked him.

What was he imagining? Huh. Would he scare her off if he told her the truth? Yeah, sure, he'd fantasized about a lot of heavily sexual things since they'd met, the content of which could fill up an issue or two of *Playboy*, but there were also few daydreams that'd crossed his mind in the past few weeks that were decidedly...well, more homey than erotic.

Bram shuddered.

Since when was he a white-picket-fence, live-happily-ever-after-with-one-woman kind of guy? Must be all the jetlag finally catching up with him.

He cleared his throat. "You're in your panties and bra. I've just tossed the silly business clothes you always wear into a pile on the floor and—"

"Silly business clothes?"

Her indignant tone made him laugh. "I mean, I've peeled off of you anything that isn't silky or lacy or see-through. And now I'm preparing to get rid of all the rest." He paused. "I plan to use my teeth."

He heard her quick intake of air on the line and couldn't keep from grinning. Those breathy little sounds she came out with made his day every time.

"Um, okay," she said. The delectable rustling of clothing being removed greeted his ears. "The *silly* business clothes are now on the floor."

"Thank you. You gonna tell me what color those panties of yours are, Shannon, or am I to assume they're red, white and blue like the frosting on the cupcakes?"

"They are not red, white *or* blue. Nor are they any combination of the three."

"Hmm. So, no pink? No purple?"

"Nope."

"Does your bra match them?"

"No." She paused. "I'm not wearing a bra."

Now it was his turn to inhale sharply. He squeezed his eyes tighter and said, "All the better. I'll deal with the panties when I get to them. For now, I'm kissing your neck, just under your chin, and then running my tongue along the soft skin at the base of your throat. Can you feel that?"

"Yes."

"Good. And, since there's no fabric to stop me, I'm sliding my kisses further down. To your chest. To the tops of your beautiful breasts. I'm just about to reach your nipples, which are inviting me to kiss them, too." He remembered her naked breasts and groaned. "What are you doing, Shannon?"

"I'm gliding my fingers up your back. Kneading those stiff muscles on either side of your spine until you press yourself against me."

Bram flipped over on his stomach, eyes still closed, and imagined Shannon's soft body on the firm mattress beneath him. "I can feel that," he whispered. "Touch me harder."

"I want to crush your lower body to me, but you're pulling back—"

"Because I'm licking your nipples, Shannon. I want to drive myself into you, but first I need to hear you invite me in."

"You're invited," she whispered.

God, he wanted to take her. Now.

He swallowed. "Okay, then. So, I'm sucking on your nipples, squeezing them with my lips until you're writhing beneath me. I hear the moans from deep inside your throat, and I hold your hands as I continue to kiss you."

She moaned. "Okay. I'm there."

"I'm getting impatient now, and my body hurts from holding back—"

"Your boxers aren't still on, are they, Bram?"

They were. "Well, uh—"

"Oh, God, take them off."

He did as she commanded. "They're off. My t-shirt, too."

"It's about time."

He laughed. In spite of his lust for her, she always made him laugh. Amazing woman.

"Where were we?" she said.

"I was holding your hands and sucking your nipples."

"Oh, that's right. Please continue."

"So, in order to get further down, to where your panties are, I have to let go of your fingers. I slide my lips to the top of your waistband where the lacy elastic is pressing into your skin. I bite against the edge of the dark green fabric—"

"It's not green, Bram."

"Ivory?"

"Nope."

"Yellow?"

"Huh-uh."

"Fuchsia?"

"Guess again."

"Goddammit, Shannon. Tell me *now* before I take the first direct flight back to the States to throttle you."

A deep, throaty laugh greeted him on the line. "My panties are black. A very sheer black. And you're successfully pulling them off with your teeth."

"Of course I am," he replied, picturing the said panties and their subsequent removal.

"So, now that they're on the floor, Bram, what are you going to do next?"

"I'm kissing you again. Can't you feel my lips against your thighs? My tongue moving between your legs?"

He heard Shannon reply with a sound that could only be described as a whimper.

"I'll take that as a yes," he said.

After a heated pause, she said, "Yes."

And in his mind, his lips were right there, against her pale, moist skin, a slant of light escaping into the room through the closed blinds. He inhaled her sweet scent, as potent from six thousand miles away as from a distance of six centimeters, and he heard her call his name.

"Bram."

He exhaled into the receiver, struggling for his usual control, but his imagination had taken over. They seemed to have entered a new realm of connection together. A place where their shared vision dictated their reality.

"Bram, I want you inside of me."

"I want that, too."

And as his cock rubbed against the smooth sheets of the Belgian hotel's mattress, he mentally plunged deep into Shannon, emitting a sound he knew she'd recognize on the other end of the line as pure desire.

"I can almost feel you," she whispered.

"Use your fingers. Thrust as I do, sweetheart. I'll tell you when to do it."

"Okay."

"Okay," he said, pulling his hips back. Then, just as he was about to thrust again, he said, "Now."

She moaned.

"And now." He thrust even deeper. "And now. And now.

THE SWEET TEMPTATIONS COLLECTION

And now again."

Her breath caught. "Ohhh, I—I'm—"

"How close are you?"

"Close."

"Then I'd better thrust some more." And he did, telling her each time and feeling her rising heat sizzling through the phone line until he heard her cry out.

With a sense of concentration he didn't know he possessed outside of his company's boardroom, he focused his mind's eye on Shannon. He let his body follow her lead, feeling her hands clinging to his back, squeezing him as he pumped, until he, too, found his release and called her name.

Bram had never been a man to shy away from bedroom games or dirty talk, but phone sex with Shannon surprised him by being one of the most erotic thing he'd ever done in his life. And he intended to do it again. Ideally, without the phone.

"How are you?" she asked once he'd caught his breath.

He pulled himself up from the now-wet bed sheet and grinned into the receiver. "I'm having a marvelous start to my birthday, Shannon."

She laughed. "Glad to hear it. I wouldn't want to leave you unsatisfied on your big day."

"Not possible, sweetheart."

She sighed. "I know this is anticlimactic, but I should probably get back to work soon. Maybe, if you want, we can, um, talk again...later..."

"Yes," he said, but he knew time differences and his packed work agenda would complicate matters. The CEO in him started to take over again as he began to strategize how to merge their schedules to his liking. "What are you doing at this time tomorrow?"

"Talking to you?"

"You'd better believe it. And, Shannon?"

"Yes?"

"I'm not gonna bother guessing the color of your panties next time. I want you to skip wearing them altogether."

Shannon hung up the phone and let herself curl into the silky sheets of the massive bed. For a moment or two, with Bram on the phone, it had really felt as though they were sharing it. She missed the sensation already.

She glanced at the clock. Hmm, nearly dinnertime. But since no guests were at the inn yet, she was alone.

Well, not exactly. *Almost* alone.

Several members of the staff scurried around downstairs. If she strained her ears to listen, she could hear the bustle of activity just below the Astaire Suite floorboards. Everyone was preparing for the big holiday weekend, and her staff had probably noticed her absence an hour ago.

But, guess what? She didn't care.

She pushed herself off the bed, dressed quickly and tugged off the sheets to send down to the laundry room. She'd deal with them later. Then she opened the door to the hallway and stepped out of the suite.

"Hello, Shannon."

She swiveled around to see Jake standing a few paces away, staring at her oddly.

"I—um, hi, Jake." She forced a wide-eyed smile at him.

"Everything okay in there?"

"Oh, yeah. Sure. Of course." Her mind raced through a list of questions: Good God, had he heard her? Could he have figured out what she was doing? Whom she was talking to? Would he have stayed to listen if he had? Jake's expression gave nothing away, so she could only speculate. "Uh, how are you?"

He laughed. "I'm fine, Shannon. I thought, I don't know, you disappeared for ages, so I wondered... You're not feeling sick or anything, are you?"

She let out a relieved sigh. "No, no. I just needed a break from all the commotion." She began walking toward the staircase. "Coming?"

Jake shook his head. "We've got a honeymoon couple that reserved the Astaire Suite for the weekend. Silvia said she made up the bed earlier, but I want to do a quick check of the kitchenette to make sure we've got enough stuff on hand for them." He pulled out his master key reached for the doorknob.

Panic came flooding back. "No! I mean, let's do that tomorrow, shall we?"

He raised a light-brown eyebrow in her direction. "Why wait? No time like the present."

"Because—" Oh, what convincing reason could she give him? "Because I was hoping to have dinner with you and, then, maybe talk about some of the activities we've got on the agenda for this weekend." She grinned at him. "I asked Margaret to send over some of Ricardo's Florentine lasagna and garlic bread. Want to share it with me?"

Jake groaned. "Oh, that guy is The Cholesterol God. I swear, every time I eat at The Ashland I put on five pounds." He patted his flat stomach. "But I'd never refuse a dinner date with you, even if it involves enough garlic to scare off Dracula and his entire extended family." He waggled his brows at her, but she didn't bother to correct his misuse of the word "date" as it related to her invitation.

Jake slipped his master key back in his pocket and trailed her down the stairs, but Shannon didn't fully relax for the rest of the evening. Not until everyone went home and she could embrace the memory—real or imagined—of Bram's arms around her, his lips creating a trail of heat against her skin, his body joined with hers.

Fantasy, when tinged with just enough reality to make it exciting, held an innate sense of safety. She had nothing to fear while in its grip.

But, in the inky black of midnight, she couldn't help but wonder: Does one adventure naturally lead to another? Does one small risk open the door to an exponentially larger one? And how long before she would be faced with a challenge she couldn't overcome?

This funneled her thoughts back to Bram again and brought with it her first real bolt of apprehension at his impending return.

~CHAPTER FIVE~

Independence Day

Shannon paced behind the reception desk, certain they'd need to re-carpet to cover up her tread marks.

She heard the fifteenth explosion. *Bang!*

Then the sixteenth. *Bang!*

Then the seventeenth. *BANG!*

She squeezed her eyes shut, clenched a miniature American flag in each fist and paced some more.

Bang! Bang, bang, bang, bang! detonated the latest blast of pyrotechnic interjections from the Crosby Room. Followed by...big surprise...*bang, bang, BANG!*

"Jeez, get me some goddamn aspirin," Jake groaned, tapping his forehead against the counter and slapping his palms on the desk in emphasis. He lifted his head, caught Shannon's eye then sniffed the air. "Uh, do you smell smoke?"

She sniffed, too. Yep. Oh, God. "This guy had better know what he's doing."

"Look, Shannon, I know you think the world of Margaret Ashland, but where she finds some of these freaking bizarre-o people—"

The Freaking Bizarre-o Person in question emerged from the Crosby Room with tap shoes on his feet and a fistful of unlit theatrical firecrackers in his hand. "Totally awesome space, lady." He did a quick Shuffle Off To Buffalo and grinned at her and Jake. "The show's gonna go super great, don't you worry a bit. I got Freddie's routine down pat, and we're all gonna have a blast." He laughed. "Get it? A blast!"

Shannon and Jake stared at him.

"Okay, then, dudes. I'm off to do a little more rehearsing in the studio tonight, but I'll be back with my buds to set up the FX on Saturday afternoon. You sure you don't want that smoke machine, lady? I can bring one in real cheap?"

Shannon was quite sure. "No, thank you."

"Well, alrighty then, I'm gone." He put his palm over his chest where his bizarre-o heart must be. "Freddie and me, we're tight. Even though he's in the spirit world and all, he's gonna be with us for the show. I guarantee it." He did a step-ball-change, spun around in place and tossed a trick firecracker to the ground with each hand. *Bang, bang!* "This inn has a super cool feel to these rooms. Totally awesome."

"Yeah, totally," Jake agreed, then said, "Who talks like that?" the instant the guy strode out the door. Jake rolled his eyes. "Did I miss Flashback to the Eighties Week or something?"

Shannon chuckled and pulled out a bottle of extra-strength pain reliever from one of the desk drawers. She lobbed it at her wise-aleck assistant. "As long as he doesn't burn down the inn, I don't care which decade he emulates." She sighed. "His voice sure doesn't sound anything like Fred Astaire's, though. Or 'Freddie's,' as the tap guy kept calling him. What did you think of his dancing?"

Jake shrugged. "Not bad. Better than mine, that's for sure. But there are bound to be guests who know every move of Astaire's classic Fourth of July routine from the movie. Don't know what they'll say."

At this point, Shannon didn't know either and almost didn't care. They'd watched the guy do the routine once without the firecrackers and, to her, it looked fine. However, she had plenty of other things to occupy her thoughts. Like the fact that guests were scheduled to start arriving the next day and, with them, so came Bram.

"What'cha doing tonight?" Jake asked her.

"My usual before a 'holiday' weekend of craziness. Bubble bath. Tall, cool drink. Good night's sleep." She winked at him. "Maybe a handful of chocolates to ensure sweet dreams."

"Ha. Something your Grandma Quinn used to say when you were a kid, right?"

She nodded. "That was one of my favorites."

Jake looked serious for a moment. "You miss them all, don't you? Your family?"

"Of course." She took a few steps away. The empty space in her heart always grew larger whenever someone mentioned them. Loss might fade, but it never disappeared. "You probably want to get home, and I've got to grab a bite for dinner and run that bath now, so—"

"Hey, Shannon, wait." Jake motioned her closer. "You need still need that tall, cool drink tonight, too, right?"

"Well—" she began.

"So, why don't you let me make one for you. Long Island Iced Teas are...awesome, lady. Totally awesome."

She laughed. "Very funny."

"Just say yes," he said in his serious tone again. "It's only a drink. Okay?"

With Bram's return on the docket for tomorrow, she could use a little something to calm her nerves. True, alcohol wasn't her usual choice of an anti-anxiety med (her tastes ran more toward Godiva truffles), but why not? She'd heard of the concoction and always wanted to try one. And it *was* only a drink, after all.

"Okay."

So, Jake rushed off to work his cocktail magic. He returned to the lobby in a flash with a couple of tall, cool drinks that seemed harmless enough, even on an empty stomach. She took a first sip, then another. "Mmm."

Jake grinned and started chatting about the warm weather and other innocuous things while drinking his own beverage.

Ten minutes later, after swallowing the last few drops of

her drink and licking her lips, she said, "This was really tasty. Kind of reminds me of a tangy lemonade."

Jake eyed her curiously. "Want another?"

She checked her watch. It was still early evening, but she noticed the beginning symptoms of sleepiness sweeping through her body. And thank God. She'd been worried that the combination of fear and excitement over Bram's approaching arrival would keep her up all night.

"I don't know…" she said. Most of the staff had already gone home, and everyone—herself included—needed a good night's rest.

"It's not that late," Jake countered before she could come up with an excuse.

She sighed, feeling her body caving to the temptation. "Well, it *is* helping me unwind, I have to admit. What goes into one of those things anyway?"

"Why don't I bring you another one? I'll tell you all the ingredients." And before she could say Long Island Iced Tea three times fast, Jake dashed off and soon returned to the reception desk with a fresh glassful. "Here you go, babe. Drink up. It'll relax you."

"Mmm, thanks." She took a few swigs. Remarkable really. The nervousness she'd been feeling for weeks started slowly seeping out of her. She leaned against the counter and let the negative energy and apprehension drift away.

So what if Bram was a hotshot, multimillionaire type who could have any woman he wanted in the Western Hemisphere by simply snapping his fingers twice? He said in his last e-mail that he couldn't wait to get back to her. He liked *her*.

Who cared how little they had in common or how lonely she'd been before meeting him? After having phone sex two dozen times, their differences melted away into ancient history. She didn't have to be tied to the past.

And why worry about risks and loss and all that other depressing stuff? She could chart her own course. She knew she'd be okay no matter what happened next—she had a job, friends, resources. From the deliciously hazy view through her tall cocktail glass, it all seemed so clear.

Jake caressed her shoulder with brotherly affection. "Good stuff, isn't it?"

"Yeah. We may need to make this a pre-holiday-weekend ritual."

Jake laughed, soft and low. He lowered his hand to the middle of her back and massaged her there. "Fine by me." He paused. "It's nice to see you so calm like this, Shannon. I can tell you've been under a lot of stress lately."

She looked into Jake's kind eyes. Something different registered in them. He wasn't being his usual flirtatious self, but she couldn't quite put her finger on what had changed, or why. Plus, her mind was starting to float away...into fantasies featuring Bram. He was at the inn with her. In the Astaire Suite. Completely naked. She heard herself moan.

Jake's fingers slid lower still. "Yeah, I feel a knot of tension right here." He rubbed deeper, more intensely.

Shannon put down her nearly empty glass, a slight glimmer of dread settling on her shoulders like a weight. This situation didn't feel quite right. What was Jake up to?

She turned to face him, his fingers refusing to break away from her body, just as the front door of Holiday Quinn swung open. Was it the tap-dance guy returning? One of the maids who'd forgotten her keys, perhaps?

With Jake's hand still planted firmly around her waist, she glanced over at the door.

"Hello, Shannon," the formidable Bram Hartwick said, his jaw clenched. "Am I interrupting something?"

Bram strode over to the counter where Shannon and Jake the Prick stood.

"Bram!" she cried, her expression and her voice indicating delight. It sounded genuine. He desperately hoped it was. She leaped away from Jake and threw her arms around him. "You got here early!"

Not early enough, apparently.

He held Shannon for a long moment, then he kissed her hard on the mouth, tasting alcohol.

With a lethal look in Jake's direction, Bram reached for Shannon's glass, sniffed the remaining inch of liquid at the bottom and said, "Mind if I have a taste? It's been a long drive."

"Sure," she said, grinning up at him. "Jake made it, but I've had *more* than enough already."

Bram took a tentative swallow. Long Island Iced Tea. With a mix of seven different kinds of liquor, those things were damn potent, but its strength was disguised by the kind of flavorful fruitiness women loved. Something every remotely intelligent man on the planet knew. Only dishonorable men exploited that knowledge, though.

He gazed into the defiant green eyes of Jake Marcolis, loathed him with every fiber of his being and knew with absolute certainty that he was going to beat the bloody crap out of the bastard. And soon.

Shannon, for all her luscious curves, was still a lightweight when it came to booze, and she seemed to be getting a little unsteady on her feet. How many of those drinks had she had?

"You hungry, sweetheart? I wasn't in the mood for fast food on the way here, so I'd planned to fix myself a little something when I got up to the room. Join me?"

"Of course," she said, laughing. "I made sure the kitchenette in the Astaire Suite was fully stocked." She paused. "Good thing, too. I never got around to eating dinner. I'm starving."

Bram shot another glare at Jake. From the guilty look in his eyes, the assistant had known about this, too. Jake would be sorry. Bram would deal with him later.

"Well, goodnight Jake," Shannon said cheerfully. "Drive home safe, and I'll see you tomorrow."

"Yeah, Jake," Bram said. "Drive home *safe*." Or not.

The assistant stood to his full height, five-foot-ten, maybe—Bram was taller so it didn't matter—and waved a farewell to Shannon. "Goodnight, babe," he told her.

Babe?

That guy was so dead.

To him, Jake continued to raise his hand, but he subtly lowered the thumb, index finger, ring finger and pinky of that hand as he turned toward him, so Jake's "wave" goodnight was a whole lot like a flip off. Bram suspected this was entirely intentional.

As far as he was concerned, the gauntlet hadn't been thrown down—it'd been hurled to the floor with a smack. And Bram was not one to let a challenge like that go unacknowledged, either in business or in his personal life.

Jake the Prick had better watch his back.

"Let me take you upstairs," he whispered in Shannon's ear once the assistant had finally left the building. "I've got a lot to show you, and you know I'm an impatient man."

She shivered in his arms then hugged him tighter. "I'd been worried, you know," she admitted, "about how it would feel when we were face-to-face again. It's been such a long time." She pulled him by his necktie down to her and planted a long, wet kiss on his lips. "I'm not worried anymore."

He led her to the stairway, aware of her slight stumbling and unusually relaxed posture as they wound their way to the suite. "I'm glad you're not worried. You have nothing to fear from me." *Except the untimely demise of your assistant.* "I was looking forward to seeing you so much, I didn't want to wait until tomorrow to get here."

She grinned at him as she fumbled with the door key. "Bram, I think I'm a little drunk."

He eased the key gently from her fingers. "I know you are, sweetheart. But, like I said, you don't have anything to fear from me. I'll take care of you until you're thinking clearly again. Okay?"

"Okay." She paused as they entered the suite, watching him as he tossed his bag on the chair and kicked off his dress shoes. He felt her eyes scanning him. "Then what'll you do? Once I'm thinking clearly again, I mean?"

He smiled at her, enjoying her warm and open expression,

her waterfall of auburn waves, her intelligent and imaginative way of just *being*, and he said, "Then we'll have wild and raunchy sex until you shriek. Sound good?"

She threw her head back and laughed. "Well, yeah."

Shannon awoke sometime after two a.m., her body curled up against Bram's slumbering form in the Astaire Suite.

It wasn't as though she didn't remember what had happened, only that the memories seemed yellowish and blurry, like the sepia snapshots her grandfather had kept in an old family photo album.

She recalled Bram's early arrival, how excited she'd been to see him and how surprisingly unafraid.

How she'd been drinking those big Long Island Iced Teas on an empty stomach—stupid, she knew—but how they'd kept the panic at bay.

How Bram and Jake had glared at each other downstairs, but then Jake left and Bram took her to the suite for ham and cheese sandwiches, fruit salad and pretzels. Hmm, and something else... What was it?

Oh, yes, the pudding. Chocolate pudding. And he kissed her and fed the dessert to her with a little teaspoon, as if she were a child. Then he made her drink some water, and he tucked her in bed.

She watched him now, watched his chest rise and fall and rise again, and she reached out to put her arm around him and snuggle closer. He was so firm and his body heat radiated onto her despite the room's cool air.

"So, did you sleep off the effects of your assistant's poison?" he whispered, his voice raspy and tired.

"The drinks? Yep. But I think I'm getting a little tipsy again just from being around you."

He laughed. "Oh, you're a sweet talker, Ms. Quinn, but I need to make sure you're really sober." He heaved himself onto his knees and lifted her to a sitting position. "Feeling dizzy? A little unsteady?"

"Nope." She hugged herself and realized she was wearing her short-sleeved work shirt but no slacks. He'd undressed her down to her pink panties, but he hadn't done more than kiss her tonight. So far. The man had real self-control, and her deep appreciation.

"Can you stand up? Walk around?"

She slipped out of the bed and moved in a circuit around the nearby coffee table and two chairs. "Seems so. When does the 'wild and raunchy sex until I shriek' part start?"

His grin shown bright even in the darkness. "Oh, so you remember that, do you?"

"My memory is excellent," she informed him, pulling off her shirt until she was clad in only her bra and panties. "And a promise from you is *especially* memorable."

He looked deep into her eyes, his expression as intense as she'd ever seen it. Not a hint of tiredness remained. "You're sure you're okay, Shannon?"

She marched over where he sat at the edge of the bed, nestled herself between his legs and waited until his arms encircled her waist before nodding. "I am. But Bram? I could be better."

He groaned and buried his face against her far-from-firm tummy muscles. He didn't seem to care about her not having abs of steel, though. With one swift and obviously well-practice movement, he unclasped her pink bra and whipped it across the room. He dragged down the matching panties and tossed them in a different direction before finally letting her tug off his t-shirt and boxers.

When they stood face-to-face again, both of them were naked. And though, in her mind's eye, she'd imagined this scene a few thousand times, the reality proved far superior.

He pushed her onto the bed, his mouth devouring hers with commanding kisses, his legs trapping hers to the mattress.

"That time when I was in Brussels," he said, pulling back a few inches, "I groaned so loudly imagining us like this—in this exact position—that the businessman staying in the room next door glared at me in the hall in the morning."

He laughed at the memory and, for a second, she laughed with him. He moved his kisses to her neck.

"I think Jake may have overheard my side of the conversation, too," she whispered. "He was in the hallway when I left the suite."

Bram pulled back again, further this time. The corners of his lips jerked downward and he stopped laughing. "What was he doing? Lurking? Loitering? Stalking you? Why was he out there?"

"Don't be silly, it was nothing like that. He just had some inventory work to do." She rubbed his shoulders. "Look, Bram, I realize you two aren't particularly fond of each other, but Jake's a reliable staff member, and we've been good friends for two years."

"Just friends?" he asked, still frowning.

"Yes. Definitely just friends."

And that was completely true, not that she'd tell Bram about some of the silly conversations she'd had with her assistant or the times Jake would proposition her in jest. At least, until tonight, she'd *thought* it was in jest. But, surely, alerting Bram to her suspicions wouldn't help relations between the two men. And, anyway, it was irrelevant.

She decided a change of subject would be the best idea under the circumstances.

"I'm not shrieking yet," she informed him. "And these kisses, they're nice and all, but there's nothing raunchy about them." She feigned a bored yawn. "Maybe I should just go back to sleep."

Bram's eyes widened in astonishment.

"Why, you little—" His exhalations turned into chuckles, and he shot back from her like a lightning bolt. A moment later, she found herself in a rather inelegant position over his knees, bottoms up.

"Um—" she began.

"You have a naughty streak," he said. "You look all nice, sweet and professional on the outside and, okay, sexy as hell, but on the inside—" He smacked her bottom once, which almost made her laugh and ruin his game. "You're a bad girl." He smacked her two more times, the last one stinging a bit. "Clearly, spanking is too good for you." He paused to kiss her shoulders and rub her bottom. "But I'm going to do it anyway."

Another few light smacks followed. She figured she ought to at least attempt to get away, so she kicked her legs a bit and put up the pretense of a struggle until Bram laughed aloud.

"What do you have to say for yourself?" he asked.

She wriggled a little more for effect. "I have a well-hidden naughty streak?"

"Damn right you do," he said, but she could hear the smile in his voice.

He smacked her bottom twice more, both times surprisingly hard, before dumping her back on the bed and lording over her with a look of triumph.

She grinned at him. "You're funny, Bram Hartwick."

"I'm *funny?*" He put his fists on his hips, his erection jutting out to greet her, which made her stop grinning. She wanted to touch him, make him take her. Right that very second. "You're, you're—" He shook his head. "Hell, I can't even begin to describe you. When did that prim little Irish lady I met on Valentine's Day turn into such a firecracker? Are you ever this brash out of bed, too?"

She considered his last question, even though she doubted he expected an answer. "No," she admitted as her hand reached up to grasp his firm cock and massage it with her palm. "I'm not."

He sank down to the mattress and conveniently positioned himself between her legs. "Then I guess I'm lucky I get to see both sides of you," he said softly.

Their eyes met and, for a full ten seconds, neither spoke. Shannon felt her whole body blazing with desire for this powerful, yet indisputably affectionate man.

"Got any plastic eggs on hand?" she asked, knowing he'd have no trouble deciphering her meaning.

He raised a dark brow and pulled a purple plastic egg out of the bedside drawer. "As a matter of fact, I do."

Her jaw dropped. "You still have the purple egg? I hadn't expected you to take me so literally."

"Glad to know I have a surprise or two up my sleeve for *you*, sweetheart." He broke open the egg and pulled out a condom. "I'll admit to liking the Easter egg carrying case better than the boring old box these originally came in." He sheathed himself and tossed the egg back in the drawer. "Now, let's see about getting to that shrieking part."

By now, Shannon knew Bram Hartwick was nothing if not a man who kept his word. His kisses ignited a flame of passion so combustible that she was convinced her limbs would burn up before he could plunge inside of her.

She didn't, but it was a close call.

After weeks of only pretending that he'd thrust deep into her, the reality was a delicious shock to her system.

"Oh, God, Bram."

He pumped hard, deep, wild. His hands gripped the backs of her thighs so tight, it felt as though all of her were being compressed by him. Into him. Parts of him seemed to touch her everywhere.

Finally, when all of her felt wet and slick to the touch, he angled his hips just a bit differently, pushing against a new boundary, thrusting into uncharted territory.

And, yes, it was as if every barrier then came tumbling down around them, and they shrieked.

Loudly.

Together.

Shannon wobbled down the stairs, fifteen minutes later than usual, but still earlier than most of the staff. Not, however, earlier than Jake.

"Morning," he said, looking up from a stack of invoices he appeared to be organizing.

"Good morning." She smiled at him but knew she'd better

sit down before her legs gave out on her. Four times with Bram before dawn. It was a wonder she could walk at all. She slipped into her office and sunk into her chair.

Jake appeared at the door not twenty seconds later.

He cleared his throat. "Hey, um, I've been thinking." He coughed into his fist. "Last night with the drinks—I, uh, guess I got excited that you liked it, so I figured if one glass was good, two would be better." He laughed a little. "I'm sorry, though. I'd forgotten you hadn't eaten much. I wasn't trying to actually get you drunk or anything." He sighed. "I really didn't think the liquor would seep into your system so quickly."

She heard him out and nodded. Maybe he was telling the truth, maybe not. Either way, it didn't matter.

"That's okay, Jake. You didn't force it down my throat. I really liked it." She grinned at him. "You make one wicked Long Island Iced Tea, though. Sometime, when I'm prepared, I'd love another. Though, just *one*."

He smiled, but it was soft, not one of his smirky expressions. "Just say the word, babe, and I'll make you whatever you want." He shot a nervous glance behind him. "Are things okay with that Hartwick guy? He still sleeping?"

Shannon felt the heat rush to her face and put her palms up to cool her cheeks. "Well, um, he, uh—"

"No, never mind!" Jake said, stepping back two paces. "Forget I asked. I think I know the answer." He chuckled and took another few steps backward. "Good for you. I don't need to know the details. Talk to you later, Shannon." He was out the door completely, but his voice floated back to her. "About *business* things. Only business things."

Shannon laughed and could, thankfully, finish blushing in the privacy of her office.

Work claimed her time for much of the day, though she did manage to steal away for a quick meal with Bram before the Friday night crowd began their mass arrivals.

Friday late night, however, proved to be a charming repeat of the previous one. Although, admittedly, they had to be a little quieter in their vocalizations, being that the inn was actually occupied by guests this time.

But Saturday brought more work, of course, and a slew of activities that Shannon was responsible for overseeing.

"I don't know what I was thinking," Bram complained on Saturday afternoon when, for a half hour, they'd miraculously arranged some alone time in the Astaire Suite. "Coming here for these holidays is fabulous, and I love this place, but I'm barely getting a chance to see you."

"I'm working, Bram. This is my job."

"I know. And I understand that, but maybe we need to meet sometime, someplace when and where you're *not* working."

The blood cells and nerve endings inside of her leaped up and danced at this idea. "I'm game, but getting you away from *your* business, even for national holidays, is like pulling a baby tiger away from its tribe." She pointed at his cell phone. "I know I haven't seen you much since the guests showed up, but why hasn't that thing been ringing off the hook or vibrating uncontrollably or something?"

He grimaced at her. "Because I turned it off."

She blinked. "Seriously? For the whole weekend?"

He sighed. "No. But during times when we're together...yes. And before you start thinking I've become some slacker CEO, I'll have you know that I spent nearly two hours this morning dealing with Zurich, Milan and Tokyo."

She laughed. "I've never thought of you as anything but dedicated to your company, Bram. And those bath oils are amazing." She studied his mouth and strong lips for a moment. "Hey, will you say something to me in Italian? I know you speak it fluently."

He pulled her into his arms. "What do you want to hear, sweetheart?"

She shrugged. "Anything. I don't care. Surprise me."

His forehead creased as he thought. Then, finally, he said, *"Tu odore di cannella."*

"What's that mean?"

"It means 'You smell of cinnamon.'"

"What?" She smacked him on the arm.

He grinned and kissed her. "Well, you *will* when I get you a bottle of the latest batch of 'Sin-amon Spice' body lotion. Not that you need help smelling delicious." He kissed her again, longer this time. She didn't want to have to pull away, but her work break was long over.

"I've got to get back," she said. "See you later, though? After the big show?"

"How about before, during *and* after the show?" he countered. Before she had a chance to open her mouth to reply, he said, "Don't stand alone in the wings tonight, pacing, Shannon. Sit by me during the performance. Hold my hand, and let's be a couple. Okay? I've got to leave tomorrow morning, and I want every second with you that I can get before then."

She nodded, loving that he'd asked this of her, that he'd even *thought* to ask it. Just being with this man made her bolder and more adventurous. "Okay," she said, squeezing his hand one more time then rushing out of the room.

How would she fill the lonely hours in this sleepy town in his absence?

More than anything else, this thought convinced her that she needed to consider more seriously the idea of getting away... Not just weekend visits somewhere, but real travel. Maybe even moving. And, quite possibly, very soon.

Never before had Bram wanted to stay in one place so much.

The thought of going on another international business trip almost nauseated him. And, though fond of the Twin Cities, his bustling hometown didn't have the quaint charm that Shannon's resort location did. Would a move to this little harbor town in Door County be possible with his business still back in Minnesota?

In truth, he didn't know, but he vowed to seriously consider it.

He clicked his cell phone back on and answered a few messages. His brother Grant had given him a newer, faster iPhone for his birthday, but Bram was still learning all the gadgetry details and, in an oddly sentimental way, still missed his old cell. Mostly because it reminded him of all the long phone calls he'd made to Shannon in the past few months.

The memory brought a grin to his face, and he was still grinning ten minutes later when he headed outside to get some fresh summer air.

It was a gorgeous summer day and, despite being bound to the business world by a pocket electronic device, he felt...well, almost free...hopeful. He liked the sensation.

His cell phone vibrated against his hip.

Damn. That was what he got for getting too comfortable and complacent. He lifted it to his ear and said, "Hartwick."

"I think we need to talk," a man's voice said.

Bram looked at the Caller ID. It displayed Holiday Quinn's main phone number. What the hell? "Who is this?"

An arrogant sigh came through loud and clear on the line. "This is Jake Marcolis."

"Ah," he said. "Shannon's employee and *friend*." He paused, letting his sarcasm sink in. "I'm standing right outside the inn, Jake. Why are you calling me on the phone?"

"Because I care a great deal about my employer and *friend*," the assistant shot back. "And I'd just as soon not have her see us trying to kill each other on the lawn."

Bram laughed. He had to hand it to the guy, Jake the Prick had balls. "Well, you've got *my* intentions right. I'd like to dismember you, piece by piece, especially after that stunt you pulled the other night. Long Island Iced Teas on an empty stomach? Why didn't you just drug her?"

There was a long pause. "Look, Hartwick, I'd only been trying to help Shannon relax. I hadn't been trying to get her drunk, but I told her I was sorry it happened nonetheless. As for you, I don't owe you any apologies. You're a man who blew in here one cold night and then blew out again. The fact that you show up once every month or two, doesn't mean you have what it takes to make a long-term relationship with her work."

Bram's jaw dropped. "And *you* do? You've been with her all this bloody time, long before I showed up, and, yet, nothing has ever happened between you two. Explain that."

"Maybe I don't look as impressive as you do on paper. But I suspect she's not seeing all of the *real* you anyway. I'll bet you've got a face you show to her when you're here or when she calls you, but the man at home is someone else. Someone obsessed by stuff she's not a part of. How long will it be before your 'mystery' wears off? How long before she realizes she's just something else you've added to your collection, and that you wouldn't alter a single important thing in your life for her?"

For maybe the first time in a decade, Bram was too stunned to immediately reply. Jake's accusations were all wrong. The kind of workaholic guy Jake had just described? Maybe Bram's brothers fit that description, but he...he'd changed.

"You don't know what you're talking about," Bram said finally, his voice as low and dangerous as he could make it. "And what happens between Shannon and me is none of your damned business. Just keep your fucking hands off her, or I'll pound you to the ground with mine."

"Fine," Jake said. "But don't think I won't be watching you, too." Then he clicked off.

Jake the Prick had hung up on him.

Bram stared at the cell phone before putting it away. He wasn't like his brothers, dammit. He was willing to make changes. He already had, with more to come. And Jake Marcolis could follow the devil down to hell for all he cared.

His phone vibrated again a few minutes later—his secretary Miranda this time—but a sense of panic strangled him, even as he answered. What if he really was stuck in this chaotic life and couldn't get out after all?

Later that night, however, as he watched a very exuberant dancer recreate one of Fred Astaire's most famous tap routines from *Holiday Inn* in the Crosby Room, Bram held Shannon's hand, and he felt liberated again.

She squeezed his fingers hard every time one of the firecrackers went off. The crowd cheered louder with each *Bang!* but, for much of the performance, Bram felt as though just the two of them were watching the routine.

After one particularly explosive display, he saw Jake across the room and his temper rose along with the crowd's feverish excitement. Nothing—and no one—was going to keep Shannon from being his, even if he had to employ every big-business technique for acquisitions and mergers to make it happen.

"The crowd loves the show," Shannon said. "The firecracker-dancing guy really came through with that amazing performance. Wow."

Bram leaned in close. "Yeah, but he ain't got nothin' on us." When she grinned at him, he added, "Let's go upstairs and set off our own sparks, shall we?"

~CHAPTER SIX~

Labor Day

Ah...freedom!

The warm, late-summer wind ruffled Shannon's hair through her car's open window, the sun beat down on her skin and her entire body sprung to life despite the confinement of her seatbelt. Fast-paced swinging tunes from the "Golden Oldies" station poured through her speakers and flooded the car with 1950s and '60s favorites. If Shannon didn't have to keep her eyes on the road, she would have closed them in bliss.

Never had she felt freer than when she'd locked up Holiday Quinn and left it this morning.

Never had a highway looked more beautiful than I-94 headed into Madison—Wisconsin's lively capital city.

Never had a weekend held more promise.

Three days and two nights. With Bram. In a hopping university town. At a tasteful Victorian Bed-n-Breakfast.

Emphasis on *Bed*.

And the best part? No responsibilities for her! Her parents had never opened the inn specifically for the Labor Day holiday, and she didn't plan to start that tradition. Plus, she'd taken vacation time away from The Ashland this weekend. So she could have "fun, fun, fun," just like the Beach Boys sang, with or without a T-Bird, and not have to worry about working at all until Tuesday.

She navigated through Madison's vibrant downtown, alive with pedestrians and just-returning UW students. What an exciting, youthful city this was!

Then, carefully following the directions Bram had e-mailed her, she pulled into the B&B's tiny parking lot, which had room for maybe five cars, and spotted his silver Lexus right away.

She grabbed her bag and all but sprinted into the lobby of the colorfully painted but well-preserved house. A bell jangled from the front door and, within seconds, a woman who looked like Mrs. Cunningham from those old "Happy Days" episodes, appeared before her with a warm smile and a plate of bakery items.

"Hello, dear, and welcome to The Lakehouse B&B," the woman said. "I'm Henrietta Tate. Scone?" She thrust the platter in front of Shannon's nose. Blueberry. And they smelled heavenly. "I just pulled them out of the oven."

"Thank you," Shannon said, reaching for one, her mouth already watering. "I'm meeting a gentleman here, Bram Hartwick, and my name is—"

"Oh, I know, dear. You're Ms. Quinn. Mr. Hartwick told me you were coming." Henrietta winked. "He's expecting you upstairs in the Marquette Room. First floor, second door to the right." When Shannon paused to stare at her, the older lady's eyes danced in merriment. "Go on up there, and why don't you bring him one of these." She handed Shannon another blueberry scone. "He seems the type to enjoy an afternoon snack."

Henrietta winked again and then, to Shannon's continued amazement, bounded away.

Shannon loved this place already.

She gathered up her bag and the scones and raced upstairs. She didn't have to hunt long for their room, though. Bram was waiting for her.

Leaning up against the doorjamb, a half smile gracing his lips, he had his long legs crossed at the ankles and his arms hooked in front of him as he watched her approach.

"Heard your voice," he said, his voice so husky it shot tremors of desire through her limbs.

"I made it here."

He nodded. "I can see that." He eased the bag and the scones away from her, set them inside the room then dragged her in also. He locked the door. "Two months apart is too long."

She stood, her back against the door, Bram's body maybe three inches away from hers, none of him touching her. Well, enough of that.

"Way too long," she agreed, pulling him toward her until his chest was pressed tight against her t-shirt and she could feel the rush of his pulse through his clothing. "I couldn't wait for our relaxing weekend away."

"Mmm-hmm." He kissed her and the room thrummed with the stirrings of their passion. She didn't have to think about any of the what-ifs that plagued her at home. What if a guest needed her? What if Jake interrupted them again? What if someone at the inn spotted them, their bodies entwined? Here, she could concentrate only on Bram. On hearing him, seeing him, touching him.

And on tasting him.

His lips consumed hers with the wild strength of an untamed leopard and, yet, there was tenderness, too, in every motion of his embrace. Few things were sexier than a powerful man capable of such infinite gentleness.

He removed her t-shirt and his. "I brought you something." He led her to the queen-sized bed and tugged down the window shades. Then he unzipped his bag and pulled out a dark-pink bottle with the distinctive Lathericious label embossed on the front. "Sin-amon Spice," he informed her, twisting the cap to release the pump. He squirted a mound of lotion into his palm. "Turn over. It's time for your backrub."

She laughed but did as he asked.

With one hand he unhooked her bra and discarded it, then he rubbed his palms together so, when the lotion first touched her skin, all she felt was silky warmth. The scent of cinnamon infused the room and swirled around her.

"I've been looking forward to doing this for weeks," he said, the pads of his fingers creating a pattern of fan-like whorls on either side of her spine. Her thirsty pores drank up the spicy cream and the as-yet-untouched skin on the front of her body craved his caress. She needed more of him against her.

Preferably now.

"Enter me from behind," she whispered.

"Not until I'm done with your back massage."

In a dexterous move, which she accomplished thanks to three years of Pilates workout videos, she reached behind her to her middle back and shackled his wrists with her hands. "This massage is officially over, Bram."

He chuckled. "As you wish."

She released his wrists long enough for him to sheath himself with a waiting condom and press his hips against the backs of her thighs. He encircled her with his arms and, a moment later, he thrust into her with the skill and the strength she'd come to expect from him.

She was wet and unquestionably ready. She'd been ready for him since last Tuesday.

"Deeper," she said as he began to increase his speed, his fingers splayed against her belly, his groans growing louder. "Harder."

God, she knew she sounded like she was reciting the script from "Daphne Does Daytona," or something as equally sexually explicit, but he brought out her wild, uninhibited side. And guess what? She liked it.

Apparently, so did Bram.

"Everything you say, every way you move...you turn me on, Shannon. Come for me."

She'd spent a lifetime accommodating people's wishes. She had no intention of letting him down.

Thankfully, Bram assisted nicely.

He rocked her until her muscles trembled from the tension of wanting him, until she cried out in passion and heard him echo it, until they collapsed against the mattress together, sated.

Bram brushed a kiss against her neck and slowly pulled his body a few inches apart from hers. "Now *this* is what I call a fantastic weekend away."

All she could manage in reply was a breathy "Yeah."

For heaven knows how long, she remained content to lie in his arms, feeling his fingertips draw designs against her breasts, her hips, her shoulders. Feeling her heartbeat race in double time against the ticking clock on the bedside table.

She daydreamed about their possible upcoming international adventures, based solely on romantic films she'd seen: Driving down a winding road on the Italian Riviera with sunshine kissing their skin. Feasting on *weiner snitzel* and *sacher torte* at an outdoor café in Vienna. Watching a Parisian opera and then making passionate love all through the night.

She stayed in the relaxing warmth of Bram's embrace, enjoying the thrill of her reveries, until hunger roused her at last, returning her to the realities of the present.

"I'm starving," she said.

He laughed. "Wanna order some carryout and eat in bed? If you're in the mood for Chinese, Greek or Italian, I know of several places on State Street that deliver."

She considered this. Maybe her fantasies of being far away were still too fresh in her mind, though, or maybe she'd been cooped up in Door County for far too long, but she couldn't help shaking her head.

"Let's go out. I don't mind where we eat—you can choose. It can be McDonald's for all I care, but I want to hold your hand and wander around downtown and window shop and do whatever strikes our fancy. Okay?"

He kind of squinted at her, but he nodded his assent. "In that case, we'd better get dressed."

Bram watched Shannon nibble on her eggroll at The Imperial Mandarin. Her fingers played with the crispy shell, peeling off little bits to pop into her mouth at random intervals. Then, with her tongue, she swiped the duck sauce off her bottom lip in one swift, luscious movement designed only, he decided, to make him insane with lust. His appetite stilled as he fixated on this intricate and mesmerizing dance between her mouth, her tongue and her hands.

After two months of fantasizing about her during dull business meetings and in the shower every morning, his recollections of Shannon's laughter had soaked deep into his skin, and her scent had invaded his consciousness. Huh. And this was when he was a full day's car ride away from her.

Now, with her sitting in front of him at long last, driving him crazy with the intensity of her presence, he could hardly handle his chopsticks well enough to eat half his portion of ginger chicken and fried rice. No way did he want to hang around this place for dessert when the tastiest treat of all would be to thoroughly devour her back at The Lakehouse. They could grab the check and a couple of fortune cookies to go.

Shannon, however, had other ideas.

"Excuse me," she said brightly to their waitress. "We're in town for only a few days. Are there any special events going on this weekend that we should know about?"

"Oh, yeah," the waitress said. "Madison will keep you on your toes. I'm not sure who's playing tonight, but there's almost always a concert at the Civic Center. I know they're showing a few indie films on campus. And someone's lecturing on travel at one of the UW conference halls."

The waitress held up her index finger in a wait-just-one-second gesture and then racewalked across the room. She returned with a folded newspaper and a handful of flyers that she thrust into Shannon's hands, a grin covering her freckled face. "There are tons of things listed in here. Check 'em out and keep whichever pages you want. You guys'll find something really great, I'm sure."

"Thanks so much," Shannon said, already flipping through the newspaper, her blue eyes glued to the seemingly endless event listings like a kid perusing Santa's toy catalog.

Once the waitress left, Shannon turned to Bram. "We're going to have a blast tonight! What are you up for? A Best of Blues concert at The House of R&B? Jazz guitarist Mickey Stern playing live at the Civic Center? Karaoke and half-priced ales at Lindsey's Pub? A chance to view—"

Karaoke? God protect him.

"—long-anticipated works from the photography collection by artist Karen Jamison? Or the travelogue series Trekking in Tibet on campus at seven tonight?" She shot him an excited look that telegraphed high expectations.

"Well," he began.

She riffled through a few more flyers. "Oh, and look!" She flashed one of the pages at him. Neon yellow. It said something about a rock group making a big comeback. "Local favorites the Scarlet Warlocks are playing. AND—" She held up another page, turquoise with jaunty black type. "The Cannes Festival hopeful 'Love Is a Monkey Wrench' is being screened tonight at nine." She squinted at the small print. "Says it's subtitled in English with the original dialogue in Finnish. Wanna go?"

"Uh..." he managed.

"Or, wait, maybe we could see—"

He couldn't take much more of this. "Shannon?"

She glanced up at him from behind a fan of multicolored flyers. "Yeah?"

"I haven't seen you in person in two months. I—" How to put this gently? "I'm not sure I want to share you with the, um, Scarlet Warlocks tonight. Any chance we could just go back to our B&B? Relax a little? Maybe listen to some music—in bed— with the lights out?" He grinned at her.

For a split second the twinkle in her eyes dimmed and a decided frown crossed her lips. Not the reaction he was hoping for.

"Oh, sure." She refolded the newspaper and straightened the papers into a single tidy stack in front of her. She smiled carefully at him. A sweet smile, but it lacked the aura of excitement that'd been bursting from her just a minute ago.

Damn. He hadn't meant to kill that.

He reached across the table to caress her hands with his. "Or, maybe I just need the rest of the day to recover from my work week. What if we take tonight off but choose something on the wilder side for tomorrow?"

Her smile brightened a notch. "Great." She collected the papers in one smooth swoop and stood up. "I'll bring all of these along then."

"Okay." He eyed the stack of flyers. Yeah, really great. There was probably a "Limbo by the Lake Contest" in there somewhere, too. Or an equally riveting evening's entertainment, like "Slides of Regency Costumes: The Form and Function of Corsets."

He sighed. Well, at least he'd bought their freedom for that night.

They left the restaurant and strolled along State Street, a traffic-free zone, with the State Capitol building in view and the warm sun sinking slowly toward the horizon. Hand-in-hand, they edged near the university's bustling Memorial Union.

"They've filmed all kinds of movies here," Shannon informed him, rubbing her thumb against his knuckles and making his body heat rise. "I know they shot 'Back to School' with Rodney Dangerfield on this campus and, also, some of 'The Prince and Me' starring Julia Stiles." She paused. "The view from the Union's back terrace is especially pretty. I haven't been in town for a while, but I know it overlooks the lake. And you can buy really delicious ice cream inside the building and eat it on benches outside."

He leaned down and kissed the top of her head. Ice cream he could do. After all, he had to agree to *something* she suggested tonight. "Why don't we aim for that then? I could go for something chocolaty right now." And he'd bide his time until he could get her back to The Lakehouse and would be able to lick her instead.

At this invitation, she tugged him down the street and into the formidable brick Memorial Union, pausing only to laugh with delight at a family of Canadian geese waddling on the sidewalk in front of them. Some of that high energy and enthusiasm was returning to her and, if pressed, he'd have to admit a few beams of it were rubbing off on him.

They ordered enormous waffle cones loaded with triple scoops of tangy, freshly made Orange Custard Chocolate Chip ice cream (one of the Union's specialty flavors, it turned out) and carried them like burning torches through the dark "Rathskellar"—the UW's popular student café—and out onto the terrace.

The waters of picturesque Lake Mendota greeted them with winks of dappled sunlight, and Bram was overcome by the illusion that, if he could glide across the lake's shiny surface, he would be in the midst of a dazzling lightshow.

"This *is* pretty," he said, taking in the 180-degree view. He'd been to Madison for half a dozen business meetings, but he'd never bothered to sightsee here before.

Shannon nodded but soon skipped ahead, passed both him and the weathered tables, toward the stairs that led downward to the lakeside walkway. "C'mon," she said.

He trailed after her, swerving around a thicket of loitering youth engrossed in the quest for end-of-summer fun. Never had he felt so old. The swarming students reminded him for one unhappy heartbeat of his brothers and the way the three of them battled through their college years. For him especially, holding Grant and Alex up as role models, he'd spent most of his university experience alternating between driving workaholism to get his career off the ground and mindless partying to blow off the resultant steam.

Memorable years? Yes.

Enjoyable years? Well, not particularly.

He watched from the distance of a few yards as Shannon paused by a tall pole, a glorified billboard with posters of all sizes and hues tacked to it. A look of longing he couldn't miss graced her face. More bands advertising their concerts. More lectures. More art shows. More book discussion groups. More Open Mic invitations. No, thank you.

But when he cleared his throat to announce he'd caught up with her, she turned away from the activity postings and gazed up at him with a sad, half smile. Her tiny indication of defeat.

Yes, he'd won their battle of wills for the night but he felt, again, like an old man in the midst of youth's joviality. Did they give out senior-citizen discounts on this campus for grouchy thirty-one year olds?

"We'll do whatever you want tomorrow," he said, staring at her mouth as she licked the top of her ice cream cone into a custardy twist.

She nodded. "Oh, I know we will." Her tongue swiped another swirl of creaminess, and he had to bite back a groan. "Tomorrow's mine to plan."

And though he didn't say anything further on the subject, he couldn't help but wonder how the hell she could think that going to some lecture on Tibet would be preferable to returning to the B&B and doing something erotic with that luscious orange ice cream. Wasn't being alone with him an exciting enough activity?

From the way she darted along the walkway that evening and back up the steps and around the Union's terrace, perhaps not. And something in Bram's gut clenched tight at this thought.

Even without a formal event to attend, she kept scoping things out and moving like a sunfish in the water. She was acting like his ex-girlfriend Angie, for God's sake. Social. Insatiable. Relentlessly curious. He'd always appreciated Shannon's imagination and intelligence, but he hadn't guessed she'd have these other traits, too, and he'd be lying if he said they didn't worry him. Not that they were problems in and of themselves, but what did they mean in regards to their relationship? And his questions didn't end there.

Without an inn to run or any other occupying pursuits, did she find herself bored in his company already?

After over a hundred hours of late-night telephone conversations and nearly a thousand sexy e-mails, did this woman not know him at all?

And, worse, did he not know *her?*

In the impeccably furnished dining room at nine a.m. sharp, Shannon yanked on Bram's collar in an unsuccessful attempt to nudge him along.

Saturday morning!

They couldn't waste away this sunny day indoors, however lovely The Lakehouse B&B might be and however delicious the full English-style breakfast certainly was.

"Want another cup of coffee?" Bram asked her as he refilled his mug.

She grimaced at him. "You're purposely dragging your feet." She crossed her arms. "Drink up your coffee and let's go already! I want to walk around the Capitol. Henrietta said they're having a farmer's market this morning."

"Hmm. Well, we'll rush right over to it in a few minutes, but I need to get a little caffeine in my system first." He leaned close, so their hostess in the other room couldn't hear, and he whispered, "You wore me out last night, sweetheart. I need to replenish my energies."

She rolled her eyes. Yes, the man was energetic enough in bed—and, okay, delightfully so—but out of bed he'd turned into a real slacker. You'd think she'd asked him to compete in the Ironman or something for all the resistance he put up whenever she suggested going to a little event, like a watercolor showing or a piano concert. What was his problem anyway?

Then it hit her.

He'd already been everywhere, seen everything.

No wonder the guy looked so bored.

Sure, art was very nice in Madison, but it must be positively spectacular in Rome. Mozart might still be nifty when played on a street corner in Wisconsin, but maybe it was just a tad more lyrical when performed by a professional Austrian orchestra at a concert hall in Salzburg.

She sighed. She'd just have to handpick a bunch of activities that would be as novel an experience for him as they would be for her. From her handbag, she pulled a few of the flyers their waitress last night had given her. When were the

Scarlet Warlocks playing again?

Henrietta slid into the room. "Hey, loves, before I put away any of the goodies, do either of you want another pecan muffin? A slice of carrot cake?" She temptingly held out a tray with both delicacies in front of them.

Bram raised an eyebrow, and Shannon saw his hand begin to rise to reach for another muffin, which would've been his third.

She clasped his hovering hand and brought it down on her lap. "No, thank you, Henrietta. After the eggs, sausages, tomato slices and all the delicious bakery items you'd prepared for us, neither of us could eat another bite." She squeezed Bram's fingers and shot him a hard look. "Right?"

He winced. "Right. But thank you," he added, sending Henrietta a genuine smile. "You've got me looking forward to tomorrow's breakfast already."

Henrietta laughed. "Ah, the way you two go on. Glad you enjoyed it." The older woman swiveled back toward the kitchen. "Have fun out on the town today," she called over her shoulder. "And if you get back after midnight, don't be shy about using the key in the hanging azalea pot to let yourselves in. That's what it's there for."

"Thanks," Shannon and Bram chorused.

Then Shannon looked at him. "Well, you heard what the lady said. It's high time for us to go out on the town. No more delay tactics."

She kissed his chin, remembering their passionate night together and how he'd rubbed that same strong chin against the backs of her knees. And against other places on her body as well. The recollection made her face flush hot.

He grinned as if he knew exactly what she'd been thinking, and then he held both his wrists out to her, palm side up. "Lead me away, my sweet. Try to be gentle."

She couldn't help but laugh. "I will, and don't worry. We're going to do lots and lots of interesting things today. Stuff you've never done before."

He shot her a worried look that he tried to cover up with a

neutral glance a second later.

"It'll be exciting," she said, trying to reassure him. "We'll have so much fun together, I promise."

Twelve hours later, Shannon was prepared to eat every syllable of that hasty promise.

They didn't have fun together, not really. Oh, on the surface Bram seemed attentive enough to her—and he valiantly put up with the farmer's market, a half hour of browsing at a New Age bookstore, the photography show, lunch at a Mongolian Barbeque (which he readily admitted he'd never tried before), dessert at an amazing Eastern European bakery, a hair-raising reptile exhibit at the Vilas Zoo and an introduction to Argentinean sweater weaving on campus. But the harder she worked to find an activity that would please and surprise him, the more tense he got. And his reaction to the Scarlet Warlocks mystified her.

Here were a group of musical artists that had won the hearts of the town. Sure, they looked a little beat-up and grungy (what band didn't these days?), but they possessed a lively, invigorating sound that wasn't derivative. They chatted it up with the crowd in a funny, personable manner. They wrote catchy melodies to accompany intelligent lyrics. What wasn't to love?

Shannon caught Bram checking his watch for the eleventh time since the band began their second set.

"Tired?" she asked him as the dynamic, student-filled crowd clapped and cheered around them.

"Nope." He shrugged. "Well, maybe a little."

"Let's go then," she said, taking a step toward the exit. "We've done a lot today."

He pulled her back. "Nah, I'm fine. I know you really wanted to see these guys." The look that crossed his face was almost sad, and it confused her. "Let's at least stay until the end of this set," he said.

So, they stayed. But the whole time, she got the distinct impression that Bram would have rather been just about anywhere else. Here they were, finally together in a city where neither of them had any pressing responsibilities and, yet, they couldn't seem to do anything mutually enjoyable together unless it took place in the Marquette Room's comfy bed. What woman wouldn't worry about a pattern like this?

In a veil of post-concert silence, they arrived back at their B&B—long before midnight, too. No special flowerpot key was necessary, which made Shannon feel irrationally depressed. There was so much to see and experience, they shouldn't have gotten back until after three a.m. at least.

When they'd trudged upstairs, Bram rubbed his eyes. "We've both got hours of driving to do tomorrow, so we should probably get a good night's rest."

Her jaw dropped. "Of-of course," she said. He didn't even want to sleep with her now? Oh, God, what had happened between them this weekend?

He gave her a slight smile and pulled her into his arms with a fierceness that surprised her. "Sleep tight, Shannon." He then disappeared into the bathroom to brush his teeth. Soon afterward, he was beneath the covers and breathing deeply. Eyes closed. His body facing away from hers.

Shannon washed up and slipped into bed herself. Questions about her relationship with Bram assaulted her from every angle, and they wouldn't let her slide peacefully into her dreams.

Who was this man sleeping beside her?

Would he ever understand her point of view, or vice versa?

What did each of them want from being a part of this couple, and why?

It wasn't until sometime around two-thirty, when shafts of moonlight angled into the room through the slats in the blinds and Shannon could no longer spin the same worries around in her head, that Bram turned and reached for her.

Though his eyes remained closed at first, he pulled her body against his, wrapped his arms around her waist and whispered her name again and again along the side of her neck. He kissed her until passion's fire consumed them.

When, finally, they faced each other and stared deep into one another's eyes, it was as if an unspoken agreement had been forged between them and the inky-black night. If any fretful questions remained, Shannon knew they'd both chosen to disregard them.

At least until morning.

~CHAPTER SEVEN~

Columbus Day

"**D**id the birthday girl get my present?" Bram asked Shannon, long distance, of course, on October seventh.

"It's absolutely lovely," she said over a line so clear she might have been only across the courtyard. But she wasn't.

Despite his original plans to return to Holiday Quinn for Columbus Day, he'd been called away to Italy on business. Venice this time, but the city's romantic beauty was killing him this morning.

He stared out his hotel window overlooking San Marco's Square, his gaze swinging toward the incomparable Grand Canal. Everywhere he looked, couples walked hand-in-hand through the bird-filled piazza or sat together in the distinctive black gondolas, which swept them off on an amorous ride. Venice was a city for pigeons and lovers.

Today, unfortunately, he was neither.

"I thought you might be able to wear it with that stunning cream-colored gown of yours, the one that has the golden straps," he said, recalling the dress she'd dazzled him with on the night of the Valentine's dance. "Every beautiful woman should have a Murano necklace to wear at least once a year."

She chuckled. "Oh, I think I'll have it on a lot more often

than that. The beads are gorgeous. I can't believe someone can make something this delicate out of glass and gold." She paused. "Bram, thank you. It was the best gift."

"You're welcome. Wish I could've been able to give it to you in person."

And he did. Ever since their September weekend getaway had ended on such an unsettling note, he'd craved an opportunity to be with her again—and at a place where they had a history of everything going well.

Holiday Quinn.

"I know," she said, her voice wistful. "Me, too. But work is work, and at least yours takes you somewhere exotic." She sighed. "I have almost two hundred guests coming this weekend, all of them expecting 'The Voyage of Discovery' that the Holiday Quinn brochure promises for Columbus Day, and I'm nowhere near ready."

"Going to have little boat races with folded-paper Ninas, Pintas and Santa Marias?"

A laugh erupted from her on the other end of the line. "Yes, in fact. How did you guess? Of course, this'll be for the Age Twelve and Under set, but still." After a moment's silence, she added, "When *might* you be able to come back?"

He heard the question beyond the question in her voice. He sensed she was really asking not merely *when* he was coming back but to what degree did he *want* to return.

In the weeks since Labor Day, their phone conversations, while sounding aloud almost as they had during the summer, now held an edge of carefulness. Maybe both of them had been out of their element when they were together in Madison. Maybe that accounted for this subtle discomfort between them...and her new questions within questions for him. Maybe that explained why, though he wanted her with a desire unmatched by what he'd ever experienced with another woman, he felt he needed to be a little more perceptive when it came to her reactions now, a little less certain of her responses.

All in all, these unfamiliar anxieties drained him and he wanted to put an end to them.

"I'll be there in a couple of weeks," he told her. "For sure. For Halloween."

"Good, we've got a fun weekend planned. Oh, and don't forget your costume."

"You're making the guests go trick-or-treating?"

She laughed. "No. But we *are* having a Masquerade Ball on Saturday night in honor of all ghouls, ghosts and goblins. And there'll be candy for everyone."

"Sounds great." He hesitated, not sure if he should tell her yet what he'd decided to do in December. But he wasn't a man accustomed to being intimidated into silence, weird vibe between them or not. "Shannon, I told my secretary that I was taking off the whole week between Christmas and New Year's. I know you do a lot of special holiday events then, and I was hoping to make a reservation for them all."

Quiet—loud and clear—met his ears.

Then, finally, "That's…that's wonderful, Bram," she said, her tone a combination of surprised, excited and (did he read this right?) worried. "I can't imagine better news."

"Then it's settled. Book me for the full week in the Astaire Suite, and you can fill me in on all the details when I see you on Halloween."

"Okay," she said, but Bram still couldn't identify the multiple nuances of emotion in her voice. If any doubts beset her about their relationship, well, he'd just have to root them out one question mark at a time.

Because, despite their different ways of spending a weekend away from home, he had only one real burning question to ask her: Had she fallen in love with him the way he had for her?

On Halloween, he intended to find out.

Shannon set down the receiver and tapped out a pattern on the back of the phone with her fingernails.

Who *was* Bram Hartwick?

An international business mogul? A passionate lover? An unlikely homebody? She couldn't pin an easy label on him. She only knew he had more sides than a decahedron, and she'd never been too fond of geometry.

She touched the delicate yet stunningly beautiful glass beads encircling her neck. This birthday token of Bram's showcased his generosity and his terrific taste in jewelry, but a ribbon of envy wrapped itself around her throat as well, making it difficult for her to swallow.

She, too, wanted to watch as the talented artisans crafted these hand-blown beads right in front of her eyes. Despite adoring the necklace Bram had selected for her, she, too, wanted to walk into a Venetian jewelry shop and be assailed by row upon row of choices. Then, after picking her favorite, she, too, wanted to stroll alongside the canals and over the quaint, centuries-old bridges, letting the wind ruffle her hair. And later, when her fingertips would brush against her new necklace, she would be reminded of that specific, joyful memory. A memory she'd played an active part in creating.

Whenever she touched that necklace now, it reminded her of Bram's thoughtfulness on this, her twenty-seventh birthday, but it also slammed home just how much of the world she had yet to see. How much she'd never experienced, despite inching ever closer to the dreaded age of thirty.

She *so* didn't want to get to thirty years old having never really lived.

Bram brought sophisticated excitement and a dash of international exoticness with him every time they were together, but waiting around for him to bring adventure to her doorstep wasn't how she'd fantasized getting it.

No, indeed.

She caressed a golden bead with her index finger then tapped a lonely rhythm on the swirled glass. With a sense of determination and restless soles inside her white sneakers, she skipped downstairs to see what it would take to put some serious change into motion.

For over two hours she'd been staring at the financial spreadsheets on the computer in her office and going over her accounts—page by page—before Jake swept in, a cavalier look on his face.

"The New World is finally fit for your presence, My Queen." He bowed deeply and twirled an imaginary mustache. Then he grinned. "Seriously, Shannon, you've gotta see the ballroom. Those florist guys finally finished with it, and it's beginning to look positively Amazon-like."

"Well, who could resist, then?" She frowned at her computer screen and stood up. "I could use a break from these accounts anyway."

Jake squinted at her. "What'cha doing with them? Tax time is months away."

"I know but—" Could she tell Jake where her thoughts were leading? If she did, how would he react? She took a deep breath. "But I'm not sure how long I want to run Holiday Quinn," she admitted. "I was just checking to see how marketable the inn might be."

His eyes widened. "Whoa. Big step."

She nodded.

"What would you want to do instead?" he asked, taking several strides toward her.

"There's the big mystery, Jake. I have no idea." She paused and pointed at her necklace. "Did you know that Venice is known for its expert glass blowers?"

He shook his head.

"And that there's a special jewelry process made famous there called *mille fiori*, which means 'a thousand flowers' in Italian, and it involves lots of tiny strands of colorful glass?"

He shook his head again.

"And that there are hundreds of bridges in the city, and when you ride on a gondola, you're supposed to kiss the person you love whenever you pass underneath one?"

He gave her a tender look. "No, I didn't know that either.

Sounds like you want to go there someday."

"I do." There, and just about everywhere else. "Oh, and I read once that some of the world's prettiest pearls are found on Majorca, an island just off the eastern coast of Spain."

"Are you looking for a good strand of pearls, Shannon?"

"No, but if I were, I'd want to go to Majorca." She puffed out some air. "And, speaking of Spain, I really think that's the best place to learn flamenco dancing."

Jake raised an eyebrow. "That's on your agenda for the coming year?"

"Maybe. I might love it or I might hate it, but I won't have any idea until I try it. And the closest I've ever come to it is watching some special on PBS a few years ago."

"Hmm," he said. "That's not the same."

"No."

He shot a speculative glance her way. "You know, I've always wanted to watch a live bull fight. I took two years of high-school Spanish and all I can say now is *Yo sera el matador,* 'I am a matador.'"

She couldn't help but chuckle. "Useful."

"Very. So, I was thinking of maybe doing a European tour sometime and hitting the highlights of the continent, including Spain, of course. You know, that way I could pick up other important Spanish phrases like 'Where is Barcelona's best dry cleaners?' or 'I have no idea how to read this menu, can you help me track down and strangle my freshman-year language teacher?' Stuff like that."

She laughed aloud this time, and he grinned at her.

"Wanderlust hitting you pretty hard?"

She nodded. "This place is really wonderful, but I don't think I can handle being here forever."

"Me either, babe," he agreed.

"Being up in Door County?" a third voice asked.

Both Shannon and Jake swiveled toward to door to see Margaret Ashland's smiling face.

"Hi, Margaret. What's going on?" Shannon said, hoping to change the subject.

"Oh, I'm just dropping off a few extra pastries for my favorite competition."

All of them laughed. It was clear to everyone in the small Wisconsin peninsula that, however popular Holiday Quinn might be, it was no competition for the multimillion-dollar enterprise that was The Ashland Hotel chain.

"Thanks for thinking of us, Margaret," Jake said. "Until the guests start arriving this weekend, I'm living on tuna sandwiches and nachos." He glanced at Shannon. "Which reminds me, I should probably spend some time in Paris learning how to cook while I'm at it."

Margaret walked further into the room. "While you're at what, Jake? From the sound of your conversation when I arrived, I got the impression you two were planning on doing some traveling. Am I right?"

"I hope so. Actually, I've been kind of saving up for some backpacking through Europe, but I didn't know until today that Shannon was chomping at the bit as much as me." He smiled one of his sauciest grins. "Hey, what do you know about the art of flamenco dancing, Margaret?"

Shannon elbowed Jake and rolled her eyes. "What he means is that we were fantasizing about all the fun things we could try if we ever traveled to Europe." She glanced down at her wool sweater, white sneakers and faded jeans. Her attire had a long, long way to go before it would be appropriate for any kind of highly specialized Spanish dancing. "But all of that is still in the idea stage."

The older woman smiled. "Yeah, I could see Shannon with a pair of castanets, couldn't you, Jake?"

"Absolutely. And in one of those ruffled pink and black outfits with the tights and the pointy shoes." He crossed his arms and scanned her from head to toe. "And don't the dancers wear feathers in their hair or something?"

Shannon had put up with enough teasing. "Out of here," she commanded to Jake. "Go inspect the New World, the boat miniatures and the pastries, will you?"

"Do I have to do it in that order?" Jake said, sliding just far enough outside of her grasp that she couldn't swat him.

"Out!"

"I'm out, I'm out. Bye, Margaret," he yelled from a safe distance in the hall.

"Bye, Jake," Margaret called back, then she turned to Shannon. "He's a good friend of yours, isn't he?"

"Yeah."

"So, why not go to Europe with him?"

"With *Jake?!*" She laughed. "Well, for starters, it's because he'll have *mademoiselles* and *frauleins* and *senoritas* trailing him everywhere, and I'd be so busy wading through his admirers that I wouldn't get in any sightseeing."

"Hmm. I don't know about that. I think that boy really likes you."

Shannon shrugged this off. "I don't. Besides, it's a moot point. I'm with Bram now, and Jake can go to Europe, Africa, Antarctica or wherever he chooses. I can't go anywhere until I figure out what to do with the inn."

"Sell it," Margaret said. "Sell it to someone who can handle it skillfully or, better yet, sell it to me."

Shannon looked into her mentor's warm eyes for a hint of some ulterior motive. As usual, she couldn't detect a single one, and she felt a flush of embarrassment for even thinking she might.

"Thanks, Margaret. You're so kind to offer, but I know you don't need to take on another venture when you've got so many huge hotels to run."

"Look, sweetie, I know you think I'm just a cute old lady with a fondness for rich foods." She patted her substantial belly. "That happens to be true, but I'm also an astute business woman. Holiday Quinn is a darling place, but I've grown rather attached to its owner." She beamed a warm look at Shannon. "I'll do what I need to do to entice you into higher management at my hotel chain. Good help is hard to find," she winked, "and you'll find me a benevolent and always delightful dictator."

Shannon laughed. "I have no doubt of that. And, again, thanks. I'll keep thinking about your offer." Although she couldn't forget how big-business-minded Margaret was and how the woman could turn a sleeper lodge into a bustling tourist spot almost overnight.

If Shannon did find a buyer for Holiday Quinn, she'd have to seek out someone who'd preserve the integrity of the inn the way her family had envisioned it. Someplace small. Someplace quaint. Someplace only open on holidays.

"You do that, honeybunch. What's holding you back, though?"

"Questions, I guess. I don't know where I'm going or what I should do next. But I'm sure the right set of circumstances will align soon, and then I'll have a better idea of the direction I need to head."

The older woman gave her a considering look. "This Bram that you keep mentioning—should I meet him? Is this becoming a serious thing?"

Shannon felt her face heat up. "I—I'm not actually sure. He's one of my big questions. We're from two different worlds, Bram and I. I'm me, and he's very sophisticated and experienced and—"

"Oooh, I see." The grin on Margaret's face broadened. "He's the body lotion guy, right? The one that lives in the Twin Cities?"

Shannon nodded.

"There's an Ashland Hotel in Minneapolis, you know," Margaret hinted. "Something you should, perhaps, consider, in light of the circumstances."

"The circumstances?"

"Your impending engagement. Surely, the man will come to his senses soon, stop jetting around the world and propose to you like he should."

Shannon gulped. "Well, I don't know if that's where he's—" She scored her fingers through her tangled mass of hair, trying to come up with a way to explain to her friend the real state of her relationship with Bram when she wasn't even sure of it herself. "I mean, I'm not sure he even wants to—"

But Margaret's imagination had gotten caught up in the

fairy tale she'd spun like cotton candy in her mind, and she didn't seem interested in being given a reality check.

"You could hold the reception in The Ashland's Grand Ballroom," Margaret suggested, "or even here at Holiday Quinn, if you'd like. Regardless, Ricardo will prepare a sumptuous feast of filet mignon, fit for a Celtic princess such as yourself, and you'll dance the night away in a gown of flowing white satin, your man by your side. Oh, you parents would be so proud." She dabbed at a tear in the corner of her eye.

She wasn't done yet. "Then, after your month-long honeymoon to all the romantic hotspots in Europe and Asia, you'll both return to the Twin Cities where you'll take over management of my hotel up there. Perfect!"

"Hmm," Shannon said.

"What? You don't like the filet idea, darling? Never mind. Ricardo's grilled salmon is excellent or, if you'd rather go the poultry route, you know he makes a phenomenal chicken marsala."

"I'm not worried about the dinner menu, Margaret. It's all the stuff that precedes the wedding and reception that has me wondering. Like whether or not Bram actually wants me to be the bride."

"Nonsense, of course he does!"

Shannon laughed. "You've never met the guy. How would you know?"

"Because I've met the girl," Margaret said simply. "How could he resist you?"

Oh, so very easily, Shannon wanted to reply, but she didn't. Her strong, capable mentor wouldn't understand the kinds of fears she had to battle. Like, despite their fireworks in bed, how would a guy like Bram keep himself from getting bored with her?

Would he want to show her all the places and things in the world she longed to see, even though he must have seen them all a dozen times before?

Would he be willing to share the ins and outs of his business empire with her, or would he act as if she couldn't be trusted to understand the details?

And, after the initial honeymoon period wore off, would he stop working so much overtime so he could spend most of his evenings and weekends with her, or would she soon become just another one of his business acquisitions?

"We're not even close to that stage yet," Shannon said to Margaret. "Besides, I have a lot of exploring yet to do. If I do sell the inn, I want to see some of the world, but Bram's plans could very well be quite different from mine." She sighed, remembering their frustrating weekend in Madison and their inability to do anything outside of the B&B together without tension.

"Fair enough, my young friend. As I've advised before, just keep your options open. And never forget that you have a job waiting for you in any city where you can find an Ashland Hotel, okay?"

"Okay." She hugged the wonderful lady who'd been her support, her guidance, her family, and she wished she could pledge employee loyalty to Margaret for life. But the truth was starting to dawn on her that, no matter how attached she was to her longtime friend, and despite her growing feelings toward Bram, doing the same things she'd always done but in a new city might not be the adventure she'd been seeking.

What would be?

Before she and Margaret made the trek to the ballroom to take a look at its transformation into "The New World," the older lady posed one more question. "Do you know what you'd find about a four-hour train ride south of Madrid?"

Shannon shook her head.

"Seville. A city known for its flamenco dancing." Margaret winked at her. "With Jake or with Bram—or without either— you ought to go there, sweetie. Take a chance...and dance a little."

~CHAPTER EIGHT~

Halloween

Shannon rose up another step on the ladder, her hands filled with the creepy remains of her old pal "Skeleton Sam." Where to hang him up this year?

She considered the window in front of her. To the left? To the right? She stepped a bit higher on the ladder and held him from his bony, plastic arms in a number of unflattering positions.

Hmmm. No.

From the ceiling, maybe?

She looped her index finger through the thin rope at the top of Sam's skull and let him dangle precariously, his emaciated body swaying as if in eternal limbo.

Yeah, she knew how he felt. If she didn't get somewhere outside of these four walls soon and take a few serious strides in a new direction, she'd probably lose all her skin, muscle and sense of initiative, too. Frustration could do that to a person.

She reached into her pocket for the screw-in hook, attached Sam to the ceiling and felt an irrational pang of guilt for committing him to a weekend of suspended misery.

"Was he misbehaving?" an all-too-familiar voice asked.

She swiveled around on the ladder step, nearly losing her

balance. "Bram! I didn't hear you drive up."

"Too busy entertaining another man, I see." He grinned and strode toward her. "If he weren't in such bad shape, I'd have to fight him for you. But, apparently, you've already punished the poor guy for his misdeeds."

God, she'd missed her hotshot businessman. She jumped off the ladder and, a second later, he caught her in his arms, encircling her with tenderness. He was all warm skin, taut muscle, hot breath—nothing bony about him.

Well, okay. That wasn't strictly true. Something decidedly solid and unyielding pressed hard against her, alerting her to Bram's intentions, not that she was unwilling to comply. The delectable kiss that followed was a happy premonition of the erotic evening to come.

And amen to that. It'd been far too long since the last time. If only *everything* about their relationship were as simple, as straightforward and as satisfying as their sexual life.

She eyed his designer garment bag draped over his monogrammed duffle near the doorway. "So, what costume did you bring for the Masquerade Ball tomorrow night?"

He lifted a corner of his lips. "Not telling, sweetheart. You'll just have to wait and see."

"What? No hints?"

"Nope. Just deal with the mystery." He paused as the mini grin morphed into one far more devious. "But don't worry. You'll end up in the right bed after the party. I guarantee it."

She kissed him again, feeling the swirl of adventure that naturally surrounded him as it spiraled to encompass her, too. He brought that effortless sense of the unknown to every one of their interactions and, while it still made her pulse race with the sheer novelty of it, she couldn't deny the thrill that this quality of his brought to her every time either.

"I'll hold you to that," she said. "But don't think you're the only one who can pull off a surprise, Bram. I expect to keep you on your toes this weekend, too."

And she did. If all went well, she hoped to tell him about her plans to leave Door County soon and to begin challenging herself with experiences away from here. Surely, he'd be excited by a change like that. He'd appreciate her decision to broaden her staid, conventional world. Her interest in taking on a life that was a little more like his stimulating and sophisticated one.

"Promises, promises," he said, as if disbelieving her ability to ever astonish someone as confident, suave and hard-to-ruffle as he.

Well, maybe she couldn't compete with him on an adventure-seeking level, but she was so very ready for something new. She could face significant change, and she *would*.

She winked at him. "All I'm saying, Bram, is be prepared for anything. Surprising a surpriser can be very exciting."

The look that crossed his face was intrigued but, if she weren't mistaken, there was a flash of apprehension, too. This was the first time since they met that she felt she might just have the upper hand in something.

Interesting.

Maybe Bram Hartwick was no longer as stony-faced or as inscrutable as he'd once seemed.

They were nibbling on a late-night fruit platter in the Astaire Suite—post-coital, pre-dawn—when Shannon decided to drop her first hint.

"You know, I'm thinking of taking some time off to visit Milwaukee. *The Phantom of the Opera* is going to be performed there soon," she informed him. "I can't remember which theater, but the show is set to run for several weeks, and I've always wanted to see it."

He gave her a blank look.

"Don't you like musicals?" she asked.

"They're okay." He snagged a couple of red grapes, popped one in his mouth and rubbed the other against her bottom lip until she opened to receive it.

"Mmm, thanks," she said, chewing. "But Andrew Lloyd Webber's songs are amazing. Wouldn't it be fun to see one of his best shows performed live onstage?"

He shrugged. "Depends. Is it a community theater production or a touring Broadway show?"

She had no idea and said so, then added, "Does it matter?"

He laughed briefly. "Well, yeah, Shannon. There are good and bad actors everywhere, but usually the Broadway standards are higher and more exacting than your average community theater ones. The voices in a Broadway cast are exceptionally well trained and can handle the dramatic musical range necessary to pull off a score like Webber and Hart's. Sure, you can find loads of young talent in any city across America, but aspiring actors and singers flock to New York City for a reason, especially if they're serious about their craft. As the saying goes, 'If I can make it there...'"

"'I can make it anywhere,'" she finished for him.

Having always had to work, either to help her parents out at the inn or to manage things at Margaret's hotel, she'd rarely gotten away for a weekend. She'd only seen a handful of musicals at her nearby college and, one memorable Christmas, *The Nutcracker* with her mom in Milwaukee. She'd enjoyed each show tremendously, but maybe they weren't as good as she'd thought. Maybe she didn't know the difference.

"So, you'd recommend seeing only a Broadway production?" she asked him.

"If you want to count on it being excellent, yes, a touring Broadway show brought in to Milwaukee or Chicago would be a strong bet. Although, you couldn't go wrong with a West End performance either—but they tend not to tour around here."

"West End?" She'd heard that term before. Where was that? Los Angeles? San Francisco?

"London's theater district," he clarified. "That's where I saw *Phantom* the first time. The cast was phenomenal."

She raised her eyebrows. He saw *Phantom* in London? The *first* time? Meaning: One of many times. God, she was so far out of her cultural league here it was frightening.

539

"I guess that would be especially great. I suppose I should try to go there sometime, huh?" she told him, reaching for a strawberry and ripping off the green stem and leaves.

Heck, she'd have to go to the top source on *everything* now just to converse with him. Forget about small-town art shows, if it wasn't the Louvre in Paris, it didn't count. Why bother with any old dance performance if it couldn't be the Bolshoi Ballet or a troupe of real flamenco dancers in Seville?

She bit into the strawberry and watched as Bram grinned at her. "Hey, why don't I take a look at what's playing in London and New York," he suggested. "Maybe we can steal away for a long weekend after the holidays and catch a few shows. I can show you around a bit, too."

She nodded but had a hard time swallowing the fruit. His indulgent smile was like that of a world-weary parent looking down at an impressionable child. Just because she hadn't had the opportunity to have these cultural experiences didn't mean that she was a dumb kid incapable of learning about life on her own. She just needed a little time to catch up.

He leaned back against his pillow and speared a melon chunk with a long toothpick. "Ahh, so peaceful here," he whispered, almost to himself. "I think I could stay in this relaxing place forever."

Boy, not her.

But she didn't tell him that, let alone mention the possibility of selling the inn, because something vague and unsettling had grown clearer: He might *like* her, a whole lot even, but it was Holiday Quinn that he *loved*.

She cringed thinking about it. Yes, he kept coming back here but not so much because he wanted to see her. Instead, it was because of this place she ran. This quiet environment he'd grown so attached to was a haven of sorts for him. When they were together in Madison, but away from the inn, it hadn't been the same, had it? Now, unfortunately, she knew why.

She decided to test out her theory. "Well, there's no rush to get away," she told him. "It's nice to spend time together right here."

"Exactly," he said with a contented sigh, kissing her on the nose then slinking down further into his pillow and closing his eyes. "Nothing's better than this."

Precisely what she was afraid of.

As Bram drifted off into dreamland, she put the fruit platter back in the kitchenette's refrigerator and snuck out of the suite, certain she was equally unnecessary to him now that he'd fallen asleep.

And the pain she felt at that realization shocked her by being almost as strong, almost as powerful as the death of a loved one. She tiptoed back to her own room to grieve the loss.

Bram adjusted his mask in the hallway mirror and let his long, black cape swirl behind him as he descended the staircase toward the ballroom.

He'd arrived at the inn with all the accoutrements to transform himself into a fearsome Count Dracula but, after Shannon's professed interest in *The Phantom of the Opera* last night, he'd managed to make some slight alterations.

Discarding the vampire teeth he'd brought along, he'd escaped this morning to one of the party shops in the next town over and procured a white, half-faced mask à la Phantom style to complete this newest incarnation of his costume. He hoped Shannon would be pleasantly surprised by the result.

He ran his fingers across the top of his heavily gelled hair to make sure it was still slicked back, as it should be. He spotted a werewolf, a lady villain in black bodysuit (Catwoman?), a Queen Elizabeth look-alike and some unfortunate guy with the ears and complexion of Spock, but none of them resembled Shannon, whatever her choice of costume.

Would she be dressed as a princess? An historical figure? A sexy librarian, maybe?

He allowed himself a slight smile at the thought. Or, perhaps, she really was a burgeoning theater aficionado and dressed up as a stage character. If her interest in musicals was more than just a passing fancy, he would look forward to taking her to a major production someday. Hell, he could fly in a halfway decent cast to perform for her in Holiday Quinn's ballroom if she so desired.

Anything to make her happy.

But, what if this weren't enough? What if this latest cultural interest wasn't really about spending time with him but more about getting away from here? From several of the remarks she'd been making recently, he'd begun to worry this might well be the case.

Last night she was fascinated with seeing musicals in some other city. But that hadn't been all.

In one of her e-mails at the beginning of the month, she'd written about wanting to learn the art of Tuscan cooking. In Italy.

Then she'd made a handful of comments on the subject of wildlife photography and asked him nearly fifty questions about African safaris and how someone might go about studying this. As if he, Former Crowned King of the Workaholics Guild, would know anything about the pursuit of such a hobby.

Then, on the phone last week, she came out with some craziness about flamenco dancers in Seville. Why would she suddenly want to go to Spain to start dancing? It was just plain bizarre.

As he strode into the ballroom and scanned the crowd of early revelers for his auburn-haired lady, a thought crossed his mind that stole his breath: What if she was saying these things only because of *him?* What if she thought these were the types of activities that he, as a big businessman with global interests, would want to participate in?

He felt the corners of his lips tilt upward another notch. He'd just have to reassure her yet again that this wasn't the case. That there was nowhere he'd rather be than with her in her beautiful inn. Maybe then she'd relax a little about this whole sophistication thing. God knew, she was intelligent and adorable just the way she was.

And he was falling in love with her and with the possibility of sharing a life together right here in the Midwest.

Yep. That was the honest-to-heaven truth. Just like Bill Murray's character in the movie *Groundhog's Day*, he was coming to realize that he didn't have to "get ahead" anymore. He could live in a small, unassuming town like this and fly out to the Twin Cities for business a day or two each week. On the other days he could work via phone and Internet. The idea mesmerized him with its appeal, and Shannon was bound to love it, too.

Wasn't she?

Bram convinced himself that, yes, she sure was.

Then he spotted her. Finally. A vision in wisps of blue tulle that matched her eyes. A silver fairy wand in her hand. Long, elegant wings fluttering behind her as she walked across the floor. Petite ballet slippers on her feet.

And Jake the Prick by her side.

Bram clenched his jaw and increased his pace.

Jake, dressed appropriately as a court jester, raised a brow at him when he approached the two. "Well, well, Tinkerbell," Jake muttered to Shannon, though loud enough for Bram to overhear. "The Phantom is crashing our Masquerade Ball. How original."

The Prick's sarcasm wasn't lost on Bram.

Shannon's eyes widened as she took in his Phantom costume. "I'm impressed," she whispered, but he'd had to read faces at international business meetings for too many years to be fooled. He got the distinct sense that some other, less enchanted reaction lay behind her words. He tried to dismiss the thought as paranoia, but he couldn't.

"I hoped you'd like it," he told her anyway, ignoring Jake but not quite able to block him out of his consciousness. The assistant edged his way closer to Shannon. To retaliate, Bram reached for her hand and tugged her toward him. "You look beautiful, Tinkerbell."

A small grin played along the curve of her lips. "Thanks."

Bram saw Jake grimace, tap her shoulder and motion her close to him again. She took a step in Jake's direction, and The

Prick pulled her the rest of the way.

"We still need to decide when to announce the winners," Jake said. He shook his head so the bells on the pointed ends of his jester's hat jingled. The guy looked bloody ridiculous but, for some reason, Shannon laughed at his antics.

Bram hadn't thought it possible, but he now hated Jake even more.

"There'll be prizes for Best Costume tonight," Shannon explained to Bram, "in the categories of Scariest, Cutest and Most Authentic."

He nodded and made a show of glancing around the room. "Well, you've got a lot good outfits to choose from. Who'll be doing the judging?"

"The Bakers." She pointed to the older couple he remembered from the Easter Egg Hunt back in the spring, and he was flooded with memories of the desire that had come to a head between him and Shannon that day.

He looked her in the eye as best he could, given the constraints of his mask, and projected his most smoldering gaze her way. He wasn't sure why it felt so necessary tonight, but he needed to remind her of the passion they'd shared. And, yes, on an admittedly primitive level, to remind her that she was *his* woman. Not Jake's.

Jake, of course, refused to take the hint and just bug off the way a second-place loser-man should. Instead, he draped his arm—*his arm!*—around Shannon, leaned in close, as if making a pretense of discretion, and said, "Shall we say ten o'clock?" He looked beyond where Bram was standing and nodded in the Bakers' direction. "That should give them plenty of time to make their final selections."

"Okay," Shannon said to her assistant. "Why don't you let them know and—"

"Oh, hey," Jake replied, too quickly. "We should go talk to them together. They'll probably have questions for you about the prizes or the—"

"Can't handle it on your own, Jake?" Bram interrupted, forcing a grin and a light laugh. Shannon might put up with

Jake's obnoxious and overtly needy behavior, but Bram couldn't take another nanosecond of it. Enough crap.

Shannon shot him a dark look before turning her attention to her assistant. "Go ahead and let the Bakers know, Jake, but tell them I'll find them in twenty minutes or so, just in case any questions arise."

Jake pulled his arm away from her shoulder but let his fingertips trickle along the edge of the blue tulle for a moment too long. The guy was contemptible. "Okay, babe," he said with that damned smirk. Then he pivoted on the heel of one of his pointy jester shoes and strode away.

The second Jake was out of earshot, Shannon faced him, one hand on her hip, the other grasping her fairy wand so tight her knuckles were pale. "What are you trying to do, Bram? Jake's a friend of mine and my employee. Your rudeness toward him is inexcusable."

"My *rudeness!*" Fury burned his lungs. "Jesus, Shannon, the jerk was practically feeling you up right in front of me. How do you expect me to react?"

She rolled her eyes. "Oh, he was *not*, and what I *expect* is for you to act like a man who's confident in my affections, not like an insecure teenage boy." She tightened her lips and glanced away.

Bram took a step back. Literally. And his jaw actually dropped. An insecure teenage boy? *Him?* What the hell...

"That's what you think of me?" he managed to say.

"You know, Bram, I don't know what to think. You come here acting all eager to see me, but maybe it's the *place*, not me, that you're excited about. Then you mock me with your costume and get all possessive and Neanderthal in front of my assistant. I've got to say, I wonder if I'm a person you actually *like* or just one you want to *acquire*."

He was rendered so speechless by this that, not only did zero words leave his mouth for a full minute, but they didn't even form in his brain. The only thing he was aware of was an absolutely disturbing pairing of emotions—anger laced with hurt—and the certainty that she was wrong. *Wrong.* He shook his head but couldn't seem to communicate any of this to her.

She crossed her arms and glared at him, eyeing his costume with an expression of suspicion and fury. What had she said? That she thought he was *mocking* her with it? She couldn't have been more off target. He'd thought it would please her.

"You're wrong," he whispered.

She raised her eyebrows. "I'm wrong? That's all you have to say about this?"

"Yes."

She threw her hands in the air, swiveled on her slipped toes and rocketed down the hall, out of the ballroom and into some "Employees Only" area. Away from him.

He left, too.

It took Bram almost an hour of sitting on the edge of his bed and mindlessly staring into space before he got his temper in check and recovered the use of his complete vocabulary again.

By the time he finally returned to the party, the Masquerade Ball was in full swing. The "Monster Mash" blared from the speakers as a collection of shirtless handymen with tool belts, naughty nurses and the usual variety of witches and ghouls danced around him.

He heard Shannon before he saw her.

"There are so many places I want to visit," she said enthusiastically to somebody nearby. "London. Venice. Seville. Zurich. And those are just the ones in Europe."

"Don't forget romantic cities like Paris and Rome," Jake the Jester Prick replied in a silky, seductive tone that made Bram want to slug him.

But he held himself back. He did not march over to them. Did not punch the not-remotely-humorous jester in the jaw. Did not tell Shannon what he really thought about her colleague.

He knew how to play corporate games better than this. She'd already defended Jake once that night and made the jerk seem like some kind of victim. Bram wouldn't give her an excuse to do it again. Still, having to witness another man putting the moves on her stung.

He got himself a large glass of some dark reddish concoction from the refreshments table labeled "Potent Potions" and proceeded to drink two of them. He identified vodka and tequila as a couple of ingredients in the mix, but decided he needed a third glass to figure out the rest. He'd just poured it when Shannon came up beside him.

"I could probably use one of those, too," she said.

He handed her a glass. "It's good." He didn't know what else to add. Maybe he hadn't gotten as much of his vocabulary back as he'd thought.

She took it from him, drank about half of it, then studied him carefully and sighed.

"Bram," she said, touching his forearm and making his heart almost stop from the desire to hold her. "I was angry, but I shouldn't have yelled at you, and I shouldn't have run away from you like that. I'm sorry."

He felt a surge of hopefulness and nodded, silently accepting her apology, even though he hadn't understood her outburst earlier. "Your fiery Irish temper got the best of you, huh?"

She half smiled. "Something like that."

"I wasn't trying to 'acquire' you, Shannon. And I wasn't 'mocking' you with my costume. I thought you'd like it, but I guess I should've stuck with my original idea—Dracula."

She smiled the rest of the way. "Really? You have vampire teeth back in your room?"

"In the garbage can, but yes." He paused. "I don't need them to bite your neck, though."

At this, she chuckled. To Bram's ears, it was like hearing the Vienna Symphony Orchestra playing Mozart.

She nudged him with her elbow. "Let's go up there. You can show me."

He didn't need to be asked twice. He hustled her out of the ballroom before she could change her mind and, when they got to his suite, he hastily removed every stitch of her flowing costume...from the blue tulle dress to the delicate wings to the soft ballet slippers.

She responded by hurriedly tugging off his mask, untying his cape—which dropped to the floor with a swish of fabric—and pulling off his black shirt, black slacks and pumpkin-orange boxers until he was standing bare in front of her.

His cock rose to meet her, trying oh so hard to bury itself within her.

But Shannon insisted on playing with him first, running her fingertips up and down his shaft, kissing his chest with her lips—still cool and red from the spiked "potion"—and making these breathy, moaning sounds every time he touched her breasts, her ass, her legs.

Bram just couldn't take it anymore. He lifted her off the floor long enough to half lay/half toss her onto the middle of the king-sized bed. Then he sank into her at the same time as he bit the tender area of skin on the left side of her throat, alternating rocking deep within her and sucking hard on her neck until he finally got the Halloween scream he'd been waiting to hear from her lips.

The next morning brought a harsh ray of sunlight, invading the room through a window blind he'd stupidly neglected to close all the way.

Shannon stirred beside him. "I should go downstairs soon," she said, her voice sexy and low with the huskiness of sleep.

"Why? Can't Jake be responsible for another hour or two?"

Bram knew he shouldn't bring up the name of that other guy but, dammit, couldn't The Prick do something useful for a change? Anything besides playing tug-o-war with him over Shannon's attention?

She exhaled heavily. "I left the party early to be with *you*," she reminded him. "I need to make it up to Jake today."

He all but growled at the thought of Shannon owing Jake *anything*, but he was proud of himself for dropping the subject. Instead, he tried to distract her. He ran his fingers down her back, holding her in place and reaching for the new body lotion he'd set on the bedside table. "Apricocious."

"Mmm. Smells like apricots and cream," she murmured, as the scent of the lotion filled the air. "It's making me hungry."

He warmed up a dollop of it in his hands and began massaging her shoulder blades, then her lower back, then the firm rounded cheeks of her delectable bottom. They'd had two rounds of flaming-hot sex during the night but, already, he wanted her again.

"It would be perfect if I could spend all day making you feel hungry. Right here in this room. So cozy, so relaxing, so far away from everything stressful," he mused.

She shifted, moving a tad closer to him, and laughed lightly. "Not for me. It would be *more* perfect if we were on the Côte d'Azur or the Amalfi Coast. Somewhere so much more interesting and exotic than...Wisconsin."

He tried to explain that she wasn't appreciating enough of the beauty of her own home state. "I've been to both of those other places, Shannon. They're really pretty, sure, but not as special as you make them seem. The coastal view out this window is gorgeous, too. You've got this perfect location right here in Door County. You don't have to travel the world to find it."

He hoped he was getting across to her that she didn't need to change a single thing about her life or her experiences to impress him. But, instead of snuggling even closer to him so he could continue her backrub, she abruptly pulled away. She all but leaped out of bed and started gathering up her clothes.

What did he do wrong now?

"That's, perhaps, easier for you to say because you've already done it." Her words came out in a chilly, clipped tone. "I'd like it if, for a change, someone didn't try to tell me what I should want or not want. What I should try or not try."

She slipped on her blue Tinkerbell dress and shot an accusing glare at him. "You've got this image of me stuck here at Holiday Quinn—a little domestic haven tailor-made for you to retreat to from the real world—but you don't seem to be as interested in being around me when we're away from here."

She crossed her arms, clutching her fairy wings to her chest. "I was right last night, wasn't I? It's this *place* you're excited about and attracted to...not *me*."

Again, he was rendered nearly speechless, and all he could think in response was to murmur, "Of course I like this place, but it wouldn't be the same without you."

"So, if I weren't here, you wouldn't ever come back?"

He blinked. "But you *are* here. This is your inn, Shannon. Aside from being gone for a vacation or something, where else would you be?"

She huffed out some air, glanced at the clock and said, "Look, I have to go, and we're not getting anywhere with this conversation. Have a good day, Bram." Then she strode out the door, slamming it behind her.

WTF? He just didn't get it.

He picked up the ballet slippers that Shannon had forgotten at the edge of the carpet and wondered if this was a not-so-subtle hint that she was rejecting the Cinderella-story ending he'd been hoping for.

Though he hadn't wanted to admit it, he'd secretly been daydreaming about Prince Charming's version of that particular fairy tale—where the guy and the girl get together, settle down and live happily ever after in the castle. Or, in this case, at their holiday cabin in the heart of the forest with occasional forays into the big city.

What wasn't to love about that? Why the hell was she being so stubborn? So unwilling to fall in with his beautiful, well-constructed plans? Granted, he hadn't actually verbalized any of these plans to her yet...but still.

He tossed his belongings into his bag, marched down to the front desk and put the slippers on the counter with a thud.

"I'm checking out," he informed Jake, the surprised but always on the verge of sneering employee, who had to have been wondering why Bram would depart several hours early.

"Okay," the assistant began. "Did you want to—"

"You have my credit card information on file," Bram said, cutting him off. "Just charge everything to that, and kindly see that Shannon gets her slippers." He stepped away from the desk. "Thanks," he added dismissively over his shoulder.

He didn't give The Prick a chance to respond and, though he wouldn't have blamed the guy for gloating a little, he didn't look back at Jake to read his expression, so he didn't know for sure.

Bram did, however, make it to his car in record time. He slid into the driver's seat and started speeding westward.

Hasta la vista, Holiday Quinn.

~CHAPTER NINE~

Thanksgiving

A month later, Bram was still ticked. He and Shannon hadn't been in contact even once since Halloween.

No impromptu visits.

No sexy phone calls.

No flirtatious e-mails or text messages.

He'd tried one night to get ahold of her, but he'd only reached her voicemail. Then, not that he'd admit this to any living soul, he'd chickened out and hung up because he had no idea what to say.

He did, however, get both a smail-mail postcard and an automated text alert notifying him of the Holiday Quinn Thanksgiving Weekend festivities. There would be a Turkey Trot Dance-Off, a Pumpkin Pie Eating Contest, a Corn Husk Doll Making Demonstration and some kind of Traditional Feast of Gratitude.

Bram wasn't feeling especially grateful.

He tossed the postcard in the trash and deleted the text, but he kept hoping—perhaps a bit irrationally—that Shannon would call him personally to talk about the upcoming inn events. And, while she was at it, she'd tell him what the hell was going on with her and explain why she'd mistakenly thought he was the bad guy in all of this. If she said she was sorry or reached out to him at all, even in some small way, he knew he'd forgive her in an instant.

But he wasn't going to be the one to fold first. In his not so humble opinion, he didn't have anything to apologize for anyway.

So, instead of driving to Wisconsin to see Shannon or celebrating the national holiday with his too-busy-as-always brothers, he accepted a dinner invitation from his favorite married couple, the Wainwrights. Gina and Trevor were both Midwestern transplants—she from the South and he from the West Coast—and they were hosting a big Thanksgiving "friends who are like family" gathering at their house.

"There'll be a few interesting ladies there," Gina informed him with a spirited laugh. "I think you'll have fun."

Bram assured her that he would, particularly since he'd be there as one of only a couple of bachelors.

He'd been downplaying his holiday visits to see Shannon, so the Wainwrights didn't know the depth of his hurt. Still, Trevor eyed Bram with sympathy when he arrived alone at the house.

"Ah, thanks for the fine wine," his buddy said, taking the bottle of white that Bram offered him. "A Viognier, I see. Delicious."

"I hope you and Gina will enjoy it." Bram glanced at the small clusters of people around the dining room table, standing in the foyer and sitting on the living room sofa. A collection of strays if Bram ever saw one, but a well-dressed and—from the sound of the conversation—a very articulate collection.

"Please make yourself at home," Trevor said. "There are munchies on the table and I can make you whatever drink you'd like. Or," he pointed toward the table, "there are glasses of warm spiced cider to combat the November chill."

"I'll start with that," Bram said, thanking his friend, and he strode over to where the cider was being served. Steam rose from each of the stoneware mugs.

A leggy blonde in a pink mini, who introduced herself as

Candy-somebody, handed him one of the mugs when he approached the table.

"Thank you," he said, appreciating not only the kind gesture but, also, her flirtatious smile. And the simple fact that someone who was hot, sweet and—best of all—available seemed excited to see him.

"You live in the area?" Candy asked, indicating with a lift of her fair, carefully tweezed eyebrow that she hoped this was the case.

"Yes," he replied, and then he asked a few questions about her.

How did she know the Wainwrights? *Gina and I went to college together.*

What was her profession? *A copyright lawyer in the Twin Cities.*

Did she have any pets? *Yes, a pair of parakeets named Romeo and Juliet.*

He laughed. She was charming and delightful, and he and Candy chatted at length and joked with ease.

Even so. Even though she wasn't hard to spend time with, Bram knew his heart wasn't in it. That fiery spark he'd seen in Shannon, the one that had attracted him to her from the moment they'd met, appearing in a way that was both unexpected and undeniable...that wasn't what he felt as he talked with Candy and the other single ladies at the dinner party.

He could recognize them as being pretty (in some cases, even beautiful), but none of them were *compelling*. None would hold his interest for longer than an evening or two.

After about three hours of small talk, Bram managed to detach himself from Candy so he could hide out in the dense shadows of the den. He just needed a few minutes away from the group to sit alone in silence, sip his bourbon and attempt to rub away an impending headache with his fingertips against his temples.

He suddenly spotted Gina lugging two heavy bags of trash and a box filled with various papers and wrappings down the hall to the garage.

Bram leaped up to assist her and said, only half joking, "Why isn't Trevor helping you or doing this for you?"

Gina grinned. "Oh, he *would* if I asked him, but when I saw that the trash bin was overflowing, he was in the middle of a conversation with his friend Liam. The two of them have been so busy with work lately that they rarely have a chance to really talk. I just didn't want to interrupt them."

Ah, that was sweet, Bram thought.

Not twenty minutes later, he walked through the kitchen to find Trevor simultaneously soaking a pot and scouring away a wine stain on the counter. Gina brought in a few more items and said, "You've dealt with so many of the dishes already, honey. I can wash up this batch—"

"Nope," her husband told her. "I've got this one, too. You go ahead and grab yourself a piece of pumpkin pie. I know you haven't had any yet." He pecked a kiss on her nose and shooed her away. "That lady works too damn hard," he told Bram with a smile.

But, although Bram didn't say anything about it, he couldn't help but recognize how thoughtful Gina and Trevor were with regards to each other. How unselfishly they both behaved. It was, Bram realized, exactly what a loving couple *should* do—both sides always keeping in mind the little ways they could help the other. Gifts of time and effort that made their spouse's life a bit easier.

And he found himself thinking about Shannon again (honestly, when had he ever stopped?) and wondering what *she* was really feeling these days. Had he actually considered her point of view? She wasn't a company he could "merger" or—as she put it—someone he could "acquire." She was a complicated woman. One who, maybe, hadn't expressed herself on this issue as well as she should have.

Still, if he were to be just like his happily married friends, shouldn't he be working harder to see the world through her lens? To give her whatever it was that *she* needed, more than what he alone knew he wanted?

Bram got the uncomfortable feeling that, perhaps, he hadn't been doing nearly enough of that.

Shannon found herself swamped with work once the Thanksgiving weekend was underway. But, when she was able to slip out for a few hours, she spent it by going no further than The Ashland Hotel to have a quick holiday luncheon with Margaret.

Her mentor was her usual lively self.

"So, when was the last time you saw that handsome Minnesota businessman of yours, hmm?" Margaret asked around a mouthful of Ricardo's famed cranberry and pecan stuffing. "Is he coming in for the weekend?"

Shannon shook her head. She'd managed to avoid spilling her guts to Margaret in the weeks since Halloween, but she realized that she could really use some wisdom and advice. She found herself trying to explain what it was that had frustrated her so much about Bram's comments last month. His quick dismissal of her travel dreams. His inability to be comfortable with their relationship anywhere outside of Holiday Quinn. His insistence that she stay in the tiny box in which he'd placed her.

Her older friend listened intently before speaking. "Shannon, there are many things I regret about your parents dying so young. Not only do I miss them as friends and neighbors, but I'm aware of how much responsibility their being gone has put on you."

Margaret reached across the table and clasped Shannon's hands in her own. "The thing is, you've handled it well, but it came at a heavy cost. I think you know the time is now to take stock of your life and where it's going. Time to look at the patterns you have in place and decide which you want to keep and which you'd prefer to change. Any man who might have a chance at being part of your world long term needs to be let in on these decisions. Much as you may wish he were psychic, you can't necessarily expect him to know what you want and what you feel without telling him."

Shannon nodded. What Margaret was saying had the deep ring of truth to it. Looking back, perhaps she had been expecting Bram to understand too much. To be able to perceptively see what she'd hoped for and dreamed of without ever spelling it out for him.

And, in truth, there had been a number of plans and ideas she'd barely acknowledged to herself. Hopes for the future that she hadn't dared to say aloud for fear they wouldn't work out...or, perhaps, for fear they *would*.

Back at Holiday Quinn that evening, Shannon found herself looking at her current life with the sentimentality of someone about to leave it. The regulars who visited the inn—like the Bakers—and the staff that worked all the major events— especially Jake—had become her surrogate family. She truly cared about them.

And she cared very much about Margaret, too. A woman who understood—in a way Shannon suspected a parent might—that, at some point, most kids needed to leave the nest in order to grow up.

If they later chose to come back, they'd know then exactly why they were returning.

On Sunday morning, as the final guests were checking out and preparing to drive to their respective homes, Shannon came to a decision. One that, on some deeply subconscious level, she knew had been made for months. Its execution, however, was going to depend on others.

"Keith? Darlene?" she said to the Bakers when they walked through the lobby with their luggage, including the massive stuffed animal (a turkey, of course) that they'd won in the Turkey Trot Dance-Off. Shannon grinned at them. "Do you have a few minutes to talk?"

"Sure, dearie!" Darlene said.

Her husband nodded. "With you? Anytime."

"Good," she replied, motioning them into her office. "Because I have a business proposition for you both, and I'm hoping my idea might appeal to you."

~CHAPTER TEN~

Christmas

Shannon stared at the blinking cursor of her computer screen and at the still unwritten message she'd been trying to compose—with a stunning lack of success—for the past hour. She'd gotten as far as:

Dear Bram,

How are you?

Then she ran out of ideas.

It was, however, two weeks before Christmas and, much as she would love to see him again and not ever have another argument with him, they still hadn't recovered from their Halloween standoff. A month and a half of avoidance on both their parts was hardly healthy relationship behavior.

Although, he *had* tried to contact her once...

She'd seen his number come up as a missed call on her phone back in mid-November. And she'd waited and waited, hoping he'd call back or send her some other kind of message.

But he hadn't.

Then it was Thanksgiving and, ever since, she'd been working sixty-hour weeks between her regular job at The Ashland Hotel and the transitioning she'd been doing to prepare for the official sale of Holiday Quinn, which would be coming up a few weeks into the New Year.

All these moments of busy insanity hadn't stopped her from *thinking* about Bram, though. A lot. But the longer they didn't talk, the more awkward it felt to try to strike up a conversation out of nowhere. Even if that conversation was one-sided and electronic.

I hope everything has been going well for you.

I've miss you so much—

No, no, no, no!

She deleted that last line.

I've been thinking about you and had wondered if you were still planning to visit Holiday Quinn during the Christmas/New Year's Celebration Week. You'd made the reservation several months ago, but...

Shannon paused.

...but you walked out of the inn without a word and, since then, we've both been too stubborn to reach out or to apologize.

Definitely no.

Not that this wasn't the truth, but it just wasn't something that should be said via e-mail.

...but I would understand if your holiday plans have changed.

Please let me know when you have a moment. I look forward to hearing from you soon.

With best wishes,

Shannon

She took a deep breath and clicked SEND.

Then she rested her arms on her desk and flopped her head down on top of them. One measly e-mail and she was as exhausted as if she'd just run a marathon.

Jake, who was at the inn helping to pull the Christmas decoration boxes out of storage, strolled by her office, glanced once in her direction and laughed. "You look like you're ready for a long winter's nap, Mrs. Claus. Need a cup of coffee?"

Shannon raised her head up just far enough to shake it. "I need more than a cup," she admitted. "A vat of peppermint-mocha lattés topped with whipped cream and red-and-green sprinkles would, actually, be perfect. Can you tell Santa to bring me that?"

He grinned. "Only if you're good." He pulled out a folded sheet of paper from his back pocket and tossed the colorful pamphlet on her desk. "Spain," he said simply. "Think about it."

Then he disappeared down the hall, whistling "Here Comes Santa Claus" as he went.

She groaned.

Jake certainly knew how to entice her. Almost every day in the two weeks since the Bakers had enthusiastically agreed to buy Holiday Quinn (with Margaret Ashland as their adviser, when needed), Jake had been plying Shannon with travel brochures—all featuring alluring places around the globe. He'd already tempted her with seductive, exotic locales in the Caribbean, South America and a number of Pacific islands, and he was now working his way through the wonders of Europe and Asia.

She flipped open the information on Spain. The sunny image of the gorgeous Costa del Sol stood in marked contrast to the snowy image outside her window. She wrapped her arms around herself—hoping the cable-knit sweater she wore would ward off some of the Arctic-like chill in the air around her—and she daydreamed about strolling along the lush, vibrant, nearly subtropical beaches of southern Spain. Mmm.

The phone jarred her out of her fantasy, and she reached for it reflexively, without checking the Caller ID first.

"Holiday Quinn," she said.

"Shannon?" a male voice she hadn't heard in six weeks said. The mere rumble of him saying that single word—her name—registered deep in her abdomen, and she realized just how much she'd missed him.

"Bram." It came out soft and breathy, but she didn't care. She felt lucky to be able to speak at all.

"I got your e-mail," he said.

"Oh, yes. Of course." She slowly exhaled. Ah. That was why he was calling. She steeled herself for his next comments, certain a cancellation was coming...and then, she knew, she'd never see or hear from him again.

"I've missed you," he said. "I'm sorry it took me so long to tell you that."

And she just melted into a puddle.

She apologized, too, for not reaching out to him sooner and confessed to having missed him a great deal. "I think we need to talk," she said, feeling the elation of hope for the first time in a long time. "In person."

He agreed and said he'd called to ask her to keep his weeklong reservation. He'd blocked out the vacation time back in early-October and fully intended to use it.

"I'd really like for us to discuss what, exactly, happened on Halloween, Shannon. To see if we can move forward from there."

"Okay," she whispered. Then she made herself add, "There have been some changes since you were last here."

The pause on the line was interminable.

"With you? Your relationships?" he asked finally. "Is there...somebody else now?"

"No!" she said quickly. "It's nothing like that." But she found she couldn't bring herself to tell him about the impending sale of the inn over the phone. It seemed too impersonal a method for someone like Bram. Someone who'd grown so attached to the place.

Fortunately, he didn't seem to require any further explanations. "Oh, good," he said, relief in his voice. And he left it at that.

Shannon knew in that moment that he hadn't gotten himself a new significant other in the interim either, and she was surprised by the power of her gratitude for that small blessing. No doubt, he would have had the opportunity, especially in a populous area like Minneapolis/St. Paul or on one of his many business trips to Milan or Tokyo or wherever.

Instead, they talked about the weather for a few minutes, determining that it was equally cold in both Minnesota and Wisconsin—hardly news for December in the Midwest—but that was the kind of easy chitchat Shannon needed after their earlier, heart-pounding conversation. Then, before they hung up, they settled on the plan to spend as much of the upcoming holiday week as possible together.

She was sweating, she noticed, as she took her hand off the receiver and saw the wetness left behind on the phone. And she had to completely pull off her sweater for a few minutes and walk around the office in just the t-shirt she'd worn underneath until she could lower her body temperature to a range closer to normal again.

All signs—physical and emotional—pointed toward one scary realization: She was far more invested in her relationship with Bram than she'd ever wanted to acknowledge and, soon, the fate of their future would be determined.

She couldn't help but hope that everything would magically work out, of course. Wasn't that what angels and Christmas miracles were for?

But she had an uncomfortable foreboding sensation that lingered deep within her and carved out little pockets of worry in her gut. She couldn't help but fear she'd been right from the very beginning on two important points:

One, that Bram's interest in her was tied to Holiday Quinn and would fade quickly without her continued connection to this place.

And, two, that she and Bram might share a steamy romance for a few seasons but, ultimately, they were too different to be destined to stay together for long.

Bram pulled into the Holiday Quinn parking lot at 6:47 p.m. Christmas Eve, turned off the car engine and opened the driver's side door, taking several fortifying breaths of the wintry air.

The scent of snow mingling with pine grounded him in the moment. And the flashing holiday lights, which surrounded the inn with color and brightened up the dark December sky, reminded him that it was, in fact, supposed to be a time of celebration.

He'd been on the road much of the day, driving with a feeling of nervous anticipation usually reserved only for big corporate takeovers or long sit-down conversations with his father. Since it had been several years since he'd experienced either, the tense edginess that had been lurking inside of him all day could only mean one thing: Shannon.

He wasn't a man prone to doubting himself or second guessing his decisions, but he'd been mentally running scenarios for hours about how it would go seeing her again after nearly two months apart. Would they fall right back into the patterns they'd begun when they first met…or had that only been an illusion? How well did they know each other *really?* And was he a fool to care so much about what she thought of him? Or to imagine that they had a shot at a life together?

Bram didn't know the answers to any of these questions, but he was determined to find out once and for all.

He stepped out of the car, grabbed his bag and, with determined strides, marched toward the front entrance.

It was like the movie set of *Holiday Inn* come to life. When he walked inside, it seemed as though they'd imported the soundstage for the film and transplanted it to eastern Wisconsin.

Guests milled around the lobby like cast members, dressed in cozy winter garments and sipping cups of cocoa with candy canes as stirring sticks.

Snowflake clings adorned every window and the soft sounds of "White Christmas," complete with jingling bells, played in the background along with the hum and chatter of the happy couples.

There was a hint of peppermint in the air (from the candy canes, no doubt) melding with the scent of pine from the large Christmas tree in the corner. A beautifully decorated blue spruce, lavishly trimmed with tiny white lights and silver and gold ornaments.

Bram saw an angel in white atop the tree, exquisite with her gossamer wings, a fur-lined cloak and glinting silver sequins, but he knew the *real* angel was dressed in a red sweater and standing behind the counter, checking in the guests.

"Ah. Hartwick, you've returned," Jake the Prick said coldly.

The chill from behind him made Bram shiver as he turned to stare down the guy. He gave his best attempt at a Machiavellian scowl. "Yes," he said slowly. "Yes, I have."

There was something different about the assistant this time, though, Bram realized as Jake stared back. He couldn't quite pinpoint what it was, but he felt a definite undercurrent of change behind Jake's expression. Almost as though the assistant knew something that he felt gave him an advantage. Jake looked bolder as a result.

The mask is fully off. The jester has gone into fighting mode.

Bram intensified his glare at the other man and watched as Jake's green eyes twinkled with a brighter light of cunning than he had ever seen.

One side of The Prick's mouth quirked upward. Then, as if laughing at an inside joke that Bram wasn't in on, the assistant said, "Hope you'll enjoy your *final* stay." There was a significant pause. "Of the year."

Before Bram could respond, he heard his name. He looked up and saw Shannon waving to him from behind the counter. When he glanced back at Jake, he found that the other man had disappeared. Odd.

He walked up to Shannon. It'd been too long since he'd last seen her in person. Not that he'd forgotten anything, just that she was *more* vibrant, *more* alluring than even he had remembered. He had to tell his heart to slow down, force himself to take deeper breaths before he could speak.

"It's good to see you, Shannon," he managed. "Very good."

She didn't reply at all at first. She just smiled at him. That was enough.

Then, finally, she said, "It's good to see you, too." She fiddled with the computer for a moment before handing him his keycard. "The Astaire Suite is waiting for you."

He took the plastic card from her, caressing her hand in the process. He could see her pause. Hold her breath. Swallow a time or two. A line was beginning to form behind them. He knew he had her attention for only a moment more.

"When will you be free?" he asked in a low voice.

"Ten-thirty," she murmured. "The evening events should be over no later than that."

Bram picked up his few items and leaned across the counter until his head was only a few inches from hers. "Until then, Shannon."

Her heart pounded in double time as she knocked on the door to the Astaire Suite. Seeing Bram again, just a few hours ago, brought rushing back every single memory they'd shared since February.

Shannon was surprised by how many there were, despite the fact that they'd only gotten together in person on scattered holiday weekends. But it was amazing how fast you could get to know someone if you were motivated...

Or, at least, *think* you'd gotten to know someone.

Nervousness made her almost turn away, but Bram was quick to open the door. Too quick.

"Hi," he said, his voice deep and husky, his eyes trained on her face. His white dress shirt was unbuttoned all the way down the front, and his feet were bare below his black slacks.

"Hi," she whispered back.

He motioned her inside the room. "What have you got there?"

Lost in the intensity of his stare, she'd almost forgotten the basket she was carrying. It was a gift of sorts, being that tonight was Christmas Eve and all.

"A present for you," she replied, setting it down in a nearby corner. "For later."

One of his dark eyebrows rose to mid-forehead and a smile tugged his lips upward. He closed the door behind them and then nodded at the table closest to the bed, where a gift-wrapped package sat prettily in wait.

"Got one of those for you, too. Thought we'd save it until Christmas morning, though." He took a step toward her and pulled her into his arms with a smooth, proprietary movement. "Unless—well, unless you aren't planning to be here then." His voice held an unasked question.

She met his gaze and held it. "Bram, my plan was to stay with you tonight. Unless, of course, you'd rather—"

But he cut her off, blanketing her mouth with a kiss so passionate she felt its heat singe her toes.

Shannon wrapped her arms around him, underneath his open shirt so she could run her palms against his bare skin, and let herself be consumed by the flames of their reunion.

"That's all I needed to know," he said in her ear, a moment before he stripped off her red wool sweater and divested her of her bra, her skirt and her panties, too.

She, in turn, tugged off his dress shirt and got as far as unfastening his belt before his impatience got the better of him. He relieved her of that task, finishing it himself with a rapidity approaching the speed of light.

And before she could blink, he was on top of her. His bare chest against hers. His lean legs entangled with her own. Their lips and tongues connecting in a dance that merged their whole bodies together.

Shannon's breath caught when he entered her with a graceful but powerful thrust. It felt destined for them to be as one. Like the fit of two interlocking puzzles pieces. And, yet, it was unsettling, too. She had already lost all notion of where her flesh ended and his began. More than ever, it felt dangerous to have her boundaries disintegrate like this. To have no control in his presence. No tangible sense of self. He effortlessly rendered her immobile, dependent and fuzzy-brained from lust.

Well, no.

It had become more than lust.

There was admiration, affection, respect, friendship and other qualities present there as well. Maybe it was too soon to confess to being in love with the man, but what Shannon felt when she was around Bram was far more than mere infatuation.

As much as she was thrilled by their physical compatibility, it was that rare feeling of oneness and contentment that he brought out in her when she was in his arms that challenged her the most. It convinced her that, for the first time in her life, she may have actually found The One.

Unfortunately, it was at exactly the time when, more than anything, she needed to be independent and unencumbered.

It was sometime after midnight when Bram awoke, having just had, perhaps, the best make-up sex of his life, followed by the deepest post-coital nap. But he wasn't above doing it again a time or two before daybreak, just to make sure he'd really and truly reached a personal record.

One thing, though, kept nagging at him about the make-up sex—and it wasn't the sex part that was cause for concern. He and Shannon still hadn't spoken a word to each other about the Halloween blowup. It was this massive white elephant in the room, which might as well have been sitting on the loveseat like a gigantic Christmas present with a big red bow on its head.

The more Shannon avoided discussing the incident with him, the more worried about it he became. Not that he'd actually given her much of a chance to talk about anything that night.

"Hey," she said, flipping toward him and smiling sleepily. "You're up."

He nestled against her, letting his hard shaft nudge at the space between her legs. "You could say that."

She laughed. God, he loved that sound.

"You're insatiable, Mr. Hartwick," she murmured, but she didn't pull away. One of her hands snaked around his hips and began to trace patterns on his butt cheeks. He felt himself getting even harder.

He moaned, but another involuntary sound competed for

attention in their bed. The distinctive rumbled of his stomach. He hadn't eaten in hours.

"You're hungry," Shannon said, pulling back. "We should get you some food."

He tried to protest so he could keep her next to him. "Oh, no. You're plenty delicious, Miss Quinn." He sent her a wolfish grin and licked his lips. "I'll make a meal out of you."

She chuckled in return but, nevertheless, managed to escape his grasp. He watched as she slipped out of bed and padded naked across the room to the place she'd left her basket. Retrieving something from it, she returned, glanced at the clock and then offered him the wrapped object.

"Merry Christmas," she said.

He took the proffered gift. "Thank you."

Shannon motioned for him to open it. "It's part one of your present. The edible part."

He made quick work of ripping off the pretty gold paper and uncovered a sturdy cake box. When he opened the box, he found it contained a dense but delicious-looking confection. Familiar somehow, but in the dark he couldn't easily place it.

"It's from that Eastern European bakery we went to when we were in Madison," she explained. "I special ordered it for you. Maybe you've had something like it before, but I thought it was interesting. It's called *Cesnica*—the Serbian Christmas or 'Money' bread. There's a silver coin baked inside, and it's considered good luck to whoever finds it."

Bram unwrapped the bread, broke off a piece with his fingers and took a healthy bite, chewing carefully to make sure he didn't swallow a coin if he should happen to come across one. "Mmm," he murmured. "It's good."

Then he broke off a bite-sized piece for Shannon and trailed it along her lower lip until she opened up for him. The look of delight on her face as she chewed was too much for him. He had to do this again.

He fed her another bite and another. She finally responded by pushing him down on the bed and dropping soft bread morsels into his mouth as she kissed his face, his jaw, his neck.

Then he got the brilliant idea of scattering breadcrumbs on her chest and devouring them one at a time—"I'm Hansel, you're Gretel," he murmured, "and this is the breadcrumb trail in the deep, dark forest"—but she returned the favor with such devilish enthusiasm that it made him pant with a different kind of hunger.

Her clever tongue caught bits of bread on its way to licking his torso clean. But he wasn't done feasting on her yet, and it was he who finally found the lucky silver coin in a hunk of crumbled bread, somewhere in the region of her bellybutton.

He laid the coin on her heart. "I don't need a token to tell me I'm a lucky man, Shannon. I already know." Then he dipped his head to taste more of her—a part of her body that looked inviting enough for a banquet.

And so they played.

Bram thought if he could just keep her right here, in this very spot, he could make her happy forever. Was it too much to hope she'd want that, too?

Christmas morning was off to a rushed start as Bram watched Shannon hastily put on her clothes from the day before and smooth down her auburn hair with a grimace.

"The brunch begins in about an hour," she told him. "I have to run back to my room to shower and dress, but I hope we can spend some time talking later today."

"Hey, I'll be here relaxing all week long," he said with a contented grin, brushing away a few breadcrumbs still hiding between the sheets. "I'll look forward to having you to myself again soon, but I'm not sure if I'll make it down to the brunch. I'm still full from eating all of that Christmas bread."

She laughed and sat beside him for a moment at the edge of the bed. "There's another gift for you over there." She waved her palm toward the basket. "You can open it up this morning, if you'd like. Sorry I have to leave so soon."

"Don't worry about it. I know it's your job."

A look of sadness crossed her face that Bram didn't quite understand.

"I have something for you, too, before you go, and I'd really like to give it to you now," he added, reaching across the bed to the table on the other side. He plucked up the wrapped package and handed it to her.

She pulled off the paper to reveal a full Lathericious gift set—shower gel, refreshing body mist, luxurious hand lotion and scented soap.

He waited and watched as she read the name of the fragrance, her eyes widening. "Bram, it says—" She pointed to the label.

"Shannon's Gift," he supplied for her. "Yes, that's what it's called. It's our brand-new bath and body line, named specifically for someone I know..." *And love*, he almost added, but he stopped himself just in time.

Her eyes grew even bigger. "Oh, Bram! You mean this wasn't just a special label you put on these four items. That there's *more* of them? And other people can order them, too?"

He got out of bed, hunted down his briefcase and pulled out the December Lathericious catalog. The "Shannon's Gift" line was featured prominently on the cover. He handed it to her.

"I've been working on this for about six months, Shannon. And, yes, other people can order these specialized products. In fact, about 500,000 units shipped internationally just last week."

She looked stunned but impressed. He grinned as she squirted some of the body mist into the air and inhaled deeply, taking in the aromatic citrus-ginger scent that had been the special blend he'd requested.

"Mmm, thank you. I love it," she said.

"And I love *you*," he whispered. He hadn't meant to say the words aloud but, somehow, they slipped out anyway.

She stared at him with those huge blue eyes. Never had his heart been on pause like it was in that instant. He'd been in countless tense business situations—where one word would make the difference between sealing a multimillion-dollar deal or losing it—but this single silent moment was harder on his nerves than any of those had ever been.

Then he heard her voice.

"I love you, too," she murmured, but she looked more melancholy about it than thrilled.

Never mind. He could be happy for the both of them. He pulled her into his arms, kissed her passionately—his heart finally beating again—and said, "That's good news, right?"

She shot him a weak smile. "Right." Then, "I should really go—"

But he didn't want to let her go. Not now. Not yet.

"How about I open up your second present real quick? Then I'll let you leave me to my quiet room and my breadcrumbs," he joked. "There's still forty minutes before the brunch."

She nodded but eyed him apprehensively as he tore off the wrapping paper and unearthed a box beneath. The words "fragile" were written in big letters on each side of the box.

"I remember getting the edible gift last night, so I'm guessing this one is *not* edible, eh?" he asked with a laugh, opening up the top of the box and studying its contents with some puzzlement.

It was a vase. A very familiar-looking one.

He pulled it out in surprise and delight. It looked just like that beautiful, curvy, stained-glass vase that was in the inn's display cabinet downstairs. "You found another one," he exclaimed. "Did you have to go to an antique shop in New York to get this one, too?"

She shook her head. "It's not a different vase. It's the same one my parents bought. You said you thought it belonged elsewhere, in a private home. Maybe above the fireplace. Somewhere more personal than the hallway of an inn," she reminded him. "I loved your idea, and I wanted you to do that with this vase."

Bram didn't entirely understand. "But this is special to you. You can't just give it to me—"

"Of course I can," she said with a gentle smile. "What else could I give the man who has everything?" She paused. "Besides, I want it to have a good home. The Bakers are going to be putting other items in the display case soon, so the vase had to come out anyway."

He was getting more confused by the second. "The Bakers? Why are *they* decorating the case now?"

He saw Shannon take a shaky breath.

"They're the new owners of the inn, Bram." She squeezed his hand but, then, abruptly stepped back. "I sold Holiday Quinn to them. They're officially taking over by the end of next month—and I'm leaving."

The ground seemed to drop from beneath Bram's feet and the air whooshed out of his lungs. He opened his mouth to speak but was unable to utter a syllable.

Shannon was already standing by the door. "I need to go, but I'll be back. We'll talk later, okay?" she promised.

He thought he nodded at her, but he was in such shock that he couldn't be sure.

When she left, he carefully set the gorgeous, colorful vase back inside the safety of its box so it wouldn't break, but he didn't have any similar protective measures for his heart.

He could almost hear it shattering inside his chest.

~CHAPTER ELEVEN~

New Year's

The week that followed was a special kind of torture for Bram.

Despite the post-Christmas/pre-New Year's Eve festivities taking place at the inn and around the scenic Door County peninsula, he couldn't have felt less like celebrating.

He was losing her. Not to another man—although Jake was certainly putting up a persuasive fight—but to an *idea*. To her conviction that the grass was always greener somewhere else and that it was greenest of all halfway around the world.

Case in point, Bram walked into Shannon's office the day after Christmas only to find The Prick already there. From what Bram gathered, based on the gift bags and wrapping paper lying about, the two of them had exchanged presents. An intense jealousy shot through Bram's body, strong enough to almost paralyze him.

Cagey Jake didn't reveal what Shannon had given him (he stuffed whatever gift it was back into its bag the second he spotted Bram), but Bram did see what Jake gave her: a thick travel guidebook entitled "The Marvels of the Mediterranean." Shannon was flipping through it and staring at the images like a teen boy might look at a particularly descriptive page from the *Kama Sutra*.

Bram scowled. "Thinking of taking a trip?"

Shannon responded with a laugh. "Who wouldn't? Just look at these pictures of Mykonos." She pointed to several alluring shots of the famed Greek isle before oohing and ahhing over some resort town on the coast of Turkey.

Jake looked too smug for his own good. What did her jerk of an assistant even *know* about foreign travel? What a poser. If The Prick was involved, it would be more like "Mediterranean Misadventures" than *marvels* of any kind.

Jake didn't bother speaking to him. The assistant just gave him one of those smirky looks, edged with a sense of triumph. Then he said cryptically to Shannon, "Just think about what I said, okay?"

She glanced up from the book and nodded. They did some kind of eye-contact thing before The Prick finally strode out of the room.

Bram wanted to say, *What the hell was that about?* But he knew he didn't have the right. If Shannon wanted to explain, she would. He didn't want her claiming that he was jealous or didn't trust her.

Still, he couldn't stop himself from asking, "Is that where you're headed next? The Mediterranean?"

She'd told him the day before that she was leaving the inn. When they talked at length last night, she confessed that the only thing she knew for sure was that she was moving out of Wisconsin, but she still didn't know where in the big wide world she was going yet.

Bram's head had been spinning as she spoke, but he remembered her saying something about that Margaret Ashland woman, who was her boss and her friend, as well as the owner of a hotel chain that spanned the globe. And that, after Shannon had a chance to see some of her dream destinations, Margaret would give her a position at whichever Ashland Hotel she wanted. There was no reason why Shannon couldn't live anywhere in the world she damn well pleased.

Shannon closed the guidebook thoughtfully. "I don't know," she said, in answer to his question. "Maybe, I'll go there.

It's sure beautiful."

He nodded. He wouldn't deny it. And, man, he would've offered to take her there himself and show her the sites *the right way*, but then she'd probably think he was only doing it to show up Jake. Which, admittedly, would have been at least partly true.

Instead, he said, "Do you have time for that walk we were going to take?"

"I could slip away for a half hour or so. Let me just get my coat."

When they were outside—the late December chill ziplining through Bram's thick leather jacket and heading deep into his bones—he finally reached for her hand. His glove grasped her mitten and held tight. To him, this felt as intimate as anything they'd done while naked in the Astaire Suite. The two of them were connected. Bonded together. A unified front as they faced the winter wonderland.

For the longest time, they didn't speak.

"I owe you an apology for Halloween," she said, squeezing his fingers a bit tighter. "Because I was reacting to the things you were saying and doing as if you knew everything I'd been secretly thinking about and struggling against. And you didn't know. You couldn't have known. I realize that now."

He was afraid to speak, but he mumbled a barely audible, "Mm-hmm."

It was enough to get her to continue. "I spent a lot of time thinking about it, though, and I can see now that what happened was really simple—we both wanted to experience what we didn't have. You'd already traveled the world, so you craved being in a place that was calm and remote. Somewhere quaint and in the middle of nowhere, like Holiday Quinn, right?"

She smiled kindly at him and, somehow, he managed to nod. She was, in fact, one-hundred percent right. Holiday Quinn was like an oasis of peace from the normal chaos of his life.

"But, see, for me, Bram, quaint, calm and remote is all I've *ever* known. And I really want...really *need* something else right now. Some of those amazing foreign adventures you speak so casually about having experienced. The day has finally come when I have both the time and the money to be able to do a little of that."

"The grass is always greener, huh?" he murmured, saying aloud what he'd been thinking for the past twenty-four hours.

"Maybe," she replied. "But, for once, I'd like to go to a place with no grass at all. Just ancient stones. Or miles of concrete. Or tropical sand as far as the eye can see."

Her wistfulness made him smile in spite of the sense of loss he felt.

"Then you really *should* go." He paused. "But there's nothing wrong with having a home base. Shannon, I love you. And you said you loved me, too. Is there any reason we can't still see each other when you're back in the Midwest? You're not going to be away indefinitely, are you?"

"The thing is, I just don't know that. I care about you too much to want you to have to put your life or plans on hold for me. And, maybe, for you, being able to relax at the inn is what you *really* want. Think about it, Bram. You may have just connected those feelings of happiness and peacefulness to *me* because I was always here, but I know the Bakers will do a wonderful job continuing all of the traditions. And Margaret's going to help them. Even if I weren't here, there's a whole lot you might still love about Holiday Quinn and this little corner of the state."

She hesitated, as if mentally weighing her words, before she finally continued. "To be honest, I'm not sure how long we'd stay together in a different environment. How interesting I'd be to you on some average weekday when you're caught up in your job and your responsibilities back at home. Our time together has always been vacation time for you."

He took a steadying breath and, because he wanted to do her the honor of seriously considering her thoughts on the subject, he refrained from answering right away, although he desperately wanted to contradict her.

To himself, he acknowledged that, yes, he *did* love being with Shannon in the calm, carefree environment of Holiday

Quinn best of all.

But he could also imagine spending time with her elsewhere—like in Minneapolis. The mental image of the two of them living together day after day, and the thought of having her to come home to after the long hours at work, brought a sense of longing he couldn't deny.

Did *she* not feel similarly, though? Was she simply not ready for that yet? Perhaps that was the real problem.

"I don't think there's any way to know that until we try it, Shannon." Bram wasn't able to suppress a sigh that fought its way out of him. "But I respect your need to travel the world and see new things. I know that's important to you. If you get back someday and want to look me up..."

He didn't finish that sentence, though, because she had tears in her eyes, and he realized, whether she'd gotten at the heart of things or not, she was hurting and struggling. For him to argue with her or try to convince her to stay with him would only add to the turmoil of her emotions and the difficulty of her decision. So he backed off.

They parted soon after that, if only for the afternoon. Shannon went inside the inn to oversee some paper-snowflake-making competition or something, while Bram found himself unable to stop walking outside, despite the frigid temps.

He ambled down the lengthy drive and along several back roads—for how long, he wasn't sure—but he tried to imagine coming to Holiday Quinn without Shannon being there. It would still be a peaceful and beautiful getaway, sure, but would he *care*? Weren't there other quaint and quiet resorts a helluva lot closer to him?

Honestly, without Shannon greeting him at the inn when he came to Door County, or maybe sitting beside him in the car as he drove up to it, he knew he'd never come back. It would be too painful. She was *the reason* he made the trip. She might not ever believe that, but it was the truth.

As for spending time with her outside of their holidays at the inn, he sincerely didn't know what it'd be like. They'd only had that one weekend in Madison to base the experience on, and it hadn't been as smooth or as successful as he would have liked. But, if she wasn't willing to try something like that again, what could he do?

He wandered around in the wintry briskness for hours. But even though his arms swung freely by his sides as he trampled down the snow-covered streets, he couldn't help but feel as if his hands were firmly tied behind his back.

Shannon could tell that the news she'd shared with Bram was tough for him to take. To his credit, though, he was being extremely mature about it and was handling the changes better than she'd expected. She knew there was still tension between him and Jake—enough that she hadn't even considered telling him about Jake's "big idea" yet—but Bram didn't criticize her assistant. At least not to Shannon's face.

Oddly, though, the fight seemed to have drained out of him. He wasn't acting competitive or proprietary with her. He wasn't rushing to make any unrealistic promises or grand romantic gestures. Bram was just respecting her wishes and seeming to enjoy this last bit of time they had together before she left Holiday Quinn. Before the patterns of their relationship would inevitably be changed.

Which was what she'd wanted from him, wasn't it? To no longer be angry with each other but, also, for her to finally have the freedom to travel and reboot her life?

Well, he was giving that to her without a single battle but, it turned out, that wasn't exactly what she'd wanted after all.

She'd hoped, perhaps, that he'd insist on traveling somewhere exotic with her. That he'd want to share in her adventures—not just give her his blessing in seeking them out. That he might chase her a little and not merely tell her to "look him up" if she ever came back.

Foolish and childish of her, she knew.

But, just because she realized her desires were a bit irrational and contradictory, it didn't mean they weren't genuine. She'd never had the opportunity to make any such life-changing choices before. She supposed she still had a lot to learn about herself.

Jake, however, was living up to her fantasy-boyfriend role with startling intensity.

Of course, he had a freedom from career responsibilities that Bram did not, since Jake was taking a three-month leave of absence from both the inn and his music-store job—starting in mid-January—to backpack through Europe and the Middle East. He'd urged her repeatedly to join him for as much of it as she was willing to share, particularly once the transition of the inn to the Bakers was completed on February first.

"So, imagine this," he told her. "We could meet in Madrid. Make a circular loop around Spain, including Seville, the Costa del Sol, Toledo, Barcelona and a little excursion to Majorca. Then, we'll go by Eurail through the French Riviera into Italy and take in the sites there—Venice, Florence and Rome for sure. Skip down to Palermo, Sicily for a cruise that'll take us to Athens, the Greek Isles and various stops in Turkey, Egypt and the Holy Land…"

He painted an incredibly tempting picture and made her feel as if she could almost see herself there. That they could explore these fascinating and foreign regions together like school kids on a field trip.

Then again, there were a few locations that could be at least as dangerous as they were intriguing. Did she know enough to wander around cities like Cairo or Jerusalem without getting herself into trouble? Jake was a very bright guy, but *he'd* never been to any of these places either. How would he know what to do to keep them safe?

Margaret Ashland had said that she thought Jake's feelings for her were real. If that was actually true, had Shannon been unknowingly leading him on? Encouraging him to create a dream vacation he knew she'd love? Or, perhaps, could it be he was the right man for her after all?

She sighed. *No.*

As convenient as that might have been, her heart

disagreed. It was *Bram* she'd unwittingly fallen in love with...but, unfortunately, despite his professions of love, he didn't seem to want her nearly as much as she'd hoped.

The Bakers were beside themselves with both delight and a hint of inebriation.

"Yoo-hoo, you two!" Darlene said enthusiastically, jogging up to Bram and Shannon in the lobby and tugging on their sleeves until they swiveled around to greet her. Darlene's husband, Keith, was just a few steps behind, carefully balancing a tray with drinks.

Bram glanced at Shannon, who was absolutely radiant that night, clad in a dazzling silver dress that shimmered and reflected every fragment of light in the place. But she smiled at the older couple with a slightly unsettled look—a gaze filled with at least as many mixed emotions as the number of liquors used in Holiday Quinn's signature New Year's Eve drink recipe.

"I see you've made tonight's first official batch of the Bing Crosby Cocktails," Shannon said, nodding toward Keith's tray, which held about a dozen martini glasses. In each there was sparkling golden liquid garnished with orange slices and a bright red cherry.

"We tasted them 'til we were one-hundred-and-fifty percent *sure* we'd gotten the recipe right," Keith said with a noticeable slurring of syllables. "But we wanted you two to try the first ones we'd perfected."

"You're both going to be so ready for this changeover at the end of next month," Shannon said with love, admiration and a touch of sadness in her voice.

Darlene squeezed her arm. "If only we could do half as well as you, dearie. And you'd better not be a stranger. We expect to see you both back here." She shot them a significant look then handed each of them a martini glass. "Drink up, lovely friends! It's New Year's Eve and the champagne will be flowing soon, too. Say farewell to the old year and hello to the new one." The older lady encouraged them both to "let the celebrations begin."

Bram had no sooner taken his first sip of the specialty cocktail when there was a loud squeal across the room, followed by an even louder shout. "YES!"

The Bakers, Shannon, Bram and, in fact, every single person milling around the lobby all turned to stare at the squealer. A woman who looked to be in her mid- to late-twenties. And, right in front of her—bent down on one knee—was a man about her age, who leaped up, lifted her and spun her around.

"Whew!" he cried. "She said 'yes,' everybody! She's gonna marry me. She's gonna *marry* me!"

An immediate cheer rose up and everyone clapped for the newly engaged couple. The Bakers scurried toward them to hand the joyous man and woman celebratory drinks. And Shannon studied the scene before them wistfully.

"Wow," she said, seemingly unable to take her eyes off the young couple. "Imagine that. Beginning your life with someone."

Bram watched her wander over to the pair to offer her congratulations as well, knowing he'd do the same in a few minutes when there were fewer people crowding around them. For the time being, though, he just thought about Shannon's comment. Oh, yes, he *could* imagine that. For the first time in, perhaps, his entire adult life, he really *could* picture beginning it with someone—provided that someone was Shannon.

When midnight came, he was alone with her in a sea of over a hundred Holiday Quinn revelers. Waltzing face to face on the jammed dance floor, they enjoyed the last few minutes of the old year before the countdown to the new one was set to begin.

"I've been thinking about your trip ideas," Bram said, though it cost him something to sound so unruffled about it. "I've gotten the sense that you might already have some, uh, plans for after February first. And I—I don't want to interfere with those." He took a shaky breath. "But I do want to make sure you're safe and able to get in touch with me or with, uh, anyone who cares about you." He pulled the smart phone out of his pocket that he'd snuck away from the inn to buy her yesterday. "So, I got you this."

He explained some of the special features and ways it could prove to be a useful tool abroad. It had GPS tracking and satellite-image maps if she ever got lost or needed directions. It had a calculator for computing currency exchanges. Internet accessibility, of course, to directly check on flight times or train departures, museum openings and closings, the cost of dining or theater tickets.

"And I have a list of some of the most popular sites in Spain, Italy, Greece and throughout the Mediterranean. Places that I think are really worth a visit. Plus, I've also included a few spots you might want to avoid unless you're with an experienced guide."

He watched as she read through his lists—wide-eyed and with a sense of innocent wonder. Damn, he wanted to protect her *so* much. Not "acquire" her. *Be there* for her. But she said she wanted her freedom, and now wasn't the right time to chain her to his side when she needed a chance to run carefree and wild, if that was what she really desired.

"Best of all," he said, "it's got an international phone plan, so if you *ever* need help with anything at anytime, you can reach me in an instant. I'm on speed dial, see?" He punched in a couple of digits and, immediately, his own phone in his jacket pocket began to ring. He showed it to her. "Shannon calling," the face of his iPhone read, while the ringtone was a somewhat heartbreaking electronic version of "Leaving on a Jet Plane."

He saw her swallow a few times. "Thank you," she whispered, holding her new cell phone tightly and Bram even more so. "I promise I'll always carry it with me."

"Good," he replied. "Then it'll be kind of like me being there with you." And though he didn't say this aloud, to himself he added, *Keep me close to your heart, Shannon. And come back to me.*

She looked like she was about to say something more, but

the crowd suddenly began to chant, "Ten, nine, eight, seven…"

"Already?" Shannon asked, glancing at her watch in surprise.

Bram nodded, grabbed champagne flutes for them both from a passing waiter and joined in on the countdown.

"Six, five, four, three…"

Shannon laughed, gazed warmly at him and chimed in as well.

"Two, one. Happy New Year!"

Then, amidst the sounds of noisemakers from the crowd, they kissed—a long, deep, passionate kiss—and broke apart, breathless.

He raised his champagne flute just as "Auld Lang Syne" began to play and everyone else began to sing. "To the people who touched our lives in the past year," he said.

She raised hers, too, and added a toast of her own—one that caused a twinge of pain in the vicinity of his heart.

"And to new beginnings for all of us," she said before clinking glasses with him and stepping back. Thus, taking her first steps of the New Year in a direction away from Bram.

Shannon kept the fingers of one hand wrapped about the phone Bram had given her. It was safely out of sight, in her pocket, as she officially checked him out of the inn the next morning. But it gave her comfort to touch it. Like a talisman. She didn't want to let go of it, and she didn't want to let go of Bram either.

"Be safe on the drive back," she said to him, trying hard to keep from crying. The month ahead was going to be insanely busy, and she knew there would be no time for get-togethers, even if he could to slip away or meet her somewhere for a weekend. She missed him already but, given the unlikelihood of them seeing each other again anytime soon, he really was no longer hers.

"I will," he promised. "I'll be thinking about you."

Then, with a final and very quick goodbye kiss, he was gone.

Shannon heard Jake exhale audibly next to her. She turned to look at him. To see if he was doing it deliberately—there was certainly no love lost between the two men.

But, no, it seemed to be an unconscious thing, much the way that Bram's neck and shoulders always seemed to stiffen when her assistant would walk into the room.

Which was why Bram's non-competitive behavior over the past week had perplexed her and had, ultimately, played a part in her decision to just let their relationship drift quietly away. She'd never liked it when he would fight with Jake for her attention, but it was far more unsettling when he didn't.

He'd just let go of her.

But, she realized suddenly—again feeling the smooth phone in her jacket pocket—it wasn't that he didn't care about her. He'd made that clear enough. It was because, as with any standard board game, like chess or checkers, it was actually *her move*. She just didn't know which one to make.

Jake interrupted her thoughts. "Wanna grab some lunch after we're done with the morning checkouts? I could really go for a cheeseburger. I know it's the last thing I should have on New Year's Day, especially after my vow not to eat so much red meat this year." He laughed. "But a man wants what a man wants." He waggled his eyebrows suggestively at her.

She smiled at him weakly in return. "I avoided New Year's resolutions altogether this year. That's the only way I can make it through January first without breaking any."

The latest cluster of guests had just stepped away from the front desk, so it was only the two of them remaining in the lobby. Jake glanced around and took an obvious step toward her. "Really?" he asked. "No resolutions? No special promises?"

She shook her head.

"What about commitments?" he said. "Any of those...with, say, someone like Bram Hartwick?"

She shook her head again, feeling an acute sadness as her memories with Bram swept over her.

A grin slid over Jake's face. "He's a big fool, Shannon. You can do better than him. You *deserve* better. Anyone with half a brain would know never to just let you go."

And, suddenly, Jake was right in front of her—his arms around her shoulders, his lips pressing against her cheek, then her jaw, then her neck and, finally, at the corner of her mouth. She was disoriented by it and didn't quite know how to react for a few seconds but, eventually, she managed to step away and stutter a question. "Wh-What are you doing?" she asked him.

"It's my second resolution of the New Year. To win you over once and for all." He paused, took a deep breath and added, "I'm crazy about you, Shannon. Don't tell me you don't know that. *Everybody* here knows it. And you'll see. With a little time and distance from this place, everything will look clearer to you. You have choices. Where you wanna live. What kind of work you wanna do. Who you wanna date."

He gazed deep into her eyes—very seriously, she noticed, for the first time in a long time. She could feel his intensity and his utter sincerity. He wasn't joking around in the least.

She swallowed. She didn't want to hurt him, but she had to say something. "Jake, look—"

"No," he blurted. "Please don't. Don't say anything now, not if you can't say yes to me. Okay? We've got time together planned. Take it. *Please* take it. I'm going to Europe in a couple of weeks, and I'll be there to meet you whenever you arrive. The closing date for the sale of the inn is the morning of February first—and you were planning to fly to Spain on the second. Groundhog's Day. I'll be at the airport in Madrid waiting for you, Shannon. If, after even one week, you don't *love* it and love being with *me*, then tell me and I won't stop you from leaving. I promise."

Too many people making promises to her today, she thought, but she held her tongue and let Jake finish.

"You can travel alone after that," he said. "Or take a train to somewhere else with a hot Spaniard. Or fly back home...whatever you want. Just give it a chance." His green eyes pleaded with her.

And because she didn't have Bram beside her to remind her heart of how passion felt, because he'd let her go…just as she'd asked him to…and because all of the changes in her life had left her feeling unmoored, with no direction, no compass, no sense of where she belonged in this incredibly huge world— or with whom—she said, "Okay, Jake. I'll give it a chance."

~CHAPTER TWELVE~

Valentine's Day...Again

The grounds of the Alhambra were gorgeous.

Even in early February, the Andalusia region of southern Spain was temperate and beautiful, and this famous, decorative palace of the Moors was especially so.

Shannon admired the architecture of the buildings, the stunning arches and intricate detailing. She breathed in the fresh air and delighted in the natural loveliness of the gardens. And she felt the late afternoon Granada sunshine warming her skin. A winter's day that was fifty degrees?! Hard to imagine *that* happening too often in Wisconsin.

Such a different climate. So much ancient history. A completely unique cultural experience and, yet...yet, she was the *same* Shannon Quinn. No matter how far from home she'd traveled, she couldn't seem to leave herself or her memories behind.

She'd brushed off the post-holiday blues by keeping energetically busy with the sale of the inn to the Bakers, but then she'd come to Spain.

Jake, true to his word, was waiting for her. And, well, even when the two of them went sightseeing until they'd nearly dropped from exhaustion, she wasn't able to escape her thoughts and emotions indefinitely. Something would unexpectedly remind her of Holiday Quinn or her favorite guests or her friend Margaret...or Bram.

It was nine o'clock in the morning back in the Midwest. What was everyone back there doing right now?

About a half hour into the palace tour, Shannon couldn't rein in her curiosity any longer. She slipped away from the group and from Jake's watchful eye, and she punched in a series of numbers on her phone.

"Yes?" Margaret Ashland's distinctive voice said from some 4,200 miles away.

"Miss me yet?" Shannon asked.

The older woman chuckled. "It's great to hear from you, honeybunch! What do you think of sunny Spain?"

Shannon raved about the country for several minutes while her mentor listened with attentive silence and a handful of encouraging comments.

Then Margaret, who was never one to avoid the heart of an issue, said, "And how is it being abroad on this grand adventure with Jake?"

Shannon paused. She'd never been quite as straightforward as her friend, but she could no longer disguise the truth. "Jake's not the problem, Margaret."

To his credit, Jake—though flirtatious as ever—had been a gentleman the entire time they'd been together. He let her set the pace of their friendship, which was still platonic, at least from her point of view, and he didn't once push her into anything more.

She was the one who was struggling.

In spite of herself, she missed huge chunks of her old life. She missed the routines she'd lived with for years. She missed the natural beauty of her home state. And she missed Bram. She tried to explain all of this to Margaret.

"The problem," Shannon said, "is that I *know* I should be here. I have so much to learn, and a trip like this was always my dream! How can I possibly go back home until I've seen something of the world? Gained some knowledge and wisdom?

Experienced everything I imagined?"

"Honey, world travel can certainly give you many of those things, but there's more than one way to 'take a trip,' you know." Margaret paused. "Education is a true odyssey of the mind. And love—well, love is a journey that never ends. It sets you on a path that never stops twisting and turning. Don't underestimate the power of those types of experiences either."

Her friend was right, as she had been so many times. Shannon knew it and thanked her. Then, after they'd said goodbye, Shannon stood near one of the walls and admired the garden flowers until, inevitably, Jake found her there.

He nudged her arm. "Saw you talking on the phone."

She nodded. "Yeah. Jake, I'm sorry. It's really not you. I'm just—"

"In love with someone else," he finished for her.

She nodded again.

He winced and swallowed a few times. "Well, damn," he murmured. "I thought I might be able to change your mind, you know? But, hey, at least I tried. And you were worth giving it a shot, babe."

Then he draped his arm around her and pointed to one of the Spanish tour guides—a shapely brunette dressed in a slinky black miniskirt with a smile as bright as the Granada sun.

"That's Juliana," he said. "She invited me out to a tapas bar tonight. Guess I can tell her yes now, huh?"

Shannon kissed him lightly on the cheek. "You may be an insatiable flirt but, deep down, you're a really good guy, *Jakey*." She paused until he chuckled, even though the laughter didn't quite reach his eyes. "Don't keep the pretty lady waiting—and good luck. With everything."

He winked at her. "Yeah, you, too."

When he finally strode away, she clicked over to the Internet. Sure, it'd taken a month since New Year's, plus a full week into her trip, but she'd finally figured out what she wanted to do, and she had a few important details to look up online.

Bram was freezing his ass off in a corporate board meeting in Minneapolis when they finally got to take ten minutes off for a coffee break. He needed it—the heat of the mug for his chilled fingers as much as the caffeine boost for his tired brain. Sitting motionless for so long, even while listening to his own shareholders praise the growth of his company, still wasn't helping his circulation any.

It'd been a year since last Valentine's Day. A year since he'd met Shannon Quinn. And far too long since he'd seen or spoken with her.

He poured himself a big cup of coffee and stared with irritation at the cutesy heart-shaped cookies his secretary Miranda had ordered for the meeting. They reminded him too much of Holiday Quinn, the Queen of Hearts Singles' Dance and Shannon in that lovely cream-colored evening gown with the gold straps.

Depressing as hell to still miss her so much. He should've been able to get over it. To move on. *She* clearly had. She was in Spain with The Prick. But, mad as he was at Jake, he was much angrier with himself. He'd let her go, and her assistant was smart enough to keep her by his side. Bram couldn't fault the guy for that.

He sighed, thinking of the text she'd sent him just a few days ago with a picture of the Alhambra Palace attached. Yeah, *a text*. Not a phone call or even an e-mail. So impersonal. It had him wishing for the olden days when people sent each other snail-mail postcards from their vacations.

Miranda saw him wandering around the office and shot him a concerned look. "Are you feeling well, Mr. Hartwick?" she asked.

He shrugged. "It's cold."

"It's February in Minnesota." She smiled. "What were you expecting?"

"Yeah, yeah, I know." He'd given strict orders to the maintenance staff to keep the building temps as warm as possible, but the winter chill had a way of seeping in no matter what.

Bram glanced out the window and noticed it was snowing. Terrific. On top of everything else, his commute home would be punitive.

"Roads are going to be treacherous in a few hours," he told his secretary. "Maybe we should close early today. Give everyone a chance to get to their houses safely."

Miranda glanced at the clock and worried her bottom lip. "Hmm," she said.

"What, you've got a problem with that? Think the shareholders will disapprove?"

She shook her head. "Not precisely," she murmured, a noncommittal response that left him confused.

He was puzzling over how to respond to this when Miranda's desk phone suddenly rang.

"Excuse me for a moment, Mr. Hartwick."

He watched her take the call, chuckle into the receiver and instruct the person on the other end of the line to come up to the fifth floor.

"I'll meet you by the elevators," he heard her say.

Bram winced inwardly. Sounded like another delivery had just arrived. More Lathericious samples to sort through. More documents to sign. More of some kind of work he'd need to do before he could finally leave the office for the day and lick his wounds in private. He turned to walk back to the boardroom.

"Mr. Hartwick?" Miranda said.

He looked at her, waiting.

"Yes." She nodded. "I definitely think you should suggest an early departure to the shareholders." She gazed out the window with an amused expression. "Right *now* would be the best time, if you want my honest opinion."

He stared at her with a niggle of suspicion. "What's going on?"

But no sooner had the words left his mouth than the elevator in the hallway, just out of sight, dinged loudly, and his secretary dashed away from him.

"Hold that thought," she called over her shoulder.

"Miranda—" he began, but his secretary had already disappeared.

He returned to the boardroom and dismissed his associates. A few lingered to chat with him so, maybe, another fifteen minutes had gone by before Miranda came bursting into the room with an impatient expression on her face.

"You're needed at once in your office, Mr. Hartwick," she informed him sternly. "It's important."

This was wholly uncharacteristic behavior for his secretary. This sternness. This impatience. The last time she'd acted remotely like this it'd been on the eve of his company's anniversary, about five years ago, when his brothers surprised him with a little party at the office. They'd gotten his secretary in on their plans so she could help set it up.

Miranda wasn't someone accustomed to keeping secrets.

He trailed after her, squinting his eyes at her fast-moving form and about to ask her yet again what the hell was going on. But she swung open the door to his private office...and the words froze on his tongue.

"Bram," Shannon said. "Happy Valentine's Day."

His mind was, perhaps, not functioning as efficiently as it should have been. It was as if the icy conditions on the roadways outside had extended their hazardousness into the pathways of his brain. Everything was moving perplexingly slow, and his thoughts were skidding perilously around inside his head with little control.

He got only as far as forming the word "Shannon" with his lips, but his shock at seeing her just standing there kept him from believing the messages his eyes were sending. He was incapable of speech.

Shannon, however, wasn't nearly as tongue-tied. She raced up to him, flung her arms around him and whispered, "It's *so* good to see you."

He buried his face in the softness of her hair and neck, clinging to her as tightly as he could without cutting off her circulation.

Miranda cleared her throat. "Well, Mr. Hartwick, I'll be heading out now. Bad driving weather and all." There was relief in her voice and enough warmth to melt half the snow that had fallen that day in the Twin Cities. "Ms. Quinn, it was a pleasure meeting you."

"You, too," Shannon said with sincerity. "Thank you so much."

Then his secretary was gone.

He was holding the woman he loved.

And they were alone.

"You're *here*," he said finally. "*Why* are you here? Not that I want you to leave," he added quickly, "but I thought you were somewhere in the middle of the Iberian Peninsula."

She pulled back just far enough to gaze deep into his eyes. "I was. But I missed you. And when I talked to Margaret, she reminded me that there was more than one kind of journey... I *do* want to travel the world, Bram, but I also want to learn a little more about the places I'm visiting and about a whole bunch of other subjects I've never had a chance to study or experience. It's time for me to continue my education, and I hear there are a few good colleges in the area."

She smiled and flashed a University of Minnesota course catalog at him. "You'll have to tell me, though, if I should check out the dorm situation or if, perhaps, some alternate housing might be arranged."

Bram stared at her, not sure he could trust his ears. All of his senses were wacked. "Wait, you want to move to Minneapolis?"

She shook her head and, immediately, his heart plummeted to his toes.

"Minneapolis, Milwaukee, Manhattan, Mozambique. The location is irrelevant, Bram. What I want is to be where *you* are. I want to take life's greatest journey of all—the grand adventure of love—with you. And, if we're lucky, if we find it's the right path for us, then, maybe, we can continue journeying onward. To see if it leads to a life together." She paused and looked at him with an equal mix of apprehension and hope. "Is that something you might want, too?"

"Oh, Shannon," he murmured and, once again, he was rendered speechless for a few moments. "Yes. A thousand times, yes. Whether or not we ever go back to our favorite inn, being with you would make *every day* feel like a holiday."

Then, before she could get away or change her mind, he locked his office door, snapped shut the window blinds and showed her with every part of his body, mind and soul just how much he loved being her valentine.

The room temperature spiked hotter than a night in July.

And somewhere in the distance—in the middle of yet another Midwestern blizzard—Bram Hartwick could have sworn he heard fireworks.

∼**END**∽

EXCERPT: PRIDE, PREJUDICE AND THE PERFECT MATCH (©2013)

Would an Elizabeth Bennet by any other name be as appealing to a Darcy?

A single mother and an ER doctor meet on an Internet dating site—each for reasons that have little to do with finding their perfect match—in this modern, Austen-inspired story. It's a tribute to the power of both "pride" and "prejudice" in bringing two people romantically together, despite their mutual insistence that they should stay apart...

Beth Ann Bennet isn't looking for love. She's an aspiring social worker using an online alias to study sex-role stereotypes. Dr. William Darcy isn't looking for love either. He's just trying to fund his new clinic by winning a major bet. Both think Lady Catherine's Love Match Website will help them get what they want—fast, easy and without endangering their hearts. Both are in for a big surprise.

Pride, Prejudice and the Perfect Match...where true love is just a fib and a click away.

That day at dawn, Beth reviewed her stereotypes list:

1. Greater size and strength
2. Goal-oriented, often highly ambitious
3. Values the rational/logical over the emotional
4. More independent, assertive, critical and competitive
5. Fast visual-attraction reactions
6. Better at spatial/mathematical skills
7. Difficulty expressing emotions

Yep. That seemed to pretty much sum up the major male stereotypes as she knew them, omitting universal truths like men's bizarre predilection toward big tools and bigger remote-control devices.

Beth laid down her pen. She was armed and ready for today's coffee "date" and planned to find as much direct, supporting evidence as she could for each point in the few minutes she and Will would spend together. She prayed she'd be able to pull it off.

Somehow she managed to get Charlie to school, do a morning's worth of organizing at the agency and pull into the Koffee Haus parking lot right on time.

The scent of warm, roasted coffee beans enticed her nostrils even before she made it through the doorway. The singles' bar of this century had cinnamon shakers and skim milk pitchers on the counter instead of vodka jiggers and salty peanuts, but the idea was unchanged.

A pair of lanky guys leaned against the counter waiting for their orders to be ready. Neither of them looked anything like Will's website photograph. Where was he?

A small table opened up near the door and Beth leaped for it. She slid into the chair and began casing the room. Mostly couples or small groups of friends. A dark-haired man in his early thirties sat alone with a newspaper. His back was to her so she leaned to the left to try to catch a glimpse of his face.

It could be him. Might be.

She leaned a little further but before she could see him she felt that roller-coaster dip in her stomach and lost her balance—hands swiping the floor, chair scraping awkwardly. Very smooth move.

The guy turned to stare at her. So did everyone else. She readjusted herself and tried to bury her head in her purse.

That looked like him. Close enough to the photo anyway to make her pretty sure. Darn it. There was no way he'd want to be approached by a klutz.

When she looked up, he was staring at her again. An assessing glance.

Yep. The game was over before it had a chance to begin. Something about him struck her as odd, though. His e-mail personality was so warm, so charming. This guy—well, arrogant seemed to be a better descriptor.

She wondered what he'd do now. Ditch her? She grabbed her stereotypes list from her purse, scanning it covertly in case he worked up the nerve to come over before she approached him. A glimpse at her watch told her it was already ten minutes past one. When she looked back at his table, he was gone.

She sighed. This wasn't good. Her final project was due in a few weeks, and she needed to cite concrete examples of Case Study #1's behavior, documented and dated over a period of thirty days. She didn't have time to start again with a new subject. As it was, she'd have to use all of their e-mail correspondence in her report, and that still left her with over a week's worth of communication to obtain and record.

And nothing she had thus far was very conclusive.

She didn't want to resort to shortcuts to complete the paper, but Charlie's future was at stake here. She stood to leave.

"So, are you the woman Lady Catherine thinks I'm destined for?" a deep voice with a laugh hidden in it whispered in her ear.

She swiveled around and stared at the man behind her. He wasn't the guy with the newspaper, but he, too, looked like Will's website photo… only better. Much better.

"If so," he continued, "I'm your Perfect Match."

EXCERPT: PRIDE, PREJUDICE AND THE PERFECT BET (©2014)

The course of true love doesn't always run smooth—not even for millionaire bachelors...

Everyone thought Beth Ann Bennet and Dr. Will Darcy had an unexpected romance in Pride, Prejudice and the Perfect Match. Now, Beth's best friend, Jane Henderson, and Will's first cousin, Bingley McNamara, begin their own unlikely love story in Pride, Prejudice and the Perfect Bet, which starts at the Darcy/Bennet wedding when they find themselves in the roles of maid of honor and best man for the newlyweds.

Jane is an interning school psychologist and a woman who wears an angelic mask in public, but she's not as sweet tempered as she'd like everyone to believe. Turns out, she may have just crossed paths with the one person who'll unnerve her enough to get her to reveal her true self.

As for Bingley, he's a wealthy, flirtatious and compulsively social guru of finance, who likes to wager on stocks and, let's face it, on just about anything that strikes his fancy. But this dedicated ladies' man may have finally met the woman who'll challenge his bachelor ways!

Pride, Prejudice and the Perfect Bet...where life's biggest gamble is the game of love.

Finally, the procession out of the church began, and Jane, as maid of honor, had to walk back down the aisle with Bingley. Oh, joy.

"Delightful ceremony," he pronounced loudly, insuring that everyone nearby would hear, as he formally offered her his arm. But he looked at her as if he'd much rather promenade with a python.

"I agree," she said, smiling tightly and playing the part.

He cast an absolutely ecstatic grin at the friends and family in attendance as the two of them took their first steps toward the church's vestibule. "Only the receiving line and the final pictures," he hissed, his lips near her ear as if sharing a secret. "And then I can start getting drunk. I plan to be pretty damn buzzed before our special dance."

She leaned closer to him and hissed right back, "So funny! I was thinking exactly the same thing."

"Yeah? I remember the last time you got your hands on some champagne, Jane. Who are you gonna be making out with tonight?"

She gripped his arm perhaps a little more forcefully than necessary. "Not you."

He winced but didn't stop walking or faux grinning at the congregation. "Oh, I wasn't offering, sweetheart. I've already been burned once. I don't do second chances."

She gulped. To her ear, he sounded hurt, which both surprised her and pissed her off. He was acting like some innocent in the whole thing. Like he hadn't been trying to take advantage of her—one way or another. That he hadn't made a bet that involved her. Ha. She'd tear him apart limb by limb, this very second, in fact, if it wouldn't ruin her dress before the reception.

Beth and Will had stopped just up ahead of them and were getting ready to greet their guests in the receiving line. Before

Jane pulled away from Bingley to dutifully take her place next to the bride, she gave the quote-unquote "best man" her parting shot. "I don't do second chances either," she informed him. "And, for the record, you might as well pay up Dustin and buy your own beer because there's no way you'll win your gamble with him. At least not with my help."

Jane had the satisfaction of seeing him freeze in his spot, a look of shock and confusion on his handsome face, as she turned her back to him.

Now that she'd told him off at last, he'd have to stay away from her, except when their attendant duties made interaction absolutely necessary. Seriously, how much more trouble could the guy cause in less than twenty-four hours, right?

Right.

ABOUT THE AUTHOR

Marilyn Brant has been told she writes with honesty, liveliness and wit (descriptors she's grown terribly fond of) about complex, intelligent women—like her friends—and their significant personal relationships. Although her favorite pursuits undoubtedly involve books, she proves she's not just a literary snob by confessing her lifelong fascination (read: obsession) with popular music, especially from the '70s and '80s, most flavors of ice cream and a variety of sensuous body lotions/oils.

As a former teacher, library staff member, freelance magazine writer and national book reviewer, Marilyn has spent much of her life lost in literature. She is the *New York Times & USA Today* bestselling and award-winning author of ten novels to date and, in 2013, the Illinois Association of Teachers of English (IATE) selected her as their Author of the Year.

Her debut coming-of-age novel, *According to Jane* (Kensington, 2009), featuring the ghost of Jane Austen giving a young woman dating advice, won the Romance Writers of America's prestigious Golden Heart Award and the Booksellers' Best, and it was named one of the "Top 100 Romance Novels of All Time" by Buzzle.com. Her second novel, *Friday Mornings at Nine* (Kensington, 2010), was a Doubleday and Book-of-the-Month Club pick in women's fiction. And *A Summer in Europe* (Kensington, 2011) was featured in the Literary Guild and BOMC2, and it became a Top 20 Bestseller in Fiction and Literature for the Rhapsody Book Club. The Polish translation of the novel was released in June 2013.

She's also a #1 Kindle and #1 Nook bestseller, who writes fun and flirty romantic comedies, like her stories in *The Sweet Temptations Collection*, that involve sweet treats, unexpected love and large doses of humor. *Pride, Prejudice and the Perfect Match* and its sequel were also Amazon and B&N bestsellers. *The Road to You*, a coming-of-age romantic mystery, was selected as one of the Top 20 Best Books of the Year (December 2013) by The Reading Frenzy. Her novels are available in ebook, paperback, and many will be released on audio as well. Look for more romantic fiction—including her new Mirabelle Harbor series—coming soon!

Marilyn currently lives in the Chicago suburbs with her family. When she isn't reading her friends' books or watching old movies, she's working on her next novel, eating chocolate indiscriminately and hiding from the laundry.

Please visit her website: **www.marilynbrant.com**